THE DEVIL IN

PARADISE

THE DEVIL IN
PARADISE

STEPHEN FRANCIS MONTAGNA

ARPress
45 Dan Road Suite 5
Canton MA 02021

Hotline: 1(888) 821-0229
Fax: 1(508) 545-7580

Ordering Information:
Quantity sales. Special discounts are available on quantity purchases by corporations, associations, and others. For details, contact the publisher at the address above.

Printed in the United States of America.
ISBN-13:   Paperback   979-8-89389-240-6
                  eBook   979-8-89389-241-3

Library of Congress Control Number: 2024906330

Contents

Dedication

This novel is dedicated to my son Stephen Francis Montagna JR. who has backed me in my dreams to become a writer.

This work explores the want to rid Cuba of Fidel Castor's rule, and the aftermath of this want and the unpredictable reactions of the proud Cuban peoples, both pro and con for Fidel Castro and the future of Cuba.

Prologue

The insurrection by Fidel Castro and his ill trained troops began inauspiciously on July 26th, 1953, when his rebel forces began their raid on the Moncada Army Barracks in the Cuban city of Santiago. This attack was a complete and utter disaster to the small band of highly motivated but ill prepared rebel invaders, and its failure quickly lead to the arrest of the leader, Fidel Castro, and many of his followers. Castro was placed in jail for a short period of time and then, after a quick mock military trial, he was exiled until he finally returned to Cuba as a conquering hero.

In 1933, a Sergeant's Revolt hit the tiny Island of Cuba. It was being led by a young upstart Sergeant who was named Fulgencio Batista Zaldivar. This small rebellion shared the full support of university students, many intellectuals and the professionals of the Island alike. This backing gave the Sergeants the power to overthrow the current Presidential Administration of Carlos Manual deCespedes. After the successful revolt, a minor provisional government was left in full command of the entire Island of Cuba. Right in the midst of the fighting, General Gerardo Machado, at the time the President of Cuba, finally fled the country by plane when he realized all was lost to his Administration.

A few days after the end of the Sergeant's Revolt, Ramon Grau San Martin was named the new seated President of Cuba. He was installed to power by the Sergeants of the Cuban Army who had taken part in the revolt. This was also supported by the intellectuals who encouraged the uprising to begin in the first place. President Grau San Martin's first order to the Army was to elevate Sergeant Fulgencio Batista to the rank of Colonel. This was done to cement Batista's loyalty to him; President Martin quickly installed Batista as the Commander in Chief of the Army of Cuba, making him one of the most powerful men in all of Cuba. President Grau San Martin then allowed the Colonel to influence many of his decisions while ruling over Cuba and reducing President San Martin to a mere puppet to Batista's whims and wants.

The United States government, controlled by President Franklin D. Roosevelt at the time, was extremely disturbed how Batista gained such control of the revolt torn Island of Cuba. When Batista installed San Martin to the Presidency, the American President was left with no other choice in the matter but to consider having little to do with this new and highly unstable Cuban government. This opened the door further and in the future to Fidel Castro, who would use it to open his quest for complete control over of the Island of Cuba, and to also enslave all her people under his oppressive thumb.

The Grau San Martin government did very little in the way of improving the lifestyles of any of the civilians of Cuba during his entire Presidency. He found he could not carry through with many of his ideas. With the growing despair of the people of Cuba, San Martin slowly bled Cuba dry, helped by his Generals and Ministers. In his short time, San Martin established the Cuban Revolutionary Party with its proud cry, "Cuba for Cubans." To take the shadow of his failure further away from himself, he attacked what he referred to as the 'Yankee Imperialism', doing business inside his country.

Grau San Martin was a physician and a part time University Professor, who was well noted for his national zeal and great passion. But his regime never contacted or was ever recognized by the United States Administration. The failure of the United States to recognize the San Martin government brought about its quick end. After weathering an attempted revolt by a second military faction, there was a loss of support by his party, and Batista's lack of faith for San Martin quickly led to his resignation. Grau San Martin's stay of power lasted for just four short months in office.

Colonel Carlos Mendieta was a very strong willed and uncontrollable Cuban, and he was also a veteran of the war of Independence for Cuba, enjoyed the full and complete support of the traditional parties who originally controlled a large membership, and he was installed to the Presidency of Cuba by Batista from the years of 1934 through 1935.

But Batista remained working in the background to allow Cuba to begin down the long road Cuba was destined to follow, and to find her true fate in the scheme of world affairs. Far from being idle though, Batista skillfully massed and organized the power of his Army. He ruled the country from behind the scenes, and he used the puppet governments he created, to carry out his wishes and commands. Batista was more interested in keeping the military of Cuba strong, than he was in openly and fairly ruling over Cuba and her proud people.

Throughout the following years of 1934 to 1940, Batista made many important contributions to the Cuban way of life. The first of these contributions were through the negotiations between Batista and President Franklin D. Roosevelt in 1934. Batista talked Roosevelt into making it possible for Cuba to sidestep the hated Platt Amendment. But the United States kept one stipulation set in place during these negotiations, and that was the United States would keep the Naval Base stationed at Guantanamo Bay in operation, enabling the United States to keep its finger resting on Cuba's pulse.

Batista's second accomplishment in Cuba came with the drafting of a new constitution passed in 1940, where he became the real President of Cuba. Batista's first political mistake occurred when he allowed Grau San Martin, now his most powerful political enemy, to remain alive, and to retake the office of the Presidency of Cuba after Batista grew bored with it.

The eight years of Grau San Martin's second rule as the President of Cuba, was about as ineffective and corrupt as his first one was. San Martin's many failures in office, soon forced him to ally himself with Carlos Prio Socarras. The Gran San Martin Administration shortly galvanized its power with Socarras, and together they organized the New Cuban Revolutionary Party of Cuba, with the help of the ruling Conservatives of the Republicianos of Cuba.

In 1952, with the new elections looming over the horizon for Cuba, and with the Reform Party expecting to overwhelmingly win the election, and the Presidency of Cuba. Batista read the signs and he quickly organized the Coalition Socialista Democratica Party, which was now composed of the Liberal Party faction. He also organized a small fraction of the Conservatives called the Democratas. The Socialist Popular Party of the Communists was as well, organized by Batista, along with the much smaller groups of the Nationals of Cuba. Once he felt he was in the proper position to strike out, Batista announced his intent and then he openly ran for the Presidency of Cuba. But he was opposed by the much more powerful Grau San Martin, who was armed with the backing of the New Cuban Revolutionary Party, and most of the Republicianos.

The future President of Cuba, Batista, feeling extremely threatened by the political power aimed directly at him, and suddenly wielded together by San Martin and Cocarras. Caused Batista to decide, and he then suppressed the elections for Cuba and in late March of 1952, he merely seized power over the entire Cuban government, by means of a military coup of the Island. Throughout the seven years of Batista's second Administration of Cuba, he tightened his death like grip over the Island of Cuba and her people. President Batista used increasingly savage means and efforts of suppression and torture, to enable him to maintain his influence and power over the military, and to remain in office.

Under this second term of President Batista's vastly corrupt Administration and rule, the economy of Cuba mainly dominated by the United States influence, caused many social services of Cuba to suffer drastically, as President Batista quickly gained complete control over the entire nation of Cuba. Poverty and illiteracy became widespread throughout most of the small Island country, with Batista taking out his revenge on the state universities who did not back his latest bid for the Presidency over Cuba this second time around. And, where the youth of Cuba were rioting, and completely rejecting Batista's military takeover of the government of Cuba.

The public and military officers quickly became flagrantly corrupt under President Batista's second rule over Cuba, and Cuba soon found itself looking for a new redeemer to come along and free them from this terribly unjust and oppressive leader. A new leader who would free Cuba from the terrible suppression her people were forced to live under, and thus allowing the upstart Fidel Castro to enter the picture for the first time in his political life, for the future sake of Cuba. The people of

Cuba were desperately looking for anyone who would free them from the brutal military rule Cuba was constantly suffering through.

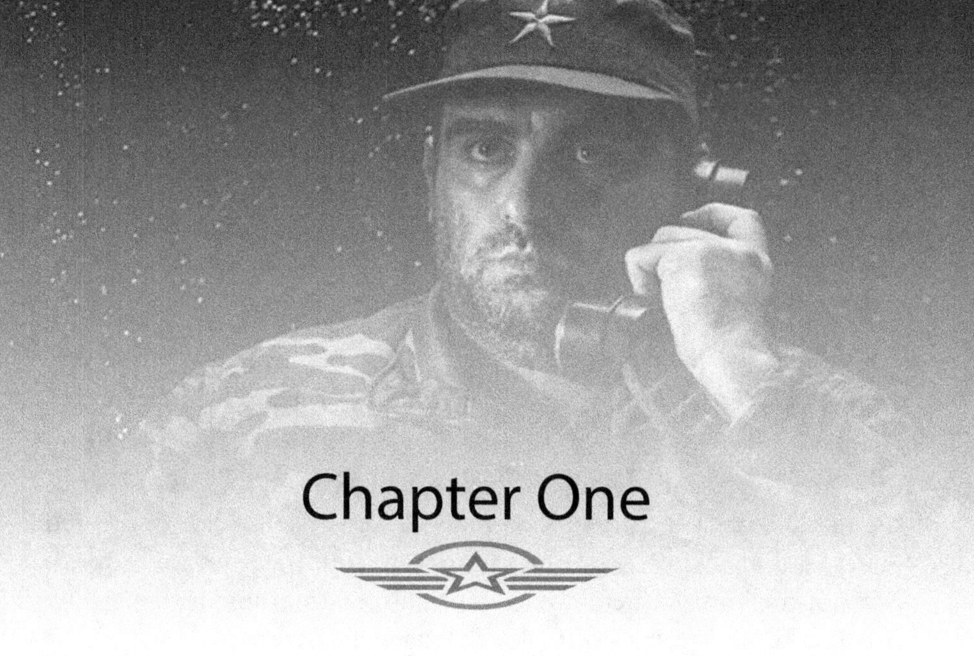

Chapter One

Cuba, which was always referred to as the Paradise of the Caribbean, suffered drastically under Batista's iron fisted rule, riots by many of Cuba's youth, and the rise in anger of the elderly citizens, rapidly lead to the decline of the country long thought to be a model for the Spanish speaking Latin American nations of Central and South America. Well before the emergence of Fidel Castro, Cuba enjoyed the highest per capita standard of living, and the lowest rate of illiteracy of any of the Latin American nations. The well developed and defined infrastructure established hospital and welfare systems that set the standard of living for other nations, including the United States to emulate. First rate road and rail systems helped to move Cuba up the ladder of success in the world's eyes.

Cuba was a tropical paradise, the land of Eden so to say, and it was blessed with the technology needed to build advanced electrical power plants, supporting a strong interest in public housing, slum clearance and good prenatal care. An advanced school system at the elementary, secondary and University levels were carefully nurtured by the government.

Cuba also enjoyed a substantial air transportation system, which included one hundred and sixty seven airports, and seventy three of them were supporting hard surfaced runways. Cuba's infrastructure and airway systems were far superior then many of those of the other

Latin countries. Cuba's spectacular shoreline was dotted with many magnificent hotels, and tourism was highly encouraged by every facet of the Cuban government. Adding to the sheer beauty of the white sand beaches was the richness of Cuba's fascinating flora and well protected reserves.

Batista was further instrumental in reforming the tax system, by ending most of the tax evasion policies much like the United States would attempt to do forty seven years later in their own tax reform movement. Everyone living on the small Island paid their fair share of the taxes. Batista instituted a national lottery system that the United States and many of the other European countries quickly copied. Most of the improvements were accomplished right under the terribly corrupt Administration of Colonel Fulgencio Batista Zaldivar. Some of the changes were started by the dictatorship of Gerardo Machado Morales. Cuba was ruled by a string of dictators, one worse than the other. But still, all these accomplishments were implemented by one official after the other, and all were trying to stay in power by giving the civilians a small offering.

Fidel Castro was born in 1927 on the eastern section of the tiny Island of Cuba in the Oriente province. Castro was the first born son of a wealthy and self made farmer of Spanish descent, and a young Cuban servant girl mother. Castro lived the life his father's wealth offered him. Cuba had been mostly dependent on the United States for many past generations. The American influence slowly replaced many of the old rule and passions of Spain, and this change worked out for the betterment of Cuba. Under the United States influence, Cuba's economic substructure rebuilt itself until Cuba became a powerful leading state in its own right. But by the time Castro's revolution finally took place, Cuba enjoyed the position of fourth place among the other leading Latin American countries of the world in economic and social advances and living standards for their civilians.

Castro rose to power in the province of his birth. The Oriente was separated from La Havana, the capital of Cuba by the rugged terrain of the Sierra Maestra and Sierra Cristal Mountain ranges that were heavily wooded, and it was almost impassable, except for a few well traveled roads and narrow goat paths. The separation of this province from the rest of the country, made it possible for Castro to instill the seeds of discontent and unrest in Cuba, and to better organize his followers. Castro pointed out the inequalities they faced by living in the poorer provinces of the lowlands. The harsh class differences between the hard working poor, and the better paid city dwellers, and the impossibility of climbing up the ladder of success while living under the present Administration, were described to the gathered.

Castro's words of discontent, along with his constant emphasis on all the government short comings, quickly caught the eye of the Cuban President, who assigned his Secret Police to keep a close eye on the young troublemaker. But the onset of the Second World War made Castro disappear into the background until he finally gathered his forces and lead the overthrow attempt against the Cuban government, and taking the Presidency of Cuba for his own.

In 1953, the appearance of Fidel Castro was introduced with an aborted rebel raid on Moncada Army Barracks. Castro's military exercise was soundly routed by Batista's well armed and much better trained Cuban troops. Castro was thus exiled to Mexico where he spent his entire time better organizing more supporters in his quest to take over Cuba for a second time. He made his second attempt at a military excursion into Cuba in the year of 1956. Castro and his supporters landed on the Island of Cuba and again, they suffered a devastating thrashing. Some of his forces fled to the Sierra Maestra Mountains, but Castro and a dozen or so of his supporters remained intact. During his second attempted overthrow, his military never grew to over a couple thousand strong, but his clever use of guerrilla tactics evened the score on the poorly trained Batista Army.

Guerrilla: one who engages in irregular warfare
Esp. as a member of an independent fighting unit.

Fidel Castro gave the true meaning to the phrase 'guerrilla war' in its scale, style, and scope and it lead to the Cuban revolution of 1956. Fidel Castro's second assault against the Cuban government which enjoyed the success of the largest military force in the Caribbean and Central America nations, landed on the tiny Cuban Island with an invasion force of just eighty two rebel followers strong soldiers who were stuffed into a small motor boat branded the 'Granma'. The poorly outfitted rebel invasion force landed on a sandy beach in the Oriente province. Fidel Castro's mighty invasion force was believed to have been betrayed from within, or his second military adventure had suffered drastically from such terrible luck. Batista's forces attacked the freedom fighters as they came to call themselves. Many of the young rebels were killed while still stationed on the beach by their small and still drifting assault boat in the surf of the waves.

The survivors suffered running attacks by the Batista forces until Castro's Army made it to the safety of the Sierra Mastra Mountains, in particular, the Pico Turquino Peak, and the highest point in the range. With twelve of his force still intact, Castro planned a counterattack on the Batista Administration. He declared his revolution a success once he had established his headquarters in the Mastra range. Using his fabulous military mind, coupled with his gift of gab and national pride, he drove the Cuban Dictator, Fulgencio Batista from office in less than two years time. Batista had been Cuba's dominant military force in the Presidency and out of office since the 1930s.

By 1957, Castro's military had grown to a staggering eighty fighters, many fighters were without any military training, and they were poorly armed with machetes or just sugar cane knives. The trees and valleys of the Sierra Maestra range, gave a natural protection for his small Army of rebels, protecting them from many of the attacks by Batista's Federal forces by land or air. Batista's soldiers were reluctant to enter the forest in search of the rebels.

This action allowed Castro's forces to hit many military and economic targets without being pursued, thus crippling the Batista government. His meager military accomplishments were broadcast over the rebel station 'Radio Rebelde' both day and night. Adding to Fidel Castro's growing strength, were the small networks who relayed news of Castro rebels, calling rebel sympathizers and malcontents, 'Bolas', who operated by spreading rumors through the lowlands of the Island. He turned his fighters from a thorn in the side, to a major threat to the second Batista Administration of Cuba.

In 1958, Raul Castro, Fidel's younger brother sent a second force of freedom fighters lead by an Argentine Doctor, Ernesto 'Che' Guevara. His orders were to attack selected prime targets scattered throughout the central sections of Cuba. This column of quick moving and hard hitting running revolutionaries, attacked substantial military and economic targets, completely paralyzing communication systems in the country, and engaging in minor hit and run battles with the Batista's forces.

Batista's Administration enjoyed major advantages over the Castro Revolutionaries. His Presidency had considerably more financial resources to draw from, and a very effective and outstanding secret police system, and his paramilitary forces were both well feared, and hated by all who lived on the beautiful Island Paradise. These forces easily penetrated some rebel cells operating in the country. The officers knew who the rebels were, and where they were hiding, but yet they were either unable, or unwilling to do much about their presence.

The Batista regime shared the general, if not the unwilling support of the present American government. Most of Batista's opposition lived in the major cities of Cuba, and they were ineffective as a serious threat to his government. The growing rebel forces were infiltrated by Batista's secret police force, and for the most part, they controlled the groups. Throughout Cuba, the anti-government faction was low. Only in Universities and the intellectual circles were the people able to understand Batista's true threat to Cuba, and they resented him for it.

Batista's Administration died more from within than from the outside pressures leveled against it by the meager forces of Castro. On January 1st, 1959, Batista was driven from the Presidency, and he fled Cuba. But he did not leave empty handed either. He took vast sums of valuables which added to the staggering wealth he successfully smuggled out of Cuba over his many years of his control, leaving the desperate forces of the revolution in undisputed control of Cuba and her citizens.

Once Fidel Castro realized Batista and many of his military forces had abandoned the Presidential Palace in Havana, and they also fled the country. Castro started the only true military action of his entire invasion. He attacked Santiago de Cuba, the main objective during his ill-fated raid on the Moncada Army Barracks. Castro left it up to his Generals to run the length and width of the Island, taking city after city under their control. Fidel Castro's revolutionary forces met with minor resistance in the larger cities before they finally fell to his rebel forces. His soldiers quickly wreaked their revenge upon their non-supporters until Castro's forces took over control of La Habana, the capital city of Cuba. By the time he moved from Santiago, the revolution was already over, and his rebel forces were victorious throughout most of the country.

The major importance of the Cuban Revolution did not lie in just the savagery usually found in most military struggles for freedom for their country. The war against Castro waged by the Batista military forces was very sporadic at best, with just a minuscule amount of military forces employed by either side against the other. The true revolution lay in the fulfillment of the dreams fostered by the Revolutionaries of the past times. The Castro rebels employing the safety offered to them by the impassable Sierra Maestra Mountains, began their Guerrilla warfare attacks, and these new tactics created a fascinating new beginning to waging wars of the future. Just a small group of ill equipped, non-military trained peasants, now calling themselves soldiers of freedom, used guerrilla tactics by fighting numerous and hard hitting and disappearing attacks on the defending troops, slowly wore down their counterparts, and rapidly encumbering their enemy's ability to wage a successful war against the small rebel forces on the Island of Cuba.

Fidel Castro's rebels soon began to act like well trained soldiers, forced to fight their war for freedom from the terrain unfavorable to them. But it was instrumental in hampering their enemy's capability of counter attacking them. This enabled the rebels to survive many battles where they were heavily outnumbered, and it attracted countless new soldiers to their romantic cause. These new bands of rebels were soon able to defeat the staggering Federal forces of the Batista regime. The rebels further enjoyed feelings of a just cause given to them by the depressed civilians of the tiny Island. He delighted in all the backing of other Latin American nations that were sympathetic to his beliefs, and the freeing of the Cuban citizens arrested by the corrupt Batista regime, added to the strength of Castro and his band of rebel's fame.

After a two year long struggle during Castro's second overthrow attempt of Batista, his small Army finally forced Batista to flee the country. Castro's acquiescence to power was not without any true bloodletting. Once he had assumed the Presidency, he used this new found power to execute Ministers, and some political followers of the Batista regime who had not backed his revolution, and his bid for power over the Island of Cuba.

Castro was merciless in dealing with all those he wished to visit his revenge upon, for their non-support of his takeover bid of Cuba. Many of Batista's backers were arrested in the middle of the night, and forcibly removed from their homes, and then they were never seen again by any of their loved ones. Castro's revenge included the families of his enemies arrested for no reason, and silently disappeared into the jail cells which were fast becoming overcrowded by the ones being detained. Castro usurped his power by eliminating certain elected officers of the previous government, and then he appointed his followers to the vacated positions. These actions were geared for one thing and one thing only, to galvanize his complete control over the Presidency of Cuba and her people.

Fidel Castro

Once Fidel Castro had assumed complete control over the Island of Cuba on January 1st, 1959, he revealed to his people and the rest of the world, just how mean spirited his future political system would be. The once beauty of Cuba was quickly transformed into a Communist satellite, removing many freedoms and enjoyments of its people. Forgotten was any thought of restoring the old Cuban Constitution of 1940. Fidel Castro cared little for what he believed to be the meaningless people of Cuba, and the oppressing stresses that weighed heavily upon the shoulders of the poor. Instead, the new leaders of Castro's revolution quickly closed ranks until they finally became known as the Elite Revolution Family, and Castro's comrades in arms soon ruled over all of Cuba and her people with an iron grip like no other in Cuba's stormy past history.

Fidel Castro's revolutionary government confiscated many properties the rebels felt were illegally acquired under the past corrupt Batista Administration. He also sought to resolve Cuba's present problems concerning himself with the well off, than the poor of Cuba by beginning with inflation and trade, by implementing radical new programs to the system. He made it hard for the poor to get any proper medical treatment, and he also made it impossible for them to receive any monetary aide such as welfare, and state aid. He made it harder for the less fortunate of Cuba to attend any university, or secondary school systems. Many of his ideas forced Cuba's youth, both male and female alike, into lives of severe degradation and prostitution, and it helped eroded the once great systems that were installed to make the lives of Cuba's people better for living.

The Castro revolution shared some success though in diversifying the rather shaky economy of the tiny Island country. His most notable accomplishment was the rapid expansion of the fishing industry of Cuba. Helping this expansion grow was the construction of seaports to handle the fleet of fishing boats and their trade. Nevertheless, the inability of the Castro government to develop a working socialist economic system, fueled by his attempt to break any and all ties with the United State, stole some of his power from him. The failure of Castro to break free of the dregs of a stagnated monoculture economy increased his steady draw towards the Russian sphere of influence over the Island of Cuba.

After June of 1960, relations between the United States and Cuba suffered many setbacks and deteriorated at an accelerated pace. This occurred as a retaliatory action against Castro's decision to nationalize over two billion dollars of the United States civilian owned factories and properties spread throughout the Island of Cuba. After many fruitless meetings held between the two governments the United States sever all relations with the revolutionary government of Castro. Tensions further increased when Castro took steps towards dealing with the Communist nations. Adding to the mounting tension was the decision of Castro to nationalize, and then takeover the three major United States oil refineries constructed on the small Island. He used the excuse the oil companies refused to process any Russian crude oil. The United

States had no other choice but to react further by eliminating Cuba's sugar quotas. This dealt a devastating blow to Cuba's main money maker, their sugar cane crops.

On December 1st, 1961, Fidel Castro stunned many of the nations of the world by announcing he was now a true follower of Marx-Leninist beliefs, and he was one with the socialist world and their way of life. His stunning announcements continued, he further declared Cuba, and all who lived under his leadership, were now part of a socialist country. He continued shocking the world by declaring all major means of food production on the Island, every commercial industry including the powerful fishing industry, and all distribution, importing and the communication systems, along with all forms of transportation and government services were now nationalized by his order. This action virtually removed any and all free enterprise from the country, and it condemned all to a dual class system of the very rich, and the very poor of Cuba.

Fidel Castro was determined to establish Cuba's independence from the much hated United States' influence. The nationalization of America's holdings inside Cuba was only the beginning. He began a campaign to export his revolutionary ways to other Latin American countries of the world, in order to bring them under the growing influence of Communism. Cuban and United States relations were on a head on collision course of hatred and dispute. Growing concerns over the rapidly worsening relationships between the United States and Cuba, and Castro's many fears of an American retaliation mounted against his Administration, forced him to lean more towards Russia for further aid, both financially and militarily.

The ever increasing dependency of Castro's Cuba on the Soviet Union, and the attempt of the Castro government to put a revolutionary fever in the usually stable Latin American governments of South America, ended the United States patience, and his actions forced the United States to react rather harshly against the revolutionary government of the tiny Island.

On January 3rd, 1961, the United States broke off all diplomatic ties with Cuba. America went one step further by imposing a stifling trade embargo on Cuba and her people, and threatening to retaliate against any allies who dared to have anything to do with this small rebel country. The United States moved rapidly in its attempt to further isolate this rebellious control of state, and a thorn in the side of the present American government, by taking her complaint to the OAS (Organization of American States). America attempted to separate Cuba both politically and economically from the other Latin American and non-Communist nations. All North and South American nations were encouraged to stop dealing with Cuba. Some of them were threatened with sanctions by the United States, in an attempt to break diplomatic ties with Castro and Cuba.

All of these moves forced Castro to react even harsher with the other Latin American countries of the world. He quickly turned his attention to destabilizing the weaker Central and South America countries. His idea was to make these weaker nations ripe for revolution. In late 1967, Castro's great General Che Guevara, was killed in a military action while assisting in an attempted overthrow of the present Bolivian government. With the well liked General's death, the collapse of the other revolutions inside Bolivia was quickly realized by Castro and the world. The United States attempt to isolate Cuba was equally as unsuccessful. The OAS suspended Cuba from the organization in 1962, but in July of 1975 the Latin America Commission passed the Freedom of Action resolution, allowing any country to deal economically with Cuba if they so choose to do so.

America's plans to dislodge the Castro regime by force were set in motion in 1960, during the later part of the Eisenhower Administration. It was President Eisenhower who broke off all diplomatic relations with Cuba, and he imposed harsh trade embargoes on Cuba on January 3rd, 1961. March 14th, 1960, President Eisenhower authorized the organization, and the military training and equipping of a large number of Cuban refugees who were forced to flee Cuba, when Castro came to power over the Island nation. He further authorized the mobilization of the Special Forces units stationed at Fort Bragg.

Twenty seven soldiers from the 7th Group were requested by the CIA to begin the training of the so called Cuban Brigade up to snuff. The Secretary of the Army and the CIA did not exactly agree on the impending invasion of Cuba which was given the code name Operation Zapata. So the Army did everything in its power in an attempt to slow down the invasion of the tiny Cuban country. The CIA reacted by going to the President and complaining at him, but he sent the Special Forces to Homestead Florida to train Cuban exiles. Other soldiers were also sent to Guatemala, where they set up a base in Helvetia that was a coffee plantation in the Sierra Madre Mountains. There the Special Forces soldiers trained seventeen hundred Cubans fighters to attack Fidel Castro's troops in Cuba.

After John F. Kennedy won the Presidential election, he was immediately briefed on all of the past Administration's dealing with the Cuban rebel leader. The newly elected President followed through with the past Administration's policies concerning the Cuban troublemaker. President Kennedy's opening salvo aimed at the revolutionary government of Cuba was fired on April 3rd, 1961 with the publication of a thirty six page special report on Cuba. In it, President John F. Kennedy condemned Castro for betraying its revolutionary beliefs, and he further urged Castro to break off their relations with the Communist movement of the Soviet Union. Unrealized by either of the past and present American Administrations, they actually forced Castro more towards the Communists. If America had tried to deal with Castro with the respect due him, then it was doubtful he would have even gone over to the Communist beliefs in the first place.

President Kennedy carried on with the ex-President Eisenhower's policies and he sent the Special Forces out to setup a communications network stationed at Eglin Air Force Base in Florida as the command center for the upcoming operation. The soldiers were instrumental in training the Cuban exiles in guerrilla warfare tactics, and in the use of automatic weapons. The original plan was for the Cuban exiles and Special Forces soldiers to infiltrate Cuba, and then linkup with the anti-Castro fighters in the country, and then secure land to be used as airports for supplying the Cuban fighters on the Island.

Castro resented President Kennedy's efforts to force him to make decisions in America's favor, and he replied to the report by leveling his own contemptuous attacks on the United States. Castro's remarks only served to widen the gap rapidly growing between the two countries, and it gave President Kennedy the resolve to continue with its adopted campaign to ouster Fidel Castro from Cuba. While the rhetoric was flowing, President Kennedy uses his time to secretly unite two hundred anti-Castro refugee organizations. On, or about March 31st, 1961, the organizations formed into the Cuban Revolutionary Council, and they elected Doctor Jose Mire Cordon to lead the Council in their attempt to ouster Fidel Castro and his Administration.

On April 8th, 1961, the so called Cuba Revolutionary Council released its first war dispatch, where they called upon all free Cubans to rise up and overthrow this Devil in Paradise, the Castro regime destroying their country of Cuba, and making it a Communist puppet of Russia. The Council also let it be known to the world they had no plans whatsoever to try and invade Cuba. Instead, they merely announced they were going to engage in multiple attacks by the refugee Council, and those who were trapped in Cuba. The Council further suggested the revolutionaries turn the tables on Fidel Castro and his government, and use his own tactics against him this time, guerrilla warfare. The Council further let it be known they would coordinate their present activities with many of the underground factions still operating inside Cuba, and to enlist their aid and organize resistance against Castro and his followers.

The CIA received the go ahead from President John F. Kennedy, and they went in action. Under Kennedy's orders, they talked the Cuban Revolutionary Council members into invading Cuba. But the talks between the CIA and the CRC were not conducted on a top secret level, so many of their plans were beset with leaks. Reports published in major newspapers throughout the United States and Latin America countries, stated the upcoming military actions were to be carried out by the CRC refugees operating in southern America. These leaks forced President Kennedy to respond to the speculation of an impending invasion of Cuba. Kennedy held his first press conference since taking office on April 12th, 1961, where he announced under no circumstances would the United States aid, nor agreed with any military intervention that might be carried out by anyone against the Castro government. He also assured the world the United States would never land on Cuba, or to take an active hand in an attempted ouster of Castro.

Despite the statements coming from Kennedy, on April 15th, 1961, sixteen hundred well armed Cuban exiles were transported from their training base in Central America. The exiles commonly referred to as freedom fighters, were transported in the outdated American merchant ships, and they were scheduled to land on the southern central tip of Cuba. This Cuban invasion force was being escorted by United States destroyers, along with an aircraft carrier shadowing the small convoy in case their support was needed in a fast hurry.

The CRC's invasion force was scheduled to land at Plata Giron at a secluded bay called Bahia de Cochinas, or the Bay of Pigs. Bahia de Cochinas was bordered to the east by the great Cienaga de Zapata swamp situated on the southern coast of the Les Villis province. Matanzas province was situated to the west of the supposed landing site, and it was skirted by the Peninsula de Zapata, and shallow waters. But before the small invasion force was to land on Cuba, the exiles were trained to pilot their own attack aircraft, and they were to hit Megar Castro airfield with American B-26 bombers. Their plan was to destroy the Castro airforce while still on the ground, opening the door for the invasion force to get a good foothold on the tiny Island of Cuba.

But, things went seriously wrong, and before the Cuban pilots launched their opening attack, Kennedy got cold feet and he canceled the air strikes. This drastic change of events left the Castro airforce intact. The Cuban government was also able to track the invasion force with the use of spies and a fleet of small fishing boats, since the American ships left the Central American port. When it was reported to Castro the invasion ships were nearing the Island, and they were within striking distance of their planes, he sent out his airforce. The nine planes Castro had in his airforce scheduled for destruction by American aircraft, attacked instead, and they successfully sank two of the invasion ships before they were even able to off load any of the ammunition and supplies so desperately needed by the freedom fighters on the tiny Island.

Before the exiled invasion force support ships arrived in the waters off Cuba, Cuban exile paratroopers were air dropped inland from the proposed backup landing site to secure the area. They were twenty four miles from the nearest city, and they were surrounded by swamp, and poor roads. Castro had at his disposal two hundred thousand volunteer fighters, and twenty thousand well trained soldiers armed with automatic Soviet weapons and ammunition. The Castro Army was being supported by fifty Soviet tanks and self propelled artillery pieces.

When Castro was certain the hated exile force was on land, he committed his forces to battle them. But before his tanks arrived on the supposed battlefield, the refugee invasion force was already cut off from any help or supplies. The exiles suffered from exhaustion and lack of ammunition and no communication with any support troops on the ships already sunk by Castro's airforce. The ships stationed off the coast of Cuba and scheduled to extract the exiled invaders if anything went wrong, were unable to communicate with the invasion force either.

Heavily outnumbered, and trapped by superior Cuban forces and with their ammunition rapidly running out on them, and without anymore back up forces. There was nothing for the already beaten exile fighters to do but to surrender to the Castro fighters. All the fighting on the tiny Island ceased by 5:30 p.m. on April 19th, 1961, seventy two hours after the sixteen hundred man invasion force had touched down on Cuba's soil. The invaders lost four hundred fighters killed or missing in the great swamp. Missing exile fighters were spotted running deeper into the oppressive swamp, never to be seen again by the living. There were one thousand four hundred freedom fighters taken prisoner by Castro's military. It was reported Castro bragged about his forces suffering only eighty dead, and some two hundred of his soldiers wounded in the battle.

Castro marched the humiliated exile prisoners' through the streets of every village they passed on the way to the prison in Havana. There, the civilians cursed and threw stones and garbage at the prisoners. Castro's first statement on the invasion by these American backed Cuban refugees came on May 17th, 1961. After an hour of America bashing, Castro finally got down to his business at hand. He offered the American government the thousand plus exile prisoners in trade for medical supplies, cash and some farm machinery. Kennedy felt he owed the prisoners their freedom, and he allowed private concerns to organize the requested materials, and he gave his permission for the trade to go through without a hitch.

Shortly after Fidel Castro had the Cuban troublemakers removed from his Island, he next turned his attention towards the Catholic Church. He opened his attacks on the Church by invalidating a religious procession, and then he expanded his assault on the Church by deporting over one hundred and thirty Roman Catholic priests on the 17th of September. Castro further announced on the 19th that all further public religious processions were now prohibited on his Island of Cuba. These proclamations caused nationwide demonstrations by the mostly Catholic population of Cuba, with the largest taking place in Havana itself. Over four thousand Cuban citizens took part in a massive demonstration that lasted most of the day.

Countless arrests and executions of counter revolutionary organizations continued without pause on the Island of Cuba, reaching their full height after the invasion of Cuba by the so called freedom fighters from America. Castro used this as an excuse to rid his country of those who did not see eye to eye with him and his rule. He widened his attack on those he considered troublemakers in his country, by declaring physicians, technicians, engineers and professionals who fled Cuba, would lose their citizenship and they would not be permitted to return to Cuba under his regime. He also included all government employees who sought political asylum in other countries, and he classified them as non-Cuban residents. Vast amounts of Cuban refugees poured into the United States in an effort to avoid Castro's wrath or worse, death.

Castro, ever being the politician he was, seized on the moment and he appealed to the Soviet Union. He used his anti-American stance to request military supplies in an effort to repel any further American attacks on his Island. He was assured the Communists were coming. The Soviet Union complied with his requests, seizing on the moment and the possibility of turning Cuba, situated so close to the United States mainland, into a massive Soviet military base.

Premier Nikita Khrushchev was not interested in Castro or his rule over the Island. He was more interested in establishing a Soviet satellite nation, and a strong military base close to the United States, his prime enemy. Nikita Sergeyevich Khrushchev saw his chance to narrow the missile gap that presently existed between the United States and Russia. After many discussions with Castro, he struck a deal with the rebel Cuban leader where he would supply Cuba with rifles, machine guns, tanks, artillery pieces and thirty Mig jet fighters, along with a number of attack helicopters. Premier Khrushchev commenced to flood Cuba with the military supplies, including nuclear tipped long range and intermediate range ballistic missiles.

Unbeknownst to the Kennedy Administration, or the rest of the world for that matter, the Soviet Union supplied Cuba with twenty four SA-2 SAM missile systems for air defense over the Cuban Island, and five SSM cruise missile systems for the same purposes. Premier Khrushchev also sent hundreds of Russian military advisors and construction engineers to help aid Castro's workers in the construction of two gun patrol boat bases, along with building Mig airfields to accept the three wings of Mig 21s Premier Khrushchev already set for delivery to the Cuban Island. The Russian leader also transferred a number of Russian ground battalions to these bases which he was constructing on the Island.

To help better defend them from any American led attacks by either air or land. Two Il-28 troop jet bomber airfields were also constructed on the Island. When most of these military defense bases were constructed, Premier Khrushchev gave his blessing for the construction of six medium range nuclear tipped, ballistic missile sites, and three intermediate range nuclear tipped, ballistic missile sites on Cuban soil. The United States never realized how long the Russian and Cuban workers worked on the missile bases, nor did it know when the first of these nuclear tipped missile systems were delivered to Cuba by Russia.

However, the Kennedy Administration picked up the intelligence on the rapid Soviet arms buildup inside Cuba through their monthly U-2 flights over the tiny Caribbean Island. More information came by means of the United States Navy and the Coast Guard, who were conducting operations in the Caribbean area at the present time. As more information on the military buildup dribbled in, President Kennedy sent out other inquires. More reports flooded in from Marine observation posts on many of the Russian merchant vessels heading towards the Island of Cuba.

Turkey was also instrumental in helping Kennedy accumulate the much needed information on Cuba's strong military buildup, by allowing United States ships stationed there, to observe and even photograph the many passing Russian flagged ships. The Sixth Fleet Carrier launched countless recon flights, taking photographs of Russian, and other Eastern Block flagged vessels sailing through the Bosporus Straits, and the Mediterranean Sea.

Other information gathering systems were pressed into action by President Kennedy. Naval air patrols based in Naval Station in Bermuda and also many air flights carried out by the Naval Air Station constructed in Jacksonville, Florida, began daily flights over any Russian ships as they approached Cuba. Photographing them, Navy intelligence quickly analyzed the pictures of the cargo, identifying just what type of military supplies was presently being sent to the Island of Cuba. Other sources of information were coming in through the American Intelligence Agents operating covertly inside Cuba itself, friendly foreign nations who had active Embassies in Cuba and American and foreign journalists helped. These groups accumulated the needed information on the Russia activity in Cuba, and they quickly passed it on to the American government.

Upon analyzing this new information on Cuba, Kennedy authorized an increase in U-2 flights over Cuba. On October 14th, 1961, the so called 'Milk Run' flights of the U-2's started in earnest. After hours of scrutiny of the pictures, this milk run flight turned out to be an intelligence coup. Kennedy now had in his hands, clear pictures that depicted Soviet made SS-4 MRBMs (Medium Range Ballistic Missiles) of offensive capability just ninety miles from the shores of the United States. The Secretary of Defense took the lead and he ordered more U-2 flights, along with low level reconnaissance flights flown by American fighters. On October 14th, 1962, photo reconnaissance aircraft noted Soviet military personnel constructing missile bases on the Island. This sounded the alarm in Washington, forcing Kennedy to react. More photos showing the Soviet made SS-5 Shean IRBM missiles had also arrived on the Cuban soil.

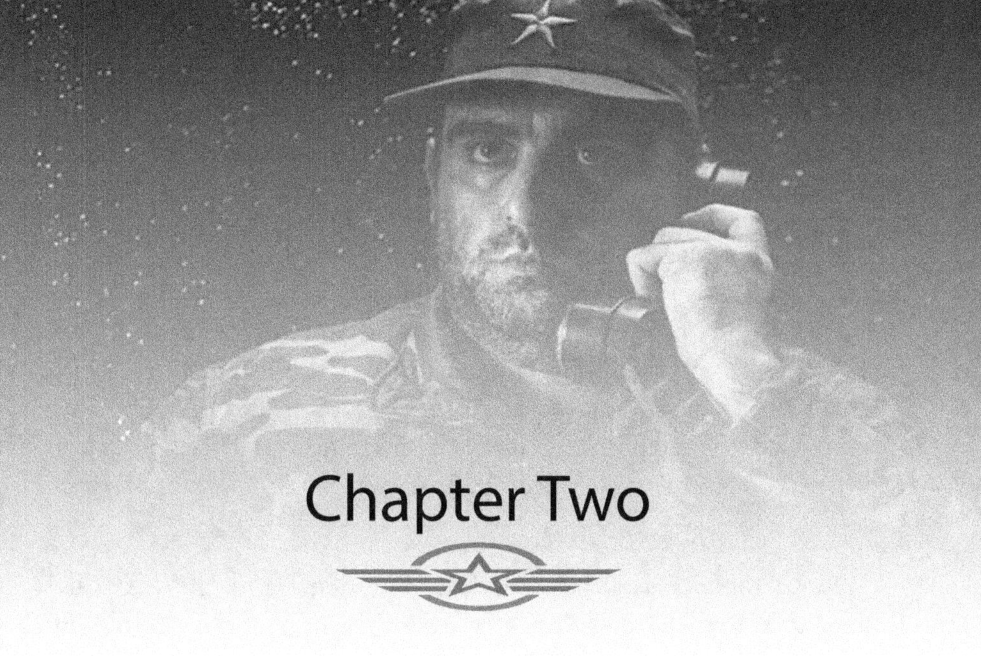

Chapter Two

At an emergency meeting between Kennedy and the rest of his security advisors and cabinet members, was being held on October 18th, 1962. Pictures clearly showing missile launch sites for two IRBM's, which were more accurate and powerful than the much longer range, but far less accurate MRBM (Medium Range Ballistic Missile) site under construction at San Critobal inside Cuba. Six MRBM sites were also located in the photos, and Kennedy held further meetings with his Joint Chief of Staff and cabinet. On the 18th, President John Kennedy met with the Soviet Ambassador and Soviet Foreign Minister, where he repeated his warning of September, and the Soviet Foreign Minister assured the American President that Russia had not and never would ever introduce any offensive nuclear weapons on the Island of Cuba.

President Kennedy realized any further conversations with the Soviet Union or the Cuban representatives were useless, and he ordered military forces to a higher alert status, Defcon Four. The USS Aircraft Carrier Enterprise sailed from Norfolk, Virginia on October 19th. Reports stated the reason for her departure was to avoid the rapidly approaching Hurricane Ella. Over the next few days, the Picket Destroyers DDR-714 William R. Rush, DDR-873 Hawkins and DDR-Fiske left Mayport, Florida, to join forces with the carrier group and her other Naval support ships. On October 20th, the Navy ships formed up to make Task Force 135, America's first line of defense against Cuba.

To further drive the point home to the Russian and Castro governments that President Kennedy was not just issuing idle threats here, he had the Joint Chiefs of Staff alert the American strategic forces, including SAC and the ICBMs missile forces of the airforce, along with the ballistic missile submarine fleet. Other Airforce and selected Army units moved to staging areas, to better prepare to battle the Soviets. Marine Corps units were called up, and they were prepared to invade Cuba.

On October 20th, the American President, and the EXCOM leaders answered the question of what to do next about the rapidly approaching Soviet ships. President Kennedy orders the Navy to stop, and then board any Russian ships believed to be transporting illegal offensive weapons to Cuba. These ships were called Task Force 136. The Base in Guantanamo Bay, Cuba, was strengthened with a flood of personnel and military equipment, including tanks and aircraft.

At Nineteen Hundred Hours on October 20th, 1962, American military units were moved up to Condition Defcon Three. Polaris submarines moved to their launch points throughout the world. SAC prepared to launch one hundred ICBM missiles slaved to hit targets stationed in the Soviet Union and other Eastern Bloc nations. President Kennedy appeared on TV and shared with the public the evidence he had accumulated on what the Soviet Union and the government of Cuba had been up to in Cuba. Kennedy also condemned all Soviet denials about the presence of any offensive nuclear tipped missiles in Cuba, and he considered the presence of these missiles to be a direct threat to the security of the entire Western Hemisphere. He announced he was instigating what was referred to as a strict quarantine on all military shipments to Cuba. The President further warned the Soviet Union any missile fired on a country in the Americas from Cuba, would be considered a direct attack on the United States by Russia, and it would result in a full scale retaliatory strike against the Soviet Union by all United States forces at hand.

When the American President's speech was broadcast worldwide, both Russia and Cuba immediately increased their alert status. The Organization of American States instantly backed the American government's stance, and Canadian and the British forces joined the defense of the Western Hemisphere. On October 23rd, President John F. Kennedy announced a quarantine of Cuba would commence at exactly Ten Hundred Hours on the 24th. He warned all international shipping to avoid the area in question until further notice, or risk being sunk on sight.

The day after the warning was issued by the American President, twenty six Soviet and Eastern Bloc ships heavily laden down with covered military supplies resting on their decks, were inside the line drawn across the Atlantic water by the American President the day before. The Soviet freighter, Leninsky Komsomol, was singled out by the United States Navy as the first test to the embargo, and the American Cruiser Newport News, and her two Sister Destroyer ships were ordered to intercept the Russian merchantman ships. The American forces were ordered to stop and board the Russian freighter, permission to use deadly force was issued. A second Russian freighter, the Kimovsk was also targeted by United States Naval ships, and the Guided Missile Cruiser Canberra, was dispatched to intercept this second Russian freighter.

By the afternoon of the 24th of October, it was clear to the American Navy the sixteen Soviet ships once heading for Cuba, were now stopped dead in the water while waiting to see what would develop next between the American Navy and their country. One Soviet ship continued through the blockade though, it was the Russian tanker Bucharest, and she slowed and identify herself to the American Destroyer Gearing, who was demanding her classification. The Bucharest allowed herself to be photographed and inspected by the American warship.

On October 25th, tensions increased more when at the emergency meeting of the United Nations. The Soviet Ambassador to the United Nations demanded the American Ambassador produced any and all proof of their complaints being aired at the meeting. Ambassador Adlai Stevenson replied by saying to the Soviet Ambassador. "Do you Ambassador Zorin, deny the Union of Soviet Socialist Republic has placed, and is in the process of placing both medium and intermediate range nuclear tipped missiles, and is in the process of constructing the launch sites for these said missiles inside Cuba at present time?" Ambassador Stevenson did not allow the Russian politician a chance to think his answer through, as he suddenly barked at him in a harsh tone. "Yes or no---Don't wait for the translation, you know what I have said---yes or no sir!"

Ambassador Zorin promised to answer later, but Ambassador Stevenson snapped he was prepared to wait until hell froze over if needed. The American Ambassador produced enlarged photographs to the members, showing the Soviet activity and deception on Cuban soil.

Late in the evening of the 25th of October, there was a stopping of a Russian merchantman freighter heading for Cuba by an American Destroyer. This move demonstrated to the world, and especially to Russia, America's resolve on this matter. The Lebanese flagged freighter Marcula signaled as planes from the Essex located the Lebanese ship sailing on the open ocean, and the American Destroyers John R. Pierce and the Joseph P. Kennedy rapidly closed in on her last reported position. In the early hours of October 26th, the USS Kennedy ordered the Marcula to heave too which she complied immediately with the order. Upon close inspection, everything was found to be in proper order and she was allowed to continue for Cuba.

The United States-Soviet confrontation came to a head on October 27th, 1962 with the Soviet tanker Groznyy. The United States thought Moscow was intending to test the line. The Groznyy failed to respond to an American Destroyer's orders to heave to. The United States ship had live ammunition loaded in their five inch guns, and orders were received to clear the guns by means of firing the rounds into the sea well away from the Russian tanker. The rounds fired were more than enough of a warning to force the Russian tanker to stop. Groznyy put about and then she headed away from the quarantine line, and the American ships waiting to intercept her. President Kennedy was further rocked on Saturday, October 27th, when a U-2 spy plane was shot down over Cuba, killing the pilot. This action informed the United States the SAM missile sites inside Cuba were operational now. Talk shifted to an all out invasion of the tiny Island of Cuba.

Russia tried to muddy up the waters even more by demanding if America remove her nuclear tipped missiles aimed at Russia from Turkey, they would in return remove all missiles from the Cuban country. This was immediately rejected outright by the American government, but a climax was seen looming on the horizon. Hopes were lessened though with the reports a second U-2 flight had been shot down over Russian airspace.

Requests were made to President Kennedy by his general staff to begin the air strikes already set up to pound Cuba on October 29th, and then, seven days later, for America to launch an all out invasion of Cuba, and forcibly destroy the missiles constructed on the Island. Kennedy rejected this request, and had his brother Robert, meet with the Soviet Ambassador, and he respond to Russia's first offer, for the United States to pledge not to invade Cuba, and in return, Russia would remove her missiles from Cuba. But President Kennedy did order units of the Special Forces to prepare to be sea dropped in Cuba by means of submarines, with orders to destroy as many of the twenty three operational SAM missile sites as possible, before the main invasion forces arrived. Kennedy hoped enough of the missile sites would be destroyed to give our aircraft a fair chance to destroy the missiles in Cuba, before any were launched at the United States.

Robert Kennedy forced the issue further by demanding an immediate response by the Soviets. If no response was forthcoming, the American government was prepared to go into Cuba and remove the missiles forcibly from the Island herself. Attorney General Robert Kennedy left the Soviet Ambassador without a commitment from him.

On Sunday, October 28th, 1962, the full might of the armed services of the United States were prepared for any crises. Soviet and Cuban forces were equally prepared and the world held its breath and waited for the shoe to fall. Unknown to United States forces, stockpiled in Cuba were tactical nuclear warheads for the Lunas or Frog missiles. The Soviet commander of Cuba was authorized to use the short range weapons to beat back any attempted invasion of Cuba.

As the world waited while holding their breath, a communiqué suddenly arrived in Washington at Zero, Nine Hundred Hours EDT on

October 28th, from the Soviet Union. The beginning paragraph made it quite clear Premier Khrushchev had accepted President Kennedy's solution. The power of the Russian Bear had blinked, and with that blink, the likelihood of a global nuclear war had quickly ended. In the days that followed, the dismantling of the missiles and anti defense missile systems commenced by the same Russian technicians who installed them on Cuban soil. All Soviet personnel prepared to leave Cuba, taking with them the military equipment they brought to the Cuban country. The world believed all missiles and nuclear warheads were removed from the Island at this time. Even though America kept a close eye on everything taking place on Cuba, Fidel Castro keep a secret from the ever prying eyes of the Americans. This secret would come back to haunt America in the distant future.

Unknown to the rest of the world, units of the Special Forces did land secretly in Cuba during the threat, but they were extracted before going operational on the Island during the missile crisis. The American soldiers operated under the code name Operation White Swan Three.

The second decade of revolution in Cuba witnessed the Castro government become even more deeply entrenched as an active member of the Soviet Bloc nations, with Castro publicly supporting the Russian invasion of Czechoslovakia in 1968. The Soviet Union takeover of Cuba was fast becoming pronounced, with the Communist party growing in both power and strength over the tiny Caribbean Island nation. Soviet and Eastern Bloc technicians arrived on Cuban soil, sharpening Castro's military might for the Cuban leader, while Castro sent his military Officers off to Russia to receive special training by elite Russian soldiers of that country.

The Soviet Union employed a number of troops from Cuba to fight many of her dirty little wars raging inside Africa for Russia's sake and desires, who had no intention of getting involved in a war much like the United States suddenly found herself trapped in. Vietnam.

The Cuban military success in Angola caused President Fidel Castro to offer her military assistance to the country of Ethiopia, in her constant and continuing conflict with the nation of Somalia. Cuba's rapid expansion was Russia's expansion in many of the African nations as well, and it continued with thousands of Cuban troops showing up in the Horn of Africa region. Smaller numbers of highly trained Cuban and Soviet technicians also started to appear in other African nations such as Mozambique to the south, and to the north inside Libya.

Cuban's relations with many of the other Latin America nations were having a much more difficult time of it though. The revolution raging in Nicaragua, along with the civil war taking place in El Salvador, quickly forced the world's attention on the small Central American nations now. Cuba was supporting the revolutionary government of Nicaragua, until it fell during the elections of 1990 when the Sandinistas lost the Presidency and their power in that country as well.

Fidel Castro's government was dealt its biggest blow to his leadership since first coming to power over the tiny Island of Cuba with the complete and total collapse of the Soviet Union. The rapid and most unsuspected demise of Russia resulted in the total cutoff of all Cuba's economic and military aid from that once mighty Communist nation. Castro heavily relied on these funds during his many years of his control over Cuba and her people. Despite many of the new movements in reforms of the current and former Communist governments, Castro had remained steadfast to the beliefs of his revolution.

His answer to the countless problems presently facing his leadership and country, was to blame the United States and the present Administration, and the continuing trade and necromantic embargo, rather than blaming some of his own shortcomings, or on his own failed governmental programs for the problems currently facing Cuba and her people. Castro blamed the United States for waging bacteriological and chemical warfare on the citizens of Cuba.

He also found it much easy to blame the country of America, just some ninety miles to his north, for everything that had befallen his once beautiful Caribbean country. From the outbreak of the African Swine fever on the Island, to the sugar cane rust, and he even blamed the United States for the tobacco mold blight attacking much of his country. He even went so far as to accuse the United States of causing the drought that was presently plaguing his nation.

Since Castro and his rebels rise to power on Cuba, three quarters of a million Cubans fled their country in search of their own private freedoms, mostly to southern Florida. The dreams of a Castro free Cuba dominated their thoughts every second of the day. Castro tried many different ways to force a quick end to the American trade embargo, except to allow free elections to happen in his country. He assaulted the United States with the influx of raft people. One could not understand how any leader of a country, could possibly sit by and allow so many of the people he was supposed to represent and protect, to sail off from the safety of his shores in shark infested waters on rafts barely able to float, during the great Maril boat lifts. The daring attempts of these proud and brave Cuban people displayed to the rest of the world the terrible living conditions taking place on the tiny Island under which the peoples of Cuba live.

Many of Cuba's children were forced into prostitution which was the only door left open to them to enable them to survive under the terrible conditions they live through on the beautiful Island of Cuba. The dreaded and well feared curse of AIDS ran unchecked throughout the tiny Island, and it was also adding to the hopelessness and desperation of the youth and poor of Cuba. Under Castro's misguided leadership, the once proud Pearl of the Antilles, had lost its beautiful luster, and only the Devil of Paradise was laughing at his people from the Presidential Palace in Havana. He was also laughing at the peoples of the world, because he knew in his heart he would never make peace with the United States, and he was going to further continue his attacks on all the Presidents who would lead America in the future.

His blind hatred for the United States, and all she stood for in the world, caused the once great military mind of Castro to be clouded over, and cause him to make mistakes while ruling over Cuba. Although he had always regretted his experience with the Russians and their military advisors who he had held in utter distain ever since the Cuban/United States missile crisis of 1962. For years now, President Fidel Castro cursed himself for the one true mistake he believed he committed in his military life, by aligning himself and his country so closely with Moscow and the Communist beliefs. He was far from being anything but a smart man with an extremely sharp and fast thinking mind. But as smart as he was, he did make his own mistakes though, and the missile crisis always made him sad because of the terrible affect it had on the relations between the two countries who were so close to each other.

Castro was further angered because he had General Che speak secretly to members of the Kennedy Administration, and he ordered Che to offer the United States everything they were demanding from him. The members Che spoke to refuse the offer that would have surely ended the hard feeling growing between the two nation, and it would have further turned the situation in Cuba around, and together, Castro and Kennedy would have gotten along.

Fidel Castro's relationship with the Soviet Union came to a crashing halt in the year of 1993, with the demise of the Russian political system, and the takeover by leaders willing to entertain such suggestions by the United States to eliminate the Communist beliefs, and to allow the Russian civilians to enjoy some freedom.

Cuban President Fidel Castro was extremely upset with his former ally for abandoning the Communist beliefs, and he became belligerent in his dealings to the new way of Russian thinking. He even tried to actually force the Soviets to continue with the programs it had supported through the good years. He would not buy the fact that Russia could no longer support Cuba or her people, and Castro's unwavering beliefs in the Communist ways no longer interested, nor concerned the new Soviet leadership. He ended up fighting openly with President Gorbachev, and the Russian President was so taken back with the upstart Castro, that he had even less and less to do with the argumentative and aged Cuban dictator.

Fidel Castro was relieved and he was supported by President Gorbachev's loss to Boris Yeltsin in the latest Soviet elections, but his illusion of the situation returning to the good old ways of the past, was quickly dashed with the first meeting held between the two leaders of the Communist nations. President Yeltsin informed Fidel Castro in no uncertain terms that he was going to cut back even more on many of Cuba's military supplies, and his monetary support of Castro's government. President Yeltsin asked, and when this did not get a response from Castro. He then demand the Cuban leader make preparations for the repayment of the nearly thirty billion dollars which Cuba owed to the Soviet Union for their passed services and military equipment dealings.

Castro was beside himself, and his anger showed in his reaction when dealing with the new Soviet President. The anger demonstrated by the aged Revolutionary President, caused the Russian politicians to grow extremely impatient with their belligerent and old ally, and his deeply entrenched and foolish ideals of world conquest, and the old ways of life and control.

The Soviet government's lack of concern for Castro's small Island fortress, and his unpredictable leadership, made the Cuban dictator grow more aggressive towards Russia. Eventually it caused him to even threaten to disallow any further relations between Cuba and Russia. Castro went over the edge with his rage, and he even dared to threaten the new Yeltsin government with more attempted intimidation, forcing the Russians to removing from his Island their hidden secret that has been long buried under the sands of the Island since the Communist heydays of 1960s. The latest threat from Castro caused members of the Russian Parliament to refer to him as the Mad Dog of the Caribbean. His new warnings so angered the present Russian President, until he was finally forced to offer to remove the particulars from years past from his tiny Island. From that day forward, President Yeltsin decided there would be no further shipments of goods or military supplies sent to the small Caribbean Island.

It did not take Castro very long to realize his government was now completely cut off from their main supporter and the cash and supplies their relationship once provided to the rebel leader. Castro's world of Paradise soon became a nightmare for him. In order to make ends meet, he discontinued many of his social programs. He also cut back most of the monies to offices of the government and military, and he had to bleed the outer provinces dry, to keep the capital city running. He did his best to increase tourism to his nation, by forcing many of the hotels to charge less money for their visitor's food and liquor.

He also ordered beaches to stay open later, and he even put massive flood lights on them, and he required bars dotting his country to remain open all night long, and to keep the booze flowing for the tourists. Because he realized a drunken tourist was more apt to spend much more money than a sober one. He even encouraged the bars to allow topless dancing, and worse, to add to the revenues from the visitors.

This new way of thinking caused the Cuban locals living in severe poverty, to sell their bodies and souls to this new flux of tourists flooding into the country. The back streets leading to beaches were overcrowded with teenage girls and boys, willing to sell their bodies to anyone who was offering them cash. These pathways turned extremely dangerous, every night bodies turned up in the streets, killed for their money and valuables.

AIDS grew at an alarming rate, forcing many visitors to the Island of Cuba to change their destinations, crippling the Cuban economy even further. Castro reacted to the new threats to his economy with a heavier hand. He sent his guards out to run the night children of the street, off the roads, and to arrest all Cuba's prostitutes. This attempted crackdown on the street walkers and child prostitutes, forced them to turn to the shadier elements who offered them the protection against the government troops, causing some open warfare on the streets at night.

The capital of Cuba, Havana, was marked with the sounds of gunfire at night, almost every night now. The few tourists that once filtered back to the luxurious Cuban resorts, soon fled. Castro sent troops out to extinguish these pockets of resentment towards his leadership of the Island. Throughout it all, he maintained his unending hatred aimed at the United States, and all she stood for, and the exiles he forced to flee to the United States and elsewhere. In late 1994, Castro forced many of the unhappy citizens into rafts and broken down boats and inner tubes once again, and then he allowed them to set sail in shark infested waters from Cuba to the American mainland in an attempt to sway American public opinion, and to gain pity for the boat people's plight, in hopes of ending the suffocating United States embargo still in effect against his country for so many years.

Instead of eliminating the trade embargo against Cuba, the United States reacted to this latest boat lift differently this time. The Coast Guard took up position between Cuba and the United States, and the ships picked up hundreds of the Cuban boat people. But they were brought to Guantanamo Bay where the Americans erected temporary tent camps. When these makeshift camps were full, the United States started to send other Cuban refugees to Panama. But soon, there were more people fleeing Castro's yoke of oppression, than there were places to put them, and the United States government soon found itself with no other alternative, but to turn the boat people back towards their own country and their leader by force, if it was need to be employed.

The Cuban Presidente viewed this move as a major victory in his ever expanding war with the United States, because he was given huge amounts of American cash, to allow the refugees back into his country. Along with the cash came a promise by America, to review the effects the embargo had on the citizens of Cuba. Talks between Castro's leadership and the American government took place over the next few months, but they never really amounted to anything, because of Castro's many outlandish demands, and his steadfast refusal to give into any of the United States demands. All further talks were canceled, and then rescheduled, and soon, no further talks were setup any longer. Castro was once again considering whether or not to force another mass exodus of the boat people from his Island.

The civilian population never did see any of the benefits of the nearly twenty five million in cash that was sent by the United States to Cuba. It was agreed the funds would be spent to help stimulate the Cuban economy, but instead, the monies ended up lining the pockets of Castro's highest ranking officials and Generals. Castro was aware of this, and even encouraged it to continue, he felt it was the only way he could be certain of keeping their loyalty during these hard times. He had no idea his days of leadership over the small Caribbean Island was rapidly drawing to a fast conclusion on him.

No matter what he tried, he just could not stimulate Cuba's economy that hit his military the hardest, by cutting their budget to less than a third of what it once was. The Cuban Army which fought many wars in Angola, Mozambique, Kenya and Ethiopia, and became military advisors in Libya, the Sudan and Mali, now found themselves sitting on their backsides, forgotten by Castro.

With the complete demoralization of the Cuban military, some of the fuming Generals contacted their once ally, the Soviet Union, begging their help from them, or to be allowed to flee Cuba for the Soviet country, so they could once again serve in a proud and well organized Army. Some Cuban Officers were allowed to migrate to the Soviet Union, but these were only the very best of the Cuban Military Commanders. The rest of them were told not to bother to come to Russia, because they had nothing of real worth to offer them. She was in as bad a shape as the Cuban Island was in at the present moment.

Other Cuban Generals and high ranking officers of the country, fled to certain Central and South America governments, offering them their loyalty and services. With the fleeing of many of his military officers, the lesser officers soon found themselves trapped in a world suffering from a total lapse of consciousness towards them. The officers felt they were the forgotten soldiers of Cuba. No matter what they tried, they just could not convince Fidel Castro to give the military the monies needed to operate, even on a much smaller basis now. This added to their ill feelings towards their once great leader. The mumbling of discontent began in earnest now.

Colonel Carlos Rafael Fernandez Alvarez, sat in the office General Renato Soto Ramon Gonzales abandoned when he fled to Russia. Colonel Alvarez read the latest communiqués, every one of them requesting something from him. They begged him for money, food, fuel for the vehicles and tanks, everything even down to paint to stop the biggest threat to all military equipment, rust. Colonel Alvarez was the highest ranking officer left in the Cuban Army, and he chose to lead. In anger, he threw the communiqués across the room and then he bellowed out. "Sergeant Regueiro, get my god dom car ready for my use. I'm going to see that sonofabitch who we call El Presidente, and get money we need to continue to operate from the fool, or I'll bring back his head on a stick."

The concerned Sergeant burst into the office when he heard his name called out by the Colonel and he snapped to attention as he saluted. He stared ahead as the Colonel made a number of serious threats against Castro. The Sergeant did not know how to react to the Colonel's sudden tirade, and he found it difficult to take him seriously.

"By the Holy Madonna, what the hell is wrong with you, you great fool you? Did you not hear what I said, Sergeant? Is there shit in your ears you cannot hear my god dom words? I ordered you to get my car ready use, Sergeant. I'm going to pay a visit to our so called fearless leader getting fat wasting his precious time sitting in his dom Palace, while the rest of his soldiers slowly starve to death. Get my god dom car ready unless you enjoy the way you have been forced to live as a once proud Cuban soldier, fool."

The Sergeant lowered his hand and he offered to the upset Colonel in a low and contrite tone. "Colonel Alvarez Sir, if you go to see our Presidente in this rage, I fear for your life, sir. As you know, Presidente Castro has not been in the best of moods lately, Colonel. If only we could have convinced the Americans to lift their dom embargo against us, all will be as it once was sir."

"I pray to the Holy Virgin Sergeant Regueiro, you live in a paradise of dreams and fools, mista. The ways of the past are as you stated, the past. The American embargo is not the real problem facing Cuba and her children. If it was lifted tomorrow, we'd still have that bearded pig to deal with, Sergeant. I fear the only true door left open to Cuba and her children now, is what the American's wanted all along, to remove that godless fool as our El Presidente, Sergeant. His time has passed, and it's about time Cuba takes a step into its own future, and the new world she will face, just as our Soviet brothers have obviously done when they turned their backs on the Communist beliefs, mista."

"My Colonel, you're talking treachery against our government and leader I fear, sir."

"I know god dom well what I'm speaking fool, and if you want to remain alive. Then I suggest you think along the same lines as I. It's only a matter of time before one of our other Officers takes it upon themselves to relieve Cuba of this fool, mista. Before someone else acts, I'll insure my own position in the new government slowly marching towards the Island of Cuba. I'll do whatever is necessary to get my beloved Cuba out from under the yoke this old man has leveled upon her people. Now get my car or leave me. I'll do it, with or without the backing of my Army. We know something has to be done the door has been opened for Castro to step down. Instead of leaving, he eliminated anyone who might be able to replace him, and start meaningful talks with the hated Americans. Get my car I told you fool!"

The force of the Colonel's order made the Sergeant flinch, as if just being struck across the face, he snapped to attention and he saluted his officer, before running from the office.

Colonel Alvarez smiled as he watched the young soldier take off. He stared at his map of Cuba and the surrounding nations. The map noted many locations of Army Units and military equipment, and also listed military manpower in numbers. There were nine hundred and seventy five thousand military forces spread out on the Island. Many soldiers were placed on the inactive list, because Castro could not afford, or would not pay their wages. The best statistics he could come up with as the count of personnel was four hundred and fifty thousand still active troops.

Colonel Rafael Fernandez Alvarez wondered how the Airforce and Navy were faring out under the stifling cutbacks to their military funds and supplies, by Castro's government. He placed a quick call over to Colonel Santiago Ramon Agramonte, the commanding officer of the Airforce.

"Yeah, what do you want of me." A bored sounding voice barked back into the phone.

The Colonel's blood boiled in his body as he snarled. "This is Colonel Alvarez, who is this?"

"This is Private Gorriaran, so what do you want of me I asked you, Colonel Alvarez."

"By the hated Priest's robes, if you want to remain alive to see tomorrow's sunrise you great fool, you better act like the soldier you're supposed to be. Get Colonel Agramonte for me."

"He has left strict orders not to be disturbed by anyone on this day, Mr. Big Shot Colonel."

"By the sacred Madonna's love of her infant children, I curse you to hell Private. I'm ordering you to march your god dom ass into his office, and let him know I'm on the dom line, and I wish to speak with him immediately, Private! If you don't do as you are ordered, I swear by the Holy Father. I shall have you hanging by your foul and worthless thumbs until the crows pluck out your evil eyes from their worthless sockets, you fool you."

"Yeah, yeah, another windbag of an Officer I see, hold on the line, Colonel Alvarez Sir."

Before the Colonel could reply to the Private's last angry words to him, he was placed on hold, and a few moments later, the Colonel was on the line. "Colonel Alvarez Sir, it's good to hear your voice again, sir. Would you believe I was planning to call to you later today, sir? What is on your mind, sir?" he rather jovial young Colonel remarked over the phone.

"The first thing I want you to do is to place that cursed Private in jail, until I can get up there and separate his skin from his foul body. I have never been spoken to in such a matter..."

"Colonel Alvarez Sir, I know how disrespectful the god dom Private can be at times. But you have to understand many of my men have not been paid in three months, and they're barely getting enough to eat to remain alert. Colonel, if I was to place all the active men and women on my base showing disrespect to my Officers in jail, I'd have no one left to carry out my orders, sir. Even my Officers show little respect for anyone, let alone a fellow Officer. I don't understand what will become of our Airforce, the miserable conditions I'm forced to operate under..."

Colonel Alvarez let out his breath in an angry hiss as he said to the other Cuban Military Officer over the phone. "In the name of the Holy Father, I see you're faring no better than my Army is at the time, Colonel Agramonte Sir. This is the true reason for my call, sir."

"I planned to speak with you about this same problem later today, Colonel Alvarez. I was going to see if you might be able to lend me some money. So I can pay my more important personnel before I lose them, or have an all out mutiny on my hands, Colonel." The upset Colonel gave out with a nervous laugh as he waited to hear Alvarez's reply to his request.

"I'm in the same god cursed condition you're in sir, maybe even a little worse I hate to admit, Colonel. I have more personnel under my Command, and my base is larger. My soldiers haven't been paid for several months and they're getting tired of operating with no pay." Alvarez turned serious as he lowered his voice and almost whispered. "Colonel, I think it's time we take matters into our own hands, sir. The fool sits day after day in his god dom office chewing on his dom cigars, and watches as his military rot from under him. I plan to see the sonofabitch, and make one final attempt to beg, or demand he do something about the predicament that his Armed Forces find themselves mired in."

Colonel Agramonte's voice showed his concern as he said. "Colonel Alvarez Sir, I beg you to take greater care in your choice of words, you're speaking treason against Castro, and you have no idea whose ears might be listening to us. I heard about a Captain at Ciego de Avila put to death for daring to speak his mind against our leader, sir."

"By the Holy Madonna, the leader of shit! The useless cochino still sits day in and day out in his dom office acting like the true Presidente of our country. Yet the great fool allows the country to crumble to dust under his worthless feet, and all he does is suck on those dom cigars of his, sir. By the white collar of the Priests, the Captain you speak of was one of my soldiers. No Colonel Agramonte, I had enough of this foolishness, and if it costs me my life to speak out the truth to our leader, then so be it. No longer can I force my soldiers to live under these terrible conditions, sir. If he cannot afford to keep his military running then he should dismantle it, and allow the troops to make a successful living on the outside. It's that simple sir."

"Be wise about your decisions I caution you, Colonel Carlos Alvarez Sir. You cannot change the winds that be, by blowing in another direction. We have to wait maybe our leader will die soon. His health is in question, I heard rumors. Maybe we can last until the hated Americans do something to hurry along his demise. Either way, we have to be diligent, Colonel Alvarez. You know if Castro disassembles his military forces, the cowardly exiles will be on our shores by morning time, taking over the country. With American backing, we'd be hard pressed to stop the traitors to our country from doing so, Colonel Sir."

"Perhaps Colonel, but at least we'll die as true soldiers. What better fate could befall a loyal soldier to his country? Besides my old friend, at least the Cuban people will be rid of this stagnation they were living through for too many years to count. Colonel, if the exiles in America attack Cuba in force, what makes you believe we'd be able to beat them back with our so poorly armed and well depleted forces, or would we really want to in any case, sir?"

"Yes Colonel Alvarez, I believe you're right sir. I have given this matter much thought lately myself, sir. If these god dom traitorous exiles elect to attack us at this time, we'd be in a terrible state to stop them. Especially if they were able to talk the hated Americans into helping them attack us again, sir. With the forces we have at our disposal, no, it's like you stated, I doubt we'd be able to stop them, or if my forces would want fight to stop them, sir. I have a feeling many will step aside and allow these foul exiles who spent their lives weakening the strength of Cuba, to walk into our capital and take it over without a fight, sir."

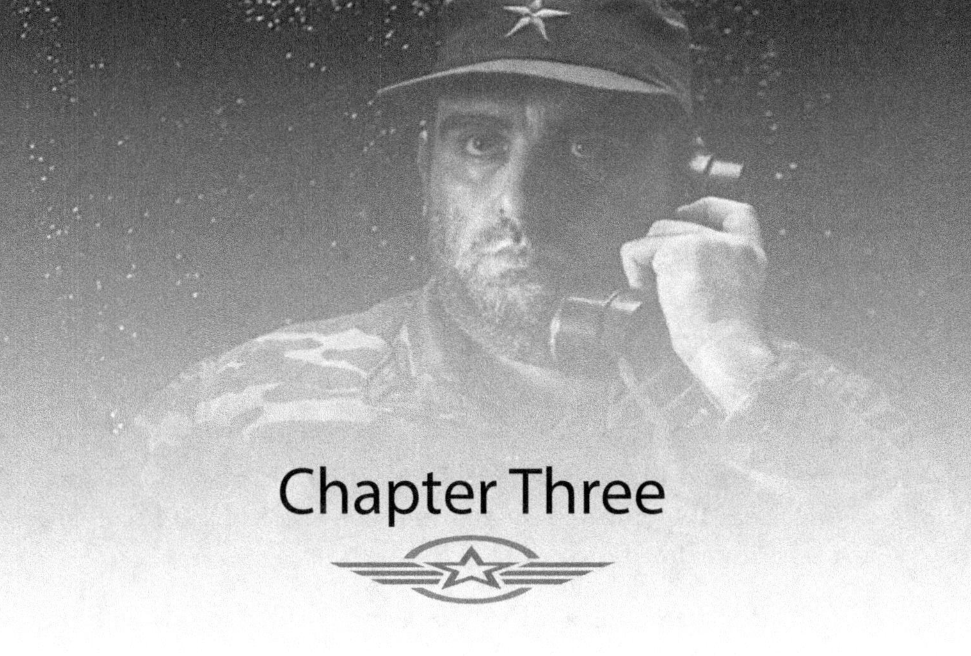

Chapter Three

Colonel Carlos Rafael Fernandez Alvarez gave out with a heavy sigh as he quickly collected his thoughts for a moment.

The silence made the Airforce Officer ask. "Are you still there Colonel Alvarez Sir?"

"Yes Santiago, but I was just taking a few moments to think, that was why I was so silent sir. There's no way of stating this more pleasantly to you, and there's no reason to put it off any longer, sir. Colonel Agramonte, we have to act, and act fast I'm afraid. Castro's lack of true leadership is forcing us to make a rash move. There's no other way to think, or to act and we owe it to our country and her people to react as quickly as possible sir. We have to eliminate the fool, and then open talks with the Americans. I believe they're Cuba's only hope for the future. The foolish Russians are useless, and even if they could help I seriously doubt they would sir. Not with the way Castro is trying to deal with them lately. Santiago, we have to talk, I want..."

"Shhh, shhh, Colonel Alvarez, I already warned you, you cannot speak in this manner over the phone sir. Your talk chills me to my bones, all I want from life is to be allowed to finish my time and retire, sir. I don't care what happens to this country Castro has broken all my passion for Cuba. I'm tired, too long have I battled only to end up like this, a forgotten soldier in a forgotten country by a forgotten leader, sir." Colonel Agramonte paused for a moment.

"I agree with you it's dangerous to speak of such things over the dom phone. I want to talk to you further about this situation, sir. But first I shall speak to our fearless leader in Havana. I want to speak with Captain Remos. If I'm forced to act, I want the Airforce and the Navy backing me, or at least not willing to come to the aide of this lowly cochino who is leading Cuba down..."

Colonel Agramonte interrupted Alvarez's anger again as he offered. "I'll see Captain Remos while you speak to Presidente Castro. If you have strength to confront our fearless leader on these matters, the least I can do is see Captain Remos, and find out his feelings of the path Cuba is heading down, sir."

"Colonel Agramonte, am I to take it you decided to side with me in this matter, sir?"

"No, you may not believe that, but you can believe I'm not against what you speak of, Colonel Alvarez. Because I too believe something has to be done about Castro, and his dom leadership over Cuba, and of his pig headed and foul beliefs, before they completely destroy Cuba. He's the last to believe in the ways of Communism. Not even the founding fathers follow them any longer. Russia has fallen in line behind the United States, and they're more powerful than we, sir.

"So why should we not do the same thing? We can allow the United States to lead the way for us, as long as we can get some money they lavished on the other nations of the world who follow their footsteps, sir. This is another way for a country who wants to destroy America, to carry out the mission. By draining the monies from them until there's none left for them by Christ, causing their foolish taxpayers to rise up in revolt against them, and then we can make our move and break relations with them. I believe the American power will only live at the top of the ladder for a short period of time, and if we're lucky enough to remain a strong nation, when this fall occurs, we'll be in the proper position to take full advantage of the demise, sir."

"You speak like you believe in my ideals my old friend. Can I trust you, Colonel?"

"I believe you can, as I just stated, I shall see Captain Remos at Villa Clare, he has taken a building by Isabela de Sague, and took the old port there to assemble what's left of his once proud Naval ships, sir."

"Why has he chosen to move his Navy there for, Colonel Agramonte?" Alvarez asked him.

"Because just as the Russian Navy lays at harbor rusting, and picked over by the scavengers of that country, Captain Remos's Navy was rusting in much the same manner while at port. He was forced to pick the best of his ships, repair what he could of them, and then move them and he has assembled them at Port Isabela."

"I hate this fool in Command of our beloved country." Colonel Alvarez hissed.

"Again, I must caution you to be extremely careful of your choice words on the phone sir. I must go sir. What time are you planning to speak to the great Presidente, Colonel Alvarez?"

"Colonel Agramonte, I plan to leave immediately, when I finished speaking to you sir."

"Then let us finish speaking Colonel Alvarez. Good luck sir, I believe you might be the only hope Cuba has left to her, before the lowly jackals move in and pick us apart at will sir."

"I hope I shall live up to your expectations sir. Good luck with Captain Remos, sir. Err... Santiago, you know sir if Captain Remos decides against our thoughts, you're going to be forced to dispatch him to silence him. We cannot possibly allow him to upset our plans before we even formulate them, Colonel Agramonte."

"I already decided on the course I must follow. If Captain Remos is not interested in a plan to eliminate our real enemy and get our country heading down the right path again. I know what I have to do next, sir."

"Thank you Santiago I knew I could count on you in my time of greatest need sir."

"Yes, you can count on my assistance in this matter you speak of, Colonel Alvarez." Colonel Santiago's voice was heard barely a over a whisper on the other end of the phone this time.

"You'll go along with everything I just spoke about on this day Santiago?" Colonel Alvarez suddenly asked his counterpart over the phone, and then he waited for his reply.

"Yes, damn you to hell and back Colonel Alvarez, yes. You're forcing me to answer you over the phone, something I did not want to do. You also force my neck to be placed in the same noose you're placing your worthless neck in." His voice was much stronger this time, alert now.

"To dare use a phrase once made popular by our soon to be late, El Presidente. 'What good is a revolution without any risk taking by the warriors, Colonel Agramonte?' One's neck is always placed into a noose whenever one is taking on a god cursed government, to be ousted by means of military force sir."

"Yes, I heard this statement said many times before Colonel Alvarez. I hope it works out as well for us, as it did for the man who had said it." Colonel Agramonte complained.

"By the love of the Blessed Virgin, it'll work as well for us, Colonel Agramonte."

"I hope it is so Colonel Alvarez." Colonel Agramonte said into the dead phone.

Colonel Carlos Rafael Fernandez Alvarez replaced the receiver, and he leaned back in his chair while listening to the many different sounds drifting from the base. He never realized it before, but the entire encampment that was usually so noisy, was extremely quiet for a military installation of its size. He opened a drawer and removed a bottle of Habana Club rum, and he poured himself a stiff shot. He downed it in one quick gulp, his body shaking from the harsh taste as the alcohol assaulted it. He placed the bottle back in the drawer when Sergeant Regueiro came back almost sneaking into his office. He looked scared to death as he snapped to attention.

"By the Blessed Virgin, yes Sergeant yes what is it? Is my car ready dommit?"

"Sir that's what I want to speak to you about, Colonel. We have a problem with your car sir."

"For the love of God, what's your problem now Sergeant? Speak up, you're wasting time."

"Sir, I'm afraid there's no fuel on the entire base for your car's use Colonel Alvarez."

The Colonel glared harshly at the Sergeant. He then leaned forward in his chair and rested his hands on the desk as he said. "I curse your worthless ass to hell, what are you trying to tell me, god dommit? We don't have enough dom fuel needed for my fooking personal car, now? God forgive you Sergeant, remove some dom fuel from a gas powered armor personnel carrier then. By the Blessed Virgin, I need my foul car. Sergeant, what do you expect me to do, walk to Havana?" the Colonel's eyes narrowed as he pointed his finger at him as if it was a dagger and then added to his angry words at the Sergeant. "By the sacred Christ Child, if you cannot find fuel then you better be prepared to carry me to Havana on your god dom back, Sergeant. Get out and get my staff car ready for my use. I intend to leave this base in fifteen minutes, mista."

"Yes Sir Colonel Alvarez I shall have your car ready in fifteen minutes Colonel Alvarez." With that said, the Sergeant spun around on his heels and nearly ran out the door.

Alvarez raised his eyes to the ceiling and complained. "God dom this cancer eating through my beloved Island of Cuba. By the Blessed Madonna, I shall skin him alive, and leave his bones for the cursed dogs to pick clean." He walked over to the window and looked out over the base. Soldiers ran to every vehicle checking for gas. In all cases, the soldiers left without fuel. His eyes went to the field where five hundred Soviet and Chinese tanks were parked in rusting rows.

For the first time in months, he realized what terrible shape the military of Cuba was in. Gone were all signs of the camouflage paint markings, leaving a new pattern of coloration for the war machines, rust. The Colonel was aware many of his tanks did not have ammunition, and the few that did, had only enough for one rack. That was thirty six rounds for the last T-80s to arrive from the Soviet Union, before their relations turned for the worse. His government owed Russia for the deteriorating military equipment. He scanned the tank dump for the newer tanks on Cuba for three years, never once having been fired. When he spotted them, he was stunned they also succumbed to misuse and neglect and were covered with rust. He shook his head as he left the office for the T-80 tanks.

The optic lenses from the infrared aiming systems were missing from many of the parked tanks, obviously stolen and then most likely sold on the black market by some of his soldiers. The 14.5 mm machine guns were also missing from the massive tanks. He knew he would find the lowly fools who did this to him, and have them stood before a firing squad to set an example for the others. Steal from his base and lose your wasted life that was Colonel Alvarez's policy.

The angry Colonel ran a hand over the fender of the behemoth machine, and it came back covered in rust and dampness, a tank's worse enemy. He saw weeds were growing between the tracks of the machine, and some hatches had been left open against orders. He moved to the rear of the tank and checked the battery compartment, they were empty. He kicked the tank out of angry for the thief as he growled. "What the hell good are these blessed tanks, if I have no ammunition, fuel, or batteries for the dom things.

"I'll have heads of all for this atrocity, whoever saw anyone stealing anything from these machines, is to report to my office and leave the villain's name on my desk." He never turned to look at any one soldier as he cursed, and then stormed around the installation in a rage. Every soldier in ear shot of him stared at the angry man cursing everyone from God, to the lowly mosquitoes buzzing all around his head. They quickly disappeared from his sight.

He scanned his military base while continuing to curse, everywhere he looked there was a bicycle laying, his soldiers main transportation now. They were leaning against a post, tanks, armored vehicles, or lying on the ground. There was a bike leaning against the next tank he inspected. Rage filled his arms, making them more powerful as he closed the short distance separating him from the bike. He picked it up over his head as he let out an animalistic roar, and then he threw it in the parade ground and he bellowed.

"What kind of fooking leadership do we have in Command of our capital who sits by and allows his fighting men to be reduced to stealing and riding god dom bicycles. By the Blessed Virgin, what kind of man I ask you..." He suddenly got control of his rampaging emotions as he realized his words drew the attention of some soldiers he knew were spies for Castro and his secret police. He headed back to his office, but not before giving the bike a kick in defiance as he mumbled under his breath at the bike. "This should be Castro's head I'm kicking, dommit."

He rushed into his office and plopped down heavily in his chair and poured himself another drink. A second later, Corporal Negrin appeared at the entrance requesting to speak with him. He lifted his drink to the well known base snitch. "Care to join me Corporal?"

"I'd be most honored to share a drink with you Colonel." Negrin moved deeper in the Colonel's office, knowing everyone was aware he had the duty to report all infractions to Presidente Castro's secret police, including words spoken against him in anger or disrespect.

The still upset Colonel was beginning to feel the booze affecting him, and his blood was now pounding wildly in his temples as he poured a glass of liquor for the snitch, and then added to him. "I guess I shall be hearing from the secret police by the end of today, mista!"

"I don't know what you mean by that statement sir." Corporal Negrin grinned widely.

"Sure you don't Corporal." The Colonel grumbled at the Corporal sharply.

"Colonel Alvarez Sir, whatever you heard said about me sir. I have no intention of reporting you, or anyone to anyone from this base for your childish outburst sir. You may not believe me sir, but I feel the same way over the situation we, as soldiers of Cuba find ourselves mired in sir. I cannot believe what we have been reduced to spend all our nights stalking about in the darkness, stealing bicycles to get around for ourselves. My belly aches from the lack of food to eat, and my wife has threatened to leave me on many occasions lately, sir. If I don't leave the Army, or demand much better living conditions and food for the servicemen and their families..."

"I take it you're still married?" Speaking to this man left a bad taste in his mouth.

"Yes I am Colonel Alvarez." The Corporal offered politely, while trying to win the Colonel.

"How the hell were you able to talk her into staying with you for so long, Corporal? I'm most interested to know of this great feat mista. As you know, my girlfriend has left me many months ago, because I'd not leave the service and seek other employ for myself and my family."

"It was simple to do Colonel. I mere beat her until she agreed to stay with me sir. I told her I'd have a man watch her and the children, and if she dared to leave me while I was on base, he'd kill her and both the boys as well." Corporal Negrin's face broke out into an ugly sneer as he stared at the seated Colonel, not noticing his expression change to someone who looked like he had just sniffed the most god awful odor in the world.

Colonel Alvarez shook his head to try and clear the cloud from the booze taking over it. "Madre de Dios, Corporal Negrin I'm busy. So I'm hoping you'll cut this visit short, so I can get on with my work. By the Holy Madonna, if you're not here to inform me you're turning me into the secret police then what is the reason for your visit? To drink my liquor fool?"

Corporal Negrin let out a quick laugh as he replied to his commanding officer. "Colonel Alvarez, I wish you and the other soldiers of this military installation would believe me when I say I have nothing to do with the secret police or Presidente Castro. I'm merely a soldier trying to live through a bad time for myself and my family sir." The Corporal suddenly turned serious as he leaned more forwards towards Colonel Alvarez, and whispered. "Colonel Alvarez, I dare to speak of this because I sense you're as fed up with Castro's rule of the Island as the rest of us are, sir. I've been trying to assemble other Officers and soldiers, to make an attempt at removing Castro from office. I could use a man of your standing to draw more men to my cause, sir."

Alvarez could not keep the smile from his lips as he growled back at the man. "By the Blessed Virgin, and who is going to lead this coup you dare speak of before me, Corporal?"

"I will of course sir. Colonel Alvarez, you're looking at the next Presidente of Cuba, sir." Corporal Negrin finished his drink and then he allowed a huge grin to cross his lips again.

"And, how many of the soldiers have you been able to muster to your cause, Corporal?"

"Enough to get the job done Colonel." He announced so proudly.

"Who are all these soldiers that you speak of? I want to know their names Corporal."

"You shall know once you agreed to join our cause, Colonel." Corporal Negrin smiled again.

"Sergeant Iglesias, get your ass in here on the double quick mista!" Colonel Alvarez suddenly bellowed out from where he was seated in his office.

The young office Sergeant rushed into the Colonel's office and snapped to attention.

"Sergeant Iglesias, you're ordered to take this motherless little bastard of a foul traitor to our country and our Presidente in custody. Then I want you to assemble a firing squad as quickly as possible. This cursed son of a milkless whore has just spoke treason against Cuba and her Presidente, by daring to threaten to lead an overthrow against our leader in Havana. I want you to send a message out to the Presidente's office, and you'll inform him of this treachery I uncovered against him that was festering on my military base. You'll then inform him further I'm putting the foul traitor to death immediately. I cannot believe this lowly dog eater had the dom cojones to make such an offer to me. I shall have his head for his foul words."

Sergeant Iglesias roughly grabbed the Corporal and forced his arms behind his back, and held him as he called for other soldiers to take charge of the prisoner. Corporal Negrin was roughly led away from Alvarez's office screaming in handcuffs, as Iglesias headed for his office to make the report to Havana.

Alvarez did not have a chance to pour himself another drink before Lieutenant Gutierrez came bursting into his office, demanding to know what he was going to do with one of his men.

At the same moment, Sergeant Iglesias reentered his office and said. "Colonel Alvarez, Command ordered you to delay putting Corporal Negrin to death before you had a chance to speak with Lieutenant Gutierrez sir. I can see he's already here sir." The Sergeant fell silent.

"Colonel Alvarez, why are you going to have Corporal Negrin put to death, sir?"

"Madre de Dios, because he just tried to enlist me in a conspiracy he has been organizing against Castro. I allowed him to speak until he said enough to condemn himself to death sir. Why does one of my Lieutenant's show any interest in this dom traitor? Could it be you're one of the conspirators he just spoke about sir?" the Colonel knew what he was doing, the base had spies, and he decided to flush them out, so he knew who his enemy was. By threatening to kill a snitch, the other rats would come out of the woodwork to save their asses, just as this Lieutenant done.

Lieutenant Gutierrez turned to Sergeant Iglesias and hissed at him. "You're dismissed fool."

The Colonel leaped up to his feet and snapped. "Lieutenant, you don't dare give orders in my office. I do! If you want the Sergeant out, ask me to dismiss him. Is this understood, I don't care who you're working for cochino, you're on my base and you'll live by my orders Lieutenant."

"Yes sir." The scared Lieutenant replied as he went to full attention before the angry Colonel.

"Do you want him out of my office Lieutenant?" Colonel Alvarez asked the lesser officer.

"Yes I do Colonel Alvarez." The Lieutenant replied as he stared the Colonel in his eyes.

"Jesus Madonna, Sergeant, it seems the Lieutenant has something to discuss over me in private, mista. I guess I shall entertain his request and speak with him in private for a moment." He made a sudden head movement at the door, and the Sergeant immediately left, glad to be away from the officers he knew were about to argue.

Once the Sergeant was out of his office, he growled harshly at the Lieutenant. "What is it you wanted to say to me Lieutenant? I have a traitor to settle up with, Lieutenant."

"Colonel Alvarez, you'll not kill my Corporal. He was merely following my orders. When you lost your temper by the tanks, you said things against our Presidente's interest, and I had to find out if you were serious or just spouting off angry words sir. I ordered the Corporal to offer you to join conspirators. If you chose to join him, it would've been you who stood before a firing squad, not him." The Lieutenant removed a security ID and handed it over to Alvarez. Colonel Luis Hector Gutierrez ITSP Internal Secret Police 114553.

"By the will of God's good grace, if you have a problem with my authority and the way I'm working on this military base, mista. Then you'll place a call to the Minister of Justice Fernando Diaz Suarez, and he'll clear up all your worries for you, Colonel Alvarez Sir."

Colonel Alvarez glared angrily at the Lieutenant standing before him, and then he threw the ID back at the Lieutenant Colonel and he barked at him at the same time. "Pick up your fooking card, and take control of your God cursed snitch, and be off my base before I have the both of you shot. By the way sir, did I pass your foul test, you son of a cochino you?"

"Yes, and if it makes you feel better, you can call me all the names you want. Names will not harm me, or Castro, but conspirators will hurt our Presidente. I'll leave because my cover has been compromised, and control will be informed you and your men are free of suspicion. I might be forced to call on you for help in the future, if I'm able to locate other conspirators."

"May God curse me to the fires of hell if I'm ever forced to help the likes of you! I shall do it, but you'll not find me a willing ally to deal with, sir." The Colonel glared at the Lieutenant.

Gutierrez grinned as he replied. "I understand if I were in your place, perhaps I'd not like working with what you have labeled as snitches. I'll be leaving now Colonel, good luck in the future Colonel Alvarez Sir."

"Remember to take your shit filled Corporal with you, sir. By the way Lieutenant..."

"Colonel." The Lieutenant looked at Alvarez while waiting for him to finish with his words.

"Yes Lieutenant, can you do me a favor, sir? See if you can find me some fuel and cash, so I can pay some of my men in this den of liars you chose to dance with, sir."

"I can't promise but I'll see what I can do." With that, the Lieutenant Colonel left the office.

Colonel Alvarez remained seated, until he heard a vehicle start and he hoped the Sergeant found fuel for his car. He rushed to the door in time to see Lieutenant Gutierrez start up a parked car, pick up the Corporal and a few other men, and then they left the base quickly.

Sergeant Regueiro rushed into the office and he yelled to the Colonel. "Sir, the Lieutenant took the car we were fueling up for your use, sir. We couldn't stop him, and he left the base. Sir that was all the fuel we found. I dispatched soldiers to head into the villages with orders to secure fuel. I have also given them orders to confiscate food and wine for us also."

"I have no problem with your decisions so far Sergeant. But, am I to take it I'll not have a vehicle for my use for today, mista?" Alvarez checked his watch, it was late, three p.m. already, and if he left for Havana right now, by the time he arrived. Fidel Castro would have left the office for the day. Everyone knew El Presidente Castro refused to talk work after office hours. "The hell with the cursed thing I guess mista. It's too late now for any meeting with the cochino, I want you to have my vehicle fueled and ready for use seven a.m. tomorrow morning Sergeant?"

"Are you planning to stay on the military base for tonight, Colonel Alvarez Sir?"

"No, I think I'll take the time to visit Maria tonight. Heaven help me but I think I need some special care on this night." For the first time in hours he allowed himself a quick smile.

The Sergeant returned his smile as he assured him he would have his car ready by seven.

"Very well Sergeant, I'll see you tomorrow morning. I guess there's nothing else for me to accomplish today mista. So I guess I'll leave." He opened his drawer and he removed the new bottle of rum, and placed it in his suitcase and left, riding the bicycle he stole earlier from the village. He felt bad for taking the bike, he was certain it was the owners only means of transportation, but his needs outweighed that of any civilians of Cuba. As he peddled away from the base, the only thought keeping him going was seeing his beautiful Maria.

Colonel Alvarez, was a young man of thirty nine, he was born in Santa Clara, of Cuban born parents. His father was a well to do sugar producer and merchant, and his mother who was college educated, taught at a local university. He had three brothers and two sisters better educated than most, because of his father's insistence. Carlos Rafael Fernandez Alvarez stood six foot five, with unmarked skin that had a handsome, true Cuban glow.

He was a lucky man, born with his father's better attributes, the strong and narrow Cuban chin, and the well formed long nose with the ever present brush of a mustache he kept trimmed perfectly. He had dark brown eyes that turned black whenever he was angered, rounded out his fine facial features. He had a well formed chest, and a good set of arms, developed by the use of free weights. His narrow waist and well shaped rear, made the women flock around when he was in a bathing suit enjoying the beach.

He loved the attention showered on him when he was around the female population. He had a fine reputation for treating his girlfriends well, and never left them wanting when it came to lovemaking. He was a slave to his passions, always hot and lying under the surface and his temper had been known to get him in trouble at times. He possessed many fine Cuban traits that helped him on his way up the ladder of success, good looks and shape, and a perfect posture that seemed to get his picture in the papers, when something of military interest was offered.

Colonel Alvarez pumped the pedals of his commandeered bike, sweating, and with every push, he cursed Castro for allowing him to be so humiliated. Some years back he remembered when he first walked into a city or village, he was treated with great respect, and the females took notice of him in his neatly pressed military uniform. But since Castro broke off relations with the Soviet Union, and he steadfast refused to make peaceful overtones to the United States or Russia. The locals now treated the soldiers as if they were the plague of Cuba, many times not even allowing any of them into their establishments for fear they would steal, or demand free meals from them. Things were bad throughout the tiny Island of Cuba, with no sign of it getting any better in the near future. This was the driving force behind Colonel Alvarez's raging passion.

He peddled the three miles from the military base in San Jose de las Lajas, to Catalina de Guines where his lover of the past two years waited patiently for him to return. He arrived on the main street and was amazed at the lack of vehicles dotting the road. He turned down Calle Street, and traveled three more blocks over until he came to a stop in front of the modest three room building Maria Ibarra called her home.

Maria was a twenty three year old Cuban beauty, who could have easily won any beauty contest she entered. She had long black wavy hair, large brown eyes and a sharp chin and high cheek bones. Her skin was absolutely flawless, with the beautiful glow of a fine, well tanned body that most Cubans exhibited. She often tanned in the nude, giving her body that all over even and rich brown color. Maria was five foot four, and she weighed one hundred and five pounds soaking wet. She was in exquisite shape with a large, perfect bust, a narrow waist and a small but rather plump rear. Her legs were also perfect, long and slender.

Colonel Alvarez considered himself lucky to have such a beauty, because he knew she could have her pick from any of the rich Cubans inhabiting the Island. He pulled in front of Maria's home, leaned the bike up against her building and he carefully chained it to the water pipe. He took nothing for chance because he could ill afford to lose his only means of transportation, and knew he would kill anyone who tried to steal it from him.

Maria was at the door before he finished locking up the bike, holding a glass of wine and a fine Cuban cigar for his enjoyment. The Colonel took both and he planted a kiss on Maria's neck, and followed her in the building. He was sweaty from the bike ride admired Maria dressed in a skin tight dress, low cut in the front and back. Her hair was up in a bun off her neck to keep her cooler. She looked hot enough to light his cigar from, and he could tell she rubbed her skin with scented oils for his future pleasure.

"You look tired my loving Colonel Alvarez, I shall run a bath for you to enjoy." She offered, and then added. "What would you like to eat? I was able to get some fresh steaks for your visit my lover."

He stared at her accusingly for a long moment while remaining silent.

The temper Maria was famous and well noted for immediately surfaced as she flew into a tirade and screamed, while swinging her hands wildly in the air at the same time at her lover. "I resent your evil look, you foul thing! I have done nothing wrong in acquiring the steaks for us, you foul pig. The seller owed me a favor and you can cook them for yourself now if you're hungry. If not leave my home at once, and I'll find a more attentive lover who appreciates what I have done for him." She was hot, and she threw the package of meat at him as she roared, and tried to slap every part of the Colonel's body at the same time.

Alvarez laughed as he easily fended off Maria's soft blows aimed at him, but when she tried to kick him between the legs, he reacted differently. He roughly grabbed her by the hands and pinned them behind her back as he pulled her close to his rock hard body. He tried to kiss her, but she turned her face on him. He tried again and this time she bit his lip, making him laugh at the taste his blood. Finally, he pinned her lips with his and kissed her until she calmed down.

Her anger turned to passion just as strong, and she returned his kiss eagerly. She raised her leg and wrapped it around his backside and wiggled her pelvis against his genitals. Her gyrations had the desired effect, because she could feel him growing rock hard under her sexy movements. She pulled away from her lover, opened his zipper and reached inside his pants until she found what she wanted. She stroked it and then she pulled it out of his pants, stepped back and looked at his growing manhood. "Hmmm... now I know why I love you El Toro."

The not so exhausted Colonel opened the front of her dress, and kissed her both breasts, making her nipples hard. He rubbed her breasts, pinched the nipples and nipped at them with his teeth. He opened the rest of the buttons on her dress, and then slid down her body, kissing, sucking, and nipping at the exposed skin as he slid further down her body and mumbled to her. "Maria, you have a body that would make the Blessed Virgin herself jealous of you." When her dress was open completely, and he was on his knees before her, and she leaned back and was pushed up against the wall as Alvarez's tongue probed her inner thighs.

She looped a leg over his shoulder, allowing his tongue easy access to her center of love making as she called it. His tongue lapped at her moistness, and as it hit the right spot, she let out with a slight moan as her eyes rolled up in her head. She wiggled her hips, grinding herself in his face. He enjoyed the offered gift she gave to him.

Maria's body shook as she let out a small cry, and then she slid down the wall to the floor. She looked up at her man as she purred. "You're disgusting my wild pig of a Colonel."

"By the Holy Madonna's sacred son Jesus, and you love me that way my lovely bitch." He retorted at her words as he flashed one of his well known smiles.

She stood and pulled her dress together and used the cord from her bathrobe to hold it closed, leaving the buttons unfastened. "I guess you apologized enough, cochino. Go and take your shower. There are oils on the shelf, use them. You smell like a wet dog in heat."

"Are you going to cook these for us?" he asked as he picked up one of the small steaks.

"I will, but only because I'm hungry, not to please you. If you ever accuse me of being guilty of such actions again, I'll skin you alive while you sleep." She glared angrily at her Colonel.

"By the sweet Madonna, woman I don't doubt that for a moment my love." He laughed as he brushed by her heading for the bathroom. He decided to take a shower rather than a bath, and he had the water running as he stripped. Seconds later, he was lathering himself up with soap. He never heard Maria come into the bathroom, and when she touched him on the shoulder, he jumped. He spun around and Maria played with him. Instantly, he was rock hard and she washed then rinsed him. It was her turn to slide her body down his. When she was on her knees she drew him in her mouth, she was planning to tease him before screwing his brains out. But she got so involved in giving him pleasure with her mouth she got carried away with her act. Quickly, she had him groaning as he wiggled all around the tub. He came in her mouth and he almost ended up sitting in the shower. He lifted her up from under her arms then kissed her, and they hugged. She easily realized he was deeply troubled and she tried to ease his worried mind a little.

"I love you very much, Maria Ibarra. When will we ever get married, my lover and friend?"

"We'll marry only when Cuba gets back to the old Cuba I had loved so much, my loving Colonel. The proud Cuba who worried about and also protected all her children from harm."

Alvarez put her at arms' length and stared in her eyes and said. "For the love of God, that could take a hundred lifetimes to come. I need you now, not when I'm too old to enjoy your pleasures daily. I say the hell with Cuba we could make it to the United States, and with the military knowledge I have, I could be valuable to them. There are many rumors of great wealth coming to any Cubans who share information with the hated Americans. By the Madonna, we could buy a home in Florida and live like royalty at their expense. I could demand a position of power, and not have to worry about the future. Remember the North Vietnamese General who defected to America I keep telling you about? The foul Americans set him up in business, and gave him vast amounts of cash, and now the sonofabitch is a multimillionaire in their foul country. Think of it Maria, we could do the same thing, bleed them for all it's worth to us.

"Then once Castro is dead, we can always come back to our country, and live the good life, with all the money we earned in the United States. Hundreds, thousands of our fellow Cubans have done the same thing I'm speaking of today. They sit in America safe, while waiting for the time to come when they can return to Cuba rich, and powerful. I'll be damned to eternal hell if I don't take advantage of what the Americans offer us. I'll be fooked if..."

Maria gave Colonel Carlos Alvarez a sexy smirk as she purred at him. "Mista Carlos Rafael Fernandez Alvarez, you'll not be fooked again if you don't stop talking like this. Alvarez, you know you'll never leave Cuba, no matter what happens to the Island. We spoke of this so many times before it bores me to death now. I'll never leave Cuba as long as I live. You'll never leave Cuba as long as you live either my lover. You'll stay and do whatever is needed to free Cuba from its bind." She suddenly pulled away from him and she quickly dried herself, and then she wrapped the towel around herself, allowing her wet hair to flow free about her head. She headed for the kitchen and the meat cooking on the gas stove.

Alvarez got out of the shower, and he used his shirt to dry himself off with, and then he left the bathroom naked. He was damned if he was going to dress in his dirty uniform again.

Maria was crying as she attended to the cooking steaks. Carlos walked up behind her and he wrapped his arms around her body. She felt his hard dick and she wiggled her rearend up against it as she grumbled at her lover. "Mista Carlos Alvarez, you're impossible lately mista."

"Is this a problem to you my love?" He said as he turned her around to face him.

Chapter Four

"Oh, you filthy pig you, you're still naked. How dare you walk around my home naked like this you filthy thing you? Have you no shame about yourself any longer, you foul cochino you? Just because you're a knuckle dragging soldier, you'll not walk about my home naked like this." She giggled as she played with his manhood again.

He remained serious as he wiped a tear from the corner of her eye, and he asked her at the same time. "You are crying my love. Why the devil are you crying now for, young lady? Are you suddenly unhappy with me and my thoughts and wants, my young lover?"

"Yes, I am Carlos." She whispered as she tried to lower her head and look away from him.

He lifted her head with his fingers so he could look right in her eyes and he asked her with concern in his voice. "Why are you suddenly so unhappy?"

"You fool you, I'm crying because of what has happened to my Cuba. Once, I had hailed Fidel Castro as the savior of Cuba and all her children. All he has offered and made me believe in has failed to come true. I would've followed him to the very gates of hell and back if he asked me to, and I would've smiled all the way, my lover. Once, I was so proud to be a Cuban. Cubans are so beautiful a people in their soul and minds. But now I fear their minds have become so clouded over by this devil that we have let loose on the Island, and I see no way of getting rid of him now. When Castro first arrived in Cuba, I wasn't born yet, but my mother told me many great stories of him, and I soon found myself wanting to meet this man who I believed to be a God.

"But now if I was to meet him, I'm afraid I'd try and kill him, and end my life as well, Carlos. I pray every night to the Blessed Virgin to take his life, so Cuba can rebuild her once greatness again. I know it's a terrible thing to ask the Blessed Virgin to take a life for me. But I fear She is my only hope of ridding Cuba of this most foul and evil of men who has lost his mind and soul. This Devil in Paradise I say he is. I have to do something in order to try and…"

"Madonna Maria, will you worry about those steaks please, and allow me to worry about this fool person we have as our Presidente. His days of ruling Cuba are about to come to a swift conclusion. I'll not allow him to harm Cuba, or her people any further. We have to step into the twentieth century if we're to ever survive as a country. To do so, we must exclude this man."

Her eyes suddenly flew open as she stared deeply into Carlos Alvarez's eyes for a moment, and she asked in desperation of him. "Are you planning to do something to remove the hated Fidel Castro from power over Cuba, my Colonel and lover?" Her body was suddenly shaking from the question she asked him, and the anticipation of his answer to her.

He took a quick breath, he was scared to confide his plans to this female he had been in love with for two years now. He was scared to trust anyone living in Cuba. What he planned to do, could cost him his life, and the lives of anyone around or helping him, or anyone who even knew him and what he planned for the future of his country.

She could not take the silence any longer and she asked him again. "Carlos, you are planning to do something about Castro's leadership over Cuba, are you not? Answer me please! I have to know this for my own peace of mind. Carlos, please tell me what you're planning to do. I want to help you I want to be a part of this new revolution, the final revolution that'll remove this foul cochino from power over my beloved Cuba. Please Carlos, you have to tell me everything you're planning to do for the sake of Cuba and all her faithful people. Please my lover and Colonel."

He let out his breath and replied. "You're right my love, I intend to start a movement to remove the lowly dog. I swear by the power of the Madonna, I'm the man to get the job done."

She suddenly wrapped her arms around him, and she kissed him with new passion and she whispered. "Carlos, I'm so proud of you and of what you're doing for Cuba. I want to help."

He tried to free himself of her grasp as he replied. "You! Madre de Dios what is this, you want to be a soldier? Don't be so foolish, you have no training. You'll be killed in the first seconds of any fighting. By the will of God's grace, I'll not allow you to fight in the war. I'll not..."

"You'll not allow me to help you! What the hell do you think I am your personal whore to be played with at your pleasure, mista? I'm a human being, one who has her own ideas of what should happen to Cuba and her future, once Castro's body lies rotting in the wet ground of Cuba. You'll not allow me to help! I don't need your permission to act on behalf of Cuba's needs, and for her people. I'll tell you this much mista high and mighty Army Colonel you. If you don't allow me to join forces with you then I'll be forced to start my own revolution against Castro. I'll have you know there are many young women who feel the same way as I do, and they're more than willing to lay down their lives for the good of Cuba and her people.

"And, as for not having any military training, that's nothing but sheer bullshit you offer me, mista. Since when in the cause of a revolution, are only the militarily trained personnel needed, Carlos Alvarez. I'll have you know throughout all history, countless revolutions have occurred, and they were even fostered by many non-military fighters as well, and I'll have..."

"For the love of God woman, you're turning into a real pain in the arse to me lately, Maria. I don't need any history lessons tonight from you, young lady. I've never understood your feeling against Castro and his foul leadership over Cuba. Okay, you win I'll find a place for you and all of your women fighters in the new revolution. But I warn you though you cannot speak to these women until after I have acted, and Castro is no longer alive and in power of the country. You must swear to this demand I make to you, Maria. I don't need any of these women exposing my plans before I even had a chance to carry them out. Do you understand me, Maria?"

"My dear Colonel Carlos Alvarez, of course I understand this you fool. Do you think me a great fool now my lover and wonderful soldier? I know you need secrecy to carry out your plan aimed against Castro. What do you think I am stupid, mista?" her eyes suddenly turned black as the night and her Latin blood rose in her body.

Carlos Alvarez just glared back at her for several long moments without speaking to her for fear of setting her off in a wild rage again.

"You better get something to wear before this little thing of yours catches cold on you, and are no longer any good to either of us for the rest of the night, mista." She gave his dick a light tug and then added. "There is a robe on the door in my room that should fit you."

"I think I'd much rather remain naked than get stuck wearing one of your flowery female robes, Maria. Besides, they'll not fit me properly my love." He replied defiantly as he rested his hands on his hips and stared at her.

"Why, you'll not look anymore ridiculous than you do right now, my Colonel. Standing there naked as you are, you cochino." She said with a smile as she turned around to tend the steaks.

"Sweet Holy Madonna, I don't care how I look here right now Maria Ibarra. I'm not going to wear a female's crazy looking bathrobe no matter what you say woman, period." He stared back at her while wearing the smile that told her he would do what she wanted.

She turned and she smiled at Carlos while lightly running a finger sexily along his chin, as she purred in her sweetest voice at him. "Baby, do you think I'd ever make you wear one of my robes with all the thrills on it, my Colonel? Nooo baby, the robe I'm speaking of hangs on the door of the bathroom is black silk, and it'll look very sexy on you, my Colonel. I'd never make you look foolish, even in front of my eyes. Now get it on before one of my neighbors sees you, and they call the police because they saw a naked man running around with his manhood standing tall and proud before him. Be off with you now my lover, before I make you use that thing waving back and forth while looking at me, mista." She slapped him on his bare butt.

"Why would you need a robe that could be worn by a man, Maria? Are you now entertaining while I'm working, my lady?" Colonel Alvarez smirked as he jumped from the slap on his can.

"I have already warned you once on this foul night about you accusing me of fooling around on you while you're working, you great fool you." She snapped as if she was truly angry with him this time, as she picked up a knife from the counter, and then she threatened him with it and grumbled at him at the same time. "Come back here you, and I'll cut it off on you and have it tanned stiff, so I'll never be without a part of you ever again, you cochino you." She growled as she took two steps towards him while lifting her hand with the knife well over her head.

"Okay, okay huh, I'm sorry Maria my lover and wild cat. I was only fooling around with you, woman." Colonel Alvarez cried as he covered himself with his hand and then he ran to the room.

She knew he was only fooling around with her, and she giggled as she finished cooking the steaks, and then she set them out on the table in dishes. Carlos came to the table dressed in the silk robe and he merely picked at the steak. She sat down, allowing her towel to slip below her breasts and she ate topless while the two talked. Twice, she tried to speak of the revolution, but he sidestepped it by changing the subject on her. When they finished eating, they shared a cold glass of wine as they headed for the roof. It was cool, and the sky was covered with stars.

He leaned up against the parapet wall while sipping on his wine and he watched the beautiful sky above him, and then he checked his watch, it was half past nine. The lights of a passing commercial airliner suddenly caught his eye. She leaned up against him with her head resting on his chest, and she hummed in a dreamy state. She looked deeply into his eyes for a moment, and then she purred at him. "A penny for your thoughts, my lover and Colonel."

"Huh, oh, nothing Maria, I was just daydreaming, that is all." He offered to her.

"It had to be something Carlos you were a million miles away from me on this lovely night. You have paid little attention to this young, hot blooded woman who is lying on your chest, naked as the day she was born, and yet you stare off in the distance on me, fool." She took his hand in hers and rested it lightly on her breast, and then she rolled his hand as she sang softly. "Hmmmmm, that feels so great to me young lady." He said lazily to her.

"Colonel Carlos Alvarez, what were you just thinking about? Please tell me of this my lover."

"You'll not let it lay for a minute, will you Maria?" he said as he let out his breath.

"Not until you tell me all of what is truly on your mind tonight, Carlos." She said back to him.

"By the beautiful Madonna, I was thinking of the many Military Officers who I'll have much need of, when I finally make my move on the old fool in Command of Cuba. I have to figure out the troops I'll need to help and also the military equipment, and all who I'll place in certain offices to run my future new government with me. I worry what the other nations of the world will do, how they'll feel about the overthrow of Fidel Castro. My mind is a blur of countless thoughts and worried and I don't know what to do first, Maria. How I should approach the men who I'll have need of and how best to use them, if they do join forces with me my love."

"What will you do if you approach someone, and he does not want to join you on your quest to free Cuba?" she asked as she once again stared into the troubled looking eyes of her lover.

"I'll kill anyone who knows of my plans, and yet they decide not to join forces with me."

"My poor poor baby, so much pressure on you on this night, Carlos Alvarez. I can understand how troubled you must be over this problem facing Cuba, and her beloved people my Colonel. When we're done here, we'll go back downstairs and then you'll tell me of all the names of the Military Officers you shall have need of, and I'll then write their names down on a slip of paper for us, my dear. Then you'll tell me of all the troops, and who has command of them, and all the equipment you'll also have need of for this new revolution of ours, Carlos. I'll write these names down as well, so you'll not forget them ever again. But first of all, there is something much more important that we must do here today, my love." With that, Maria lowered herself on his body and drew him in her mouth, and she worked him until he was hard as a rock again. She then got up and straddled him, and they made love in full view of the stars and moon and soft breeze.

When they finished making love together, they picked up the blanket and glasses, and they headed back inside Maria's home. She refilled the glasses with wine and she picked up a writing pad. She sat down at the table across from him, but before she started, she asked him. "Carlos Alvarez, Colonel are you going to spend the entire night with me tonight, please?"

"For the love of the Virgin, not the death of Castro would cause me to leave you on this night."

She smiled, and then she asked him. "What Officers do you want to speak to first, Carlos?"

"By God, come on baby. I don't want to do this all night long now you know, Maria. I want to enjoy you on this night, I want to drink in your beauty all night."

"I'm not going to let you forget your pledge to me, to remove the fool Fidel Castro from power in Cuba and over her people, my lover. What Officers do you think you should speak to first, I asked you Carlos Alvarez?" she lightly tapped the pencil on the table impatiently while waiting for him to speak to her again, and offer the names to her so she could write them down for him.

"Madre de Dios, you're a real pain in my backside on this endless night I see, my young woman. Blessed Lord Jesus, I already spoke to Colonel Agramonte from the Airforce, and he's going to speak to Captain Remos of the Navy for me. So they're both covered at this point I guess. I shall also need to speak to Cienfuegos, he's in Command of the First Armored Division, a Colonel as well. I'll also have need of Gonzales of the Infantry, so I can lock up the troops stationed in and around the capital city of Havana, honey. I'll also have much need of Lazaro Prio Socarras Cabrisas, if I'm ever going to get any help from the people in office. I think I'll use this man as my Vice Presidente if I'm successful with my attempt to rid Cuba of..."

"Holy God in Heaven Carlos Alvarez, I have never given it a second thought before this time I'm afraid. But you're absolutely right you can become the next El Presidente of all Cuba and her people, Carlos. And, I'll then become the First Lady of Cuba, just like the First Lady who lives in the United States with her President of a husband, my love. You'll take me with you to visit the United States whenever you have to go there to greet that great government leader, my Colonel and lover?" She asked her Colonel with a wide eye gleam lighting up in her beautiful eyes, as she stared back at Colonel Alvarez with great anticipation.

"You bet your sweet life I'll take you along with me anytime I have to visit the United States, or any other country in the world for that matter, young lady." He offered as proud as he could be of the sudden offer from his lover.

The pencil she was holding in her hand suddenly went flying across the small room, as she unexpectedly charged at Carlos, knocking him out of the chair and down to the floor as she ended up lying right on top of him. She kissed him wildly all over his face and neck, the mere thought of her becoming one of the most important and powerful women of all Cuba just thrilled her to no ends. Maria Ibarra once again took him into her mouth until he was rock hard, and she then mounted him and make wild, passionate love to him. She got off his lap just before he came, and she finished him off with her mouth with great delight, knowing he liked it this way. But all the while they made love together. Carlos kept complaining at her she was milking him like a cow.

Maria's only comment to him was. "Not like a cow, like El Toro, the mighty bull Carlos."

Their wild lovemaking nearly destroyed the kitchen of her home by turning over the kitchen chairs, along with the small kitchen table. A dish crashed into many pieces on the floor, and the silverware went flying all over the place. Once she finished making love with him, she again looked for the pad of paper and the pencil also lying on the cluttered floor. Finding them she asked Carlos to continue with his needs, but he was in no condition to speak any longer, because he was sound asleep lying on the floor of the kitchen.

She quickly cleaned up the kitchen, and then she woke Alvarez from his most uncomfortable sleep on the floor, and carefully led him over to the bedroom. Once he was lying in the bed and comfortable, she tried to raise his interest in her again. But she failed at her attempt to try and arouse him again. So she covered him with the light sheets, and then she snuggled up alongside him and also fell fast asleep lying against her loving and warm Colonel's body. All the while they slept, she never moved from the side of her lover and Colonel. She needed his feel and touch all night long.

Colonel Carlos Alvarez was up by four the following morning, his mind was set to wake him at that time every day of his life, to give him the hours needed to bike to the military base. He looked at the sleeping beauty lying beside him, and he smiled. He got up and dressed as quietly as possible and he was about to sneak out of the house when Maria woke and called out to him in a sleepy voice. "Carlos, don't you dare try and leave me without saying goodbye, you heel you."

He entered the bedroom filled with Maria's fine fragrance, and he kissed her, and she tried to pull him back in bed. But he immediately begged of her. "By the Blessed Virgin my little one, I have to get back to my base. Today is going to be a big day for me honey, and hopefully, a much bigger day for the people of Cuba. Wish me luck baby."

"You know I do. Carlos, promise me you'll be very careful today, please my lover."

He smiled back at her as she lay back in their bed, and then he left for the military base.

TUESDAY, AUGUST 27th, 1996. 5:30 A.M.

As Colonel Carlos Rafael Hernandez Alvarez entered the military base, it was in the first throngs of wakening up from its sleep of the night before. It was the height of the hurricane season, and Cuba was currently being threatened by the fifth hurricane of the season already. The fourth one just missed the tiny Island of Cuba, but Hurricane Ellen was aimed directly at the Island this time. The latest weather report indicated the storm might turn away from the Island at the last moment and follow the same path as the last two hurricanes and turn north again. He took nothing for granted, and he issued a number of orders for the large Cuban military base to prepare itself for Ellen's possible assault on them. Just in case the storm did not turn towards the northeast as it was predicted to do as of the last reports, and the hurricane hit the Island.

Before he entered his office, he scanned the area and noticed his car in its usual parking place. His driver leaned against the front fender smoking. "Is my car fueled and ready?"

The driver instantly ditched the cigarette he was smoking and snapped to full attention as he replied to the angry sounding Cuban Colonel. "Yes Sir Colonel Alvarez Sir, it is ready to go for you at this time, sir."

He said nothing more to the young soldier as he entered his office, only to find Sergeant Regueiro sitting in his chair with his feet propped up resting on his desk, and he was enjoying one of his cigars. When the Sergeant spotted the Colonel enter his office, he tried to jump up to his feet and he almost ended up tumbling backwards as the chair he was sitting on suddenly moved out from under him. "Sir, I was not expecting you until a little later on today, sir."

"I see that mister. Were you enjoying yourself sitting in my chair, Sergeant Regueiro?"

"Yes sir, err... please excuse me Colonel Alvarez, sir." The Sergeant said in his own defense.

"No need to apologize, there has been many a time I chose to sit in the General's chair when he was out of the office. Sort of gives you the feeling of power, right Sergeant?"

"Yes Sir Colonel Sir." Sergeant Regueiro replied with the widest grin plastered on his lips.

"Sergeant, you did well, but I'll not embarrass you by asking where you located fuel. You did, and that is that. You're dismissed I have to prepare for my meeting with the El Presidente."

The Sergeant made no move to leave his office, causing Colonel Alvarez to place his hands on his hips and ask him. "Madre de Dios, is there something else on your mind today, Sergeant?"

The Sergeant shifted his weight from one foot to the other as he struggled with his words.

"Come man, spit it out Sergeant." He growled, growing impatient with him now.

"Yes Colonel Alvarez Sir, I'm aware of your intention of today sir, and I want to assure you Colonel I'm behind you one hundred percent no matter what happens, sir." The Sergeant tried one of his best smiles on the Commander, but it did not soften Colonel Alvarez's stance.

He allowed himself to relax a little bit and replied to the concerned looking Sergeant. "You are a true friend to me. It makes me feel good to know I have your approval, Sergeant. Can I trust you to organize the ones who share your same feelings as us?"

"Yes sir. I know many who are as fed up with Castro, and his misunderstandings, sir."

"Good then you'll have them ready for anything, even an attack on the capital itself, if I have need of them for this action. They'll be fighting brother against brother I fear though, Sergeant."

"I'm aware of this possibility Colonel Alvarez, as I'm certain they are as well, sir."

The Colonel decided to go all the way with him this time as he offered the Sergeant. "By the Blessed Virgin, of course you know. Anyone who is against my plans will be placed under base arrest, until we have accomplished our goals, or worse. We have killed Castro." He stared at the younger Sergeant.

"I understand this also, it was needless to warn me of this fact, sir. Not every order has to be spoken. There are some things a Sergeant understands without being told, my Colonel."

Colonel Alvarez walked the few feet that was separating them, and then he actually hugged the Sergeant to him. The Sergeant's chest swelled with great pride over the display of trust and feelings. He struck him on the shoulder and said. "I believe you have things to do."

"Very well then Colonel Alvarez, I'll have your car moved up for your use, and sitting just outside the door for you, sir. You need not inform me when you leave sir, I'll know it sir."

"Err... Sergeant, I cannot tell you how important it is that I have your full support in this..."

"And the support of many other soldiers from the base Colonel Alvarez."

"Yes, you know my chair fits you. It'll be yours when I move to the Presidente's office."

"Then you're planning to ouster the troublemaker living in Havana, Colonel Alvarez?"

"He should've never assumed such power over all Cuba from the very beginning. He has caused more harm to befall Cuba, than all the foul plagues that had ever visited our country, combined. I lose sleep thinking it's only a matter of time before we ouster this Devil in Paradise. Now be off with you Sergeant, I have more important things to complete, before I leave base."

"Is El Presidente Castro expecting your visit on this day, Colonel Carlos Alvarez Sir?" The Sergeant asked him with some surprise in his tone of voice this time around.

"No, I'm going to surprise the great and foolish bastard by my visit to him on this day."

"Some surprise that'll be for the fool, Colonel Alvarez!" the Sergeant replied.

"Be gone with you before I curse you to hell, Sergeant." The Colonel threw a slip of paper at the Sergeant. When he was alone again, his thoughts quickly returned to Maria and the night they shared together. He was not very pleased with himself, because he refrained from telling her he scheduled a meeting with Presidente Castro, and he was intending to give him one last chance to do something for the military and the civilians of Cuba. If he failed to convince Castro to help the military, he would put his plans into motion. He was sorry he withheld this from Maria, because she was so pleased with his plans to act again Castro. He was wondering how she would feel if he and Castro were able to come to a solution.

He looked at his watch, it was almost six a.m. and he had to get going, if he wanted to be at Castro's office when Fidel arrived for work. He figured it would take him an hour to make the drive over to the capital, and another fifteen minutes to get to the Presidential Palace. He added in the time needed to locate parking, clear security, and then get to Castro's office. He knew Castro was a creature of habit, and he always arrived at his office by eight o'clock every morning, and he had no thoughts the man would ever change his habit today. He planned to be sitting in the outer office as he arrived, and follow the Presidente in his office. Although he had no appointment, he felt if he was able to get in Castro's face, he would have no alternative but speak with him, and even invite him in his office.

He believed Castro would not be so rude as to ignore one of his Colonel's, who had traveled so far just to speak with him. He raised his arms and then stretched, looked at his lovers picture, and then he placed his revolver in its holster. After checking his office to make sure he had not left any incriminating items behind, he left. He passed some soldiers who upon seeing him, instantly snapped to attention and they saluted him. He ignored their courtesy as he stormed by them while heading directly for the car and driver. He saluted the Corporal and then said to him. "Abelardo, it's time we leave for the capital and the foul fool there."

Corporal Abelardo Alegret snapped to attention as he returned the Colonel's salute. He opened the door for Carlos, and then he waited for him to get comfortable before shutting it on the Colonel. He jumped into the driver's seat, started the engine that loudly backfired before coming to a rumbling idle. He revved the engine and slammed it in gear and popped the clutch.

MARIA'S HOME IN CATALINA DE GUINES

Maria sat in her room remembering the evening of lovemaking with her Colonel. She was naked except for a transparent black bed jacket she had draped over her shoulders. Her mind filled with the pleasures they shared the night before, as she searched for ways to help Alvarez overthrow the Presidente of Cuba. She prayed he would kill this malignant cancer that was draining the will of the Cuban people. She slowly scanned her room in hopes of finding what she was looking for, an answer. She smiled when she saw the list of names she made of the soldiers and military officers Carlos believed would back him. A thought hit her and she sprang up to her feet. She realized she just found a way to bring all of the players in one place for a special meeting free of any investigation from the secret police shadowing the moves of the military.

Maria wrote feverishly, planning to send a copy to Alvarez's office at San Jose de las Lajas. She threw a robe over her shoulders, and then she ran out to place the letter to Carlos in the box. Coming back to her bedroom she collapsed on the bed exhausted, she smelled the faint odor left by her lover and Colonel. "Hmmmm." She moaned as her thoughts returned to the night before.

HAVANA, THE PRESIDENTIAL PALACE, 7:35 A.M.

Colonel Carlos Rafael Fernandez Alvarez allowed Corporal Alegret to park the car for him, as he went through the security precautions in the Palace. He left his weapon at the front desk, before being allowed to go up to the third floor to Fidel Castro's private suite. He was ushered over to a leather couch, and then offered a cup of coffee by Castro's secretary. He was sipping his steaming coffee, when a soldier he did not recognized, suddenly came over to him and he offered him his hand and said. "Colonel Carlos Alvarez Sir, I cannot tell you what a pleasure it is for me to meet you, sir. I have gone over the report filed by Colonel Gutierrez. He's one of my men. Oh, I can see by your expression you have no idea who I am. Please allow me to introduce myself to you. Colonel Alvarez, I'm General Adolfo Hernandez Boada, the head of the Secret Police in Havana, sir."

He nodded as he admitted he heard his name mentioned before.

"This is good for me to hear from you Colonel Alvarez Sir, and you'll know what I offer you, I offer very few in all of Cuba, sir. Colonel Alvarez Sir, I liked the way you handled yourself over that test I ordered of you, to check where your loyalty truly lay, sir. Colonel Alvarez, tell me truthfully sir, would you have killed my Sergeant, if Lieutenant Colonel Gutierrez did not inform you he worked for me, sir?" the concerned General gave Carlos a quick smirk while resting his hands on his hips while waiting his response.

"Yes sir, I would've most certainly ordered his death for two reasons on that day, General Boada Sir. One: I thought he was truly trying to betray our great Presidente of Cuba and I..."

"And, the second reason for ordering his death Colonel Alvarez." The General interrupted.

"The second reason was because I didn't like the sonofabitch in the least, sir." He glared at the General as he thought to himself, 'It would give me great pleasure to kill you when the proper time comes' General'.

The General's smirk suddenly turned into a wide grin as he replied to the military officer. "To hell and back again, I can see what you mean Colonel Alvarez Sir. I don't like him sitting in the seat of power in Havana myself, sir." The smirk instantly disappeared and he turned serious as he cautiously eyed the taller and good looking Colonel, and then he added. "I must warn you sir it was some of your foolish remarks that caused me to instigate this check on your loyalty in the first place, sir. You spoke some dangerous words against our Presidente, and I had to check out your true feelings on him, sir. You have passed my test perfectly Colonel."

"Not wishing to show any disrespect to you, General Boada Sir. But you said something about an offer for me, sir? I was wondering what that offer might be, General."

"Ahhh that is what I like to see from all the military soldiers on this Island, tenacity sir. Colonel Alvarez, I was wondering if you might be interested in joining my outfit, sir. I could certainly use a good man such as you, especially since you have already passed my test, sir. That makes you a very special person in my eyes, sir. Well, what do you say to my offer Colonel? Will you allow me to steal you away from the Army and move you here to the capital and work form my office, sir?" the much older General grinned that was more of a sneer at the Colonel.

He smiled back at the ugly looking General of the secret police, as he offered to him. "I'm afraid not General Boada, sir. I'm quite comfortable where I am at the moment, sir."

"Of course you realize I can just order this of you, if I so choose Colonel Alvarez."

"I understand you can sir, but I don't believe you'd do that to me, General Boada."

"Oh, you believe this true sir, and why is it that you believe this thought, Colonel Alvarez?"

"Because I believe you're as good a soldier as I am sir, and I'd much rather have one of my soldiers join me out of respect for my accomplishments, sir. Than to be forced to order him to do so, sir." He allowed his expression to show that he was getting very bored.

Again the grin returned to the General's lips as he replied to the smug looking Colonel. "Yes, you're so much like me, yes very much so, and I to would much rather have someone I was interested in, join me voluntarily, Colonel. I thank you for your honesty, but I warn you, I'm going to keep my eye on you, and try to steal you from the Army every chance I get, Colonel Alvarez. You're too much like me to allow you to escape my needs, sir." General Boada checked his watch, it was half past eight and he remarked. "The Presidente is a little late this morning, oh yes, I remember now. He's waiting until I finished speaking with you."

No sooner did he announce this, than did Castro come charging into his outer office. Both of the Officers immediately snapped to attention. Fidel Castro hesitated before returning their salutes as he growled at his General. "Well, how did you make out with my young Colonel here, sir? Is he going to join you organization General?"

"No El Presidente Fidel Castro Sir. He much rather remain a Colonel in your service, sir."

"Oh. Do you want me to order him to join your office, General Boada?" Fidel Castro offered as he cast a cautious eye towards the saluting young Colonel standing by the General's side.

"No El Presidente that'll not be necessary sir. I believe he'll come around in due time sir, once he realizes his chosen field will lead him no further than he has already accomplished, sir."

Colonel Alvarez took this moment to announce to Castro he wished an audience with him.

"I'm much too busy to meet with you today, Colonel Alvarez. You should have gone through the proper channels if you wished to have a conversation with me, Colonel. General Boada, were you aware this Colonel wished to speak with me on this fine morning, sir?"

"No sir, I never did get the chance to ask him why he was here at your office today, sir. I thought perhaps you might have sent for him, because of my recent test, El Presidente Sir."

Castro turned back to the Colonel and announced in not so friendly a term. "I cannot spare the time to meet with you today, Colonel. I suggest you speak with my private secretary and she'll setup a meeting in the near future. Maybe we can have lunch I'm pleased when one of my Officers are willing to put to death anyone who threatens me, sir. If you'll excuse me Colonel, I have a lot of work to do." He started to push his way passed the two military officers.

"By the Madonna, I must see you, my Presidente. It is that important I speak with you sir."

Presidente Fidel Castro suddenly glared angrily at Colonel Alvarez as he barked at him this time. "Was that a threat you have just leveled at me, Colonel Alvarez?"

"No sir, I'd cut my tongue free of my mouth before I dare threaten you, Presidente. But it's most important I speak with you. I, my Army have many needs and I must beg for their..."

"Colonel Alvarez, everyone has needs to attend to in Cuba, sir. I'm aware of your Army's countless needs, and I'll see to them the first moment I can. You must leave I told you I have work I must attend to. Thank you for coming to visit me, Colonel. Until the next time we meet again." Castro went to enter his office, but the Colonel dared to speak again.

"El Presidente Sir, I must speak to you today sir." He offered to Castro's back.

Castro did not turn back as he snapped at Alvarez over his shoulder. "You must speak to my secretary and request a meeting be set up between us, Colonel. I cannot help you today." The Cuban Leader entered his office and closed the door behind him.

General Boada smiled at Alvarez, as he smirked and offered. "You see Colonel, if you had joined my office, Castro would have found the time to speak with you."

"I cannot believe he could not spare a few moments to see me." He moaned.

"I suggest you do as ordered by your Presidente, and be careful using religious remarks around him. He has been known to put the user of such remarks to death. Now Colonel Alvarez, speak to his secretary and she'll let you know when Castor will meet you, sir."

He turned to the secretary who gave him the cup of coffee, and asked her when he should return. He hoped he might be able to see Castro this afternoon, or no later than the next day.

The secretary checked her book, and offered. "Colonel Alvarez, Presidente Castro is busy for the next three weeks, and then he is scheduled to leave for South America for a three week vacation. I could not set up a meeting with him until..." She fumbled through the calendar book. "Three months from today. Do you wish me to put you down on the calendar? I must warn you sir. If I do, I cannot promise the meeting will take place. He could change his mind, and you might be bumped from the list of those who wish an appointment with the Presidente."

He could not disguise the disappointment etched in his eyes as he replied to the secretary. "No, that'll not be necessary Ma'am. I believe the problems I come to discuss with Fidel Castro, will have worked themselves out by that time. Thank you though." He turned to leave, but he was forcibly stopped by the General who grabbed him by his arm and he said. "You see Colonel Alvarez, this is how Presidente Castro eliminates any problems facing his soldiers and constituents. This is also how he has been able to remain in office for so long. Colonel, I remind you once more, if you decide to join my office, I could intervene on your behalf, and you'll be able to meet with the Presidente. I feel I must ask you again before you leave if you care to join my office. I can use an Officer like you."

He was too angry to be polite this time as he barked at him. "I told you already I have no intention of joining your crew of liars and snitches, General. By the hand of God, I am a soldier, not a bastard who makes his living by bringing down good soldiers and citizens, sir."

General Boada was just as hot as he fired back with stinging words of his own. "Colonel I already warned you to take heed in the words you address me with sir. I can as simply turn my office loose on you sir, and I'm certain my den of liars and snitches given enough time, could come up with some kind of evidence, that'll bring you down to your knees before me, Colonel. I suggest you leave the capital at once, and do not return to the city until you have a scheduled appointment with the Presidente. I warn you further Colonel I'll be keeping a close eye on you. I swear sir, step one foot over the line just once Colonel and you'll find your fooking ass sitting in one of my cells so fast your head will snap off of your foul shoulders, Colonel Alvarez!"

The buzzer rang in the outer office, it was Castro and he was ordering his secretary to send in General Boada. As he entered, he was offered a seat as Castro asked, "well General, what do you think? Did the Colonel come here as I expected to ask me for monies for his Army?"

"Without a doubt that was his intent Fidel," he offered with a smile to Castro.

"Do you think he's a possible threat against me and my rule over Cuba, General Boada?"

"No definitely not my Presidente. I believe you can trust this Officer to keep the Army in its place for you, sir. If anyone can be trusted, I believe it is this fine Officer, sir."

Castro leaned forward in his chair while staring at Boada. "I hope for your sake you're correct General Boada. I need not remind you of the rumblings we've been monitoring lately, sir."

"Presidente, you should consider raising this Colonel up to General, and placing him in Command of your Army. If you're concerned about the grumbling we've noticed lately. I believe this Colonel Commands enough respect from the Officers to keep them in tow, sir."

"Maybe so General Boada, but I have no such intention of giving my Army Officer this much power. This man will remain a Colonel, until I feel it is the proper time to give him a raise. How are you doing with your plans to sell drugs to the foolish Americans, General Boada?"

"Presidente, we have made contact with two of the toughest drug kingpins in America, and they're happy to get the cocaine and heroin we're offering them. Of course they're trying to get it for less than the agreed price. We have been successful making contact with the Russian gang, and they too are interested in getting some of the shipments of the drugs."

"Just how much money are we speaking about, General Boada?" Fidel Castro asked him.

"Err... to the Americans, we're speaking of about two hundred and seventy million American dollars, Presidente. The Russians have offered three hundred million dollars in cash, sir."

"Are these monies from the Russians going to be paid in American dollars, General Boada?"

"Yes, of course they are American dollars, Presidente." Boada announced proudly.

"Good then I suggest you speak to our allies in Colombia, and get these cursed drugs in transit as soon as possible General. When we get these needed monies, I want some of it going to our military. I have to keep them strong in case the American Coast Guard gets nosy and we have to react properly to protect our, err... interests." He gave his General an ugly sneer.

"I agree with your last assumption Presidente." The General replied calmly.

"General Boada, how soon can I expect to see any of this money coming into my hands?"

"Presidente, the American drug lords are willing to give us half of the requested monies in advance, as soon as we can give them an exact arrival date for the cocaine, sir."

"How soon can we ship the merchandise out to them then General Boada?" Castro asked him.

"Within the week it should be safely on its way to the fools, Presidente Castro."

"Good, I want all that money. I have need of it I swear this is Russia's god dom fault General. Turning me into a lowly drug runner to keep my dom country alive, until something with this American embargo happens. I'm tired of it all I tell you, and all the hardships it's causing to my country and my people. I wonder what history will think of me for selling these drugs to keep my country breathing."

"They'll refer to you as what you truly are, El Presidente Castro, a great leader willing to dance with the devil, to help his beloved country survive, sir. I ponder how many other Presidents of the world would do the evil dance for their country's sake sir."

"Thank you for your kind words General, I needed that. I want to know the first moment when the American money arrives in Cuba, General. I wish to give our military half of it, so the Officers can pay their god dom soldiers for a few weeks longer. Be off with you now General." Castro watched as the General quickly left his office.

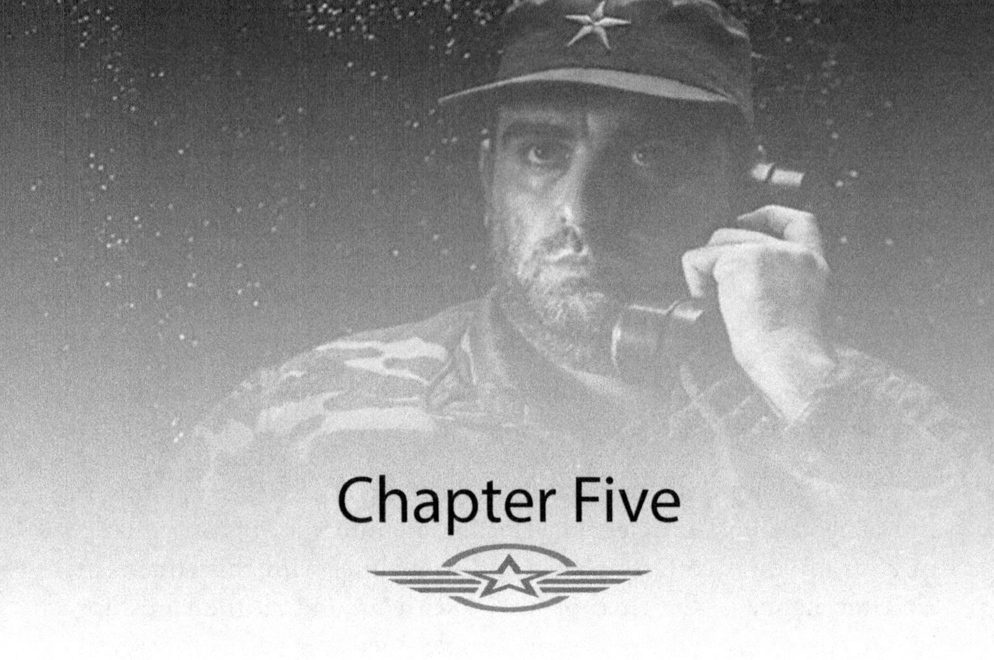

Chapter Five

COLONEL CARLOS RAFAEL FERNANDEZ ALVAREZ

Colonel Carlos Alvarez left Fidel Castro's office in a huff, slamming accidentally into a young female worker walking towards him, and knocking her down to the ground in the process. He never offered her his hand to help her back to her feet as he nearly ran down the stairs to work off some of the growing anger within him. He charged through the double doors, and then he looked for his driver. He spotted him enjoying a tortilla, and jawing with a young woman of dubious standing. The woman was dressed in a rather short dress and a blouse open to her waist, allowing her ample breasts to show clearly to all, and the fuming Colonel called out to him. "Corporal, where the hell is my god dom car at, mista?"

Corporal Alegret jumped while dropping his tortilla on the floor as he looked in the direction of the Colonel yelling at him, and he immediately replied. "Colonel Alvarez, I'll have it for you in a second, sir." He instantly ran off, leaving the young woman staring angrily at him, and then at the Colonel who snapped nastily at her. "By God's good grace woman, be careful or I will have you investigated."

Not knowing who this young military officer yelling at her was, she immediately turned and quickly disappeared in the maddening crowds walking around the streets of the capital. Moments later,

Corporal Alegret appeared with the car and he jumped out of it and opened the door for the still fuming Colonel Alvarez as he offered to his Commanding Officer. "Sir, I was able to fuel up at a military stop. I even fueled up the two five gallon reserve cans and stored them in the trunk of the car, sir. If you feel like…"

"I care not a bit of my sweat about fuel, get me back to the god dom base, I'm wasting my god dom time trying to talk any sense to this old and worn out man leading our country right to the very gates of hell, Sergeant."

The Corporal limbed into the vehicle and they headed off for San Jose de las Lajas. The one hour ride was done in complete silence, with Colonel Alvarez still fuming in the back seat. The traffic was light, there was no one on the highway, it was ten o'clock in the morning and everyone who had a job, was already working.

The Colonel's vehicle pulled through the gate and he immediately growled at the driver. "Drop me off at my dom office." He got out of the car and found Sergeant Regueiro waiting on the steps for him. "Colonel Alvarez Sir, were you able to see the Presidente of Cuba, sir? How did it go? Were you able to make him understand he's turning his back on the Army?"

Colonel Carlos Alvarez said nothing more as he stormed passed the Sergeant, and he slammed his door behind him, and then he proceeded to rip apart his office. He knocked pictures down from the walls, kicked over the garbage can, and he even ripped the map of Cuba off the wall and he tore it to shreds with his angry hands, and then he threw a bust of Castro through a window. All the while he cursed anything he touched in the room. As angry as he was, he was smart enough to refrain from using Fidel Castro's name, or even cursing him in his wild tirade.

Sergeant Regueiro carefully opened the door hanging by one hinge, and entered the destroyed office slowly, afraid of being hit by a flying object. He was holding the bust of Castro that went flying through the glass. He smiled at the raging Colonel, but he got cursed at for his trouble.

"Madre de Dios, what the fook do you want with me, mista? May God curse you and your entire family to hell for all of eternity, if you keep on bothering me today Sergeant. Leave my office at once, I want to be alone, god dommit. Leave before I place my foot up your ass mista. Get out of here, god dommit!" Colonel Alvarez was a long way from calming down any.

Sergeant Regueiro saw the Colonel in a tirade before, so this was nothing new to him and he did not get insulted by his angry words aimed at him either as he offered to his Commanding Officer. "I guess you did not get to see our Presidente?"

"By the loved Madonna, the son of a milkless whore could not spare the god dom time to listen to me for one dom second of his god dom time. Not for one dom second, I tell you Sergeant. The sonofabitch was too dom busy to see his Military Officer on an important matter such as this one is. No wonder so many of Cuba's fine Officers have fled our country as if there was a foul plague raging throughout the entire Island. Sergeant, I see no fooking future for Cuba if Fidel Castro is allowed to continue his worthless rule over the god dom Island. He's locked into the old ways, and even the foul Russians were smart enough to abandon these very foolish ways of before, Sergeant."

"You speak the truth Colonel Alvarez. I'm here to inform you every Officer and Junior Officer on the base is behind you if you choose to do something about the problem in Havana."

The Sergeant's words immediately calmed Colonel Carlos Alvarez down a little as he asked his young Sergeant. "You were able to speak to all the other Officers for me already, Sergeant?"

"Yes Colonel Alvarez and they all happen to agree with you and your new cause, sir."

"What about the other Officers I need? Are they as willing to back me, err... us, Sergeant?"

"I believe every soldier on the base is fed up with Castro and his stupid antics of late, anyone of them would be willing to pull the trigger to end the old fool's worthless regime, sir."

Carlos Alvarez stood up his chair and then he plopped down heavily in it, and he grumbled at the young Sergeant again. "By the blessed Virgin Mary, this is more than I have dared to believe, or have ever expected. You have done very well Sergeant, and I shall never forget the fine effort you have put forth here. I think it's time I start conducting some interviews with my soldiers, to see how far they'll follow me in this. I'll have to get in touch with other Officers in the country I'll need, if I'm to be successful in ousting this old fool we call El Presidente."

"If you care to make a list, I'll get in contact with them, and set up the meeting for you, sir."

"Madonna save me from the devil's eyes, you're the second one in the last few days who has asked me to make up such a god dom list for them. I'll have all the names for you later. I guess I better clean my office if I'm to invite the Officers here to speak with me, Sergeant."

"Why do you not go over to the mess, and have yourself something to eat, Colonel. I can have one of the orderlies repair your office while you're gone, sir." The Sergeant offered to Carlos.

"No, I don't want any of the orderlies in my office at this time, Sergeant. No one is to enter my office any longer except for yourself, and any of my Officers who stand behind us, mista. I don't want someone coming across something they should not see lying around in here. I shall handle this foul mess for myself. My driver was able to fill two five gallon reserve gas cans in the back of my car. Take the fuel and divide it in the other Officer's vehicles for them. At least they'll be able to travel in their cars for a few days before they're forced to go back to their god dom bikes for their transportation. I hate that old fool for this terrible insult to us soldiers."

"This is good to know sir, I'll handle it my Colonel. I'm certain the other Officers will be happy to see the improvements we're creating already, sir. How much fuel is left in your car?"

"I believe I heard the driver complain we were down to half a tank of fuel already. Why?"

"Do you not think you should hold the fuel in reserve for yourself, Colonel Alvarez, sir? After all Sir, you're going to be doing a lot of traveling in the near future for us I believe, sir."

"By God, you have given me something to think about, Sergeant. I should give my Officers the god dom fuel, but on the other hand I'm going to need it for myself, Lord Jesus help me."

"Then I'll take the decision out of your hands, Colonel Alvarez. I'll hold the fuel in reserve for your use only, sir. The other Officers seem to be getting rather use to riding their bikes sir, and we should allow them to continue to do so, until you're finally installed in the Presidency. It's a minor hardship we'll have to put up with for just a while longer, my Colonel."

"Ahhh, you take better care of me than my own mother does, Sergeant. Thank you for your concerns, Sergeant. I want you to assemble all my Officers in the mess in half an hour. You're to have the other soldiers out of the way for this meeting. By the will of God, I don't want any interruptions, or anyone else around to listen in on our conversation, Sergeant. I had one run in with the Special Police and General Boada already, and I don't want to tangle with him for a second time, before I'm ready to do proper battle with the god dom great fool. The General is a smart sonofabitch to be forced to deal with."

"I understand this and I have teams sent out to care for all the tanks. I'll have them scraped clean of rust, and oil all moving parts, as long as the used oil holds out, sir. The rest of the soldiers will be busy policing up the entire base, Colonel. Guards will be placed around the mess hall to keep anyone from coming too close to it, sir. I'll start a rumor that the Officers are discussing some leave time for them. That should keep the foul troops willing to stay away, sir."

"Sergeant Regueiro, you're my right hand man on this base. Get it done for me soldier."

"Yes sir. Err... sir you said something moments before that has troubled me a little, Colonel. You said something about making the list of Officers you'll need for someone else sir, but you never told me who you did this first list up for, Colonel Alvarez. Do you mind telling me who you were referring to before, Colonel?" the worried Sergeant looked at Colonel Alvarez cautiously, as if he was hurt by being forced to actually ask him this question. The last thing he wanted to insinuate was he did not trust the Colonel or his judgment for that matter.

Colonel Carlos Alvarez's face broke out into a wide smile as he offered back to his concerned looking young Sergeant. "It's no problem Sergeant Regueiro, my girlfriend has asked me to make up a list for her as well, the last time I was with her. She's aware of my future plans for this new revolution of ours, and she also wants to be a part of them, Sergeant." Colonel Alvarez suddenly looked for the small framed picture of Maria dressed in a black dress that always sat on the corner of his desk. It was missing, and he looked around the mess, the floor was littered with all sorts of broken debris and papers from his desk. He made a move to rise from his chair and start looking for the missing picture of his girlfriend, but Sergeant Regueiro spoke up first which caused the Cuban Colonel to sit back down in his chair and listen to his words.

"I forgot about it Colonel Alvarez. But a letter from Maria Ibarra addressed to you has arrived earlier today on the base, sir. I was at the base post, and the Corporal gave me the letter for you, sir." Sergeant Regueiro fumbled in his pocket until he found the small light blue envelope, and then he added as he handed the concerned Colonel the envelope. "Ahhh Colonel, here it is sir. I'll leave while you read the letter from your girlfriend, Colonel Alvarez."

"Nonsense, I have no secrets to hold from you, Sergeant Regueiro. You'll stay in my office while I read the dom letter for my lady, mista." Colonel Alvarez cleaned the shattered glass away from the desktop, and then he look for his letter opener. It was nowhere to be seen, so he merely ripped the end of the envelope off with his fingers, and then he pulled out a card. It was an invitation of some kind that was printed on hard blue paper. There was a short note included with the invitation, he unfolded it and read the words from his lover.

The letter was printed out on plain white paper, and it was lightly scented by Maria's favorite perfume, which forced him to remember their lovemaking of two nights before. He smiled over the fond memory held in his mind as he began reading the letter.

Dear Carlos.

'I was so happy when you proposed marriage to me last night. I waited so long for you to ask me to marry you. You made me the happiest woman in the world, my dear Colonel'.

Colonel Alvarez stopped reading and he searched his mind, trying to remember if he ever did really asked her to marry him that night, but he could not remember it ever coming up in any of his conversations with her on that night. He shrugged and continued reading.

'I made a list of those I'd like to attend the engagement party announcing to the world we'll marry. I love you and I have included the names of all those I want to invite to my home for the party. If you think of anyone else you might want to add, please, add them to the guest list, and I'll make sure they receive an invitation. I included one of the invitations I'll send out'.

'I love you dearest'.

Maria Ibarra, the future Mrs. Alvarez.

The Colonel was really confused he did not remember asking Maria to marry him, even though he wanted her. She was the one who always put him off. But now he wondered what got into her. A thought suddenly flashed through his mind, maybe she was pregnant. He quickly laughed that off because it was too soon for her to know that. The thought of her fooling around had never entered his mind.

He opened the second page with the list of guests Maria wanted to invite to the party, and a smile started to spread across his lips. Reading the names off, he realized what she did. The list contained the names of every officer he recited to her the night before, the men and women he would need if he was serious about ousting Castro. He laughed as her plan cleared in his mind's eye. What could be a better way to assemble the officers he needed in one building, than to invite them to an engagement party, not even the Secret Police would find this out of the ordinary?

"Madonna, she is great." He said as he handed the pages to the Sergeant Regueiro. He read them while Carlos looked at the professional type of invitation included with the letter.

The Sergeant handed the list back as he offered. "Colonel, I see your lady is going to be quite the asset to our cause. This is quite a plan. No one would ever think we're going to have a meeting to form the future of Cuba. One thing I don't see through is my name on the list, sir."

"You don't then watch this Sergeant." He picked up a broken pencil from the floor and he wrote his name on the list as he offered to the Sergeant. "I guess I have to ask you Sergeant Regueiro. Are you coming to my engagement party, mista?"

"Nothing could stop me from being there and seeing you with your lady, Colonel Alvarez Sir."

"God must be protecting me from all harm. Now, do as I have just instructed you Sergeant. Get the troops busy working on the base. I want to meet with my Officers, but first, I shall speak with Maria. Out Sergeant."

"Yes sir." Sergeant Regueiro saluted and then he left the Colonel's office. As Colonel Alvarez looked around his all but destroyed office for the picture of his love, he heard his Sergeant screaming at the other soldiers, making sure they all had something to keep themselves busy. He found the picture he was searching for tucked under some papers, and he brushed it off and then placed it in its usual spot, he then dialed Maria. After the third ring, a tired sounding voice responded in the phone. "Yes?"

"Maria, Carlos here and I have to ask you a question. Will you marry me young lady?"

"Hmmmm... I thought you would never ask me Colonel Alvarez. I believe you have received my invitation, and you approve of it. Am I allowed to send one to all the guests on the list?"

"By all means my love and future wife." He said into the phone calmly.

"Thank you, and are there any other names you wish to add to the list? I need to know if you wish them to know about our party, so they can make the proper arrangements to attend."

"I have a few more names to add to the list, but they can wait until I arrive tonight."

She immediately perked up when she heard him promise to spend the night with her. "Good, then we can settle on a date for the party. I'll have a lot to do to prepare for our party, I need some more wine, snacks, and extra food. I'll have to buy myself a new dress, and make arrangements with my neighbors, so they don't become alarmed when they see so many soldiers and friends showing up. I hope I have enough room for everyone. I have to..."

"By the Virgin, I swear you'll do fine Maria, don't worry about your neighbors. I'll give you the money I have, although it'll not be very much. It has been three months since I received any pay, and it costs money to live, even on base. I'll be of little financial help with the party."

"Carlos! Listen to yourself. Next, you'll threaten to eat bugs on me. I'm well aware of your situation, and I don't remember asking you for any money. I have plenty of money set aside, you know I've been working for the past three years, and I own my home thanks to my beloved father. You worry about who you want to invite, and getting here yourself. I'll worry about the rest. I hope you'll have something else to wear other than that filthy military uniform."

"For the love of God, what the devil is this about young lady? I thought you like me dressed in my uniform, woman." He suddenly laughed as he hung up the phone, and then he called out and ordered his Sergeant to bring him the only civilian suit he owned, while he went over the list of names to make sure no one was missed needed by him and the others. The Sergeant returned with his civilian suit, it was filthy and wrinkled up. "Err... Sergeant, do you think it at all possible for you to get my suit cleaned and pressed mista?"

The Sergeant held the suit aloft with one hand and he rubbed his chin with the other. "I'd stand a better chance of having it buried. What did you do, eat dinner on it and then sleep in it sir?"

"Funny mista, get it cleaned and have it back here by no later than tomorrow night, mista."

"I'll do that for you Colonel." The Sergeant spun around and left his office.

The Colonel checked his watch, it was nearing four p.m. and he was amazed the time had flown by at such a pace. It felt like it was only an hour since he was with Castro. He stood up, and stretched and groaned as he gathered his list of names and checked his bottom drawer, cursing as he found it empty. Now, he had to pick up a bottle of wine for them. He walked out of his office and headed for his bike, he decided to save the fuel in his car for when he really needed it. He took time to threaten Sergeant Regueiro that he would lose his nuts if the fuel in his car disappeared. Carlos then headed off base for the first time, not upset at having to ride a bike again, because he understood this chapter in his life was fast approaching a conclusion. He whistled over the thought of spending the night with his lover, and the possibility of becoming the next President of Cuba. He smiled as he thought of sitting in Castro's chair.

The bike ride to Maria's home was completed quickly, but he forgot to stop and pick up the bottle of wine though. Maria did not allow his troubling thoughts to linger for long, because she rushed out and wrapped herself around her man. They kissed, laughed and then walked hand in hand into her home. The show was for anyone who might have been trailing the Colonel. Once inside she offered him a chilled glass of rum. Alvarez downed it in one gulp, and she quickly poured him another glass. This time he only sipped it as he offered her the new list of names.

She checked it against the other one, and she realized she had to make up two more invitations. After he relaxed, she ordered him to shower. When he finished, he came walking into the kitchen and found Maria naked and waiting for him. They made love on the kitchen floor, and then they had something to eat, before they talked of their future plans.

It was seven thirty p.m. on August 27th, 1996, when the two of them formulated their final draft of the list and their plans for the celebration in earnest. She began by asking her lover. "Carlos, when do you want to have this party?"

He checked his watch as if he was going to find the answer there and then replied to her. "We'll have to give the Officers time to make their plans to attend. I think we should put it off until around September 18th, no?"

"Yes, you're right. We have to give them some time to respond. I hope everyone will come."

"They'll all come, I swear by the sacred Madonna they will, over the years, all those on the list have offered to attend my marriage, just to make certain I'd go through with it. I'm extremely certain not one of them had changed their minds." He laughed at Maria.

"And, why is this mista?" she guffawed with a smile as she stared at him.

"By the Blessed Virgin, it's because they're all jealous of me. I was always playing with all the women, and they were married, and they had to sneak around to do what I was doing freely."

She suddenly reached out and grabbed a hand full of Alvarez's chest hair as she moved her face close to his, and she warned him with burning eyes. "And, this sport will stop when we're married, right Mista Colonel?"

Carlos grinned as he hesitated for a moment, causing her to tug even harder on his hair. "Hey, yeow, yes, yes, huh. I'll stop screwing around on the beach I swear it to you Maria."

"You promise me you'll stop chasing all the young women of Cuba around, mista?"

"Yes, yes, I promise Maria. By the Holy Father, let go of my hair please, you're killing me lady." He said as he went with the pressure as she pulled even harder on his hair.

"Yeeeaaaooowww, for the love of God woman. Yes I promise you, let go please Maria."

"You better, or I shall have these little babies here for my new pair of earrings, mista." She warned as her hand went from his chest hairs down to his nuts, and she tugged lightly on them.

The two lovers spent the entire night going over the complete list of name, and searching their minds to make certain they included everyone necessary for their plans to be successful, to be there when they were needed. It was Maria's idea to actually invite Fidel Castro and General Boada as well to their party. Both of them knew the two men would never attend the party, but this would eliminate any prying eyes with the offer. Who would waste their time keeping an eye on a party they were invited to? Carlos Alvarez kissed Maria lightly on the forehead for her idea, one he would never have come up with himself. By the time they finally finished, and figuring a way to break his idea to the other military officers, it had grown late on them. When he saw Maria yawn, he noticed it was quarter past eleven, and he felt thoroughly exhausted as he said to her. "Maria, you want to go to sleep?"

She checked the clock, and then agreed as she slid her hands through her lovely hair then she rubbed it vigorously until she looked like the rear end of a sheep with her hair sticking out all over her head.

He reached over the table to take her hand in his, and making her stand as he did so. He then undid the buttons on the straps of her dress, and allowed it to fall to the floor, and he cupped a breast and kissed her nipple. He scooped her up in his arms and carried her to the bedroom, where he laid her down on the bed. He kissed her belly, and then he worked his way down her body until he finally reached his goal. He worked her over until he was certain she came, he then mounted her and took his time while making love to her. When they finished, they laid on the mattress, sweat covered and exhausted. In seconds, they were both snoring away.

Maria woke in the middle of the night to pull the sheets over their naked bodies, deciding to make love to her man once more by taking him in her mouth. In seconds, he was hard as a rock, but he was too exhausted to take full advantage of it, so she finished him off with her mouth.She was the first one to rise on this morning, and she was full of vigor. She started the bacon cooking and took a quick shower, dressed and was cooking eggs by the time he woke and came strolling into the kitchen. She was singing and when she saw Carlos standing there hard as a rock, she immediately took advantage of the situation. They made love on the kitchen floor again. Satisfied, they both ate and felt the world was a good place to live in, and they were glad to be alive. She assured Carlos she would have the invitations in the mail that same day. Then she cleaned the dishes, pulled Carlos to his feet and led him to the bedroom to get dressed.

She tapped him on his rearend as she ordered him to dress, and then she told him to leave because she had so much to do. She wanted to speak with a few of her female friends, to make sure they were really serious about causing Fidel Castro's overthrow. She also wanted her friends involved in the new revolution, so she had some people close to her she could rely on herself. If she was going to be Cuba's First Lady, she would need ladies in waiting. She decided to offer her two best friends the opportunity to be her bridesmaids, and with this, she could breach the subject of Castro with them.

When Carlos was dressed, she quickly ushered him out of the door. She kissed him good bye but he was very reluctant to leave as he cupped her breast. She giggled and purred at him sexily. "Oh no you don't mista, I swear by the Blessed Virgin, you're not going to get my motor running, and then run away on me. Leaving me to handle what you have started by myself. Beat it before I change my mind and rape you."

"For the love of God, that is exactly what I wanted you to do to me, Maria." He smirked as his hand tried to work its way into the thin nightdress Maria wore.

"Carlos please what will the neighbors think about what you are trying to do to me here?"

"By the Holy Madonna, they'll think me one of the luckiest bastards in the whole world, making love to the most beautiful woman who lives on the god dom planet, Maria." He slid his tongue in her mouth.

She nipped at the tip of his tongue as she giggled, and then she complained at him again. "You really have a way with your god cursed words my dear Colonel, Carlos, Alvarez. Now I understand why you were so lucky with all the beach babes. I warn you mista, if I ever catch you using these lines on anyone else but me, I shall skin you alive and then allow the ants to pick your carcass clean on you. Go before I make you earn your morning meal again." She tugged on his stiffening dick while purring once more at him. "Carlos, you better be very careful riding your bike with this little problem of yours here, my foolish lover. I'd surely hate to see you hurt yourself because of this, mista."

"Hey, hey, what do you mean by my little problem? It was not a small problem last night."

"Ha, that was before I wore off an inch of it on you, mista. Now, be off with you so I can start the work I need to do. You're beginning to make me angry with you." She glared at him.

Carlos won on the receiving end of this look before, and knowing she was serious he finally gave in and left her. They kissed and he headed off for the military base, as happy as he could ever be. His whole world was taking great shape, Cuba's future was shaping up, and he would soon become the most powerful man in all of Cuba.

Colonel Carlos Alvarez saw many of his soldiers working hard on a few of the newer T-80 Russian built tanks. They were attacking the machines with wire brushes, and rubbing the rust free of them. A second team of soldiers ran the ramrod down the bore of the 125 mm cannon. A third team of troops worked inside doing God knows what to the machine. He could not see, but he heard them complaining. He spotted the Sergeant and he motioned him over to his side.

Sergeant Regueiro saluted and said, "I have the men inside removing the stagnated water to stop the breading of God cursed mosquitoes, Colonel. One man found a six foot snake hiding in tank three. They killed it, and we had fresh meat for the morning mess. Later, I'm having a work crew work on the tracks and rollers of the undercarriage of the tanks. I know many tanks have not been oiled in this manner for a year."

"What the hell are you using for oil for the god dom machines Sergeant Regueiro?"

"Colonel Alvarez, we're using the old oil from the mess cooking pots sir, the grease from their cooking Colonel, sir. I know it is not right to use this, but it is better than nothing at all, sir."

"You are right, carry on." He saluted his best, and Carlos headed for his office. To his surprise, he saw his suit cleaned and pressed and hanging on a hook. He looked for his Sergeant, but he was nowhere to be seen, yet he could still hear him screaming at the make work crews outside.

Carlos smiled as he went over the latest reports lying on his desk. Most of the reports were requesting something from him. Ammunition, fuel, paint, oil, and money, every report he read had a plea for money with them, for soldier's pay, money to enable the cooks to buy meat for the troops, money to buy more supplies, money, money, money, always money.

"As God is my judge," he bitched as he chucked the stack of requests into the waste paper basket. "Do any of these fools realize I'm aware they need god dom money? I too need money." He paced the room to walk off his anger, he checked his watch. It was nine thirty, his stomach growled and he griped he would kill for a cup of hot coffee. There was a tap on his door.

"Enter!" He growled at the person who was standing on the other side of the closed door.

Sergeant Regueiro came in the office with a coffee pot and some small cakes that the cooks made fresh that morning. The Sergeant smiled to his commanding officer as he said to him. "It was getting around the time I usually have myself a cup of coffee, and I hate drinking it alone, sir. Besides sir, after spending the night with that wildcat of yours, I thought you might need something sweet to help replace your energy I'm certain she had depleted on you, sir. That is why I stole these cakes the cooks planned to hand out for afternoon mess. Hungry Colonel?"

"Dom right I am Sergeant, place that tray right here in front of me," he cleared an area on his desk and then added to his Sergeant. "You have read my mind, I was just bitching to myself I'd kill for a cup of coffee."

"I hope you'll not kill me sir." Sergeant Regueiro chuckled at the grinning Cuban Colonel.

"Not a chance in hell of that happening, Sergeant Regueiro. To kill you would be like me cutting off my own right hand to suit my arm, my dear friend." Colonel Carlos Alvarez laughed as he poured himself a cup of coffee. If there was one thing not lacking in Cuba, it was coffee.

The steaming brew quickly filled his nostrils and he drooled as he sipped it. It burned him going down. "Ahhh that is great," he announced pleasantly as he leaned back in his chair.

The Sergeant seemed like he had something on his mind, and he shifted his weight in his chair until the upset Colonel snapped at him. "What is it? You're acting worse than a virgin on her wedding night."

The Sergeant calmed down. "Sir, I was hoping you'd tell me how it went last night."

"With Maria? You want to know how she was in bed from me, you great fool you? Sergeant Regueiro, I didn't know you were nothing more than a dirty old man with evil thoughts, mista."

Regueiro's face turned red as he replied to his Commanding Officer. "No, not that sir, I just wanted to know if you came up with a plan. I'd not pry into your private life, sir. I swear I would never do such a foul thing sir. I was only..."

Colonel Alvarez laughed as he stared at his Sergeant who realized his Colonel was busting his horns. "Arr... you're something Colonel. Give me back my god dom coffee and get your own."

"Calm down a little Sergeant, what is it you wanted to know from me, mista?"

"I wanted to know how good Maria truly was in the old sack with you Colonel Alvarez, sir." This time around it was the Sergeant who was trying to get the best of his young Colonel.

"May God curse you to hell for asking me this, Sergeant? Well let me tell you Sergeant, Maria has the best tits in all Cuba, mista. She has an ass that only God Himself could have shaped, and a waist I can squeeze with both of my hands. And, let me tell you something else, she can suck your eyes out of your head right through the end of your dick, if you allow her to mista. She can make love all night long and never get tired, and always want more." Colonel Alvarez could see he was making the Sergeant excited, and he kept it going until he could finally get even with him.

"Yeahhhhh?" The Sergeant said, getting even more involved with the conversation.

"Yeah, may the Virgin curse me to hell, but she has the best lips to slip your dick between, and a dry mouth, and she humms while she does you with her mouth, this is to increase a man's pleasure, Sergeant." He spoke lower and lower, forcing him to lean closer to hear his words.

"Yes, I believe Maria could take care of ten men, and leave none of them wanting more."

"Yeahhhhhhhhhh?" the Sergeant said again, as he was getting even more excited over what the Colonel was telling him.

"Yeah, and a rearend, oh Madonna, let me tell you about her lovely rearend, Sergeant. It's so round and firm that it fits in a man's hands like this." He held his two hands apart before him.

"Yeahhhhh?" the Sergeant said, now grinning from ear to ear as he stared at him.

"Yeah, and she weighs next to nothing so you can pick her up, and move her around to increase your pleasures, mista. She is so light you can hold her in the air and finish her that way."

"Yeah?" the Sergeant cried as he swallowed his saliva, and he wiped the side of his mouth.

"Yeah, may the Madonna protect me, but there is one more thing that you must know about Maria's fine lovemaking abilities. Come here, closer, no closer than that Sergeant. Yes, that is it, nice and close, I want to whisper this to you so no one else can hear my words. There that is close enough. Here is the last thing you have to know about Maria, when she is coming, she does this little thing with her hips that heightens a man's ecstasy to new depths on him, Sergeant."

"Yeahhhhhh, and what is that little thing Colonel Alvarez, sir?" the Sergeant asked him excitedly once again.

He did not speak any further to the excited Sergeant. Instead, he hesitated for a second or two as his face suddenly contorted into a mask of what looked like pain to the Sergeant. The terrible look of strain caused the Sergeant some concern until the Colonel let out with one of the loudest and longest farts the Sergeant had ever heard in his entire life, actually making him jump back and curse at the Cuban Officer at the same time.

"Why you sonofabitch you, you really had me going there for a little while Colonel. Blessed Lord Jesus, all this was nothing more than bullshit. You have to remember you're talking to a poor man who has not had any loving for over a month now, sir. Christ Almighty, will you look at this please, I almost came in my god dom pants Colonel, and I would've been pissed if I did, and found out all of this crap you have been peddling me, was all bullshit, sir." The Sergeant rubbed his crotch, and he added to his complaint at his Commanding Officer. "Shit sir, my dick nearly burst through my god dom pants. Look at me Colonel." He complained as he rubbed the mound his stiff dick made in his pants.

The Colonel laughed all the more harder, as he saw the effect his little trick had on him. "Sergeant, everything I told you about Maria is true, everything for the fart that is, you fool you."

"You really had me going for a minute there, Colonel. You should know better than to drive a poor foot soldier crazy like this sir, especially one who is not getting any for himself for quite a while, sir. Now, I'm forced to spend my evening trying to bed something, even if it has to be a god dom chicken, Colonel." The young Sergeant complained at Colonel Alvarez.

They shared a laugh over the Sergeant's last remark. It was a good moment shared by close friends. Then Colonel Alvarez turned serious as he went over the rest of the plans both he and Maria had formulated. By the time he was through, he was as hot over the plan to eliminate Castro, as he was about Maria's body.

"Your plan is flawless and it should succeed. But I fail to see where I fit in your future, sir."

"Sergeant Regueiro, you're turning into quite the baby on me I fear, mista. By the good grace of God, I have already told you there is a place for you in my future, mista. You'll take over this military base and work with me. Once I'm in place as the new Presidente of Cuba, you'll be heading all my security forces for me and the country also. On your head will fall my safety, and the safety of all who are placed in office with me, mista. There'll be plenty of work for you in my new Administration so fear no more, Sergeant." The Colonel carefully eyed his friend.

A smile slowly spread across the young Sergeant's lips, as he milled over what the Colonel had just told him. "You mean I'll be in control of all the security forces for the Island, sir?"

"Madre de Dios, let us not jump ahead to fast here. For the time being, you shall have to be content to be in command of my personal security, while I'm on this base or in the area. Once I am the Presidente, I'll form a private security force in which you'll be an intricate cog Sergeant."

"Will I still be a mere Sergeant with all of these new duties of mine, Colonel Alvarez?"

"Madonna, you jest with me unwisely, you fool you. How could you possibly remain a Sergeant if you're part of the Presidente's security force? At the least, you'll be a Colonel, and if all goes as planned, you could even become a god dom General. I shall need countless trusted people surrounding me. Can I rely on you mista?"

Sergeant Regueiro jumped up to his feet and punched himself in the chest as he replied. "You can trust me with your life, Colonel. I'll die before I allow anything to happen to you sir."

"Let's hope nothing that drastic will take place Sergeant. Another cup of coffee please?"

"Please." The Sergeant replied as he held his cup out to the grinning Colonel now.

The long stretch of days before the scheduled, supposed party/meeting, passed slowly for all concerned. Colonel Carlos Alvarez filled the rest of the days by paying a number of short visits to Maria, during which they made love and formulated the rest of their plans together. The rest of the days were spent with preparing himself, and the few who knew of his plans. His depression over the condition his country was in was fueled by many daily reports that kept flooding into his office, and more requests for any of the basic necessities. Day after day, Colonel Carlos Alvarez's anger increased against Castro, because all he was able to do was sit in his office, and act like he was making plans to help the people of Cuba. Yet day after day, nothing new ever came out of Havana that showed Castro had any interest in helping Cuba get out of the deep depression she was slipping deeper and deeper into with each passing day.

Each night when he visited Maria at her home, she informed him of the many responses to the invitations coming in, so far one of nineteen of the invited officers, declined to attend their party, stating personal business would not allow him the luxury to get away from his duties at the time requested of him.

Chapter Six

THE PRESIDENTIAL PALACE, HAVANA CUBA.
SEPTEMBER 4th, 1996

Presidente Fidel Castro showed up a little late to his office on this day, it was the third time it had happened to him that year. He enjoyed a relaxing morning, after he shared extra time with his mistress the night before. When he entered his office, the mail was already lying on his desk, and General Boada was sitting in his chair waiting for the Presidente to finally arrive.

General Boada instantly rose from his chair and he quickly bowed slightly as Castro entered his office, surrounded by his ever present horde of bodyguards. He bowed again to Castro as he walked by him. The guards took up their protective positions on either side of the door, and one by the window of the office. Castro did not acknowledge the General's presence in the office until he made himself comfortable in his chair. After lighting up a cigar, he leaned back deeply in the chair and blew the smoke up towards the ceiling. Then he turned to the General and looked at him, he then smiled as he pointed towards the empty chair with the end of his cigar. Once the General was seated, Castro asked him politely. "Would you care for a cigar to enjoy while we carry out this unscheduled meeting between us, General Boada?"

"Please El Presidente." The General nodded toward the seated Presidente of Cuba.

Castro offered him the box, and the General took a Havana as Castor started to speak. "I see this is going to be one of those meetings that I don't like to attend. When my General calls me El Presidente, there has to be a problem. You have my undivided attention General. Begin."

General Boada exhaled the thick smoke and then he watched it drift slowly up towards ceiling, and he began the meeting by removing a letter from his breast pocket. He handed it to Presidente Castro and then he waited until he had the time to read the paper.

"It's an invitation to one of my Colonel's wedding party, General. Don't tell me my greatly feared Security General has become concerned over a simple wedding party now, sir?"

"No my El Presidente, I'm not concerned about this party at all, or the dogs who are invited to it. It seems this young upstart has amassed a bus load of important friends though, and I was..."

"Then he's worth your watching of him General Boada. No?" Castro interrupted the General.

"No Fidel, not really sir." The General offered as he took another drag of the fine cigar.

"That is better General Boada. I no longer feel so threatened." He made a quick movement with his hand, and the bodyguards quickly left the room and then the Presidente growled at the General. "You may continue speaking in private because I must know what causes you concern."

"The interest I'm displaying is for this young Military Officer, not against him at this time..."

"Is he in danger of being assassinated General Boada?" Castro interrupted again, showing his concern for the young officer, and referring to American agents operating inside Cuba.

"No my Presidente, but this is the same Officer who was here a few weeks ago, and he was requesting to have an unannounced audience with you, sir. He's also the young Officer who had his loyalty tested by me, at about the same time as he had appeared here to speak with you, sir."

"And how did he do with this little test of yours General Boada, sir?" Castor asked him.

"He wanted to have my Agent shot, and if it was not for the fast intervention of Lieutenant Colonel Gutierrez, my stupid Agent would've been put to death before I was able to place a quick stop to it my Presidente." The General replied as he took another drag from the cigar.

"Then he's one of my true and loyal soldiers you're speaking of, General Boada?"

"Yes my wise leader." The General replied as he stared back at the seated Castro.

"Then why have you brought this man up to my attention again General? I warn you General Boada, I'm fast becoming bored with this little game of yours, and you're wasting my time with it. You better get to the point quickly, before I lose my patience with you and you pay dearly for it, General." Castro suddenly glared at the now very uncomfortable General.

"Presidente Castro, I spoke to you before about this young Military Officer, sir. We even discussed him at length a few days ago, and I informed you I still wish to enlist this Officer into my police unit, sir. I felt he would be very valuable to me and the service, sir."

"General Boada, why are you bothering me about this god dom Colonel? As I already stated, you're wasting my time over him. If you want him, order him to show up. Is this not so simple?"

General Boada let out his breath mixed with cigar smoke as he added. "If only it was that simple, sir. I already offered this Colonel a position in my staff, but he refused my offer, sir. I'm powerless to order him to enlist because of his military rank and position on his military base, sir. I'm sorry, but you're the only one who can order him to enlist in the Secret Police, sir. This is why I'm still wasting your time with this ongoing situation, my Presidente. I spoke to you many times of this lack of power on my part to deal with this young upstart sir, and you promised to consider this and change it for me, sir."

"It's the way it should be General Boada. I'm the only one here who should have the god dom power to order this of one of our loyal soldiers, General. And, as I told you before this, I shall not increase your power any further than it already is on this Island. You have enough power for one man to enjoy in Cuba General Boada. But I'll consider your reques..."

Castro's attention went to his desk. He just noticed the same type of envelope lying between his letters and he smiled as he offered to his powerful Secret Police General. "It seems you're not the only one who has received an invitation to this pain in the arse Colonel's party, General. You said he has important friends, like who?" Castro said, showing more concern now.

"Well, my leader..." The General started, but he was cut off by Castro as he snapped at him.

"Fidel." Castor interrupter and he said to his trusted General in an angry tone of voice.

"Yes Fidel, it seems some of the Officers from all branches of our service have received this same invitation, sir. Every ranking Officer on Cuba has been invited to this god dom party."

"It appears not only the Officers have received an invitation to this upcoming wedding of one of our Officers. Both you and I have one as well."

"And, so does the Vice President of the Council of State and Minister Lazaro Prio Cabrisas have one, sir." General Boada added with some slight concern lacing his tone this time.

"Hmmm... it seems this young upstart has surrounded himself with a number of extremely important friends. Well General, what do you think? Is this man up to something? Or is he trying to get gifts from the people who can afford to give them."

"I believe this man is to be trusted, Presidente Castro Sir. If he's pulling something here, attack you in anyway. Then why the devil would he invite us to the god dom party? He has to know we'd both arrive there with enough bodyguards to foil any attempt against our lives, sir. No Fidel, I see nothing threatening about this party, sir. I believe, at least I hope the reason he choose to invite us to his party, is so can announce he's joining my Secret Service, sir. I can sure use a man who has been tested, and has passed my test as this one has.

"He has also invited many of my loyal Officers who would immediately foil any attempt on your life, Presidente. The only thing I believe a little strange about this offer, was to invite us both, but, on the other hand, sir. If he wanted to join my service then what better way to announce it than at his wedding party in front of so many of these very important people of Cuba, sir? Taking a young bride means he'll need much money to support her, ahhh, this has to be the true reason for the invite, sir. So he could join my forces with me, sir."

The Cuban President did not like the idea of this man enjoying such powerful friends in his government, joining forces with his second in command as he grumbled at his General. "General Boada, I came to a decision on this young Colonel you speak so highly of. I have decided to enlist him myself, in my private group of special bodyguards. If he's so well trusted by you and all these powerful friends of his then he should work directly under me, General Boada. I thank you for bringing this young Officer up to my attention once again. When is this god dom wedding party scheduled to take place?" He looked at the invitation and then added.

"Ahhh, here it is, September 18th. Very good sir." Castro checked his calendar and noticed he had a prior engagement that would take his entire day, and most of the night also. So it was impossible for him to attend the wedding party, and he was forced to do some quick thinking and he offered to his General. "Are you free on this god dom day, General Boada?"

General Boada quickly checked his pocket calendar and then announced he was free as he smiled at the Cuban Leader.

"Good then I want you to head for Colombia and check on the next shipment of drugs for our new friends in the hated United States, General. Plan to be gone from Monday the 16th, until Friday the 20th, General Boada." Fidel Castro snapped harshly at the General as he held him in his angry stare for the moment.

"Yes, I'll be out of the country between the 16th, until the 20th then, Fidel." General Boada announced as he looked at his watch. "I better get back to my office, so I can clear off my calendar so I can be free for this trip. Am I allowed to take a partner to Colombia with me?"

"Your spouse?" Castro smirked in a mocking tone, knowing who he wanted with him.

The wise General smiled back at the Cuban Leader, but he said nothing more to him though.

Castro realized the General was asking to take his young mistress along with him on this mission and he added to him. "Ahh, I understand now General Boada. Yes, you may take a friend along with you if you please, General Boada." Presidente Castro had no intention of allowing this man to speak to this Colonel before he could, and being he was already involved on the day of the party, the Cuban Leader decided to eliminate General Boada from the playing field. But before he was able to leave his office, Presidente Castro spoke again to his officer. "General Boada, I truly hope you're going to make your apologies to this young Military Officer and his future wife, and you'll also send a gift to the two young people, a cash gift to him would be nice to help celebrate his pending marriage to this young Cuban woman, General Boada."

"Yes Presidente, I'll send them a cash gift to help the two young ones celebrate their pending marriage and their future life together, sir." General Boada added in a rather upset tone of voice to the President of Cuba.

"Very good, all newly wedded children need a little extra cash. But make it a rather substantial cash gift at that, General Boada." He remarked to his General.

General Boada let out his breath in a rush, underneath, he was seething because he was aware why Castro chose to get him out of the way as he replied to the Cuban Leader. "Of course I'll send the Colonel a good size cash gift, sir." He nodded slightly, and then he left Castro's office steaming. By the time he reached his office, General Boada was looking for something to break. He slammed his office door, but that did little if anything to relieve his anger. He took a stiff shot of booze, and then headed to the jail to see who his people were questioning. He entered and saw them working on a naked young woman, and he barked at one of his soldiers. "Sergeant, have you been able to get any information from this lowly bitch?"

"No sir, she's still being very difficult today against us I fear, General Boada Sir." The young Sergeant announced with an ugly sneer on his lips to the General.

"This is good for me to hear, I need a good work out today, because I'm extremely angry on this foul day myself, Sergeant." He walked over to the young woman hanging by her wrists, her legs were pinned down to the floor by the heavy chains, and she was forced spread eagle. He rubbed her breasts as he picked up a bull whip with the other hand and he spat at her. "I hope you are very strong today, and you'll dance for a very long time for me, my little pretty." The Cuban General stepped back until he was sure the very tip of the whip would find its mark correctly. He then swung it with all his might, but the first hit only drew blood and some strained twisting from the young girl, but no screams came from her lips.

"Ahhh Sergeant, it's as you stated to me, mista. She's obviously very strong and hard to loosen her foul tongue, but I'll break her of this foolish pig headedness quick enough today I believe." General Boada hissed nastily as he swung the whip a second time. It cracked with the sound of thunder, but still no scream came from her lips. "Good, good, don't give up on me too quickly, before all of my anger subsides and I'm calm again, young woman."

General Boada swung the whip twice more, causing more nasty welts and a trickle of blood from each of the terrible wounds on her body, but still no screams came forth from her mouth, just the stare of hatred emitting from her burning eyes, and it was directed right at him.

General Boada took a second whip from the table it was the same as the first one, but with one difference though. This whip had a number of long strips of rawhide at the very end of it. He swung it once but still no scream, but by the second hit the girl let out with a soul ripping scream, and from then on, each strike brought a new blood curdling wail from her tortured young body of the woman. It was over for the young girl, his anger had the best of him, and the only thing that would stop General Boada now, was the death of this woman who had no real information to share with him. Each of her blood curdling screams brought new delight to the angry General, and it also added new strength to his body as the fuming General strove to reach the perfect scream from her failing lungs.

On the twentieth strike, the screams stopped, but this did not stop him as he laid ten more strikes on the now limp body of the young female, and he would have continued with the beating if it was not for one of his men grabbing his arm while in motion, and then he offered to him in a concerned tone. "General Boada Sir, I believe the filthy pig is dead sir. You have done very well today General. This will serve as a good example to the rest of the lowly pigs of this Island."

General Boada shook his head to try and clear it a little. Then he carefully examined his handiwork on the limp and still bleeding naked young female body. The woman hung limply from the chains that held her body firmly, her body was crisscrossed with a number of terribly ugly welts still oozing blood. The powerful Cuban General stepped back a little bit, and then he stared at the dead woman's face for a few seconds, whose body had been virtually ripped to shreds by the heavy whip, and now not looking anything like a human being. Then he ordered the two soldiers who started interrogating the woman. "Cut her worthless body down and return this pile of filth to her foul parents. Why was she arrested Sergeant?"

"General Boada, she was arrested because it was believed she had witnessed two young children stealing a loaf of bread from a local store. But she refused to identify them for us, sir." The Sergeant sort of sneered at the General as he allowed the information to sink in on him.

"Good, then maybe this will help set an example to the foolish others of this country, steal, and you'll be treated like the dog they are. Witness it, and yet refuse to give us any evidence of the crime so we can rid Cuba of all criminals, and the same treatment will befall the witness." With this said, General Boada quickly left the interrogation room without a second thought to the young woman left hanging from the chains dead by his hands. She served his purpose well for the General, because he was now in the state of mind to deal properly with anyone on the Island.

He breathed deeply proud he was able to work off some of his anger. After returning to his office, he wrote out a check for five hundred American dollars. A sum he was certain Fidel Castro was not going to meet. He called in his private secretary and he ordered her to have the check cashed for him. He had no intention of sending a check down to this young Colonel. He was looking forward to going to the wedding party. The Cuban General never knew what young and pretty and unattached women might be hanging around at the little get together, along with the rest of the young people supposed to be showing up for the Colonel's party. He had no way of knowing Fidel Castro was a step ahead of him already though.

The Cuban President had one thousand American dollars removed from his wall safe, and he issued orders for a special messenger to hand deliver his gift for him, along with a letter instructing the Colonel to report to his office on the twenty third day of September, a Monday. He smiled to himself, allowing this young Colonel five full days to enjoy his new spouse, before having him report to Havana for his new duty in his private group of well trained and trusted bodyguards.

He was vastly pleased with himself, and he thought about having this young Colonel Carlos Rafael Hernandez Alvarez get married at the Presidential Palace for a brief moment. He even considered allowing him and his new bride, to use his private suite on the top floor of the well renowned Havana Hilton that overlooked the Atlantic Ocean for their honeymoon. He was that satisfied he was able to offer this great prize to the young man and his new wife he was hoping to cultivate as an ally to him. A soldier he knew he wanted standing at his side, a young military officer he might have once feared, and did not realized his fear if this officer was not brought up to his attention by his wise General, something he will be forever beholding to General Boada by ordering this young military officer before him.

General Boada was just as pleased with himself, thinking he was one upping Castro over this young Colonel. The same Castro who always boasted he never makes a mistake at his own game, and this thought gave him great pleasure. He was weary and growing as tired as the other important citizens of Cuba, over the lack of action coming from the once powerful President's office lately. He did not give a care about the poor and unemployed of Cuba, they all meant absolutely nothing to him or any of his future plans. The General heard the rumblings coming for the upper class though, and he played close attention to these complaints.

General Boada felt Presidente Fidel Castro had the power in his hands to put a quick stop to Cuba's constant punishment by the United States, and the other nations who followed their lead when dealing with Cuba. He knew all it would take was Castro merely making some friendly overtones towards the United States. So the Americans would end the effects of the strangling trade embargo still set in place since the early days of the Kennedy Administration. The wise and understanding Cuban General knew full well the time was fast approaching when the Castro issue would have to be addressed, one way or the other, by him and the rest of the military fraction of the Island of Cuba, if there was to be any hope for Cuba's future in this world. The crafty and wise General questioned himself on this subject many times in the past, and he was positive he would be able to stand up and answer this question of the fate of Fidel Castro, and the future of Cuba when the proper time finally came for him to answer the call.

General Boada also knew in both his heart and mind if he was the one who ended Castro's life, he would take over the Presidency of Cuba. He would be the only one who will finally come to terms with the United States, and bring lasting peace between the two nations. He suddenly let his breath out while still thinking of Cuba's future fate.

SEPTEMBER 18th, 1996. MARIA IBARRA'S HOME IN CATALINA DE GUINES

The day finally came when Colonel Carlos Rafael Fernandez Alvarez would be able to speak to some of the most important citizens, and also the most powerful military men and women in all Cuba. The time had come to lay out his plans for Cuba's future, a future that had no place left in it for the old ways of Presidente Fidel Castro and his likes.

Carlos spent the night before with Maria, and he helped her prepare for the wedding party, he was the first one to wake up on Wednesday morning, and he made the morning meal for the two of them. They ate in silence, with Maria absentmindedly picking at her food until Carlos took her dishes and he cleaned them while she checked on a few of the last-minute preparations for the upcoming party. The Colonel was being a real pest of himself and Maria finally snapped at him. "Will you leave me alone and get dressed will you please, Carlos. Stop acting like a filthy pig and trying to force me to make love to you, mista."

She was busy preparing all the variety of dishes she planned to serve her visitors at the upcoming party, when there was a sudden knock on their door and a young male messenger stood before her, and he instantly offered her a sealed letter. She took the letter from his hand and then she called Carlos over to her side as she closed the door behind her.

"Well my dear Colonel Alvarez, we have a letter from the great Presidente himself, my lover."

"Really?" Colonel Alvarez said as he stared back at his lady with surprise etched in his eyes.

"Yes, you open it Carlos." She immediately handed him the unopened letter.

The surprised Cuban Colonel was shocked when he saw the American cash stuffed in the envelope, and he handed it over to Maria, and then he read the letter with the money. "It seems we're ordered to appear before our fearless Presidente on the 23rd of this month."

"The both of us?" She asked the stunned looking Carlos, with some concern in her tone.

"Yes of course the both of us, Maria." He replied to his lover and future wife in a snappy tone.

"What are you going to do now Carlos?" Maria asked as if she was suddenly scared.

"By God, we are going to go. If everything goes well today, I'll know where I stand, and I'll take action at this meeting. If I cannot talk sense to the old fool, I'll kill the bastard."

"Oh Carlos, I'm so proud of you my Cuban lover." She cried as she hugged him close to her body, and then she added to her soldier barely over a whisper. "You are a true leader, the only one who Cuba needs to lead her out of the dark ages."

"Yeah, how much did he send us, Maria?" he asked as he struggled from her.

She quickly counted all the cash and then she cried. "Oh my God my love, he has sent us one thousand American dollars, Carlos."

"Sure, he's the only one on the entire Island who could afford such a vast sum of money as a gift, without going to the poor house. We can use the cash to help finance our revolution. The fool is actually paying for his own overthrow."

They both shared a quick laugh together until there was a second knock on the front door, and a second messenger offered a letter. It was from General Boada. Carlos opened it and he removed the cash and handed it to Maria, and then he read the letter. General Boada also invited him and his bride up to Havana. He reminded Colonel Alvarez he was still holding a position open for him in his special police service.

The smirking Cuban Colonel looked at Maria and she said to him in an ex cited tone of voice. "Five hundred American dollars."

"Great, put the new cash in with all the rest of it, Maria." He suggested to his lover.

"You get dressed while I take care of the kitchen. I'm expecting guests to arrive at noon."

Cuban Colonel Carlos Rafael Fernandez Alvarez went back into the small bedroom, and he dressed quickly in the only civilian suit he owned. When he came out, Maria stopped what she was doing and she gave him a little whistle as she shook her hand, and then she growled like a cat. "Arrr... I warn you, you look hot enough to eat right where you stand, mista."

"What do you want me to do for you, Maria?" He asked of his beautiful young lover.

"Keep an eye on the stove while I get dressed, you fool." She said as she left the kitchen.

"Will do Maria." He replied over his shoulder, as he took over duties at the stove for her.

It took her fifteen minutes to get dress, and when she entered the kitchen, she caused Carlos's mouth to hang open as he stared at her in disbelief. She was stunning, dressed in a black slip dress that went to her ankles, but it was slit up to her rear end on the right side. He was able to tell that she had no panties on, and he could see the top of her nylons through the wide slit. The front of her dress was cut low, barely covering her beautiful breasts in the fine silk like fabric.

She realized what he was looking at, and she bent low, so he could enjoy himself more. His mouth snapped shut, and he found it rather hard to swallow. Maria noticed the problem between his legs and she grabbed him through his pants as she purred at him. "I think you better breathe before you pass out on me, mista. My my, we do have us a little problem here, do we not?"

"What do you mean my little bitch?" he snapped back at her this time as he faked anger.

They laughed together as the pot suddenly boiled over on the stove, causing Carlos to offer to Maria. "I know just how the stove feels, honey. Do you want to screw around a little Maria?"

"You're impossible, our guests are about to arrive and all you want to do is make love to me. Be off with you while I attend to my cooking duties, mista." She warned him angrily.

Carlos was having none of it as he reached for Maria's exquisite body. She screamed and laughed at the same time, while she tried to fend off Carlos' wild advances aimed against her. Maria was responding to all of his attention when there was another knock on the door. Both of her breasts were out of her dress, as Carlos tried to hike it up over her waist, when Anita Hernandez Morales came walking into the kitchen after she let herself into Maria's home.

Maria saw Anita standing behind Carlos and she was staring at them and complained at her. "Oh, thank God you're here my little sister. Maybe you can help me control this wild Cuban man attacking me here. He's absolutely crazy Anita."

Anita walked around the two as Carlos ignored her and he finally got his head down between Maria's slender legs. When he did, she let out a small cry as he found the right spot he was searching for with his tongue. Anita watched what he was doing with his tongue, and then she announced in an excited tone to her girlfriend. "Maria, you have never told me how talented his tongue was. My, he's good at it. You're a very lucky woman to have such a fine and vigorous lover here, I'm envious of you Maria. Will you look at him go at you, will you please."

"Never mind that, get him the hell off of me before the other guests arrive at my home, will you please. Hmmm... Carlos please hmmm... you stop that or I'll kill you. Hmmmmm..."

"Look at you, you're going to come, have you no shame Maria?" Anita laughed at her.

With a slight shudder of her body, she finally pulled free from Carlos. She was a mess, her breasts were out, her dress was pulled up exposing her to Anita and Carlos, her hair was undone, and her makeup was smeared, and she complained at her Colonel. "Look at what you have done to me. I have to fix myself all over again, you filthy pig you."

"By the Madonna and you loved it my little wild cat." He said as he rubbed her breasts while she stood with her hands resting on her hips while still glaring at him and she turned to her friend and moaned at her. "Will you look at what he has done to me, Anita?"

"I see, if only I was so lucky. Do you think I might borrow him for a little while, to see if he can repeat his act on me, Maria?" Anita offered, only half kidding with Maria and Carlos.

"If he does, I shall cut his tongue out from his filthy mouth. That baby is all mine Anita."

Carlos looked at the two women, and then he slowly ran his tongue along his lips and he grinned and said to Maria. "Hmmm, you taste good."

Both girls snapped back at Carlos. "Oh God, you're disgusting you filthy cochino you."

Anita suddenly reached out and she cupped one of Maria's breasts, and she rolled it gently between her fingers as she offered. "I think you better go and fix yourself again, I'll take care of this crazy stud of yours and what you need done in the kitchen, Maria."

"You better be careful with him, when the fool sees two women with each other, he gets really nuts and he wants to join in with us." Maria warned as she wiggled in the front of her dress.

"That is a shame for me to hear Maria because I'm horny myself on this day from seeing you two go at it like two filthy dogs in heat, Maria. Go and get dressed will you please while I attend to the cooking for you, my little Cuban sister." Anita announced proudly as she walked over to the stove and then she started to attend to the cooking for Maria, as she left to get dressed again.

She smiled at her two friends as she headed off for the bedroom, with Carlos following after her like a little puppy. She placed her hands against his chest, and then she hit him in the arm and snapped at him at the same time. "Carlos Alvarez, I just told you, you we were not going to do anything right now. It's too close to the beginning of the wedding party, and I'll not be caught making love to you by all our guests, or being placed in disarray by you either, mista."

"No, it is not that at all my love, I wanted to talk to you, privately Maria." He told her.

"Don't trust him Maria, he only wants to get in your pants, and once he's done with you, he'll not give a damn." Anita called out from the kitchen as she stirred the pot boiling.

"Mind your own god dom business Anita." He snapped back at her angrily.

"See, I told you. He's nothing more than a lowly pig. Don't give him any until you have a ring on your finger. At least you'll have something of worth to sell, once he is done with you."

Carlos glared at Anita and Maria pulled him in the bedroom and she warned him in no uncertain terms. "Remember, only talk mista."

Once inside, Carlos closed the door behind him and grumbled at Maria. "Madonna, what the hell was that about? Her playing with your breasts like that and you allowing her to do so."

She laughed as she replied, "what's the matter Carlos, are you jealous suddenly?"

"Me? No, err... yeah. I don't know. What was it about Maria?" he demanded of her.

"We're just close friends, nothing more than that Carlos." She said as she fixed herself.

"Lovers?" Carlos asked her as he stared into her lovely eyes for a long moment.

"No! Don't be such a damn fool! How could we be lovers when I love you, Carlos Alvarez, you fool? True, Anita loves women, but I only love men. One man, you, you big fool you."

"By the grace of God then how come you have allowed Anita to touch you like she did?"

"My, but we are a little jealous Carlos. I allowed Anita to give me a little pleasure once in a while, but I never returned the pleasure to her. But now I'm sorry I never did. How dare you interrogate me like this, mista? We're not married, and I'm not one of your soldiers, and what I do with my body is my own business, now, and later on as well. If I want to take a female as a lover, I will mista. You're more than free to take a male lover if you want to, Carlos."

"That'll be the fooking day I ever do something like that, Maria." He snarled back at her.

She laughed at the look that was on Carlos's face, causing him to chuckle with her.

"Maria, if you chose to make love with a woman, will you do me a favor please." Anita asked.

"What is it you want of me Anita?" she asked of her girlfriend from the bathroom.

"Invite me to give you pleasure one day," She called out from the kitchen. "I'll make love to that clout if you let me make love to you at the same time, and you return the favor to me Maria."

"You have very big ears my little sister Anita." She complained as she stared at Carlos.

"You know I'll do anything to have you sleep with me one day, baby." Anita added to her.

Carlos stared at Maria, causing her to snap at him. "You have given me something to think about, girl. Can you imagine the present we could offer this big dumb soldier, honey? To enable him to make love with two women at the same time while they made love to each other.

Hmmm... Maybe for a wedding gift, are you game for any of that kind of action, Anita honey?"

"As I always told you, I'll do anything to bed you Maria. You know how long I've been trying to have an affair with you, my love. I'll throw everything out of the window to have you for one night, even if it means making love to that big pig of yours, my little Cuban sister." Anita announced proudly as she continued to stir the pot resting on the stove before her.

"Baby, you can call me anything you want, as long as you let me to be part of the game."

"I told you he was nothing more than a filthy cochino all along, Maria dear?"

"Who is a filthy cochino?" Rita Jose Majal asked as she entered Maria's home, and got right into the conversation going on between the two. "Am I missing something here girls?"

"Rita! Maria, Rita's here." Anita and Rita hugged and kissed, with Anita trying to slide her tongue into Rita's mouth but she quickly pulled away while saying. "Always trying, huh Anita?"

"Be careful with her Rita, Anita's horny on this day." Maria warned as she smiled at Carlos.

"I picked that up already by myself Maria." Rita replied as she smiled back at Anita.

"What did she try to do to you Rita?" Maria asked as she stared to fix herself up again.

"Nothing yet, but she has that look in her eyes again Maria." Rita warned Maria.

"You're very lucky she offered to make love to Carlos, if I allowed her to make love to me at the same time, Rita." Maria called out from the bedroom this time while still dressing.

"What did you say to the offer from her, Maria?" Rita giggled at her girlfriend now.

"I'm going to take her up on it, maybe on our wedding night. Should be some fun Rita."

"Can I take pictures of the action when you do, Maria?" Rita asked her.

"Only if you join in on all the fun honey." Carlos added with a smirk on his lips.

"Who was that, that just spoke to me Maria? Do you have someone in there with you honey?"

"The filthy cochino, now he wants to make love to a gaggle of women on the same bed, Rita."

"I told you he was nothing more than a filthy pig, Maria." Anita offered once more to her.

Maria came out of the bedroom while combing her hair, and she kissed Rita on both cheeks. Carlos followed and Rita asked Maria. "Is this the man we'll be following, honey?"

Carlos glared at Maria. "Yes Carlos, I told both of them. They're my best friends, and both of them are as upset as I am over Castro. We want him out of office, and we'll do anything to accomplish this feat. So stop looking at me in that manner before I lose my temper with you."

The Colonel shook his head, and he looked at the angry Rita.

"You don't want to hurt her feelings, or I'll bleed you and then leave you for dead, mista." Rita snapped as she glared hotly at Carlos.

"These two are the women I told you about, my love. I have two other girls I shall approach, but not until after you acted, and rid Cuba of Castro." Maria placed her hands on her hips.

"What can I say? Welcome aboard ladies." He said as he spread his hands apart before him and smiled at the two other women.

Maria smiled broadly as she formally introduced Carlos to the other two women in her home. "Rita Jose Majal, and Anita Hernandez

Morales, please allow me to introduce you to Colonel Carlos Rafael Fernandez Alvarez. The next Presidente of Cuba ladies and he's the one who'll make long awaited friends with the hated Americans, and all her people for us, ladies."

Carlos bowed to the women with Anita offering, "does the deal we made still count, Maria?"

"What deal?" she barked back at her, not remembering what they just talked about.

"The one between you, Maria and myself, my sister." Anita said as she looked at Carlos.

"I'm afraid you had to ask her, Anita." Carlos growled as he took a beer from the ice box.

Anita turned to Maria with pleading eyes and she stared back at her for the moment.

"It's a deal Anita, I had to open my big mouth though, and you'll not let me back out now."

Anita let out her breath in a rush of delight as a smile quickly crossed over her lovely lips.

There was another knock on the door and Anita opened it and saw a soldier standing there.

"Hello lady, I'm Colonel Ricardo Fernandez Cienfuegos of the 5th Armored Division, and I don't know if I have the right house. I'm looking for Colonel Carlos Rafael Fernandez Alvarez, I have an invitation in my hand to come to the party. See it here young lady?"

Carlos rushed passed Anita and bellowed at the stranger standing at the door. "Why you old sonofabitch you, I'm so pleased to see you made it here without getting lost for yourself, my old friend." The two men hugged, and then they punched each other in the arms.

Maria looked at Anita and she mumbled to her. "This must be a male thing, I guess. We kiss, and they beat on each other's body with their hands. I guess it makes sense to me somehow."

"Do you really think I would've dared miss you getting married, Carlos? Not on your life my young friend. I would've given my left nut to see you walk down that aisle, knowing all the women of Cuba can finally breathe a little easier, when you at long last joined the ranks of the married slobs of Cuba, Carlos." Again, they beat on each other as the other Colonel offered. "Carlos, one thing I have to know though, how come the invitations didn't include our wives?"

Carlos whispered to his other military officer. "All this will be explained to you in good time, Colonel Cienfuegos, sir."

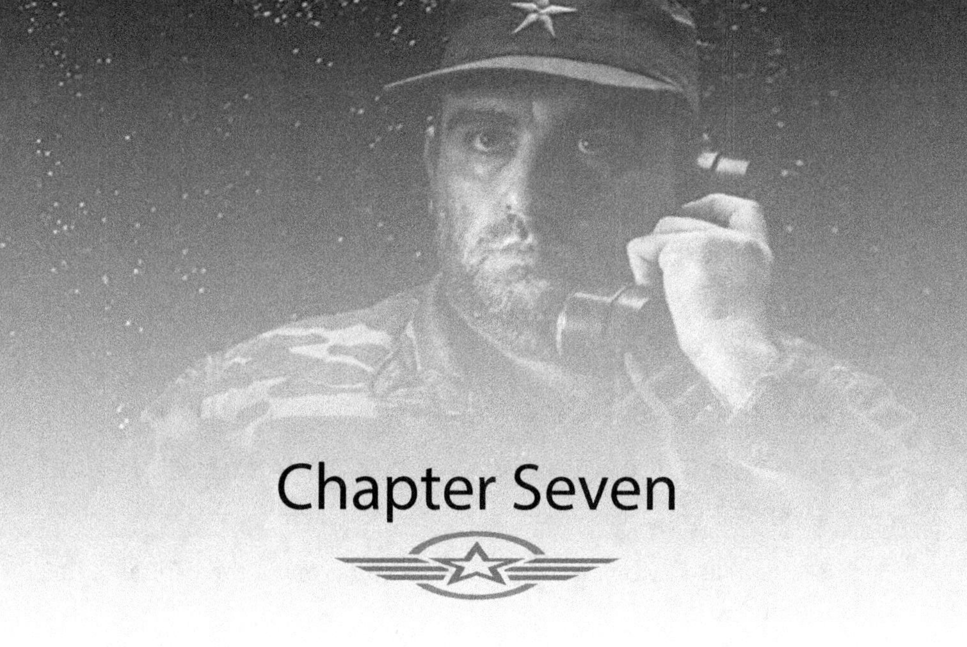

Chapter Seven

"Don't tell me you have some strippers coming to this little party of yours, Carlos Alvarez. I should've known you had something up your sleeve like that, you old dirty dog you." Colonel Cienfuegos laughed as he tapped Colonel Alvarez lightly in the guts with his hand.

"I have a lot more friends coming to the party. How did you get here Ricardo?"

"When I got your invitation, I had my base rat commandeer fuel for my car to get me here, and back to my military base. I told you I wouldn't miss this for all the gold in Castro's rotted teeth."

Another knock on the door, Alvarez opened it to see Captain Fabio Hernandez Gonzales from the 2nd Infantry Division standing alongside Colonel Santiago Ramon Agramonte of the Airforce. Both men smiled and they hugged Colonel Alvarez, as they offered him their envelopes.

He held up his hand and then offered to his future wife. "Maria will take those from you. Did you have any trouble finding the place?"

"Yes." They both offered to Carlos at the same time with a grin.

"Carlos, where are your manners, invite them into our home please." Maria offered as she passed by and she took the soldiers hats, and then she lead them in her home. Even before Carlos closed the door, another person showed up outside while calling out his name to him.

Carlos saw Captain Aguero Portal Remos coming up the walkway.

"Aguero, I'm so pleased you made it for my little party, sir." He offered him.

"Made it? I wouldn't have missed this party for all of the gold in..."

"Yes I know, in Castro's rotten teeth." Colonel Alvarez added as he cut the Captain off.

"I see you also heard the latest joke going around the capital." The two shook hands.

The party got off the ground when Anita and Rita dressed in clothing accenting their fine attributes, served the soldiers their drinks. Each girl made sure they bent over enough to cause the men to sweat, by giving them the show of their lives. Maria brought out the food, and Alvarez introduced the soldiers to each other, telling colorful jokes and giving the women lingering leers while he was at it. The Latin music was too loud to carry on any conversations.

Another knock on the door and Colonel Alvarez rushed to cut Maria off as he reached the door first, and he opened it. There was Lazaro Prio Socarras Cabrisas, the Vice Presidente of Cuba, and the Council of State and Ministers. He had a smile on his lips and he held a gift in his arms as he offered to the man standing in the doorway before him. "Colonel Alvarez, sir?"

Colonel Carlos Alvarez's mouth snapped shut as he nodded to the Vice Presidente.

Cabrisas offered him the package, but Carlos was frozen in place, and all he could do was stare at the powerful man. Cabrisas smiled as he realized the officer was in awe of him and he asked. "I believe this party is being held inside this home sir?"

Colonel Alvarez shook his head yes, as he sidestepped and allowed the Vice Presidente of Cuba to walk passed him. All conversations instantly ended inside the home as everyone rose, and then they bowed towards well respected Vice Presidente Cabrisas as he complained to the gathered soldiers. "My, I didn't know I'd be the cause of this fine party ending so quickly. Please gentlemen, carry on and have some fun, I'm here only to enjoy myself, and to make sure this scoundrel is truly getting married."

The women closed in on the Vice President, offering him drink and food. Maria offered him one of Cuba's best cigars. Cabrisas nodded to Maria. "I take it you're the lucky young woman?"

"Yes, Vice Presidente Cabrisas, I am sir." She gleamed at the Vice President of Cuba.

"Please, not so formal, you may call me Lazaro, young lady. This night is for you and my young Colonel, not for me. Allow me please." He took Maria's hand in his and he kissed the back of it and added to her, "I must say my Colonel has excellent taste, but, on the other hand, it was going to take a woman of exquisite stature and looks to land such a man as he." Again, the Vice Presidente kissed her hand, making Maria blush and bow as she giggled, and then she thanked him for his fine compliment.

Vice Presidente Cabrisas now turned towards Colonel Alvarez and took him by his shoulder and said to him. "You have landed yourself one fine woman here. If I ever hear you been unkind to her, I'll cut your balls off. She is too nice a woman to be abused by anyone in Cuba, mista."

Alvarez was a taken back by Cabrisas's sudden warning. "Yes sir, you have nothing to be concerned about in that area, sir. I'll treat her as my sister, my wife, lover and friend, sir."

"You better, because I have a responsibility to the other female population of Cuba. As long as I know you're married, then and only then will I assure them they're safe from the likes of you constantly chasing after them day and night, mista." Cabrisas's face turned to a grin, and he laughed at Colonel Alvarez as he held on his shoulder, and he sucked on the tip of the cigar. "Ahhh, a fine cigar, and fine looking women."

Colonel Carlos Alvarez was relieved the Vice President was only kidding about the threat that Carlos considered was overstepping his bounds a little as he offered back to the man. "Vice Presidente Cabrisas, I had no belief you'd attend this party sir. I know you're a very busy man sir. You have bestowed upon me a great honor by attending, sir. Thank you sir."

"Colonel Alvarez Sir, I wouldn't have missed this party for all the gold in Castro's teeth." The group broke out in laughter over Cabrisas's remark as he continued on without missing a beat. "Besides, I owe it to your great father. On his death bed, I promised him I'd keep a close eye on his only son, and not allow any harm to befall him." Vice Presidente Cabrisas leaned a little closer to Colonel Alvarez and he said to him almost in a whisper. "I have promised him I'd never allow you to marry the wrong woman. You see Carlos, your father knew of your many womanizing ways, and he was deeply concerned by this. But I'm certain he's at rest over your fine choice for a wife. She's stunning and very obedient, and she looks like she'll bear you many fine and healthy sons, sir. You done honor to your father and myself, Carlos. It's good to see he has raised a man, not a child, your father would be pleased."

Cabrisas slapped Carlos on his shoulder, as took a drink from Anita, who bent low, allowing him to get an eye full of her breasts, almost flopping out of the top of her dress.

"Young lady, you have just caused a stirring where a stirring has been hiding for many years now I'm afraid. I might wish to speak to you in private a little later on, after the party that is." Cabrisas grinned as he enjoyed the offered view.

"You're much too kind Vice Presidente Cabrisas, sir." Anita replied kindly to the man.

"Lazaro. Please, everyone here please. For tonight, you may all call me Lazaro. Thank you."

The soldiers gathered around the Vice President, and assaulted him with questions ranging from the direction the government was heading in, to which team he thought would win the World Series in the United States. Cabrisas was beginning to relax a little he enjoyed some conversation, some good liquor and cigars, and the finest looking women who seemed to be flocking around him.

Another knock, this time Maria answered the door. It was Major Pipi Enrique Cardona who commanded the 9th Infantry Brigade stationed at Guanahacabibes on the southernmost tip of Cuba at the Peninsula de Guanahacabibes. The Major was in a strategic position, and the keeper of a terrible secret, he was accompanied by Captain Vittorio Francisco Varela, who was in command of the 17th Infantry, and the Light Armor Brigade stationed at de las Vegas, Havana.

Two other officers stood behind them. Colonel Alfredo Casas Vidali who commanded the well feared and respected 34th Infantry Brigade stationed at Campo Florido on the outskirts of Havana, and Captain Domingo Rivero Bernardo who commanded the 27th Mechanized group stationed at Guanajay in the capital, Havana. A fifth officer walked up behind the group of fine looking soldiers waiting to be invited into Maria's home, and he identified himself to the young woman standing in the doorway. He was Captain Fernando Diaz Suarez, the commander of the 19th Infantry Brigade stationed at Barreras Minas, also situated on the outskirts of Havana.

Maria ushered the other soldiers into her home to get them out of her neighbor's eyes, and she introduced them to the rest of the guests in her home. Maria and the other women watched as the soldiers greeted those there with slaps on the backs, and breathe robbing bear hugs. She remarked to her two girlfriends it looked like a bunch of children getting together for the first time.

There was another tap on the door, and Maria found herself staring at a tall and slender looking soldier, who looked like he was angry at the world as he stood with his hat tucked neatly under his arm, and he barked loudly at her. "Young one, I'm Carlos Calvo, Captain. I'm the Commander of the 1st Paratroopers Brigade stationed at Camague woman, and I've been invited to a party supposed to be celebrating Colonel Carlos Alvarez's upcoming marriage, woman. Am I at the right location, woman?"

"Location Colonel Calvo Sir?" she asked him, not really knowing what this ridiculous acting and looking man with the massive mustache was talking about to her.

"Young lady," the Captain snapped harshly as he gave out with a deep sigh, and then he added. "Is this the location where the party is to be held, woman? For Christ sake woman, use your head for more than a hairdo. I suggest you get some more clothes on as well young lady, before you invite an attacked by one of the lowlifes on the Island while you're at it."

She could feel her cheeks flush as she fought to control her mounting temper. She thought to herself, who was this pompous man barking at her as if she was a scatterbrained female and she snapped. "Who the hell do you think you are, yelling at someone you don't even know, mista?"

"I told you already who I am young lady, I'm Captain Carlos Francisco Vega Cal..."

"As God is my judge, I don't give a shit who you think you are. What gives you the right to come to my house and criticize my dress, you old stuffed shirt you. If I offend you, turn your ass around and march off my property. What is the matter? Do you not like looking at a woman's breasts?" She snapped as she pulled down the front of her dress, and she allowed her breasts free of the restricting fabric. "Or do you prefer to look at little boy's penises. Get the hell off of..."

Cuban Colonel Carlos Rafael Fernandez Alvarez rushed to the front door of Maria's home to see who she was arguing with. He instantly recognized the proud Captain and he rushed passed Maria as he clamped the feared Cuban Officer into a bear hug as he offered him. "I should've known it was you causing my future bride all this grief already, sir. I should've warned Maria about you and your dry sense of humor, sir." Carlos Alvarez turned to Maria and he said to her. "Maria, this is my close friend Carlos Calvo. Captain Calvo, this is my soon to be wife, Maria Ibarra from the well known Marcus Ibarra family of Cuba."

"I think you better choose your friends more carefully then, Carlos Alvarez. Do you really want to know what this great bore has said to me, mista? If I was a man I'd demand satisfaction from his foul being. The dirty old cochino actually told me I should put on more clothes, because of the way I'm dressed must have offended the great clod and I..."

"And, you should at that young lady." Captain Calvo added without a smile on his lips.

"Why you old sonofabitch you!" She growled nastily as she tried to jump passed Alvarez to get at the angry looking Captain. She was a flash of arms, kicking legs, and a mouth of stinging curses as she tried to get the smug Captain, but Alvarez grabbed her around the waist, and he actually held her in the air as she continued to kick and swing her arms at the young Captain, who merely took a step back to avoid her legs. "Colonel Alvarez Sir, I see you picked yourself out a real spitfire to marry, sir. I always knew it was going to take a powerful woman to land you, and I see that you located one, sir. Look at her. Her breasts are out of her dress, if she was my wife to be, I'd beat her for such an insult to myself Colonel Alvarez, sir."

"And, I'd never be your wife, you filthy swine you. I don't understand how any woman could ever be your wife. I warn you, if you ever lift your hand to me, I'll bite it off for you."

"Yes Carlos, I see you have picked yourself quite the spitfire here, sir. I'm thirsty does this party serve any liquor here sir? Or should I have brought my own with me, sir?"

"Why you filthy cochino you, you just wait until I get my god dom hands on you." Maria snapped angrily at this new insult as she again flailed her arms and legs at the smug looking military officer with her arms and legs with new anger and she yelled at him. "Carlos, if you allow this pig in my house, I'll kill him."

Carlos placed Maria down, but he did not let go of her as he whispered a warning in her ear. "Maria, I have much need of this powerful military officer and all his forces, if I'm to succeed in my quest to rid Cuba of Castro. Please honey, I know what a bore he can be to you, baby. But I'm begging you, put up with him for me and the good of Cuba please. At least until I can get him to cross over to my side of this thing, honey. I'm going to let you go now, and I don't want you to attack him again with anything but kind words, honey."

"But he's such a..." She started to complaint, but she was instantly cut off by Alvarez again.

"Do you understand me honey!" he suddenly snapped at her in a very low whisper.

She calmed down as she lowered her eyes and then replied to her lover. "Yes, I understand you, but if the sonofabitch doesn't join you, then I'll take care of him myself."

"Join you in what Colonel Alvarez?" Captain Carlos Calvo asked him with concern in his voice, as he overheard Maria's warning aimed solely at him.

"Later my friend, right now I'll get you something to drink, sir. Please come in Captain Calvo and join the party, sir. Maria, would you be a honey and get the Captain a drink please?"

"In a cochinos ear I will. If this foul dog wants something to drink, I'll pour water in a bowl, and he can lap it up like the dog he is." She growled as she tried to get around Alvarez.

Captain Calvo stiffened his back up straighter, as he glared harshly at Maria's back, and Carlos snapped at her in an extremely angry tone of voice. "Maria, I just told you to get the Captain something to drink, now do it!"

She spun around and glared into Carlos' eyes, as she pointed a finger right at his face, as if it was a weapon. Then she turned and joined the party. Carlos gave a laugh as he remarked to the Captain. "She's being impossible today. She's under pressure, the party, the marriage you know how it is sir. You're married."

Captain Calvo placed his hand on Carlos' shoulder as they walked into the room. "No need to explain to me, maybe it's that time of the month, Colonel Alvarez. I shall get my own drink..."

Their conversation was suddenly interrupted by Rita who offered both of the new officers something to drink. Carlos cringed as Rita bent low before the Captain so he could see all she had to offer. He cringed again, but he was glad Maria did not hear the time of the month remark by Captain Calvo. He knew he would not have been able to control her if she heard the rude comment, and he actually started to fear for the arrogant Captain's life, if Maria ever got at him for real. She was like a wild badger once she latched onto a target she wanted.

Once everyone was introduced to each other, the party really got down to the business at hand, drinking and the telling of nasty jokes and tall stories. No one noticed every officer was a Commander of an Army or Naval Unit on the Island. No one realized every military unit in Havana, or on the outskirts of the capital city, was represented at the party. If everyone had agreed with Alvarez, he would be able to cut Havana off from the rest of Cuba, in just a matter of moments when it came time to act.

The three beautiful and scantly clothed young women and the booze did their intended job for Carlos and his future plan. After two hours of some rather heavy drinking, all the men were much freer with the women, and they were grabbing at them whenever they brought more drinks to the waiting and grinning military officers and politicians. Carlos Alvarez knew the time to unveil his future plans to the other soldiers at Maria's home was rapidly nearing.

Maria at long last allowed herself to relax a little with Captain Calvo who had appeared to have made a form of peace with her. Colonel Carlos Alvarez noticed Captain Calvo was speaking privately with her, and he smiled when he noticed the Captain take her hand in his, and then he kissed it kindly for her.

Vice Presidente Cabrisas worked his way over to Colonel Alvarez, and he suggested they share a toast to the future Mrs. Alvarez. No one noticed when Sergeant Regueiro entered the party, and he was making the best of it, by helping the women with the drinks and the food.

Carlos was feeling a bit tipsy, and he was not paying much attention to Vice Presidente Cabrisas and his suggestion. He was trying to look down Rita's dress as she bent low while offering Agramonte a refill. She had almost as nice breasts as Maria, and he saw both as she held her bend while Colonel Agramonte took his drink. For a moment, Alvarez thought he was going to actually reach down the front of Rita's dress.

Vice Presidente Cabrisas tapped on the rim of his glass with a spoon and he suddenly bellowed out to all at the party. "Okay you Rogues now we have eaten most of Maria Ibarras's food..."

"Not to mention drinking all her liquor while we were at it, sir." One of the other officers remarked to the laughter of all paying attention to the Vice President now.

"Yes, and her booze as well, but we have to remember why we are here. It's because we want to wish Carlos and Maria all the best." He lifted his drink, "to Carlos and Maria, may they live forever, and may Maria give birth to many healthy boys. Good luck to the both of you two."

"Here, here." The officers replied as one, as they lifted their drinks, and then they toasted the two young people, one of the officers shoved his way to the center of the room.

"Speech, speech, speech." Some of the other officers chanted as they stared at Alvarez.

Maria squeezed Carlos's hand as she leaned closer and whispered. "Carlos now is a good time to speak to them. They're paying attention to you now. I'll stand behind you through it all."

Carlos looked deeply into Maria's eyes for a second, and then he said to her. "Yes, you're right as always my love of life. It's time I see if I'm sticking my head into a noose with these other Military Officers, honey." Carlos raised his hands to all the chanting. Once everyone quieted down for him, he asked them all to take a seat, and then he told them he had something to discuss with them. When Colonel Carlos Alvarez was sure everyone was comfortable and paying attention to him again, he began to speak to the gathered soldiers. "To all my very dear friends who made their way here today, announcing my wedding plans wasn't the only reason I asked you all to attend this party on this day with me." He had to stop speaking for a moment as Captain Gonzales held up two of his fingers, and Rita quickly crossed the room while carrying two more drinks, one for the Captain, and the other for Colonel Cienfuegos. Once he had his drink, he motioned for Carlos to continue with his speech.

Colonel Alvarez glared at him, informing him he was upset at the interruption. "Yes, as I was saying, the reason I invited you all here today is to discuss what is happening in Havana."

"And, what is it you'd like to discuss about it, Carlos?" Vice Presidente Cabrisas said as he quickly turned serious, while placing his drink down on a table, and staring at his friend's son.

"By the Blessed Virgin sir, I'm speaking of Fidel Castro. All here know what I mean." Carlos Alvarez barked at the Vice Presidente of Cuba before he realized who he was speaking to, and then he put on a contrite look as the young Captain interrupted his words.

"I know what you mean and I warn you Carlos, you're speaking treason here Colonel Alvarez. I for one will not listen to this shit a moment longer. I should turn you in, and have the police take you away. Is this motherless whore involved in these treasonous beliefs of yours also, mista?" Captain Carlos Calvo snapped, as he suddenly threw his drink angrily to the floor, and then he assumed an extremely threatening stance aimed at Carlos.

Maria snapped at the angry Cuban Captain. "For the love of the Holy Madonna, yes I am, and I'm not afraid to back Carlos in his future quest, we know he's only saying what we're all afraid to say. For the sake of Cuba, I suggest you sit down and listen to what he has to offer us, before you overreact and create a scene, sir." She placed her hands on her hips, and then she glared at him as she moved to her man's side.

"Why you filthy little pig of the mud you, how dare you speak to me in this mann..."

"Calm down Captain Calvo, sir." Vice Presidente Cabrisas growled and then added. "Let us hear what this traitor has to offer to us first, before we condemn him for the words he speaks."

"But I'll not stand..." Calvo went to complain, but he was cut off by the Vice President again.

"Then sit down and be quiet Captain Calvo." Vice Presidente Cabrisas snarled, he waited for the Captain to be seated and he turned to Carlos and said. "Colonel Alvarez, you were saying."

"Yes, I gave this problem much thought for the past few years now, sir. We all know it's only a matter of time before someone takes matters into their own hands, and he deals with Fidel Castro in his own way. I fear the longer we wait to react, the lesser the actor will be."

"What the hell are you talking about here Carlos?" Gonzales hissed while staring at Alvarez.

"Madre de Dios! What I'm trying to say here is, the longer we sit on our foul asses, and we wait for something to finally happen to the old fool running our country to the ground. Or we hope another Officer would end his worthless life. The more people will feel the same way as I do, and before we know it some lowly peasant will finally react to his foolish instincts, and he'll take out the sonofabitch for us. This lowly commoner will then proclaim himself as the new Presidente of all Cuba, and before we all know it.

"All the miserable and angry peasants will unite behind this foul person, and back a person who is not in the Armed Forces to be our new Presidente of Cuba. The United States will be greatly relieved they no longer have to deal with Fidel Castro, and they'll also back this new leader of Cuba without question. Then the rest of the hated Latin American nations will also fall in behind the United States, not wanting to go against their great will and military. And, before we know it, this ignorant peasant will be the new Presidente of Cuba, and we'll be powerless to stop it and him after that time."

"What makes you believe there is some fool waiting in the wings to take out Castro for us, sir?" Captain Varela asked, feeling much the same way Colonel Alvarez did, something had to be done about Fidel Castro, before it was too late for the sake Cuba and her people.

"For the grace of God are you truly deaf Varela? Have you not been listening to the people of Cuba over the past years, you fool? Have you not listened to your own soldiers, man? If your men are anything like the soldiers on my base then they complain constantly about the rapidly deteriorating conditions they're forced to operate under lately. The complaints of no pay, no fuel for our tanks, no ammunition for weapons every Officer here has to ask himself what would happen if any of the exiles attacked our island again. What will their forces do if this happens to Cuba? What would have happen if the Americans waited until today to launch their Bay of Pigs invasion against us? I'll tell every one of you what would've happened. We would have a new President of Cuba, and that Presidente's name would be Doctor Jose Cardona, sir.

"All of us gathered here today know full well what is happening to Cuba, and who the blame for it is. If only Fidel Castro would simply make some peaceful overtones to the hated United States, this wouldn't be being discussed here today. Look at what Russia had to do in order to survive in this rapidly changing world lately. The Soviet Union has stepped back, and they're now following the United States. Yet, here we are, still sitting on our asses while Castro sits in Havana, and he continues to curse the United States and all her people.

"Fidel Castro is the only man cursing the Americans, and Cuba is the only country not receiving any help from them. For the love of God, look at what is happening throughout the rest of the world. The Americans have finally made peace with Vietnam, and that same government is now sharing in all the prosperity this new peace agreement brings their country. The Bosnian war is coming to a fast conclusion, and Chile is fast becoming a world financial power.

"Mexico is strong because of their new agreement in trade with the worthless American fools. Every other nation in the world is becoming powerful. Why? Because they have formed their own agreements with the hated United States, yet here we still sit cursing them, as we slowly starve to death because of our own foul words and foolish anger. I don't fully understand how we can possibly be happy with ourselves while sitting on our god dom thumbs like we're doing, while our country is slowly being starved to death right before our eyes.

"There are no new revolutions we can possible start to help Cuba, Central America has made peace, and South America is only interested in making deals with the United States and Canada. Japan is offering many South America countries deals, deals that'll make them strong while they continue to turn their backs on us Island of fools. Look at the terrible condition that has befallen our great nation in the past years. A nation once feared and looked up to by many other countries of the world. Look at Africa, they're eating themselves for god dom food, and what makes you think this will not happen to the people of Cuba in our future. If we continue down the same foolish path we allowed our Presidente to follow over the years?

"Look at the terrible condition of Cuba at the present time, her children are forced to sell their bodies to the god cursed foreigners we were able to talk into visiting our country. What a legacy we're leaving for our future children. To fook foreign pigs just to make money to support their parents or children. I cannot sleep while I think of our babies, and the way they're forced to live under Castro's foul influence and command. We forced our own people into the Ocean on pieces of wood to flee their own god dom country. Look at the only ones who have money to buy food for their families. The only ones who can afford meat are the ones running our government."

"Traitor!" Captain Calvo suddenly snapped at Colonel Alvarez. "You miserable traitor..."

"Shut up you fool! Colonel Alvarez only speaks what we have been afraid to speak of, sir."

"He speaks the truth. We have to do something about Castro." Agramonte cried out as well.

"What do you intend to do, Captain Calvo Sir? Sit on your god dom ass, until Cuba no longer exists in this world, sir?" Captain Varela growled as he physically threatened the larger man.

"What is this I hear being called out by you fools? You dare to threaten me over this traitorous Colonel, sir? I have a good mind to dispatch you where you stand, sir. You're no better than this lowly traitor is who stands before you, and he spewing all this filth about Fidel Castro and his Administration, sir. I'll no longer be part of this shit, I'm going..." Captain Calvo was complaining until he was interrupted by the Vice Presidente of Cuba.

"Captain, you're going to sit down and remain with your mouth shut as well. You're interrupting the Colonel, and I wish to hear more of what he has to say before I react, sir." Vice Presidente Cabrisas snapped as he rose and he glared at the Captain.

"Am I to believe you're even considering what he's speaking of?" Calvo barked at him.

"I'm one of the leaders of this great country, and I rose to this position by listening to everything citizens have to complain of or offer to us, sir. You, being a good Military Officer should know what I'm saying to you, sir. Now, sit down and be quiet for a moment so the Colonel can finish with his words of wisdom to us. Then we can decide what to do with him and his ideas, sir. Sit down I just told you Captain!" Vice Presidente Cabrisas suddenly exploded at the stunned looking and upset Cuban Captain.

Captain Calvo stared back at the Vice President for a long second, trying to think of something else to say to him that would carry on his argument for him. Finding nothing more to say at this time, the still fuming Cuban Captain returned to his seat and settled down.

Vice Presidente Cabrisas turned to Carlos and told him with a confident tone of voice. "Colonel, continue with your words. But I warn you sir, what you speak can cost you and your bride your very lives, sir. I shall promise you this much sir, I'll have the both of you buried in the same grave, so you can spend all eternity together if I don't believe what you have to say is the truth. Continue speaking Colonel Alvarez, and be quick about it while you're at it, sir. What future does Cuba have lain out before her, if we allow this lowly mongrel to continue leading our country the way he does?" The Vice Presidente's words gave Carlos the strength to attack Castro outright, something he was refraining to do, before Cabrisas's speech moments before.

"Everything Castro has done while he's the Presidente of our great country of Cuba, has only served to harm Cuba and her people, rather than to help them, sir. Castro's stance of anti-Americanism is slowly strangling Cuba to death. What future sir? What future does Cuba have lain out before her at this time? If we continue to allow Castro to lead us down the path he treads upon, I shall tell you what future lays out before Cuba and her people.

"None! None at all sir! Cuba will have no future at all to look forward to but a slow and very agonizing death. If this foul pig is allowed to continue with his foolish ways, every other nation in the world will soon turn their foul backs on Cuba and her proud people. We have to accept that for the moment, the United States is the power of the future, and we cannot continue to turn our back on her. Need I remind you all that Castro's Cuba is the only nation in this entire world that is still trying to battle with the United States? What the devil is wrong with that great fool anyhow I ask all of you? We have to ask ourselves why it is he's still there."

These comments from Colonel Alvarez caused some of the other officers to mumble at him.

Colonel Alvarez continued with his words as if he did not hear any of their concerns. "I know my words are very hard and most displeasing for you to digest, but they're words that have to be spoken if we're ever going to consider trying to shape the future of Cuba as a country for her civilians. The way our children and future children will have to live under Castro's continuing rule is hard for me to accept. And that my friends, are the only concerns I have, the future of Cuba and her dear people. I have to consider this now, now I'm planning to take a wife and bring some children of my own into this world, to live in the only country I love, and will ever love.

"I cannot sit idly by while the only country I love rots beneath my very feet, and I do nothing whatsoever to stop it but sit on my worthless hands. I'd much rather be dead than to watch this happen any longer people. I'd rather be dead than bring children to this country, to know the only life open to them, is a life of selling their bodies and souls to the devil and hated foreigners. I cannot bring my children into a world like this. I cannot, and I will not do this." Carlos took a quick, deep breathe his voice was breaking with emotion and anger on him.

"Madre de Dios Colonel Alvarez Sir, you have our undivided attention, sir. Please continue with your words of great wisdom, Colonel Alvarez, sir." Vice Presidente Cabrisas snapped, not wanting to miss a moment now, because he too knew something had to be done with Fidel Castro and his Administration and rule over Cuba, and soon at that.

Colonel Carlos Alvarez took a quick moment to himself to sip from his drink, and then he continued with his words for the others who seemed like they were now hanging on his every word he spoke now. "I'm speaking what everyone here knows deep in their heart and soul has to be said, and I might as well say it in the words that'll leave nothing to the imagination, nothing for you to waste your time with thinking about. May God curse me for saying this to all of you, but we have to remove Castro from office, in any manner open to us.

"Even if it means killing him and then we'll appoint a new Presidente, one who'll make it his goal to open talks with the Americans, and get the United States to lift their dom embargo and trade with Cuba. This is what we must do right now. As leaders and future leaders of Cuba, we owe it to our people to accomplish what I speak of here today, gentlemen. We have to react, or we should eliminate ourselves for our lack of action for Cuba's sake. We have to do something!"

Colonel Alvarez stopped speaking, and he glared at each officer, daring them to respond.

Captain Calvo stood with his face covered with a mask of sheer hatred, as he openly glared harshly at Colonel Alvarez as he hissed at him as nastily as he could speak. "You god cursed traitorous dog, who would you put in place over Cuba once you have killed our Presidente?"

Alvarez glared back at Calvo just as harshly for a moment, and he shouted back at him. "Me!"

"Why you lousy pompous ass you, Colonel Carlos Alvarez! Why should any of us back you for the new Presidente of Cuba? What the fook makes you believe we would think you any better than Castro is, who has earned his seat of power over Cuba by his past deeds and efforts, sir. Why not offer us Vice Presidente Cabrisas to takeover power of our country, mista? If you truly want to be fair about it Colonel Alvarez that is. No, that thought has never entered you evil mind, and now you want to come along and kill the rightful Presidente of Cuba, and then you want to assume his seat power, just because you're able to sneak up behind and kill him like a dog in the middle of the night, I'll be damned to hell if I allow this to happen to my Cuba, Colonel." Captain Carlos Calvo reached for his pistol, drew it and aimed it right at the chest of Alvarez.

Maria moved over to Colonel Alvarez's side while actually placing her body between him and the weapon the angry Captain was aiming at him. She was stopped by Alvarez's arm, as he put his hand against her chest, and he shoved her away from him.

Captain Remos reached out and he grabbed her by the arms and pinned her arms down by her side, and he held her out of harm's way. All the while, Maria pleaded with Captain Calvo not to kill her lover and Colonel.

Captain Calvo turned to the begging young woman with madness etched in his eyes, and then he snarled at her. "Lowly bitch of Cuba, you're wasting your god dom tears on this lousy traitor to Cuba standing before me, woman. I suggest you cry more for Cuba and for our Presidente Castro, than the things this foul madman had just tried to talk us into, woman. Look upon this traitor standing before you one final time before I kill the lowly son of a filthy dog, who has just wanted us to turn our backs on the rightful Presidente Castro and our country, woman."

Three other Cuban Military Officers suddenly sprang to their feet, also removing their pistols as they rose, and they all aimed their weapons at the Captain standing in the center of the room, and threatening to kill Alvarez. It turned into a standoff, with Colonel Alvarez not moving, and the Captain threatening to kill him, and with Colonel

Cienfuegos, Gonzales and Colonel Agramonte threatening Captain Calvo with their weapons.

Vice Presidente Cabrisas laughed as he suddenly placed his hand on Colonel Agramonte's pistol, and he forced his hand down as he remarked. "Ahh, so this must be the way Castro's revolution had started, with his fighters threatening to kill him for daring to demand a change in our government. My, my, where would we be now if he and his men had chosen to be much the same way we have been over the last many years of the past? Captain Calvo Sir, lower your god dom weapon immediately, I tell you to do this sir."

Captain Calvo stared opened mouthed back at the Vice Presidente of Cuba and he grumbled at the second most powerful person in all of Cuba. "Cabrisas, please say this is not so sir. Tell me you're not going to back this pack of cursed traitors here, sir."

"It is and I am Captain Calvo Sir. For countless years now, I have only dared to dream of what this man standing before us speaks of today, sir. I have only deceived myself into believing one faithful day Castro would wake up, and he'd finally see the error in his foul ways of thinking, and make things right for all the people of Cuba, sir. So far, this has not taken place, and I see no reason why it will happen in the near future as long as Castro remains the Presidente of Cuba, sir. My eyes have been opened to the plight of the Cuban people by this young man. Now, I see what must be done, and I back this young Military Officer and his rash ideas, and I see a new evolution quickly taking shape in the wings for Cuba.

"I see a new idea that'll surely set Cuba free, and free of Castro and his narrow ways of thought and actions and leadership. Colonel Carlos Alvarez Sir, on behalf of the people of Cuba, I must thank you for opening my worthless eyes, and showing me the true path we must take in freeing Cuba of this Devil in Paradise, sir. Something that should have been accomplished many years ago I'm afraid. We should've taken the message from the worthless Russians as you stated when they moved down the second path to their future, sir. We should've taken the road that includes the United States, and all who follow her ideals. Captain Calvo Sir, I understand your feelings and commend you for them, sir. But you must consider the future of Cuba and her people. Now sir, lower your weapon so we can speak further..."

"But Vice Presidente Cabrisas Sir, why the hell should we back this young rebel, and then install him to the Presidente's chair of Cuba for us, sir? Why should he not be fair about it, and offered to install you, as the next in Command, as the new Presidente of Cuba, sir? I cannot swallow the fact he wants to be the next leader of Cuba, sir. Are we to follow any young upstart who wants to kill the Presidente, so only he can become the next Presidente over Cuba himself? What happens when the next god cursed rebel comes along, and he wants to kill him so he could become the next Presidente of Cuba? What message are we sending to the rest of our youth of Cuba, sir? If you want to become Presidente of Cuba, just kill the seated Presidente. What message will we be sending them? What message I ask you sir?"

Vice Presidente Cabrisas crossed the few feet separating him from Captain Calvo, and then he actually rested his hand on his weapon, forcing it down as he rested his other hand on the angry Captain's shoulder, and he quickly offered to him. "I swear by the sacred Madonna, I understand how you must feel Captain, sir. But I find myself agreeing with Colonel Alvarez on many of his points he has made here today, sir. If he was to carry out his new revolution, only to install me as the new Presidente of Cuba, and then what would the people of Cuba think? I'll tell you what they'll think sir. They'll think it was I who has led this new revolution for them, because I wanted to become their new Presidente of Cuba. This thought alone will force all of them to believe there shall be no new changes in the running of the Presidency of Cuba.

"They'll also believe nothing new will be different in the rule of Cuba, sir. No Captain Calvo Sir, Colonel Alvarez is most correct in demanding he becomes the new Presidente of Cuba, and it is up to all of us to stand behind him and support him and his efforts at this time sir." Vice Presidente Cabrisas stopped speaking as he turned to face Alvarez, and he pointed his finger right at his face as he added. "You, Colonel Carlos Alvarez Sir, I warn you right here and now where you stand, sir. If you're to ever have my full support of this new revolt, sir.

"You're going to have to be the difference to Cuba and her people, Colonel. If you dare to slip back into the old ways of Fidel Castro iron fist in ruling Cuba then I'll be the one who'll organize the next revolution of Cuba against you, Colonel Alvarez, sir. Total revolution, it's the only true way Cuba will ever be able to shape her own future for herself, by the gun and the death sir. What have we done to this poor Island nation and to all her beloved people and children, sir? We've offered them nothing but slow death and fighting in the past, sir. What a poor future do we offer to Cuba's future children and existence, sir?" Cabrisas shook Captain Calvo by the shoulder lightly as he bowed sadly over his words.

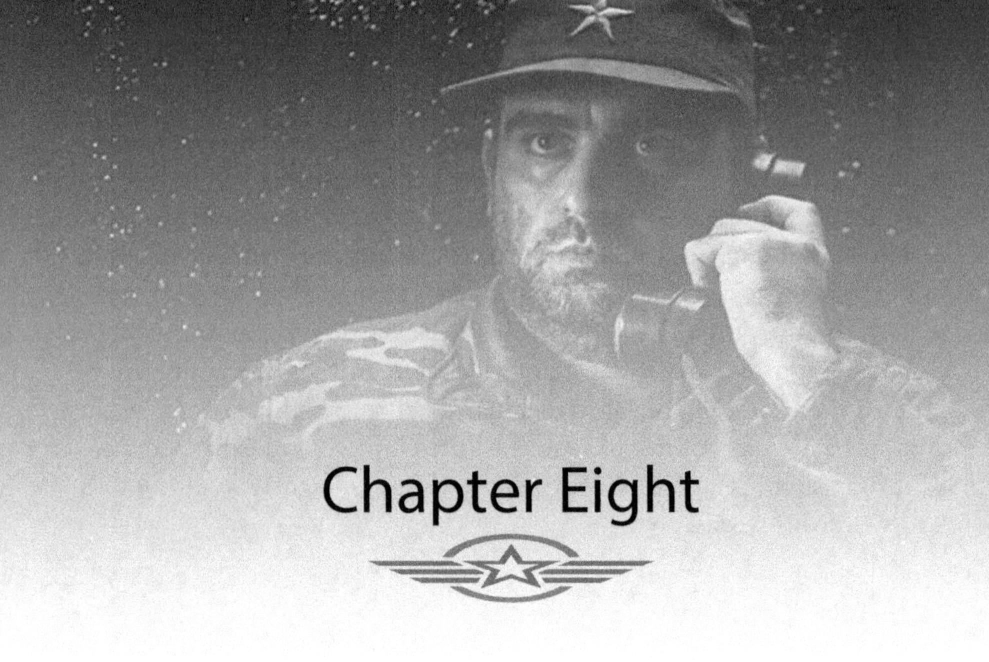

Chapter Eight

Maria suddenly broke free of Captain Remos's grasp, and she quickly ran over to Colonel Alvarez's side, and she hugged him to her while turning him away from the still angry looking Captain's view. She started to lead him away from the center of the room, but she was stopped by the Vice Presidente of Cuba, who had suddenly pulled Carlos Rafael Fernandez Alvarez by the shoulder back into the middle of the room. He then reached for Captain Carlos Calvo's arm, and he pulled him over to Colonel Alvarez. Vice Presidente Cabrisas remained standing between the two powerful men, all the time he was pulling them a little closer to each other. He then turned to Calvo and said to him. "Captain Calvo Sir, Colonel Alvarez is Cuba's only hope for the future sir, and you being an Officer, must offer your hand to the next leader of our country, sir. You must sir." Vice President Cabrisas put more pressure on the Captain's arm, nudging it forward.

Captain Calvo looked at the Vice Presidente for a few stunned and long moments while he went deep in thought.

Vice Presidente Cabrisas smiled at the still angry looking Cuban Captain, as he tilted his head to the side, and then he made a motion to Colonel Alvarez, standing an arms distance from him. Maria stood behind Alvarez and off to his right for protection, out of the way of the two powerful Cuban Officers.

"By the Almighty hand of God Captain Calvo Sir, I see your wise father did not raise a child, he has raised a god dom man here I say to you, sir. You must do what is right for the sake of Cuba and her people Captain Calvo, sir." When the Captain made no move to speak up, Vice Presidente Cabrisas added to him in a sharp tone of voice as he continued to stare at him. "I and all Cuba's children wait for your final decision to be made, Captain Calvo Sir." Again, he made the slight head movement. This time, the angry Captain allowed his arm to be moved forward by the Vice Presidente. Soon, he found himself standing there with his arm extended all the way out towards the waiting and smiling Colonel Alvarez.

Colonel Carlos Alvarez slowly extended his hand forward as well, and then the two very powerful men of Cuba shook hands, and then Captain Carlos Calvo pulled Colonel Alvarez closer to him and he locked him up in a hug as he said to the colonel in an agreeing tone. "I'm only doing this for Cuba's future, sir. Dare not betray it or me sir, or you'll have a most terrible enemy who'll be stalking you for the rest of your life, Colonel Alvarez Sir."

The Captain then kissed Colonel Alvarez on both of his cheeks, and then he held him at arm's length and added to him. "Colonel Alvarez, for many years now sir, I have also believed the same as you, that something must be done to get Cuba back into the new world order of things to come, sir. But I must add this to you also sir I have always felt Presidente Fidel Castro should be included in the future of Cuba, Colonel Alvarez. I know this is impossible to do at this time sir, and I'm willing to do whatever is necessary for the sake of Cuba and her people, sir."

Colonel Carlos Rafael Fernandez Alvarez's chest was swollen with great pride for his fellow Cuban Military Officers as he replied proudly to the military officer who he had once feared so much in life. "Captain Carlos Calvo Sir, dear friends. I shall do whatever is right, whatever it takes whatever is needed for the sake of Cuba and her faithful people, or I shall lay down my worthless life in my efforts. Every man here will be included in my new government, so each one of you will have a say in the way the new government of Cuba will be ran by me. I cannot express in words how I feel at this very moment, to have your backing for this new revolution for the sake of Cuba and her children. The last revolution for Cuba I say, people."

"Am I to take it you're offering free elections for Cuba, sir?" Captain Varela asked him.

"Certainly, I am sir. That is exactly what I'm offering." Colonel Alvarez replied.

"Then you have my vote, and you can depend on my total backing of your future plan, sir."

"Great. This is great for me to hear these words of respect, loyalty and friendship to be spoken by all Cuba's most powerful Military Officers." Vice Presidente Cabrisas said happily, and then he turned to the rest of the officers with him and said to them. "What about the rest of you fools, are you going to stand up and back this new revolution of ours, for the sake of Cuba?"

Each of the officers took a step forward, and one by one, they answered yes to his question.

"It's settled then, and we gathered here today, agree it's to be Colonel Carlos Rafael Fernandez Alvarez, who shall lead the new revolution, later to become the next Presidente of Cuba, if we're successful." Vice Presidente Cabrisas offered as he stood proudly by the side of Alvarez.

"All this is great to understand for Cuba and her children's future, but what will happen to you after all of this unfolds before your feet, sir? What will you're value be to this new revolution we are speaking of here, sir? You'll still help us after the revolution, is that correct, sir?" Captain Hernandez of the 11th Infantry asked the Vice Presidente of Cuba.

"I shall step down from my office and then put my faith in the hands of the civilians of Cuba. If they feel I have backed Castro and they want my worthless head for this and their revenge then so be it, sir. They'll have it to use as a soccer ball if they will with me, sir." The wise Cuban Vice Presidente replied to the concerned military officer.

"The hell they will Vice Presidente Cabrisas Sir. By the Holy Madonna sacred smile please, if my revolution is to be successful. Then it'll be successful only because of you standing by my side, and I'll not allow the people of Cuba to forget this for one moment, sir. Vice Presidente Lazaro Prio Socarras Cabrisas, I'm offering you a position in my new government, sir. Of course, you'll accept the office I offer you right here and now, sir?" Colonel Alvarez said as he held the arm of Vice Presidente Cabrisas, and he stared back at the man with much concern.

"And what is this new position you offer me today, sir? Dog catcher, Colonel Alvarez Sir?"

"No sir, it's the office of the Vice Presidency of Cuba, sir. The same exact position you're currently occupying in Castro's Administration, sir. But with one major difference though sir, you'll now serve in my new government as my Vice Presidente, sir. Will you please accept the new position I offer to you on this day, the new Vice Presidente Cabrisas of Cuba, sir?"

There was not a sound in the room as every one of the officers waited for Cabrisas's response.

Vice Presidente Cabrisas suddenly pulled Colonel Carlos Alvarez close to him with surprising strength, and he hugged him as he did this and he replied to the Colonel at the same time. "I'll be most honored to assume the Vice Presidency of your new government, Colonel Carlos Alvarez Sir. I thank you kindly for the offer, but first, I think you should clear this with the others assembled here tonight, sir. One of them might have eyed the position you offer me themselves, and I don't want to be the cause of any dissension in your forming ranks, sir. I'm not a military man as you well know, Colonel Alvarez."

The two men pulled apart, only to find themselves instantly surrounded by the other military officers in the room everyone of them was nodding and patting them on their shoulders.

"Hmmm... then I take it your people agree with your first unwise decision you have just made Colonel Alvarez Sir."

"Vice Presidente Cabrisas Sir, they're not my people at all, sir. They're our people of Cuba sir, and they're only concerned with Cuba's future fate, and they're willing to do whatever is demanded of them to insure Cuba's successfully future here today, Vice Presidente, sir." Colonel Carlos Alvarez said as he smiled back at the pleasantly grinning Vice Presidente.

Everyone quieted down as Maria walked over to Colonel Alvarez. They remained quiet as the two kissed, then Maria pulled free and she walked over to Captain Calvo, offering him her hand.

The Captain smiled as he kissed her hand tenderly. But she suddenly pulled her hand away from his lips, and she pulled him to her and she kissed him on both of his cheeks as she whispered so only he could her words spoken. "Captain Calvo Sir, I thank you so much for backing my Colonel in his quest to free Cuba of Castro, sir. We have gotten off on the wrong foot before when you had first arrived at my home sir, and I just wanted to clear it up by..." her words were suddenly cut off as the Captain said to her in a very calm tone this time.

Captain Calvo put his finger up to Maria's lips and he shushed her with a soft smile as he said just above a whisper back to her. "Please young woman, I'll be most proud to back your brave young soldier, just as long as he continues to have Cuba and her children's best interests in both his mind and heart, young lady. But I warn you of this as well young woman, I shall kill him in a blink of an eye if he ever forgets his sacred oath for one second to Cuba and her people. Other than that, we have nothing else to clear up between us, young lady." The Captain suddenly smiled at her for a brief moment, before adding to his words for her. "Though I still think you should have some more clothes on your body, young woman." The smile remained as the Captain stared at Maria for a brief moment longer.

Her eyes suddenly flashed a moment of sheer anger, before she finally realized the Captain was only kidding around with her this time, and then she replied to his last comment with a rather devilish smile on her own lips. "Why Captain Calvo Sir, I was always led to believe that every true Cuban soldier of Cuba enjoyed looking at a young beautiful woman's naked body, sir." With that said, she purposely bowed real low this time, allowing him a view he would not soon forget. When she stood straight up again, she saw his face and the sheer appreciation of the view his eyes had just beheld of her exquisite breasts. She smiled back at the Captain before turning to her Colonel who was also wearing a grin from ear to ear now, as the rest of the soldiers congratulated him and each other of the group of new rebels for Cuba, over their plans to do away with Castor and his rule over Cuba.

Both Rita and Anita quickly joined Maria who was now standing along with her Colonel in the center of the group of soldiers, and the three women watched as the other men slapped each other on their backs. They were all speaking at once to each other at the same time, so none of their conversations could really be understood by anyone who was really listening to them speaking.

The three women smiled pleasantly amongst themselves as they watched the rituals currently being carried out by the men in the room, rituals that would have embarrassed most women of Cuba. The men's attention suddenly turned on the three young women.

The girls saw the men swaying from drink, and they all had that certain look locked in their eyes, and the three women immediately ran for their lives, laughing and easily outrunning the obviously drunken soldiers falling over themselves, as they gave weak chase to the fleeing women. Everyone at the party was suddenly filled with a joy that was lacking ever since Fidel Castro had taken over the leadership of Cuba. Even though many of the proud Cuban soldiers would not have done anything with the only women at the party, they continued to try and chase them around. Laughing all the while they continued to give weak chase to them.

Maria cut away from the other two women and she quickly made her way back to her Colonel Alvarez's side. He was still standing with Vice Presidente Cabrisas and Captain Carlos Calvo, the only three men not trying to bother any of the young women at the party now. She got back to Colonel Alvarez and she smiled warming at him as she held him in her proud gaze.

Vice Presidente Cabrisas offered to her kindly. "Young lady, I fear we have just destroyed your engagement party on you and your fine young Colonel Alvarez here, Ma'am.

She just smiled tenderly back at the kind elderly Cuban Vice Presidente. The party ended when all the soldiers agreed on their soon to be leaders, and the necessity of this new revolution to free Cuba from Fidel Castro and the rest of his cohorts foul hands. The men sobered up as they laid out the future plans together. Each officer searched their minds as to which soldiers under their Command were most trustworthy and loyal to them. They all made lists of the soldiers who they could count on, and who was needed to be eliminated. Plans were devised on how to secure the capital of Havana in the opening attack on Castro, while they eliminated him.

It dawned on them that each of the military units stationed in Havana was represented at the gathering. It was decided which units were designated as the security units. It would be their responsibility to close roads leading in and out of the capital until the revolutionaries secured the government, and eliminate anyone who disapproved of their action. If the officers and politicians at this meeting got their troops and men into position, they would move on Castro on the 23rd of September. This was the date of the meeting to be held between Castro and Alvarez.

The securing of Havana fell upon the shoulders of Captain Varela, and his 17th Infantry and his Light Armor Brigade. Colonel Cienfuegos, and his 1st Armor Division would park their military equipment on the main roads leading into Havana. The initial thrust of the new Revolutionary Army on the Presidential Palace was to be carried out by Colonel Carlos Alvarez, the Vice Presidente Cabrisas, and the combined forces of Gonzales and his 2nd Infantry Division currently stationed in Havana. Captain Suarez and his 19th Infantry Brigade from Barreras Minas, Colonel Vidali and his 34th Infantry Brigade presently stationed at Campo Florido, and all the military units from Hernandez and his 11th Infantry Division would come from Santiago de las Vagas and they would help Alvarez with his troops.

Colonel Alvarez ordered the forces of Colonel Agramonte, who controlled the Airforce, along with Captain Remos who controlled the Navy, and Cardona and his 9th Infantry Brigade, stationed on the Peninsula of Guanahacabibes, to help secure the rest of the entire Island. The combined Armies of Captain Calvo's paratroopers, and Bernardo's 27th Mechanized Group of soldiers stationed at Guanajay on the south side of Havana, were ordered to secure the streets of the capital city of Havana. Once Colonel Alvarez's plans were set forth, each of the military officers knew where their responsibility lay. As they all came to agreement, the meeting finally broke up. Each of the proud and overly excited Cuban Officers vowed to make certain all the soldiers in their Command to be eliminated would be, and the rest of the soldiers would know of their future plans and responsibilities.

The last people to leave Maria's home were Vice Presidente Cabrisas and Captain Carlos Calvo, who were hitching a ride back to his military base with Cabrisas. The greatly pleased Vice Presidente shook Colonel Alvarez's hand and he kissed Maria on her both cheeks. Before he left, he thanked Colonel Alvarez for bringing the problems facing Cuba to a head for them. He felt as if the weight of the world had just been lifted from his shoulders, as he waited for the Captain to finish speaking with Colonel Alvarez now.

Captain Calvo shook Colonel Alvarez's hand as he offered to be in position when he was needed. Alvarez thanked the officer for his help against the attack on Havana, and Castro. He watched as the last of the large group of Cuban officers left Maria's home. Captain Calvo opened the door for the Vice President, and then he got in and the driver started up the car with a backfire and bucking, the old car soon rumbled down the road.

Maria, Anita and Rita, all spoke to Colonel Carlos Alvarez at the same time.

"Alvarez, it looks like we are going to start the last revolution in Cuba." Maria cried to him.

Anita's words overlapped hers, "I know other women who'll join your forces, Colonel Sir."

Rita's voice crossed over hers as she almost ended up arguing with her friend. "Anita, we have to know who they are first, before they might be allowed to join us in this new Revolution. I think we have more than enough people already involved with it. I'm quite certain the Colonel would be most willing to enlist more people, when and if they're needed by him. He'll let us know in due time when to bring them in at the proper time, honey." Rita looked at Anita as she glared angrily at her for voicing her opinion to her.

Colonel Carlos Alvarez smiled at Rita as he said to her. "By the grace of the Madonna Anita, Rita is absolutely correct. The fewer people who know of our future plans for Cuba, the better off we truly are. Now, you three women are more than enough for our beginning Revolution. We must sit pat and wait for the rest of the Officers to check in with us to inform us that their troops are in position and ready to act when needed."

Anita removed her glare from Rita, and her eyes softened as she looked at the Colonel and she offered. "You're right. After listening, I understand. I'm sorry for offering these other women."

"Don't be sorry for any offer for help for us, just keep the others in mind and when the proper time comes when they can then come and help us, Anita. I know we shall need all the help we can possibly organize later on, if we're forced to defend our new revolution once it has been successful. Don't be sorry for offering any possible help to us. I have a feeling we're going to need all the help we can muster, once the fighting starts."

It was Maria's turn to ask, "Fighting? I didn't know there was going to be any fighting. I thought once Castro was dead, the soldiers following him would not fight. Why would they?"

"Mother of God Maria, you're truly the romantic. Of course there'll be fighting, we're going to fight the ones who agree with Castro. No doubt we'll fight soldiers who don't believe in our just cause, those who think we're trying to take over the country for our own means. Then, we'll probably have to fight the exiled forces the United States organized over the past years..."

"Why would they attack us? Was it not they who wanted Castro to be removed in the first place? Is not that what we intend to do? Why would they attack us? I don't understand this."

"Of course the filthy exiles will attack us. I believe they'll attack us the moment when they realize Cuba is in the midst of a new Revolution and at her weakest times, woman. If they don't attack on their own then I'm most certain the hated United States will talk them into attacking us, and if they fail with words. Then they'll probably force the foolish exiles to attack us under their orders. Everyone knows the true time to attack your enemy is when he's the least able to defend himself against those attacks. If we're forced to fight with Castro's troops, we'll be less able to defend ourselves from any other invasion mounted against us." Carlos Alvarez stopped speaking and he stared at Maria while waiting for her to respond to his last words of warning.

Maria could not hide the surprised look stuck on her face as she shook her head, and then she milled over Colonel Alvarez's last upsetting words to her and she replied. "I had no idea this might happen to us with this new revolution of ours, Carlos. I thought, no, I had always believed that once Fidel Castro was eliminated from Cuba, the rest of the world would be so greatly relieved. And, this new relief would help serve to aide all those other nations who were waiting to open up talks with the future new government of Cuba, Colonel Carlos Alvarez."

"I hope this would truly come to pass for us. But you have to understand one thing here Maria, if the other nations of the world, especially the United States agree with our new Revolution and elimination Castro one way or the other. Then they'll back us with the needed arms and money as well. But they have to agree with us first honey, but you have given me a new idea though, I think I'm going to send Vice Presidente Cabrisas to the United States secretly.

"He'll be instructed to make contact with the CIA operating inside Cuba. He can inform them he wants to speak directly to their President of the United States on our behalf, honey. Once he's there, he can inform the American President of our future plans to enlist his help. Or at least have the American President promise not to intervene until the fighting is completed. If he does this successfully, we'll be assured of winning our new revolution. Once we're in power over the Island then who cares what the worthless United States thinks of or believes of us. We can put them off until we finally make peace with the rest of the world first. What other choice would the Americans have but to make peace with us, and lift their god dom embargo against us?"

Maria's chest swelled as she stared at her lover, "I've been of help to you, my Colonel?"

"More than you'll ever know Maria." Colonel Alvarez replied with a smile on his lips.

"You'll inform me when and I'll be able to bring in the other women, Colonel Alvarez?"

Colonel Carlos Alvarez turned to Anita and then he smiled pleasantly at her.

Rita moved over to Anita's side and said, "you must let Anita know when she can bring in her favorite girlfriends, so she'll have someone else to make love to." Maria and Rita laughed.

"You better be careful with her or you might fall victim to her pleasures you know, my dear Rita." Maria warned her other girlfriend with a warm smile. No sooner did she say this though, than Anita slide her hand in the front of Rita's dress, and she fondled her breast.

Before Rita knew what was happening to her, she was quickly getting turned on by Anita's skilled hands, and now her tongue sliding over her body, and if it was not for Maria calling out her name to her. She might have even forced Anita down to the floor just to see what it was that had captured her dear friend into this world of making love with only other women.

"Rita, Rita. Err... Rita. You better be very careful with her Rita. You're quickly beginning to respond to her advances of you all of a sudden. Err... Rita, come back to the real world will you please. Rita..." Maria was staring at her two friends when she saw Rita look up at her.

Rita suddenly pulled free of Anita's grasp as she tried to work her hand down between her legs now, and she then held her off at arm's length. She shook her head no and she smiled pleasantly at both Maria and Alvarez, they were taking in the scene with his mouths hanging open.

Rita saw Colonel Carlos Alvarez's dick was rock hard and she felt thoroughly embarrassed by it, but she still refused to be intimidated by any of her actions, or the stares coming from both Maria and the stunned looking Cuban Colonel as she snapped at the both of them. "What the hell are you two fools looking at? As for me getting turned on by Anita and what she is doing to me, Maria. I suggest you check your own man's thing out please."

She turned and looked down at him, and then she slapped him and she hissed angrily at the same time. "You dirty cochino you, you want something to get turned on by, mista? You like it when two women make love to each other I see? Then watch this if you dare, fool." She moved over to Anita and she slid her straps from her shoulder. She cupped her breasts and lapped at the hardening nipples. She then rolled Anita's breasts slowly in her hands as the dress slid down her body to the floor. All the while Maria kept asking her soldier. "You like what you see do you mista? You're nothing more than a filthy cochino you."

Colonel Carlos Rafael Fernandez Alvarez said nothing as he continued to stare down at the two young women locked in each other's arms and they were really going at it now. But when Maria slid her hand down between Anita's legs and her body until her head soon replaced her hand, he suddenly reacted. Carlos grabbed Maria by her arms and he tried to pull her up to her feet again, but she refused to budge for him as her tongue now probed Anita's inner regions.

"C'mon Maria, you have proven your point to me loud and clear, god dom you woman. I'm sorry I got turned on by the two other women making love to each other. Knock it off will you please. I'm not enjoying this woman!" the Colonel growled angrily at his girlfriend.

Maria said nothing she grabbed him between the legs and felt he was hard. She removed her head from Anita's thighs and snapped as she held onto him. "How could you say that when your dick is ready for action mista? You must like this, or you wouldn't be so turned on by it mista."

It was Anita who pulled free from Maria's grasp, she was the one feeling embarrassed now.

Rita piped in this time. "Maria, I'm getting turned on by the two of you making such fools of yourselves, and I'm feeling rather left out of all the fun and games between you two."

Maria did not look to Rita as she waited for the Cuban Colonel to respond to her last words.

Colonel Alvarez knew he had to say something even if it was wrong, and he offered. "Maria, I don't know why this turns a foolish man on with watching two women make love to each other, my love. All I know is that it does, and it always will baby. What can I tell you honey?"

Anita laughed as she wiggled into her dress and Maria got up to her feet and she replied to the Colonel. "You want to know why this turns men on so much, fool? It's because there's nothing as beautiful as two women making love to each other. It interests men because a woman can satisfy a woman completely, and she does not need a dirty smelly dick to do it with. Why man watches, is because he wishes to learn our secrets. He's turned on by this, because he knows he's incapable of pleasing a woman as well as another woman can, and that scares the hell out of him. The pleasure of seeing a woman turned on by another woman drives you men wild."

The three girls looked at him and he shrugged and laughed. "Guilty on all counts I guess."

Rita added, "I thought you were going to allow Anita to join you two on your wedding night?"

Maria turned red as she hesitated and then she shifted her feet while trying to avoid Rita's grin.

"Come on Maria will you please, you promised me that, you cannot possibly change your mind on me now, girl." Anita cried as she stared back at her girlfriend with sadness in her eyes.

She looked from Colonel Carlos Alvarez and back to her girlfriend Anita, staring back at her, looking as if she was going to cry if Maria changed her mind on her and she offered. "I didn't change my mind in the least Rita. She's invited, if she still cares to join us that is, honey?"

All eyes instantly went over to Anita standing there and nodding her head yes rapidly, and she was also grinning wildly back at Maria and her boyfriend.

Now it was Rita who cried out, "once again I'm feeling a little left out around here, people. I don't want to have a lesbian relationship, but I must admit I'm a little more than inquisitive about this now. Oh what the hell, if you three are going to play around, I want to play too."

"You mean I might have three women to share my bed with on my wedding night, Maria?"

Rita smiled and then replied, "No stupid, I don't want to have a dumb man right in the middle of the three of us enjoying each other. I want to experience this on a one to one basis with only women. Would you make love to a man if he was in your bed with two other men, mista?"

"No way in hell, I only do women." Colonel Alvarez announced proudly to the three women.

"Then stay the hell out of my bed will you please." Rita snapped back at the grinning man.

Anita turned to Rita and then she offered her services to her. Rita smiled and she replied to her girlfriend. "Okay baby you won me over, you have worn me down girl. I give up to you, and hand my body over to your hands, honey. Where and when do you want me, Anita darling?"

"The night is still young, tonight, now, my place." Anita said, not believing her luck.

"Okay, let's go over to your place then, Anita. After seeing all I have seen on this puzzling night, I'm afraid I'm more than horny in places that no man is going to be able to satisfy for me, honey." Rita announced proudly as she smiled in the concerned looking eyes of Anita.

Maria felt slightly jilted this time as she watched the two girlfriends leave her home. Rita saw the look in her eyes and said to her. "Don't worry so much Maria, I'll leave you some of Anita to have your fun and games with along with your dirty cochino. Who knows, if this works out for all of us, we could tell the men to get fooked." Rita closed the door behind her to the Colonel calling out to them. "That'll be the day. No matter how good she is with you in bed, you'll always need a man to scratch that certain itch she could never reach on her best day for you."

Anita's voice was the last to be heard, "you want to bet on that, my dear Colonel Alvarez?"

Colonel Alvarez and Maria made love that night with a new passion, Alvarez because of the talk of sleeping with two women at the same time. Maria was turned on because Castro's days in office were fast coming to a conclusion, and Cuba would finally be free to elect the next Presidente to lead the Island of Cuba and her people.

The night passed by rather quickly for the two of them and Maria was the first one up. She prepared the morning meal when she heard Alvarez taking his morning shower. She looked at her clock it was 6:25 a.m. on the 19th of September. She counted off the days left, five days until the meeting between Castro and her lover and soldier. She smiled to herself, because she knew on that day, Cuba would be set free at long last.

The water stopped running, and Colonel Alvarez came walking in the kitchen naked again.

"Look at you, you filthy cochino you!" Maria exclaimed as she reached out and began playing with him and then she asked, "You want to make love to me?"

Alvarez did not answer, instead he pulled her down to the floor, and they enjoyed each other once more. When they finished, Maria purred at him. "What a beautiful way to start the day."

"Yes, err... Maria, I have to think about leaving and getting back to my military base and see what is happening there, baby. I have an awful lot I have to prepare for and accomplish young lady, before my meeting next week with Castro, honey."

"I know that you do Carlos, but first you'll have something to eat. It's almost done honey."

"By the Lord sweet Jesus, no! I have to leave right at this moment if I want to get started with all my plans, Maria." Carlos Alvarez got up, and he started to look around the room for his suit which was scattered about the room, and he quickly dressed himself. Before he left though, she had his meal resting on a plate and she refused to move out of his way until he ate some of it. Colonel Alvarez quickly choked down the food, and he swallowed his coffee as he headed for the front door of her home. He used his car to get over to the party last night, and he was amazed to see Sergeant Regueiro was sleeping in the front seat, protecting the car from thieves who would siphon off his fuel to see on the Island. He rapped on the glass of the car door and the Sergeant's eyes opened and Colonel Alvarez ordered him. "Sergeant, let's get back to the base."

The drive back to the base seemed much quicker than usual. As they entered the Army military base, activity was high, as if the soldiers knew something was afoot. Carlos Alvarez ordered the Sergeant to drop him off by his office, and he was to take charge of the men. He also informed the Sergeant he wanted them busy so they did not have time to think. He told him he wanted to send in one man after the other, but not to send in anyone he thought would be against their plans for Cuba's future. The Sergeant did as he was ordered, and the first man appeared in the Colonel's office.

"Ahh, Lieutenant Fernardo Calderio Sir, will you take a seat please sir. I have some important matters to discuss over with you today, sir." When the Lieutenant was seated and comfortable, Colonel Alvarez went over what had been decided the night before with the other officers at his wedding party. The young Lieutenant could not keep the smile off of his face, as he swore his allegiance to the plan, and then he left the office with a new skip in his step.

Next was Lieutenant Eulogio Marinello, and when Colonel Alvarez finished with him, he also agreed with the strategy. So did the third officer, Captain Mango Jordan Padilla. Captain Gerardo Lopez Baquero and Lieutenant Renato Granados both agreed also, and they completed his roster of officers he needed on the base. Everyone knew who among their men, could be depended on. Each of the other officers agreed to eliminate the few that they did not fully trust. Every officer also agreed Castro was no longer good for the sake of Cuba.

Colonel Alvarez decided to start with his noncommissioned officers next, and he ordered Sergeant Granados to send Sergeant Aguero Crespo into his office next. When he informed the Sergeant of his future plans, the stunned Sergeant immediately sprang up to his feet and he took an extremely threatening stance with the Colonel. But he was prepared, and he also realized this man could not be depended on to be part of the new revolution of Cuba.

Colonel Alvarez did not allow the Sergeant to get too worked up on him before he fired twice with a silenced pistol, striking him both times in the chest. He then dragged the body over to his bathroom, and sent for the second Sergeant. Sergeant Virgilio Garcia entered the Colonel's office next, and he quickly agreed with Alvarez's plan. The next two Sergeants entered, Armando Guerra then Agostino Chenard, and they both were more than happy to follow him to hell if need be. This left just the Corporals on the base to deal with next, the last of the noncommissioned officers to be questioned by the excited Colonel. Corporal Ernesto Gonzales, and then Corporal Heberto Cardona were sent for, and they went along with his plan as well.

Colonel Alvarez breathed a deep and exhausted sigh of relief, knowing only one of his NCOs did not fully agree with him, and all his officers could be trusted to follow his new revolution. He checked his watch after his stomach growled at him, and he was stunned to discover it was after three p.m. already. He was starving and headed off for the mess hall on the base. After the cooks fixed him two sandwiches, he quickly choked them down and went back to his office. He ordered Sergeant Regueiro to remove the body of Sergeant Crespo from his bathroom, and have it buried. He checked his sleeping quarters, and then he spent the night on base in order to stay close to the phone. He waited for the other officers who were part of the new revolution to check in.

His only hope was they were as successful as he was with all his officers and NCOs. His attention was drawn to the sound of a sudden weapon fire on base. Sergeant Regueiro was in the office in a flash, and he immediately informed the Colonel it was Lieutenant Marinello, who shot one of his men because he threatened to expose their plan. Throughout the rest of the day, the base was the source of sporadic weapon fire. Even some of the enlisted men who agreed with the plans, shot ones they knew would be against the new revolution in Cuba.

Of the fifteen hundred men and women stationed on Alvarez's military base, only ninety of the soldiers were killed. A few others were placed in jail because they were not too sure if they agreed or not with the Colonel's plan to take overpower in Cuba, and rather than kill these few soldiers, it was decided to keep them alive and hold them in the stockade for the time being.

It was after eight p.m. when the first report carried by Sergeant Regueiro was offered to the concerned Colonel, assuring him that his entire military base was secure, and free of any soldiers still loyal to Castro. Colonel Alvarez relaxed and enjoyed a cigar. The phone rang, it was Maria. She said she was scared and driven to tears when he did not come home. She admitted that she had feared the worse when he did not show up at her home.

Colonel Carlos Alvarez laughed as he joked, he was going to remain on the military base until he heard something from the other officers of his plan. He promised Maria he would be home on Sunday, and he would bring her up to date on what was happening with the beginning of their new revolution. The Colonel promised he would spend the night with her it was the only way he could get her off the phone. Once Carlos hung up with her, Alvarez turned in for the night, he was exhausted. But sleep did not come to him for the entire night. His mind went over the day's happenings, playing over the officer's words, as if his mind was trying to find some betrayal in them. His mind refused to allow his body to rest.

FRIDAY, SEPTEMBER 20th, 1996

Colonel Carlos Rafael Fernandez Alvarez awoke to the sounds of a slight commotion taking place on his military base, and he rushed over to the window, and he saw three fuel trucks parked by the row of tanks, and his soldiers pumping fuel into the massive steel monsters. He looked around until he noticed Sergeant Regueiro standing with Captain Padilla, and the Captain was issuing a flood of orders to the men fueling up the war machines. Colonel Alvarez jumped from the steps and ran over to the two soldiers.

"What the hell is going on out there god dom, Sergeant Regueiro?" he barked at him.

"Colonel Alvarez Sir, glad to see you are up, sir. Last night a few of us hit the fuel refineries stationed at Caibarien. We discussed it with the Captain, and he agreed we need our war machines if we're going to be successful carrying out our new Revolution. We have five fuel tanker trailers full of fuel on the way over to the base as we speak, sir."

"What about any god dom ammunition for the god cursed war machines? Has anyone given any thought to locating some ammunition for us, at least for the machine guns on board the foul tanks?" Colonel Alvarez asked the Sergeant angrily.

Captain Padilla immediately spoke up and offered to the excited Cuban Officer. "Yes Sir Colonel Alvarez Sir, I was able to locate five hundred rounds of heat or high explosive rounds, and another three hundred Sabots, or anti-tank and armor rounds for all our tanks Colonel, sir."

"Good work Captain, but what about any ammunition for the god dom machine guns, sir?"

"We have plenty for them, always had sir. When we stopped getting paid, the Officers and myself thought it wise to remove the machine gun ammunition, before anyone got the wrong idea. I have a feeling we hid rounds for the main mounts on base. We're going to be in good shape when we go into action against the fools in the Capital, Colonel."

"I see our revolution is beginning to take good form for us, Captain. I shall leave you to carry on with your orders that you seem to have everything under control here, sir." Colonel Alvarez saluted the two soldiers and then he headed back to his office. The moment he entered the room his phone rang. "Yes, Colonel Alvarez here."

It was Captain Carlos Calvo on the phone, and he immediately began to inform Colonel Alvarez that he nearly had a small mutiny on his military base a few hours ago, and to end all the possible fighting, he had to order half of his base to attack the one soldier's who had disagreed with him and their new revolution. He then informed the worried Colonel it was really touch and go there for a little while, until his men were finally able to get control of the ones who wanted nothing to do with the new revolution of Cuba.

"How many men did you lose in the fighting on the base, Captain Calvo Sir?" Colonel Alvarez asked him with concern.

"Five hundred men in the first attack, and another hundred on the second one and I was..."

"All these men were from your side, Captain Calvo?" Colonel Alvarez asked him excitedly.

"No, no sir, this was a total. From my forces I have lost only two hundred and seventeen soldiers, Colonel Alvarez Sir. The rest were loyal to Castro, sir. I expected some trouble, but I never expected this much resistance from them. Most of my military equipment is still intact though, and my men will be ready to move out on the 23rd as scheduled, sir."

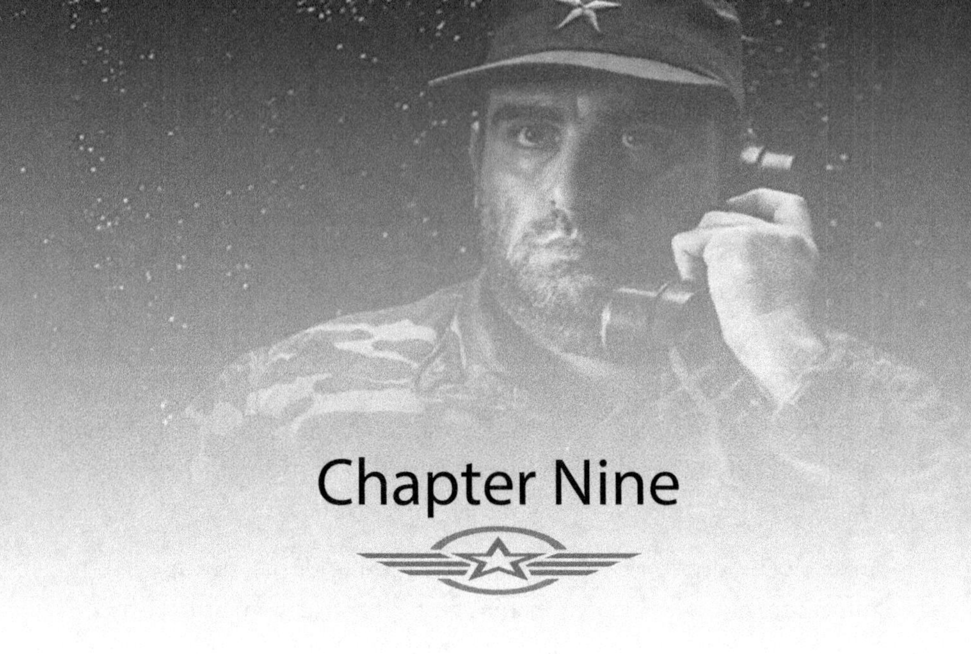

Chapter Nine

Colonel Alvarez checked his calendar, it was Friday, the 20th, he had three days left before the meeting. "Captain, have you heard from anyone else? I didn't, and I'm getting worried sir."

"Yes sir, I have heard from Colonels Cienfuegos, Gonzales and Agramonte. They all reported they had no problems with their men, they were only forced to eliminate a few of them, sir."

"It would be wise if the god dom fools would've reported to me you know, Captain. Everything is well coordinated off of me for the new Revolution, sir. I'm the main key to the whole thing, Captain Calvo Sir."

"I understand this Colonel Alvarez Sir, and I'll instruct the other foolish Officers to report to you immediately. I'm still a little concerned about Captain Remos. I have not heard a sound from him, and I know many of his men were for Castro, sir."

"I better get in contact with him then. I'll be back to you once I found out how he's making out with his base and soldiers." Colonel Alvarez hung up with Captain Calvo, and he took a quick breath and then he dialed Captain Remos' number. The phone was picked up on the fifth ring. Captain Remos was out of breath, and Colonel Alvarez could hear heavy automatic weapon fire going off in the background as he asked him. "Captain Remos, Colonel Alvarez. What is happening on your base? I hear much weapon fire sir."

"Madre de Dios, I'm in the middle of a fooking war, that is what is happening here Colonel Alvarez, sir. The ones backing Castro took over the barracks, and my men are trying to root them out of it by force. We are Navy men, used to fighting on the water, Colonel. Fighting on the ground is new to us, and it really sucks, sir. You ground stompers can keep this crap, sir."

"Never mind all that shit, do these god dom soldiers holding the fooking barracks have access to any radios, sir? I don't need them blowing the whistle on us before we even start our revolution, sir." Colonel Alvarez warned him.

"This action took place so quickly that I assure you Colonel Alvarez, a fooking radio was the least of the problems that was on their or my mind, sir." A heavy explosion suddenly interrupted the conversation.

"Remos, Captain Remos Sir, are you still there sir?" Colonel Alvarez roared into the radio.

Captain Remos ducked because of the power of the blast as he responded to the worried Colonel. "Yes, that was one of the barracks. Our demolition people are very busy I see, sir. I wish I had a few tanks with me, so I could drive them out of the god dom buildings, sir."

"I'll send three tanks to your base immediately, sir. You are thirty five minutes away from my base. Can you hold them until the tanks arrive at your base sir?"

"Yes. Of course I can Colonel Alvarez, sir." The Captain replied confidently.

"Good, help is on the way to you, sir." Colonel Carlos Alvarez hung up and then he went outside and got Captain Padilla's attention by waving at him. Captain Padilla saw Colonel Alvarez trying to get his attention, and he ran over to him. "Captain, I need three tanks to get over to Captain Remos's base, ASAP sir. Sent two armored vehicles with a full complement of our best fighters, he's having some trouble securing his base. I'm going to check with the rest of our friends, to make sure that nothing like this is happening on their bases. We might have to put off this new revolution a might, if the fighting between ourselves gets too serious."

"I understand this, I shall have all the tanks on their way to you immediately Colonel, sir."

Colonel Alvarez watched as Captain Padilla gave the orders and three T-80s with ammunition rumbled off, followed by two armored vehicles. The machines left to the cheering of the other soldiers on base they were happy, and used this as a sign of the beginning of the next revolution.

Colonel Carlos Alvarez ducked back in his office and he quickly placed a call to the other officers involved in the new revolution for Cuba. Every one of them reported they had some minor problems, but they assured Colonel Alvarez they had everything under control, and their forces would be set in position when needed. The Colonel informed the others he was in command of the fuel refineries, and he would send fuel for their vehicles. He told them to inform Sergeant Regueiro how much fuel they needed, and he would see to it they received it. Sergeant Iglesias rushed in and he reported they discovered more than a thousand heat rounds for the 125 mm main guns for the T-72 battle tanks. This meant every tank on his base would have at least ten rounds of heat rounds for each of the vehicles.

"By the Holy Madonna, this is great news for my ears, where was this ammunition located?"

"It was stored in the old Russian military mess hall that was constructed back in the year of 1962, when the loathsome Russians were all over our small Island sir. And, the great fools were busy building their god dom missile site that had almost cost us all of our lives, sir." Colonel Alvarez's excited Sergeant offered him.

Colonel Carlos Alvarez had no idea as to the time of day it was, because things were happening so quickly around him. Reports from his other forces kept flooding in for the rest of the day. It was not until well after five before Captain Remos finally reported in that

Colonel Alvarez's tanks had arrived on his base, and his base was now completely under his full control. Every base involved in the new revolution reported quiet. It was then Colonel Alvarez allowed himself to relax a little and in doing so, he realized how hungry he was. The worry Cuban Colonel looked out of the window, night was showing, and the bats were flying.

"Sergeant Iglesias! Where the hell are you at, mista? Get in here this instant before I set the dogs out on you, mista."

The Sergeant quickly appeared in the doorway, standing as if he had just done something wrong, and he was caught while doing it. He was staring at the suddenly irate Colonel screaming for him and he asked. "Sir?"

"Where the hell were you mista? I'm starving you know and you were to look after this matter for me, fool. How could you allow me to go all day without any food to eat, you great fool you? You better get me something to eat before I nibble on your god dom arm, mista. Sergeant, if this happens again, you'll go a god dom week before you're allowed any food to eat, mista. Get out of my sight and get me something to eat right now, mista."

"Yes sir, I'll get on it right away for you, Colonel Sir." He disappeared as the sun slowly went behind the mountains, and a chill soon filled the darkening air. Colonel Alvarez listened to the sounds of his military base, and for the first time in many months, if not in years, he finally heard normality. Soldiers were singing or whistling, while others played their radios. The clanking and noises accompanying the soldiers working on their military equipment also filled the air. The smell of fuel oil, and cooking food floated through his window again. Soldiers cursed, while others talked about their love life and families. Sergeant Regueiro's voice could be heard screaming out orders at the other soldiers. It seemed they were going to be ready when called on for action, to defend the new revolution of Cuba.

Sergeant Iglesias rushed into Colonel Alvarez's office while carrying a tray of pork chops and beans along with some bread. He placed the tray down in front of the Colonel, and he then removed a chilled bottle of red wine and smiled.

"That is much better Sergeant. I better not have to scream for you the next time I'm hungry mista, or it will be your ass I'll chew on, Sergeant Regueiro. Do you understand me mista?"

"Yes sir." The young Sergeant said as he snapped to attention and he saluted the Colonel.

"Good, be off with you then mista. I'm starving and I want to eat in peace, Sergeant." After he ate Colonel Alvarez called Maria and finishing with her, he turned in for the troubled night.

SATURDAY, SEPTEMBER 21st, 1996

Colonel Carlos Rafael Fernandez Alvarez woke to the sound of the telephone ringing, it was Captain Remos, and he was reporting he just dispatched three small patrol boats to monitor the Port of Havana, so when they finally made their move against the capital city, it would not be strange to see a number of his small Naval boats floating off Havana Bay when they began their opening attack against Castro and his supporters.

Colonel Alvarez was not fully awake yet, and he responded with the word 'good' to everything that the excited Naval Captain reported to him. Sergeant Iglesias suddenly appeared at his door while holding a plate of eggs and bread and he announced proudly. "Sir I heard you up and I thought you might be a little hungry this morning, sir."

"Sergeant Iglesias, I didn't even brush my god dom teeth yet, fool. Look you pain in the ass you, being too early is just as bad as being too dom late for me, mista. Madre de Dios man, use your dom head once in a while, man."

The Sergeant's smile instantly disappeared, and he looked like a man who was just slapped across his face.

Colonel Alvarez shook his head and then he added. "Sergeant, it's no big deal I assure you. Leave the dom food and get out."

"Yes Sir Colonel Sir." The Sergeant replied, while picking up some of his strength again.

Colonel Carlos Alvarez quickly brushed his teeth and the smell of the cooked eggs was making him hungry, as he splashed cold some water on his face. He ate and then he dressed quickly and went out onto the front porch of his office, to observe his men working on the base. Two of the fuel tankers were parked near the rows of parked tanks and armored vehicles. Every machine was red flagged, indicating they were fully fueled up, and even their reserve tanks were likewise full of fuel. His soldiers were also busy attacking the rust, and dirt caught up in the tracks of the tanks. Many of the massive war machines had their camouflage paint mostly repaired. He spotted his Sergeant and the Colonel immediately motioned him over to his side and asked him. "Where the hell did you get the paint from for the tanks?"

"Sir, we raided a local hardware store in the middle of town sir, and we had the..."

"That is enough, I don't want any more mid-night raids on any of the civilian buildings or their stores. The next thing I'll know is the police will be poking their slimy noses around on my base while looking for their foul missing merchandise. Is this understood by you Sergeant?"

"This is understood very well Colonel Alvarez, sir. No more mid-night raids sir." The Sergeant replied to the angry looking Colonel.

"Fine, then make certain that everyone else on this god dom military base knows of my last orders for the pack of fools, Sergeant. I'll make the next offending soldiers work for the man who he steals from, for a full year without any pay, mista. Get going and relay this cursed order to the other soldiers throughout the base for me Sergeant."

This day went by rather quickly for the worked up Cuban Colonel, with all his forces steadily checking in and stating they were well prepared for the opening attack. Colonel Alvarez was thrilled to all ends every one of his vehicles and war machines had enough fuel and ammunition needed for the upcoming engagement. Before he knew it, it was time for him to call Maria again, he assured her he would be home the following night to be with her, and then he hung up and went to sleep.

SUNDAY, SEPTEMBER 22nd, 1996

Colonel Rafael Fernandez Alvarez was up before any phone calls came in. He placed a call to the private number of the Vice President of Cuba. He did not know if he would be there or not, he was the only conspirator he had not heard from since his organizing of the new revolution. The phone rang five times before a sleepy voice answered. It was a female voice.

"Err... excuse me, I'm Colonel Carlos Alvarez, and I was hoping to speak with Vice Presidente Cabrisas for a moment please. Is this his residence Ma'am?" the young Colonel asked her.

"Yes, Colonel Alvarez Sir, but I'm afraid he's still asleep, sir. Do you have any idea what time of the morning it is right now, sir? Huh, wait a minute will you please Colonel Alvarez, sir."

Colonel Carlos Alvarez could tell she just covered over the mouthpiece of the phone with her hand for the moment, and she was now speaking with someone else obviously in the room that he was certain was Vice Presidente Cabrisas. A moment later he heard his voice over the phone as he said to him. "Yes, Colonel Alvarez Sir, it's about time you finally returned my call to you, sir. Is there any reason it took you so long before you got back to me Colonel Alvarez, sir." A very sleepy but rather strong sounding voice demanded from him.

"Madre de Dios, I wasn't aware you had called me, sir. With all that is going on with my base, someone obviously did not inform me of your call, sir. Who did you speak to, sir?"

"No one at your base, I spoke to Captain Calvo the day before, and he told me he was going to inform you know I wanted to speak with you, sir. How are things going at your base, Colonel? Are you going to be prepared to move out by tomorrow morning as scheduled Colonel Alvarez?"

"Yes Sir Vice Presidente Cabrisas Sir, all my forces will be set in place by tomorrow morning at the very latest, sir. Everyone who is concerned with our movement is in full control of their base sir, and all their surviving personnel sir. What about you sir? Are you going to be safe until I finally arrive at the capital, sir? I need your influence in dealing with all the god dom politicians who we'll want working on our side, once we have been successful on our mission, Vice Presidente Cabrisas Sir."

"I already spoke to everyone I want or need and the rest of the fools can be mere fodder for your soldiers when they attack, sir. Colonel Alvarez Sir, I don't want you to be worried about me, sir. I'll take very good care of myself and those of concern to me. You have to be successful in this new Revolution, or all is lost to us, and Castro. If he survives, will wreak a terrible toll on all those who followed you, and anyone else he wants to eliminate, me among them. Good luck Colonel and keep me informed if anything goes wrong with our plans, sir."

"I will, I was thinking of dispatching a unit of soldiers out to protect your life if we fail, sir."

"No need to worry about that Colonel Alvarez. If you fail on your mission sir, I'll be one of the first to know about it, and I'll be on a plane heading for the United States, before your body cools on the ground, Colonel Alvarez Sir." The Vice President of Cuba gave a nervous laugh into the phone receiver at Colonel Alvarez.

"Understood, and I'm very pleased you have taken certain steps to protect your life, sir." There was no answer, only the dial tone. Colonel Alvarez laughed to himself as he hung up his phone, and a thought suddenly hit him. He remembered he told Maria that he was going to spend the night with her, but he realized his support troops would be on the move that night. It was much more important for him to be available in his office, just in case something went wrong with any of their plans for the opening of his new Revolution. He checked his watch and he decided to make a quick run over to Maria's place, and be back by twelve. He walked over to his car parked between two of the massive Russian made tanks.

Colonel Alvarez could tell every eye on the base was glued to him and his every move as he started up the car, and then he quickly drove off the base. He pulled up in front of Maria's home, and even before he killed the engine, she was outside and hugging him. They entered the house together, with Maria already pulling at the clothes on his back. She stripped and they made love on her bed, and when they finished, he told Maria to make plans to accompany him back to the military base for the rest of the night. He told her he wanted her safe when the fighting started to free Cuba of Fidel Castro's oppressive Administration.

Maria complained, but she quickly packed up her most needed and wanted items in a suitcase, taking special care of the high fashion dress she was planning to wear when her Colonel Carlos Rafael Fernandez Alvarez became the next Presidente of Cuba. She pulled the main fuse from the electric box, and then she placed it inside her pocket, she then turned off her gas and locked the box to keep anyone else from stealing any of her cooking fuel. She also locked the rest of her belongings inside a huge trunk, and then she slid it in her closet, and she chained it down to the floor of her home. She was now ready to leave her home, and to be with her Colonel and lover.

Colonel Carlos Alvarez checked his watch, time was very important to him on this day, and it was nearing eleven a.m. already. He was pleased to return to his base before twelve midnight. The trip back to the base was completed mostly in silence, with Maria not wanting to speak to him for fear of distracting her Colonel as he drove. Colonel Carlos Alvarez was so deep in thought he did not even think of speaking to Maria. They pulled onto the active military base, and the Colonel immediately spotted Sergeant Regueiro, and it looked like he had something on his mind. He drove right over to the Sergeant and then asked the man with anger lacing his tone of voice. "What is wrong now with you, Sergeant?"

"Colonel Alvarez Sir, I just heard from Captain Calvo, and he has reported his men were moving out to begin their part of the Revolution at this time, sir. I asked Captain Padilla if he thought it might be a wise idea to start preparing the men also, sir."

"You did very well with asking the Captain that question Sergeant Regueiro, where the hell is the Captain?" the concerned Colonel asked him.

"He's taking Command of the first column of tanks to move out, Colonel Alvarez, sir. He's over there with his tanks by the mess hall, Colonel." Sergeant Regueiro pointed over to a number of tanks slowly moving from their spaces.

"Arr... it's too late to speak with him now. Maria, go to my office, I'll send for you when I'm ready to head out for the capital city of our country to begin our new revolution, young lady."

Maria said nothing to her lover as she rushed for his office as she was told to by Alvarez.

"Sergeant Regueiro, where the hell is Captain Baquero and Lieutenant Calderio at?"

"The Lieutenant is busy handing out the weapons to all the infantry soldiers, and Captain Baquero is taking control of the second squad of tanks ready to leave our base and head out on their opening mission, Colonel Alvarez Sir."

"Fine, I want you to have them report to me when they have completed their orders, Sergeant. I want you to keep the infantry units at bay until we're ready to head out. Make certain they are fed and have plenty of dried food to take with them to hold them over until our Revolution is over with and they'll have access to food after that point, Sergeant."

Colonel Alvarez headed for his office next, and there were many notes scattered all over the surface of his desk, most of the reports were from his other officers, all of them stating they had started their men in motion. Some of the reported unit of soldiers were moving into Havana at this time, and these troops would deploy where they would be the most effective to help us better defend the revolution when it started, and also protect the other soldiers assaulting the capital city of Cuba. With every report he read, Colonel Carlos Alvarez's smile widened on his dry lips.

Maria saw the smile on his face and she asked him. "What is happening now my lover?"

Colonel Carlos Alvarez looked back at her and then he replied, "by the Almighty and sacred God, the future of Cuba is about to change for us, honey. All our troops are going to be set in position before we have any need of them. By God the capital city will be secured before I even enter the city. The rest of Cuba will be in our hands by this time tomorrow night as well. Everything is set in place and waiting to erupt. By tomorrow night, Cuba will finally be free of Castro's iron fisted rule, and I shall be leading the country."

Maria rushed into Colonel Alvarez's arms, crashing into him with such a force she almost made him lose his balance. He hugged her to him, and she kissed him and she cried into his eyes. "I have so long longed for this day to come. To think that Cuba's freedom is just a few hours away for us, Colonel Carlos Alvarez."

"And you're going to be my first lady when it finally happen Maria, and I then become the new Presidente of the Island of Cuba my love." Colonel Carlos Alvarez said with a grunt to her.

"I never dared to dream such a thing possible for us. I have never thought I, Maria Ibarra, would ever be the leading first lady for all Cuba, my love. I'm so proud of you, Carlos Alvarez, Colonel." She said as she smiled very warming at him as she stared into his eyes now

Sergeant Regueiro came into the Colonel's office in a rush, and he quickly announced the first of the troops and armor left the base for their positions in and around the capital city of Havana.

Colonel Carlos Alvarez and Maria walked over to the front door of his office, and then they both looked out just in time to see Captain Padilla riding past them, his head was sticking out of the hatch of the massive Russian made T-80 tank turret he was riding in. Captain Padilla smiled to himself as he saluted Colonel Alvarez proudly. Colonel Alvarez stood at attention as each of the fifteen monstrous tanks slowly rumbled passed him on their way off the large military base. Once the machines passed, Colonel Carlos Rafael Fernandez Alvarez looked to where the second squad of tanks were parked, the last of the massive

T-80 tanks under the Cuban Colonel's control. They were in the process of starting up their powerful engines, to his pleasant surprised, the next vehicles to move out were a column of his light armored vehicles. He looked to the excited Sergeant who was standing right by his side.

"Colonel Alvarez Sir, we decided to stagger the tanks leaving the base over fear of drawing any special attention aimed at their moving off the base, sir. We're going to allow the armored vehicles to leave the base next, and then an hour later the next of the tank squads will begin to move out and taking a second road for the capital city of Havana, sir. Don't worry about it sir, all our armor and infantry will be set in their positions by midnight, Colonel."

"Very wise thinking on your part Sergeant, when do you think I should leave the base, mista?"

"Colonel Alvarez, you should be prepared to leave by nine o'clock tonight at the latest for Havana, sir. I'd like to have you in the capital city by one, so you'll have all the time you need to get oriented, and know how to get to the Palace. The worse thing that could happen is to attack only to find out you're stuck in traffic and out of position, sir. Or worse lost in the capital, sir."

"I agree with you Sergeant, I'd hate to be throwing a party, and not show up for it, mista."

"Hmmm... you think I'd ever allow you to miss this little party of ours, my lover? Not on your life, my Colonel." Maria purred as she looped her arm in his, and she stared in his eyes.

"You devil born female you, come with me please, I want to better prepare to leave for the beginning of our new revolution now." The two entered Colonel Alvarez's office and he stuffed some more papers into his briefcase. He took care with some of his files while others he carelessly stuffed into the already overflowing briefcase. Once he was sure he had everything he needed, he removed his pistol from the top desk drawer. The weapon was checked to make certain the clip was fully loaded, and one round was in the chamber, and then he holstered it under his shoulder.

Colonel Carlos Alvarez knew he was going to turn in his weapon to the security guards when he entered the Presidential Palace, but he also knew where the one Presidential guard they already enlisted in their revolution hid a second weapon for his use against Fidel Castro. Colonel Alvarez was going to make an excuse to the escort, and he was going to use the bathroom. There, he would remove the pistol hidden behind the second commode in the bathroom. He reminded himself to check the weapon before he continued on with his plans to kill Presidente Fidel Castro if he needed to kill the man. Colonel Carlos Alvarez could not trust anyone, not until they have proven their real worth to him and the cause.

Colonel Carlos Alvarez made certain he had his medals pinned on his chest properly. All his uniform buttons were buttoned correctly, and his scarf was folded and set in placed, and his shoes were highly polished. He then placed his black beret just right on his head. He looked in the mirror and he felt good about himself, the model of a fine looking young Cuban soldier. He hoped he would have the inner strength to live up to the look he extruded in the mirror. He was a bundle of nerves and tense as he paced back and forth in his office while waiting for the time to move out. Outside, he could hear the revving of the last column of T-80 tanks as they prepared to leave his base now. Colonel Alvarez's base was the center of activity which served to surge his adrenaline to new heights in his body, and causing his muscles to tense up and ache him.

Maria could tell he was having a problem relaxing, and she did something about it. She walked over to her now sitting lover and she unzipped his zipper as she said in her sexiest voice. "You look like you're a little troubled here my love and I have just the right answer to all your worries and stress my love. This was taught to me by an old gypsy by the light of a full moon, Carlos."

By the time she was able to get his dick out of his pants, it was stiff as a board and ready for action and she drew it into her mouth. Within seconds she had him shifting all around in his chair. She added to his great pleasure by humming, and then using her teeth, nipping the tip of his member, and then running her tongue up and down the full length of it. By the time he came, he looked a mess and he had to fix himself up again. His shirt was out of his pants and his beret was off and lying on the floor right next to his scarf, and his pants were a mess also.

"They're my mighty and great warrior of the night that should put your mind at ease a little."

"Yes, but you should have done this before I was dressed. Look at me, I am a mess again."

"My my, there is no pleasing you anymore I see, mista." She laughed as she dressed in a military uniform.

"What is this?" Carlos Alvarez asked her as he watched her quickly dress into the uniform.

"Huh, do you think I'm going to fight in the dress I was saving myself to wear when you finally climb the great steps to the Presidency. Don't be so foolish, my dear Carlos Alvarez."

"And, what makes you think I'm going to allow you to be involved in any shooting, Maria?"

She placed her hands on her hips as she growled back at her lover with a snap in her tone. "I don't really think you want to start this argument over with me again at this time, mista. I have already told you I was going to be part of this new Revolution, and I will be Mista Alvarez. I have a pistol and an AK-47 rifle, and I know how to use them both as well, I assure you my Colonel." Her eyes narrowed and she glared at him again and then added to her angry words. "I'm going to be part of this new revolution, with, or without your help. If you try to stop me, I'll hop aboard one of those armored vehicles, and fight my way to the capital myself. I'm not afraid to die Carlos. All revolutions need their martyrs. Now mista, who am I going to be traveling with? You or your troops, my Colonel?"

"God dommit, you're getting to be a real pain in the ass, lady." He moaned as he let out his breath and then continued with his words. "Arr... You know you have to go with me, if not for the fighting, for the safety of my troops, my lady. I don't think they're ready for a snapper like you. Look at you with your hands resting on your hips like that, and your breasts sticking out the way they are, woman. By the Holy Madonna, I need my men ready to fight, not drooling over themselves while staring at your body. You know I could use you for a secret weapon if my Revolution fails. I could always have you march through the streets of the capital dressed as you are, and you'd be instrumental in single handily disarming all of Castro's hated troops for us."

Maria buttoned her blouse and then she barked back at her Colonel. "Ha, Ha. Then I'm to take it I'll be accompanying you to the capital city?"

"What other choice do I have in the god dom matter, woman?" Carlos Alvarez replied as he let out his breath in a rush.

"None at all I fear my lover and future Presidente of Cuba!" she said while grinning at him.

Sergeant Regueiro rushed into the Colonel's office, and he announced. "Colonel Alvarez Sir, we just received reports from Colonel Cienfuegos's 1st Armored Division, he's declaring all his forces made it safely to their assigned position unobserved. Sir, it seems he started his troops before any of the other forces moved out, sir."

"That is great news for the both of us, but what about the other armored divisions, Sergeant?"

"From all the reports we're currently receiving on the inter-squad radios, they're in position also Colonel Alvarez. We're the only Armored Division in the process of shifting our positions."

"How long before we're set in positions, Sergeant?" Carlos demanded to know from him.

"Another hour or so I believe sir, and then all our troops will be set in position by that time sir, or near enough to enable them to attack from where they might be stationed, Colonel Alvarez. The only outfits we have received little information from, are the troops from the 9th Infantry that are stationed on the Peninsula." The Sergeant saw the concern look locked in the Colonel's eyes and he quickly added to his words. "I don't believe that Major Cardona is having any problems with his troops in the least, sir. I told you this to inform you that he's probably operating under constant radio silence for the beginning of the revolution, sir. Something I think we should do as well Colonel Alvarez, sir."

"Why have you not voiced this concern to me well before this time, you fool? Order it done at once Sergeant, radio silence from this point forward for all our troops to observe mista. I cannot risk any soldiers loyal to Castro monitoring the troop's internet and listening to our plans. Inform all these latest orders come directly from me, Sergeant."

"I believe it's time for the two of you to leave for the capital city of Cuba at this time, Colonel Alvarez Sir." The Sergeant offered to his commanding officer as he stared at him.

"It's not nine yet, it's only eight ten, Sergeant." Carlos snapped as he looked at his watch.

"What is the difference in time, Colonel Alvarez? So you get there a little ahead of your planned schedule, sir. Colonel Alvarez, you have to realize this sir, it's you who sets the schedule for all the other soldiers involved in this revolution, sir. You owe no further excuses to anyone but yourself, sir." The young Cuban Sergeant replied to his Commanding Officer.

"I cannot argue with you there, Sergeant. Have my car brought around for my use. I'll be leaving to joining my troops within fifteen minutes. Have Sergeant Iglesias come in to place all my belongings in the trunk of my vehicle, Sergeant."

"Will the Colonel's companion be accompanying you on the beginning of the last Revolution ever to be fought on Cuban soil, sir?" the Sergeant asked his Commanding Officer politely.

"Yes. Make dom sure all her stuff is secured in the trunk of my staff car as well, Sergeant."

Time crawled along at a snail's pace for him, as Colonel Carlos Rafael Fernandez Alvarez gave his office one last look over, to make certain he did not leave anything of important he might need later on behind. He understood if his new revolution was a successful one, he would never return to his old office ever again. Once he was satisfied, he had everything he needed with him and already packed up properly, he turned to Maria and said to her. "Well, my lover. What do you think so far? Are you ready to start our new revolution against Fidel Castro, honey?"

Maria instantly ran into his arms and she replied to her Colonel in a dreamy tone of voice. "Hmmm... I have never looked forward to anything in my entire life before, as much as I'm looking forward to this one dream of mine, my love. The last Revolution Cuba will ever be forced to live through, Carlos Alvarez."

They kissed again, and only stopped when they realized that Sergeant Regueiro was still standing in the doorway of his office. Once he was recognized, the Sergeant said to his Colonel. "Colonel Alvarez Sir, Sergeant Iglesias is here for your briefcase, sir. He'll carry it out to the waiting car for you sir, so you'll only have to worry about your personal belonging, sir."

"Fine, it's resting over there on the chair, Sergeant." The Colonel and Maria followed Sergeant Iglesias out of the office, and they waited until Sergeant Regueiro closed the door behind them. Colonel Carlos Alvarez looked in his car and he saw no driver. He turned to Sergeant Regueiro and complained at him. "Where the hell is the god dom driver? I don't want to be held up waiting for him, Sergeant."

"Colonel, your driver went out with the armor column, sir. I chose to be your personal drive for this mission, sir. I'll protect you better than he ever could do for you, Colonel Alvarez Sir." Sergeant Regueiro proudly bragged as he smiled back at the Colonel sitting in the car.

Colonel Carlos Alvarez leaned forward and then he placed his hand on Sergeant Regueiro's strong shoulder and he mumbled at him. "Ahhh Sergeant Regueiro, what the hell would I do without you looking after me all the dom time, mista? Get in the car so we can leave Sergeant."

Maria broke up the moment between the two military soldiers by pulling on Colonel Alvarez's arm, and then she led him over to the car.

Moments later, they were off for the capital, Havana. Colonel Alvarez's car made good time on the almost empty lesser highway, and in what seemed like only a matter of minutes to them both, they were on the main Central highway running the full length of the Island. Maria looked out of the window, and Colonel Alvarez seemed lost in deep thought as his caravan slowly traveled along, a very fine mist of rain began to fall.

Forty five minutes into the long drive to the capital city of Havana, Colonel Carlos Alvarez and Maria were harshly shifted sideways as his vehicles suddenly turned sharply onto the Avenida De La Independencia, that lead directly towards the massive Presidential Palace right in the heart of Havana. Moments later, Colonel Alvarez saw the great Palacia de la Revolutions constructed in the center of the city, where the road forked into Avenida Rancho Boyeros, and the wide Avenida Carlos M. Decespedes. The Palacia de la Revolutions was the building Presidente Castro took over for his private use, and it now served as his Presidential Palace.

The massive building grew more in size and structure as his caravan quickly approached it, until he thought his driver was going to drive right through the middle of the large structure. His car suddenly veered off to the left, and then it headed down Decespedes Road until the vehicle turned down the side road of Avenida De Colon, and then onto Panorama Road, where the car stopped, and the other four vehicles following continued on by the now parked car.

The Sergeant got out of the vehicle and opened the door and let the Colonel out of the car. From where they parked, they could still see the Presidential Palace, hauntingly lit up in the black night. The building looked like an old construction right from a horror flick. The mist was still falling, and it only served to strengthen the eerie look of the massive and very aged building.

The Sergeant quickly ushered Colonel Alvarez and his female friend into a private home. He did not knock instead he just opened the door and walked right in. An older woman stood in the living room, and she looked scared to death as she stared at the sudden intruders to her home.

"Colonel Alvarez Sir, we have decided to take over this small house for your private use for the time being, sir. So you're well within walking distance of the Presidential Palace when the fighting starts in earnest, sir. I suggest you try and catch up on some of your much needed sleep while you can Colonel Alvarez, sir. Tomorrow will be your day to enjoy, sir. I'll be on guard all night long right outside your door for your protection, sir. So, you can lay your mind to rest for now, sir. I have many trusted soldiers who'll accompany us over to the Palace, and taking up position around this building, Colonel Alvarez. No one will get at you while you're here and under my protection, sir."

"You seem to have thought of everything, Sergeant. Have you heard anything from the other troops from our base, mista?" the Cuban Colonel asked of his Sergeant with much concern in his tone this time, as he stared at the young Sergeant while waiting for his reply.

"Yes, Sir Colonel Alvarez Sir. All our tanks are set in place as of this time sir, and the armored vehicles are in position also, sir. Most of our troops are set in place sir, and the few who are not ready, will be by midnight at the latest, Colonel Alvarez Sir. From all the reports I'm picking up already sir, they all state they're set in position at this time, Colonel Alvarez Sir. None of our troop movements have been noticed or detected by any of the Havana security guards, sir. I believe sir that we shall take the bastards by complete surprise, Colonel Alvarez."

Colonel Carlos Alvarez said nothing more to his Sergeant as he allowed the scared and much older woman lead him and Maria to a bedroom in her home. The woman quickly turned down their bed without uttering a single word to either of them. Carlos could actually smell the coffee brewing in the kitchen and he snapped at the old woman. "I think I'd like two cups of coffee brought up to this room just as soon as you can look after this request for me please."

She barely looked up from the floor as she bowed her head, and then she instantly rushed out of the small room. The Colonel looked at Sergeant Regueiro, and then he gave him a quick smile and a slight nod.

"She's scared to death of everything that's happening around her lately my Colonel Sir. She's even afraid to speak to anyone any longer, sir. But I just dare anyone to try and get passed her while she's in this home, sir. She's one of our best fighters for the new cause for Cuba, Colonel Alvarez Sir." The rather young Sergeant said proudly to the concerned looking Colonel.

Maria squeezed Carlos Alvarez's hand as she looked up at him with pleading and loving eyes.

"Now what? By the Holy Father, please don't tell me that you now want to enlist her into your bunch of bitch fighters, Maria? I think you have more than enough of your female friends who are already involved in this dom thing, honey." Colonel Alvarez moaned at Maria as he wiped sweat from his forehead.

"No need to do that Colonel Alvarez Sir. She is already one of us Colonel. In fact sir, she has killed the true owners of this home herself, so we would have a safe house so close to the Palace to work from, Colonel Alvarez Sir." The Cuban Sergeant said with a certain air of confidence in his tone as he glanced back at the door that the old woman had just walked out of.

"You'll make certain that she's very well taken care of for her loyalty to this last Revolution of ours and to myself, Sergeant?" Colonel Alvarez warned the Sergeant, he did not want anyone he felt he could not trust around him.

"Colonel Alvarez Sir, all you'll have to do is look to your left, and she'll be there, sir."

"What is her name Sergeant?" the Colonel asked his Sergeant as he looked at him.

"Melba Jose Hernandez Guevara, Colonel Alvarez Sir." He replied as he grinned back at the Colonel. Then he waited to see if the Colonel was going to ask him another question.

"Why does she have such strength to our cause, Sergeant Regueiro?" Carlos asked, keeping the conversation going between them, because he wanted to know everything about this woman.

"Colonel Alvarez Sir, she has lost a younger sister to the hated prison cells of the secret police of Havana operating under General Boada's direct orders a few days ago, sir. From what she has told us about the loss, her sister was taken into custody for no reason other than she might have witnessed a minor crime being committed in the capital, sir. Melba told us her sister didn't really witness anything happening though, sir. It was she who saw the crime truly happen Colonel. She was deathly afraid to come forward and inform the police of what she had witnessed, sir. Because she thought they'd think she had something to do with the crime as well, sir.

"Now, she blames herself for the death of her younger and well beloved sister, sir. She has vowed to herself to get even with all the hated cochinos who work for the Castro Administration, Colonel Alvarez Sir. She buried her sister just yesterday in fact, sir. But she opened up the coffin, and she was shocked by what the secret police had done to her sister's body, Colonel. She has so far refused to tell any of us what the murderers had truly done to her lovely sister. But she's still very bitter over the fact of her death and the way she died, Colonel Alvarez Sir." Sergeant Regueiro offered to his Colonel as he smiled at him this time.

"Madre de Dios Sergeant Regueiro. I want you to keep her far away from the two of us then, mista. I don't trust anyone operating on pure vengeance and anger anywhere near me mista. Sergeant Regueiro, vengeance quickly leads to blind hatred, and blind hatred leads to foolhardiness, which could be the very cause of our new Revolution collapsing on us, mista." Colonel Carlos Alvarez warned his Sergeant nastily as he stared back at him.

"Consider it done for you, Colonel Alvarez Sir." The Sergeant snapped back at his Colonel.

"Very good Sergeant Regueiro, now if you don't mind, I'd dearly like to be left alone with my lady until tomorrow morning. Make god dom sure you wake me well before the time I have to leave for my scheduled meeting with the once great and feared leader of Cuba, Sergeant Regueiro. I'll hold you personally responsible if I miss the start of my own revolution, mista." Colonel Carlos Alvarez said with much concern lacing his tone to his Sergeant. Then the Cuban Colonel waited for the Sergeant to leave the room so he could finally be alone with his love. When the door closed behind the Sergeant, Colonel Carlos Alvarez looked at Maria, and then he smiled at her as he stepped towards the also smiling young woman. They made passionate love together with a new and heightened vigor that neither of them had even enjoyed before in their young lives, as they both waited for the night to pass by for them.

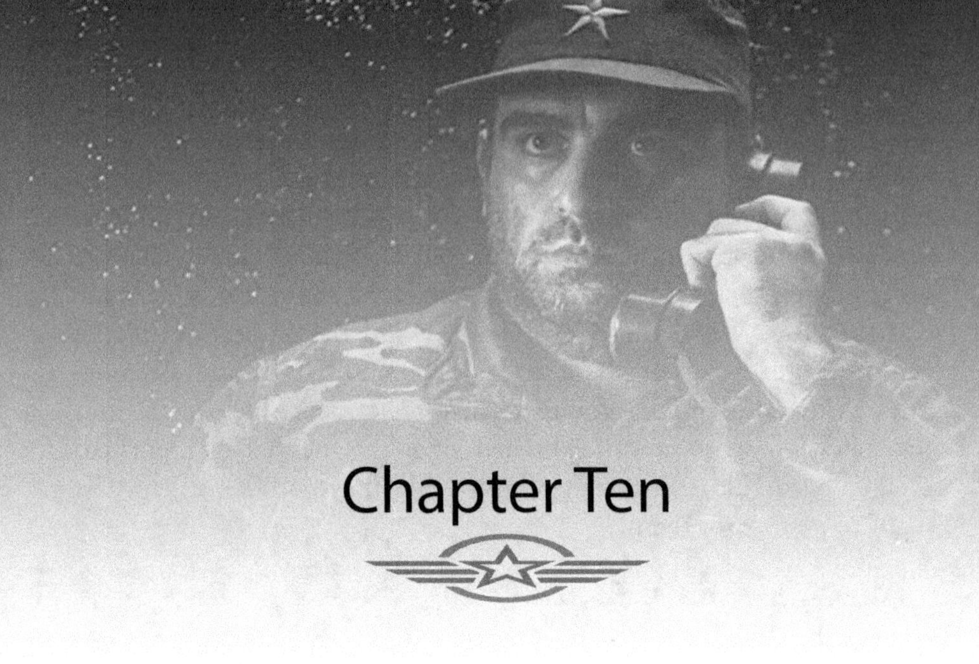

Chapter Ten

The beautiful Maria Ibarra heard a light tap on the bedroom door and she looked at the clock. It was five a.m., the knocking continued until she finally called out from under the covers at the person in the hallway. "We are up, thank you."

The knocking immediately stopped, and she heard someone walk away from the door.

She gave Carlos a slight shove, but he was still sound asleep. She took a second to remember their lovemaking of the night before, and the deep passion they both reached. It seemed fear and excitement had elevated them both to new heights of passion and need. She snuggled under his arm for protection again.

All her moving finally woke up the still exhausted Cuban Colonel, and he instantly bitched at her. "For the love of the good Christ Child foolish woman, how much of the god dom bed do you need for yourself to sleep in, god dommit?"

Maria got up on one arm and she purred back. "It's time we wake Carlos. They tapped."

"How long ago did they knock my love?" Carlos asked as he looked at the clock.

"Just seconds ago, would you care to make love to me while you're still a mere Colonel?"

"Please woman, leave me some of my god dom strength to enable me to carry out my new Revolution with. How would it look to the other soldiers if I fell asleep while talking to the great Fidel Castro, and I ended up sleeping right through the new revolution taking place all around me, woman?" Colonel Carlos Alvarez complained at Maria as he swung his legs off the side of the bed, and he stretched his hands over his head and he yawned loudly.

"Hmmm... I'll let you off of the hook this time I guess, mista. It'll be fun the next time we make love, you'll be Presidente of Cuba and I the First Lady. Hmmm..., that sounds wonderful to me, no more Castro."

"Maria, you should stay here at the safe house until I send for you to come to me and then..."

She immediately complained, but she was instantly quieted by Carlos resting his hand across her mouth. "Shush, my love. Maria, I have to be in top form for today, and how can I be if I'm more concerned about you and your welfare? I couldn't keep my mind on my discussion with Castro, if I'm worried about you. If I'm forced to kill the great fool, that should be the only thing on my mind. I hope you understand it's not like I don't think you're a good fighter. I believe that you're equal to anyone of my soldiers. It's only I want you safe until I finish with the great fool. I fear there will be plenty of time for you to join fighting Castro, Maria."

"What do you mean by that Mista Carlos Alvarez, Colonel of Cuban soldiers? I still believe, once Castro is dead, all those who once protected him will flock to your side in droves, Carlos."

"I hope you're right with those thoughts of yours, woman. But I fear I don't share your same view, Maria. I fear there will be plenty of fighting for the capital city, woman. I hope I'm wrong with these troubling thoughts of mine, but I seriously doubt that I am, young lady. Can I depend on you to stay here until I send for you?"

She wiped a tear from the corner of her eye as she stared at Carlos Alvarez, and then she finally gave in and agreed with him. "Yes, I'll stay here until you send for me my love. What other choice do I have in the matter, Carlos?"

"None, but I promise you that you'll play a very important part in our new revolution, my lover." Colonel Carlos Alvarez kissed her, and then he got out of bed and quickly dressed. All the while he dressed, Maria watched him until he finally snapped at her. "Well, are you not going to get dressed and see me off on the start of our new revolution to free Cuba, young lady?"

"I am dressed for want I want to do right at this moment, my Colonel." She giggled as she put her best face on, and then she threw the sheets from her body and she laid on the bed naked.

"If you're going to walk around like that all day then I'm not going anywhere today, Maria."

Maria sprang up from the bed and she immediately wrapped her arms around his neck and she cried at him. "Oh yes you will my hero to all Cuba, Colonel Carlos Rafael Hernandez Alvarez. You have a date with your true destiny on this most wonderful day for Cuba, my love. To set all of Cuba free from Castro's deadly grasp, and to destroy the devil that has made Cuba a living hell for all of us to bear for so long. He's the true Devil in Paradise, Colonel Carlos Alvarez my dear." She suddenly slapped him on his rearend, and then she quickly gathered up her clothes and began to dress herself.

Carlos Alvarez went out of the room and he bumped right into the elderly maid preparing his meal for them. The concerned Colonel leaned close to her and he said. "Melba, I want you to promise me you'll protect Maria's life from all harm, and if I fail in my quest to free Cuba of Castro and be taken prisoner, you must promise me you'll get her out of the city, and then out of the country safely. You must promise me this Melba." Carlos looked deeply into the pitch black, lifeless eyes that were now staring back at him.

For the first time since he arrived at the safe house, Melba spoke to him. "Colonel Alvarez Sir, you'll have nothing to worry about concerning her safety, sir. I shall protect Maria with my very life for you sir. I'll be there, I owe it to my dear sister, dead because of my fear of Castro, sir. Never again, will I ever allow a loved one of mine to die for my weakness of body and soul, sir."

Colonel Alvarez rested his hand on her shoulder and added. "Melba, I'll find the foul ones who did this to your sister. I'll have them chained the same way they bound your sister and allow you to wreak their punishment out on them."

Melba's eyes showed the first sign of any feeling and compassion in them, as a forced smile slowly crossed her lips, and then she replied. "You'll do this for me Colonel Alvarez Sir?"

"And much more, I'll help you punish the guilty who has committed this crime against you."

"You can put your mind to rest concerning Maria and her life, Colonel. I'll look after her very well for you Colonel Alvarez, and if anyone leaves this Island safely, it will surely be her." Melba turned back to the stove, and then she flipped the eggs, hiding her tears from the Colonel.

Maria came out of the bedroom, and she joined the two of them. They ate in silence then Carlos checked his watch. He stood and stretched again as he looked at Maria and smiled at her. She jumped into his arms, imploring him to be careful today. Colonel Alvarez laughed then he kissed her, nodded to Melba who immediately took hold of Maria's hand as he pulled free of her. Alvarez left to Maria's sobbing behind him.

Outside, a car was already waited with Sergeant Regueiro the lone occupant and the Colonel asked the driver. "Where are all the other cars?"

"Good morning Colonel, how are you today sir?" the Sergeant replied to his Commander.

"Fook that bull shit, mista. I asked you where is everyone set up in for the start of this fooking Revolution, Sergeant?" Carlos barked right back at him.

"Colonel Alvarez Sir, they're all set in position. Certainly, we cannot simply pull right up in front of the god dom Palace with a line of military vehicles containing armed soldiers, sir. We wouldn't get out of the vehicles before the guards would be all over us, and our plan destroyed on us. Everyone is set in position sir."

"I hope they are mista. I guess it's time we leave to answer the call, Sergeant Regueiro."

MONDAY, SEPTEMBER 23rd, 1996.SEVEN A.M. HAVANA, CUBA

The vehicle with the colonel and his driver pulled away from the curb, and it headed down Panorama drive to Avenida De Colon. No matter where Colonel Alvarez looked, he noticed members of his new revolution watching his vehicle past them. They were all trying to make themselves inconspicuous as possible until the time to act finally came. He nodded at a few of the soldiers when they recognized him as his car slowly passed by the soldiers milling about the capital city streets. Colonel Alvarez's chest swelled with great pride when he saw so many of his soldiers willing to die for his beliefs and for the freedom of Cuba.

His vehicle carefully turned onto Avenida Carlos M. Decespedes, and then the vehicle cut across the six lane highway and slowly pulled into the massive Palace's courtyard, and then it headed right for the visitors parking of the complex and parked. As he got out of the car, Carlos was instantly intercepted by two well armed and concerned Palace guards. A second pair of guards armed with attack dogs was in his sight as well, as one of the guards demanded to know why his car was parked there. Colonel Alvarez showed the guard the orders from Castro, telling him to report to his office on this day.

The guard handed him the papers back and then he instructed him where to go. The instant he entered the doors of the great Palace, he was assaulted by other guards who pulled him to a metal detector. Another guard held out a basket and he nastily ordered him to put anything of metal in it. Colonel Alvarez placed his pistol on top of his keys and change. The gun drew a harsh stare from the guard who placed it in a drawer and then he locked it, informing Colonel Alvarez the weapon would be returned to him when he left the building. The guard standing behind Alvarez kind of roughly shoved him until he went through the metal detector. Once on the other side, a third guard led him to Castro's outer office on the third floor.

When they exited the elevator, Colonel Carlos Alvarez announced he had to visit the bathroom before his scheduled meeting with Castro. The security guard led him over to it, and then he waited right outside the door for him to finish. Colonel Alvarez's blood was pounding in his ears as he cautiously entered and headed right for the stall where he hoped the pistol was hidden for his use. He reached up and behind the toilet and fumbled around until his hand finally touched the handle of the nine millimeter, American made Colt weapon. He pulled it free from its hiding place, ejected the clip and saw it was full and then he checked the chamber to make certain there was a round set in place to go, before inserting the clip back in the weapon. It had a round ready to fire. He hid it under his jacket and then the worried Colonel wiped the sweat from his brow and he went over to the sink and quickly washed his hands.

The escort entered with his weapon at the ready, feeling Alvarez was taking too much time in the bathroom, seeing him standing by the sink made him relax and say. "Colonel, you're not the only Officer who had the piss scared from him when he was sent for by Presidente Castro, sir."

Both men laughed as the young soldier waited for Colonel Alvarez to finish up. Then he escorted him to Castro's office, and the guard instructed him to wait for Castro to request him to enter his office. He warned Colonel Alvarez if he was to leave his seat, the secretary in the room would blow his head off his shoulders.

Colonel Alvarez stole a quick glance at the young blonde working behind a desk. She looked up and winked at him and then she went back to her business. The escort saluted the higher ranking officer, turned and left.

Colonel Alvarez heard voices coming from another office, but he could tell it was not the voice of Castro. A door suddenly opened and General Boada stepped out of the room. He stopped and stared right at Colonel Alvarez for a brief second, before saying to him. "Ahhhhh… Colonel Carlos Alvarez Sir, how good it is to see you once again, sir." The powerful Secret Police General quickly crossed the room and offered him his hand.

Colonel Alvarez stood and he shook hands with the grinning and extremely dangerous Cuban General, but he looked at the secretary who stared at the both of them. The Colonel motioned to her with a quick head movement at her and the General, seeing the source of his concern, laughed as he said to her. "Gina, you're scaring my young Colonel here, woman. He's okay, you may return to your work please."

She nodded, but she still refused to take her eyes from the stranger in the office.

"Pay no attention to her she's the office pet, Colonel." General Boada smirked as he gave Colonel Alvarez a quick wink. He did not let on in the least that he was as afraid of this extremely dangerous young woman as he continued his words for the military officer. "Colonel Alvarez, I know why you are here, and once you are finish with Castro, stop by my office, sir. Maybe, you could be of use to me yet, sir."

Their conversation was interrupted when Fidel Castro marched into his office without even noticing the two of them. Gina sprang up to her feet while keeping a close eye on the stranger as Castro breezed past them without showing any recognition to the two officers. General Boada was about to disappear in his office when the intercom buzzed, and Gina called out to General Boada. "General Boada Sir, Presidente Castro will see you now, you may go in, thank you sir."

Cuban General Boada could not help the conquering smile coming from his lips as he walked past the young Cuban Colonel now, feeling he had just one upped the young officer by being asked into Presidente Castro's office first. Moments later, the intercom buzzed again, and this time Gina told Colonel Alvarez he was expected inside the Presidente's office immediately.

Colonel Carlos Alvarez stood as if he was walking to his death and he took a quick breath in, felt for the weapon with a movement from his arm, and then entered Castro's office. He quickly scanned the room that stank of old stale cigar smoke and body odor. Castro was sitting behind a huge antique oak desk, and he was already enjoying a cigar. A fresh bottle of rum and three glasses sat on the desk. General Boada was seated a few feet away from the desk to Castro's right. The elegant drapes were opened, exposing the magnificently carved woodwork surrounding the glass window, but the rest of the office was empty.

Upon seeing Colonel Alvarez enter his office, Castro motioned him to a second seat with the end of his cigar. Once he was comfortable, Castro offered him a cigar which he took, but he did not light it. Colonel Alvarez left it resting in the ashtray because he knew he did not want anything in his hands if and when he was forced to act. General Boada being in Castro's office complicated things a little for him, but he made up his mind when he acted, he was going to take Castro out first. If lucky, he would then kill the General before Boada assaulted him. The Colonel dared to check the General's person for a weapon, there was none. He breathed easier, knowing this would make his job a whole lot easier, the only one left to worry about was the secretary and obvious bodyguard working in the outer office.

Castro took no notice of Colonel Alvarez placing the cigar down in the ashtray. He kept a close eye on his General, knowing he was taking something that General Boada wanted away from him. He liked the feeling of this power he held over the extremely dangerous General, and he had convinced himself it was very good, because it was putting this most troublesome General in his place. Fidel Castro knew he would have General Boada killed in the near future, because he was fast becoming too powerful a man in Cuba and a serious threat to his Administration. Castro finally turned his gaze to the young Colonel, and he found the man who would soon replace General Boada, once he was forced to act against this threatening man.

Colonel Alvarez shifted his weight nervously, locked under Castro's stare until Castro felt the strain and he offered him calmly. "Colonel Alvarez Sir, I trust you have received my little gift?"

Colonel Carlos Alvarez stiffened up as he replied to the feared Presidente of Cuba. "Yes I did Presidente Castro, and I thought it was too generous of you, sir." Colonel Alvarez bowed to him.

The pleasant way this Colonel said 'Presidente', pleased Castro, and the display of total respect shown by the young man seated before him, served to reinforce his decision to have him replace the General.

"Good, I guess you're wondering why I have summoned you here before me on this day, Colonel Alvarez. Am I right?" Castro grinned.

"El Presidente Castro, I must admit to you, this thought has crossed my mind before and I was very surprised you have sent for me sir. But I felt the reason would be explained to me soon enough if I wait patiently, sir."

Castro bellowed with laughter for a moment as he turned to General Boada and announced. "Ahhh, young, intelligent, fine looking, and a very good sense of humor at the same time, something that has been missing from this office for much too long a time, General Boada."

"Much too long I agree with you Fidel." General Boada replied, feeling slightly threatened by this officer now.

Castro turned his attention back to Colonel Alvarez again and offered. "Colonel, I have sent for you, because it has come up to my attention you're a well trusted and loyal Officer who'll support me at all times, sir. I need not tell you this is an attribute that is fast becoming hard to find, what with the troublemakers both on and off this Island, always trying to stir up trouble every day against me, Colonel Alvarez. I grow very tired of all this constant complaining lately." Castro stopped speaking while he went into thought before adding.

"Colonel Alvarez, I have summoned you here today to inform you that I want you to give up your Command of the military base and take a new position on my personal staff. I need men like you, loyal soldiers surrounding me at all times. I grow tired, and I must think of the next person who'll run this country, one man who'll carry on my fight with the hated United States. Colonel Alvarez, they are not to be trusted, never. I warn you sir, the moment we trust those lowly dogs that fled Cuba for the United States, it'll be the beginning of the death of Cuba. America!

"The god dom exiles have done nothing but cause the good and loyal people of Cuba unending pain and embarrassment. Bah, never mind this for the time being Colonel, this is something for the next Presidente to worry about, not you nor myself. Colonel Alvarez, what I want to know from you, is if you'll join my staff. I'd like you to do it voluntarily Colonel. Don't think too hard and long over this offer, this decision is totally out of your hands. I want you on my staff, and you will be there Colonel, period!" Castro stared at Alvarez.

Colonel Alvarez was angry over the way Castro just ordered him to leave his command, and join his staff. 'Just like that, huh, you pig. Just like that I'm supposed to leave my soldiers and join your god cursed staff', he thought to himself. His eyes hardened a little as he knew what he had to do now. He stared back at Castro without speaking, causing the Presidente to snap at him.

"Colonel Alvarez, what I'm offering you is no big deal. You're needed here in Havana for the sake of Cuba. I need you. Colonel Alvarez, your people demand this from you as a soldier. I expect you to report next week to the Presidential Palace Barracks on this site. Is that clear?"

Colonel Carlos Alvarez shook his head in an effort to get his mind working again. He looked from Castro to General Boada, and then back to Fidel as he slowly stood up. Neither man reacted to his suddenly motion though. Colonel Alvarez shifted his weight from one foot to the other while quickly searching his mind for the right way to phrase his next words to the two dangerous men. Settling on something Presidente Castro just said, he looked at him and then he began. "Presidente Castro, you're right in stating this offer is for the sake of Cuba that I should join your personal staff, sir."

"Ahhhh… You see General Boada Sir, who says the youth of our country are a bunch of thick headed fools who don't know what they want from life. This young officer seems to know right where he wants to end up in his career in the service. Continue with your words to me Colonel Alvarez." Castro smirked as he turned back to the officer. Instantly, Castro's mouth hung open as he realized he was now staring into the barrel of a pistol, and then he hissed at the young military officer standing before him. "Why you ungrateful little bastard you, how dare you point a god dom weapon at your Presidente of Cuba. I'll have you put to death very slowly for this terrible insult you level against me, fool. Where the devil did you get that weapon from, you could not have entered this floor with one on your person, you god cursed dog you."

Castro went to stand up, but Colonel Alvarez instantly motioned him back to his seat with the barrel of the weapon. He pointed the weapon right at General Boada, and ordered him not to do anything foolish. The General sank back into his chair as well, and then he folded his arms to show he was no threat to him.

"That is better. You see General Boada, who says the great Fidel Castro does not listen to any of his people when they speak out. Look at the old fool sitting there almost human now."

Castro did not speak he just glared back at the Colonel, waiting for the chance to destroy him.

Colonel Carlos Rafael Fernandez Alvarez tried every trick in the book he knew, to try and get control of his wildly beating heart. He never expected to get this far with his life still intact. He looked into Castro's eyes and growled at him. "Presidente Castro, you raised my spirits when you first spoke of the next man who shall run Cuba. I'll save your life, if you're smart enough and you're willing to step down, and appoint me as the next Presidente of Cuba. I'll promise your safety sir, and you'll be delivered safely to any country you wish to be exiled to. I shall allow no harm to come to you, if you merely step down from your office peacefully. As you have just stated, for the sake of Cuba I offer you my services, sir."

Castro said nothing he just stared at the Colonel as if he was trying to burn a hole through him.

General Boada finally saw his chance and he tried to throw his weight behind Alvarez by saying. "Colonel I too have been trying to talk Presidente Castro into stepping down and he..."

"Shut your filthy mouth, I care nothing for any of your lying words you foolishly offer me, General Boada. There's no god dom place for the fooking likes of you, or him either for that matter in my new government, General Boada." Colonel Carlos Alvarez made a quick motion at the seated President with his gun.

General Boada glared, but he did not notice Castro had turned and harshly glare at him.

Colonel Alvarez was amused by both Castro and General Boada who were now locked in a stare down of pure hate, he broke the trance. "Castro, I must know what you plan to do, how you'll react, sir. I don't want to harm you, but today is your last day as the Presidente of Cuba, sir. This I promise, you must step down if you wish to live a day longer, sir."

Colonel Alvarez's words were cut off by the sounds of automatic weapon fire suddenly going off just outside the Palace walls. He knew he had just run out of time and his revolution had begun, and he had to take control of the Presidency if the revolution was to succeed. He was about to ask Castro one last time, when his secretary suddenly rushed into the office, her weapon held in her hand, she was going to protect her leader. He immediately fired twice before the woman's eyes fully focused on what was happening in the office. She tumbled to the floor, hit twice in the chest she was dead before coming to a full stop at his feet. Her eyes stared up at him, her mouth agape as if it was caught in the middle of words.

Castro instantly jumped up to his feet and he suddenly made a wild lunge at Alvarez, but the Colonel was too fast for the old man and he hit him twice with two rounds he fired at him, once in the face, the other in the chest. Castro slumped across his massive desk dead. The desk was the implement that caused his death, because it was too wide for him to reach across it to get his hands on Colonel Alvarez, before he dispatched him. Fidel Castro's body slowly slid down to the floor, with the Colonel staring at it in stunned disbelief.

If it was not for General Boada's sudden movements, if only he would have moved a little slower, he would have got to Alvarez before he was able to spin around and aim his weapon at his chest. The Colonel caught the movement out of the corner of his eye and he spun around while leveling his weapon at the General's chest that had not cleared his seat. Seeing the weapon, he lowered himself back in the chair and stared at Colonel Alvarez.

"Colonel Alvarez Sir, I beg of you don't do anything rash here, sir. Think before you act again Colonel Alvarez, think of all the help I could be to you and your troops, sir. Think of what I know, where all the money is hidden in Cuba, where all the troops are stationed across the entire Island, Colonel Alvarez, sir. Where all the special operatives are working within this country and any of the other countries we have successfully infiltrated as well. You must think of everything you'll never know if you react foolishly Colonel Alvarez, sir. All the help I can offer to you and the rest of your people, sir. Why together, we could rule this tiny Island the way it should truly be ruled all along, sir. I can be a ser..."

A fifth shot rang out, striking the sneering General right in the face, sending his blood bone and brains flying. The General's body flung back, knocking the chair one way, his body the other. It came to a tumbling stop against the door frame the secretary used moments before.

Shots were fired in the Palace and Alvarez could hear countless footsteps running up steps now. He dared a quick look out the window and he easily saw what was taking place below. He spotted his tanks moving into the parking lot and firing at the Palace police. A number of large explosions drew his attention, he could tell some of the tanks fired, and he saw fires instantly breaking out in various places of the capital. He spotted a number of soldiers firing at the fleeing palace police. He bit his lip as he saw two civilians drop from weapon fire. He did not want that, he did not want any civilians who had suffered too long under Castro's oppression and the United States embargo, to suffer any longer. He cursed over their death.

Just then, three men came rushing into Castro's private office, causing Colonel Alvarez to spin around and aim his pistol right at them. He instantly lowered his arm when he recognized it was Sergeant Regueiro, and he was leading the two other soldiers from his base. He flashed a quick smile at Alvarez as he chucked him a loaded AK-47 assault rifle and then he announced in an excited voice to his Commanding Officer. "by the grace of God, we have taken complete control of the Palace. Where is the filthy pig at, sir?"

Colonel Alvarez motioned with his head towards the side of the desk. He rushed over and checked the prone body and grinned as he offered. "Castro is dead! Long live our new Presidente of Cuba, Viva Carlos Rafael Hernandez Alvarez!"

The three soldiers lifted up their weapons and they fired at the ceiling as they cheered him.

Colonel Alvarez blushed as he issued his first orders of the new regime. "Sergeant Regueiro, take your men and get downstairs and make certain this entire fooking building is secured. Oh, and find Vice Presidente Cabrisas at once for me while you're at it, mista. I want him protected at all cost and brought here to me at once, Sergeant."

"Colonel Alva, err... excuse me sir. El Presidente Alvarez, the Vice Presidente of Cuba is safe and secured sir. He's secured and surrounded by a number of our soldiers and he's in his office just three doors down the hall from this very room, sir."

Colonel Alvarez let out his breath in a rush and he ordered the out of breath Sergeant. "Bring him here at once to me."

"Right away Colonel Alvarez Sir." The Sergeant rushed out of the office and a few seconds later he returned while leading Vice Presidente Cabrisas into the room right behind him. He carried an AK-47 also, and he held it as if it was a foreign object locked in his shaking arms.

The two men hugged each other and wiped tears from their eyes. But their friendly reunion was suddenly interrupted by a young soldier who fired his weapon, shattering one of the huge ornamental windows. The shooter and the second soldier then picked up Castro's body and they dragged it over to the broken window and then they harshly threw the body of the deposed Cuban Leader out of the shattered window. Then the two soldiers cheered until the corpse struck the pavement with a sickening thud heard on the third floor. Colonel Alvarez's cheeks flushed with anger as he glared at the two soldiers yelling at the soldiers below.

"Madre de Dios, why the fuck did you two fools do that for, you dom fool you? Blessed Lord Jesus, where the hell are your god dom brains at, god dommit. May God curse you both to hell for all these foul actions. I'm ordering you two to go downstairs and find his body, and then you are to guard it and treat it with the utmost of respect. By the Holy Madonna, I don't want to stoop down to his level of savagery. Christ Jesus, we're much better than that. Now get the devil out of this dom office and do what you were told. Now you great fool you, god dommit!"

Colonel Alvarez stared at the two young soldiers, until they were completely out of the President's office. Vice President Cabrisas walked up behind the shaking and fuming Colonel, and he rested his hand lightly on his back, causing him to take his attention away from the two soldiers, and he turn to the Vice President.

"Presidente Alvarez, for the love of God we have started it, sir. We have started our new Revolution god dommit, and with all the grace of God and His guidance, the final one our beloved country will ever have to endure again. Think of it, you're the new Presidente of Cuba my son, and as such, you'll be able to repeal the laws we don't believe were passed for the good of the Cuban people and the country. Sweet Lord Jesus, we shall free Cuba from Castro's deadly influence. Cuba is free, free, free at long last, by all the Saints in Heaven, she is free. Is it not beautiful Colonel Alvarez? Cuba is free, Colonel Alvarez, free!"

Colonel Carlos Alvarez cried as he listened to the Vice Presidente announce Cuba's freedom to him. He too was smiling from ear to ear, but he also knew there was much more work to be accomplished before he could finally agree with Vice Presidente Cabrisas's last words. He had to ensure all Cuba was secure before the celebration truly began for him and his supporters. Castro was the crime that struck Cuba down, the Devil of Paradise, but before Colonel Alvarez could call his revolution a success, he first had to go through the baptism of reality first. As Colonel Alvarez and Vice Presidente Cabrisas spoke together, their conversation was suddenly cut short by a thunderous explosion just off of the parade grounds of the Palace, to the east side of the Plaza De La Revolution. They rushed over to the broken window and they looked out of it.

The new Presidente Alvarez was stunned at what his eyes beheld. An ugly mob of angry Cuban citizens had just attacked five of his massive Russian made T-80 tanks with anything they found. Some of the women even kicked at the machine with their bare feet. Behind a slow moving tank was a destroyed tank burning out of control. Its ammunition stockpile cooking off inside the massive war machine and sending sparks of molten steel soaring into the brightening sky. The monster's turret lay fifteen feet away from the main body of the machine lying on its top. The tank's Commander hung half out of the turret, his body burned beyond recognition.

Another wave of fast moving horde of civilians moved against the tanks as they picked up some speed on them. Colonel Alvarez stared in shock, as a mob of countless civilians tried to stop the massive machines by standing right in front of them, and the tanks did not hesitate in the least to run right over them. The tankers then opened fire with their 7.62 mm co-axial machine guns as well, mowing down many of the rampaging civilians as they continued to try and attack the massive and deadly war machines.

A cloud of gas bombs next flew through the air next, landing on many of the moving tanks. Two of the massive machines were smothered in flames, and then a second explosion ripped through the night air as another massive tank exploded, leaving only the undercarriage of the huge machine still intact, and still burning.

"What the devil is happening here, god dommit? Don't these dumb shits know that we're setting them free of Castro's rule over them? I cannot believe this." Colonel Alvarez said as he flinched when a third machine erupted into a ball of flames.

His foot soldiers moved in now, shooting many civilians in their backs as they fled from the soldiers. A hundred added soldiers ran over to the marching grounds, chasing the horde of civilians. Many of them ran to the rear of the complex with the soldiers in rapid pursuit. The civilians dropped down to the ground and then a second group jumped up and they fired on the soldiers. It was rapidly turning into a bloody ground battle between the soldiers and the rampaging civilians. The soldiers used the bodies of the fallen civilians and dead comrades for cover, while the civilians used drainage ditches for their own protection now.

More of the huge tanks charged into the fight now, using their heavy cannons to fire on the civilian hordes wildly attacking any soldiers of the new revolution they came across. It looked more and more like the soldiers were losing their patience with the civilian attacking against them, and they were not so willing to engage the civilian forces using just small arms fire against the soldiers. Colonel Alvarez turned to the Vice President with questioning eyes. He could not force his mouth to utter a single word to him as he found himself just staring back at the elderly Vice Presidente of Cuba.

Vice Presidente Cabrisas placed his hand on Alvarez's shoulder and he said to him calmly. "Could we have made a possible mistake here, Presidente Alvarez? Could we have been so arrogant as to imagine that everyone living on this Island felt as we? That Castro was a plague. I hope this reaction to our takeover is just an isolated incident, and not happening all over the Island. Could we have underestimated the desires of the Cuban people? Could it be they were actually happy living under his foul leadership, sir?"

Both men looked out the window just as another explosion took place. This time it was a civilian vehicle targeted by one of the tanks. The truck lifted high off of the ground and it did a cartwheel while flying through the air, and then coming to rest on its roof and erupting in flames.

The second column of tanks made its way over towards the compound, moving in to support their foot soldiers who suddenly found their backbones at the appearance of the additional tanks. The soldiers jumped up and they moved towards the drainage ditch. But, before they make good their attack, another wave of civilians charged onto the parade grounds from the left side. This group of over three hundred civilian fighters attacked the tanks using gas bombs again.

Both soldiers still standing in Fidel Castro's private office on the third floor of the Palace, stared at the terrible blood bath rapidly unfolding right before their stun eyes on the large palace grounds. The civilian mobs swarmed all over the seven attacking tanks, obscuring them completely from Alvarez's view momentarily. Flames from their gas bombs quickly engulfed one of the massive tanks, as the angry mob then turned their attention on the other tanks with all their anger, hatred and revenge.

Hordes of wildly running civilians attacked the tanks by firing bullets from old and outdated weapons, only to become frustrated when the bullets merely bounced harmlessly off the thick, steel hide of the monstrous war machines. Their weapons did as much damage to the machines as a person throwing tomatoes at them. Yet, the peasants continued their wild attack on the steel monsters, and when their ammunition ran out, the hordes resorted to attacking the tanks with sticks, rocks, leather straps, feet, fists, and then a flood of curses.

Little by little, Colonel Alvarez's troops soon got heavy handed with the rampaging civilian mobs. At first, the soldiers were content with just firing over the heads of the civilian hordes. Tankers took to closing up their tanks and armored vehicles to ward off the attacks, but when gas bombs started causing the death of their tanks, they reacted differently against them. When the firing did little to stop the massive hordes, the troops lowered their aim until they fired into the very heart of the crowd, the tanks fired round after heavy round into the center of the civilians.

Colonel Alvarez realized he had underestimated the hold that Castro had on his people, because on every civilian's lips that attacked his tanks in a wave of humanity was the cry of, "Castro, Castro, Castro!" Colonel Alvarez along with the Vice Presidente were further stunned as a tank fired on two tanks covered by a mass of humanity. Men, women, and children were blasted away from the tanks, their bodies falling before the tanks and ground into the earth by the steel treads. The air was filled with shrieks of the dying. The terrible odor of burning flesh made its way up to the office on the third floor of the palace.

A sudden movement off to the left caught the Colonel's eye, more tanks now moved into position, and they immediately opened fire at anyone running, sometimes hitting their own soldiers as the civilian mob got behind the war machines for cover.

Countless gas bombs flew, landing across the front of the tanks. Soldiers setup a number of tripod mounted 14.5 mm machine guns, and they began to spray lead into the masses as they ran across the open grounds attacking the tanks. Tens and then hundreds of bodies soon littered the vast expanse of the great parade grounds of the Palace.

Slowly, Colonel Alvarez's ground forces gained the upper hand against the rampaging mod of civilians. The tide quickly turned when troops from Captain Calvo's 1st paratroopers suddenly surrounded the parade ground, stopping any other civilians from joining the ones forced together in a tight area.

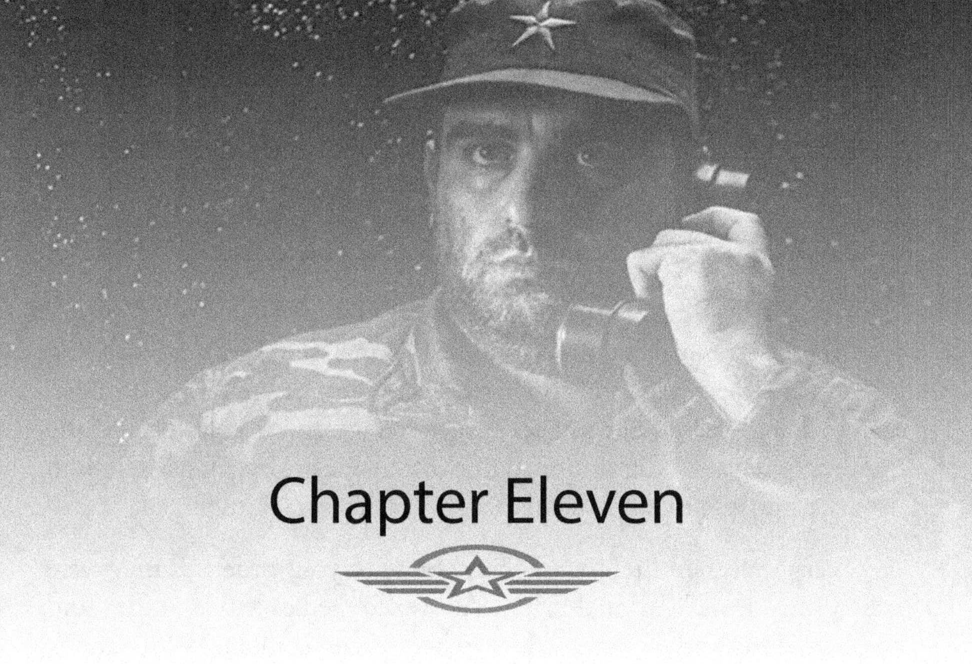

Chapter Eleven

Captain Carlos Calvo arrived at the site of the fierce fighting taking place outside the Presidential Palace, and he was infuriated over the civilian's reaction to their new revolution. He severely overreacted by ordering his troops to let loose on the rampaging civilians with hand grenades and heavy automatic weapon fire. He jumped down from his jeep and moved out with his soldiers as they tried to take control of the rapidly deteriorating situation. The fuming Captain had not walked very far onto the parade grounds before he cursed at the civilians running wildly amuck against him, and the rest of his troops who were not engaging them properly. The angry Captain tried to urge his men forward. Many of the soldiers were reluctant to open fire on the civilian crowds until Captain Calvo finally removed his sidearm, and then he shot at some of the hordes of civilians himself, causing his soldiers to do the same thing.

None of the soldiers hesitated this time as the quickly advancing paratroopers made their way onto the bloody parade grounds, viewing this unruly mob as loyal soldiers for Castro. The slaughter started in earnest now, with the soldiers used grenades, automatic weapons and pistol fire on the attacking civilian hordes. The excited soldiers shot into the masses of humanity indiscriminately hitting men, women or children anyone who was caught out in the open was fair game to the soldier's weapons. Captain Calvo's troops moved on against the civilian groups with a savagery that Colonel Alvarez had only read about in fiction novels. A young officer suddenly rushed into the office as he reported to his new leader of Cuba.

Colonel Alvarez turned from the window and looked at the officer. "Give me the report man."

"Yes sir, I was ordered to inform the Colonel that the Palace building is completely secured at this time, sir. Every floor of the Palace has been searched and cleared already, sir. You're free to go into any part of the building safely, sir. The troops stationed outside are engaging in a mop up situation against some civilian assholes that attack them, sir."

"Very well then Lieutenant, carry on with your orders as they were issued to you, sir." Colonel Carlos Alvarez looked out the window and he became instantly angry as he watched fifteen civilians wildly attack two of his armored vehicles with firebombs. He watched as the two machines exploded in a thunderous eruption. He saw a few soldiers trapped inside the machine try to flee it, the clothes on their bodies burning furiously. The screams from these poor soldiers were horrible, and making the scene even worse, were the civilian attackers were actually cheering as the burning men tried to put the fires on their bodies out by rolling on the ground.

This was the straw that broke Colonel Alvarez's back, he suddenly pulled out his pistol and he fired from the window at some of the cheering civilians watching his men die. He roared as he fired until his pistol was empty. "Give me more ammunition for this god dom weapon!"

A young Cuban Corporal stationed as a guard outside the massive room, instantly rushed inside and he handed him his weapon and three extra clips for it. Colonel Carlos Alvarez did not respond as he took the weapon from him, and then he fired at the some of the fleeing civilians who attacked his armor vehicles. All the while he continued to roar angrily at the civilians.

Massive explosions were going off throughout the entire city proper now, with one explosion worse than the other, and when the fuel station just a few blocks away from the Palace building suddenly exploded in a enormous fireball, with the flames reaching well over a hundred feet into the air. Colonel Carlos Alvarez knew he was going to be forced to use even stronger measures against the rampaging civilian mobs to try and gain some kind of control over the hordes, and the capital and the rest of the country.

As Alvarez stared out the window, he heard the whomp of mortars fired, as other troops setup M-140 and 160 mm mortars. The rounds rained down on the quickly scattering civilian hordes.

The parade ground became dotted by smaller explosions from the mortars that sent plumes of earth, blacktop, cement and human parts into the air. The mortars were the weapons that broke the strength of the rioting civilian hordes. When the first few rounds struck in the midst of the crowds, they ran away from the soldiers. The civilians did not realize to avoid this new wave of soldiers and the death they were dealing out, they would have to run right into the very teeth of the original attacking troops.

Colonel Carlos Alvarez smiled as he watched the civilians finally break off their attack and run off in separate directions, but his relief was short lived though. The civilian mobs ran right into a wall of lead being fired at them from well dug in revolutionary troops, and he roared out the window. "What the hell is wrong with all those lousy sonofabitches? Why the hell are they attacking those god dom civilians for? Order them to stop this crime at once, so they can get away from all the death surrounding them, god dommit." Colonel Alvarez suddenly bellowed as he turned away from the window and he then headed for the staircase to the ground floor of the Palace. The fuming and running Colonel was taking two steps at a time, leaving his guard and the Vice President behind him and he charged forward and out of the building.

Colonel Alvarez jumped down the last few steps and he then ran out the brass doors, and continued to run out to the middle of the parade ground. He was instantly set on by other soldiers who immediately recognized him, and they restrained him from putting himself in any further danger. The small group of soldiers actually wrestled Colonel Alvarez down to the ground in order to stop him. The Vice Presidente made it down the staircase and he rushed over to Alvarez's side as he continued to struggle with the soldiers. He rested his hand on his chest and when Colonel Alvarez made direct eye contact with him, Vice President Cabrisas ordered. "Colonel Alvarez, pardon me, Presidente Alvarez Sir, you're much too important to allow you to place yourself in danger. I beg you think about the revolution before you act foolishly here. I'm going to let you up now, but I'll instruct the guards to drop you if you react foolishly."

Colonel Alvarez nodded in compliance as he tried to see what was going on again.

"Very well then Presidente." He then nodded slightly towards the two guards and they quickly released the Colonel who immediately jumped to his feet as if he was in danger of missing something happening around him. The mortars continued their attack on the civilian hordes, but their explosions were suddenly interrupted by a number of hand grenades popping off. Colonel Alvarez tried to see what was happening, but he was too low to the ground to make any clear observations. The sounds of the explosions, machine guns and the small arms fire, combined with the occasional tank round was deafening. But through it all Colonel Alvarez heard the terrible cries coming from the dying civilians. It seemed the women's terrible wails actually drowned out the deafening sounds of war taking place in the heart of the capital of Cuba.

Colonel Carlos Alvarez's blood was pounding loudly in his ears as he mumbled angrily at a young soldier staring at him. "This is all wrong mista. What the hell have I done, god dommit? I just wanted to set all the people of Cuba free, yet all I have succeeded in doing is becoming the god dom instrument of their cursed death, and more pain to them also."

The stinging words of the Vice President suddenly rang loudly in his mind, because the Vice Presidente of Cuba now realized they were all untrue. Cuba was far from being free of any military rule my Presidente. Cuba could never be free as long as so many of them believed differently than the way he did.

The extremely worried Vice Presidente led Colonel Alvarez over to the safety of one of the parked tanks as they tried to see into and onto the massive parade grounds. Vice Presidente Cabrisas actually shoved Colonel Alvarez to the side of the massive war machine, as the entire area was suddenly being racked by heavy automatic weapon fire coming from where some of the rampaging civilians had just taken cover from the bullets near them. The heavy machine gunfire was pinning them down by the parked tank.

Carlos Alvarez spun around just as Vice Presidente Cabrisas slowly sank down to his knees while clutching his side, blood was seen seeping from between his fingers, and he was having some trouble with his breathing. As the color started to quickly drain from his face as the Vice Presidente of Cuba continued to try to breathe properly, and to also get the pain he was suffering under some kind of control in his body. The Vice President ended up lying on the ground

The Colonel instantly leaped over to his side and actually dragged him behind the protection of the massive war machine, as the cluster of bullets from the attackers continued to bounce off the tank's side. "Medic, this is Colonel Alvarez, I need a medic up here right now. The Vice Presidente has just been wounded. Get that god dom machine gunner before he kills all of us!"

Men screamed to Colonel Alvarez's right, while repeating his orders frantically to the other soldiers with them. More heavy mortar rounds quickly turned the entire area of concern into a ring of flames, and the soldiers sprayed the earth with their deadly rounds. The heavy machine gun fire finally ended from the civilian fighters. Then a wave of soldiers under his command charged Colonel Alvarez's position, lifting him up from the ground and they actually carried him and the wounded Vice Presidente back in the Palace building. Vice Presidente Cabrisas was laid down on the floor as some of the medics quickly attended to his serious wound. One medic had to actually shove Colonel Alvarez out of the way, so he could work on the injured man in peace.

Moments later, one of the medics reported to the new Presidente of Cuba. "Colonel Alvarez Sir, the Vice Presidente is going to survive his wounds and be okay, but he'll be rather sore for quite a while, but he'll do fine sir. The bullets passed right through his body, and neither one of them has struck any of his vital organs or any bones, sir. I'll have him transferred over to the compound's hospital, until all the fighting is over with sir."

Alvarez glared harshly at the young medic as he hissed at him. "Get it done fool." His anger was still hot, and he ripped an AK-47 from the arms of a guard and growled. "Follow me."

The Colonel stood by the set of heavy brass doors to the Palace entrance, and the Cuban Colonel waited there for a lull in the fire to momentarily take place, and then the fuming Colonel made a dash for the safety of the tank again. When he was alongside it, he started to fire into a crowd of civilians fighting with the paratroopers. As he fired his weapon at them, Colonel Alvarez screamed angrily at the civilian attackers. "You bunch of dumb shits do you not realize we're trying to help you, god dommit? How the hell could you bite the very hand of the one who offers you equality in your foul lives? I, the new Presidente of Cuba, order all you fool's to stop this fighting at once, and then you're to go home where you'll be safe. I order you to..."

His words were instantly cut off on him by a loud chorus of, "Castro, Castro, Castro!" That was coming from many of the civilian who were still attacking the revolutionary soldiers.

These angry and ugly shouts only served to infuriate Colonel Alvarez even further now, and he fired in the direction of the chants in a wild rage. More of his soldiers quickly moved out until they had completely surrounded him, and then they fired at the fleeing civilian crowds.

Colonel Alvarez let up on his firing just long enough to see a young woman run towards a tank with a flaming bottle of gas. She reared her arm back as she prepared to throw the homemade deadly weapon at the tank. Suddenly, her body was racked by a stream of bullets. Her body, caught up in the light coming from a sudden explosion of the gas bomb was an easy target for the soldiers firing at her. Many bullets ripped into her torso, causing her to perform the dance of death as chunks of lead tore her body apart.

The Colonel was close enough to see the bullets doing their deadly job. Adding to the gruesome scene, a bullet struck the gas bomb still held in her hand, causing the flaming gas to pour all over the young woman's body. No matter how many bullets found their mark, the woman refused to die. She crumbled down to the ground in flames as the bullets continued to rip into her body, making it jerk along the ground. All the while she wailed a terrifying scream as her body rapidly burned and continued to be assaulted by the rounds fired at her.

Her screams shook Colonel Alvarez to his very soul. Never, in all of his days on earth, had he ever heard a woman scream so agonizingly long and loud. He aimed and fired at the woman's head. She finally stopped screaming as the bullet mercifully ended her torment.

The tank the soldiers were trying to protect suddenly exploded. Some of the civilian fighters had got their hands on a number of RPGs from one of the armored vehicles they destroyed. It took three of the deadly rounds to kill the massive war machine.

"Radio, I want a fooking radio! Dommit, I need a fooking radio now god dommit!" Colonel Alvarez bellowed out at some of his soldiers near him.

A young trooper ran up to Colonel Alvarez's side, and he offered him a headset.

Colonel Alvarez keyed the mike, "Colonel Cienfuegos, where the fook are you, dommit?"

Colonel Ricardo Fernandez Cienfuegos was in Command of the 1st Armored Division, and his responsibility was the security of Havana, and to control all the civilians. "I'm right here sir."

"Where the hell is right here, god dommit. Tell me where you are standing fool!" Colonel Alvarez roared at the other Colonel on the radio.

"Where I was assigned to be stationed sir, I have secured all god dom roads leading into the city of Havana from the south and southeast side of the capital, sir. I'm running into moderate resistance from a bunch of crazy acting civilians attacking my god dom armor with anything they can get their foul hands on. I've been forced to open fire on the god damn fools. I'm waiting for my infantry to catch up, and help me with these dom civilians, sir. I need…"

"Madre de Dios, I don't give a shit what you might need, Colonel Cienfuegos. What I want from you is are you going to be able to free up some of your tanks and armored vehicles, to help us out here? God forgive me, if I don't receive your help, all will be lost. Sweet Jesus, I have underestimated the god dom fools and how they're reacting to our new Revolution, god dommit. It seems the fools must have been happy living under Castro's heavy thumb all these years."

"That is totally impossible at this time Colonel Alvarez Sir. I need all the armor I have at hand and more even, sir. These god damn stupid civilians… Shit sir here they come again on us, Colonel Alvarez Sir. I have a mob of hundreds of civilians attacking my column of tanks, and I'm hard pressed to ward off their foul attacks against us, sir." As if to emphasize they were under heavy attack, there was a loud explosion over the radio, and then it went dead on him.

"These god dom fools, they have caused what has happened to them." Colonel Alvarez barked as he threw the head set aside and he turned to Captain Padilla, working his way over to him. Captain Padilla made marks in the dirt with a stick as he offered to his Commanding Officer. "Colonel Alvarez Sir, I have backup troops stationed here and here waiting to be committed, with other forces hunkered down here and here, sir. If I pull them in, that'll leave our southern flank exposed, and if the civilians attack here, they'll split our forces in half, and we'll then find ourselves locked in the fight of our lives, sir. But on the other hand sir, if I commit these troops being held in reserve and have them attack from here and here, they could catch these lowly troublemakers at this point and then we could rip them apart here. I never expected this sir."

Colonel Alvarez attentively studied the marks were carved into the hard ground. A mortar suddenly round exploded nearby, and it made the both of them duck as the Colonel complained angrily. "These fooking asses, the fools are forcing me to kill them. Captain, do it. I'll have troops from Fabio's 2nd Infantry move in to fill any gap in your forces that might develop from these moves. I decided to secure the Palace and parade grounds first, and then use this as our main headquarters and move out to secure the rest of Havana one street at a time, sir.

"Once I'm certain Havana is safely in our hands then we'll spread out and secure the rest of the cities, towns and villages one province at a time, until we have secured all Cuba, sir. Then, we can take over the government, and rule Cuba the way she should be ruled, with a free and open and soft hand. I wish these spineless devils would have shown Castro such god dom resistance. If they did then he never would've come to power in the first place, god dommit."

Captain Padilla slapped Colonel Alvarez on his shoulder and remarked. "Then we, as soldiers would've had nothing to do on this most wonderful day, my Colonel. I'll have my men move out. Are you going to have the other troops held in reserve, move up for support as well sir? There is something about an Army moving out, and leaving their flank hanging open out in the breeze like my troops will be doing once they start moving out, sir."

"I'll have all the troops there before your troops leave their present positions, sir. I shall never leave your flanks unprotected for one god dom moment sir, not for the shortest of time I assure you, Captain Padilla Sir. Get going sir and good luck with your attack against these god dom foolish civilian mobs, and try to get some kind of control and sanity over these dom civilian fools while you're at it, Captain Padilla."

"I have all the god dom luck I need in my soldier's hands, sir. And, Fidel Castro is dead Colonel Alvarez Sir." Captain Padilla saluted, and then he made a dash from behind the tank, and he headed back to his men.

Colonel Alvarez took the radio and he ordered Gonzales to move a platoon size unit of infantry soldiers up to the south gate of the wide parade grounds, to help relieve Captain Padilla's troops as they quickly changed position to better support the bogged down paratroopers. The Colonel waited for his troops to move out. It seemed to him as if there was a slight lull in the fighting that made it much easier for Captain

Padilla's forces to move up uncontested. He saw the Captain's forces circling a horde of wild acting civilians.

Once these troops were set in their position, Captain Padilla's men attacked with a suddenness that surprised even him. The attacking soldiers must have coordinated their attack with Captain Calvo's troops, because when Captain Padillia's men attacked the center of the civilian fighters, it easily split the non-military forces in two. Two groups of soldiers from Captain Calvo's forces attacked downwards, ripping into the separated non-militant Armies. Captain Padilla's troops suddenly reversed themselves, and they quickly added their bulk to Captain Calvo's forces, while successfully destroying the unorganized civilian Army now. In just a few minutes of heavy fighting, over a thousand civilians were trapped and then eliminated, or they were arrested and forced under the control of the soldiers loyal to Colonel Alvarez.

Captain Padilla's forces continued on with their opening attack against the rampaging civilian hordes, until they were able to hook up with Vidali's 34th Infantry Brigade who had just attacked the parade grounds of the Palace from the west side of the massive compound. The fighting for the grounds was rapidly coming to a fast conclusion, with Colonel Alvarez's forces easily wiping out any of the pockets of civilian resistance they encountered. Hundreds of civilians from the surrounding area quickly disappeared back to where they had come from. Although most of the fighting for the Palace and parade grounds was largely over with at this point, it did not mean the capital city had been entirely secured by any means. The besieged city was far from secured, and the fighting for the capital had just started in reality.

A heavy cloud of blue haze from the countless spent rounds, hung over the parade grounds like a morning fog, with all the fires they had caused still burning out of control, adding to the thickening haze on the soldiers. Colonel Alvarez came out from behind the tank, and he quickly surveyed the scene laid out before him. Everywhere he looked, he saw bodies sometimes they piled two and three high. Men, women and children lay spewed about on the ground like some kind of child's discarded toys. The bodies were in all manner of dress and half dress, Colonel Carlos Alvarez even noticed a few of them were almost naked individuals, who had nothing but a stick, or an old gun as a weapon still locked in their hands.

It was a very sad sight to observe for the new President of Cuba. Colonel Alvarez looked at the body of a small child lying before his feet, whose face was locked in an angry mask of hatred. He had been shot right through the throat, but the bullet did nothing to hide the child's anger for Colonel Carlos Alvarez's new revolution. Sadly, he slowly shook his head over what he was seeing displayed all around him on the new battlefield.

Colonel Alvarez rested his hand lightly on the side of the parked tank for some added strength to his exhausted body, as he carefully studied the battlefield before him. He could not understand why all these civilians had backed Castro, the bastard who made their lives a living hell to endure. Why did they honor Fidel Castro so much, and go against him as they have done on this night? The Colonel tried to reason with himself as he fought to understand this. He asked the soldier standing by him. "Did the fools not understand we were trying to set them free?"

The young Private's face was covered with grime and dried blood, but he replied by merely sneering as he spat on the dead body. "These lowly bastards were too stupid to realize what we're trying to do for the fools. Don't allow it get you Colonel Alvarez Sir. There are many more crazy bastards we'll fight before we can finally claim complete victory for the revolution, sir."

Colonel Alvarez did not respond to the Private's words of wisdom aimed at him. Instead, he snapped at the young soldier in an angry tone. "Radio! Get me a god dom radio mista."

It was immediately shoved in his hands by another soldier standing just behind the Colonel.

"Captain Padilla Sir, Colonel Alvarez here, sir. Where the devil are you at, sir?" The Cuban Colonel barked into the radio at his other military officer.

"Colonel Alvarez Sir, I'm engaging in a mopping up operation by the west gate of the parade grounds, sir." The Captain reported back to his commander.

"Forget about all that shit and get back to me at once, sir. I'll wait for you by the side of the parked tank." Colonel Alvarez ordered the other officer over the radio.

"Very well Colonel Alvarez Sir. I'll be right there as soon as possible, Colonel." The Captain replied in the radio.

Captain Padilla appeared seemingly from out of nowhere. Colonel Alvarez slapped him on the back as he told him he did well with his attack against the rampaging civilian hordes. Captain Padilla's face broke out into a wide grin as he tapped a cigarette out from the pack, and then he offered the Colonel one of them.

"I have no time for that shit right now, sir. Captain Padilla Sir, you're now in Command of the cleanup of the parade ground area, sir. Order the bulldozers over to that empty field, and have them start digging ditches to throw the god dom bodies in. I want this fooking place cleaned up before the hated Americans find out what has taken place here, and send in their god dom spy planes to take pictures of this mess, sir. Set some tents up over the dom ditches so we can work in private, sir. I want to get these bodies out of here before the rest of the city, and the world finds out what has happened here. Speed sir, you can use all the hands you have need of, to accomplish your orders, sir. If you need more help, call them in, use my name to cut through any hassle you might get, grab some of these stupid civilians to help your troops out also, sir."

Colonel Alvarez checked his watch next, and he was stunned to see it was already after ten in the morning. His opening attack had begun at exactly seven a.m., three hours of heavy and uncontrolled fighting had occurred, and he could not believe it. "Captain Padilla Sir, get the god dom engineers out here to help you with those fooking ditches, I want all these bodies out of here quickly, sir." Colonel Alvarez glanced up to the sky, and then he added to his orders to his other officer. "With the way my luck has been running so far on this foul day, for all

I know. The god dom American spy planes probably made flights over us already, sir." A moment of thought, then he turned to the Captain and added. "Captain Padilla Sir, has anyone thought to secure the god dom radio and television station yet? Maybe, with a little luck this time, we might be able to hide some of this slaughter from the ever prying eyes of the dom Americans."

"Colonel Alvarez Sir, I believe the responsibility of the radio and television station fell into Captain Calvo's jurisdiction, sir. I can check and see if he had some of his men secure the stations for us yet, sir."

"Then do this moment Captain Padilla Sir!" Colonel Carlos Alvarez barked angrily at his military officer, and then he waited for him to act on his last orders.

"Err... Colonel Alvarez Sir, what do you want me to do with Fidel Castro's body, sir?"

"I have not given a second thought to it, Captain Padilla Sir. Do you have any idea where it might have ended up, sir? I remember giving an order to have two soldiers protect it, sir."

"Yes, Colonel Alvarez Sir, I had the fool's body moved to the first floor of the Palace, sir. The body was placed in the male's bathroom there. I ordered it guarded at all times from any harm sir, at first, I thought the god dom civilians might be after his body, so I had it secured there, sir."

"Good thinking on your part Captain Padilla Sir. I want Castro's body dumped into the same fooking pit as the horde of dead civilians. I don't want anyone digging up his body and doing who knows what to it, sir. Yes Captain, the same pit is good enough for the likes of him and his terrible memory to all Cuba and her citizens, sir."

"This order is understood Colonel Alvarez Sir. Errr... what about General Boada's body, sir? I had his body brought in and placed by Fidel Castro's side, Colonel Alvarez, sir."

"Wrap Castro's body up in a clean blanket and then you're ordered to place it in the ditch with great respect. The General can be dumped naked in a heap for all I care about him, along with the rest of the troublemakers here, sir. I have no intention of offering him any dignity, even in his foul and hated death, sir."

"Very well Colonel Alvarez." Captain Padilla quickly carried out his first order, and he made contact with Captain Calvo. After a moment he reported to the new Presidente of Cuba. "Colonel Alvarez Sir, Captain Calvo has just informed me he had a unit of his soldiers sent out to both of the communications stations in Havana, before he started on his mission sir. He has stated to me he had electronic jammers setup to knock out all radio, television, short wave transmissions, along with any cellular and microwave communications, Colonel Sir. He has assured me nothing is getting off the Island unscrambled at this time Colonel Alvarez, sir."

"Blessed Lord Jesus, at least this much of our plan has gone well for us. I think you better get on with the cleanup of the parade grounds. Inform Captain Calvo I want to see him in Castro's office as soon as possible. Inform him I want a radio and television hookup set up in Castro's..."

"Pardon me sir, but do you not mean your new Presidente's office now, Colonel Alvarez Sir?"

"You're correct Captain. Inform Captain Calvo I want communications set up in my office immediately. Just in case I have to go on the air to counter any lies the hated Americans might spread about our revolution sir, and all the actions we're forced to engage in, dealing with this crap here. Captain, I shall wait patiently to address the people of Cuba, to inform them of what has happened to them on this day, and what will happen in the future to benefit them in the coming days of my taking over command of Cuba, Captain. Get going on my orders, sir."

"Yes Sir Colonel Alvarez." Captain Padilla laughed as he slapped the new Presidente of Cuba on the back, before heading to carry out his orders as instructed. Captain Padilla was screaming at any soldiers he laid his eyes on, to start hauling the bodies to the lot across the street from the Palace grounds. He also ordered digging machines onto the field, and then he ordered his soldiers out, and they were armed with canvass rope ties, and standing polls. So, they could start setting up the tents over the area the machines were digging to hide their actions from the view of any American satellites or spy flights.

215

Chapter Twelve

Republican elect Albert Cole was read the morning paper when he received the first report from his CIA Director, John Raincloud. The President immediately sent out for his National Security Director, Norman P. Griffin so he could be part of the situation taking place in Cuba. He smiled, knowing the last President was the one who opened the door to negotiations between the United States and Cuba.

President Cole let out his breath as he milled over sending for the Chairman of the Joint Chiefs of Staff, General William 'Rockjaw' Weidenbacher. He respected the man and he relied heavily on his opinion, but his answer to any question was. 'Bomb the sonofbitches into submission', and the new President always had to step on the General to keep him in line

Most of the time the General's opinion was hard to agree with, but he had such an uncanny ability to sniff out any possible threat against the United States. He knew what had to be done to countermand these threats no matter where they came from. The American President suppressed the intercom button and said into it. "Joan, I think you better invite General Weidenbacher over here for me please. Where's Mary?"

"Yes sir, Mary's in the reading room, sir. You want me to inform her that she's needed, sir?"

He grinned because this was the second time he caught her going to the bathroom now. "Yes."

Mary Hirshfield was a strong woman who brought the President the Jewish vote. She was a no nonsense type woman who stood as strong as the male members of his cabinet, as she did to all the females. She was the best thing to have happen to President Cole, she worked tirelessly for his election, and he would never forget her face when he asked her to join his ticket. She was a young woman, a widower. President Cole admitted she was his second choice for Vice President, but General Powell could not be talked into running yet. He did vow he would find a place for the respected ex-General on his staff, because he understood he would be nuts not to. The man was too good to allow him to take a back seat.

President Cole's thoughts were interrupted by Mary who came steaming into the office and she asked the President. "What's this crap about Albert? You have the bathrooms monitored or something, sir? Every time I take a dump now, you want to see me."

"Cuba. Did you wash your hands Mary?" the President asked her with a smirk on his lips.

"Ha, ha, what did they do now, find their backbone and do away with that bearded bastard?"

"Maybe so I believe at this time Mary." The President replied to her last remark calmly.

"What? You really believe someone on that Island took matters in their hand and did away with him?" Mary snapped, surprised at the President's response to her comment about Cuba.

Their conversation was interrupted by Norman Griffin, the Security Director, who reported that General William Weidenbacher was on his way over to the Oval Office, and he looked like he had a bee trapped in his jockies.

The President laughed, but that stopped the instant when General Weidenbacher arrived at the Oval Office and he immediately barked at the American Leader. "Who the hell needs me to hold their stinking hand this time for them, Mr. President Sir?"

"General, I suggest you take a seat, sir. We might have a slight problem on our hands, sir."

"Where this time Mr. President Sir?" the large General grumbled back at the President.

"Cuba. We're waiting for Director Raincloud to arrive with his reports, sir. He's the one with the information. For the moment, I know as much as each of you do. Anyone care for coffee?"

Director John Raincloud came in carrying a plastic file box with him in his arms. He plopped down in a chair, and then he placed the box between his legs and he looked at the President and nodded pleasantly to the American Leader.

"Glad to see you were able to attend the meeting with us, John." The President offered him.

The President's attempt at a joke went right over the serious CIA Director's head. The Director was the one who requested this meeting happen.

General Weidenbacher shot a sharp and angry glare at the full blooded Native American, he was pissed off he did not report to his office before sending the report over to the boss. He hated meeting with the President not knowing the reason why first.

Director Raincloud nodded while taking a number of folders from the box, and then he laid them out on the desk before the President. As he placed them in the order taken, he allowed the others to view them as he began the President's briefing. "Mr. President, members, something tragic has just occurred in Cuba. From the information I was able to gather on it so far, I believe a revolution began early this morning. My office was flooded by reports of fighting taking place on the Palace grounds, with tanks and other heavy weapons equipment involved. I've lost communication with my god damn operatives because whoever the hell's running this damn revolution is jamming everything coming out of Cuba. I can't get anything in, or out of it, sir."

"If the Cuban Army's involved in this mess then I'd assume that Castro's still in power over the Island, Director Raincloud." The President offered.

"I agree with the President, Director." Security Director Griffin offered with a pleasant smile.

"In a damn pig's ear he is." General Weidenbacher growled back at Director Griffin in a huff.

All eyes immediately went to him as the President snapped at the military officer. "Perhaps the General has some inside information that's not privy to the rest of us here. Would you care to elaborate a little further on your last statement to me, General?"

"With all due respect Mr. President Sir, I don't know about the rest of you guys, but everything I read about Cuba so far sir, clearly points to a god damn military revolution happening..."

"You mean the Army's attacking the Presidential Palace, General?" Director Griffin snapped.

"I agree with the General this time around, sir." Mary added to the conversation confidently.

Director Griffin turned to her and he grumbled at her. "You would Mary, the two of you are as thick as thieves' lately young lady."

The General smiled, but the Vice President got hot and she replied at the Director in a heated tone of voice. "You better watch your tone of voice whenever addressing me mister, or you could find yourself on the outside wishing you were back inside, sir."

The President saw this look in Mary's eyes many times before, and he knew he had to step in before things got out of hand on him with the meeting. "Calm down a little, Mary. I'm certain Director Griffin did not mean anything by his last remark. But I happen to agree with him this time myself. I believe if General Weidenbacher would offer the moon was made of green cheese, you'd agree with him, and go off trying to set up support to prove him right, so relax please."

Mary Hirshfield let out a sigh as she sat back in her chair and she crossed her arms. "I see no problem agreeing with our fighting men, someone has to back the men standing post for us, sir."

General Weidenbacher looked around the room, causing the President to ask him. "Is there something wrong sir?"

"The way Ms. Hirshfield's acting, I expect to see that pain in the ass Manning come in, sir."

"Take care I warn you General Weidenbacher Sir. I know damn well how you feel about my civilian advisor, sir. But I'll not tolerate any disrespect aimed towards him at any meeting, sir. And sir, if you have to know, I sent for him, sir."

"There goes the whole god damn meeting." Director Griffin moaned at everyone in the office.

"Am I going to start having some problems with you here now as well, Mr. Griffin Sir?"

"With all due respect Mr. President Sir, you know what that man does to our meetings, sir. He's always using one of our discussions to turn it around for his platform. If we need a military operation, Manning complains. If we need monies for the services, or a humanitarian operation, he grips. Christ sir, I think he'd complain about a god damn blow job, sir." Even as Griffin spoke the words, he blushed because he forgot about the Vice President was sitting to his left.

The instantly upset President jumped to his feet and roared at his Security Director. "Mr. Griffin Sir, how dare you, I can't believe you just said such a terrible thing right in front of my Vice President, sir. I think you owe her an apology sir."

Before he could offer it, Mary laughed as she looked from Director Griffin to the President, before adding herself. "Mr. President Sir, I happen to agree with the Director in this case, sir. I believe he would complain about that, sir."

"Agree with the Director about what?" Manning asked as he entered the office as if he owned the world, and he was just putting up with them, as he looked at General Weidenbacher. He saw the disgusted look on the General's face and he smiled, pleased he already caused him distress.

"Mr. Griffin was just informing us about how much a pain in the ass you are." Mary snapped.

Manning was stunned by the Vice President's angry words aimed at him as he looked at the Director for a moment.

"Good morning sir, and have a seat please Mr. Manning Sir." The President ordered him.

"But sir..." Manning went to complain, but he was instantly cut off by the President.

"Never mind that for the time being, take your seat and pay attention so you can catch up on what we are discussing at this meeting, sir. We have a problem so listen so you can catch up with us. Director Raincloud Sir, you had something else to add, sir. I'm sorry for the interruption; please continue with your presentation, sir."

"Thank you Mr. President, err... I was able to determine there was a major engagement currently taking place between the soldiers and civilians on most of the Island sir, before all the communications were blocked off on us, sir. I was unable to ascertain if it was a civilian revolt, or a revolt by the military, sir. The action taking place in Cuba is massive, almost nationwide from the looks as much as I was able to ascertain, sir."

"What have you done to get your Spooks (CIA Operatives) noses working for you again, John?" General Weidenbacher barked at the Director from his seat, drawing a nasty glare from the President for his callous words.

The powerful Native American Director paid little attention to either person as he replied. "Quite a bit, I'm afraid I requested an emergency flight of the SR-91 for a recon flight over the full length of the Island. I also ordered all emergency channels opened, these are impossible to scramble. I'm sure the information will come in within the next hour or so, Mr. President Sir."

The new President offered. "Mary, before Director Raincloud requests it from you, I want you to send a memo out to the Air Force Chief, General Clarence Claiborne, and order him to authorize as many SR-91flights over the Island of Cuba as John needs. Mr. Raincloud, you're authorized to communicate with Claiborne. Coordinate all your needs directly with him, sir. It'll save you some time. Is that all you have for me at this point, sir?"

"Thank you Mr. President. Err... before my communications went down across the board, I had some other reports that came in of heavy explosions taking place right on the Palace grounds itself, sir. Combine this information with the reports I received of troop movements throughout the Island, and I see a serious revolution taking place there, sir."

President Cole cut Director Raincloud off, by suddenly standing and pacing the office. Everyone understood when he did this he wanted all the conversations stopped, until he had a chance to clear his head some. He stopped his pacing, and then he leaned both his hands on the surface of his desk and he asked. "Director Raincloud, what's your off the shoulder assumption of the present situation taking place on the fucking little Island, sir?" He turned red as he looked at his Vice President and offered her. "Err... sorry Mary."

Mary ignored his apology as she turned to the Director to hear his response.

"Mr. President Sir, I believe this mess is a civilian action, sir. I think something down there has just happened, that forced the civilians to attack their leader and his Administration, sir."

"Bullshit! Bullshit!" General Weidenbacher hissed and then added, "that's a load of tripe, sir. This action has to be a military attempt to overthrow that lousy bastard down there, sir. It has to be, are you out of the loop? Did you receive reports about the civilians being upset with the ass running the place? I haven't seen any on my desk. Besides, if anything was happening, one of my ships would have reported the movements to the Pentagon, before this crap took place. I have the command ship, err...err..."

"The Mount Whitney General Weidenbacher Sir." Director Griffin offered to him calmly.

"Yeah, the Mount Whitney is down there supporting our present operation in Haiti, and if there was any possibility of any civilian unrest taking place inside Cuba. They would've been the first ones to sound out the alarm for us, sir. If I remember right, the Whitney's position is right between Haiti and Jamaica, close enough to pick up any of this action before it got so far along, if the damn civilians suddenly went nuts on that damn Island. John, how many civilians would have to be involved in this thing to be a large enough force to attack the Cuban Armies as you have reported? John, the Cuban groups operating on the United States shore, working for this very type of action have been rather silent about it, sir.

"If this was a civilian action taking place down there, they would've surely been in touch with the Cuban groups back in the States, begging their support from them, sir. We would know in advance if the civilians planned something on the Island. Christ John." General Weidenbacher moaned as he shook his head, adding to the anger of the CIA Director, who did not like the General chose to embarrass him before the President.

President Cole noticed Director Raincloud was blowing himself up in order to respond to the General's last remarks to him, and he cut him off before the meeting got a little out of hand on him. "John, I know you don't really have gathered enough information to respond correctly to our questions yet, sir. So, I'll not hold you to anything you have to offer me at this time, sir. But I do have to agree with the General here though, Director. Have we heard anything from the Cuban groups here in the States, sir?"

"Immediately sir, the Cuban Anti-Castro League was in touch with my office immediately, sir then we received the first reports of this action taking place in Cuba, sir. The Cuban Revolution Council, ran by Jacinto Adolfo Miret Cardona, the son of the late Doctor Jose Miro Cardona, has been in touch with me as well, Mr. President. You do remember Doctor Cardona, he committed his life to the ouster of Castro from Cuba. His son requested to be allowed to form up his members, so they could invade Cuba sometime in the future, sir."

"Are they trained in any military terms, Mr. Raincloud Sir?" the President asked him.

"They've been engaging in some half assed training program, ever since his father organized the group. It's the largest Cuban American group of a military nature in the United States, sir."

"Where have they been carrying out this training, and why wasn't I informed of it before this time, sir? I don't like any military forces training in the United States without my knowledge. I don't need this crap coming to the surface, and biting me on the ass around election time, sir." President Cole glared at Director Raincloud and then waited for his response.

"Mr. President Sir, this program was authorized by the late President Kennedy, and it had never been dismantled by any of the later President's sir, so you have nothing to worry about there." CIA Director Raincloud took a quick breath and then he added to his words. "The group's training is being carried out in the everglades in Florida, sir."

The President turned to General Weidenbacher and he asked him seriously. "What do you think about these damn Cubans, sir?"

"Christ Almighty sir, I don't think they could fight their way out of a stinking paper bag by themselves, sir. I'd trade the lot of them in on one lone Girl Scout who'll take orders properly, sir. Why do you think Castro never remarked about them, sir? He's well aware of this program it's not as if it was being kept a secret. He has no fear of them, they're such an unorganized bunch of assholes, and their military wherewithal's flat as a pancake, sir. They don't know what they're doing, and I don't think they give a shit about what they are being trained for, sir. I think they're taking their training as a damn joke, using it as a means of getting three squares a day, and living off our government who spares no expense on them. I don't believe they'd ever be used to free Cuba of Castro, sir. It's a stinking game to them."

"Options?" President Cole snapped at both men sitting before him.

Director Griffin responded first. "Mr. President Sir, I suggest we sit tight and see what's happening next down there, before we commit ourselves to any course of action against it, sir."

"I agree with the Director and his beliefs, Mr. President Sir." Manning said as he rose.

"If Manning agrees with me then I want to change my opinion, sir." Director Griffin snapped from his seat, drawing the President's harsh stare before Manning had a chance to respond to it.

"Mr. Griffin Sir, I already warned everyone here that I'd not tolerate any such disparaging remarks leveled at Mr. Manning expense, sir. I warned everyone I need and rely on his opinion, and I shall react to anyone who is showing any disrespect whatsoever towards him. I don't expect any personal attacks here, sir. Mr. Griffin, I think you owe Mr. Manning an apology sir."

Director Griffin glared angrily back at Manning, but he simply refused to apologize.

"Well, I'm waiting Mr. Griffin Sir." The President demanded of his security director.

"Sorry." Director Griffin said the word as if it was a four letter word for him to use.

"That's a little better sir. Mr. Manning Sir, you were saying something sir."

"I agree we should stand pat and see what takes place first. We have to stop supporting these countries, until they prove to us they're willing to ally themselves with the United States..."

"Cuba will never ally itself with us, no matter who is running the damn place for them." The General snapped, still wearing the smile placed there by Griffin's request to change his opinion.

"General Weidenbacher will you please, sir!" the President warned his military officer in no uncertain terms this time.

Manning ignored his remarks but he still did not change his approach to the conversation either. "I know what's on the General's mind here, what's always on his mind, sir. He wants to flood the Island of Cuba with his soldiers, do a military operation involving all the services, just to feed his over inflated..."

"Why you little piece of shit you. I have a good mind to eat you up and shit you out of my god damn ass the next morning, mister. Who the hell do you think you're speaking to here buster? If I had you in the service, I'd have your ass hanging from the barrel of a tank, and have your innards splattered all over the god damn place. I'd...." General Weidenbacher was absolutely furious at the civilian, as he rose from his chair to his feet. Then he angrily pointed a finger at Manning as if it was a gun and cursing up a storm at him.

President Cole suddenly yelled at his officer. "General Weidenbacher! You'll return to your god damn seat and be civil here! General, I am ordering you back to your seat, now sir!" the President was scared General Weidenbacher might be hot enough to attack Manning as he added to his demand. "General! Get hold of your temper please, or I'll have you removed from my office and meeting immediately, sir. General, dammit sir!"

President Cole's screaming caused General Weidenbacher to stop his attack on the civilian, and turn to the President who was making his way to stand between the two of them. Once President Cole was sure he had the General's full attention again, he calmed down some and ordered him back to his seat.

General William Weidenbacher plopped down in his seat rather heavily, and he was still mumbling a hot stream of curses at Manning, who was now the brunt of the President's fury as well. President Cole turned to Manning and he quickly pointed his finger at him. "Mr.

Manning Sir I just yelled at Mr. Griffin because he showed you little respect sir, and then what the hell do you do? You attack my General, knowing how he feels about having a civilian taking part in any of these meetings or military briefings. I can't believe you done this sir. Dammit, I'm growing sick and tired of all of this constant bickering every time I call for a god damn meeting to take place by any of you people. I had it this time I assure you mister.

"I'm warning everyone here, I'll not stand for anymore of this childish behavior. The next person who acts like a baby will be treated like one, and I'll have his ass removed and make him or her, stand in the god damn corner. I promise the next offender will be looking for a new job by morning. I don't care how important he or she is to my Administration, the next person who causes an outburst at this meeting, will be fired. We're here to discuss this new development occurring in Cuba. We're not here to see who is going to get away with the harshest barb against the other, people.

"I will not stand for this any longer. We're all adults here or are supposed to be adults, and we better start acting like adults dammit. I heard all I want to hear from you Mr. Manning Sir. I shall only listen if you have something more constructive to add to this meeting, sir. If you can't agree to sit there and be quiet then I suggest you leave before I'm forced to act against you. Do I make myself perfectly clear to everyone attending this briefing?"

There was a collective yes from all the members attending the meeting.

"Very well then, I suggest you warn anyone who wasn't here to hear my warning. The next one who acts like a child will be fired plain and simple." President Cole turned his back on everyone as he walked back to his seat. Plopping down he let out his breath and stated. "General Weidenbacher Sir, what is it you suggest we do?"

"Mr. President Sir, I suggest we take full advantage of the situation, and train the Cuban exiles in earnest this time. Look at what we have at hand here we have a Cuban force we can send to fight another Cuban force. Something's happening, and we must take complete advantage of it if there's half a chance of us gaining some influence over the Island. I'm damn positive Director Raincloud and my staff will agree. Mr. President, even if a revolution isn't taking place in Cuba at present, with the right amount of pressure applied, it could easily turn into one. If we play our cards right, this action might not cause us to involve our own fighting boys."

"But you have just finished saying that these damn Cuban fighters couldn't fight their way out of a bag to us, General Weidenbacher Sir." The President said back at his military officer.

"Not now they can't Mr. President Sir, but if you give me another two weeks with the damn asses, they'll be trained, and they'll be ready to bite their own damn arm off, and then eat it if they had to, Mr. President Sir." General William Weidenbacher smiled at the funny facial expression that both Manning and the Vice President put on their faces over his last remark.

"Once again, I'm afraid you're contradicting yourself a little here, General Weidenbacher Sir. Didn't you just finish telling me we might be able to pull off this god damn action without involving any of our fighting soldiers, sir? You must remember I already inherited two damn military involvements as it is, sir. One of them in Haiti that'll be over by the end of this year I'm hoping, and the second one, that major fiasco that's still taking place in the former Yugoslavia country sir. Every time we come up with a damn cease fire from one side, the other side breaks the damn thing, and neither side's any better than the other one is, sir.

"The damn Serbs and their miserable ethnic cleansing bullshit are killing thousands of innocent Muslims, when they had the upper hand in this ongoing situation. Then when the damn Muslims gained the momentum, what the hell did they do, the same fucking thing the Serbs did, killing thousands of the damn Serbs, General Weidenbacher Sir. It's a damn rat race over there, and I don't know what's to become of them. Maybe we should pull back and let them have at each other, and see who comes out the victor in the end…"

President Cole turned to Manning as if to drive the point home, before looking back at General Weidenbacher. "I'm sorry General, you were saying sir?"

"With all due respect Mr. President Sir, I believe you might have misunderstood me a little, sir. The exile Cubans had been going through some sort of military training for a number of years now sir. The damn basics are there alright sir, and within a few weeks I'm quite certain I could round them out into well trained fighting units, sir. The American soldiers I was speaking about were the few troopers I'd need to complete the Cubans military training sir, and maybe even accompany them to the damn Island if they're allowed to invade Cuba that is, sir. Our involvement in this possible mess will be minimal at the very worse, sir."

"Who would you use as the Cubans trainers, General?" Director Raincloud interrupted him.

"I don't know right off hand, Director Raincloud Sir. But I'm certain I can locate a few real fuckups who are good, and can get the job done for us, sir. I'll have to check the 201 files, sir."

"You have such people in your ranks, General Weidenbacher Sir?" the President asked him.

"Many I'm afraid, Mr. President Sir." The General replied with a smirk on his lips this time.

"Would these few special soldiers of yours be forced to engage any enemy, if they happen to accompany the exiles onto the Island of Cuba, General Weidenbacher Sir? I happen agree with you on this one General Weidenbacher Sir, about us having to do something about this mess while all this unrest is occurring in Cuba, sir. We all knew that sooner or later we'd be forced to do something about Fidel Castro, and all this action might just be the answer to what we have been looking for all along, General Weidenbacher Sir." Security Director Griffin offered.

"I think it'd serve us well if we allowed the few American soldiers, we need to train the Cuban exiles, to tag along with them, Mr. Griffin

Sir. Sort of run the damn invasion for them and us, we have to keep our finger on all the happenings down there sir. Or we just might find ourselves on the outside looking in, as we did when we first allowed Castro to take over down there, sir."

"You I believe you talked me into this mess, General Weidenbacher," the President moaned, and then added as if it was a second thought. "What's the extent of the action we'll be involved in, with this Cuban action currently taking place, sir?"

"Mr. President Sir, taking out Castro would be anti-climactic to all the damn trouble he has caused us over the year's sir, unless we take out all his damn followers and Administration officials at the same time, sir. To do this, we have to enter a civil war that we'd be instrumental in actually instigating, Mr. President Sir. Not eliminating Castro, we'll be forced to starve his country until his own people revolt against him, and then we'll move in, not knowing what might be left or how the damn civilians would feel about us, if we're forced to carry out this second plan sir. So far, it hasn't worked out very well for us sir."

President Albert Cole suddenly held up his hand, and then he offered to his military officer. "Okay General Weidenbacher Sir, I heard enough of this shit to last me a lifetime, sir. This is what I want, give me a complete list of names of the soldiers you think you might need for this advance training of the Cuban exiles, sir. I'll allow you to pull the troops from any branch. Pick the ships you'll also need to get them to the Island and the support ships and aircraft. If we decide to go, we'll go all the way this time around sir. I have no intention of losing to Castro a second time. I want this information by this afternoon General, because I'm going to call for a full staff meeting in the Situation Room tomorrow morning, starting at eight o'clock sharp, sir. I trust you'll have the demanded information for the briefing by then Mr. Raincloud Sir?"

"Yes sir." The CIA Director replied as he sat up in his chair and he looked at the President.

"Okay gentlemen, I guess that just about wraps it up here." President Cole announced as he clapped his hands together and rubbed them. "Mr. Manning, you'll remain a moment sir."

Manning looked stunned as he stared back at the angry looking President.

General Weidenbacher got up and he walked past the civilian advisor, snickering just loud enough for him to hear it. The General could not wipe the pleased expression off his face.

HAVANA, CUBA. 11:35 A.M. MONDAY, SEPTEMBER 23rd, 1996

Most of the heavy fighting had finally come to an end around the Presidential Palace parade grounds. The first report on the dead civilians came to Colonel Carlos Alvarez. Five thousand three hundred and twenty-seven civilians killed in the street heavy fighting. Eight hundred soldiers were killed in the battle as well. The Vice Presidente was taken over to the military hospital, and Colonel Alvarez was now waiting for the first report on his condition to come in.

Cuba Captains Calvo and Padilla were in his office, and they were going over the multitude of reports quickly flooding in from the units. Heavy fighting was still raging in many sections of Cuba, mostly from the capital and all the way down to Santa Clare. Captain Carlos Calvo informed Colonel Alvarez he was certain the fighting was light, because the outer provinces did not know what was taking place in the capital as yet.

Colonel Alvarez was concerned about how they were treating Fidel Castor's body. Captain Calvo assured him they left him fully clothed, and his body was placed in the grave and then carefully covered over with sand first and then dirt. This relieved most of Colonel Alvarez's fears, all he needed was for someone to find Castro's body, and then drag it through the streets, or even worse, steal it and use it to create more problems for him and his new revolution. The Colonel quickly thumbed through the many reports as his officers informed him how the fighting on Cuba was going. All but one he realized. Colonel Alvarez looked at Calvo and barked at him. "Captain Calvo! How come I don't have a fooking report from Major Cardona?"

This Major was a cousin of Doctor Jose Cardona, but he didn't share the same views on Cuba.

"That is because he has not checked in with you as yet I believe, Colonel Alvarez Sir?"

"I have no report from him, do you have one Captain?" Colonel Alvarez asked the Captain.

"I'll check for you Colonel." Captain Calvo replied as he looked through all of his reports.

Moments later. "He hasn't checked in Colonel. Could be he ran into stronger resistance, sir."

"I don't know what the reason is, but you better find out right now, Captain."

"Right away Colonel." Captain Calvo turned and he quick left the Colonel's new office.

He looked out of the window and saw the many crews working on removing the bodies from the palace grounds. The parade grounds looked like a beehive of activity with many armored vehicles moving around at will. The massive tank retrievers picked up the burnt out corpse of the huge war machines and dragged them away. Alvarez wanted everything looking normal, before the first American spy flights he was certain were on the way, flew overhead. He looked to where the mass grave was constructed. Everything looked good and if he did not know better, he would swear an Army decided to pitch tents. He smiled feeling sure he was going to keep the amount of death from the eyes of the Americans. He was going to keep every form of communications jammed for next three days, until everything could be made normal again.

Colonel Alvarez turned away from the window when Captain Calvo rushed in the office and started his report. "Colonel Alvarez Sir,

Major Cardona and his troops are entering the city at this moment, sir. He informed me he had not run into any hard resistance, but he maintained radio silence until he could speak directly to you, sir. He wished me to inform you he had something important to share with you, sir. He said he had to show you rather than tell you about what he found. He wants me to inform you to be ready to accompany him someplace, Colonel."

"He didn't tell you what this was about, Captain Calvo?" Alvarez snapped at the officer.

"No sir, he didn't say Colonel." Captain Calvo rumbled with a trace of anger in his tone.

"I wonder what the hell he's up to. Knowing him, he has probably found a naked woman hidden somewhere, and he wants to have some fun and games with her, the dom fool that he is." Colonel Alvarez laughed at his attempt at trying to be funny.

"If this is a fact, I wish to accompany you, sir." Captain Calvo said with a smirk on his lips.

"I had every intention of taking you along with me, Captain. I'll not keep anything from my trusted and loyal friends..."

Their conversation was interrupted when Major Cardona walked into the office and he instantly complained at the new Presidente of Cuba. "I had no idea the god dom civilians backed Castro so strongly, sir. I thought they would've offered us flowers and songs for liberating them from this dom madman. Just goes to show you cannot please everyone, sir."

Colonel Alvarez agreed with Major Cardona, and he asked him what his secret was all about.

"I cannot explain it for you sir, I have to show you the secret I was ordered to maintain, Colonel. Then, you can decide for yourself what we should do about it. It'll take us an hour for us to get to where this secret is housed sir. I have an armored vehicle fueled and waiting for us."

Colonel Alvarez looked to Captain Calvo and then he asked him with a snap in his voice. "Shall we get going and see what the Major has found for us, Captain?"

"By all means Colonel Alvarez." Captain Calvo said as he fell in line with the other officers.

The three of them walked down the stairs engaging in small talk. All the while, Major Cardona took in all the destruction caused by the fighting to the Palace, and the dead bodies he past lying in the streets. He turned to Colonel Alvarez and asked him with concern. "Castro?"

"Dead. He's one of many in the grave, sir." Alvarez pointed to the tents across the street.

"How many have died here, Colonel Alvarez?" Cardona asked the new President of Cuba.

"You don't really want to know the true number of all the dead here, Major Cardona Sir."

Major Cardona put a serious look on, and then he headed for the waiting vehicle in silence. When they were inside the vehicle the machine moved out, led by two others armored vehicles, and followed closely by two more. Each of them had twelve Cuban Marines riding inside them, for the safety of the new Presidente of Cuba.

After fifteen minutes of being bouncing around inside the hard riding machine, Alvarez snapped with anger. "By the grace of God Major Cardona, I don't like being kept in the dark like this sir. I'd like to know where I'm going, and what I'll find waiting there for me, sir."

Major Cardona merely smiled back at the angry looking Colonel, but he maintained his silence of what he had found.

"I warn you, you smiling jackal you, I better be impressed or I'll have my first execution."

"You'll be extremely impressed by it, of this much I promise you Colonel Alvarez, sir."

Colonel Alvarez shrugged and then he settled back and tried to make himself comfortable.

THE PENTAGON, WASHINGTON D.C. 11:45 A.M.
MONDAY, SEPTEMBER 23rd, 1996

The Chairman of the Joint Chiefs of Staff, General William Weidenbacher looked over the 201 personnel files of his soldiers. He knew where to start looking for the few special troopers he needed to train the Cuban exiles. He removed the first file and then read it.

Walker, Robert F., Corporal Third Marine Division, Third Forced Recon, Company A Age, 25 Weight; 210: Height; 6 foot 3 inches. Religion; Roman Catholic. Schooling: Twelfth year GED. Years in the active service: six. Military actions at this time: Operation Desert Storm.

The Chairman of the Joint Chiefs of Staff, quickly read over Corporal Robert Walker's past history and smiled to himself. This soldier was a much better enemy than he was an American soldier. Over the first five years of his service, he and another young Marine were in every bit of trouble any soldier could possibly get into and still remain alive, from stealing a General's air-conditioner and then installing it in their own tent, to molesting just about every adult woman who had ever lived in Hawaii where his outfit pulled R&R during their last war games experiment. There was a special note in the file that stated Corporal Robert Walker was not allowed back on the Island as a military man, or as a civilian either.

The General shook his head as he read on. Every fitness report written by the Commanding Officer of this livewire stated this soldier was one to keep an eye on. He was the type of trooper who would save a battalion of soldiers single handed, that special type of soldier every officer puts up with, because there was something that raised him above the other soldiers. A born leader who could never be a true leader because he was such a livewire.

The list of charges he read continued throughout the file, and they were staggering in their scope. But no matter how many charges were filed against him, this soldier always seemed to have the uncanny ability to beat them, another sign of a true future leader of soldiers. General Weidenbacher laughed as he read the other complaints, he felt he was reading a criminal report rather than a soldier's 201 file.

On one of the other reports in Corporal Walker's jacket, the writer, a Lieutenant John Slattery, had requested a General Court Marshal be convened for this soldier, but this request was rejected by the then Commanding Officer, with no further explanation given to the report or the request. General Weidenbacher realized someone had taken a special interest in this young soldier, and he must have taken it upon himself to look after him a little. The report from the Lieutenant went on, explaining the trouble Walker got into, the Lieutenant referred to this soldier as Road Kill.

"Ahhh, so this crazy bastard has a tag name does he?" General Weidenbacher mumbled to himself as he read on in the file. In this same report, the Lieutenant referred to a second soldier, as Walker's partner in crime, and he called this one the Mutt. The Chairman went on until he finally found this second man's name, Frank Hall, Private. General Weidenbacher put Corporal Walker's file aside for the moment, and he dug until he came up with Hall's file. The file was as thick as Walker's but was far worse in many of his actions.

This soldier was in the service seven months longer than Walker was, but he was still only a buck Private, not even First Class. Something was wrong with this one, and a little further examination of his 201 file, informed the General the reason why. It seemed every time this one increased his rate, he went off the base and then he got messed up and was busted right back to Private again. The General laughed as he grumbled at the new file. "Well, at least this one made use of his extra time in the service. Heaven help me, but I think I just found my trainers for the damn Cuban exiles." General Weidenbacher said while looking to the ceiling as if seeking word from higher up for an answer.

The General knew the reason he picked these two soldiers out to help with the training in case the boss gave the okay to invade Cuba.

These two troublemakers were most expendable, and from what he read in their 201's, it did not seem like anyone would miss them if they were killed in the invasion. General Weidenbacher searched his mind to see if he could put his finger on the many problems with the Cuban training. After a while he solved the riddle, it seemed the exiles were lacking the heart of a true soldier. The heart sometimes referred to as the killer instinct needed by any soldier, if he was to survive for any length of time on the battlefield. In war, only the fast and the dead will remain.

General Weidenbacher flipped the cover page of Corporal Walker's 201 file open for a second time and reread it again. He knew Walker was the soldier he was looking for, the type of soldier who had ice shoved up his ass, and it was the only way he could keep sliding in and out of trouble. General Weidenbacher was positive the young and troublesome soldier and his crazy friends were the answer to many of his problems, they would fill in all the answers from the exile Cubans who were just wasting their time with the training they were doing down in Florida.

General Weidenbacher laughed again as he thought these two soldiers would toughen up the Cuban exiles until they were ready to go at the enemy, even though they were fellow countrymen, and rip their hearts out and drink their blood, and then ask for some more. He threw Walker's file on top of the Mutt's after vowing he was going to find out why this one was called the Mutt. He was sure there must be an explanation, and he was curious enough to dig around until he found it.

He pressed the intercom and then ordered his secretary Mary to have the Liaison Officer report to his office immediately, as he looked over the Mutt's file again. He quickly realized where he had received his tag name from. In his 201 files, it was stated his father's nationality was listed as African American, and his mother's was listed as Italian American. "Sonofabitch, now I see where the dumb little fucker got his god damn tag name from, his father's black and his mother's white. A good name for the dumb dick like this one is, dammit."

Moments later Colonel Brendon McCormick came into the General's office out of breath.

"Relax a little Colonel McCormick Sir I have a special mission for you to carry out for me, sir. I want you to report over to Camp Lejeune immediately, and inform the Commandant there to have these two soldiers transferred over to a special unit I'm putting together. Their banner's going to be the 199th Marine Forced Recon unit." He threw the two 201 files across the desk at the other officer.

"You're making up a new unit, General? Something up sir?" he asked as he read the names.

"Yes Sir Colonel McCormick Sir, but I'll explain it to you when you return to Washington, sir. This new unit will be sent over to Fort Bragg for this special training I want for these soldiers, sir. I have two other soldiers I pulled from the Rangers special training station at Fort Bennings, Georgia sir, and another one from the Tenth Special Forces Unit from Fort Devens, Massachusetts, Colonel McCormick Sir. Here are their damn 201 files for you to enjoy reading, sir." General Weidenbacher handed the Colonel over the other three files.

Colonel McCormick scanned the names, and he was surprised by some of the picks.

"I see by the expression on your face you know some of these men, Colonel McCormick Sir?"

"I do indeed General Weidenbacher Sir, the one from Devens, Irvington, and the other shit from the Rangers, sir. Both of them should be shot rather than be given a special unit to operate from, sir. The black one's particularly bad, and he should be erased from the face of the earth before he's allowed to breed and bring forth a son for us to worry about, sir. The reason this one enlisted was because it was this or jail, sir. I think…"

"Colonel McCormick, I don't give a rat's ass what you might think about any of these damn soldiers, sir. I read their jackets myself sir, and know all their short comings, but these few damn shits fill the bill for me perfectly, sir. I'll give them a chance to prove themselves one last time before I straighten their asses out but good for themselves, sir. Get going, I need this unit set up PDQ, they might be going into action within the next two weeks, sir."

The Colonel snapped to attention, and he saluted the General sharply and headed off.

General William Weidenbacher picked up his receiver of the phone and placed a call to the Marine base stationed at Camp Lejeune. After the third ring, a young Lieutenant Bruce Leadbetter answered it with a growl. The General ignored his disposition and informed the Lieutenant of his future plans to build a unit combining a mix of soldiers from many different services, and one unit of Cuban soldiers presently training in Florida.

Lieutenant Leadbetter was in the service long enough to realize trouble coming at him, and with the mere mention of the Cubans in Florida, he instantly recognized where the fighting was going to take place. "Trouble in Cuba I take it General Weidenbacher, 'bout time we do something about that bearded wonder down there, sir."

"You're smart Lieutenant, don't be too fucking smart or you'll find yourself accompany these birds to that damn Island, sir. Prepare your problem children to be ready to move out today, sir. Their training starts as of tomorrow."

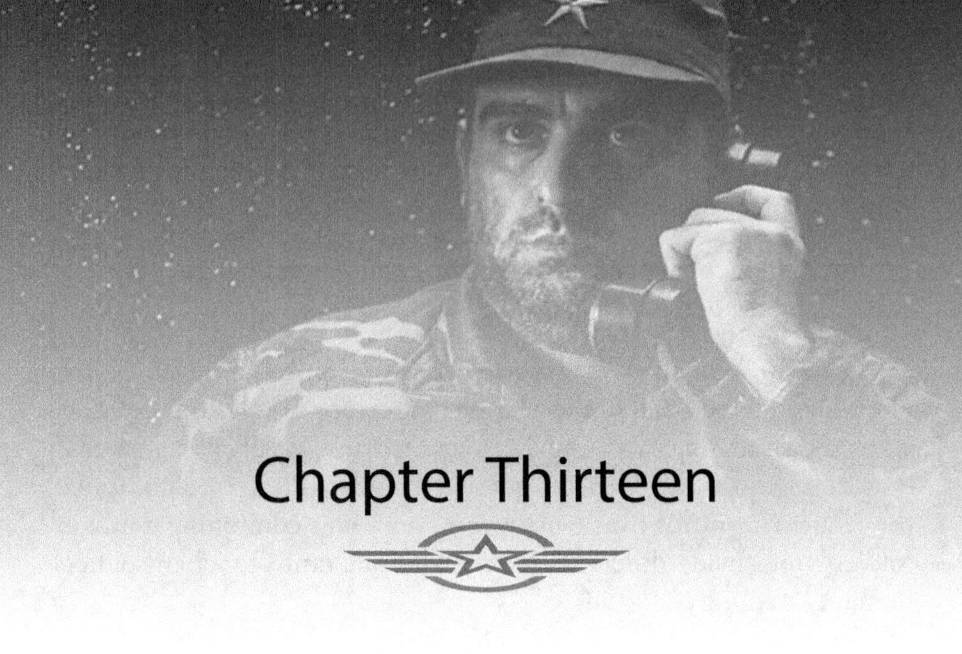

Chapter Thirteen

Lieutenant Bruce Leadbetter immediately sent for the requested two soldiers, Robert Walker and Frank Hall, they were both on base restriction for setting fire to his tent on their last maneuvers. The Lieutenant was trying to decide on their punishment when this order suddenly came about on him.

Corporal Robert Walker was the first one of the two to arrive at his office while wearing a smile and walking as cocky as he always acted.

"What's so fucking funny with you scumbag? I'm setting up a damn firing squad for your stinking ass right this minute, wise guy. Then we'll see just how fucking funny you really are, mister." Lieutenant Leadbetter warned the Corporal as he glared harshly at him for a moment.

"Hey Homes, just make damn sure they hit the target the first time, sir. Right here is my stinking heart you want me to trace it out for ya, sir." Walker pointed to his chest. "I'd hate like hell to be jitterbugging all over the stinking floor while waiting to die, sir."

"You're too funny around here mister. But I have something better than a fricking firing squad waiting for your stinking ass now, mister.

You've just been assigned to a new unit. You two shitbirds are ordered to report to Fort Bragg for some kind of special training crap. Let me warn you mister funny man, you might be engaging enemy forces within the next few weeks, and I'd be thinking about you fighting for your ass while I'm sitting in my damn office nice and safe and sound, buster. Now who is the fucking funny man around here, buddy?" Lieutenant Leadbetter warned Walker again, this time with an ugly sneer on his lips.

Before Walker could reply to the Lieutenant's last threats against him, the Mutt came into the office and Walker turned to greet him and both of the young soldiers' slapped hands together. The Mutt was holding his two hands low with their palms up, and Walker coming down with his as he quickly informed the Mutt of what was happening to them. "Hey Homes, it looks like we're getting our fucking asses offa this chicken shit base, man. It looks like they need some fricking real men to fight for them. The king of chicken shit here is gonna remain behind where his ass is safe and sound man."

The Mutt looked directly at the Lieutenant as he suddenly jumped up from his chair behind the desk and then he roared at the two young soldiers. "Chicken shit, I'll show you two shitbirds just who the hell are the chicken shit bastards around here, mister. I'll rip the both of you apart at the same fucking time, and then mix all the damn parts together on you two so you can't possibly reassemble yourselves again." Lieutenant Leadbetter started to make his way around the desk while hunching up his shoulders and preparing himself for a fight, but Corporal Robert Walker immediately put up his hands and he offered back to the angry acting Marine Officer.

"Hang in there for a sec. will ya Lieutenant Leadbetter Sir. You win sir I'll take your word for it sir. Look at me sir I'm shaking in my fricking boots from fear of you, sir. Besides Lieutenant Leadbetter Sir, we have to report to another stinking military unit, and how would it look if we both showed up there all bloody and bruised up, sir. Even thought it would be your blood we would be covered with, Lieutenant Leadbetter Sir." Corporal Robert Walker smirked at the angry looking and fuming Marine Lieutenant, showing absolutely no fear of him whatsoever.

Corporal Robert Walker's words stopped the fuming Lieutenant dead in his tracks, because he knew Walker was correct. He could not beat on them right now. The Lieutenant put his personal anger for these two soldiers on the back burner for the time being. He then pointed his finger directly at the both of them as if it was a dagger, and he hissed at the pair of them. "I don't know how the hell you two shitbirds have pulled this off on me, but you two scumbags have been saved again from me and my wrath. I warn the two of you, someday, somehow, you'll fall under my Command again. Then I'll finally get some of my satisfaction against the both of you one way or the other, especially for that little fire of yours. Get the hell out of my damn office before I have a change of heart, and go through with my threat of a fucking firing squad, dammit."

"But Lieutenant Leadbetter Sir, I was just getting kinda use ta this here fricking place, sir." Corporal Walker grinned back at him as he stared at the angry looking military officer.

"Get the fuck out of here and off my damn base before I kill the both of you dumb little shits!" Leadbetter barked as he hit Walker in the back with the pencil he sent flying.

They left the Lieutenant laughing with the Mutt adding to Walker. "Hey Homes, I never saw the Lieutenant so damn pissed off at us like he was this time around, man."

"Yeah, Homie he really turned a lovely shade of purple in there, didn't he Homes?" Walker moaned as he fell in line with the Mutt, and then they headed for where they were ordered to be.

"He sure did pal. Man, the stinking Lieutenant was sure dissing the living shit outta your stinking ass in there, Walker." The Mutt replied to Walker's last words to him with a grin.

"Dissing my ass, didn't you see the way he mad dogged your fucking ass in there, man. If he had his stinking way, he woulda chewed you up and shit you out of his ass." Walker laughed.

"He woulda fucking tried to do it to us, Homes. But the stinking service woulda had one less fucking set of stinking Railroad Tracks (slang for Lieutenant) in this man's Marines Corps to fucking worry about, if he tried to do it Homes." Corporal Frank Hall warned Walker as he suddenly turned serious with him, and then he faced his longtime friend for a moment, while he waited for him to say something else. When he didn't, the Mutt added to his words at Walker.

"Hey man, you gotta calm down some there, Homes. I was fucking round a little with your stinking mind on ya for a minute, that's all man. Hey Walker, where the fuck do you think we're gonna end up this time around, buddy?" the Mutt asked Walker as he stared back at him now.

"Beats the crap outta my ass dog man, all I know is I heard some stinking scuttlebutt about something happening down in Cuba a little while ago, man. But I really think all the fricking trouble is more in Bosnia, and that dump might be heating up on us again man. Who the fuck knows buddy? Who the fuck really gives a flying shit about it anyway man. All I know is that we're finally getting our lazy asses the hell offa this damn military base for the time being, man. That'll give the stinking dumb shit back there a god damn chance to fricking cool off a little on us man." Walker complained to his friend as they continued heading for their next destination.

"You're on the beam with that line of shit, man." The Mutt snapped back as the pair of soldiers banged fists again, and the Mutt added. "Who gives a shit where the fuck we end up man. Just as long as we're together and protecting each utters backs as always Homes."

"You got that right, I guess we better get some of our stinking packing done for ourselves before it's too late, old buddy. I hope this thing isn't just another game of mind fuck around here that the Lieutenant's playing on our damn asses again, man. Getting our hopes built up, just so he can pull the stinking rug out from under us at the last moment, and then he changes our damn orders on us again, and we're still stuck back here again, man. Just as we thought we're getting off this stinking base for a little while, and get the fuck outta his hair as well, Mutt." Corporal Walker complained at the Mutt as he flashed him one of his quick smiles.

"No way in hell on that one happening to us here, Homes. The big number one prick back there doesn't want our stinking asses hanging around him for any longer than we hafta be in his damn puss, Homes." The Mutt offered Walker with a smirk, and a wink of his eye.

The two young soldiers walked back to their barracks laughing and joking with each other, neither one of the two young soldiers showing the least bit concern over where they might have just been sent off to, or who they might be fighting with in the near future. Nothing bothered the two young and confident soldiers as they walked on so proudly. They both entered the barracks together and they immediately checked in with fire watch trooper, and they informed him they were ordered to pack up their gear for a quick move out of the other military base.

The barrack fire watch soldier demanded to see a copy of their new orders before he would allow either of them to enter the building on the off time period. But when Corporal Robert Walker threatened to take the young soldier apart with his bare hands, if he continued to bust his horns like he was doing, the fire watch soldier finally relented. He allowed the two soldiers to enter the barracks to pack up their belonging and gear. But he kept a close eye on them though, hanging around them all the while they packed up their stuff. The security of the barracks rested solely on the fire watch soldier, when the Master at Arms was out of the building, along with the rest of the soldiers who used the barracks as their home. The Master at Arms was called over to the barracks Commander for a conversation with him.

The two young soldiers packed up their gear as quickly as they could, and then they went over and collected their back pay from the Paymaster wasting his life marking time off on the calendar until he reached the big Two Oh retirement time. Then the two soldiers headed for the debarkation center on the base, and they waited for their names to be called out. Both soldiers had orders Lieutenant Leadbetter handed them in their hands, and they were ordered to give them over to the officer on duty at the train station. He read the orders, and told them where to stand. After about an hour, they heard their train coming for them. The Mutt griped at Walker. "If you got my stinking ass involved in another god damn dumb mission man, I'm gonna fuck you up real fricking bad on this one man, I really swear it this time Homes."

Corporal Robert Walker laughed at his long time friend as the duty officer made certain they knew which train to get on. The Corporal spat angrily on the train platform as his final act of defiance against the service, before leaving the military base for what he hoped was the last time in his life. He had no idea what he was heading for, and he cared even less about it. The train jolted in motion as he looked around for the drinking car with the Mutt in tow behind him. It was going to take them less than an hour to get over to Fort Bragg which shared the massive military base with Pope Airforce Base in North Carolina.

Corporal Walker knew his destination already, and he was really pissed they had to ride all the way there on the rail to get to their new base. The least he thought the service could do for them was to put them in some go fasts (jets), and get them to the new base a lot quicker than this, instead of sticking them on this metal snake bound to the iron rails on the ground. Walker was steamed, because he felt he deserved better treatment from the service he so proudly worked for so long. He was in the service for over five years, and he wanted the respect he felt was due him. He was thinking he was going to spend the rest of his life in the service, so when he retired, he would have a good pension to live off of for the rest of his days, and he could always do something else to make some extra money for himself. In the back of his mind he was thinking more lately about getting married and rising a family, but he did not dare talk to the Mutt about his ideas, for fear of what he would say about them.

THE PENINSULA OF GUANAHACABIBES, CUBA.
MONDAY 1:30 P.M. CUBAN TIME, SEPTEMBER 23rd, 1996

The heavy armor vehicle carrying the new Presidente of Cuba, Colonel Carlos Rafael Fernandez Alvarez, along with Captain Carlos Francisco Vega Calvo, and Major Pipi Enrique Cardona, reached its destination. During the last fifteen minutes of their long journey, Colonel Alvarez did nothing but complain at the other two soldiers for allowing Major Cardona to talk him into leaving the capital city so quickly after his victory over Fidel Castro and his foul Administration and supporters.

During that time, Major Cardona assured Colonel Alvarez he had done the right thing by coming along with him. But he never once let on to their final destination, or what they would find once they had arrived at the location. All the Major kept saying was it was the find of the century, long ago buried on Cuban soil by the fool commanding the people. The small convoy rumbled to a halt at La Bajada, the center of the top of the peninsula.

Colonel Alvarez was the second one to crawl out of the machine while stretching and lifting his arms over his head as he let out with an angry growl while enjoying the fresh air. "Okay Major Cardina, I allowed you to drag me out here to the middle of nowhere to view this extraordinary find. Where is it? I see nothing here."

"Please Colonel, follow me and you'll see for yourself, why you had to come here, sir."

Major Cardona walked towards the water, and when they could see into it, the excited Major pointed out the large concrete covers five feet below the crystal clear water. The six covers were hard to locate at first because all the marine life making the concrete slabs their home.

"I see two of what you're calling concrete slabs, Major. What the hell are they covering sir?"

"Silos sir, that bastard Castro had constructed the underwater missile silos long before the nosy Americans had located the Russian missiles stored on our Island back in 1962, sir."

Colonel Alvarez and Captain Calvo leaned further out over the water and they tried to locate the other four covers. Captain Calvo picked up and then pointed out another slab, and Alvarez located two more before he turned to the Major. "I see five, but I shall take your word there is six of the god dom things, Major Cardona. I must ask what good do these god cursed silos do empty? They are empty am I correct, Major?"

"For the time, the silos are empty Colonel Alvarez." The Major said confidently with a smirk.

"What do you mean by that remark, Major? There's no way we can possibly get missiles from Russia to fill them. Not after the way Castro has allowed relations between Russia and ourselves to deteriorate."

"Colonel Alvarez Sir, what makes you think we'll have to rely on the blasted Russians..."

"Don't play any games with me Major Cardona Sir, I'm thoroughly exhausted and my sense of humor was lost long ago on this cursed day. If you have something more to show me then do it while you still have my full attention, and I don't throw you into the sea for the fish to nibble on." Colonel Alvarez gave a tired laugh, as he tapped his foot on the rail that stopped them from falling into the water.

"I'm sorry for the delay if you will follow me, I'll be pleased to show you what has me so excited about this discovery, Colonel Alvarez." Major Cardona walked over to a pile of sand dunes. There the concerned soldiers came out before a pair of heavy steel doors. Major Cardona picked up a length of pipe and he rapped loudly on one door, and after the fifth hit the door slowly opened. Colonel Alvarez leaned forward and looked into the great void. The air smelled stale but he saw lights. There was a set of steps off to one side, with a wide slide on the other.

"You may go down if you please, Colonel Alvarez Sir. I have some men stationed downstairs protecting our discovery, sir."

Colonel Alvarez lead the way for the other officers with him, the concrete walls he leaned on were damp to the touch. Ocean water had seeped through the concrete long ago. The constant whine of a sump pump was clearly heard inside the bunker. When they went down the steps, the room leveled out, and the soldiers stood in a vast opening. To one side of the massive room were a long bank of computers and many stacks of wires, and a good number of file cabinets in the room. The rest of the room was taken up by six massive cylinder shaped covered objects.

Alvarez rushed over and examined one of the cylinders and then he cried to the Major. "Major Cardona, please tell me what I think I'm seeing is not what I am seeing, if that makes any sense."

Major Cardona replied as the Colonel's words confused him for a brief moment. "Huh?"

The excited Colonel stood by one of the massive cylinders, his hands feeling the object hidden by the heavy canvas. They explored the huge cylinder until they came across a fin. "They are, they are god dom missiles. What type are they Major?"

Major Cardona removed a clipboard and then read from it. "Presidente, they are Russian SS-19 Model 3 missiles, sir."

"They're some of their new missiles you say, sir?" Colonel Alvarez asked the smiling Major.

"They were built in the year 1979, Presidente Alvarez Sir." The Major said proudly to him.

"How the hell did they ever get here on Cuban soil, Major?" Alvarez asked in a stunned tone.

"They were smuggled onto the Island during the 1980s. Castro was instrumental in getting the missiles and Russian workers here to covertly construct the underwater silos. From what I read about their efforts, the missiles were smuggled onto the Island in a number of cargo ships. The missiles were broken down to their smallest pieces and then reconstructed once they were smuggled onto our Island, sir."

"The warheads, what about the god dom warheads, Major Cardona? How many are there, and are they nuclear warheads, sir?"

"Sir, the missiles were constructed in late 1979, there are six MIRV, (Multiple Independent Reentry Vehicles) with a yield of 250 Kiloton apiece, each weigh around one thousand five hundred pounds, thus making it nearly impossible to enable them to launch from a cold start..."

"Meaning what to me, Major Cardona?" Colonel Alvarez snapped hotly, not knowing what the Major meant by cold start.

"Meaning to you Colonel Alvarez Sir that the missile requires a fifteen minute heat up time, before it can be launched at its target, sir. Thus, giving us plenty of time to abort the mission if we so choose before the launch is completed, sir."

"Also giving the hated Americans the time to get at our missiles before they're launched at them, sir." Colonel Alvarez suddenly snarled as he diverted his gaze from the Major's grinning face to the missile again.

"Quite right Colonel Alvarez Sir. So we'll be forced to make up our minds, and start the heat up of the god dom missiles, long before the god cursed Americans know we're preparing to launch our missiles at whatever target we have picked out for them, sir. Err... do you wish me to continue on with the report I have put together for you at this time, Colonel Alvarez, sir?"

Colonel Alvarez gave him a mere wave of the hand to continue, and the Major began his report again. "Sir, the missile has a range of five thousand, four hundred nautical miles, putting Washington and other major American cities within range. The missile is propelled by a liquid fuel, the other reason we need a hot firing..."

"I don't give a god dom about that shit Major Cardona Sir. Now, I have the means to force the hated Americans to deal with us whether they want to or not, sir. I want to know how we're going to get the god dom missiles into their silos without the Americans picking up what we're doing first, Major. This is great." Colonel Alvarez moaned as he rubbed his hands on the ice cold metal skin, and then he added to his words. "Uncover them I want to see all of it. Uncover all of the fooking thing. This is great. I guess I must thank Castro for his secret it enables Cuba to become a world power overnight, sir. The fool, I cannot understand why he did not play this card while he was alive and trying to bend the American's will to his favor. Ha, I'm glad he did not." Alvarez looked at the Major until he shrugged to the Colonel's question.

The soldier Alvarez left in charge of the radio came in the cellar, and he instantly stopped in his tracks as he stared at the white missiles with the red markings as they were uncovered.

Colonel Alvarez saw him enter and snapped at him. "What is it now Private? Trouble?"

"Colonel Alvarez Sir, I received word from Havana, Sergeant Regueiro reports rioters fled to their homes, and the supporters of our revolution begun to come out. They are taking revenge on the troublemakers, killing many as they fled from the parade grounds. Sergeant Regueiro has reported the city was flooded with sporadic weapon fire, and his troops had to engage a major threat. I'm afraid one thing he stated is going to upset you..." He stared at Alvarez for a second, as if begging him not to make his report to him.

Colonel Alvarez quickly lost his patience and he growled at the young soldier. "Don't make me ask you for a second time."

"Sorry sir, Sergeant Regueiro has reported the bastard son of Castro, Justo, was found by some of the supporters of the new revolution, and they savagely put him to death by hanging him in the market square before Sergeant Regueiro, or any of his troops with him had a chance to act to it."

The Colonel was staggered as if just struck across his face with the back of a hand. He rubbed his chin and drew in a huge gulp of air, and then he growled at the young Private. "God dommit, god dom bastards! Why in the holy name of God did the foul fools have to kill Justo? He was not like his father. He was a good man who was working against Castro in every manner. He was instrumental in getting me vital information, to make my revolution a success. I liked that man, and I planned to find a position in my government for him." He had to sit on a table to get control and the soldier in him came to the surface. He glared at the messenger. "His body! What has Sergeant Regueiro done with Justo's body? Did he take command of it, god dommit?"

"Colonel Alvarez Sir, the Sergeant has reported he had the body in his custody. He brought it to the Palace for safe keeping until he found out what you wanted done with it, Colonel Alvarez."

The Colonel suddenly stomped around in a circle as he snarled. "Madre de Dios, I want you to get on that cursed radio and give Sergeant Regueiro these orders, mista. You'll inform him these orders come directly from me, and he's to carry them out to the letter. Have him prepare Justo's body for a full military burial. He'll be treated as the first hero to die for the new cause. You're also to order Sergeant Regueiro to clear out the parade ground at once or all civilian fools. I don't want anyone doing nothing there. He's free to make arrests of anyone who he believes to be a Castro supporter, or any of the other foul troublemakers. He's further free to make arrests of anyone loitering on the streets looking to create problems for my Presidency as well. I want everyone to get used to staying in their homes until we're in complete control of the entire city and the rest of Cuba, and we know how the god dom Americans and the rest of the world are going to react to our new revolution..."

Their conversation was interrupted by a second soldier who stood at the top of the steps to the bunker and called out in an excited voice. "Colonel Alvarez Sir, contrails sir! Contrails, high up in the sky, and they're not from any of our aircraft, sir."

Colonel Alvarez, Captain Calvo and Major Cardona immediately rushed over to the door and they stared in the sky, long vapor streams were clearly visible high overhead, and they were heading from north to south across the entire Island. Colonel Alvarez turned to Captain Calvo and barked at him. "Americans?"

"I'd be more than willing to bet a year's pay on it, Colonel. What did you expect from them Colonel Alvarez Sir? We knew it was only a matter of time before they started some of their dom spy flights over our country to try and out what is happening in our country, sir." Captain Calvo checked his watch, it was two thirty p.m., they had been downstairs for over an hour and he added. "I'm rather surprised it has taken so long for the first flights to begin, sir."

"What type of plane do you think it might be?" Colonel Alvarez asked the Captain with much concern lacing his tone, as he stared at the soldier while waiting for his replied to him.

"Who knows, could be one of their god dom U-2 planes like the one we shot down during the 62' missile crisis, but I seriously doubt the hated Americans would commit another mistake such as that one was, sir. If I was forced to bet on it, I'd place my money on that plane being one of their SR-91 aircraft we heard about."

"Is there any chance of us shooting the god dom things down, so as to serve as a warning to the Americans to stop these unwanted flights over our country, Captain?" Colonel Alvarez inquired.

"Not a chance in hell of that happening sir, that plane can easily outrun any of our missiles we have in our arsenal, sir. It can probably outrun any missile made, sir. The only way we could possibly get it, is by waiting until it ran out of fuel, and forced to land, and then we get it on the ground, sir. But why would we want to attack the plane in the first place sir? I thought we were going to try and approach the Americans in the near future, sir. You cannot approach someone who you just shot down one of their spy planes on, sir." Captain Carlos Calvo offered sarcastically, adding a sarcastic laugh to show how much of a chance there was of that happening. The two officers watched until the twin streaks slowly began to break up in the bright, cloudless afternoon sky.

"That plane has to be over Honduras already, sir. Its speed is astonishing." Calvo offered.

"I care nothing for the accomplishments of the Americans, sir. Private, as I said just before this last interruption." Colonel Alvarez turned back to the young soldier and then added to his words. "I want you to inform Sergeant Regueiro to clear the streets of all unessential personnel, mista. This way, we can stop any rioting from reoccurring. I want a peaceful night, so the foul American spy planes will have nothing to report back to their god dom leaders with. Inform the Sergeant he has the power to use deadly force if he deems it necessary to accomplish this last order. I want, no I demand the dom streets of Havana be peaceful tonight, even if I have to kill every god cursed troublemaker who dares to venture out on this upcoming god dom evening.

"I need full control over the entire city! I cannot believe there are so many god dom ungrateful bastards who live in the capital city. You would think they would be glad we set them free of Castro's rule. Look at how the god dom fools have repaid us, by making trouble, and giving the god dom Americans something to hang their foul hats on. I want some shore battery supports and military bases set on full alert. I don't need any Americans, or the god dom Cuban exiles they so love, sneaking a force of hated soldiers on the shore of Cuba, and then join forces with these pack of troublemakers disrupting the Island. Get going Private!" Colonel Alvarez began to ramble some, but he was smart enough to catch himself, before he went too far, and he ended up sounding just like Castro did.

THE PENTAGON, WASHINGTON D.C.MONDAY SEPTEMBER 23rd, 2:45 P.M.

Colonel Edwards came marching into General Weidenbacher's office with his cover tucked neatly under his arm, and he handed him a stack of photos just taken by the SR-91 spy flight over the Island of Cuba. The high altitude pictures clearly showed hundreds of bodies dotting the parade grounds of the Palace and surrounding area, with military personnel loading the dead into trucks and hauling them off.

General Luther (Nails) Claiborne, the large black officer from Alabama looked over the General's shoulder at some of the photos. He pointed to the sea of military tents erected just to the side of the Palace parade grounds and he asked. "What the hell do you make of these? Could Castro have pulled up so many of his troops so quickly?"

"Luther, I don't think the troops are pitching the tents on the parade grounds. Look, there's a road between where they're setting up and the marching area. Strange, I'm sure if Castro was still in Command of the Island, they would set up on the grounds. Even if the asses are the troops who pulled off the coup of the century, why aren't they setting up on the marching area? It doesn't make any sense to me, dammit. If I just pulled off a coup, and I took over control of the country, I'd want my damn troop's right under my nose, not a few blocks away from where I'd need them. No Luther, I think something smells and it ain't a pail of fish or dirty diapers, sir." General Weidenbacher went over the pictures with a powerful magnifying glass, paying close attention to the tents and the troops milling about nearby. He stopped and stared at one position.

"Whatdaya got going there, General?" General Claiborne asked his Commanding Officer.

"Don't know for sure sir. Here, you take a look see and tell me if you see what I think I see."

General Claiborne chuckled as he took the 8x12 picture and the looking glass, and studied the area indicated to him by General Weidenbacher. As he carefully studied them, he offered."Err... it looks like an open truck with some bodies making its way under one of the tents, Billy."

"That's what I saw Luther. What do you think they're up to under the damn tents, sir?"

"There's some more Bill. If you go a little further up the photo and off to the left of that parked truck, you're gonna see something that's gonna make you think you have just traveled back in time, and the Nazis are operating in the world again, sir. Here, take a look at this shit, General."

The Chairman of the Joint Chiefs of Staff followed the line of Luther's finger on the photo until he stopped, and he instantly drew in his breath and exhaled with a hiss. "Oh God no, not again, am I looking at an open pit being filled with dead bodies, sir?"

"Fraid so, those tents weren't set up to house any troops, sir. They were set up to keep us and the rest of the world from knowing how bloody this latest coup was, General Weidenbacher Sir." General Claiborne hissed as he started to pace the room. He was one of the few men who was still alive, who was with the leading elements of the liberating American troops who first entered the Auschwitz-Bickenau Nazi murder camp in Poland.

General Weidenbacher saw the hurt and pain etched in his eyes. He remembered reading his report when he picked him for the position of Chief of Staff of the Airforce. The report stated how Claiborne lost control as he entered the death camp, and he soiled himself as he broke down and cried over a body of a small starved child not even five years old yet. He remembered the report filed by his Commander, requesting

General Claiborne immediately be relieved of his present duty, and sent back to the rear. The experience devastated him, but when he was told he was relieved, General Claiborne refused to leave. General Weidenbacher remembered some of the conversations he had with him over this subject, to discover why it so devastated him.

General Claiborne told him he had seen death in the south where children, black children, and old black woman and men were allowed to starve to death, because no one cared about them. The adult men were making a living and fighting off segregation. General Weidenbacher remembered Claiborne's sad boast he witnessed death before, but never on the scale he witnessed in Europe. To think civilized men sat around on their thumbs and did nothing while so many millions of guiltless, innocent souls were tortured then murdered in cold blood, still baffled his General.

"You okay Luther? You want a drink or something sir?" Weidenbacher asked him.

General Claiborne stopped his pacing, but the sad expression was still etched on his face as he looked back at General Weidenbacher, and then he snapped at him angrily. "Yeah! I think I need something to drink if you don't mind, General Weidenbacher Sir."

General Weidenbacher removed a bottle of scotch from his bottom drawer, and he poured a good hit for both of them. General Weidenbacher saluted General Claiborne with his glass, but he wasn't to be appeased. "Christ Billy, am I missing something with this big picture around here, sir? Why is it always the damn innocent who have to pick up the tab for the aggression of a few? Haven't we learned a thing over all these years? Look at what happened and is still happening in Europe, in Bosnia sir. Hundreds no correct that sir, thousands of civilians put to the sword because they were different. Believed in another God, now here in Cuba, it looks like the civilians are going to be forced to pick up the tab for freedom again. I can't believe it sir. I wish there was some way to preserve the terrible things I saw in that camp.

"If there was, we could have marched the next generation of asses who wanted to act like Hitler through the nightmare he created. Force them to see what some asshole let loose on the innocent of this earth, and see if they were still interested in continuing their march of death to hell. If they were, then they shouldn't be allowed to leave that nightmare alive. Arr... I don't know what I mean anymore. How could anyone accept such a thing without fighting against it with his last breath? I don't think we learned a thing from that war, sir. I wished every mother's son and daughter saw what I did, before it was allowed to be erased from the face of the earth as if it never took place. I think everyone should've to walk on the destroyed remains of that camp once a year, every year. If it could stop one ass from repeating what that asshole did. Then the death of those Jews wasn't in vain." General Claiborne plopped down in a seat, and put his hand to his eyes to hide he was shaken by the photos.

General Weidenbacher moved to the front of his desk while resting his hand on the man's back, and he offered him in a much calmer tone. "Say Luther, you saw enough death in your life for three men to live through, sir. Try man to erase it from your mind if you can, sir. Look General Claiborne, I need your head clear on this one sir. Are you going to be there for me, soldier?"

Luther looked up and replied. "Only death could erase what I saw from my mind, sir."

"Perhaps another drink sir?" General Weidenbacher offered to refill his glass for him.

Luther held out his glass and he refilled it. "What's our next move my old friend?"

"We should inform the President of what we found in Cuba, sir. Maybe he'd be willing to react in force, before anymore civilians pay for what a few assholes want, sir."

"You're right." General Weidenbacher grabbed the phone and asked Mary to get the President on the horn.

Chapter Fourteen

GUANAHACABIBES PENINSULA, CUBA

Colonel Carlos Alvarez stared at a fifty five foot long, thirty six inch wide, white missile and its warheads resting on the transport carriers. Their presence offered pure, controlled power, and they made him feel like he stood on the same field as the Americans. They would soon be forced to listen to him now he possessed the power to destroy much of their country before they could act against him. He thought if the Americans were content to slowly destroy his country by keeping the embargo in place, he might as well expedite Cuba's death, and in hastening it, take some of America to the grave with him. All the while these thoughts of power and confrontation flooded his mind as he ran his hands slowly over the cool metal skin of the missile. Rubbing it much the same way a young man would massage the coat of wax he had rubbed on his first car's finish. His thoughts were interrupted by Major Cardona.

"Err... uhummm sir." Major Cardona cleared his throat to get the Colonel's attention.

Colonel Alvarez broke his trance by shaking his head rapidly, and then he turned to face the younger officer and said. "You want to speak, speak to me now Major Cardona Sir!"

Major Cardona let out his breath as he offered. "Colonel, moments before you spoke of how we would get these missiles to their launch position, under the very noses of the Americans, sir."

"You have a solution to my new dilemma, Major Cardona Sir?" Alvarez asked him.

"No, my Presidente, but I do know how Fidel Castro's people planned to get this done, sir."

Colonel Alvarez's eyes narrowed as he glared and then he hissed at his officer. "This is twice now Major Cardona. Don't keep me waiting any longer this time, sir." Colonel Alvarez had not taken any notice of how he was acting, but he was the only one who did not. The other soldiers and officers felt he was acting the same way Castro had. Showing no patience with his subordinates and ordering the deaths of civilians as if ordering men in the fields to kill locusts.

"Err... I'm sorry sir, but I thought you were well aware of the documents we located inside this installation, Colonel Alvarez Sir. They show Castro had organized a solution..."

"Obviously he did Major Cardona, but obviously I have not been privy to this god dom information, or I wouldn't be asking you for it, sir. I wouldn't find myself waiting for you to finish, and get on with what you have to offer me. Major, if you cannot get to the point more quickly, I'll have you relieved of your duties, and find someone who can fill me in on what you have uncovered here, sir. If you wish to enjoy your position, I suggest you inform me of all you discovered here, before I lose my patience and take measures in dealing with you, sir." Colonel Alvarez was hot and he glared angrily at Major Cardona as he placed his hands on his hips, and then he waited for him to make his report to him.

Major Cardona bowed slight and then he continued. "I'm sorry for wasting your time sir..."

"Not sorry enough I see because you continue to waste my time needlessly, Major. I don't need niceties here. I need answers, and if you'll not give them to me, I'll find someone else who will. Report you son of a dog, before I..." Colonel Alvarez caught himself, he looked at the faces and he cleared his throat and continued. "Err... you'll excuse me please, Major. It has been a trying few days, and I'm extremely tired. Perhaps, I realized how tired I am. Major Cardona, I'm sorry for my reaction, sir. I hope you'll be kind enough to forgive me for it, and overlook the intolerable way I spoke to you." This time it was hw who bowed towards Major Cardona. No one realized he already made up his mind to have Major Cardona replaced. He convinced himself anyone named Cardona, was not to be trusted when it came down to the future of Cuba.

"Sir, think nothing of it please. I realized how much pressure you're under since the beginning of the new revolution, Colonel Alvarez. If this is your worst lapse in judgment, I shall consider myself extremely lucky, sir."

Everyone inside the bunker laughed, glad all the tension was suddenly relieved for them, even if it was only for the time being though. They realized Colonel Carlos Alvarez did irreparable damage to his leadership, and his position in the new revolution before them.

He stopped laughing as he focused his eyes on the Major's face and realized he never laughed with the others, and said. "Major Cardona, I believe you had a report to complete for me, sir?"

"Yes sir, we searched the entire interior of this bunker, and we came up with documents on how Castro planned to get the missiles in the silos. Each of the silos has a protective ring which is raised when anyone wants to get in them, without having the water enter the tubes, sir." Major Cardona easily picked up the boredom in Colonel Alvarez's eyes, and knew he was not interested in particulars, only the heart of the manner, how Castro was going to get the missiles in the silos without the move being detected by the Americans.

Again, Major Cardona bowed slightly towards the new Presidente of Cuba as he said. "Colonel, it seems Castro planned a number of military actions throughout the Middle East and elsewhere to cover his move."

Colonel Alvarez's eyes showed the questions that he had not asked of the Cuban Major yet.

"Colonel Alvarez Sir, Castro prepared quick strikes in Israeli, Lebanon, Syria and Jordan..."

"Why was he planning to make problems in that region of the world for, Major? They're talking peace there, and I believe it'd be rather hard to stop this motion towards peace, sir."

"Castro planned to cash in on the anti-rhetoric aimed against the Arabs, the United States and the Jew nation, even though everyone in the Middle East had been speaking of peace lately, sir. Peace is the last thing any of these worthless fools really want. Add this to the strong anti-Arab feelings of the Americans after the Trade Center bombing, the bombing of their railways, and the erratic ways of the Arab Muslims, sir.

"Their capability of creating anger wherever they go in the United States, has kept this anger alive and well in the United States. Castro has found a way to capitalize on these ill feelings, sir. For the past few years, Fidel Castro had trained a number of our soldiers in the ways and mannerisms of the Jews and the Arabs. The soldiers speak Hebrew and Arabic better than most of the Jews and Arabs do, sir. From what I have read, it seems these special soldiers had surgical procedures done to alter their appearances, to look just like Jews and Arabs."

The reports made all in the bunker attentive to his words as the Major continued with what he had located hidden inside of the concrete bunker. "Colonel Alvarez, as I stated. Castro had planned to create a number of diversions in these countries, so he could work in the open and getting the missiles inside the silos. Other papers state once the missiles were set, he planned to launch them at the United States without warning, sir."

Stunned at what he just heard said from his Major, Colonel Alvarez barked at him. "Why was he planning to do that for Major? It would've surely drawn the wrath of the United States down upon all of us living in Cuba, sir."

"Sir, other reports state he planned to attack at the same time the United States and Russia were doing their talking peace. When Russia relented and they gave into the Americans, and they surrendered all her nuclear weapons, Castro and a few Russians aimed to launch the missiles, hopefully, causing the Russians to launch theirs, rather than talk to the Americans, sir."

There was some mumbling inside of the bunker by the other soldiers, but Major Cardona ignored it as he continued with his words. "As you can see, this didn't take place, sir. It seems Castro couldn't get the Russian technicians to Cuba to get the missiles set and ready to fly. This is why he and the Russian leaders were having so much trouble, and what led to the breaking of relations between Russia and Cuba. Castro was willing to sacrifice the entire Island of Cuba to force Russia to attack the United States."

"The old fool, now I'm glad he's dead sir." Captain Calvo hissed his hands balled up in fists.

Colonel Alvarez gave Captain Calvo a harsh look before ordering the Major to continue with his report. "Very well sir. Fidel Castro planned these attacks in the countries I mentioned…"

"Is there any information in this bunker explaining what the attacks consisted of, Major Cardona?" Colonel Alvarez asked him angrily.

"Colonel Alvarez, Castro planned to have these special groups of soldiers educated as Arabs, to attack the Club Med vacation area inside Israel situated in Haifa on the Mediterranean, sir."

"What the hell do you mean they were going to attack this resort, Major? It's not a military target. Why the hell would he attack a non-military target? It's not the Cuban way to wage war against other nations by attacking their civilian population, sir." Colonel Alvarez offered.

"Sir, Castro planned to do whatever was necessary to accomplish his plan, sir."

"Madre de Dios, what the hell would these soldiers done to this Club Med resort, sir?"

"Colonel Alvarez Sir, the strike force orders were to hit the civilians hard and kill as many of them as was possible, before leaving the resort. Each attacker has a grenade and they were ordered to take out the pin if the soldier was wounded, so his body would be blown apart, forever hiding his true identity from them."

"Why the hell would they do that for, Major?" Alvarez asked in a stunned tone.

"Evidence sir, Castro wanted to leave a few of the Jewish civilians left alive, to report Arabs must have attacked the resort, sir. The soldiers were ordered to rape the women and then torture them before putting them to death. Their orders were to kill the males in the most hideous of ways, to hack them to death then set them ablaze and dismember them, sir. The attackers were further ordered to do anything possible to cause the public of other countries to raise their voices against the Arabs. The attack against the Israeli resort was to be carried out first, and then Castro would send out his supposed Jew attackers to hit other targets in the Arab nations.

"Most of the attacks were going to be leveled against Arab civilians, in, or around Mosques. He believed attacking the Arab Mosques would force all Arabs to band together, and then go after Israel with all their fury, thus forcing the hated Americans to place their god cursed attention and troops towards the Middle East. This diversion would enable Castro to move the missiles out of the bunker and into the silos, sir."

Colonel Alvarez let out his breath in a low whistle as he milled over Fidel Castro's plans.

Captain Calvo stepped a little closer to one of the missiles, and then he asked the confused looking Colonel. "What are we going to do with the devil's firecrackers, sir?"

Alvarez smiled over the Captain's remark, and then he replied. "By the Holy Father, what do you suggest we do with the dom things, Captain Calvo?"

"That's an easy question to answer, I suggest we ready the god dom missiles for installation into their silos, and then we'll inform the Americans we have the god dom missiles in our control, and we're not to be messed around with." Captain Calvo wiped the sweat from his brow with the sleeve of his uniform shirt.

Major Cardona shoved Captain Calvo away from the missiles as he grumbled at the new leader of Cuba. "Colonel Alvarez Sir, Captain Calvo's wrong, dead wrong sir. I say we destroy the terrible weapons and never use them under any circumstances. Never consider for an instant, using them in any manner, sir. Cuba was once used in the past as a puppet on a string for the loathsome Communists by the threat of these god cursed weapons. I say Cuba will never survive another attempt to threaten the United States with them.

"As for allowing the hated Americans to know we have such deadly weapons in our possession, this is foolishness, pure foolishness. If we inform them we're in possession of these God awful weapons so close to their country, sir. They Americans would immediately set all their military resources in gear for one thing, and one thing only. To destroy the weapons, and take Cuba with them, I don't think they'd hesitate for one second. I say we destroy these god dom things and get back to what our revolution was truly about. We're speaking about opening peaceful talks with the United States, getting them to lift their god dom embargo, and then openly trade with Cuba and her people. That is what we should be concerning ourselves about, not these god dom weapons of mass death, sir."

Colonel Alvarez held up his hand to silence the excited Major, and then he grumbled at him. "Major Cardona, think of your worthless words you offer me for a moment, sir. You just stated we want to open talks with the United States, and get them to lift the embargo. Well Major, what better way do you know to open up talks than to aim our newly discovered missiles at the fools to get their attention. If the foolish Americans realize we have nuclear armed missiles aimed at their god dom shores, and we're serious about opening up a dialect with them, they'll trip all over themselves to speak with us, sir. Especially if we offer to allow them to take the cursed missiles and nuclear warheads from our Island, if they lift their god dom embargo."

"Colonel!" Major Cardona interrupted as he added. "Since when has any other nation who has ever dared to threaten the United States with mass destruction, been able to engage in talks with them, sir? What was America's response in the past to threats from Castro? What did they do to Libya when they attacked that airliner, sir? What did she do to Iraq when Iraq went too far sir? They destroyed Iraq as a nation. Never in the United States history did she ever succumb to any threats. Instead, the aggressors always found themselves destroyed, and left on the outside looking in. Colonel Alvarez, you have to remember Russia, at least the Russia we once knew, no longer exists. I fear if we try to take on the Americans, we'll do so alone. I don't believe we could expect some help from any other nation, sir. I believe the other nations of the world would go against us and allow America to destroy us, if we threaten her sir."

"Perhaps so Major Cardona, but what would happen if we were to carry out some of Castro's plans, so we could at least get the missiles into their proper firing position sir. Then we can..."

Major Cardona could not cover up his disgust to Alvarez's last suggestion as he fired back at him. "You would not dare attack any civilian targets, just so we could place these God hated and cursed weapons into their firing position sir. What has happened to you, Colonel Alvarez Sir?"

"What has happened to me god dommit? Madre de Dios, I have just become the new Presidente of Cuba, and as such, I must act in the best interests of Cuba and all her people, sir." Colonel Alvarez suddenly hissed at Major Cardona as he openly glared back at him.

"What interest of Cuba? Colonel, do you plan to sit by while Cuba is leveled by America's nuclear weapons, because you want to set these missiles in their silos? Alvarez, I beg you to consider what you're thinking, and the ramifications these thoughts would bring to Cuba..."

"It's El Presidente Alvarez to you sir, if you don't mind, Major Cardona, and I have done a lot of thinking about what we have been speaking of here. Remember Major, it was not me who had introduced these God cursed weapons of mass destruction to Cuban soil. But they're here, and by God, as the new Presidente of Cuba, I must put what weapons I have at my command, to their best possible use for us, sir. Major Cardona, you know I'm not really planning to launch the god dom things at the United States, I only plan to use them as a bargaining chip.

"I'm telling you Major Cardona, the fooking Americans will trip all over themselves to remove the cursed weapons from our nation when I inform them they are here, and I want them off our Island, but only as a trade off, sir. That trade is the United States lifts their god dom embargo, and then she trades with Cuba on open and equal terms, sir. I'll tell them I have no idea how long the god cursed missiles were resting on Cuba soil. I'll make them believe I'm appalled at the discovery of these foul weapons on Cuban land, sir."

"By all of the Saints Holy Presidente Alvarez, what'll happen to Cuba if the Americans don't believe you, or if they demand to come to the Island and remove them, and they still refuse to lift the embargo against us? What happens if they react to your threats by an all out invasion of our Island, not taking the time to ask us any questions, sir? Who is left to stop them from doing whatever they may choose to do..."

"I am, dom you Major Cardona! I'm here to stop the Americans from doing whatever they chose against our Island!" Colonel Alvarez screamed as he pounded his chest as he continued with his angry words. "I'm here to stop them sir, and if I'm forced to do so, I'll employ these weapons to my best advantage in stopping them once and for all. I'm here to stop the arrogant bastards' sir." Colonel Carlos Alvarez screamed at the top of his lungs while pointing at himself.

Major Cardona saw Captain Calvo move over to Alvarez's side and he thought he was going to kill him, because he felt Alvarez had lost his mind, and his heart lifted. But it immediately sunk just as quickly when he saw Captain Calvo suddenly slapped Colonel Alvarez on his back.

"God forgive me for saying this, but I agree with you all the way, Colonel Alvarez. We have to keep the god dom Americans in their place, and with the power of these god dom missiles and their nuclear warheads at our disposal to do so." Captain Calvo slapped the side of the first missile with his hand and went on with his words. "We now have the power to do so. Not even the all powerful Americans are so fearless that they would allow their country to be destroyed by the nuclear weapons, sir. They'd stand to lose far more than we would in a war against us, sir."

Major Cardona could not believe what he just heard said by Colonel Alvarez, and he warned him in no uncertain terms as he stared deeply in his cold eyes. "What the hell would the god dom Americans be risking if we attacked them with these few missiles, dommit? They would risk a few cities. Look at what we'll be risking in an exchange with the United States, the total destruction of our entire country sir. There would be no hope for anyone on Cuba, no place for them to run and hide. Everyone would be dead, sir. You must give this matter some..."

"God curse you to the devil, you bore me Major Cardona." Captain Calvo screamed at the raging Major Cardona as he leveled his AK-47 at him, and he fired a shot burst of rounds into Cardona's chest, sending the surprised man tumbling backwards over a crate lying on the floor.

Colonel Alvarez stopped laughing and he stared at the Captain Calvo, as he leveled his weapon at the two soldiers from Major Cardona's troops, and he fired on them before they had a chance to react against his crime.

Outside, small arms fire broke out as the soldiers from Captain Calvo's troops saw what happened inside the bunker, and took their cue and opened fire on the rest of Major Cardona's troops, before they could come to his aide. It was wise Captain Calvo insisted many of his own troops accompany them on this mission.

Captain Calvo drew his pistol and turned and pointed it at the technicians from Major Cardona's troops working in the bunker and he growled. "Madre de Dios, I trust every one of you sonofabitches witnessed the sneak attack that took place against our convoy. We were attacked by a horde of civilian troublemakers. In the fight, the loyal Major Cardona and his brave men were killed. Is this not the way Cardona lost his life, as a brave and new fallen hero to the last revolution of Cuba?" Captain Calvo glared at the technicians, waiting for their response.

One of the workers stepped forward his face was a mask of hatred as he announced angrily. "I witnessed no such thing, Captain. By God, I shall tell the world what has happened here today and what was spoken inside this bunker, sir. You! Captain Calvo, you have just slaughtered my Commander, and I shall not rest at peace until I have avenged his death against you, sir."

"Then it looks like I'll have to make you rest sooner than you expected, and visit your God." With that, a shot rang out, striking the technician in the chest and sending him into a desk. Calvo turned to the other technicians and growled. "Is there anyone else who is tired of living?"

The remaining technicians shook their heads no, and aimed their eyes at the floor of the room.

"Very well then you will continue to follow all your dom orders as received without hesitation. I want these fooking missiles prepared to be set in the god dom silos at a moment's notice." Captain Calvo's eyes narrowed as he pointed his finger at the workers and added. "You people better do your work, and do it well. If I uncover anyone of you changing any of your reports or stalling this project, you, your wife and children will be put to the most savage death I can devise against you fools. Does each of you understand my threat?"

They all nodded yes as they remained staring at the floor and being scared to death.

"Good, then I'm certain you wouldn't mind if I took it on myself to place my soldiers in your groups, to ensure there are no mistakes committed by you pack of fools." This time he did not wait for an answer as he turned to Alvarez and requested from him. "What are my orders, sir?"

"You're doing very well making up your own orders, Captain. Carry on please sir."

Captain Calvo turned as one of his men came to the head of the stairwell leading into the bunker and he called out to him. "Captain Calvo! Are you all right in here, sir? Captain, do you need assistance?" the soldier adopted a threatening on guard stance with his weapon aimed down into the blackness of the bunker, not knowing what he might find below, or who might take it on themselves to fire up at him from the darkness from within. The last sound this concerned soldier heard from inside the bunker was the single shot fired moments ago, and nothing else since.

Presidente Alvarez was hot as hell this soldier was only interested in the Captain Calvo's fate as he bellowed at the soldier. "By the Holy Madonna, what is wrong with you, fool? Do you not understand your Presidente is down here with your Captain? Why are you solely interested in your Captain's wellbeing? You're taken down to Private for your stupid mistake, soldier."

The soldier took a step backwards, and he instantly snapped to attention and then saluted the Colonel as he realized Alvarez was now making his way up the steps and coming directly at him.

The glaring sunlight forced Alvarez to put his hand over his eyes for a moment until they grew accustomed to the light. Captain Calvo was at his side in an instant. He was not an unwise soldier, and he realized if he played his cards right, he might end up as the second most powerful man in all of Cuba. Then, all he would have to do was wait for his chance to take the President's chair. He knew it would be only months before someone killed this young pup, and if it was not him, it would most likely be one miss-guided civilian. If no one stepped forward, he would see to it someone was forced to carry out his bidding.

Twenty five of Major Cardona's loyal troops were scattered dead all over the area. Five more of his soldiers leaned up against an armored vehicle with their hands behind their necks, and they were stripped to the waist. Some of Captain Calvo's troops stood guard over them, while others dug holes to drop the dead in.

The new Presidente of Cuba, Colonel Carlos Rafael Hernandez Alvarez walked over to the five soldiers from Major Cardona's unit and he ordered. "Your dom Commander is dead. The reason the Major is dead is because he chose to go against my will. I did not enjoy, nor did I want to put him to death. I need soldiers like him in my service, he was a good man. I need loyal soldiers like you men are. Therefore, I shall offer you your lives, if you swear an allegiance to me and my new government. If any of you have a problem offering me your full allegiance, I'll have all of you put to death. There is a position for all of you in my new government. I wait for your decision." The Colonel walked over to Captain Calvo as his soldiers lifted their weapons and aimed them at the prisoners, in case one of the other soldiers tried something foolish.

The prisoners looked from one another. The elected soldier, a Corporal took a step forward and nodded towards the new Presidente, as he waited for permission to speak.

Alvarez turned to him. "May God curse you you're the elected one are you not?"

"Yes Sir Colonel Alvarez Sir." The soldier said as he tried a smile on the new President.

"Speak! But you better only speak the words I want to hear come from your foul lips, fool."

"Thank you, my Presidente. Me, and my fellow soldiers don't understand what it was that caused our Commanding Officer to go against his Presidente wishes. We don't condone, nor do we agree with what he done against you sir. We discussed this matter between ourselves, and we come to the conclusion he received what he deserved. Anyone who disagrees with the Presidente of Cuba and his beliefs, does not deserve to live in Cuba, sir."

When the Corporal finished speaking, the rest of the soldiers snapped to attention before the new President of Cuba.

Alvarez saluted, and then he instructed each of the soldiers to split up and join the other different groups of Captain Calvo's paratroopers.

He had no intention of allowing these five soldiers to remain together. He knew Captain Calvo's soldiers would find some reason to put them all death, and this suited his plans just fine. The Colonel felt he owed something to Major Cardona for his past loyalty, and offering his men life, made him feel he had fulfilled his duty to his dead friend. Colonel Alvarez was upset Captain Calvo killed Major Cardona before he had a chance to try and change his mind, he like Major Cardona. He decided he was going to keep a close eye on Calvo, and not give him a chance to betray him, and he was going to order his death before the man became too powerful, and a real threat to his new position.

The Colonel watched as the Major's soldiers mixed in with Captain Calvo's troops. He leaned to Captain Calvo and ordered him to have the five soldiers help the others dig the graves for the dead soldiers. The Presidente asked Calvo if he knew how many men he lost in the savage action.

Captain Calvo stared at the soldier the President ordered busted down to Private and said. "By the hand of God Private, how many men did we lose in this latest action, mista?"

The Private snapped to attention and replied to the Commander. "Captain Calvo! Eight dead, and three wounded, sir. I'm afraid one of the wounded will not make it past the hour, sir."

"Very well, have the new members of our outfit join the grave diggers." Captain Calvo turned back to Alvarez and replied. "You heard the report sir. Do you wish me to repeat it for you, sir?"

"Jesus Madonna no Captain Calvo Sir!" Colonel Alvarez said in a low voice as he checked his watch. It was five twenty p.m. and he added. "It's getting late Captain. It'll be dark by the time we return to the capital city, sir."

"I realized this already. Do you think it would be a much better thought if we were to remain here for the night, sir? I have no idea what might be happening on the roads leading back to Havana in the dark, sir. We could fall into an ambush, or even worse, be taken as captives by any of these god dom civilian fighters, sir." Captain Calvo offered with concern to Alvarez.

"God No! I cannot possibly be away from the capital for the entire night so early into our revolution, sir. That is totally impossible and out of the question, Captain Calvo. If there is a problem then I must be back there for my troops, sir. These dom civilians, I have a good mind to erase them all from the capital, and then turn Havana into an entire military city where all will be safe to live and work in peace, sir."

"What about this installation, Colonel Alvarez? How do you want to secure the bunker until we decide how to make use of what we discovered, sir?" the Captain asked him with concern.

"How many men do you still have to help guard me and the others with, Captain Calvo Sir?" Colonel Carlos Alvarez asked with concern as he held his Captain in his gaze for the moment.

"Presidente Alvarez Sir, I have twenty two able bodied and well trusted men with me, sir."

Alvarez did not respond right away, instead, he headed for the lead armor vehicle, he reached inside and removed the receiver and barked in it. "This is Presidente Carlos Alvarez, and I wish to speak to the Commander of the 9th Infantry Brigade stationed on Guanahacabibes. Over."

"Yes Presidente Alvarez Sir. This is Lieutenant Jules Soto Estrada, sir. I was left in command of the military base when Major Cardona left us, and he headed off for the capital city, sir."

"I must report to you that your Major Cardona is dead Lieutenant. He was killed when we came under attack at La Bajada by some of the foolish civilian rebel forces constantly attacking us, sir. How many soldiers do you have stationed on your base at this time, sir? I have need of some extra soldiers for protecting me and what we can protected while I return to the capital." The new Presidente of Cuba asked the young military officer over the radio.

"I'm sorry to hear about the new of Major's death, sir. Presidente Alvarez Sir, I took the precaution to order three hundred soldiers here to help support this military base for you, sir."

"Are they armed and do you have any means of transportation with them Lieutenant?"

"Yes sir they're armed and we have vehicles and jeeps to transport the entire company, sir."

"By all the Saints who dwell in Heaven you done well, Lieutenant here is your orders. I want you to send two hundred soldiers to Bajada. They're to stand guard over the installation here..."

"I was unaware that we had any operational military bases in that area of Cuba, El Presidente Sir. Are you certain there is a military base where you are reporting one to be and should..."

"By the Holy Madonna, you will shut that worthless hole of yours and you will pay close attention to your god dom orders as I issue them to you, or I'll have you put to death for insubordination to my orders, mista. I want two hundred of your soldiers armed, and they're to be stationed here at this base until I get back to you with any further orders. You Lieutenant are now a Major, and the security of this god dom installation is entirely in your foul hands, sir. God forgive you if anyone harms this base in any way, shape or form on me mista. I'll hold you and your entire family personally responsible for that harm if it takes place against this installation, sir. The troops you are dispatching are ordered to start out immediately for this base. The rest of your troops will deploy on, err..." Colonel Alvarez unfolded the map before him and he quickly checked for a section where the troops could wait for him until he hooked up with them.

"The rest of your troops will assemble at La Fe on the Central highway, Lieutenant. These soldiers will be prepared to accompany me back to the capital and they'll take up now positions surrounding the Presidential Palace for my protection, sir. They'll be responsible for my security and safety at all times while I'm in Havana. I'm forced to leave the bulk of my security force behind to help protect this god dom installation from any attacks from the god dom civilians causing me all these problems. I cannot impress upon you how important this installation is to the security of all Cuba. Do you have any other questions of me at this time, Lieutenant?"

"One sir. What about my base sir? If I move out will all the troops under my command sir, the civilians will immediately move in and take over the base, sir."

"Good point Lieutenant, you're instructed to abandon your base, but before you leave it sir. You're ordered to remove all weapons. Any weapons you can't remove or transport with your troops are to be rendered useless before your troops pull off the base. I want you to set mines throughout the base. If some of the dom civilian troublemakers are blown apart, maybe the rest of the fools will not advance further onto the base. Either way, I don't care about your base any longer, it's expendable to us. Look at it this way, your base is now being moved out to Bajada."

"Yes Sir Presidente Alvarez Sir, I shall follow my orders as I have received them, sir. I'm prepared to leave the moment we end this communication, sir."

"Very good Lieutenant, excuse me, Major. When do you think your troops will leave, sir?"

"Presidente Alvarez, as we speak, I given out orders for the troops to assemble. I can have them heading for the installation within ten minutes at the very latest, sir. The troop's who'll be meeting you at La Fe for escort and protection duty, will be there in plenty of time before your arrival at that position, to secure the entire area before you arrive and your safety afterwards, sir."

"Very good Major, I suggest you don't waste further time talking to me, sir." Alvarez broke off the communication and turned to Calvo and ordered him. "Captain, you're now a Colonel. Before we leave this installation, I want you to find the list of soldiers specially trained by Castro for these selected attacks on the Jew and Arab countries, and you are take the list along with you, Colonel. You're to accompany me back to the capital. Once there, you'll locate these troops and have them assemble on the parade grounds sir. Set up a base there for them. I think I shall take advantage of their training. We know the foul Americans will be all over our skies, and if we're to move these god dom missiles into their silos, we'll need a window of time in which to operate freely from, sir. These soldiers will offer us this window sir."

"Right away sir." The new Colonel Calvo snapped as he stormed back inside the bunker. Five minutes later he returned with a yellow folder and he announced proudly. "I have the names sir. One thing sir, they're already stationed in Havana on a base constructed just for them. I checked with that Base Commander from below, and he informed me they were at the base. I instructed him to have these soldiers remain until he heard from me."

"Outstanding Colonel! Let's get on the road. Do your soldiers know what is expected of them once we leave them, sir?"

"Yes Sir Colonel Alvarez Sir, I'd like to see anyone who doesn't belong on this base, try and get on it now after the orders I have issued to the soldiers we are leaving behind to protect this base, sir. They'll not know what hit them if they dare try it, sir." Colonel Carlos Calvo boasted proudly to Colonel Alvarez as he stared back at him for a long moment.

Alvarez smiled as then turned and headed for the vehicle. He was taking his life in his hands heading out in a machine with only four guards for his protection, but he had no choice. He had to secure the base, and there was not enough time to wait for the other troops to arrive, before he left for the capital city. He cursed for not having more soldiers with him. If only Cardona would have informed him of what they found at this installation, he would've ordered a fully armed Army to accompany him. They boarded the vehicle and the soldiers saluted when they walked by. Then they rushed to their positions and waited the arrival of the 9th Infantry making their way to the new base.

The armor vehicle jerked forward in motion. Colonel Calvo ordered the driver to travel at maximum speed, and not to stop under any circumstances. He further ordered the four guards to keep their attention glued to the gun ports of the war machine. He told them he wanted them to return fire if they came under attack. Colonel Calvo also took an extra AK-47 for himself and he also gave one to the new Presidente of Cuba.

The drive to La Fe was completed within twenty five minutes of some hard bouncing around inside the armored vehicle for the Presidente and new Colonel. Presidente Carlos Alvarez kept his eyes glued to the bulletproof windshield of the old and outdated war machine, and he watched as the rapidly fading light soon gave way to the dark of night.

This section of the road had no lights on, and the heavy undergrowth was feet away from the edge of the road, with many branches of trees and bushes actually hanging over the road itself.

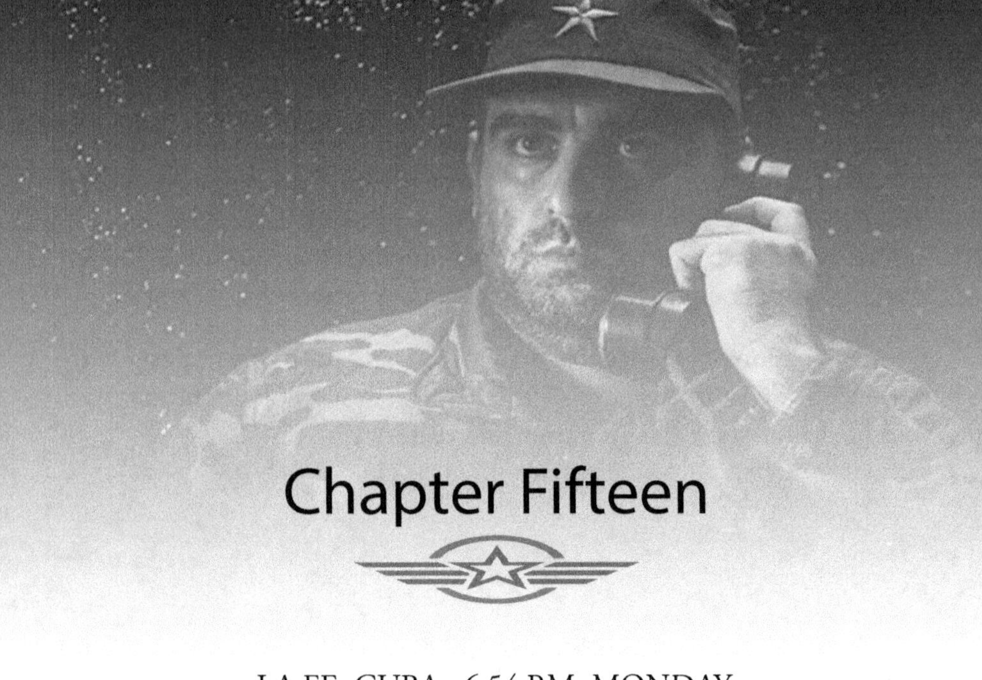

Chapter Fifteen

Colonel Carlos Rafael Fernandez Alvarez's vehicle came to a sliding stop at the beginning of the main Central Highway that ran from one side of the Island to the other. From this section of the road, he could get to any other part of the Island he wanted to visit with little trouble and with great speed. The extremely upset new Presidente of Cuba twisted his neck while looking for the troops ordered to meet him at this point. He snarled when he did not see any of them waiting.

"I don't see any sonofabitches I ordered here as yet. I swear by the Holy Madonna's crown I'll have their heads taken for this failure, mista. Where the hell are those bastards at dommit? I'll have Estrada's neck for this failure. Driver, I order you to turn around and get me back to that installation immediately. As God is my judge, I should've known better than to trust that lousy bastard of a Major to protect my life. What the hell is wrong with you, you great fool you? I just told you to turn around didn't I and that…" Colonel Carlos Alvarez yelled at his driver until that driver dared to interrupt him by saying.

"Yes Presidente Alvarez, but I'll have to find a place opened enough for me to turn around, sir. All available space is taken by the other military vehicles sent to pick us up for protection, sir." The driver smirked as he announced he located the other soldiers sent out there to protect them from this point on.

Alvarez reached forward and then he slapped the driver on the back of his head, as he complained angrily. "By all the Saints Holy, why the hell did you allow me to make an ass of myself, mista? You're not making any points with me. If you're not much more careful when you're dealing with me in the future, you're going to find yourself cleaning out the alleyways of Havana with only a stick for your own protection from the hated criminals that prowl the night, fool." Colonel Alvarez was not very unhappy with the driver. But he was pleased the soldiers were where they were ordered to be, and at the time they were supposed to be there. Colonel Calvo suddenly slapped Colonel Alvarez on his back, and he said to him.

"Presidente Carlos Alvarez, you have to have a little faith in your new Army I'm afraid, sir. Are you not one of us sir, and are you not now the new Presidente of all Cuba, sir? There is not one soldier here who wouldn't go to his grave protecting your life, sir."

Colonel Alvarez grunted as he stared at the thirty or so military vehicles parked on both sides of the highway in the shadows and off in the underbrush on the sides of the road. The vehicles were originally hidden from his view by all the heavy undergrowth along the highway. His vehicle then inched forward, and when it reached the center of column of vehicles, they started off, trapping Colonel Alvarez's machine right in the middle of the long column of military war machines, offering him the most protection from the soldiers there.

Alvarez's machine was surrounded by jeeps, encompassed by a ring of armored vehicles. They all moved as one, all turning when one turned, and slowing down when one slowed down. When the vehicles entered the wider main part of the highway, their speed increased, and they spread out across the highway, blocking other vehicles from getting anywhere close to Presidente Alvarez's vehicle. His caravan took up the four lanes of highway, forcing any civilian vehicles off the road if they did not want to be rammed off the road by the heavy military vehicles.

All civilian cars pulled off the road, and they remain there until the caravan of speeding military vehicles passed by them, if any civilian vehicles did not move out of their way fast enough, they were merely bumped off the road by the leading military vehicles.

HAVANA, CUBA. 7:19 P.M. MONDAY,

SEPTEMBER 23rd, 1996

Alvarez's caravan of vehicles pulled onto the parade grounds of the Presidential Palace, just as all hell broke loose in the area. The civilian's who attacked the Palace the night before, were attacking in force again on this night. The sky was filled with bottles of burning fuel, exploding in the ranks of the soldiers protecting the Palace from their attack, and on the tanks sent out to repel the attacking civilian hordes. The Colonel grabbed the radio and he ordered the soldiers in his caravan to prepare to engage the rioters. Presidente Alvarez without hesitation gave the shoot to kill order. He was determined to break the backs of the civilian troublemakers, or he would kill everyone involved in the attacks against him and his new Administration.

As the soldiers rushed out of the Palace and circled the vehicle containing the new Presidente of Cuba, and Colonel Calvo. The two officers were roughly pulled from the machine and dragged in the building for their protection. Presidente Alvarez gave a quick look around and he noticed more tanks in and surrounding the compound than when he left the capital city earlier in the day.

"Who is inside the god dom building?" Alvarez noticed the steel plating placed over the windows of Castro's private office on the third floor of the Palace. He rushed to the desk and removed a bottle and poured a drink. The liquor made his body shiver, he poured a second glass as he thought over the happenings of his day. That morning he killed Castro, and he watched as his soldiers fired on the rampaging hordes of civilians. He was then dumped in an armor vehicle, and his body banged around until he ended up at the installation at Bajada, and he found the nuclear tipped missiles. After that, he had to fight Cardona and he witnessed his death. The trip back to the Palace added to the abuse to his exhausted and battered body, until he ended up where it all began, under the same circumstances, killing civilians again. "What a god dom day." He moaned as he plopped down in his chair.

The concerned Vice Presidente Cabrisas entered the office in a rush, and he hugged Alvarez as he reported. "Colonel Alvarez..."

"El Presidente Sir." Carlos fired back at the Vice Presidente of Cuba nastily as he waited for him to correct his error.

"Excuse me my El Presidente Sir. We've been forced to engage the civilian hordes throughout the entire day, sir. They probed our defenses, but they only attacked in force when the light of day faded out, sir. I allowed more troops to enter the capital city to have them ready to help with these asses who think they can drive us from this building with curses and sticks, sir. We killed over eight hundred of them already which displeases me greatly, sir. The civilian attacks forced us to stop burying all the dead of earlier in the day, and forced our energies to fending off their constant probes. This was until I pulled Varela's 17th Infantry and Light Armor Division from positions stationed outside the capital city as extra security, sir. I had them come in and engage these miserable dogs, sir."

Presidente Alvarez sat down, and he rested his elbows on the desk, as he made a steeple of his fingers. He sat his chin on his hands and he drifted off, deep in thought for a moment before offering. "We had four Armies move into this city to help secure the capital. By the Holy Madonna, do you mean to tell me five thousand armed soldiers cannot crush these cochinos, and gain control over the dom city?"

"Colo... err... Presidente Alvarez Sir, no one expected the civilians to react as they have done on this day, sir. You have to understand at times, we're being pressured by more of the civilians than we have soldiers at the ready, sir. You should realize these soldiers are not stationed on the Palace grounds, but they're spread throughout the entire city. If we had these troops in this one region, there would be no problem with the civilians. I..."

"I don't really care if we have one thousand soldiers. They're trained men and women, and they're being backed by armor and artillery. There is no reason for us to allow this civil unrest to continue, and I have no intention of putting up with it for a minute longer. The American spy planes are flying over our country as we speak, and I don't intend to provide live entertainment for their bastard President. I'll not become the laughing stock of the United States government. I demand our soldiers break the backs of these civilian troublemakers. I'll not tolerate further unrest from them!" Alvarez screamed as he rose and he lifted his fist in the air, making a threatening move at the Vice Presidente with it.

Vice Presidente Cabrisas was stunned as he stepped back a few paces and then he offered in his defense while suffering a shock of pain from his wound. "Surely Presidente Alvarez, you don't tell me you'd unleash artillery on these misguided peoples. Think of what you're saying. Think of what this act would mean. The death, it would be unbelievable. No, I cannot conceive the outcome if you allow troops to use of artillery. I beg you reconsider your words. Presidente Alvarez, allow me to reason with the masses. I'm willing to address them, to point out the error in their foolish beliefs, and warn them of consequences, if they continue on the unwise path they have chosen for themselves. Sir, I know I can bring them to their senses, I just know it."

Alvarez did not respond he just glared at Cabrisas who appeared recovered from his wounds. Vice Presidente Cabrisas continue with his words in a rush. "Presidente Alvarez, if you allow the Army to use artillery on the civilians, you'll be doing something Castro never dared. Do you want the people of Cuba and world to think you're worse than Castro? No, you must reconsider."

Presidente Alvarez's blood boiled within his body and his shoulders tightened up, as he suddenly roared at the wounded Vice Presidente. "I must! I must reconsider! Who the hell are you to tell me what I must, and I must not do. I'll do whatever is necessary to gain control over this dom Island, and I'll not have any subordinates trying to control what I must, and must not do. Cabrisas!" Alvarez hissed as he moved around the desk and stood face to face with him and he continued with his anger. "You and the troops had the day to get control over the rampaging bastards, and you failed miserably. The night is going to serve to bring out more of the fools. The thing I must keep in mind is the rest of Cuba is watching what's happening here. If I intend to gain control over the Island, I'll have to start with its capital. Does this not make sense?"

Vice Presidente Cabrisas did not answer Colonel Alvarez immediately as he continued to struggle with a new wave of pain suddenly wracking his entire body.

"Does it not make any sense to you I just asked of you, Vice Presidente Cabrisas Sir."

The Cuban Vice Presidente flinched from the force in Presidente Alvarez's voice as he replied to him. "You're correct El Presidente Sir." He said as he tried to get his breathing under control while also ignoring the stabbing pain tormenting him in his side.

"By the Blessed Virgin Vice Presidente Cabrisas Sir, you are god dom right I'm correct, I am always correct and don't you forget it for a moment, sir." Colonel Carlos Alvarez snapped nastily as he headed back to his seat, continuing to drill the weakened Vice President. "What about the rest of my dom military forces, sir? Are they having the same problems with the civilian mobs as we're having here, sir?"

"El Presidente Sir, the 19th Infantry Battalion under the command of Suarez successfully severed the Island in half at Ciego de Avita. All his troops have joined forces with Colonel Agramonte. Together with Colonel Agramonte's aircraft, they have gained full control over the central land of Cuba from Camaguey all the way to Santa Clara. But from Santa Clara to Havana is anyone's guess at this point, sir. We also control most of this region, but our convoys come under constant attack from the rebels hiding in the jungle, sir. They make fast attacks against us, and as quickly, they disappear back in the brush. Captain Remos is intending to join these forces by placing all his attack boats off shore in the more troubled areas, and he'll employ his heavy weapons to strike back when the rebels attack. I believe it'll only be a matter of a few days before we can secure this area between Havana and Santa Clara..."

"What about the area that is below Camaguey? Is there any trouble there god dommit?"

"No my Presidente, and I'm at a loss as to understand why there is no trouble there, sir. The only reason I can think of, is they have not found out what has happened in Havana, sir."

"Are you telling me you're expecting trouble even in this region of the Island, Cabrisas?"

"Some, sure, there has to be some. I'm positive not all the Cubans believe Castro was the villain we believed him to be, sir. And, they're willing to fight for what they believed in, sir."

"Then we should immediately begin to make plans to get all the troops needed in the area to squash any trouble there before it happens."

"El Presidente Sir, I have taken that into consideration, and I issued orders to have Captain Remos transport an Army on his ships down to Holguin, so they can spread out and get to their positions in a hurry, sir."

"I'm please someone was able to make some intelligent god dom decisions around here on his own accord besides me, Cabrisas. What about the god dom western end of the Island where I just came from, sir. Is this section at lease possibly secured properly for us, god dommit?"

The concerned Vice President of Cuba overlooked the anger he felt at Alvarez for his omission of Vice President or the mister before his name. He felt he earned the respect of this minor courtesy. "Presidente Alvarez Sir, the forces from Major Cardona's 17th Infantry have completely secured this entire region for us, sir. There have been few reports stating that some minor skirmishes had occurred between our troops and some of the foolish civilians living in that area since we have taken this action, sir."

"By the way Cabrisas, Major Cardona is dead, sir. The Major was killed in one of these minor skirmishes that you keep referring to, sir." Colonel Alvarez said matter of factly.

"Dead? Major Cardona is dead sir?" The Vice President mumbled more to himself as he suddenly turned green, and he looked as if he was going to be sick to his stomach, as he held onto his injured side and took a deep and painful breath.

"Yes, Major Cardona is dead Cabrisas. By the Holy Madonna, he has brought his own fate down upon his foolish head by failing to take the obvious into account, sir. He had allowed his defenses to slacken, and it has cost him dearly, sir. One other thing I shall demand from our troops, even if we lose the rest of the dom Island, we must remain in complete control of the Guanahacabibes Peninsula region. We have to maintain our command over this one section of Cuba at all costs, sir. This order is not to be questioned, just followed by all our troops." Colonel Carlos Alvarez warned him angrily.

The words Alvarez chose to use in explaining the death of Major Cardona, sent sirens off in Cabrisas's mind. He now knew Alvarez ordered Cardona's death. It informed him he had backed the wrong man for President as he moaned. "Oh, what have I done? Have I placed a man in office that is going to make Castro look like a Saint? My Cuba, what have I done to you my Cuba?"

"Cabrisas! By the Holy Saints, are you still alive man? If you remain standing like that, flies will land in your worthless mouth, sir. I think you better take a seat before you fall to the ground, sir." Alvarez allowed the injured Vice President a few moments, because he knew how close he and Major Cardona were. When the color returned to him, Alvarez demanded, "what about the rest of our god dom troops? Do we have anymore who we can pull from?"

Vice Presidente Cabrisas slowly shook his head in an attempt to try and clear the fog that was rapidly clouding over his mind as he replied. "Yes Presidente Alvarez Sir, we have pulled all the troops of Varela from their security positions sir, and we had them join forces in the heart of the city. I tried to move some of Captain Calvo's paratroopers from their present positions to help us as well, but they have refused to do anything without Captain Calvo's direct orders, sir. This refusal has forced me to pull some of the armored vehicles and tanks from Major Cienfuegos' 1st Armor Division, and I have them move up to support the tanks and armor units from the 17th Infantry and Light Armor, sir. This moves left Major Cienfuegos very weak in his present position of security on the roads there. He has complained constantly to me of this fact every chance he was able to communicate with me, Presidente Alvarez Sir."

"By all the Saints that are Holy, I bet he is complaining to you a might, sir." Colonel Carlos Alvarez grinned back at Cabrisas, and then he added to his words to him. "By the way Cabrisas, Captain Calvo is now Colonel Calvo. What about Bernardo's 27th Mechanized Group? Could you not pull some of his armor and troops from him?"

"I considered that, but thought better of it. Bernardo's forces are taking heavy losses from the civilians. He has requested help on a number of occasions, and I was unable to support him sir."

Alvarez searched his mind and then he ordered the Vice President. "Have troops from Hernandez's 11th Infantry support Bernando's troops. I can ill afford to lose his forces to us. Order troops coming under attack to consolidate their positions and pull closer to the Palace. Cabrisas, I considered your warnings of employing artillery against the attacking civilian mobs and I shall use it." Colonel Alvarez raised his hand to still the Vice President and ordered him. "Only if there is any danger of our forces being overrun by the civilian fools. Will this make the order a little more palatable for your ideals?"

Vice Presidente Cabrisas let out a deep sigh of pain as he relented, and agreed and said. "Who shall make the decision to use artillery? Who'll decide when and how much will be used, sir?"

Presidente Alvarez's stubble covered chin twitched slightly as he barked at the injured man. "You will! It'll be you who'll decide which group will be saved, the civilian hordes going against our rule, or the soldiers laying down their lives while carrying out our orders. Yes Cabrisas, you, the one who was so concerned about the use of the artillery on any of the cursed civilian troublemakers, will decide where and when it will be used against them for us." He laughed at the stunned Vice President.

Vice President Cabrisas's temper grew as he glared back at the laughing man sitting at Fidel Castro's old desk.

Presidente Alvarez continued to laugh as he added to his angry words aimed at the Vice President of Cuba. "My dear Cabrisas, don't try and tell me I might have just hurt your feelings, sir. That is the least I wanted to do against you, sir. I just wanted to prove to you that sometimes, one has to take a very heavy hand in dealing with any civil unrest in his nation, sir. Sometimes, that one might even have to choose between the wild acting civilians, and the good soldiers and loyal people of that country. I'm not the least bit sorry I have burdened you so heavily on this day, I'm quite certain you'll make the proper decision when it's needed to be made by you, sir." Once again, Presidente Carlos Alvarez laughed, disturbing Vice President Cabrisas even further.

The meeting between the two Cuban leaders was interrupted by Major Cienfuegos, who stormed into the office and plopped down in a free chair.

Colonel Alvarez nodded at the exhausted looking Cuban officer as he stared at him for a few seconds sitting in the chair.

"Alvarez, I am..." Major Cienfuegos began but he was immediately cut off by Alvarez as he snapped angrily at him.

"Presidente Alvarez if you don't mind, Major Cienfuegos." Alvarez snapped hotly at the exhausted looking Major.

Major Cienfuegos completely ignored his gripe as he continued with his report. "Alvarez, I have gained control over my sector of the Island, but the losses are staggering on both sides, sir. I cannot believe these god dom fools have dared to attack my armor with god cursed fire bombs and sticks for weapons. I was actually forced to turn my machine guns on my own tanks, in order to blow the attacking civilian fools off the top of the dom tanks, sir. When this action was finally finished, I moved some of my troops into the other trouble areas of the city, sir. I know we have to gain control over the capital city if we ever intend to control all Cuba, sir.

"The god dom troops I moved up, have received very heavy resistance from the western area as well, sir. When I ordered more troops into this region, the fighting actually intensified, forcing me to commit even more of my troops to the region, sir. It seemed the dom troublemakers who were being driven from the parade grounds, have chosen to take up position in this area against us, sir. As I was preparing to move in the new armor, it was brought up to my attention that the safe house you were waiting in, was also in this area sir. It was then I remembered you ordered your lovely young lady to remain there until you sent for her, sir."

Presidente Alvarez slowly rose to his feet as he stared back at the young Major reporting to him, dreading the next words he thought he was going to speak to him.

Major Cienfuegos saw the pained look etched in Alvarez's face and he laughed at him, as he stated. "No sir, she is well and at this moment, she is being brought here to your office, sir."

"Oh, thank God for that much sir. Who was the one who saved her life, sir?"

"Me you great fool you. Do you think for one moment that I would've ever allowed any harm to befall the romantic interest of my new El Presidente? Colonel Alvarez, you hold little faith in me I see, sir." Major Cienfuegos grumbled, he was able to speak to Alvarez in this matter because they were such old friends.

Colonel Alvarez hugged his old friend to him, feeling rather foolish that he tried to force the man to use Presidente when he was addressing him. When he finished thanking him, Alvarez stepped back and sat down on the edge of the desk, and then he told Major Cienfuegos to continue with his report for him.

"Alvarez, when my soldiers first entered the area of civilian homes off Lombillo Avenue, I quickly realized this was where you had stayed waiting to launch your new revolution, my Colonel. I remembered you left Maria behind. Realizing this, I sent some of my soldiers to surround the building to ensure her safety, sir. I was with the soldier who banged on the door, and that maid Melba Guevara actually shot at us right through the god dom door, sir. I had to leap into a bush to avoid being hit by her. She wounded one of my men before she finally stopped firing at us, sir. That woman is a tiger Colonel Alvarez, sir."

Alvarez interrupted as he laughingly asked him about Maria. "Major Cienfuegos, although I find all this very amusing, I'd like to know more about Maria. Is she safe sir?"

"I'm sorry sir, once we stopped this crazy maid from firing at us as we entered the god dom building, not knowing what we might find in there. We found Maria hiding in the basement under a mattress. She complained about the way the maid forced her to hide there, sir. I informed her I was going to take her to the safety of the Palace. She made me wait until she packed all her things, ignoring the problems raging outside. She's a very cool one sir. Anyway, once she packed, I placed her inside an armor vehicle, and had her driven here to the Palace sir. The crazy maid would not leave her side for an instant, and she would not allow us to lead Maria around with us. She insisted she'd look after her, sir."

"Mother of God, never mind that garbage sir, where is she now?" Alvarez barked at him.

"Sorry Presidente Alvarez Sir, we escorted her to the Palace, and when I told her you were waiting for her in your new office. She insisted she be given time so she could fix herself up for you, sir. When I insisted, she delay that and accompany me directly to you, the crazy maid started in again and I had to relent. I left some guards behind to protect the bathroom and escort her to your office when she is ready." Major Cienfuegos leaned closer to Alvarez and said in a whisper. "Sir, we're going to have to do something about this dom maid of hers, sir. Especially for your sake, that is if you intend to have any private time with your lady." Major Cienfuegos gave Colonel Alvarez a quick wink which set him to laughing again.

Major Cienfuegos was the only man on the Island who would dare speak to Colonel Alvarez in this manner. He would speak bluntly to his friend no matter how powerful or erratic he became. The two grew up together, with Alvarez's mother treating Ricardo Cienfuegos as her second son. They were inseparable as children, and got in all sorts of trouble youth brings, stealing, fishing, giving the female population fits, not wanting to work. It was Alvarez's father who talked the two into thinking about the military life. Major Cienfuegos was the first one to enlist he was a sad child who lost his parents in a farming accident, thus giving Alvarez's mother the responsibility of rearing him.

Both of them were enjoying a good laugh, with Colonel Alvarez saying as he wiped the tears from his eyes. "I think I'm going to appoint Melba Guevara as Maria's private bodyguard, sir."

"With her guarding Maria's body, not even you'll get at it, Colonel." Ricardo laughed.

"Hmmm, maybe that is not such a good idea after all I see, my old friend." Alvarez replied.

"What is not such a good idea?" Maria asked as she entered the office with an armed guard standing on either side of her, and Melba, who was looking like a female bouncer while standing to Maria's right side. She adapted a very threatening stance, almost daring anyone to try and approach either of them.

Major Cienfuegos had to swallow as he stared at Maria with his mouth hanging open, while Colonel Alvarez slowly stood looking dumbly, and not removing his eyes from her as he rose.

Maria was thrilled to death from the response she received from her lover and the new Presidente of Cuba, as she swaggered her way into the office, crossing from left to right, and stopping right in front of Alvarez. She stood with her toes a foot apart, and her hands resting on her hips. She was dressed in a snow white, body fitting chiffon slip dress that was open to the bottom of her breasts. He shoulders were draped by a transparent white silk scarf. The dress went all the way down to the floor, but it was slit up the both sides to her hips. She wore lure white nylons which did not need a garter to remain in place.

The slits went passed the top of the nylons, adding to the thrill of seeing a work of God draped as such. The dress left very little to the imagination, and anyone who stood to either side of Maria, had a clear view of her breasts from the sides of the opening, and the slits in the dress made it impossible for her to wear any underpants and when she walked, the dress flared on her. If one was quick enough, he would assure himself that she had no underpants on. Her hair was up on the crown on her head, held in place by what Colonel Alvarez referred to as a monster claw, a hair clip with teeth that looked like it would rip right into her head. A spray of small pearls draped down from her hair across her forehead and the sides of her face. She suddenly licked her lips as she stared back at Colonel Carlos Alvarez. He looked at her as if he was staring at a ghost.

"Hmm, I see you do approve of my choice of dress, my new Presidente." Maria purred in her sexiest voice, as she slowly ran her hands down the full length of her exquisite and hard body.

"And what is in it as well." Major Cienfuegos said as he continued to stare at her breasts.

Colonel Alvarez punched his best friend in the arm as he continued to stare at Maria.

"You better breathe before you pass out on me, my dear El Presidente Carlos Alvarez." She warned the new Presidente of Cuba as she smiled back at her lover again.

"Out god dommit! Madre de Dios, everyone out of my office at once, now! Get out all of you fools!" Alvarez barked as he actually pushed Major Cienfuegos, and he then took Maria's hand and lead her around the massive antique desk. Alvarez looked at Ricardo and then barked at him. "Will you get the hell out of here please? We want to be alone."

Ricardo put a pout on, forcing Alvarez to add. "No! You cannot watch us, get out you fool."

The President's words made the three soldiers laugh as they quickly filed out of his new office. Colonel Carlos Alvarez laughed as he listened to the soldiers passing some rather crude remarks at what they knew he and Maria would soon be doing behind the closed doors of his new office.

"Hmmm." She purred as she smiled at her man, as Alvarez sat down and he pulled her to his lap. She wrapped both arms around his neck and cried. "My Presidente of Cuba." They kissed.

While Alvarez kissed her he picked up a suddenly slight movement in the corner of the office and he jumped over it. He was still rather ill at ease of his new position and the problems the civilians were causing him, and he would remain that way until all of Havana was fully secured by his troops. His eyes shot open and he instantly found himself staring right into the set face of the female bodyguard Melba. She had obviously moved close and Alvarez did not know if it was so she could see what was going on, or if it was to protect her newly assigned ward. Colonel Alvarez suddenly pulled free of Maria's embrace and he whispered to her. "Maria, if you don't mind, your watchdog, please honey."

"Hmmm." She whispered back as she tried to kiss him again while ignoring his words.

"No Maria. I mean Melba is still inside the god dom office with us, honey. May God curse her, she is staring right at us, my lady." Carlos Alvarez mumbled into her ear a little louder this time as he gave her a slight shove with his shoulder.

"What?" she snapped as she finally opened her eyes, and then she looked around the massive office until she spotted Melba still standing in the room. She was staring right back at her as if she was her disapproving elderly mother, and she did not approve one bit of what they were about to do together in the room. She wiggled off Alvarez's lap, causing his problem to grow even more. She walked over to Melba and then she placed her arm on her shoulder, and she tried to move her bodyguard towards the door of the office as she told her. "Melba, there comes a time in your life when you'll be forced to leave my side, and this is one of them my dear friend."

"But my lady, the Presidente has left you in my charge, and he has ordered me to protect you."

"Yes, and you have carried out his orders faithfully to him on this day, my dear. But I need to be alone with him right now, until I had the chance to show our new El Presidente just how proud I am of him, honey." She offered to the concerned looking older woman this time.

"But my orders I must follow my Lady." Melba exclaimed at Maria as she stared at her.

She let out her breath in a rush as she quickly realized this was going to take her some more explaining. "Melba honey. Who was the one who has issued those orders to you my dear?"

"Presidente Alvarez of course, my dear lady." The older woman cried back to her.

"And, who do you think is sitting in that chair over there waiting for my pleasure, my dear?" She pointed a slim finger at Colonel Alvarez, as she put on her most sexy smile at her.

"Why Presidente Alvarez, my lady." Melba replied with a stunned look on her face now.

"Exactly Melba honey, and who would you be protecting me from if you remain here, dear?"

"Err... the Presidente of Cuba, my lady?" Melba replied as she suddenly realized what Maria was saying.

"Exactly. And, why would you need to protect me from the El Presidente, the man I love?"

Melba's face instantly lit up as if she had just seen the light of day and she cried. "Oh, my lady, I shall leave you, but I'll be standing right outside the room, and no one will get in to cause you any harm. This I swear my lady."

"Very good Melba, you do that honey." Maria said as she led the older woman towards the door. "Now honey, you stay out here and make sure no one interrupts us until I'm through with the new El Presidente, honey. Then, if he's still alive he can begin to run the country for us."

The two women shared one of their special laughs together, with Maria kissing the cheek of her new maid and bodyguard. Then she closed and locked the door behind her, when she left the office. Colonel Alvarez instantly jumped up from his chair, and with one arm he swept everything off the top of his massive desk. He then charged at Maria, pulling her into his strong embrace and lifting her off the ground.

"No, no, not yet you don't, mista. Hold on here a second will you please." Maria said as she placed her hand up against Alvarez's powerful chest, and she held him off her for a moment.

"What? Why? I want you right here and now, Maria." Alvarez complained as he went at her.

"I want you to go back to your chair, and wait there until I'm done with you, El Presidente."

"But..." Alvarez began to protest again, until she said in an angry tone. "Go on. Go!" Maria waited until he was seated again behind the desk after he put her down. Then she started a little striptease show for him, slowly removing her dress. She made the most of it as the fabric sexily slid away from her breasts and then her hips. She left the scarf in place though, and her nylons on as she wiggled her way over to his chair again. She straddled and then moved her body over his, allowing him to grab what he wanted to, but not letting him to get carried away though.

When she felt she had him at just the right temperature, she wiggled again and then she slid her body along his until she ended up kneeling before his legs and she offered to him. "I'm here to give you pleasure, great pleasure my El Presidente." She purred as she unzipped his pants while running her tongue sexily over her teeth, and she pulled them down, she then drew him in her mouth. In no time she had him squirming all around in the chair, and when he felt he could no longer take it, Alvarez scooped her up in his arms again. He placed her down on the desk and they made love together. The sporadic gun and cannon fire drifted off until it was no longer heard by either of them, as they entwined their bodies to make one.

Once they finished making love together, Colonel Alvarez fell back into his chair naked and thoroughly exhausted. Maria made herself comfortable resting on his lap, and they slept that way for the entire night.

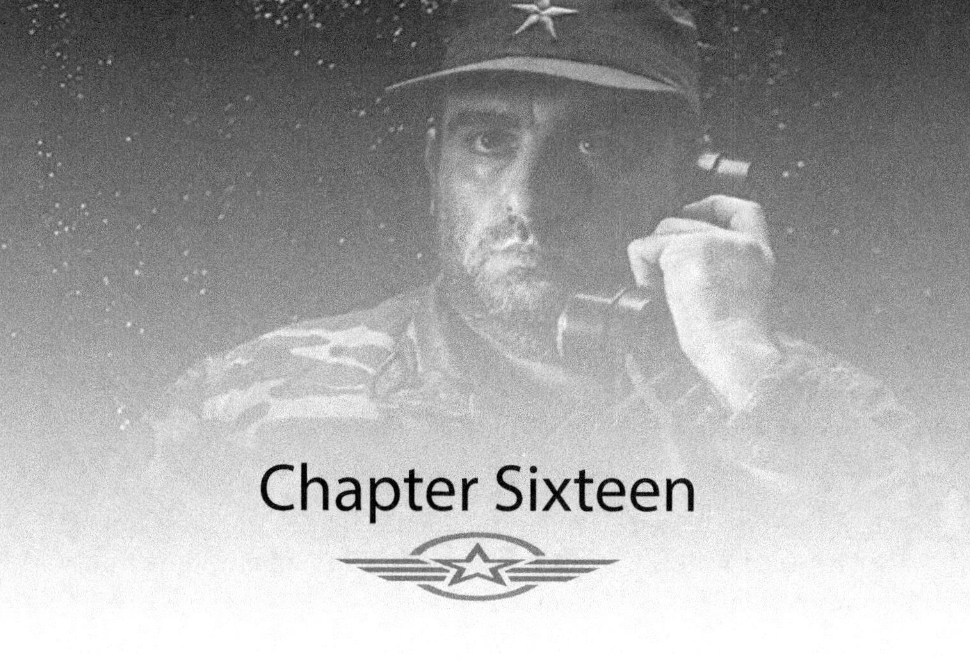

Chapter Sixteen

FORT BRAGG, NORTH CAROLINA.
2:30 P.M. MONDAY, SEPTEMBER 23rd, 1996

The trip from Camp Lejeune over to Fort Bragg went quickly, and Corporal Robert Walker, Road Kill, and Frank Hall, the Mutt, found themselves standing at attention in an outer office waiting to see the Colonel for their orders. While they waited, three other soldiers entered the office, and were ordered to take seats.

Corporal Walker eyed the three soldiers cautiously, and then he recognized one of them, it was Corporal David McKinnon. He nodded and McKinnon responded by saying. "Hey man, do you have any idea why the fuck they have drafted our damn asses on us, man?"

"Nope," Walker replied. "You fricking birds are in the same stinking boat we're in pal."

"What stinking boat is that Grunt?" Irvington snapped back at him as he stared at Walker.

"What's up your fucking ass, Blood?" Walker shot back as he glared at the black soldier.

"You, a fucking honkie prick trying to talk like a stinking brother bugs the living shit right outta my damn ass, friend."

Before Walker could reply to his words, the Mutt was on his feet and growling angrily at the new dick. "You got a stinking problem with me talking like a fucking brother, Homie?"

"Plenty fucker, you're as white as the utter mutherfukka over there is man, and I don't..."

"Hey Homes, he's part nigger himself, man." Walker warned while wearing a smirk and glaring at the other soldier.

"Nigger! You called me a nigger, I'll cut you real bad for that scumbag word, buster." Irvington suddenly jumped up to his feet and then he asked Walker. "You wanna dance a little with me mutherfukka? Come on man, let's do it right here man."

Delorenzo grabbed Irvington by the arms and he gave him a serious warning. "Hey pal, if you wanna go home in a mummy sack, (body bag) then I'm gonna let go of you, shitbird. You're cutting a big gut fellow, in case you don't know who the fuck you're trying to trade fricking blows with, that big guy in front of you is the famous Road Kill. I think you betta step back some and take a breath, before it's too late for ya and you end up a blood spot on the floor, Homes."

Irvington stared at Walker as if he was trying to recognize him. What he saw was a man who showed absolutely no fear whatsoever, something his instructors warned him about. Never attack a man who shows no fear unless you intend to kill him. "Later sucka." He barked as he sat down.

"Road Kill, I thought that was you, dickhead. What are fuck we doing in Officer's country, man? We're ground pounders and we don't belong in this office, friend."

"Dunno it seems like they have scrapped the bottom of the barrel for this mission when they picked the likes of us to carry it out for them, man."

The five soldiers laughed and then McKinnon introduced Walker to his buddy, and he offered. "Hey Road Kill, this puke here is Neil Delorenzo, better known to the rest of us as Wire."

"Wire?" the Mutt asked, confused over the soldiers tag name as he stared back at the man.

"Yeah Homes. That's because I mastered the fact of killing any shits with a stinking wire."

"Got ya man. I'm Frank Hall, but my friends call me the Mutt. Who is the cherry?"

"Cherry mutherfukka." Irvington hissed, angry as hell at being referred to as a new recruit.

Delorenzo, who knew Irvington for a quite while, laughed over the Mutt's remark as he said. "C'mon man, you betta back off some sucka. These fricking pukes are real square cruds man. Mutt, Road Kill. This puke here is Theodore Irvington, better known as Glue."

"Theodore? Theo, like Teddy man? Now ain't that sweet, Homes." The Mutt laughed, causing Irvington to jump up to his feet and threaten him again.

"Why you shit you, you gots a problem with my name? I'll cut you for dissing me man."

"Knock it off Mutt. Can't you see the stinking puke's a little sensitive, man? Next thing you know it, he's gonna be crying all over you man, so back off." Walker growled as he stared at Irvington.

"What the fuck's the matter with your half ass, you gonna allow that honkie man to rule your stinking life for you buddy. Like all the honkies try to do all the time to the Afro-bros, man."

The Mutt got really angry at being called half ass, which meant the same thing as the mutt though but he did not like the way this dude said it.

Walker laughed as he offered to the other soldier. "Theo, you'll do us fine. Welcome to the damn club, whatever that stinking shit we got caught up in is." Walker's words defused the tension as Mutt and Irvington sat down with Mutt still glaring at him.

McKinnon leaned forward until he was able to see Irvington's face clearly. Once he was sure he had his full attention, he asked him. "Hey Theo, why the tag name of Glue anyhow, man?"

Irvington laughed this time as he sat up and replied to the question. "Well Homes I went and gots myself busted for running a private little home shopping channel of my own, man."

"Whatttt, a home shopping channel, I gotta hear this one pal." Walker grunted with a laugh back at the grinning soldier.

"Yeah I gots myself busted by the heat for running a stinking home shopping channel without a license. This is how it happened man I stole a box truck full with computers, radios and TVs from Radio Shack. Once I had me the truck, I backed up it against a phone booth and made some calls. If I had another two hours I woulda sold off the load. What happened was someone dicked me out to the heat and I gots busted. The Judge was a cool dude and offered me a second chance. He gave me the choice of jail or the service. Well." Irvington spread out his hands. "Here I am."

Everyone in the group laughed as the Mutt added. "That still doesn't explain the tag of Glue."

"It don't huh? When I enlisted, the DI (Drill Instructor) knew of my bust record with the stinking cops and the reason why I had to enlist in the service. He was the lousy turd who tagged me Glue, because he was always getting on my frigging ass, and telling everyone I had sticky fingers, and to be careful of me."

"Makes sense to my ass Homes." McKinnon laughed at his friend this time around.

"Makes my stinking boat float man." The Mutt added as he sat back in his chair.

"And, what are you into here, dog man?" McKinnon asked the Mutt as he looked at him.

"B and B, Beer and fucking Bondage Homes, just Beer and Bondage, man." The Mutt snickered at him.

The door to the Colonel's office opened and a booming voice bellowed out. "You shit eater's better drag your sorry asses in here on the double quick, before I come out there and start kicking your sagging asses all over my office. It's a damn good thing no one started a fight out there, or I would've been forced to shoot the lot of you asses and have my Sergeant get rid of your bodies."

Walker was the first one to enter the Colonel's office and he grinned at the seated officer.

"You piece of shit you, stand where you are, you're making me sick to my guts looking at you standing so close to me. The rest of you shits stand by his side." Once the soldiers were inside his office, the Colonel ordered the last one to close the door. "I guess you pukes are wondering why you assholes were sent here to train. I'll start by introducing myself to you assholes. I'm Colonel John Governali, and I'm the one who pulled the pleasure of forming you shit talkers into soldiers and gentleme... Arr fuck that, you shitbirds will never be gentlemen. You shits were picked to train and lead a group of worthless Cuban troops in an invasion of their stinking homeland.

"Something has happened down there on that little Island and I don't know what the hell it is at this point, but for the past fifteen years we have been training. Arr... at least trying to train these dumb shits in the ways of soldiers. Everything we did so far has failed miserably to date. I don't know why, either these damn shits are too dumb to retain what we tried to train them, or they just plain outright don't want to learn. Either way, their pleasure trip on our government's expense is coming to a fast conclusion, as yours is. For years you scumbags have been wasting your time taking a free ride on your government and taxpayer's ass. Now, you shits are going to earn some of your pay. Any of you shits speak Spanish?"

McKinnon and Irvington raised their hands in response to the Colonel's last question.

"What about you Corporal Walker? I know you speak Spanish mister."

"Yes sir." Corporal Walker replied as he continued to grin back at the angry looking Colonel.

"Well then why the fuck in the name of the good Christ Child didn't you raise your hand and inform me you know how to speak Spanish, asshole?"

"Dunno why I didn't raise my hand, sir." Walker replied while still grinning at the Colonel.

"You don't know why? I believe we have a failure to communicate here. What the hell's wrong with your bone dome, mister? You stupid or something, are your oars not in the water?"

"Yes sir." Walker snapped and causing the rest of the group to burst out in laughter.

"Don't fuck with me on these new orders, mister. You'll lose every damn time pal." The Colonel pointed a finger right at Walker's chest as if it could kill him and then he snarled at him. "I'll let you get away with it this time, but I assure you not again buster. I trust you got it out of your system now. Try it again and you'll be in the field looking for your balls and a medic to help put the damn things back together, asshole. Do I make myself clear turd?"

"Yes sir." All five of the young and proud soldiers responded together.

"Mutt, you keep eyeballing me like you are asshole, and I'll rip the things out of your noggin and have them served to you for lunch. You're here for training, not drive me nuts. Got it?"

"Yeah sure sir." The Mutt said, showing the Colonel he did not believe his threat against him.

"You're damn right it's yes sir, and don't any of you shitbirds forget it for one damn second either. I know all about each of you dumb shits and I'll get the respect I'm entitled to, or I'll have your heads for my damn trophy room. Now, this is what I want from you people, you're to train these non English speaking types we're putting you in command of, in the excellent ways your government trained you jerks in. Remember, the better you train them, the better the chance you'll have of living through this mess. For some reason unbeknownst to me, the powers that be picked you stinking pukes, thinking you're any better than we're in training these damn assholes.

"Your training of these dumb shits will begin tomorrow morning at exactly Oh, Four Hundred Hours on the 24th, of September. You'll have no more than two weeks to whip these non English speaking types into top notch soldiers. These shits will probably hate your guts for you, but it's up to you to make them respect you, and respect is enough. I can't give you too much in the way of any added information on your mission. What I have I'll share with you and when I find out anymore, so will you people. Any questions from you shitbirds?"

Corporal Robert Walker's hand immediately shot in the air before him.

"I should've known there would be one of you assholes who are going to bust my horns. Yes, yes what is it? And it better be a damn good question, mister."

"Yes Sir Colonel Sir, if we're gonna be in command of all these Cuban puds training crap. Then does that mean we're all gonna be made Officers, or something like that sir?"

The Colonel laughed and it took him a second to gather himself as he replied. "God in Heaven forbid that from happening. Ahhh... Walker, I must say, that was a real good question though there mister. You're a real funny puke mister, just what is it that makes you believe you and the rest of these slobs with you should be lifted up to damn Officers, mister? Man that last question stuck right in my stinking throat on me, buster. Just the mere thought of it, wow."

"Well sir, I was led to believe any stinking time someone's in command of a unit, he's usually a stinking Officer, and if we're going to be in command of this unit of stinking Cuban assholes. Then I feel we should be made stinking Officers, sir. Simple sir." He offered with a smile.

"Nice try there asshole, but let me break this down in terms that even you can understand, buster. There ain't no way in unholy hell you shitbirds are going to be appointed to Officers over this mission so fuhgedaboutit."

"We ain't even going to get a stinking rate increase outta this fricking shit, Colonel?"

"To what buster? What the fuck could I possibly lift you up to, Major pain in the ass, mister?"

"Sergeants at the least I guess, Colonel." Corporal Walker grinned back at the officer again.

"That'll be the day you have to have brains to be Sergeants, mister. Look, this isn't negotiable so get off it will you. If I had my way about it, all you stinking shitbirds would be civilians serving out your service time in the fricking can. Look, the only reason any of you shitbirds were picked to lead this other mess of shit in possible battle, is because someone much higher up than I am, felt you asses might be able to communicate with them on their terms..."

"And, because we're fucking expendable on this mission as well, right Colonel?"

"Yes, you slobs are expendable for this mission you got that one right, mister. But one thing you said was wrong, Walker. This entire group you referred to as a unit, was way off base, mister. You're going to head a new Division that's being formed for this mission. The damn thing is going to be branded as the 199th Cuban Infantry Division, and it'll consist of a force of one thousand and forty four miserable men and women who think of themselves as soldiers. That's right, you shitheads heard me correct, I said damn women too, busters."

"Colonel, the only place for a woman's ass is on my face." Walker smirked while causing the rest of the soldiers to break up, as the Mutt rapped fists with him over his last comment.

"That'll be enough of that kind of talk, scumbag. Let me warn you shitbirds, I catch any of that crap going on and I'll skin the lot of ya.

These women fighters are to be treated with the same respect as the rest of the soldiers. It's only a matter of time before your government comes to its damn senses, and finally realizes women are every bit as good as any of our male fighters, maybe even better in some instances."

"Which is none, Colonel?" the Mutt added, referring to the remark about respect being shown to the women at all time, and causing the rest of the group to break up again.

"Okay funny bunnies, can the crap before I lose my temper, and I have you all shot for sport. These soldiers are serious in fighting to set Cuba free from Castro's grasp. Arrr... enough of my telling you what I don't know about, I can see by your expressions that none of you shits are paying attention. Get out of my office and head for barracks One Eighty Four, that's yours. Your troops will arrive throughout the rest of the day, and they'll be ready to begin their new training program at time set. Get out."

"One question if you don't mind my asking you, Colonel." McKinnon asked the Colonel.

"Dag gum it, shoot Wire." The Colonel snapped angrily at the other soldier this time.

The five soldiers were rather impressed by the Colonel knowing their names and tag already. "Yes sir. Have any of these Cuban peckers we're gonna be training starting tomorrow, have any formal military training yet sir?"

"Yeah, they have the infantry part down pat at this time, and they're also performing pretty well as a working unit, but they don't know jack shit about any military tactics, and that's where you pack of shitbirds come in, mister. Command believes you shitbirds have enough military tactics down pat, and they want you to try and train the rest of these asses in that art. I'll remind you shitbirds again, the better these shits fight, the better chance you have of making it home alive from this mission. Simple?"

"Too simple sir." Walker snapped as he headed out of the door with the rest following him.

The Colonel watched as everyone turned and followed Walker out of his office, causing the officer to bitch at himself. "So that is the one who'll be leading this mess. Someone in personnel hit the nail on the head when they picked him for this damn duty."

HAVANA, CUBA. SEPTEMBER 24th, 1996. 6:30 A.M.

Presidente Carlos Rafael Hernandez Alvarez woke to a painful cramp working its way through his right thigh, and he was naked and freezing. He looked for Maria and found her lying on the floor, she found their clothes on the floor and she used them to snuggle under. She obviously slid off his lap sometime in the middle of the night before.

Alvarez stuck his feet out from under his chair as stood and paid the price for it. There was a stabbing pain in his back as he raised his hands over his head, and he stretched and yawned. He then rubbed his back as he stifled a moan, and he ran his tongue over his mouth that felt like something just died in it, and he wished there was a sink in the office. He decided to send a guard outside to fetch them some drinking water and something to eat. He could still hear some automatic weapon fire and explosions going off as he painfully walked over to the double doors. He opened the left door and stepped out, almost tripping over the sleeping form of Melba as he looked at the guards standing on either side of the entrance. When they saw him, they immediately snapped to attention with their rifles held at port arms. The Colonel shook his head as he looked at the sleeping woman and smiled over her loyalty.

Melba opened her eyes when he kicked her in the rump, and she jumped to her feet, staring open mouthed at the naked and young Presidente of Cuba smiling at her.

"Melba, I need something to drink. Water, and some food too, can you help me out please?"

Melba shook her head yes as she continued to stare at his nakedness so near her.

Alvarez followed her gaze and smiled as he scratched his dick, almost making her cry out.

"Go and get us some food and water please." Colonel Alvarez repeated to her a second time.

Melba started to leave Colonel Alvarez's side, walking backwards as she left him and then to her side. All the while she kept her eyes glued to Carlos Alvarez's rock hard and well tanned body. When she was out of sight, Colonel Alvarez laughed as he closed the door after flashing a quick smile at the pair of security guards staring ahead. He knew he found someone who would relieve some tensions when Maria was unavailable. He laughed again as he thought of Melba who was not too hard to look at. His laughter woke Maria and she was getting up on her elbow when he returned to his seat and he pushed her rearend away from the chair with his foot.

"Sure, you're like all the rest of you pig males. When you get what you want from us women, you just shove your woman aside with your foot." She stood and wrapped his too large a shirt around her and then she sat on the edge of the desk.

"And, just how many men do you know well enough to wake up with the next morning naked as you are, my little minx?" Presidente Alvarez jokingly snapped back at her as he smiled.

"Wouldn't you like to know the answer to that question, mista." Maria purred back as she stuck her tongue at her Presidente.

"Ha, I thought so." Alvarez struggled into his clothes, actually taking his shirt from Maria's shoulders. He hated getting dressed in a dirty uniform, but there was no opportunity to try and locate a clean one. Maria dressed in the new clothes she obviously hidden out of his sight. She looked good and refreshed. As they talked, Melba entered the office carrying a tray of bread and eggs, and a pot of coffee. She rushed over to the desk, and placed the tray down on it and then quickly dashed out, but not before looking to Maria to see if she needed anything. Once out, the two ate. Vice President Cabrisas came in and spoke.

"Presidente, we successfully secured the Palace complex, and our control of the city reaches out the shore now, sir. We have control over Canal de Entrada from both sides of the water, and over the Port. We'll soon extend our control over the entire western section of the city, and have that area secured as well. This is where Castro chose to live, and most of his fanatical followers chose to settle there also sir. We've been forced to practically level this entire section of the city, but the fighting there is starting to even off some for us, sir. Overnight, I had pulled in more support troops and equipment from Bernardo's 27th Mechanized Group, but this move has left the entire southeastern section of the capital city mostly unprotected, and we're getting..."

"What is happening there?" Colonel Alvarez asked as he pointed at him with his fork now.

"Sir, this section is our most controlled area of the entire city, sir. That is why I chose to move most of his troops to the other sections of the city that is still in question, El Presidente Sir."

"When will we finally have control over the entire fooking city, Vice Presidente Cabrisas?"

He did not reply, forcing Alvarez to bark. "I asked a question and I expect an answer."

The Cuban Vice President looked embarrassed over the slight reprimand, causing Maria to grab Alvarez's arm in order to stop him from speaking to the Vice Presidente in such a harsh manner. She was stunned when Alvarez forcefully yanked his arm free of her grasp without even looking at her as he snarled again at Cabrisas. "I'm waiting for a fooking answer from you, dommit." He threw his fork across the room as he glared at the man.

Maria leaned away from the steaming and extremely angry Colonel Carlos Alvarez.

"Presidente Sir, I fear we'll never gain complete control over the city, or the entire Island sir."

"And why not Vice Presidente Cabrisas? Why would you dare to make such a response to me, your Presidente?" Alvarez spat back at him with anger in his tone.

"Because I believe we might have underestimated how many of the god dom citizens of Cuba would continue to back Castro, and fight against us in this new revolution. We knew there was going to be some resistance aimed at us, sir. But no one had thought it would dare reach the proportions they have here, sir." Vice Presidente Cabrisas looked directly at Presidente Alvarez, and then added to his words. "Carlos, I cannot believe how many civilians we have killed so early in our new revolution, sir. Many of our soldiers are growing weary of all the god cursed killing of civilians and are starting to complain to their Commanders, sir."

Presidente Alvarez moved as if he was going to say something, but he was stilled by Vice President Cabrisas who raised his hand and offered. "Presidente Alvarez, I issued orders to all Commanders and Sergeants to move the disgruntled soldiers to the rear of their columns. I just instructed these soldiers to be watched carefully, sir. I don't need any of them creating new problem in our flanks, sir. I know many of the tankers are following their orders without question, sir. But we're having some problems to the northwest and moments ago, I allowed the soldiers attacking that section of the city to employ artillery if it was needed."

As if on cue, the thunder of artillery boomed. The whistle of finned artillery rounds from 122 mm cannons roared on their way to their targets. Alvarez went over to the steel plates and tried to look out the crack. Not being able to see what was going on in the city he turned to the Vice President and ordered him. "By the Holy Madonna, get this god cursed metal down! I want to see what is happening in the city."

"Right away Presidente Alvarez, but if you want to see what's happening in the city. You can move to the next office while I have the workers remove the armored protection for you, sir."

Without a word, Colonel Alvarez headed for the other office. But before leaving, he looked at Maria who was still seated by the desk, using her fork to play with her food. She sat sobbing.

"Maria, I guess I have to ask, are you coming with me woman?" he barked at her.

She looked up and she stared back at Colonel Alvarez with tears rolling down her cheeks.

"What the hell is wrong with you now? You better dress before you come with me, woman."

She refused to answer as she picked up her clothes and then wiggled into them quickly.

"Look, I don't have the time for this god dom shit right now, Maria. I want you to come with me. I don't want to leave you alone any longer while the workers are removing the dom plates away from the foul windows, woman." Alvarez snarled at his lover and girlfriend.

"Why? Are you afraid I might do something with any of them, Carlos?" She snapped at him.

Vice Presidente Cabrisas saw where this conversation was heading and he left the room.

Alvarez glared harshly at Maria and he snapped at her. "And what do you mean by that shit?"

"It's you Carlos Alvarez. I don't recognize who you have become any longer, my love."

"Whattt? For the love of God Maria, what the hell is bothering you now? Look at all the god dom pressure I'm under here, god dommit. I don't need any of this from you at this time."

"You have changed so much on me ever since you took over the Presidency of Cuba, my lover. The Carlos Alvarez I have grown to love and respect wouldn't dare speak to his good friends and supporters as you have just spoken to Lazaro, especially within my presence. Carlos Alvarez, did you see the painful look on his face when you yelled at him in front of me? He was so hurt, so crushed by your angry words. You've never spoken to anyone in that manner yesterday. What the hell is wrong with you all of a sudden? What happened to you? Alvarez, I don't know you any longer. I..."

"You! You! You! It's always fooking you! Look Maria, I'm still the same man you have fallen in love with years ago, woman. It's with this god dom pressure and these miserable rampaging civilians challenging my takeover of the Presidency of Cuba. Once I broke the backs of these dom civilian troublemakers, you'll see the old Alvarez return to you with a smile on my face."

"You see my love of life. This is exactly what I meant Carlos. These troublemakers you're speaking of are civilians, Cuba's civilians and you so coldly speak of breaking their backs and crushing them under your military units and might now. How are you going to accomplish this? By turning your artillery loose on the civilian next? Alvarez think, please think about what you are doing, and how you're accomplishing it. You're acting no better than Castro has done when he was in command of Cuba. Carlos, I fear what you're becoming my love. You're becoming like Castro was. Are you beginning to enjoy killing the defenseless civilians of our great country, as he has done over the many years he was enjoying control over all Cuba, Carlos? Are you getting drunk on the..."

Alvarez lost his temper and he crossed the distance separating them in three quick strides, and slapped Maria hard across the face as he hissed at her savagely. "How dare you, you bitch you! How dare you compare me to that crazy man I was forced to kill? I'll kill you if you ever put me up against Castro again like that. I'll kill you I tell you, do you hear me bitch!" Alvarez slapped her once more, before grabbing her by the front of her blouse. He pulled her to her feet by it as he hissed right in her face. "I just told you to accompany me, and that is exactly what you are going to do, bitch. I told you I don't have any time for this crap. I don't care how you may feel about me right now, my only and main concern is getting control over this country, and you're going to help me whether you like it or not. Now let's get going you bitch!" Carlos Alvarez roughly shoved her hard towards the door.

Maria walked in a stunned stupor while rubbing the side of her face and still sobbing a little.

"May God curse you to hell, get moving. I have to see what's going on in my city, woman."

The way Alvarez just referred to Havana as his city made her shiver and hug her body. She saw how men reacted whenever they gained power, and Alvarez was acting just like a wild madman. Her mind screamed at her. 'You have stood by this man's side, and you gave him the strength to finally overthrow Castro who was a madman destroying Cuba. Now you have to watch as the man you love turns into the same kind of madman as Castro was. Cuba, my poor Cuba. What will ever become of my poor Cuba once he gains control of you and the Island?' She sobbed to herself as she slowly reached for the doorknob so she could leave the massive room.

Colonel Alvarez slapped her in the back of the head, and then he snarled at her as he roughly shoved her again forward. "You'll not allow anyone to see you crying, you filthy witch. If someone happens to ask you why you're so unhappy on this foul day, you'll tell them it's because the dom civilian troublemakers of Cuba misunderstood what it is I'm trying to do for the dom fools, and for their country. You're sad the troublemaking civilians chose to make this trouble for me, their new Presidente of Cuba. Do you understand you fooking bitch?" Colonel Carlos Alvarez barked nastily as he grabbed her by the hair, and then he growled right in her face.

She refused to speak or even look directly at him she just nodded yes at Carlos.

"That is better bitch." He let go of her hair and then he growled angrily. "Now, let's go." Alvarez snarled as he shoved her through the door. He had to grab her by the arm and pulled her into the office to his left. She went to her right and he roughly pulled her in the room, and shoved her over towards the window.

Vice President Cabrisas was in the room with Major Cienfuegos, who Cabrisas had sent for when Alvarez let him know he wanted to see what was going on in the city. Colonel Calvo was on his way up to the room also.

Presidente Alvarez nodded to Cienfuegos as he headed for the window. He could not see any artillery, but he was able to see deadly shells pounding the area he wanted destroyed. The entire area of this section of the capital city from the Avenida De Los Presidentes northwest to Paseo, was being heavily pounded. Alvarez watched attentively as a shell hit a luxurious home, collapsing it in on itself, and sending sections of walls flying into the air. The crippled structure turned into a ball of flames that tumbled to the ground in a cloud of dust and flames. Two more shells hit the same structure which caused Alvarez to realize someone was obviously directing the artillery fire. The shells completely leveled what was left of them all but destroyed building.

Maria went over to the window and she joined the two soldiers standing there as they stared out to the northwest of the capital. She was stunned to see so much of the capital ablaze. It reminded her of the news clips she saw of the cities of old Europe after they were bombed to destruction by the Ally aircraft laying siege to the Nazi cities of Germany. Hordes of civilians were fleeing the burning area carrying their belongings on their backs. She drew in a breath as she watched soldiers move in and take aim at a number of women and children, and open fire at them. She bit her lower lip as a moan escaped her, the women they were killing were no threat to the soldiers, yet they killed them for nothing more than the hell of it. Other soldiers attacked more of the civilians fleeing the shelling of this section of the city, shooting and beating them. There were other soldiers going through the belongings of the dead, taking what they wanted from them, and left the rest for whomever.

Colonel Calvo entered the room while cursing as he complained. "All these godless civilian bastards, they're taking my soldier's time to stop the fools from rioting, god dommit. We don't have the time to get the miserable services back on line for the dom city. We had to get more fuel for the dom generators of this building, to keep the lights on here Carlos. I have tanks moving up from your 1st Armor Division, Major Cienfuegos. I sent a number of your troops in to take over the Tank

Reserve stationed at Matanzas for me. These troops were ordered to kill anyone who gives them any sort of trouble, sir. I'm getting very sick and tired of dealing with all these god dom civilian mobs out there, sir." Colonel Calvo lit up another cigar as he stared at an explosion in the northwest section of the city. The flames made shadows dance across the Colonel's face.

Colonel Alvarez had a heart pain, and he found himself asking the new Colonel Calvo if he felt they were using too much deadly force in dealing with the wildly rampaging civilian hordes.

Calvo stared back at Presidente Alvarez, and he took a drag on his cigar and blew the smoke out as he asked with concern lacing his voice. "And, what the hell do you suggest I do in dealing with these god dom civilian sonofabitches, sir? As you just bitched at me, ever since we started this new Revolution, we have to gain control over the city before we can control the rest of the god dom Island. The dom civilian troublemakers have been dealt with by force and brutality for so long, I believe it is the only thing the dom fools understand any longer, sir. A little bit longer, and I shall break the motherfooker's backs on them, sir. This much I promise you sir." Colonel Calvo held up his fist and he then shook it to emphasize his proud boast to Colonel Alvarez.

"Yes Colonel Calvo, you're right, but hear this as well. I'm going to allow you to be mean spirited on these poor souls for so long, before I put a stop to it. I warn you Colonel Calvo, if you allow this to continue unchecked until I have to step in on you, you'll pay dearly for your failure, sir." It was Presidente Alvarez who now glared at Colonel Calvo. His stare was interrupted as he snuck a quick glance to Maria, to see if she approved of his last words to the new Colonel.

She ignored the confrontation raging between the two soldiers, as she kept her eyes glued on what was happening in the northeastern section of the city. A huge fireball was roaring hundreds of feet in the air. The sheer force of the explosion rattled the windows of the Palace nearly a mile away from the massive explosion, shattering many of the windows. The fireball was so far away, yet everyone inside the building, actually felt the sheer force and heat of the explosion.

Alvarez spun around, the first fireball was slowly breaking up, but a second one was rapidly working its way in the air. It felt like the ground under them was rumbling. "What was that god dommit?"

"Hmmm, it looks like it might be the aviation tanks stored on the private airfield. I guess one of the shells hit them by mistake." Colonel Calvo said as he stared out of the window.

"By mistake my ass, Colonel Calvo!" Cienfuegos growled at him as even he moved closer to the window and then added to his complaint. "You have many spotters out there, and one of them must have called a round in on the fuel tanks. What is truly going on here Colonel? Are you trying to wage a war of fear out there, sir?"

"No Major Cienfuegos Sir, I'm waging a fooking war for the control of the dom city, and an end to all this civil unrest the dom civilians are creating for us. Do you know how many soldiers were killed fighting these crazy ass people, sir? I'll do whatever it takes to stop these madmen, and I'll not allow anyone, whether civilian or military, to create further problems for our new Presidente and our Revolution. We're fighting a just action, an action that'll eventually set Cuba free, so she can join her rightful place in the world that for too long has been held from her. This fighting will stop when we break their back's, it's only a few of them creating this unrest against our soldiers, sir."

"Only a few of them you say huh? Then why do you have to use artillery on the dom fools? If it's only a few civilians causing this unrest why can you not stop them, and leave the city and her civilians alone? You're hurting so many for so few, Colonel Calvo." Maria snapped as she turned away from the window to confront the angry sounding Colonel standing right behind her.

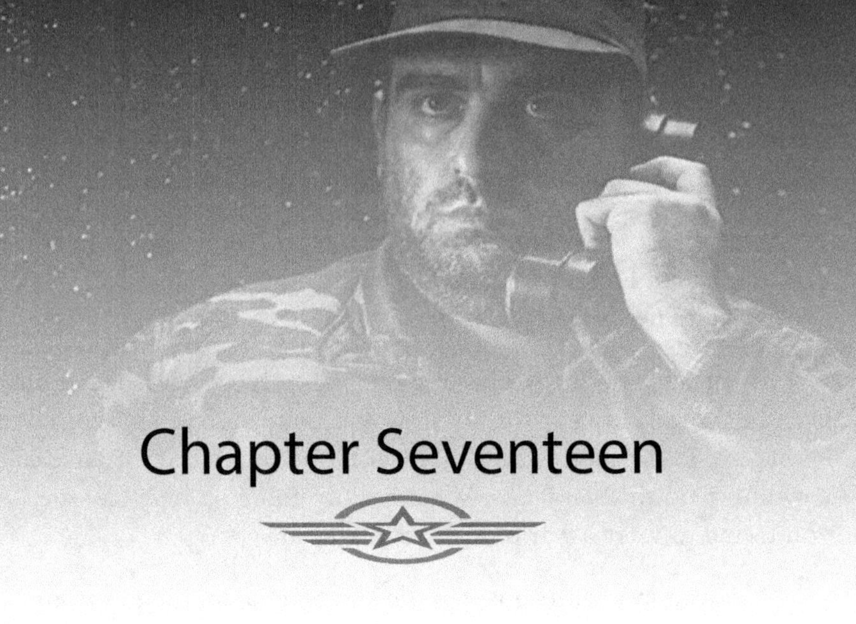

Chapter Seventeen

"What is this? I have to answer to a dom female who thinks of herself as important to our new Revolution? What next will I hear? Will I have to answer to a war tribunal next, dommit? Let me explain something to you my little lady, what I'm doing here I do for the good of Cuba and her people. I'll not allow you or any other fooking female to question my actions until that woman picks up a weapon, and she steps on the battlefield with my soldiers. Once you done this then, and only then I'll allow you to question my ways of handling these dom civilian troublemakers, woman." Calvo glared making her shudder from the force of hatred he displayed in his eyes.

Alvarez resented Maria challenging his soldiers, but he also knew he had to come to her aid as well. He rested his hand lightly on her shoulder as he said something to Colonel Calvo, but when she angrily shook his hand off her body, Carlos Alvarez boiled as he instantly growled at his new Colonel. "Colonel Calvo enough, do whatever you have to do in order to get control of the civilians and stop all this crying and unrest the civilians are causing my new revolution, sir."

Maria glared angrily at Alvarez, she was stunned he agreed so easily with Colonel Calvo's heavy handed treatment of the civilians of the city. Her look was more than enough to force him to react against her, and he snarled at her. "Maria, your place is standing by my side, and not making trouble for my soldiers hard pressed to stop the rampaging civilians for causing unrest. I'm your Presidente, and I'll not allow anyone to look at me so, woman." Colonel Alvarez suddenly slapped her hard across her face.

She was stunned to her soul, not so much he slapped her face. It was not the first time he done so. She was shocked because he slapped her in front of everyone standing in the room with them. She was mortified and tried to flee his side, but Alvarez took her by the hair, and accused her of being foolish. He told her she did not understand what was happening to his new revolution.

She cried from rage, she wanted to kick the arrogant and new Cuban President between his legs, and then run from him. But she also feared he would kill her if she dared to do so against him. She trembled from the terrible look locked so deep in his raging and wild eyes, as he glared harshly at her, fearing he would kill her if she did not act the way he wanted her to act. She cried for what she allowed to happen to Cuba, hating herself for backing this new madman, this new Devil of Paradise, Colonel Carlos Rafael Fernandez Alvarez.

"Don't dare to look at me in that manner or I'll have you taught in the proper ways of an obedient woman, Maria." Alvarez looked around the massive office, and he saw Melba standing by the door and he motioned to her to him with a quick head movement and look. In a flash, she was standing by his side. He roughly shoved Maria to her and he barked at Melba at the same time. "Melba, Maria is indisposed at the moment, and I believe she needs some looking after, before she harms herself. I'll expect to see her in my office at exactly, err..." He looked down at his watch and then he added. "By six p.m. and I'll be looking for some food and servicing at that time." He gave Melba a quick wink of his eye to which she smiled back in response, and then he ordered her. "You may go with your troublemaking ward now Melba."

Melba clamped a rather masculine hand made more powerful from her many years of working hard in the fields on Maria's slender arm, and then she then led her roughly away from the room. Her head spun on her shoulders, she could not believe what was happening to her, to Cuba, and to Alvarez, her lover in such a short time. She could not believe how much Carlos changed. Just days before, he was looking to rid Cuba of Castro, and set Cuba and her people free of his once terrible oppression.

But now, under Alvarez's control, Cuba was meant to suffer in the ways Castro never thought possible. She allowed herself to be led down the stairs leading to the kitchen area of the Palace where she was shoved into a corner, and then she was given and large pot of potatoes, and she was ordered to peel them harshly by Melba, as the older woman glared down at her so nastily.

Maria labored under the harsh eyes of the staring Melba for the day, until it came time for her to dress properly for her private meeting with the new Presidente of Cuba. This dressing was to be accomplished under the staring eyes and control of Melba as she waited for Maria to go to be with the new Presidente of Cuba. Melba even picked out the clothes she was to wear for the Presidente for the evening of pleasure. Everything Melba picked out was served to drive the passion in Alvarez wild with desire and wanting. When Maria was finished dressing, Melba again grabbed her roughly by the arm, and led her out the small dressing room and she escorted her up to her waiting lover who was five floors above where Maria was dressing for his pleasure.

SEPTEMBER 24th, 1996 O800 HOURS. THE SITUATION ROOM UNDER THE WHITE HOUSE, WASHINGTON D.C.

President Albert Cole was seated by the time CIA Director John Raincloud entered the room. The Chairman of the Joint Chiefs of Staff, General William Weidenbacher, was present with the rest of his staff. The President ordered the Secretary of State, Maria Hernandez, National Security Director, Norman Griffin with Secretary of Defense, Jerry Levenhagen, along with the Civilian Advisor Raymond Manning, to attend the meeting.

They sipped coffee and engaged in talk until the Native American stormed into the bunker. He slapped his briefcase on the polished cherry wood conference table, and then let out a groan as he plopped down in his chair. Director Raincloud stretched and then he looked at those gathered and nodded at the President.

"Director Raincloud, I'm not going to beat around the bush with you at this meeting, sir. You called for this meeting and I need not tell you I had to rattle a number of trees to get everyone here so early. I think you should begin with your presentation for us, sir."

Director Raincloud stood and smiled as he started. "Mr. President, ladies and gentlemen. I called for this meeting so I could bring you up to date on the situation taking place on the Island of Cuba, sir. As you're aware Mr. President, yesterday as of Oh, Seven Hundred Hours a force of unknown soldiers attacked the city of Havana, and other cities throughout most of Cuba. At first we believed it was Castro who ordered the troops to the cities to check a overthrow attempt aimed at him. Since that time, it came to my attention this attack on Castro's government has been led by a soldier known as Colonel Carlos Rafael Fernandez Alvarez. Here's his picture."

The CIA Director removed a color photo of Colonel Alvarez, and he handed it to a Marine Lieutenant who immediately mounted it on a projector. The image of a young and good looking Cuban Officer instantly appeared on the screen, and all eyes went to it.

"He's a young bastard isn't he sir?" General Weidenbacher mumbled at the large Director.

"Yes, evidently he's being backed by most of the military units stationed on the Island, sir."

"Do you know how many troops are under his control, sir?" Defense Secretary Levenhagen asked Director Raincloud.

"No official number is known as of yet, but it's believed to be over sixty percent of them, sir."

The Security Director let out with a whistle as he milled over the meaning of Raincloud's words, and replied. "Then we're to take this as a viable threat against Castro's rule over Cuba."

No one dared ask the question on everyone's lips. The President adopted the tact of most Commanding Officers, by allowing his lesser officers play the inquisitors, while he weighed Director Raincloud's responses. His face was set in a mask of armor as President Cole asked the question. "What about Fidel Castro? What's he doing about this Army attacking his city sir?"

"I don't know, but you can bet the bank on it he's not a happy camper, Mr. President Sir." Manning smirked as he entered the conversation now.

Manning's comment was overlooked by all as everyone waited for Director Raincloud's reply.

"With all due respect Mr. President Sir, you have to understand, I'm working with extremely weak information. Anything coming out of Cuba is being transferred by word of mouth only at this point. Everything else is being knocked right out of the air, sir."

"Director Raincloud, you seem to be stalling me. I don't care how you gathered your damn input. What have you gathered on Castro's response to this attempted military coup, sir?"

"Mr. President Sir." Director Raincloud paused for effect and added to his response. "It's my belief Castro's dead, and his government's in the process of being purged by the military."

Maria Hernandez rose up on shakily feet she was so stunned by Director Raincloud's words you could see the deep concern etched on her face. Lately, she was having some problems with her legs, and she did her best to hide it from her political friends. Only the President noticed she had a slight problem. The Secretary of State had to lean her hands on the table for added support as she cried. "Whatttt?"

Director Raincloud looked to his favorite politician and replied. "Ms. Hernandez, I believe Castro is dead, and many members of his government are paying the price for their support of him." He felt bad, because he knew she lived her youth growing up in Las Tunas on the northern coast of Cuba. She and her parents fled Cuba when Castro first came to power, and he killed or drove the intellectuals on the Island out. She made it known throughout Washington she longed to return to a Castro free Cuba.

"Yes Ma'am, it's believed Castro was killed in the opening attack on the capital, Ma'am. I gathered a number of reports stating the battle for the city was carried out on the Palace complex, Ma'am. I have two separate reports stating Castro was killed in the building, and his body was thrown from the third floor window..."

Director Raincloud's briefing was interrupted by the President pacing behind his desk cracking his knuckles at the same time. His hands were behind his back sapping his knuckles and he was mumbling. President Cole stopped and stared at Raincloud for a few seconds, and then offered. "I hated that sonofabitch, hated him bad for so many years, but I didn't want to see this happen to him. I thought we come out of the middle ages for Christ sake, but I see we didn't. Couldn't they have just killed the bastard and then buried his body, and let him lay in peace for God sake?"

"What about this other popinjay? Is this prick that has obviously led this Revolution on the Island, is he going to be any better than Castro was, sir?"

"General Weidenbacher Sir, from all the reports I gleaned so far over this situation on Cuba, they all state this guy is a real hard nose bastard, but easier to speak and deal with than Castro was. I had a report stating this chap said it was time to open talks with America to end the embargo and help Cuba grow, sir."

"That's great." President Cole announced, allowing a smile to flash across his face as he thought over the last words of Raincloud. For the first time in years, the United States and Cuba might be on speaking terms. The President's good spirit was destined to be short lived though.

Director Raincloud's pager danced in his pocket. He knew President Cole went wild whenever a pager went off at a meeting and he, like the rest of the staff, went to the vibrating kind to avoid his anger on the subject. "Mr. President, I have to get to the console I have an incoming call, sir."

President Cole did not respond he motioned towards the communications console with a nod. Raincloud rushed for it, and the Marine guard manning it asked who he wanted to speak with.

"Lieutenant, I have a call coming in please." Raincloud snapped as he checked his pager.

The Marine Officer pushed the proper buttons, and then he stepped away from the machine to give the Director privacy. After a few moments of conversation, Director Raincloud turned to the Marine and growled in a low voice. "How the hell do you work this damn fax thing, sir?"

"Here sir, allow me to get that for you, Director Raincloud." The Marine offered the Director.

They stared at the page as it tumbling out the machine. A series of reports soon followed a number of photos in succession. Raincloud organized the reports as they came from the machine, and he read them while the rest of the people attending the meeting had another cup of coffee, and continued small talk. Director Raincloud turned his attention back to the pictures and he began to sweat. When the fax shut down, Raincloud set the pictures in their proper sequence, and headed for his spot at the table.

President Cole allowed him to get settled in and then he asked him in a concerned tone of voice. "Well John, what the hell do you have for us, sir?"

"Some rather upsetting news for you I'm afraid, Mr. President Sir." The upset looking Director replied to American Leader.

The President put down his cup and stared at Raincloud. He was crushed, he thought things were turning out for the better in Cuba, and now he could tell by Raincloud's expression there was terrible information to relate. "Go ahead John you might as well fuck up the rest of my day, sir. I thought this was too good to be true. What happened on the Island of Cuba, sir?"

"Mr. President Sir, we knew a horde of civilians attacked the Palace complex in response to the reported Revolution by the military on the Island, sir. At first, we thought they were the ones going against Castro. But now we know better, and the fighting's not restricted to the capital. I have a number of communiqués stating the fighting's going on throughout the width and breathe of the Island, and in some instances it's getting out of hand. The soldiers who attacked Castro, has resorted to turning their tanks and armor vehicles on the attacking civilian hordes. There are dispatches reporting hundreds, and maybe even thousands of civilians have been killed or wounded in the heavy fighting taking place on the Island already, sir."

The fax turned out more papers, and Raincloud informed President Cole he left orders with his office to transmit any dispatches on the Cuban crisis to the Situation Room when they were received by his intelligence gathering systems. Raincloud handed the Marine pictures and ordered him to place them on the gizmo he called the projection machine, so everyone would see them at the same time.

The group stared at the photos which showed hundreds of civilians and soldiers lying on the ground as tanks and armored vehicles passed by, and sometimes driving right over the dead. Other shots showed fires raging throughout large sections of the capital, and the soldiers now throwing the dead in the burning buildings. Other troops were shown leading civilian prisoners off. In addition, there were other dispatches reporting sightings of mass murders and bodies being dumped into the open pits.

The Marine handed the Director the latest pictures transmitted to his terminal. Raincloud quickly studied them and he held his breath.

"What is it now, dammit Director Raincloud Sir?" the President demanded. "You seem upset all of the sudden, Director Raincloud."

"Mr. President Sir..." Director Raincloud handed the new batch of pictures to the Lieutenant and demanded them be place on the projector as he went on with his words to the American Leader. "Obviously the new government resorted to using artillery on some sections of the capital against the civilians trying to stop their Revolution, sir."

Both the President and Secretary of State Hernandez jumped to their feet and snapped at the same time. "Whattt?"

"Sir, the new government's using artillery against the civilians." Director Raincloud repeated.

The President motioned Hernandez back to her seat as he replied to Raincloud's report. "How dare their military turn artillery loose on a bunch of unarmed civilians? Surely, this Colonel Alvarez can gain control over civilians without resorting to artillery..." President Cole's tirade was interrupted by the flashing of the latest pictures displayed on the screen.

There was a gasp as they studied the picture. "Where the hell was these pictures taken, sir?"

"Mr. President Sir, these latest photos show the north section of Havana. This is the section where Castro and other elite officials lived." Raincloud fell silent as the President's attention returned back to the picture.

It was terrible what the pictures captured, a number of massive explosions occurring with numerous fires raging out of control in the residential section of the capital. Many civilian dead were pictured lying on the ground. It was a clear shot, too clear. Secretary Hernandez wept openly as she stared at the picture as if she was trying to will the explosions to stop on them.

General Weidenbacher got up and he walked around the table, and then he rested his hand on Hernandez's shoulder. She immediately covered his hand with hers as she looked up at him and he offered her. "We'll get the sonofabitch."

The second picture went up and the President immediately ordered it removed from the screen. It was disgusting and showed half of this section of the city engulfed in flames. Bodies were displayed burning in the streets. More explosions occurring and the telltale streaks from artillery rounds were visible as it burned through the night sky. President Cole was in a rage as he began to pace his office a second time. All the while he was raving at his military men. "General Weidenbacher! What the hell are we doing about these damn scumbags? We have to stop the killing before Cuba turns into another Bosnia, sir. We have to do something, and do it fast, sir." He stopped pacing and he glared at his General, waiting for his response.

"Mr. President Sir, we have the Cuban troops going through their training over at Fort Bragg, and I was goin..."

"You're right, I forgot all about them. How are you planning to support them, General?"

"Mr. President, we plan to sneak the Cuban soldiers on the Island at night, and let them fight their way to the capital. I believe the exile Army's more than enough to make the difference in the outcome of the fate of Cuba..." The General's explanation was interrupted by the President.

"For Pete's sake, I know that god dammit. I want to know what American troops and equipment you plan to commit to this damn fight, General!" the President snapped at him.

"Mr. President, I wasn't planning to use our troops, except for the few we used for training."

"Yes, but that was before we learned about this mess. General, I'm giving you permission to use two of our Aircraft Carriers, and their complement of ships to break this Colonel's rule before it gets entrenched in the government of Cuba. You can have three tank and Marine Divisions to support the Cuban Exile Forces. I want you to allow them to do most of the fighting, but they're not to lose this engagement, General? I won't stand for another failed Bay of Pigs nightmare, General."

"Understood Mr. President, they'll not fail on this mission I can assure you Mr. President Sir."

"No matter what, they can't lose on this one, General Weidenbacher Sir! No matter what sir!"

"No matter what, the Exiles will be in command of the Island within two days after their landing on the Island, sir."

"Very good General, this meeting is ended! I don't want to see any of you again until Cuba's a free nation, and the Exiles are in control of the country." With this said, President Cole stormed out of the Situation Room without another word. Before Weidenbacher and his staff left the room, Secretary Hernandez got his attention and mouthed the words. 'Good Luck sir,' to him.

Weidenbacher nodded to her and he quickly disappeared in a sea of military uniforms.

HAVANA, CUBA.SEPTEMBER 24th, 1996. 9:30 A.M.

The second major artillery barrage released in the capital was coming to a conclusion as Presidente Alvarez turned away from the window. It seemed the artillery was enough to turn the civilian hordes. Wherever he looked, there was no one to be seen out in the open. Many fires raging in the northwestern section of the capital burned out of control. The Colonel searched the faces of his closest officers until his eyes came to rest on Colonel Calvo's face.

"Colonel Calvo, I want you to put Castro's old plan in motion right away, sir."

"You mean the squads creating the diversions?" Calvo spoke in code, because he did not know if the Vice President and Major Cienfuegos were aware of what they discovered at Guanahacabibes, and he had no intention of giving it away. It was up to Alvarez if he wanted the others to know about the missiles and nuclear warheads. Calvo let out his breath surprised Alvarez wanted to start this action as he replied. "Presidente, why are you rushing things? We're barely in control of the capital as it is, and you want to extend our control to other countries, sir."

Major Cienfuegos cocked his head to the side as he asked. "Presidente Alvarez, I don't know what you're speaking about, and I'd like to know what it is about, sir. Especially if it's going to involve any of my soldiers in future operations you are planning sir."

Alvarez was hot and he replied to the Major's demands angrily. "Your soldiers, since when are soldiers of Cuba your soldiers, Major? If they belong to anyone, they belong to me and as such they'll carry out my bidding as ordered, Major Cienfuegos."

"But sir, they have to know what is expected of them, if they're to be successful in any..."

"Without fooking hesitation or thought I say, Major Cienfuegos" Alvarez roared.

Cienfuegos resigned himself to this fact by responding. "Yes sir, as you wish done, sir."

"That is better Major, I'll speak with Colonel Calvo privately, Major Cienfuegos." Presidente Alvarez waited as other soldiers filed out of his office, and he began speaking to Calvo. "By all the Saints that are Holy Colonel, the reason I want to implement Castro's plans of attacking the Jewish and Arab States, because I believe it's only a matter of time, before the Americans attack us. They must know we're in a terribly weakened state, and if they have any brain cells they'll make plans to attack our government before we can get a foothold over the dom civilians. For all I know, the Americans might have started their plans in motion." Alvarez took a quick breath.

"That makes sense if I were the Americans, I'd put together an attack force to make matters worse for us. But this plan, it's a serious strategy that should warrant thought and discussion."

"God curse discussions, I want to give the American fools something to worry about, so our problem is put on the back burner, and it giving us time to better organize our government, and set up our coastal defenses. Now, everything we have is pointing to the center of our country as you know, and we cannot fend off any attack with our weapons facing inland. Any attack from the Americans will come from the water. I hate them." He snarled as he plopped down in a chair.

"How do you wish me to proceed with this then, Presidente Alvarez Sir?" the Colonel asked.

He ran his hands through his hair. "Colonel Calvo, meet the leaders of the assault teams, sir."

"How soon do you wish for me to carry out your last orders, Presidente Alvarez Sir?"

"Right now, were you able to locate any of their secret training grounds, Colonel Calvo?"

"Yes as I told you, the soldiers are stationed in Havana. They should report to the Palace in fifteen minutes after being ordered to, sir."

"Good, get it done Colonel." Colonel Alvarez ordered his new Colonel.

Calvo headed for the office Sergeant Regueiro set up for himself on the first floor of the Grand Palace. The Sergeant was doing a good job of security for the Palace. He entered the office in a huff and saw the Sergeant and two other soldiers reading over new dispatches and he ordered them. "Out! I want everyone out of this room. I have a call to placed, and I need privacy to do it."

Sergeant Regueiro glared at the Colonel for invading his office and he barked at the officer. "By whose authority do you take over my office, sir?"

"By the order of Presidente Alvarez, fool." He growled at the soldier.

The other soldiers looked at Sergeant Regueiro and he nodded for them to leave. Once they were out of the office, the Sergeant complained. "Colonel Calvo, I'm in command of the security for the country, and nothing occurring on this Island is to be kept from me. I'll com..."

"You assume much, if you wish to remain in command of your security you'll leave this office before I have you broken to Private. Then you'll find yourself running the security at the great swamp of Zapata. Get out you!"

Sergeant Regueiro glared, but it did not stop him from leaving as he replied. "I'll be stationed outside my office if you have need of me, sir."

"I won't have need of you, fool." Colonel Calvo waited until he was out then picked up the phone and dialed the number and then waited. Moments later a voice growled. "Fishery."

"The sun is cold on this day." Calvo said in the phone in a flat tone of voice.

"I'll connect you right away sir." The voice replied quickly. "Special Condition Forces."

"Yes, this is Colonel Calvo Sir, and I wish to speak to Sergeant Enrique Esteban Quintana." He read the name from a list of names he recovered from the hidden missile bunker.

"Who is it requesting to speak to this man again please?" the voice asked him.

"I'm Colonel Calvo working with orders from the new Presidente of Cuba, Carlos Rafael Hernandez Alvarez."

"There is no such Presidente Alvarez of Cuba I'm aware of. Presidente Castro is the only Presidente we respond to. I know of no Colonel Calvo, only Captain Carlos Fernandez Vega Calvo, in command of the 1st Paratroopers at Camague." He too was reading from a printed page.

"I'm running out of patience with you, and I have no time to engaging further in worthless words. Any other time and I'd be pleased to settle our differences in any fashion you choose. But right now, I'm working for Presidente Alvarez, and if you doubt this true, you can have this call traced and see where it's originating from, fool. If you wish to speak to Castro, you'll have to be dead, and this I can arrange for you. As I stated I wish to speak with Sergeant Enrique Quintana."

After a long silence the voice growled again. "I shall get him for you presently Colonel, sir."

After a moment a voice answered. "Sergeant Enrique Esteban Quintana. Who is this sir?"

"Your dom code name is to be told to me first before I speak any further with you, Sergeant Quintana?" the Colonel demanded of him.

"Who is this I'm speaking to sir?" the sergeant asked hotly once again into the phone.

"I ordered you, your code name first Sergeant, dommit?" Calvo demanded hotly this time.

"Abdul Jabbar Abdul Agazadeh, sir." The cautious Sergeant replied in the phone this time.

Colonel Calvo checked his list of names and replied. "Sergeant Quintana, I'm operating under orders of Presidente Carlos Rafael Fernandez Alvarez, and I was instructed to order you, Joaguin Adolfo Pena, Jacinto Crabb Mella, and Ricardo Carlos Serantes to report to the Palace for orders. Do you understand your orders Sergeant?"

"Ahhh, so this Colonel Alvarez is our new Presidente is he? I heard Castro was overthrown, and I was wondering how long it would take for this new Presidente of Cuba to get to us. How is this man to work with sir?"

"The best, but I warn you he's particular in how you address him. I'd take care in my tone when dealing with him until this is over. He's a good man, but impatient and short tempered."

"I understand, and your warning will be taken in the light it was offered. Now, if I'm to believe you're who you say you are, when and where do you wish the men you spoke of, to report to the Palace? As you know, we're not fond of having anyone see or know about us. How would it look if the Americans snapped a picture of us in Havana? If we end up dead in some country, it wouldn't take a surgeon to figure out who sent us, or who we're working for, Colonel Calvo."

"I understand and that is why I took the precaution of sending an armor vehicle to pick you and the other soldiers I demanded to come to the Palace up. The machine will have its gun ports batten down, and it'll pull into the loading dock of your building. The garage doors will be closed and you'll be covertly led to the machine in hoods as if criminals. The same precautions will be carried out on this end. The vehicle will pull in Castro's private garage under the building, and it'll be sealed before you leave the machine. Then you'll be taken to Castro's private elevator and ushered here to meet with the new Presidente of Cuba, Sergeant."

"When will this machine arrive for me and my people?" Sergeant Quintana asked the voice.

Calvo detected the change in the pitch of Sergeant Quintana's voice, and realized he was excited over the prospect of being sent in action as he replied. "The vehicle should be pulling up to you as we speak. Do you see it yet, Sergeant?"

"I shall check." Sergeant Quintana looked out the window. "No sign of it yet Colonel, sir."

"Strange, it should've been there by this time, Sergeant." Calvo's conversation was interrupted by Sergeant Quintana, and he waited while he spoke with someone else who obviously entered the room. After a moment he was back. "Colonel Calvo, your vehicle has arrived, and it's parked in our loading dock, sir. I shall leave for the Palace immediately as ordered, sir."

Calvo hung up and he headed out of the office almost bumping into Sergeant Regueiro and he growled at the soldier. "The office is yours again." He pointed over his shoulder with his thumb, and stormed past him without another word. Calvo rushed to the third floor to make his report to Presidente Alvarez.

"Presidente Alvarez..." Colonel Calvo started to say as he was interrupted by Colonel Alvarez.

"You may call me Carlos when we're alone in the office, Colonel Carlos Calvo."

"Thank you for that consideration. Carlos, I found a woman in the Palace, she is hot. Now, I understand why Castro arrived early. This bitch walks around wearing almost nothing, and she does little to hide herself. It's a shame you're stuck with Maria. This woman is enough to make you forget any woman like that." Colonel Calvo snapped his fingers while wearing a huge grin.

"Hmmm, I can use someone to get my mind off Maria, Colonel. She hasn't turned out to be the one who I want to spend the rest of my life with. Besides, there are a lot of other females I haven't sampled, and I think it's about time I get myself back in the game." Both men laughed.

"What has happened to the two of you, Carlos?" Colonel Calvo asked Presidente Alvarez.

"Arrr... she's not backing my rise to power as she once was any longer, Colonel Calvo Sir."

"You'll not mind if I ask you a questions then sir? Is she as hot as she looks in bed, sir?"

"Hotter. When she's in the right mood, you can light a cigar off her dom rearend, sir."

"Hmmmm, I'd like to try her out for size one day in the near future myself, sir."

"I shall arrange it for you Colonel Calvo, for your loyalty to me. About those men sir?"

"Huh?" Colonel Calvo lifted his head and he looked at Alvarez as he complained. "She'll never fook me my friend. She hates me, my Presidente. I have the men you requested to speak with, arriving at the Palace momentarily, Presidente Alvarez Sir."

"She'll fuck you if I order her to do so, and I will for supporting me. If she doesn't please you, you're free to beat her till she carries out your wishes. It'll teach her not to go against me now and in the future, Colonel Calvo."

"Where is she being held my Presidente Sir?" the Colonel asked with a sneer on his lips.

"She's with Melba in the kitchen, I'll call down to see how she is, and what she's doing down there. Where do you want her, and how do you want her, Colonel?"

"Hmmm, have her brought to my private office on the second floor of the Palace, Presidente Alvarez. I want her naked and tied to my desk, spread eagle I think would do nicely, sir." Colonel Calvo smirked with a terrible sneer on his lips to Alvarez.

Alvarez made a call, and after a few moments of speaking with Melba, he hung up and then told Calvo she would be waiting for him by the time he got to his office.

He did not speak, he just shot out of the room and rushed to his office. He stared in awe as he saw Melba, and another woman holding down a kicking and swearing Maria on the desk while a third woman tied her legs to either side. In moments she was tied down and completely helpless. Once they were done, Calvo ordered the three women out of his office. He closed the door and then walked over to the defenseless female and rested his hand on her breast, and then he fondled her breast as if made of dough.

She cursed the pig in a roar. "How dare you do this to me? Alvarez will have your head for this insult to me, his First Lady of Cuba. But not before I cut your balls off and make you eat the damn things yourself. I order you to untie me and bring me to Alvarez immediately."

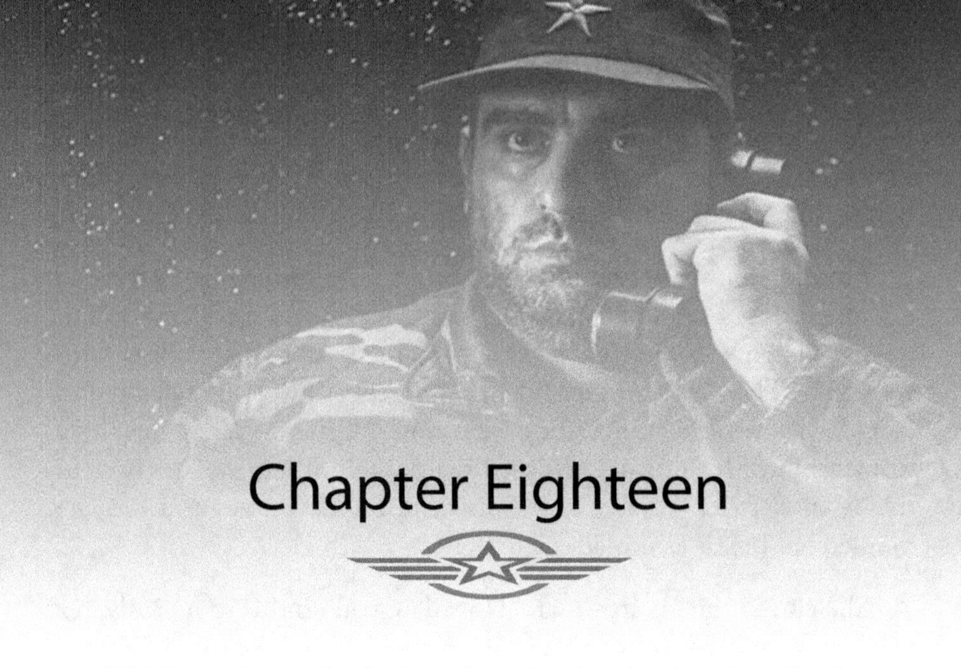

Chapter Eighteen

"Well, so this is the high and mighty bitch who thought she was too good for me a few days ago. Let me tell you something bitch, it was your precious Alvarez who ordered you delivered to me like this, woman." Colonel Calvo's hand went from Maria's breast to between her legs.

She was shocked Alvarez would allow this pig to treat her in this manner. She tried to wiggle out from under his probing hand, but it only increased his pleasure and Calvo slammed his other hand on her stomach, knocking the wind from her lungs. She fought to catch her breath while he continued to probe her more. When she got control she again tried to wiggle away from under his hands. This brought another blow to her stomach, and then another one across her face.

She looked in the eyes of Calvo and she knew he would beat her to death if she tried to fight him longer. She decided to lay there and not move. She was determined not to allow him enjoy her body, and she thought if she lay there like a dead person, she would rob him of his prize.

Calvo was grunting like a pig as he continued to probe her beautiful body. When he unzipped his pants and removed himself, and began to rub his penis on her breasts, she grew angry, but she was helpless to do anything about his attack on her body. The Colonel removed his knife and placed it under her neck as he snarled at her. "If you bite me, I shall cut your throat, bitch. I'll live, but you'll die slowly and painful death while you bleed to death, bitch."

Tears slid down her cheeks as she waited for the final insult. He straddled her head, and locked it between his legs. He grabbed himself and tried to force himself in her mouth. She refused to open. He lifted the knife until the tip dug in the tender flesh under her chin and he warned her again. "You'll open your cursed mouth and you'll not bite me, and do me good or I'll cut you, and fuck you through the slice in your throat. Do you understand my warning, bitch?" Calvo lifted the knife, pushing the point of it into her flesh a little harder to finish off his warning.

"Yes, yes, I understand, you're hurting me please." She cried to the angry Colonel.

"Then open your lovely little mouth nice and wide bitch." He snarled at Maria.

Sobbing, she opened her mouth slowly for the angry Colonel threatening her.

"Wider bitch, I said open your mouth wider!" he snapped at the shaking woman.

She did as she was ordered and in an instant, his member was stuffed in her mouth.

"Suck on it bitch real good! Let me show you how I treat a woman around here, pig."

She did as she was ordered. Calvo enjoyed himself, but Maria's final indignity arrived when he came in her mouth, and he would not allow her to spit it out. When he was done with her, he rested his hand on her chest and warned again. "My dear high and might Maria Ibarra, it looks like we'll fast become the best of friends. But once you stop pleasing me, you'll find yourself giving pleasure to my troops as their private play toy. The only chance you have is to make me happy. Your boyfriend has lost interest in you. Why may you ask me? Because he feels you no longer back him so willingly. To do so means signing your death warrant. Since you lost his pleasure and gained mine, be nice before you find yourself whoring for the Army, until you're worth nothing to any man on the Island." Again, he bellowed as he wiped his dick across her face, and then he merely left without giving her a chance to speak.

Melba was back in a flash, and she untied Maria hands and legs as she begged her to release her so she could flee. Melba paid little attention to the crying woman as she harshly shoved the naked woman to the clothes, she had stripped from Maria's body still lying on the floor. Then Melba hissed as if she could no longer stand to be within Maria's presence. "You'll dress quickly godless pig, and then you'll come down to the kitchen where you'll be put to work until another soldier has needs of servicing from you."

Maria protested until she received a slap across her face, and Melba continued with her warning against the frightened Maria. "I don't feel sorry for you pig. You brought this down upon yourself. Presidente Alvarez freed us from the yoke of Castro's persecution of the civilians. It's a bad thing you chose to do, to withdraw your backing of him when he needs it the most, and I shall make sure you live long enough to see the error in your ways. I'm willing to lay down my life for the new Presidente who sacrificed so much for the good of Cuba, and her children. Get to the kitchen for your chores before I have you beaten." Melba shoved the much smaller Maria forward as she was still struggling into her blouse. She was shoved in the hallway half naked, and Melba kept pushing her and not allowing her to finish dressing either.

Maria had to walk past soldiers who grabbed at her, or they made disparaging remarks at her.

Calvo hurried to Alvarez's office and he rushed his time with Maria, because he wanted to be in Alvarez's office before any soldiers from the special unit arrived there.

Alvarez laughed when he saw Calvo so soon. "What is wrong my old friend? You could not get Maria to spread her legs wide enough for your liking, Colonel Calvo?"

"I didn't take the time to poke her, I allowed her to show me how good she was at giving pleasure with her filthy mouth, my Presidente." Calvo giggled as he settled down in a free chair and he rubbed his crotch with his hand as he grinned at the new Presidente of Cuba.

"Whoa, don't tell me you dared to place your foul dick in her mouth? She's to be feared like a shark my friend. It took me over a month to, and that was after she announced she loved me. Let me see how much she left you to piss with, you dom fool." He smirked at him.

"I have all and more than when I started with the pig, sir." He boasted to Alvarez.

"This is strange to understand, Colonel Calvo. I would've thought she would've bitten it off on you for daring to probe her mouth with it. Colonel, you must tell me how you accomplished this great feat, and yet you remained whole as you say. Maria was always good at making love with her mouth, but it was understood you took your life in your hands, if you tried to force her to give pleasure in this manner my old friend."

Calvo removed his field knife and then he placed it under his chin and he explained. "It was a simple matter to make her give pleasure to me in this manner. You must first place your knife under her chin like this, and warn her if she bites you, she'll end up with her throat slit." Calvo shrugged at the laughing President this time.

"Hmmmm Colonel Calvo, I must try this on her one day. I'd like to see her face once I force her to do me. It'll be interesting to observe." Alvarez mumbled and the conversation was interrupted when Sergeant Quintana entered the President's office and he snapped a sharp salute to Alvarez. He completely ignored Colonel Calvo.

Sergeant Quintana stood before Alvarez dressed in the black uniform of the Shiite Muslim Hezbollah fighters. There were no markings of any kind on the uniform to tell what rate of officer this uniform represented. Presidente Alvarez did not return the salute.

"Err... Sergeant Enrique Esteban Quintana, code named Abdul Jabbar Abdul Agazadeh, you have accumulated quite an impressive file for yourself, mista." Alvarez studied the facial features of Quintana. He looked more like an Arab than Cuban, from the set of his eyes down to the shape of his beard. He wondered if his face had been surgically altered for the future missions he was going to be dispatched on.

Quintana saw the look and replied. "Yes Presidente Alvarez, Castro had my face surgically altered years ago, as he has done with the rest of us involved in this operation, sir."

"I thought so, I must say, even your accent sounds Arab. Where are the rest of your men at?"

"In the hall they decided to wait there in case you put me to death, and they were next in line. They didn't want to clutter up your office with their bodies, El Presidente Sir."

"You mean they wouldn't have put up a fight for their foolish lives, Sergeant Quintana?"

"No sir, none of us will, we've been trained. Presidente Alvarez, for the past ten years, we've been eating, sleeping, and living as part of this operation, and have vowed loyalty to Castro. If you intend to continue with the mission then we'll offer the same loyalty to you, sir."

"But not fight for your lives? I don't understand this mister." Alvarez said, bewildered.

"Presidente Alvarez, it's been long accepted our operation was a suicide one. We're prepared to die carrying out our orders. We accepted there may come a time when the United States and Cuba come to some sort of peace agreement, and when it happens, we knew the Presidente in term at the time would have no recourse but to put us to death. No Presidente of Cuba could acknowledge such a plan ever existed. We accepted this and knew sooner or later, we'll be killed in battle or put to death for security reasons." Quintana straightened up his stance some.

"I cannot believe there are soldiers such as you in my ranks, mista. Allow the rest of your force to enter. I assure you Sergeant, they're in no danger of losing their proud lives here today."

Quintana poked his head out the door and snapped his fingers. Instantly, the three other soldiers in the hall appeared in Alvarez's office. The Sergeant snapped to attention, followed by the three other soldiers as he stated. "Presidente, the man to my left is Sergeant Ricardo Carlos Serantes, his code name is Shmulik Buzali, and he's responsible for Jordan. To his left is Sergeant Crabb Mella, his code name is Bin Yamin Aloni, and he's responsible for Syria, and the soldier to his left is Joaguin Adolfo Pena, his code name is Moses Sharuit, and his responsibility is Lebanon, sir.

As you can plainly see sir, these three soldiers have Jewish code names, this is because their forces will attack Arab targets while I attack only Jewish ones, sir. Our mission is to capitalize on the era of friendship growing between Jews and Arabs of the Middle East, sir. With Israel giving up the Gaza Strip and West Bank to the Palestinians, and the constant bickering raging between both the Jew and Arafat Administrations in the name of peace.

"No one will be looking for attacks on the Jew soil, sir. This is why my action will take place first, we targeted these problem countries for an attack, and with Israel blaming Syria for the setbacks in the peace talks plays right in our hands. We're sure the hated Jews will overreact as they usually do whenever these attacks occur, and they go against Syria. This overreaction could be the cause of the final destruction of the Middle East, and all who live there, sir. I'm certain you're well aware of Israel's development of nuclear weapons sir, and also their willingness to use them against the Arab nation's sir, as I'm equally sure our mission was to take place to allow Castro, now Presidente Alvarez, the time needed to move the glow sticks into the safe..."

"Glow sticks? Safe? What the hell are you talking about Sergeant? Explain these new words to me, mista!" Alvarez snapped as he sat up in his chair, and openly glared at the group of soldiers standing before him in the office.

"I'm sorry Presidente Sir, I had no idea you were unaware of what it was Castro has hidden on the certain secluded Peninsula on the Island. Perhaps we should speak privately sir, so I can inform you sir."

Alvarez leaned his arms on his desk as he responded. "I take it you're part of that operation as well, mista?"

"Yes sir, we're the soldiers who helped smuggle the err..." The Sergeant hesitated for a second.

"Missiles." Alvarez spat out sarcastically at the concerned looking Sergeant.

Sergeant Quintana did not respond to the Presidente's last words, he just stared back at the Colonel seated in the office with them.

Alvarez saw the glance and he snarled at the man speaking. "Colonel Calvo uncovered the missiles on the Peninsula, and reported this to me. Anything you have to tell me can be said in front of him, Sergeant." Alvarez lied because he already knew it was Cardona who located the missiles, but he was not going to explain he had that officer put to death. He motioned with his hands for the Sergeant to continue with his words again.

"Yes sir, I've been trained in the ways of the Arabs, and studied their ways of attacks on the Jews for years, sir. The others trained in the ways of Jew fighters, and how they'll retaliate to any attack against Israel. We don't want anyone to miss the fact the Jews attacked Arabs for their attack on the resort, sir? We copied the Jew uniforms perfectly, and the Jew team members act more like Jews than the Jews do, sir. The mission is to set the Jews and Islamic militants at each other's throat, and start them on their way to a military collision, by causing escalation of any hostilities in the region, sir.

"This plan is an absolutely foolproof way to create the diversion necessary to give us the time we need to have the missiles set in place and prepare them for launching. This was how the mission was to go when it was conceived, and is what we were trained for. Err... sir, evidently, you're aware of the missiles, and are equally aware of what our mission consists of. If the new El Presidente wishes to save time, I suggest you ask questions, and I'll do my best to answer them."

"I need no further information from you on the missiles, and that part of your mission Sergeant. What I'm interested in though, is how soon you can begin this mission, mista. Err... saying that we might go through with it that is, Sergeant." Presidente Carlos Alvarez suddenly sat back in his chair and he waited for the young Sergeant to respond to his last question.

"Err... Presidente Alvarez, we can be ready to implement the mission in twenty four hours after receiving our orders to do so, sir." Sergeant Quintana replied in a very haunting tone.

"Is that twenty four hours from here? By that I mean on Cuban soil, Sergeant." Calvo asked.

Quintana looked at the Colonel questioningly, but he did not respond to him though.

"I mean, in twenty four hours after you have received orders, you'll leave Cuban soil mista."

"No sir, I mean our operation will be well under way within twenty four hours' time, sir. You must remember it'll take twelve hours for us to get to our targeted countries sir, and a few hours longer to set up for that mission, sir. But we'll begin our attack within twenty four hours after receiving the initial order to being that mission, sir." Quintana allowed a quick smile to cross his lips. He knew he had impressed the new Presidente of Cuba.

Colonel Alvarez let out a whistle. "Whew, that is fast, you have everything you need at hand."

"No sir, our weapons have already been placed inside our target countries sir, and they await our use of them, sir. We visited these target countries on numerous occasions, and on each visit, we smuggled more of our equipment and weapons needed to carry out this operation in that country, sir. We're well prepared, and that is why we'll be operational so quickly, sir."

"How long have you been preparing for this attack, mista? I mean with all these trips overseas to your intended countries you have mentioned, Sergeant Quintana." Colonel Alvarez asked him.

"For the past five years each unit made four trips a year to our intended targets, sir. That makes twenty trips a year for each attack cell, sir. Every weapon and piece of equipment we'll possibly need is already stored in the host country of our targets. We made many contacts over the years, and enlisted local fighters to draw from if needed, sir. As I said before sir, we're well prepared and well trained for our operation, sir." Another smile crossed Sergeant Quintana's lips.

"Hmmm... I see, and I'm impressed with your professionalism as you stand before me, Sergeant. But I have a question for you Sergeant. Let's say I send your cells to the four countries targeted by your fighters. Do you have to attack independently, or if I send your cells out to the countries, will I control you before you attack, Sergeant Quintana."

"Why would you want to do that for, Presidente Alvarez? All our training was set, so when we finally went active, we wouldn't have a need to report to any command. It was felt in this manner we wouldn't endanger our cover or our origin, sir. Why would any Arab or Jew attackers be communicating with Cuba, unless Cuba was behind the attack we're carrying out, sir? It makes no sense at all sir, and it could also cause people to get nosy, if you know what I mean Presidente Sir." Sergeant Quintana stared back at Presidente Alvarez.

Alvarez allowed the Sergeant to question his words, because now he needed his opinion, and he needed it unrestricted as he asked another question. "Sergeant, the reason I asked you this, was because I was thinking of allowing your teams to get set in place, but I was unsure if I was going to have you act. Sooner or later, you'll carry out your mission, but for now I think I'd like all your teams in their host countries, and I'd like to be able to send out a message, to set the mission in action, or have it stopped. I guess what I'm saying is, I'd like the final word before you act either way, Sergeant. In this manner, it'll be me making the decisions, not you or the teams."

"Why not wait to send us in then El Presidente, until you're certain you want us to attack, sir?"

Alvarez let out his breath in a hiss, warning the Sergeant he was growing impatient. "Because I want all your teams set in position, but I don't want you to attack until I give you the final word to do so, mista. Because I might want you to attack, and a twenty four hour window is a little too long a time for me to wait for your attack to begin, Sergeant. If your attack forces are set in position and I give you the word to attack, how long would it take to go into action then, mista?"

"Within minutes from receiving the order to do so, Presidente Alvarez." Sergeant Quintana replied extremely proudly to the new and young Presidente of Cuba.

"Exactly, now you can see why I made this request," Alvarez snapped, "can it be done?"

"Certainly sir, I guess anything is possible if you really want it to be so, sir. The only reason I hesitated sir, was because I was fearful about making radio contact with Cuba from Israel..."

"I swear by the Holy Madonna you're thick. It doesn't have to be by any radio conversations. It could be as simple as us playing a certain song over the radio. I'm sure the foul Jews will not believe it strange some of their people might listen to Cuban music, would they Sergeant?"

"It shouldn't be that much of a concern to anyone I'd guess, sir." The Sergeant replied.

"Then that's exactly what we shall do, Sergeant Quintana. I want all your fighters to start carrying a radio that'll pick up our music stations. We'll broadcast a certain recording you'll pick out, so you'll know when it's time for you to start your attack, this recording will be played at the beginning of each hour. If you're ordered to go active, another song will be played at the end of each hour if your mission is canceled. In this fashion, your teams will be able to attack in an hour's notice, rather than the twenty four hour window you offer, Sergeant. Does this make more sense to you, Sergeant Quintana?" Alvarez snarled back at him, showing his anger and disgust at having to take this time explaining himself to the young Sergeant.

"Certainly, does make sense, sir. I guess that'd work, Presidente Alvarez Sir."

"What do you mean you guess it'll work, mista? Of course it'll work for you as I stated. Has not any of your training sunk into that thick head of yours by this time? Have you not been trained time and again, the simpler the orders the better the chance of them being carried out to their finality, mista?" Presidente Alvarez snorted at the Sergeant.

"Yes sir." He responded as he drew in a breath and then he held it for a moment.

"Very well Sergeant Quintana, I want you to do a complete workup for your attack on these other nations, using the addition of a song as your off and on button. You'll pick out the song you wish will be your go ahead order. If you don't hear this song played then you'll not begin your attack, Sergeant. Then I want you to pick a second song out that'll end the mission for your proud fighters, and if you hear this recording played. You're ordered to leave your host country immediately. I don't want anyone taking it on yourselves to start this attack without my direct order, Sergeant Quintana!"

"I'll carry out all your orders as I received them Presidente Alvarez Sir, and I'll be back to you a little later on today with all my reports completed, Presidente Alvarez Sir."

"Very well Sergeant Quintana, I'll be waiting your response. You're dismissed." Alvarez waited until Quintana and his men were out of the room, before he spoke to his other military officer. "Well Colonel, what do you think of it sir?"

"Presidente Alvarez, I believe the attack cells should leave for their host countries by tomorrow morning at the latest, sir. Then they should set themselves up to carry out your orders by that time, sir." Calvo replied to the new Presidente of Cuba.

"I happen to agree with that suggestion Colonel Calvo. But I'd like to know exactly what your reasoning is for this quick a deployment of these terrorist cells to the host nations, Colonel Calvo?" Alvarez asked as he stared back at the Colonel.

"Presidente Alvarez, I believe you know the only thing the United States recognizes and understands is strength, and the only strength our tiny Island can offer against them sir, is the threat of these missiles we discovered on our soil. Sir, we can install the missiles but we don't have to install the warheads on them if this is your true concern sir, but I advise against this move at this time. I believe if we're to set these missiles in their silos. The warheads should be attached, and they should be prepared for an immediate launch, Carlos. In case the foul Americans will not join us in peace talks and we're forced to repel any invasion by their, or the exile forces they trained over the past years against us, sir." Colonel Carlos Calvo took a quick breath for himself.

"What the hell do you mean the Americans are training the loathsome exiles against us? Is this true, Colonel Calvo Sir?" Carlos asked his Colonel as he stared at him in stunned disbelief.

"Yes Carlos, I have tangible proof the Americans are still training the cursed exiles against us again, sir." The new Colonel replied to Presidente Alvarez in a sharp tone.

"I thought they stopped the training of those godless cowards after suffering that disaster on the Bahia of Cochinos (Bay of Pigs) invasion. What the hell does it take to make the United States realize they're wasting their time, and sticking their noses in Cuba's business again? How many of these so called exile troops do you think the Americans have trained against us, sir?"

"I don't know the exact number of exiled troops they trained against us, sir. The last report I read, placed the number at over seven hundred exile fighters, sir. The degree of their training is not truly known to me at this time sir, and I'm not sure if the dom Americans are still continuing with the program. It has been so long since I had last read anything about this training program for the hated exiles, sir. El Presidente Sir, I feel you should not rely on this information very heavily, when one takes the time to examine the changes that occurred in the United States..."

"Such as what Colonel Calvo Sir?" Alvarez barked at the staring Cuban Colonel.

"The cut backs to their dom military, sir. We have to also take in consideration the cutbacks in the American Medicare system, also to their Social Security system, schools, monies to the cities, other stuff like that. The increased tax burden placed on the worthless people of the United States has caused many foolish Americans to scream for more cutbacks in the size of their government, in any attempt to defray some cutbacks, and the increases to their taxes. It's a shame the black one thinking of running, is not going to this time, sir.

"If he had won, it would be a simpler matter to speak with him, and have him lift the dom embargo for us. This General Powell stated he was in favor of this sir. We wouldn't have to resort to Castro's plan, sir. Anyway, once the Republicans take the big chair, they'll be unwilling to spend a nickel on worthless programs, and turning these lazy exiles into fighting men would be a waste of their tax money for sure, sir."

"As God is my judge upon this earth, sir. I see what you're saying Colonel Calvo. I happen to agree with you on this subject, as you offered sir. Even to the point where we should have our terrorists set in place as early as by tomorrow morning, sir. I want you to handle all that for me personally, Colonel Calvo. You're their only control they have sir, and you shall advise them as to when and where to move at all times. You'll control the radio stations that'll broadcast the songs that'll start, or stop the attack, Colonel Calvo. I want you to take over control of this..."

Their conversation was interrupted by an explosion outside the Palace walls. Both men rushed to the large window. Alvarez was furious as he saw one of his T-80 tank engulfed in roaring, rolling flames. The bodies of the tankers could be seen being burned in the turbulent flames. As the officers stared at the ugly scene before them, a second explosion ripped apart another of his mighty tanks, followed by a third and four powerful explosions, each taking out another massive T-80 tanks, before the war machines reacted to the latest civilian attack against the soldiers.

"What the hell is going on out there dommit? How the devil are the dom civilians killing the best of my tanks, mista? Where is my artillery, and why are they not responding to this latest attack against us, Colonel? Why are they not destroying these dom civilian attackers?"

Alvarez roared at Colonel Calvo as he glared angrily at the military officer for a long moment.

Major Cienfuegos came rushing in the room screaming wildly at the Colonel of the Revolution. "Presidente Alvarez, the civilians attacked one of our lesser protected military bases, and they're now armed with the AT-7 Saxhorn man-portable, and wire controlled antitank missiles built by the god dom Russians, sir. The dom troublemakers are also armed with a number of heavy machine guns, and even have some light armor in their possession as well my Presidente. Sir, it has also been reported to me many such similar attacks are under way on a number of our other smaller military bases spread throughout the rest of the Island sir.

"A number of military bases we left unprotected while fighting these dom civilians have been taken over by these same troublemakers. There were other reports coming in reporting many numbers of our soldiers have went over to the civilian's side because they don't agree with your Revolution, and they're attacking our forces, sir. Presidente Alvarez, we're in for the fight of our lives for the takeover of Cuba, sir. It looks to me if we wish to control the dom Island of Cuba, we have to start fighting the civilians as we do any other Army attacking us, sir." The excited Major ended his report to the new Presidente, and then he waited to hear his reply.

Major Cienfuegos's words underestimated the impact of what was occurring in Cuba. Attacks on smaller military bases left undermanned because of troops Alvarez's Revolution employed, increased. The civilian's meager power was enough to overrun many bases, giving arms and ammunition to the once unarmed civilian fighters. Alvarez's worst nightmare was coming true.

The civilians organized their attacks on his new government soldiers. Civilian leaders took control of the massive civilian Army quickly growing to help free Cuba of all military leaders. Hundreds and then thousands of civilians joined, gathering arms and taking sections of eastern Cuba under control. The entire southeast sector of Cuba fell to civilian fighters from Santiago De Cuba to Camaguey, and was in civilian hands. They even put pressure on the huge American

Naval Base stationed at Guantanamo Bay, but eased up when the Americans freed the Cuban refugees held there for years. They were on the base since the final boat lift. The civilian turned to the next area they wanted, Ciego de Avita.

The capital of Cuba was under organized and was being attack from three sides by hordes of civilian fighters, allowing a small route of escape for the revolutionary soldiers, if they chose to run for their lives. Alvarez's second nightmare became a reality. In certain sectors of Cuba, his troops pounding civilian fighters with artillery and tank fire grew sick over their orders, and they began to refrain from firing rounds at the rampaging civilian hordes. Once the civilian fighters realized the soldiers were no longer firing at them, they attacked the military bases in mass. In instances, the soldiers abandoned their positions, some of them even joining the civilian hordes. When the mobs organized, there were stronger attacks leveled against larger military installations of Cuba. Ciego de Avita fell, along with most of the surrounding villages and towns.

Soon, many roads leading to the capital were flooded with Alvarez's retreating troops. They fled their positions, and were being driven towards the capital. Their fleeing columns were under constant sniper fire as they deserted the towns being overrun by the civilian mobs.

Alvarez's forces rushed for the safety of the larger cities of Santa Clare and Cienfuegos, and were instructed to take a stand and beat back the civilian fighters attacking them, before the civilians threatened the capital. Alvarez's forces tried to hold on to their country's capital.

The defense of Cienfuegos was Alvarez's main concern, mainly because of the two 440-megawatt pressurized water nuclear reactors built in this city by Russia, and then taken over by the Cuban workers in the final stages of construction. The VVER 440 V318 units came on line in 1992 and 1995. These units were crucial if Alvarez was going to keep electrical power going in the capital. He knew Cuba expected to ratify the Treaty of Tlateloco that bound Latin American countries to a non-proliferation commitment, and open their nuclear program to the IAEA inspections.

This would result in unannounced inspections of Cuba's nuclear facilities. Alvarez understood he would not sign since he found the hidden missiles. Especially if he intended to announce Cuba processed the weapons of mass destruction, and he would use them in the defense of the country. He realized he had to do everything in his power to protect the reactors at all costs, and ordered his forces to develop strong skirmish lines of defense in this city using his infantry to man the forward lines, and backing the defending soldiers with tank and artillery units. The soldiers dug in and waited for the ocean of civilian fighters presently marching against them to arrive.

The revolutionary forces were scared, and they soon took to firing at anything that moved in their sights, killing a number of cats, squirrels, dogs, and sometimes, even falling branches from trees. The civilian fighters took over the lower hills, and soon they scouted out the well dug in Revolutionary Armies. They studied their enemy's defenses, and they quickly and easily realized the strategy they would need to employ for their upcoming attack against them.

The civilians numbered five hundred thousand men and women and growing. They grouped together in the foothills waiting time until enough of them were gathered before they attacked.

Alvarez screamed in his radio at Captain Sanguily in command of the forces stationed at the Cuban city of Cienfuegos. He understood if this city fell, his dream of ruling Cuba would be lost and Santa Clara and Cienfuegos were the turning point. If the civilian fighters got control of both cities, they would control over fifty percent of the Island, and a major hub of the country. From here, the civilian fighters could board trains and gain access to the major highways of Cuba, and making it impossible for Alvarez's forces to defend these positions, let alone beat back the charging civilians.

Alvarez ordered reinforcements to troops defending the two cities, and make his stand there. He ordered Captain Remos to organize his Navy, and position ships parallel to Santa Clara. He knew his ship's five inch guns would never reach the city, but ordered Remos to transport his Marines to the area, so they could reinforce the troops defending

Santa Clara. The ship's guns could be used to delay reinforcements using coastal roads, to get around the defense of the cities.

Nine thousand well trained Cuba Marines were packed onto Remos's ships, and they were transported to the port city of Caibarien. This city had facilities Remos' support forces needed, and they would use them to get his Marines on shore. The facilities at Caibarien were situated on the crossroads of the northern main highway, which lead right to the very heart of Santa Clara.

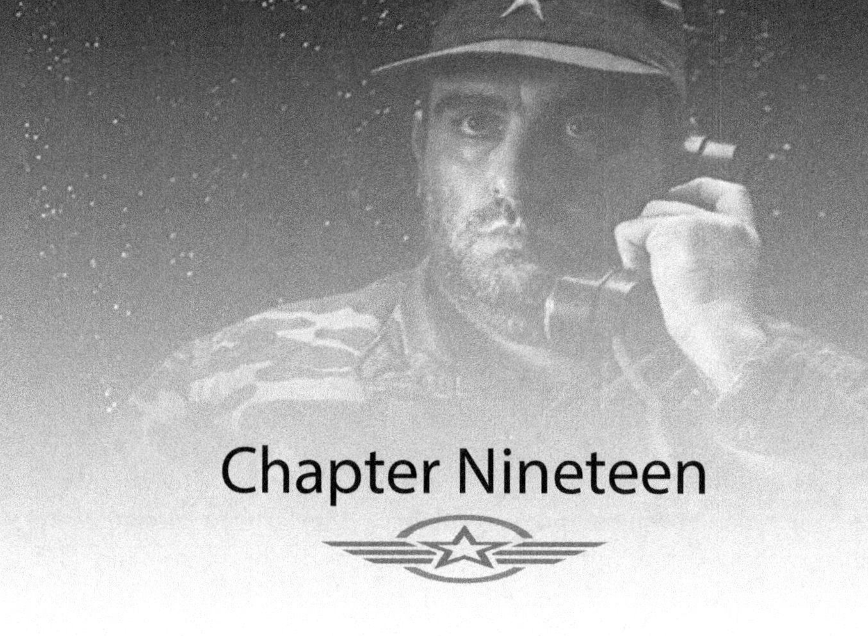

Chapter Nineteen

Presidente Alvarez got in contact with Colonel Agramonte who controlled what was left of the Cuban Airforce. He ordered him to pull back his air support of other troops, and commit his airforce to the defense of Santa Clara and Cienfuegos. He was intent on holding these two cities.

When Alvarez hung up with the officer, Agramonte made contact with his active main airforce bases. He ordered his complement of twenty seven Soviet built Mig-25 Foxbat, and seventeen Mig-23 Floggers stationed at the airbase outside the capital of Havana, up. Both wings of aircraft were interceptor planes, but they were easily converted to ground support bombers and attackers. The fighter aircraft were ordered in the air, armed with Russian built AS-7 Kerry Air to Surface missiles, with a one hundred and thirty two pound high explosive warhead, and the AS-9 Kyle Air to Surface missiles, with four hundred and forty pound high explosive warheads. The Kyle was more than capable of delivering a nuclear response if it was needed and available to them.

After making these arrangements, Captain Remos contacted the bomber base in Sale, before the Peninsula de Hicacos. On this base were stationed Cuba's fifteen Russian Tu-22 Blinders, and twenty two Tu-22M Backfire bombers. Each wing was capable of reaching areas for defense. The Tu-22M Backfire bombers could deliver ten thousand pounds of bombs, and resort to ground support using AS-4 Kitchen missiles with two thousand two hundred pound high explosive warheads. The heavier Tu-22 Blinder could deliver a payload of twelve thousand pounds of high explosives to target, and turn to ground support by using the aircrafts 23 mm gun, and AS-7 Kerry missiles.

The twenty two Backfire bombers were ordered to support revolutionary troops defending Cienfuegos, while the fifteen Blinders ordered out to support the troops defending Santa Clara.

Remos ordered seven Mig-21 Fishbed tactical fighter/bombers used for reconnaissance and surveillance. The Fishbed aircraft were armed with two thousand pounds of bombs, with one 23 mm gun, and four AA-2 Atoll radar/infrared air to air missiles for the defense against fighter attack. The other Fishbed aircraft were ordered to fly support and protection for the bombers.

Captain Remos reported back to Alvarez, informing him of his present plans to attack the hordes of civilians marching on the two large Cuban cities. Alvarez agreed with Remos' plans, and gave him the okay to use his attack aircraft for the cities defense. His defense forces were coming under heavy and constant attack from the civilian fighters stationed in the foothills surround his base, when the Fishbed fighter aircraft showed up, and made many passes over the foothills surrounding the two besieged cities. The soldiers yelled at the planes, because they knew the formidable size of the enemy forces that were massed in the lower hills against them.

The civilian fighters were surprised the plane did not outright attack them, they just continued making passes over the area. There was a slight drizzle falling under overcast sky, and it hid the bombers aligning themselves to begin their attacks against the civilian hordes. Without seeing them, the entire area of the foothills erupted into a rolling mass of flames and thunderous explosions, as the bombs exploded in the strongest concentration of the civilian enemy forces.

The civilian leaders had their forces move to the plains and tree lines. What was thought to be a deadly blow against the civilians, only amounted to a glancing sting against them, with many bombs landing in the abandoned areas. The bombs forced the civilians to begin their attack earlier against the revolutionary soldiers. The civilian fighters wanted to wait until they enjoyed the cover of darkness to attack, but with the appearance of the bomber aircraft on the battlefield forced them to react sooner then was planned.

The leaders of the civilian attackers knew with the bomber planes attacking them, the fighter aircraft would not be far behind, and their only hope of success was to get the bulk of their forces close enough to the revolutionary defenders, so the aircraft could not attack them. At that point, the fighter planes could not attack without hitting their own forces. The leaders urged the civilian fighters forward, but not many were willing to make the first attack on the revolutionary defensive lines. When the civilians started forward, the ground in front of them erupted into flying earth and spinning chunks of shrapnel coming from the wall of mortar rounds pounding the ground before them.

The Mig fighters moved in next, they were circling the area waiting for the order to attack. They raked the civilian fighters with machine guns as they fired air to ground missiles, trying to break down the frontal assault carried out by the civilian forces. Despite the estimates placed on the size of the attacking civilians, they did not come near the number who did attacked.

The revolutionary forces could not shoot their weapons fast enough to make any difference in the massive numbers of civilian fighters attacking them. Hundreds and then thousands of screaming men and women firing weapons and throwing stones, charged in a sea of humanity. Hundreds were killed, yet they continued to charge. The bullets were as thick as the charging humans, yet they came at them. Quickly, the fighter planes and then the bombers were rendered useless in supporting the defenders any longer, as the civilian fighters mingled in with the defenders locked in hand to hand combat. Once the planes were put out of commission by this tactic, the massive tanks moved in to fill the gap.

The revolutionary defenders of the city of Cienfuegos were being backed by three hundred of the outdated Russian built T-10 tanks with inaccurate 122 mm cannons. This was followed by the T-55's with

100 mm cannons then the T-62's, followed by T-72's with 125 mm cannons, the first of the newer tanks fired at a target while in motion. Then came the last line of defense, the Russian built main battle T-80 tanks with a 125 mm rapid fire cannons, and anti-personnel rounds, all of them were aimed to stop an attacking Army in their tracks.

The first T-10 and T-55 tanks did little to turn back any of the attacking civilians. But when the T-72s mixed with T-80 tanks started to pound away at the civilian front line, they had to run for cover. For a time, everything seemed to stop on the battlefield, as the civilians were forced to turn and found themselves running into another wave of attacking civilians. The confusion that ensued stopped both forces from firing, and allowed the revolutionary troops to pick them off with ease. It took five minutes before the civilians turned and ran for the hills. Their plight was not over yet, when they created a distance between themselves and the revolutionary forces, the aircraft swooped in again. First the fighter aircraft attacked, mowing down hundreds of fleeing civilians. When the fighters spent their weapons, the bombers who reloaded came in next, dropping their deadly cargo on the fleeing citizen fighters.

Nearly a thousand bodies joined the hundreds, if not thousands lying on the ground. Finally, the action was over and only occasional firing from the tanks continued. Captain Sanguily was one of the first soldiers who came out of his foxhole to scan the battle scene. It was horrible, with men, women, and children lying scattered about on the plain he defended. With the thunder of battle subsiding, the cries of the wounded and dying replaced the explosions and weapon fire.

"Okay people, let's get out there and see how many of the god dom civilians we can save."

A wave of troops headed on the battlefield, and began to check the wounded. Each person found alive was marked with a small flag. A white flag signified the wounded person was not badly hurt, and could be helped last, a yellow flag meant the wounded needed immediate attention, and a red flag mean for the medics not to bother, the wounded one was beyond help.

Sporadic weapon fire was heard and the defending Captain knew it meant either a soldier found a person too severely wounded, and he put the poor soul out of his misery, or a soldier ran into resistance and took it out. As he stared out over the field of battle, fighter planes streaked the sky, sometimes dipping their wings at the soldiers toiling below them. Captain Sanguily's tanks changed positions, ever on the alert to protect their troops from attack by the civilians. He placed a call for machinery to be brought to the site, to start the unpleasant task of burying the dead.

A Private ran up to him and reported they took six thousand civilian prisoners and were in the process of transporting the captured to Isla De La Juventud that had been turned into a penal Island under the revolutionary forces' command. The ones brought to Juventud were to have a trial and would be allowed back on the mainland if the trial went in their favor. If not, the arrested ones would be put to death. No prisoners were scheduled to spend time waiting in a cell.

Captain Sanguily was not interested in the fate of the captured civilian fighters. He was concerned with making contact with Major Trujillo, in command of the revolutionary troops stationed at Santa Clara. When he finally made contact with the Major, Captain Sanguily discovered his troops fared no better than his.

Trujillo reported he sustained two hundred soldier's dead, and another five hundred wounded. Sanguily informed him he sustained twelve hundred killed, and a thousand wounded, and his forces were nearly overrun at one point. If it was not for the arrival of the Naval Marines, his positions would have been overrun by the civilians attacking them and he would not have been able to hold onto the city.

The Captain was stunned Trujillo's forces came so close to being overrun, until he reported on the civilian losses. Trujillo said his forces killed nine thousand civilians, and had no idea how many wounded were on the ground. He had not taken any action to help the wounded he was too busy preparing his troops for the next attack from the civilians.

Sanguily had not given a thought to a second attack. He believed he successfully crippled the civilian Army, and they could not regroup and set up for another attack. His stomach growled, and for the first time in a while he realized he was starving. The light of day was failing and he caught a shiver down his back. He thought Major Trujillo was right in preparing for a possible second wave attack from the civilians. What better time to attack an Army than at night.

The exhausted Captain called his troops back to the lines of defense. Then ordered ammunition to be brought to his artillery and tanks, and he further ordered his troops to be fed and rearmed and rest and ready to defend the base. He was rushing, because night was moving in quickly and from the looks of the sky, it would be a pitch black night, a perfect night to attack one's enemy. Captain Sanguily screamed at his troops, forcing them to quickly regroup. Whatever he tried or threatened, nothing worked on the stunned soldiers.

Many troops were too tired to react to the threats. Whether they were weary from battle or tired of killing did not interest him, all he knew was he had to get his troops ready to fight off another possible attack by the civilians. He convinced himself it was coming. It was eight p.m. already by the time he was satisfied his troops were ready to defend themselves not a moment too soon, because he caught glimpses of civilian forces massing in the foothills again.

HAVANA, CUBA. THE PRESIDENTIAL PALACE. 11:30A.M.

Alvarez issued orders for his troops in central Cuba to make a stand at Santa Clara and Cienfuegos. He ordered reinforcements to help with the defense of these two so important Cuban cities when Colonel Calvo strolled in as if nothing was taking place outside. "Where the hell were you hiding, all hell broke loose on this dom Island and I need your help sir." Alvarez growled at the smiling Colonel.

"Presidente Alvarez, do you not remember you ordered me to set the Special Forces of Sergeant Quintana into motion for you sir, and that was exactly what I have done for you sir?"

"Yes, it was just so much shit has taking place lately, and I was beginning to think I was losing control over the entire situation, sir. How did you do with the special units, Colonel?"

"They soldiers are on their way now Presidente Alvarez. Sergeant Quintana's group will make first landfall in Israel by late afternoon or early this evening, sir. The other three groups should land in their host countries throughout the rest of the night. Quintana has orders to send out a message over the open air, requesting to know who is going to play in the American baseball World Series. When our operators pick up this request aimed at an American station, we'll understand then that his forces have landed safely in Israel, and they're prepared to attack. The other units will coordinate their attacks with Quintana. He's not to send his message until he has knowledge the other three groups arrived in the host countries, and are prepared to attack, sir."

Alvarez smiled as he replied to his Colonel. "Very good, I believe I shall hold these forces in check until I have need of them, sir."

"Then you're still planning to set the attackers in motion, Presidente Alvarez Sir?"

"Don't be foolish, of course I am, if anything, what a ploy to set Jews and Arabs at each other's throats. With the fighting these countries engaged in over the past years, who'd think a different country might be behind the attacks. Why should we not capitalize on the ill feeling raging between these fools? Every non-Arab nation hates or mistrusts the Arabs, and it's not the Arabs have brought these ill feelings on themselves. So why should we not use this sentiment against these nations to further us. As I stated Colonel Calvo, this is a fool proof plan concocted by a military mind. We knew Castro had a brilliant mind, there is no denying that."

"That he did, and I'm dom glad he had shaped this plan before we moved against him, sir."

Alvarez was about to respond when the radio operator rushed into his office. He glared angrily at the intruder. "What is the meaning of this? I left orders not to be disturbed."

The Corporal immediately snapped to attention and then he saluted his new Presidente.

"Blessed Lord Jesus, come on speak before I kick you in your ass. God curse you mista, the damage is done already. You're here, so tell me why it was so important to override my orders."

"El Presidente Alvarez, I received reports from the defenders of Cienfuegos, and Captain Sanguily is reporting a mass of civilians are grouping in the foothills south of the city. He reports the group is over three hundred thousand strong and still growing at an alarming rate, sir."

Alvarez jumped up to his feet and he suddenly roared at the scared looking young Corporal. "What the hell is this shit dommit? As God is my Judge, I'll find out where all these scumbags are coming from, dommit. Why have they not reacted before this? Christ hate them all, why did they wait until I finally rid this country of Castro control? Why do they rise up against me now, and yet they did not rise up against Fidel Castro's rule. I cannot believe they have waited for someone else to go up against Castro, before they went against their newly forming government. I cannot believe this for one dom moment. Is this all that the dom Captain defending Cienfuegos has reported to you?"

"Presidents Alvarez, Captain Sanguily has stated his forces are set in position, and more soldiers are arriving and he heard aircraft overhead, but had no contact with them so far sir."

"Why cannot he see the god dom planes yet?" Calvo barked angrily at the Corporal.

The soldier turned to the second officer and said. "Sir, the Captain has stated there is a drizzle and fog rising from the mountains and it's rapidly rolling into the valley, severely limiting their field of vision on the defenders, sir."

"Are they able to see any of the enemy forces yet, Corporal?" the Colonel snarled back.

"I asked the Captain this same question, and he said he sent an OP and LP (Observation Post and Listening Posts) sir, so he could keep an eye on them. He stated when the attack occurs, he's going to pull back these posts, and would defend the city blind from there."

"What about the god dom planes? Are they going to be able to hit their targets in this mist?"

"Without a problem sir, our attacking aircraft are weather adaptable, Colonel Alvarez."

"The bombers too? I don't want those sonofabitches dropping their bombs on my god dom troops because they're unable to see the attacking forces." Colonel Calvo snarled again.

"Sir, the bombers can see through the fog also. The troops will control the bombing runs, sir."

"Is that all you have to report to me then, Corporal?" Alvarez snapped at the young soldier.

"Yes, sir my El Presidente Sir. That is all the reports I have for you at this present time, sir."

"Very well, you did right to interrupt me and I'm instructing you to do so again, when further reports come in from Captain Sanguily, or any other defenders. I have to be kept abreast of what is taking place in the two cities. The future of Cuba is hanging in the balance. You're dismissed."

Alvarez waited until the young soldier was out of the office and then he stated. "Colonel Calvo move more of your soldiers to Guanahacabibes. If I'm forced from the capital, I want everything left to me defending this one section of Cuba. I need this base if I want to hold on to what I have, and I want control of the dom missiles and nuclear warheads. If I lose everything here I shall destroy this country by launching the missiles at the United States. Then I'll allow the Americans to retaliate by annihilating this Island of ingrates. We'll hurt the United States before we're reduced to a nuclear cinder, Colonel. I cannot believe these bastards are too blind to see what I'm trying to do for them for the love of God, sir."

"Are you going to make plans to escape Cuba before you launch the missiles at the United States? I mean if you're forced to resort to this action, Presidente Alvarez." He asked.

Alvarez smiled and replied. "Of course, I might be angry but I'm far from a stupid man."

The Colonel did not say anything more as he grinned at the new Presidente of Cuba.

Alvarez read his look and responded immediately. "Of course I'm going to make room for you, and the rest of my loyal Officer's to come with me. I have supporters who live in Guatemala. We'll be safe there if we're forced to flee the Island, sir."

Alvarez's words made Calvo smile more as he followed the Presidente's latest orders. He planned to use Major Cardona's 9th Infantry Battalion to defend the secluded Peninsula at all cost, he want to pull the bulk of the armor from Cienfuegos's 1st Armor Division. He also made plans to create a fall back situation. The defending troops would be ordered to pull away from the capital city, and then fall back to the Peninsula area to defend it to the last man.

THE WHITE HOUSE, WASHINGTON D.C. 1:30 P.M.WASHINGTON TIME SEPTEMBER 24th, 1996

General William Weidenbacher, the Chairman of the Joint Chiefs of Staff was in his office when CIA Director John Raincloud placed a called to him. "General, it looks like Cuba has erupted in total war, sir. I have reports showing fighting taking place between two opposing factions raging all over the Island."

"How sure are you of this report, Director Raincloud?" the General asked the CIA Agent.

"Positive General Weidenbacher, do you think I'd be bugging you if I didn't have the proof I needed to convince you of what's taking place in Cuba?" John griped at the powerful General.

"Yeah, sorry. Okay, I guess I better hit the panic buttons. Meet me at the White House in half an hour. Better bring in the troops you're going to need, so I can convince the Boss we should step up the training of those Cuban exiles, it looks like will need them sooner than I expected."

"Will do General." Director Raincloud broke off communications with the General.

General Weidenbacher remained on the phone and when his secretary cut in, he growled at her. "Mary, you better get me a line to the President, looks like it's going to be a long night."

"Very well General Weidenbacher. I'll inform your wife not to expect you for dinner sir."

"Good, better get me the President on the horn first young lady." He rested the receiver in its cradle and then waited for the call back. A moment later the phone rang and a sweet voice announced. "Please hold the line for the President of the United States, sir."

"Yeah General Weidenbacher, what can I do for you?" a jolly sounding President asked him.

"Mr. President, I'm afraid I have a need of a Level Two meeting with you A-SAP, sir. The meetings about the situation raging in Cuba, sir."

Silence, and then the American President replied in a low voice to his military officer. "A Level Two request sir, what the hell has just happened in Cuba, General Weidenbacher Sir?"

"The fighting's spreading throughout the entire Island now, Mr. President Sir."

"General Weidenbacher, you really know how to fuck up my day every time, sir. I'll have the Vice President and Secretary of State here by the time you arrive, which will be when?"

"I should be at the Big House within fifteen minutes at the latest, Mr. President Sir."

The President whistled and then replied in a flat tone. "General Weidenbacher, I don't think I can possibly get the Secretary of the State Hernandez here by that time sir, the Vice President's already in the building though. But we might get stuck waiting for Mr. Griffin and Mr. Levenhagen some, sir. I don't know where Mr. Manning's at either, sir. What about your team General Weidenbacher? Are you going to get them here in this time, sir?"

"My people will be there when I arrive at the White House, sir. They know what will happen to them if I call and they're out of position, Mr. President Sir. When this mess with Cuba first started, I gave them strict orders for my people to stay nearby, sir."

"Good orders, I think I shall issue the same orders, General Weidenbacher. I better let you go so you can contact your people, sir. I'll see what I can do about speeding up my team, sir."

"Very good Mr. President, I'll see you soon sir." The General broke off the connection, and then placed a call to General Luther Claiborne, the Secretary of the Airforce. "Yeah Luther, Billy here sir. You gotta get your ass over to the White House on the double quick sir. Better bring the rest of the team with you as well sir. It's Cuba again General Claiborne, sir."

"Very well General we'll be there sir. What's our clock time sir?" the General asked him.

"I told the President we'll meet with him at the big house in fifteen minutes or sooner, Luther."

"Fifteen minutes! Gees man, you damn white people really like to do things in a hurry."

"Luther, there's no option for this one. Fifteen minutes General or I'm going to look bad before the Man, and you know what that means." Weidenbacher warned the other General.

"Understood, I'll have everyone there, but I can't vouch as to how they will be dressed, sir."

"I don't care if they're naked Luther." Weidenbacher laughed as he hung up. Mary entered his office and offered. "General, I have Marine Three waiting on the south pad. I assumed you'd be heading for the Big House immediately sir and I know how you like to get there in a hurry sir."

"You're right on the ball as usual kid." General Weidenbacher grumbled at Mary as he quickly gathered up his papers and shoved them in his briefcase. Then he headed for the North parking lot of the Pentagon and the spooling helicopter waiting for him. When he was strapped in his seat, the chopper lifted off the ground. In three minutes, it was already preparing to land as he noticed Director Raincloud's car pulling onto the circular drive, and it stop before the main door of the White House.

Director Raincloud saw the helicopter landing and he waited for Weidenbacher before entering. The General saw him and he ran across the grass and slapped Raincloud on his back and asked. "You have all the papers and pictures you're going to need for the briefing, John?"

"Everything's with me General." John countered as he slapped his briefcase with a huge paw.

"Better get in there then sir. I don't want to keep the big guy waiting too long for us, sir."

As Weidenbacher and the large Native American entered the main doors, the Chief of Staff Aide of the White House Staff was waiting for them. "Gentlemen, the President will be holding this meeting in the Oval Office instead of the Situation Room. It seems he has a slight head cold, and the air down there only makes it worse. If you'd be so kind to follow me please, gentlemen."

Weidenbacher entered the Oval Office and he remained standing as he began speaking to the American Leader. "With all due respect Mr. President, it has come to my attention the fighting in Cuba's getting out of hand, sir. It seems there's not one damn city on the entire Island free of fighting any longer sir. It looks like Cuba's breaking herself apart, sir."

"What's it you want us to do about this present situation then, General Weidenbacher Sir?"

"Mr. President Sir, we have a large number of Cuban exile soldiers going through that special training in the States, and I wish to move up their education course on them some at this time, sir. Then have them air dropped on Cuba so they can gain some form of control over the present situation there, before it really breaks down on us, Mr. President Sir."

"Why? Do you think this fighting's going to spread throughout the entire Island, General?"

"Mr. President, as I stated it already has gone that far sir. I took the liberty of looking at some pictures John gathered on the fighting, and they look pretty serious to me, sir."

Raincloud went to remove the pictures from his briefcase, but he was stopped when the President waved him off while offering. "I saw many of the photos, and I know what's taking place in Cuba, sir. I want to know what you want to do about this situation, General?"

"Mr. President, we have to get our troops on that Island. From the Intel we put together, it looks like there's no side strong enough to take control of the other. Now is the time to step in. We believe the civilians will muster behind our troops, and place them in position of winning the Island. Think of it we could eliminate the opposition to the exiles rule in a hurry. We know the exiles if they gain control, will be open to our concerns. We'll be able to bring Cuba back in the fold, sir." General William Weidenbacher dared a quick smile at the upset looking President.

After some thought, the President replied. "I agree with all you offered, General Weidenbacher. Do you think the Cuban exile troops we're training are enough to get the damn job done for us, sir? I don't want to get trapped in a position where I'll be forced to flood the damn Island with American kids, sir. I don't want my first official act after taking over the office of the Presidency to be putting our soldiers in harm's way again, General Weidenbacher Sir."

The conversation was interrupted by the Security Director and Defense Secretary, as they both entered the room. The President pointed to chairs for them. "Pay attention gentlemen, I want you up to speed here." He turned back to the General and spread his hands. "I'm waiting General."

"Mr. President Sir, it's believed these exiles are enough to get it done, if it comes to that."

"Did I detect hesitation in your reply, General? Your last words weren't spoken with enough conviction for my comfort." His words caused a laugh from some of the members of the meeting.

"Sir, I went over the reports time and again, and I'm not too crazy with this situation. I don't think anything short of an invasion of Cuba will be successful. There are too many groups who want the power. If we want to gain control over Cuba, we'll have to send in troops and we'll be forced to leave an occupational force, one that'll be large enough to beat back any attack."

"And, you think these attacks will be coming against our troops, General Weidenbacher?"

"No matter who gains control over the Island, Cuba will be ripped apart by civil war for years to come. Unless employ the necessary troops to maintain control over the civilians, this will be necessary until a strong government is established, hopefully by the exiles we send in to control the Island when the fighting's completed. Mr. President, if we're not committed to carry it to its completion, I suggest we break up the Cuban fighters we're training, and not bother with any invasion, and allow Cuba's future be decided by the forces running unchecked on the Island, sir."

"Err... let me see if I got this mess straight, General. Are you telling me this problem we're facing in Cuba is an all or nothing situation, sir?" the President asked as he shifted his weight.

"That is exactly what I'm saying sir. Mr. President, you're the next leader of our country, and as such it'll be up to you to set the course of our country for the next four..."

"I don't need you to point out what my duties are, General Weidenbacher. Get to the point in a hurry it up, please sir." President Cole almost stood he was so angry at the General.

"Sorry Mr. President but I was about to say I'm getting tired of sending our soldiers in action with their hands tied behind their backs and one eye shut lately. It's time we start acting like soldiers when our troops are sent to keep the peace, Mr. President. I'm still haunted by the sight of that American flyer being dragged through the streets of Somalia with them sonofabitches standing on his naked body, sir.

Mr. President, we successfully tied the hands of the police, and we made them ashamed to be Officers in our country, sir. We allowed asses to attack them until no one trusts the police, and we're doing the same damn thing to our soldiers as well, sir. How the hell do the people of the United States think they'll possibly remain safe at night in their damn beds if they don't get behind the god damn police, let alone the soldiers fighting for our country? Sir, I think that..."

President Albert Cole quieted the angry General by raising his hand before him and saying at the same time. "I know we stuck it to our police officers, and I'll do something about it and soon, General Weidenbacher. We placed the police on trial and made them look worse than the damn murderers. We held court, condemning our FBI, and ATF, and then we order them to put their damn lives on the line again for us. I'll tell you this much General Weidenbacher, for weeks after that damn trial I was scared to death the LAPD would say the hell with all you people. If we're so bad then you go and protect your damn selves for a change. When it didn't happen, and to this day I still don't know why it didn't, I have breathed a lot easier, sir.

"But on the other hand General, we're not here to discuss the police, I'm afraid that situation's for another meeting. I'm more interested in the problem facing me at the present time, sir. You just said you still don't believe these damn Cuban troops in training here in the States will be enough to get the job done, sir. Then you went on to say you didn't want to engage them in battle, unless we're willing to follow through by committing enough of our own military troops to take over complete control of the Island of Cuba, General Weidenbacher."

"Sir, that's not exactly what I said, Mr. President. I was only trying to point out the..."

"That's what you meant though, right General Weidenbacher?" President Cole snapped at him, this time standing up and he leaned on the desk with both hands as he glared at the General.

"Sir, I was only trying to..." The General was cut off in mid sentence by the angry President.

"Is that what you were trying to say to me, General Weidenbacher?" the mere force of the President's angry voice caused many attending the meeting to flinch slightly from it.

General Weidenbacher straightened up in his chair and replied to the angry looking President calmly this time. "Yes sir that's exactly what I was saying, sir. That we shouldn't commit any troops unless we're willing to do whatever it takes to back them, and to ensure their safety in the field of battle, sir. With all due respect Mr. President Sir, we have to stop burying American troops in the name of peace, yet allowing that god damn peace to be the cause of their death, sir.

"We have to stop telling the parents and loved ones they died in the name of peace. I'm tired of losing soldiers during peace time activities. What happens when the real thing comes along, the real war? Will we remember how to fight a war? I'm losing sleep over troops we're sending to Bosnia to check the slaughter of the innocents there, sir. How many of these soldiers will die before we pull them out or we get the backbone to support them as the soldiers they are, sir?"

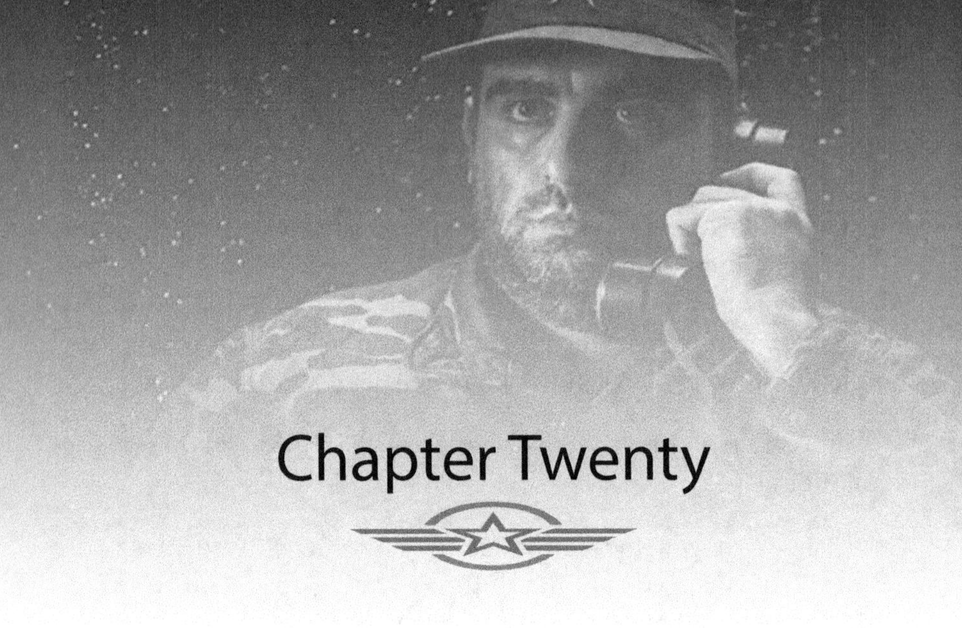

Chapter Twenty

"Enough! You're stepping over your bounds, General Weidenbacher." President Cole bellowed and then he went on with his words. "I guess I kinda asked for that response, General. What I'm about to tell you may shock you, but it's about time we stay on our own damn shores for a change, or we show the backbone which made the United States strong in the past years, sir. Yes, I happen to agree with protecting our troops in the field of battle better when we ask them to protect our shores, sir. General Weidenbacher Sir, here is what I want..."

The Civilian Advisor Manning just entered the President's office, and he immediately took a seat and then stared directly at the seated President.

"General, prepare these troops and have them ready to move out, sir. Pull up the Atlantic Fleet of sixty six ships headed by the Carriers... err..." Cole looked to the Secretary of the Navy.

"The CVN-75 United States is the one we're using, sir." The Secretary replied quickly to him.

"Fitting, the United States. I want the Carrier Washington to join this battle group also. General Weidenbacher, you're to use these ships as you see fit, sir. I believe this Strike Force will be enough to level that entire Island, right?"

"Yes, Sir it is Mr. President Sir." The General replied proudly to his Commander in Chief.

"Damn right I am General Weidenbacher! I'm going to stay that way sir. You have the amphibious ships to draw from, and I'll place the entire First Marine Expeditionary Forces at your disposal. General, now you have the forces you'll need at your disposal to insure the success of this operation, sir. I don't want you engaging them unless they're absolutely needed General. Stick with the first part of this mission, let the Cubans exiles get in there and take some of the heat off us for a change, before you commit our troops to any action, sir. Don't make me blow this one, General. What about aircraft, you have any idea what you might need there, sir?"

General Weidenbacher turned to General Claiborne who jumped up and he stood at attention.

"Mr. President, this is General Luther Claiborne, sir. He's the Chief of the Airforce sir, and he'll give you a quick rundown on what he has available for our use on this one, sir."

"Mr. President it's a pleasure to meet you sir and congratulations on winning the election, sir. I'll make a fast run up of the squadrons I have within striking distance of the Island of Cuba, sir. I shall commit what's needed, and then I'll run the operations from my Headquarters at Air Combat Command from Langley Air Force Base Virginia, sir."

Manning stood up and spoke before being recognized by the President. "What I'd dearly like to see from this African American General, is a complete rundown on all the aircraft and the troop forces he'll be committing to this one operation, sir. The President is entitled to know how much money this operation will cost the United States and her taxpay..."

"I take exception to that last remark, buster. I don't know who the hell you are mister. But you white critters burn my ass to no end." Claiborne snapped and then continued with his words. "No matter what we do for the United States, no matter how many of my people lay down their lives for this country, we're still referred to as African Americans. Just once, I wish one of you white guys could refer to us black folks as Americans. Dammit, I'd love to be called an American for a change. Christ sake, you never hear my people referring to you white folks as Caucasian Americans. Why do you have to refer to us as African, we know we're Africans sir, and we don't need you people reminding us of our roots. You know I wish you'd give us the right to be called Americans, what we are, and what we earned. When do we earn our part of this country, sir?"

Weidenbacher rested his hand lightly on General Claiborne's broad shoulder and he told him. "Okay Mr. America, you made your point and you have opened my eyes to it, sir."

"Mine too." President Cole added, causing the rest at the meeting to nod in agreement with him. "I see your point General Claiborne, and it makes good sense to me, and I'll remember it always, sir. How long will it take you to get these ships and troops in gear, General?" President Cole allowed the officers to run on, so he could judge who he would keep, and who he would let go in the future. Manning was his man, he met Weidenbacher when he was a Senator, and it seemed this man was constantly trying to talk Congress to commit some of the troops to some kind of military action someplace around the world.

"No longer than a week at the most, Mr. President." The Secretary of the Navy offered.

The President looked at his watch, it was late. "What are the forces on Cuba doing sir?"

Raincloud spoke in a pocket radio and then reported. "With all due respect Mr. President, it looks like both these forces decided to make two cities in Cuba, Santa Clara and Cienfuegos, a test of power for themselves, sir. The government reinforced their troops stationed on these two cities, while the civilians are assembling in the foothills of the Escambray Mountain ranges and preparing to attack the government troops defending these two cities, sir. There has been one major engagement so far, with the government forces beating back the civilian fighters, using tanks and aircraft against them to force them back, sir."

"What's happening right now?" Levenhagen, the Defense Secretary asked the CIA Director.

"It seems an impasse has taken place on the Island at this time, sir. The latest pictures we were able to get our hands on, shows both sides are sitting back and are licking their wounds, and reinforcing their damn positions while they're at it, and doing who knows what all else at this time, Mr. Levenhagen." Director Raincloud offered him.

"Who do you think will come out on top in this next engagement, General Weidenbacher?" Ms. Hernandez asked. She snuck into the meeting almost unseen by everyone there.

"That's a hard question to answer, Ma'am." The General offered calmly, coming to the CIA Director's aide. "We have many reports coming in, and some stating the revolutionary forces are turning and they're now joining the civilian's lines. If enough of the military go over to the other side then no matter how well the damn revolutionary forces are armed, they'll not beat back the civilian fighters for long. How many people can you kill before you're overrun by them, Ma'am? There are other reports stating the civilians are better armed because they have attacked some of the military bases and looted their arsenals."

"You're not answering my question, General Weidenbacher and I want it answered." The Secretary of State snapped at him.

"Well Ma'am, sooner or later the civilian fighters will overrun the military forces on the Island without question. It's a matter time before they take over the Island. This is why I want to get our forces on that Island before it's too late for us to change the outcome of this situation, Ma'am." The powerful and well respected General offered to the Secretary of State.

"I seemed to have missed that part it seems you plan to send troops in to take over Cuba, sir?" The Secretary of State remarked to him.

"Yes Ma'am. That's really what I want to do on this one if I can, Ma'am."

"And, who'll these troops answer to, General Weidenbacher?" she asked this time.

"Us Ms. Hernandez, I'd like to end up with a good size occupational force set in place in Cuba, much like the one presently involved in the Haiti operation, Ma'am. Until we can assure the people of Cuba there'll be free elections offered them, and they'll have the power to elect the man all civilians want to lead their country for a change. This way Ma'am, Cuba will join the civilized world again." The General offered to the Secretary of State.

"I agree with what you stated, General Weidenbacher Sir." Was all she said.

"Oh, and you agree with the General here do you, young lady. Well then, that settles it for me Ma'am. If I knew you'd go along with the General so quickly I would've saved myself one helluva lot of time and trouble by inviting you and him to this meeting, Ma'am. But I do agree with the both of you on this one though, and I'll commit the necessary troops and any other military assists to better ensure the outcome of this latest Revolution raging in Cuba. General, I believe it's time you get your troops and assets in gear, sir. You're dismissed." The President smiled at him.

No one spoke until the two Generals left the Oval Office and the meeting.

THE DEFENDERS OF SANTA CLARA AND CIENFUEGOS, CUBA.9:30 P.M. TUESDAY, SEPTEMBER 24th, 1996

The night attack by the hunkered down civilian fighters had never taken place, much of the fighting stopped in fact. The revolutionary commanders were at a loss as to explain why though. The civilians were throwing away a perfect night for an attack, and if they understood how demoralized the defenders of the two cities were, they would easily overrun the defenses without much problem. The reports of the failure of the attack reached Alvarez. He was afraid to respond to the situation though. On one hand, he hoped the fighting came to a conclusion, and the civilians allow him to take command of Cuba. But he knew of the heart of the Cuban people, and if they felt they were right then they would fight to the death, no matter how the deck was stacked against them.

Presidente Alvarez and Colonel Calvo sat nervously in his office while waiting for the other shoe to drop. Neither of the two Cuban Military Officers tried to deceive the other in the least on how badly hurt their forces truly were out in the field. Calvo gave out the order for all his most nonessential troops to leave the capital city, and then to re-deploy to the southwest of the city. These troops were to secure the area of the Guanahacabibes Peninsula. This would be Alvarez's last stronghold if Cuba fell to the rampaging civilian fighters.

The revolutionary forces defending the two cities were scared to death as they hid in their foxholes, and waited for the attack by the civilian fighters to begin. They were forewarned by their forward observers who marked the massing mobs of civilian fighters with their night vision apparatus. They tried to get an accurate numbers on the civilian fighters, and they stopped counting them when they went over a half a million souls. The defenders were outnumbered by twenty five to one, and every defending soldier knew it was nearly impossible for each one of them to kill at least twenty five of the non-military attackers before the horde of civilian fighters breached their defensive lines against them, and killed the defenders trying to stop their attack on them, and their positions.

The night dragged on until the first signs of daylight announced the start of another day. The sky brightened slowly, allowing the revolutionary soldiers to realize during the night, the civilian Army had grown to uncountable number against them. Still, they were at a loss as to why they had not attacked the two cities or their lines of defense as yet. The revolutionary command decided if the civilian fighters were not going to attack. Then they would not give them any reason to do so either. The Command decided not to attack the mass of civilian humanity with warplanes. But this order did not stop the command from preparing for the attack though.

The military defenders used this lull in fighting to flood their defenses with ammunition and armor and any free soldiers. Command had most of their aircraft moved from the Island, and had the planes concentrate in the area surrounding these two vital cities. The Navy continued to pour Marines in Santa Clara, and they even sent in a number of sailors, arming them and putting them on the defense lines. Everything that could be done to help the military defenders beat back the hordes of civilian attackers was now being done by the revolutionary command.

The Command sent observation flights over the civilian fighters' main lines which hunkered down, and they stayed in place as soon as they saw the planes flying overhead their positions. Pictures showed the civilians were not anxious to attack the defenders at this time. The photos showed the civilian fighters were busy hunting while occupation buildings hastily constructed. One of the pilots announced it looked like the civilians decided to sit down and wait for some reason. Maybe they had taken enough of the Island to satisfy their wants for the time being.

This report made its way to Presidente Carlos Rafael Fernandez Alvarez's desk, and he was steaming about it as he screamed at anyone he saw hanging in and around his office. "How dare these miserable lowly civilian bastards carve up my dom country for themselves? When I have control over the central and western section of this dom Island, I'll commit the rest of my reserve forces, and I'll drive these sonofabitches into the sea where they belong, and let them drown in the waves. Or I'll allow them to swim to America and allow them take care of these ungrateful pigs for a change, dommit."

Alvarez checked his forces position throughout the Island, represented by small blue pins stuck in the huge map of Cuba hanging on the wall in his office. He ordered the 19th Infantry under the control of Captain Suarez, to support the besieged Cuban city of Cienfuegos. He was more than willing to lose the smaller city of Santa Clara for the sake of hanging on to Cienfuegos, and the twin nuclear reactors constructed in that city. Because he understood if he lost electrical power to the capital the civilians would riot, and they would attack his forces stationed in Havana.

The Presidente felt good there had not been much trouble in the capital the night before and there still was no sign of many civilians milling about outside their homes earlier that morning. His curfew was taking effect with the civilians, and he considered allowing some factories to open on this day for their daily work. He wanted things to get back to near normal in the city, in hopes a busy civilian would be too occupied with his work to give him further problems, until his takeover of the Cuban government was completely realized.

Alvarez looked out of the window of his office, and smiled at what he saw being displayed below him. There were many civilian vehicles moving along on the streets and the artillery was silent, and the lights in the industrial section of the capital were back on. He knew better than to allow any artillery shells to land in that section of the city, because he was banking on it to bring some semblance of normality back to the situation he was mired in. The disconcerting thought of the civilian masses rejecting his revolution never occurred to him when he first decided to begin his latest Revolution to Cuba in the first place.

Alvarez actually cursed himself aloud as he continued to look over all of what he could see remaining of the mostly intact center in the city of Havana. Fires still raged out of control in the high class residential section of the capital. But he refused to allow any fire fighting vehicles, and other emergency equipment to enter this section of Havana for the time being. That was because of the sniper action occurring throughout the night in that section against his troops who tried to patrol and secure that section of the capital. He watched attentively as some of his soldiers tried to retrieve one of the burned out hulks of three of his once deadly and massive tanks, while some of his other repair crews worked in an attempt to get one of the damaged tanks in commission for the rest of his forces, before any civilian fighters attacked again.

Alvarez knew he had to stop by any means possible, the masses of civilian fighters, if he wanted to stay in power over the Island, and he could start galvanizing his hold over the country and his budding Presidency at the same time. The young Cuban Colonel was desperately searching for some answers to the many problems facing him and his command over the Island. He found himself wishing he never started this Revolution in the first place, and chose to remain stationed on his military base as a mere Colonel, and allowed someone else to begin the Revolution against the rule of Fidel Castro. That was so these hard decisions would have fallen upon someone else's shoulders, and he could have either come to the other leader's aide, or remained on his base in silence and safety.

The early morning sky over the Cuban city of Cienfuegos was dotted by smoke from hundreds of campfires, as the civilian hordes ate. It was believed when they finished eating the attack on the defenders would begin. But as time crawled by to eleven a.m., it was clear the civilians had no intention of attacking that morning. Suarez's troops arrived on the defense lines, but Suarez had not been ordered to replace Captain Sanguily in command of the defenders. When the first meeting between the two officers took place, it was decided they would try their best to make contact with the leaders of the civilian Army in an effort to talk sense to them. They were hoping to find out what it was they wanted from the government, and what they intended to do about it.

Captain Sanguily asked for volunteers to go under a white flag to speak with the civilian leaders. It was discovered the leader of the civilian masses was, Emil Hernandez Nicaro who was willing to come to Sanguily's tent for peace talks. A meeting was set for two p.m., and Nicaro promised there would be no further attacks on the cities until their talks were completed. Sanguily saw this as an opportunity to lift the siege. The longer they talked, the stronger the revolutionary's hold on Cuba would grow.

TWO P.M. WEDNESDAY, SEPTEMBER 25th, 1996. A TENT ONTHE OUTSKIRTS OF THE CITY OF CIENFUEGOS

Captain Sanguily and Suarez were seated when Emil Nicaro and Nicanor Hector Navea arrived in the tent. The Captain offered him his hand and they shook. Navea glared at the seated Suarez but did not recognize him.

"Would you care for a cup of coffee, sir?" Sanguily asked him politely.

Nicaro started off right away by demanding to know who was leading the revolutionary government installed in the capital, and what the leader intended to do with the country.

The Captain tried to assure Nicaro given half a chance, Presidente Alvarez was going to erase many problems created by Castro. He informed Nicaro, Alvarez intended to allow free elections, and would get Cuba on her feet. He further informed the civilian Alvarez was going to open talks with the United States and enlist their help in reconstructing the country, and lift their embargo.

Nicaro listened in silence, because he heard this rhetoric before. He did not believe it then, and he did not believe it now. He had a driving force in speaking to this Captain. He was appalled at the heavy losses his forces suffered, and was unwilling to engage the defenders once more for fear of losing control of the civilian fighters. At one point, Navea whispered to Nicaro, and he in turn said to Sanguily. "Is there a way we can meet with this new Presidente of Cuba? I know I have a lot to offer him, as he has to offer me and the people of Cuba, Captain."

The Captain thought, weighing the ramifications such a meeting could produce, let alone the time he would gain for reinforcing his troops, by promising to have a meeting set up in the week.

This seemed to appease the civilian leader, and he assured Sanguily he would refrain from further attacks on their defenses until he heard from the President. He warned him he would give Alvarez until October 1st, to meet. If a meeting had not taken place by then, the defenders of Cienfuegos would not see the light of day from October 2nd. With this warning issued, the civilians left the tent without further words. They made it possible for the two leaders to make contact with one another, when Sanguily gave Nicaro a radio to contact him if questions arose.

The four men shook hands, and Sanguily watched as they walked back to their defensive lines. For the first time since the revolutionary forces started their overthrow of Fidel Castro, there was silence over the Island. The Captain listened, and he could not hear a single shot being fired anywhere in ear shot. He made contact with Major Trujillo, and informed him the civilians were not going to attack until after a meeting between Nicaro and Alvarez, and only if their differences could not be worked out.

He placed a call to Alvarez to explain he set up a meeting between himself and Nicaro. Alvarez was fuming he took it on himself to set a meeting without his permission. He assured the Captain he had no intention of meeting with this civilian, unless it was between his Army and their forces, or he was surrendering and willing to accept his leadership.

Sanguily was horrified, because he believed he worked out a good meeting that would have stopped the fighting between the civilians and the government soldiers on the Island. He could not understand why Presidente Alvarez was so set against meeting with this rebel leader, a civilian who might help him and his takeover of Cuba. Sanguily tried twice more to persuade the new Presidente to meet with Nicaro, but he was forced to back off when Alvarez threatened to have him relieved of command and shot for insubordination against him and his rule.

Alvarez hung up and turned his wrath lose on Colonel Calvo who was enjoying a cigar. "Madre de Dios, what is happening to my command? Since when do my Officers tell me what to do? By all the Saints, I'll have that ass' head for scheduling this meeting without consulting me first."

Calvo sat in silence until Presidente Alvarez finished his angry tirade.

Sanguily moved more of his troops to the front line. He had them shift their positions slowly, so as not to draw attention to themselves by the civilian spotters working against them. He did not want the civilian hordes to become alarmed by the sudden movements. He knew the civilians were keeping a close eye on all they were doing.

The next few days went by as promised by the civilian fighters, and there were no further attacks on any of the revolutionary forces. In some places, the civilian and revolutionary forces even ended up talking with each other peacefully, and sharing food with each other. Cuba, for the first time since Presidente Alvarez started his new revolution on the

Island, was at peace for the time being, though it was a rather shaky peace at that to be enjoyed.

Nicaro, the unofficial leader of the ever growing civilian forces, made contact with Sanguily on a number of occasions, once to challenge him on some of his troop's movements.

Captain Sanguily tried his best to relieve Nicaro's tensions by informing him the sudden troop movements he observed were some of his rear guard troops relieving the defenders on the front line since his forces had advanced on the city.

Nicaro knew better and ordered Sanguily in no uncertain terms to stop all movement or he would attack immediately.

Sanguily ordered his troops to stop their advancing in large groups, but continued to move some soldiers in pairs, and small groups. He knew when his time ran out he had to have his troops set in place. The thought of Alvarez's refusal to meet with the civilian was eating at his guts out, because he knew he and his men were going to pick up the tab for the President's stubbornness. The Captain did not like the fact they were going to die for this man in Havana. He continued his over flights of the civilian encampment, and every time he looked over the photographs, he drew in his breath. The masses continued to grow at an alarming rate. He placed a call to the civilian leader, and demanded he end the reinforcement of his forces.

Nicaro laughed as he replied. "Captain, I have little control over what the civilians do. I don't know how, but more come in hordes looking to help us in our quest, or their safety. In case you are unaware, numbers of your soldiers attacked towns and villages, killing healthy males and raping women. This happened before in our history, and you know the outcome. Your forces put to death the leader of that revolution some days ago." The civilian disconnected while laughing.

Captain Sanguily placed calls to the other Commanders, begging supplies and anything from manpower to the more powerful weapons to defend his lines surrounding Cienfuegos.

HAVANA, CUBA. FRIDAY, SEPTEMBER 27th. 8A.M. HAVANA TIME

Presidente Alvarez began to gain a false sense of security from the lack of attacks by the civilians on his forces. It was early when he first looked over the massive parade grounds of the Palace. He smiled as he noticed his troops were relaxing in the sun and enjoying their down time from fighting. Everywhere he looked his soldiers were working, but something else pleased him. Some civilians stopped walking and they spoke to some of his troops. Havana was getting back to near normal, shops and factories were open and nearly full manpower. Civilian cars traveled the streets of the capital, and the fires in the residential area were out, and the construction crews moved in to start rebuilding the section.

The seaport of Havana operated at full steam and fresh fish were showing up in the open air markets. Life begun anew under his control, the damaged or destroyed tanks were removed from the complex and city, along with damaged civilian vehicles. The graves in the fields across from the Palace were filled over. Tents removed, and grading machines leveled the field. Alvarez ordered the area to be turned into a baseball field, when the machines finished their work.

He listened and swore he could hear music. He looked around until he spotted young women and they had a radio on a block, and danced provocatively in front of soldiers. "Ahhh what better way to bring peace back to Cuba than by sex?" He mumbled as he left the window.

Alvarez went over to his desk and he pressed the intercom button, and he ordered his meal brought up to his office. The thought of sex stuck in his head and he promised himself he was going to treat himself to a little tonight. He ordered Maria to be sent to up his quarters on the fifth floor of the Palace. He was going to order Melba to have her dress in her finest dress.

He gave a quick thought of having the maid join them in his planned night of sex with Maria. He convinced himself it was Maria who suggested he share two women in the first place, and he was going to follow up on her offer. His attitude changed, he was happy and looking forward to that night. He realized the last time he made love, was the night before they began the Revolution. That was when Maria loved and still backed his decisions. He could not believe she changed so much so quickly. Now, he had to actually force her to love him, and he was getting back at her by having his officers rape her whenever he got angry over thinking about her. His food arrived in his office.

THE WHITE HOUSE, WASHINGTON D.C. 9:30 A.M.FRIDAY, SEPTEMBER 27th, 1996

General Weidenbacher appeared at the Oval Office at nine thirty a.m. sharp. He was surprised to bump into CIA Director Raincloud already standing on the steps of the big house.

"You were ordered here I guess Director Raincloud?" the General asked him.

"Yep, and you as well General Weidenbacher?" the Director in returned, asked the General.

"What got the Boss so hot today?" the General questioned the Director.

"He informed me he wanted the latest briefing on the Cuba situation, General Weidenbacher. I hope he's not getting cold feet on us about sending in the damn invasion force, sir."

"It's too late for that, the training's going well and they'll be ready to deploy in the next few days. I'm not going to pull them back now sir. I'll find some way to get them into Cuba, even if I have to have them smuggled there on some Russian ships, Director." The General warned.

CIA Director Raincloud stopped walking and then he stared at his friend for a brief moment.

General Weidenbacher laughed as he slapped him on his back and added. "Relax John I was only busting your horns on ya. It's what the President wants, always has, and always will be."

They entered together. President Cole sat speaking with the Vice President and the National Security Director, Norman Griffin. He stopped and nodded as he asked. "Coffee? Cup of tea?"

Both men declined the offer of coffee as they entered the office.

"Very well, I guess you're wondering why I asked you to appear before me today."

Both men nodded in agreement to the President's remark.

"I want to know exactly what the hell's going on down there on that Island at all times, sirs. The reports coming across my desk are thin at best, and contain no new information at all. Am I to believe the new Cuban government is starting to be accepted by the masses of that country, sirs?" President Albert Cole growled as he gave a sarcastic snort.

CIA Director Raincloud began with his report. "That's not the fact sir. We have information the civilians are waiting for a meeting between the new President, and the leader of the civilian Army, Mr. President Sir."

"When is this meeting supposed to take place? And, what do you think the outcome of it will be, sir? I warn you, I read the reports from the Security Director and he feels this Alvarez chap's not going to be the worst thing to happen to Cuba. He feels this guy might be approachable sir."

"That's hogwash Mr. President." Weidenbacher barked and then went on with his bitch. "This little prick is no damn better than Castro was. Look at what he has been up to since he took over the Island militarily. He turned artillery lose on the civilians, attacked them with tanks and automatic weapons, and he's stacking his troops up in the southern section of the Island, making it a heavily defended installation, sir."

"Well sir, are you in possession of any new information we're not privy to, General?"

"No sir, that's it on my part I'm afraid, Mr. President." The General offered back to him.

"Then why do you think this man is so much a threat to us?" Griffin asked, speaking this time.

"Because this lousy sonofabitch is up to something in that undeveloped section of the damn Island where he has been busy assembling many of his special troops, Director Griffin Sir."

"Why do you think he's doing this for General Weidenbacher?" President Cole asked with concern in his tone.

"Because he's a smart asshole, I don't know sir. But it's not for a good reason though Mr. President Sir. Maybe he's going to turn this section of the Island into some kinda slaughter house, or prison. Using so many troops as he is, it only strengthens my beliefs he's going to do something that's not in the best interest of Cuba, or for us for that matter, sir."

"Then I take it you still want to go through with sending your troops to Cuba, General."

"Yes Sir Mr. President Sir." General Weidenbacher replied confidently to the President.

"I'll allow you to continue with plans to invade the Island then, sir. But I want the last word before you go active against Cuba, General Weidenbacher. I must warn you sir, if I think this new joker is going to work out as well as if we go through with our invasion. Then I'm going to put the kibosh to your invasion plans, and I'll not stand for any lip from you, sir."

"I have no problem with that sir. I'm in no hurry to put our boys in harm's way again."

President Cole allowed a smile as he replied. "That's good I see you and I will get along fine if you stay on that line of thought, sir. How are you doing with getting the support ships and people in position for the invasion, sir?"

"Fine, I have the entire Atlantic Fleet assembling in the Caribbean, I'm using Haiti as their organization point. We're using this position because we already have troops stationed in Haiti, and no one would find it alarming if our ships group up off that Island's coast, sir."

"Good thinking on that point General Weidenbacher, continue please if you will sir."

"I refrained from pulling in anymore troops because Task Force Eleven has over seventeen thousand Rapid Deployment Marines on board its ships. There are six thousand troops on the Aircraft Carriers, when you include Marine and Army units mixed up on the Amphibious and other support ships. We believe we have enough troops to get the job done, or give us enough time so we can pull up more troops if needed, sir."

"Let me get this right General Weidenbacher." President Cole moaned as he stared at the military officer. It's your intention to use just the troops you have on the damn Task Force, sir?"

"Yes Sir Mr. President Sir." Weidenbacher fired a quick smile back at the President.

"Don't you think it'd be wiser to have more troops than we need before you start, sir?"

"That's the ideal scenario. But if I was to start calling up troops with the problems we're facing in Cuba. It wouldn't take anyone much time to figure out where these troops are headed for, Mr. President Sir. For now, I believe the surprise element's more important than flooding the entire country with our troops, sir. It seems everyone on Cuba's adopting a stand down approach to the new government, and this is great news for us. I'd rather attack an enemy when they least expect it, than attacking in numbers when they're waiting for us, sir."

"I agree with that remark." Director Griffin added, getting back into the conversation now.

All eyes immediately went to Director Griffin, with the President saying while smiling at him. "Why Norman, I didn't know you were up to date on any of the military techniques, sir."

"I'm not really sir, but the General's making sense to me sir. I'm uneasy at what's happening on that Peninsular, and I can't help but feel I'm waiting for the other shoe to fall. I know the new governments up to something, but I'll be dipped in shit if I can figure out what it is though."

"Interesting Norm." President Cole grumbled, thinking over the ideas brought out by his staff he added. "Gentlemen, here's what I want. General Weidenbacher, you'll continue with your invasion plans. Mr. Raincloud, you'll continue to compile all needed information for us. I want you to see if you can figure out what this guy is up to before we go active against him. I want to know what kind of trap we're walking in on this one."

Everyone at the meeting nodded in agreement with the President's last remark.

"Okay gentlemen, that's it for now, I guess. Norman, I want you to stay for a moment. The rest of you, have a good day please. Oh, err... General Weidenbacher, I want you to remember my warning sir. You don't go active until you get my personal go ahead for the operation, sir."

Weidenbacher snapped to attention as he saluted the President and replied. "Yes sir."

When out, General Weidenbacher grabbed Director Raincloud by the arm and said. "I want all the information sent to my office, a copy to me, the other to the Boss. I don't want him knowing more than I do on this one, sir."

John stared at him without responding to the General's last orders.

"C'mon John, I need to know what the hell's happening down there first, sir. I just got caught with my dick in my hand in there, because I wasn't aware of the troops being moved around to the southern section of the damn Island. Don't you think I should've been informed about the new troop movements in Cuba, if I'm going to invade that country within the next few days sir?" General William Weidenbacher growled in a low voice as they made their way down the long hallway leading towards the main section of the White House.

"I guess you got a good point General. I'm sorry I was asleep at the switch on you. I'll send all copies of any information to your office, the moment I send it to the President, sir."

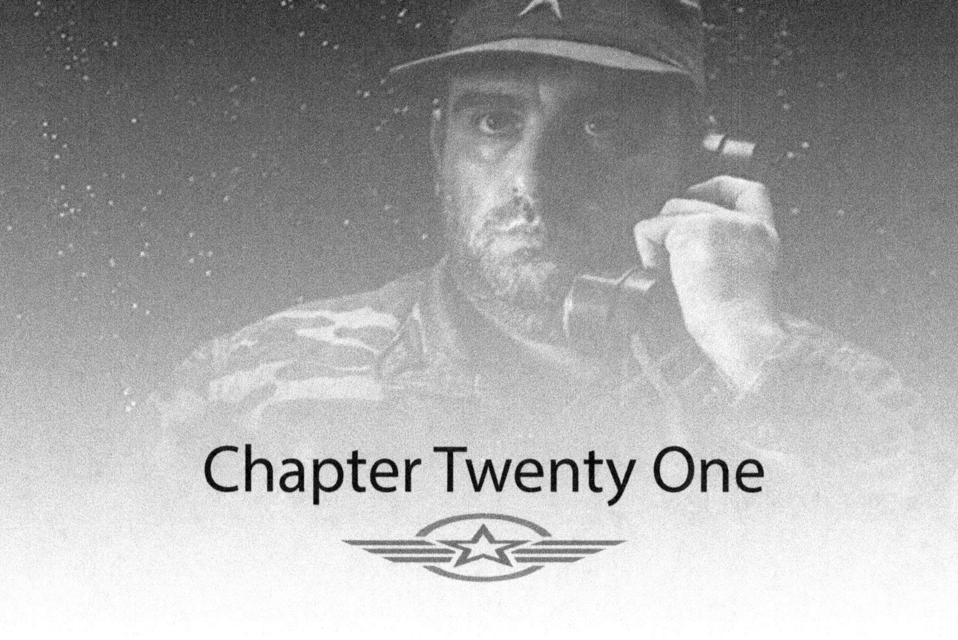

Chapter Twenty One

The day became overcast as Presidente Alvarez went over the countless dispatches covering his desk, all arising from the Guanahacabibes Peninsula area. Some troops pouring into the area had begun to overlap other troops already stationed there. They were trying to cram as many soldiers as humanly possible in this small area of the Island of Cuba. Colonel Carlos Rafael Hernandez Alvarez laughed, stating the troops would have to work out the problems for themselves, and stop dumping everything on his shoulders.

Colonel Calvo came in and plopped down in the chair and bitched. He did not want to inform Alvarez he ordered Colonel Cienfuegos to the Peninsula because he was beginning to mistrust the Colonel. He was finding something to gripe about the way everything was being handled, and when the Colonel bitched, he was sick over all the killing, Calvo moved him out of the city. The last thing he needed was one of his officers questioning his orders. "Presidente Alvarez, civilians were reported milling about the Havana Port. I took it on myself to send a number of soldiers to break up the troublemakers before they're able to stir up more problems for us. I don't want them gathering in large groups. Before you know it about any group will be able to give us a problem."

"By the Holy Madonna, you have done well Colonel. Don't be afraid to arrest anyone you think might cause us trouble. Things are good, and I don't want anything screwing it up."

A new serving soldier came in the office carrying a tray of coffee with cake for them.

"Put it down there will you please." Presidente Alvarez ordered as Colonel Calvo asked him.

"Mr. Presidente, it might be a wise idea for you to meet with this dom civilian leader? Even though they're untrained, these uncivilized troops are a serious threat to us sir. I believe it could work out in our favor if you speak with him, sir. We can use him to control the civilian fighters until we're too powerful to be attacked by the civilian Army. Once we're in that position of power, we could always kill the bastard after he served his purpose for us, sir."

"Colonel Calvo, I told you I have no intention of meeting with that sonofabitch now, or in the future. The only way I shall ever meet him, is when my troops beat back the civilian hordes surrounding Santa Clara and Cienfuegos, and I hang the dirty bastard in front of his once civilians troops I chose to leave alive, Colonel Calvo. They can see him meet his end before they're hung themselves, sir." Colonel Alvarez hissed angrily.

Neither man paid attention to the servant listening to their conversation. When the servant felt he heard enough, he asked. "Would the Presidente want me to serve him something to eat, sir?"

Alvarez's head spun around as he glared harshly at the servant. "You, what the fook are you still doing in my office? By the hand of God, are you listening to our conversation mista?"

"No my Presidente, I was setting up the coffee for you sir. I wasn't paying any attention to what was being said, sir. I'd never do such a thing sir. I back you with my life, I..."

"Enough." Alvarez snapped back at him nastily, and then he continued with his words to the soldier. "Madre de Dios, I said enough and that's what I mean, get out of here you fool, before I have you waiting on the whore who'll service my soldiers when this Revolution is done."

"I'm sorry forgive me if I caused you problems. I'd rather cut my fingers off than be the cause of any stress to you, sir." The servant said as he bowed and backed out of the office.

"Enough, get out." Alvarez said as he waved him out. When he was gone, Colonel Calvo asked the Presidente with concern lacing his voice.

"Do you want me to have the dom fool checked out since he s a new soldier, Presidente Alvarez?" Colonel Calvo requested.

"God curse him to hell for eternity. What the hell good would it do him? What could he have heard? We discussed nothing of true importance while he was in the office, sir. Did you see the ass when I yelled at him, he was scared to death sir. He's no real threat to us Colonel Calvo."

"Nevertheless, Presidente I think I shall have him checked out, one can never to be certain of loyalties. No need to take chances."

"Suit yourself Colonel that is why I have you in the position you occupy. If the man doesn't check out, you're free to have Sergeant Regueiro relieved of his command, and executed for his failure to detect this potential threat, and possibly putting my life in danger, sir."

"I'll be pleased to do this, because I don't like that fook. He reminds me of a sneaky little bastard, always sniffing around looking for someone he can rat on or complain about. I'll be the one who pulls the trigger on that one." Calvo gave a sneering laugh that caused Alvarez to shiver.

Alvarez took a second for himself. Calvo scared him, and he did not trust him, and he intended to have him eliminated once he controlled the Island. He knew he had to say something because Calvo was staring at him. "Why Colonel, you don't like anyone in my new government but yourself, sir."

"Oh now you done it Carlos, you hurt my feelings, sir." Calvo said while chuckling and he stood and added to his words. "That's not true sir I like most of the soldiers and civilians who are involved in our government, sir. But on the other hand though, if you asked me if I trusted anyone, I'd have to say no. I don't trust anyone until they have proven to me they're trustworthy sir. My mother didn't raise a fool who lived, and I have no intention of allowing one to sneak behind me, and plunge a knife into the middle of my back sir." Calvo glared at Alvarez.

Presidente Alvarez stared back just as hard at the soldier leaning on his desk, he then growled. "I swear by the Holy Madonna, I do believe you don't trust me either, Colonel Calvo."

Calvo stood back as a sneer crossed his lips as he offered. "Presidente Alvarez, you have given me plenty of reason to trust you, sir. I'd have no fear of standing with my back to you, sir."

"Ahhh, spoken like a true diplomat, you'll do fine in my new government, Colonel Calvo."

"Yes, but there is one question that has not been asked, and it must be, my Presidente Sir."

"And, what might that one question be my friend?" Alvarez asked of his Colonel.

"The question is. Do you trust me with your back, sir?" Calvo barked with concern lacing his voice as he moved closer to the desk.

Alvarez smiled and he laughed, but he really did not respond to the question though.

"I didn't hear a reply to my last question Presidente Sir. Am I to take that as a no, that you don't trust me with your life?" he asked as he leaned on Alvarez's desk with his two hands.

Alvarez stopped laughing and he stared at the Colonel as he snapped. "Colonel Calvo, I assure you if I didn't trust you with my back, you wouldn't be standing in this threatening manner before me. Blessed Lord Jesus, you'd be buried along with the civilian troublemakers, and the soldiers who didn't support me. Does that answer your question good enough for your likes, sir?"

"Completely." Calvo straightened up and then he smiled back at Alvarez again.

"Fine, now if you don't mind Colonel Calvo, I have some work to do and I need my privacy."

When the Colonel did not move, Alvarez added. "Do you not have troops to check on sir?"

"I'm leaving now to make certain the troops are properly ordered and stationed, my Presidente Alvarez Sir." The Colonel said as he turned and then he left the office quickly.

"Good!" Alvarez watched Calvo until he was out of his office. "Pain in the ass Officers, the world would be better off if we didn't have to rely on soldiers. Arrr, I'll handle your hash once I'm firmly in control of this country, and that you can bank on my dear Colonel Calvo."

No one in the Palace kitchen took particular interest in the young infantry soldier, when he returned from the President's office with the empty cart. He stripped his serving apron and then he put on his uniform jacket, he gathered up his belongings and silently slipped out the kitchen door leading to the back courtyard where the delivery trucks dropped off the food.

Before he left the kitchen, he looked to Maria Ibarra. She sat in front of a table working on the tray of vegetables piled before her, preparing them for the meal. She was crying and it seemed she done nothing else since she was brought to the kitchen. He knew she was being punished, but did not find out why. He was captivated by her beauty and wished he could do something to help.

The Private jumped on his bike and peddled off as quickly as he could. He passed three different armed checkpoints, but the guards did not bother him because they recognized the soldier, and the guards simply waved him on through the checkpoints. He secretly worked for the civilian movement, and he was dying to send out the information he gathered to his leader laying siege to the two Cuban cities. He rushed over to the southern section of the capital area while heading for the safe house in Cerro. He peddled his bike across the narrow streets, repeating everything he heard said in the new President's office over and over again. The Private turned onto Arzobispo Street while heading for San Salvador on the last leg of his journey for Cepero. He was sweating and grew tired as he pumped away. When he turned onto San Salvador Street, he paid no notice to the car quickly closing in on him from behind.

The vehicle and its two occupants rapidly closed the gap on the soldier, until they were yards from him. Just as the Private slowed his bike to turn onto Cepero, the car increased speed, hitting the bike and sending the Private flying across the road. His tumbling ended when his shoulder hit the curb of the sidewalk with his head and upper back area. The car spun around hard and headed up the road at breakneck speed, it veered, hitting the man lying half in the road a second time.

People rushing out of their homes to help the lad were driven away. The body got caught under the car and the body was dragged fifty feet before it came free, and the car sped away.

A crowd gathered around the moaning and dying young man. Eduardo Carbo made his way to the crowd and when he recognized the injured man, he rushed to help him. He enlisted the help of three other people staring at the bleeding and dying man. Together, they carried the broken man down the block to the house next door to the safe house. They worked quickly, because they were afraid the ones who tried to kill the spy were still in the area. No one wanted to give up a safe house to the secret police of Cuba.

The four men carried the injured youth to a bedroom where an elderly woman examined him. She cut away his clothes, cleaned the many cuts and scrapes and then she tried to find his major injuries. The bleeding from his head and the side of his face caused her the greatest concern. Upon examination, she turned to Eduardo and shook her head sadly.

Eduardo pushed her out of the way and grabbed the soldier by the shoulder and shook him until his eyes fluttered opened. He hissed close to the man's ear. "Maximo Fuentes, report!"

The dying youth tried to say something, but all he ended up doing was cringing out in pain.

"Fuentes, you cannot give up on me now. Report god dommit, I need your report, so I know what this new Presidente is planning against us, mista."

Fuentes's eyes fluttered and then opened them again as he focused on the man growling at him. He looked at Eduardo Carbo and gave a weak smile and moaned. "I... coming to see you. Information... must find... way to Nicaro. He's waiting for... meeting... never take place. This pig... having Nicaro waste... time waiting to meet... until he's... able to strengthen his control over... Island and his forces strong enough to defeat... forces in... hills. Carbo, promise... get... word to Nicaro. I fear I... not live long to set eyes on Nicaro... I'll not live... see... free Cuba."

"Come on Fuentes, you speak nonsense, fool. You're not hurt badly young man. A little cleaning some bandages, a glass of Cuban wine and a good woman to love your pain away, are all you'll need to get back on your feet and well again. I'm afraid you'll be here long after Cuba is set free of all the military want to be leaders." Carbo smiled at the swollen, bloody face of one of his young soldiers.

"Now who is... dreamer, Carbo? How many times... you call me... dreamer. Now... you're the dreamer as I once was... I know I'm... to die, nothing on... earth will... stop it. I'm too hurt to live." As if to emphasize he knew he was going to die, Fuentes body suddenly stiffened up as it was being wracked by a searing wave of pain. His back arched mightily in an effort to get higher than the pain assaulting his broken and terribly battered body.

Blood gurgled out of the corner of his mouth and Fuentes fought desperately with his body, in an attempt to keep his eyes open and his words coming. He slowly went over everything he heard spoken between the new Presidente Alvarez and Colonel Calvo.

The car wildly sped off to get out of the area before anyone recognized either of the two men in the vehicle, or got their description. The car shot down San Salvador Street, taking the turn onto Chapel on two wheels. After bouncing off the back end of a parked car, and mowing down some garbage cans, the driver gained control of the vehicle again. He held his foot on the accelerator, making the engine roar as the vehicle tore down Chapel Street with its wheels leaving the ground heading for the secondary highway of Via Blanca. The car slid again as the vehicle turned onto Via Blanca. The driver slammed his foot down, straightening the car out on the highway. They traveled at seventy miles an hour in no time, and the passenger keeping his eyes glued to his rear view mirror, to make certain no one was pursuing them.

When the driver got far enough away from the scene of the crime, and he was certain no one was trailing them, he dared his first words to his co-driver. "Manolo, do you think it's good for you to report to our control, to inform him we were successful and are reporting back to base?"

Manolo stared at the older driver as if he was afraid to speak to him, causing the driver to take a weak back hand swing at him, bringing him out of his sudden stupor. Once the driver was certain he had Manolo's attention, he repeated what he said to him.

Manolo did not respond, instead he reached into his pocket and he removed the small portable radio, he keyed it then mumbled into it. "Dispatch, the letter was returned to the sender, sir."

A gruff voice replied to him. "Driver, this is dispatch. Are you sure the letter was destroyed?"

"Positive dispatch. We saw the sender destroy it with our own eyes, sir." Manolo replied.

"What did he do with the letter he was carrying, you great fool you?" The operator asked.

"It was left lying on the street where it had fallen to the ground, sir." The passenger replied.

The voice growled. "Are you sure no one picked it up before it was completely destroyed?"

"Not understood your last words dispatch." Manolo asked as he stared at the small radio now.

"Listen to me you fool you. Are you certain he was dead before you left him? I don't want anyone picking him up and getting a chance to speak to him if he wasn't dead, you fool."

Manolo began to sweat as he lied to the angry sounding voice on the radio. "Yes sir dispatch. We're positive he was dead before we left sir." Neither man was making any pretense over the matter now as they continued speaking to each other over the tiny radio.

Colonel Calvo sat back in his chair staring into the mike as if he could actually see the speaker over it, and then he snapped at his agent in the field. "I hope for your sake he was dead, you great fool. If I find out otherwise, I shall have the same act carried out on you two fools, and you'll be left lying in the gutter to rot. Is this understood mista?"

"Very sir." The passenger in the car responded to the Colonel's angry words aimed at him.

"Good, you're instructed to take the longest path possible before you return to the nest." Calvo did not wait for Manolo's response as he broke off the connection, and then he threw the radio mike onto his desk before him and he relaxed a bit.

Manolo did not let go of the mike when he turned and looked at the driver, terror filled his eyes. Without a word, the driver spun the wheel hard, causing the car to slide again. He fought the wheel as the car jumped over the road divider, and it headed east on the highway, back towards Via Blanca.

Carbo remained holding Fuentes's hand as his life slowly left his broken and battered body. When he was sure he was dead, he called to the old woman. He ordered her to find two men so they could remove the body from her home. When the men arrived, Carbo instructed them to pick up the body and help him take it back where he was rundown. He ordered them to place the body half on the sidewalk and half in the street, just as it had laid when first ran down. The crushed bike disappeared. Carbo knew when he left the body the scavengers would come out of the woodwork and would pick Fuentes's body clean. It was not a fitting end for someone who gave his life for a cause, but he was sure Fuentes would forgive him. He knew Fuentes would have done the same thing if the roles were reversed, and it was he who had been rundown by the speeding car.

Once Carbo was satisfied with the placement of the body on the ground, he ordered his helpers away from it. He took one last look at his friend before disappearing in the shadows of the buildings. He stayed lurking in the darkness and sure to form, a few children came out and cautiously approached the body. In seconds they were rummaging through Fuentes' pockets. Carbo purposely left the small gold chain around his neck, and he smirked as he saw it was the first thing to disappear from his body.

He picked up the sound of screeching tires and saw the dark blue car speed down the road. The car slid to a stop inches away from the crushed body, causing the children robbing it to scatter. The driver looked out the window, satisfied the body lay where it ended up when he ran the man down. The driver spat on Fuentes's body, and slammed the car in gear and floored it, causing the tires to scream in protest as they struggled to grip the pavement. The car slid and spun in the middle of the road and in an instant, it was heading in the direction it appeared from.

Carbo heard the screech of the tires and the roar from the engine as the car tore wildly down the road. He was not the least bit surprised hardly anyone came out of their homes to try and help the dying man. Most of the civilians knew if someone was killed in this fashion in the middle of the streets, it was usually done by someone working secretly for the government. He cursed the dimming tail lights of the car as they disappeared in the night. He then headed for his safe house and the radio waiting there for his use.

Manolo turned to the driver and he asked him. "Do you think our target was heading for his safe house, or turning down that road heading for his home or girlfriend?"

"Who gives a shit, all I know is the sonofabitch is dead, and we almost ended up like him, stupid. You better understand if Colonel Calvo asks us if we think the target was trying to communicate with someone, we must tell him no, or it'll be our skins he'll seek for not locating his contact and getting him also. I don't think the sonofabitch was working for anyone. I think his death was a mistake he was just some poor slob heading home to meet a female. From what I know of this soldier, he was too stupid to be involved in anything wrong against us."

Carbo wrote down all of what Fuentes told him, he read his report over twice, making sure he did not omit anything from it. Once he was satisfied with the report, he made a call to Nicaro. He set his radio on the frequency and then held the key down for three seconds. When he released it, a voice was on the other end. "This is the sea and I want to speak with the earth."

"This is Nicanor, Emil is busy at the moment. What do you have to report to me sir?"

When Carbo explained what his agent told him, Nicanor ordered him to hold on until he got Nicaro to speak with him personally. While he waited, he went over the report in his mind. Moments later Nicaro was on the line, and he repeated what Fuentes overheard at the meeting between the President and the other officer in the room.

Nicaro was fuming because he felt he was hoodwinked into believing this Presidente was better than the bastard he dispatched. He could not believe he was foolish enough to stop his march on the two Cuban cities, and now he sat on his ass losing his momentum, while the government troops took time to strengthen their defenses against him and his attacking civilians.

"What a dom fool I have been for all this time dommit! Navea, get my leaders gathered at once, we have new plans to make. By this time tomorrow we'll own Santa Clara and Cienfuegos, and we shall march into the heart of Havana, so I can put my foot up this new guy's ass, before I shoot him between the eyes. Carbo, you done well and I'm sorry you lost a man. Fuentes' death will be avenged by me personally. Organize the civilian fighters in the capital, and once you have your forces set in place, I want you to make random hits on the revolutionary troops.

"I want you to stop them from resting, I want you to drive them crazy day and night, so they'll have little time and peace to prepare for our attack to begin against them. We shall show these sonofabitches we're not a force to be taken lightly. I want to know when you have your forces ready to act. I'll attack the two cities at the same time you probe the defenses of Havana. I want your people to begin tonight. I'll attack by then and I'll be waiting your return call, sir."

Carbo smiled, because he knew the honor just bestowed on him by Nicaro. He was elevated to lead the attack on the troops defending Havana as he replied to his leader. "Emil, rest easy, I'll be ready to begin our attack by twelve tonight."

"Are you sure your forces will be in position at that time to attack when I say so, Carbo?" Nicaro asked as he stifled a yawn, while straightening out his weary and aching back.

"Emil, if I say they'll be set in position, you can rest assured they'll be set and ready."

"Very well Carbo, I'll make plans to attack at that time. Good luck, may we meet at the Palace gates safely, sir." Nicaro broke off the connection, and then he issued orders to the leaders who assembled in his tent while he spoke with Carbo. They left and issued their own orders. Within minutes, hundreds then thousands of the civilian fighters moved to positions to prepare for their attacks on the revolutionary troops.

An observation flight picked up the sudden movements on the civilian lines, and the pilot reported this information to his command at the city of Cienfuegos. Flares were fired off for the government defenders to see when hordes of civilian fighters began their attack against them. On the land separating the two massive Armies, everything remained peaceful. The revolutionary Commander, Captain Sanguily was sent for, and he was briefed about the enemy movements. He placed a call to the leader of the civilian Army. In moments he was speaking to Emil Hernandez Nicaro. Both men were angry at each other.

"Nicaro! What the hell are you doing with your people? Why all the movement? I thought we had an agreement." Sanguily hissed as he squeezed the life out of the plastic mike.

"You're no different than any other military worker. You're all a pack of fooking liars. It's true, I thought we had an agreement, but that was until I learned you were deceiving me..."

"What the hell do you mean by that statement? Deceiving you? How? Where? How?"

"You know what I mean, I learned your new Presidente has no intention of meeting with me, yet he's using this time to reinforce his defense of the city. We agreed not to attack each other until after the meeting, and only if we couldn't work out our differences. I have no intention of sitting on my ass and allowing your forces to become stronger. I already told you..."

"I don't know what the hell you're talking about Nicaro. As far as I know, we're making preparations for a visit from our Presidente scheduled to arrive on Sunday, the 29th of September. I don't know who is feeding you these lies, but I tell you they're that, lies. The Presidente hasn't made plans to attack your men. I was told he was willing to work with you to ensure peace comes to Cuba. I don't know what you're talking about..."

"Lies! You speak the lies of your fooking Presidente, just as they were spoken by Cast..."

"They're not lies I swear to you I'm not lying to you, Nicaro." The Captain said to him.

"Lies! I'll not be caught unaware I warn you I'm preparing to attack." Nicaro hissed.

"You cannot attack me at this time! You have to wait until I can find out what the hell is going on here, sir. Nicaro, I implore you to think what will happen if you attack. You must think of the massacre that'd take place on both sides. Nicaro, I swear I don't have any information on what you're talking about sir, but I swear. If you refrain from attacking my troops until I get back to you, and the words you speak are true. I'll lay down my weapons and allow you to march into the city unopposed, sir."

Lieutenant Rafael Casas Sanchez grabbed Sanguily by the arm and he shrugged, showing him he did not know what he was attempting to do with the civilian fighter leader.

Sanguily pulled his arm free and glared at him, as he raised his hand to stop him from becoming too concerned with what he was doing, as he went back to his conversation with the civilian. "Nicaro, you have to understand I'm not fooking with you sir, and if what you say is so. I've been as deceived as much as you were, and I'll not put up with it for a moment, sir. If this is true your troops will have the city given to them and my troops will join forces with yours, sir."

Nicaro hesitated, in his heart he prayed he could put off an attack on the Cuban soldiers.

Sanguily covered the mike and then he ordered Sanchez to prepare the defenders.

Sanchez smiled. "Then you're merely giving this civilian ass a line of shit to eat, Captain?"

"Don't be a fool did you really think I was going to give this ass the city without a fooking fight? Not on my life. Alvarez doesn't have much of a sense of humor so I'm told."

"You're a crafty one. I'll have our forces move carefully so as not to draw attention."

"Get it done." Sanguily's conversation was interrupted by Nicaro.

"Captain Sanguily, you have given me something to think about longer. Perhaps, and I'd like to believe this so, you might not know of this deceit being played out against me by the ones who command you. If I could only believe you'd go through with your offer not to defend the city if you were lied to, Captain. The lives that would be saved on both sides, it'll show me there truly is still hope for the civilians of Cuba, and the military to work out their differences together, sir."

Sanguily felt he had Nicaro as he said. "I swear I'll not oppose your troops if I was lied to."

"Hmmm... I believe you for some reason. I'll give you another twenty four hours before I begin my attack against your positions. If I don't hear from you by this time tomorrow, I'm coming at you and if your defenders are stupid enough to oppose us and our will. I shall not leave one of you alive to speak of this deceit in another breath."

"You'll not attack any of my troops for another twenty four hours then, Nicaro?"

"That's correct, but I'll continue to move my forces. As you done over the days, I'll relieve the men on the front with my reserves. I'll not use this time to reinforce my fighters."

I bet you won't Sanguily thought to himself as he replied in a calm tone to Nicaro. "I'll be back to you before that time is up, sir." The two men broke off their communication.

Navea was standing by his leader's side all the time and he had a surprised look on his face.

"What the hell are you looking at so foolishly Navea?" Nicaro snapped at him angrily.

"I sent all my forces in motion, now I'm going to be forced to have them step down."

"Please have a little faith in me will you please. I have no intention of giving these government forces any more time than I already gave them. I told you before, I intend to attack the military troops by midnight tonight, and that is exactly what I'm going to do, my old friend. For once, the dom politicians are going to find out what it feels like to be lied to, and then the slaughter will begin in earnest. How the hell are you doing with getting our fighters ready for the attack against the lying fools?" Nicaro asked his second in command in a sharp tone.

"The last communiqué I read stated the civilian Armies are anxious to get on with it Nicaro. Many have complained they have crops to get in the ground, if they want to harvest next year. I can't blame them, because most our fighters are nothing more than farmers and the likes, sir."

"They might have to forfeit this year's crops for the freedom and safety of Cuba, you fool."

"This is understood by them, but have you ever tried to tell a true farmer he was going to miss the planting season, sir? It's not a very pretty sight to behold I'm afraid." Navea laughed.

"The next one to complain about it, you tell him to think of how pleasant it would be to plant next year's crops in the free Cuba soil. This should stop all the complaining about it."

HAVANA CUBA. THE PRESIDENTIAL PALACE, 4:30 P.M.FRIDAY, SEPTEMBER 27th, 1996

Captain Sanguily made contact with command in the capital to inform Colonel Calvo his troops were going to come under attack in twenty four hours by the civilian hordes. Calvo told him he had all the troops he would get, and he would have to do the best with what he had at hand. These words did not make Sanguily feel better, because he was hoping to get more troops and armor to beat back the civilian attackers.

The Colonel knew he would lose many defending the cities from Nicaro, but hoped his troops would be strong enough to stop them at the line drawn in the dirt cutting Cuba in two. He was brazen enough to ask Captain Sanguily if he thought his troops were going to be able to stop the civilians from overrunning his positions and taking command of the two cities.

Sanguily fought desperately not to lose his temper with the Colonel as he said. "In case you're unaware of it. The latest reports put the number of civilian fighters massed against us at over seven hundred and fifty thousand strong. That means each of my soldiers will have to kill at least seventy five attackers, if we have any hope to hold our position for a day longer. If no one has informed you, this is impossible sir. There's no way in hell my soldiers could possibly kill this many fighters, no matter what he's firing, unless the attackers are kind enough to pile themselves up in buses, and allow our artillery to pick them off before they reach our lines of defense. I don't think I'll be able to maintain con..."

"Captain, I suggest you take a little more care when you're addressing me, sir. Your sarcasm is completely unnecessary, sir. Need I remind you we are both on the same side? I don't know what I can do for you at this time, but I shall try to find some more soldiers and armor, and get them down to you before the deadline arrives, sir." Calvo offered to him calmly.

The fuming Captain continued speaking as if Calvo had not interrupted him. "We'll have a snowballs chance in hell to beat back the civilian attacks. The best I can hope for is holding onto my position for three hours, before my positions are overrun. The only hope my troops have of surviving this attack, is if the Presidente meets with Nicaro. I'm at a loss as to why he still refuses to meet him. I think this civilian might be the best thing to happen to our government. Maybe the Presidente might be able to enlist the services of this man to help him run the government..."

"Do you mean to inform me you think Colonel Carlos Alvarez is incapable of running the new government without this civilian? How would you feel if I informed the new Presidente of what you just offered me sir? I don't think your situation would improve. Captain, don't concern yourself with the running of the dom government. Your duty lays with your defending the government and putting down all those who oppose the leadership of your new Presidente, sir. We're more than capable of running the government without your help. Now, if you're so concerned with this civilian then I suggest your duty is to defeat him before I order you replaced, and then have you shot as a traitor to the new cause of Cuba. Do I make myself clear to you sir?"

"Yes sir." Was all Sanguily hissed at the Colonel on the other end of the radio before he slammed the radio mike hard on the table, and mumbled. "I hope I broke the motherfooker's eardrums." He snapped savagely at the operator.

Calvo smiled over the angry outburst from his Captain as he went upstairs to visit Alvarez. He was undecided whether or not to tell him what Sanguily reported. When he set off for the Presidente's office, he was still hot as hell and he wanted to tell him, but by the time he reached the office, he cooled off enough not to bother Colonel Carlos Alvarez with this latest threat until it became a real problem. He banged on the door.

"Come in." Alvarez barked and upon seeing Calvo, he griped at him. "Oh, it's you sir."

"It's good to see you as well sir." Calvo said curtly as he took a seat and grinned.

"Why have you decided to bother me at this time sir? I was beginning to enjoy myself with thoughts of visiting Maria. Colonel Calvo, since you paid her a visit, she has become more willing to please me. I was thinking of allowing you to pay her another one of your visits in the near future, Colonel." Alvarez grunted as he opened the bottom drawer and then he removed a bottle of rum and two glasses.

"It was simple to accomplish Carlos, all the desire to please a man was there, sir. All I did was show her how best to use the assists she had available in her possession. A sharp knife helped I must add, sir." Calvo replied with an ugly sneer on his lips.

They shared a laugh as Alvarez poured them a drink. Calvo did not volunteer he was seeing Maria every day. He did not know if Alvarez would approve or not, but since he made love to her, it seemed he could not get enough of her pleasures. It was simple to make a meeting, all he had to do was give Melba the word and she would have Maria where he wanted her, and ready to perform for him. Calvo was thinking about bringing another officer along him on the next visit, he felt he owed a favor to. Besides, he liked to watch as two people made love, especially when one was not a willing participant to the act." His thoughts were interrupted by Alvarez.

"Colonel Calvo, I'm certain you didn't come to my office to daydream before me like a fool in love. To what do I owe to this visit of yours, Colonel?"

"Well I wasn't going to tell you this, but after giving it more thought I decided to let you know what is taking place in Cienfuegos, sir. But before I do though, I must take a bow, because I believe the soldier who served us earlier today, was responsible for the situation sir."

"What the hell are you talking about?" Alvarez snarled at him as he sat forward in his chair.

"Well Carlos, the civilians found out you weren't planning to meet with them, and we were using the time for reinforcing our defenders' lines against them. It seems the dom civilian leader is not happy with this situation, and is threatening to attack our soldiers now."

"I cannot believe this shit, when did this take place?" Alvarez growled at the Colonel.

"I just got off of the radio with Captain Sanguily, he's at the city of Cienfuegos and he was..."

"I know where he's stationed Colonel. Don't think me a fool, I know what's happening in my government as much as you do. Do you think our soldiers are going to be able to fight the civilian troublemakers off? Or are the two cities going to fall to the civilian hordes, and I'm going to end up fleeing the capital in disgrace, sir?" Alvarez mumbled this time.

"How could you suggest that to me, Colonel? You could never leave the capital in disgrace, not with what you have sitting on the Peninsula at the far end of this country. The only disgrace I can see is in the way the fooking civilians are treating its new Presidente, sir. If we're forced out of Havana Colonel Alvarez it'd be for only a short period of time, once the civilians realize what we have at our disposal. The fools will flock to our side and then beg us their cursed forgiveness, sir. I'd not worry much if the two cities fall, they're not the make or break situation you might believe they are, sir. We'll only be forced to fall back to your old base, and then defend the capital and is easier for us to defend than the bigger cities are, sir. If we're forced to pull back, it shall be the last fall back we'll do in this war. This I promise you Presidente."

Alvarez was silent as he stared at the bragging officer sitting before him, and then he hissed savagely. "Colonel Calvo! Would you care to wager your life on that last boast of yours? I'm going to hold you to this boast. If we're forced to pull back to Mantanzas I'll ship you there, and allow you to command the defense of that dom city. If you fail to hold it, don't bother making your way back to the capital, because I'll order you shot on sight if I see you again, Colonel." Alvarez glared harshly at him.

Calvo did not know what to do, and decided to laugh this threat off as he offered. "I have no fear of being sent to Mantanzas, because I have no reason to believe the troops defending the cities will fold before we have the missiles set in place, and we let the world know of it, sir."

"Am I to take this as your answer to my question, Colonel Calvo? When I first asked you if you thought our troops were going to be able to hold the two cities or not Colonel?" Alvarez asked his officer a second time.

Calvo knew he was now caught in the middle. If he answered yes to the Presidente's question, he would have a few days before he was called on his statement, and if he did not back his boast to the hilt. Then the Presidente would never trust his judgment again as he replied to the Presidente glaring at him waiting his reply.

"Err... how could I answer that question sir? I cannot see into the future my Presidente. I have no way of knowing if the dom troops defending these two cities will run or fight to the last, sir. I have no way of knowing if by just sheer luck and that is all it'll be, sir. The civilian fighters will overrun our defenses. I have to say this much, I don't know at this time. But the way I see it, I don't believe there's anyway the dom civilian fighters will be able to overpower our forces, but there is..."

"Enough of this bantering back and forth of foolish words without any answers to them, Colonel Calvo! It would've been much simpler if you said you didn't know the answer to my question, sir."

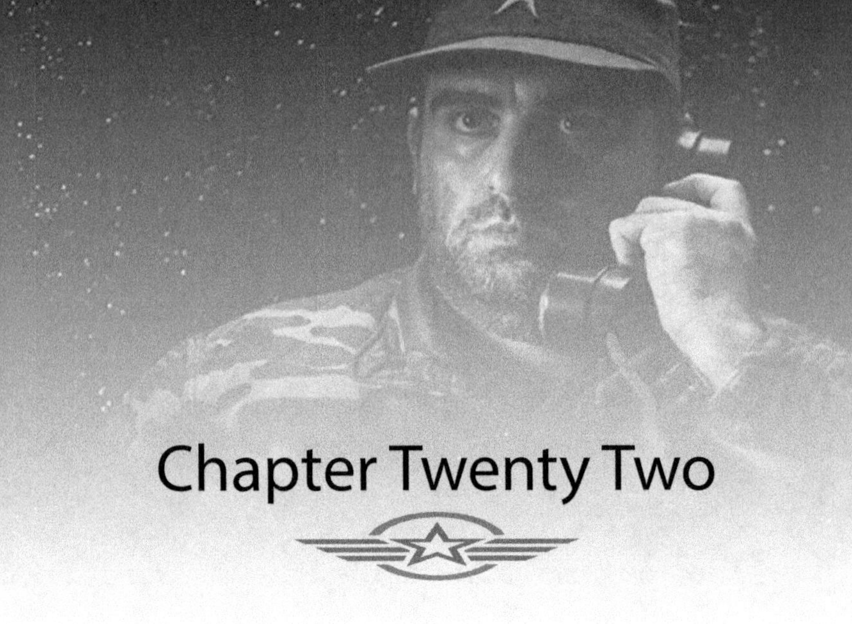

Chapter Twenty Two

THE CIVILIAN FORCES SURROUNDING
THE CUBA CITY OF CIENFUEGOS

Nicaro watched as his fighters moved closer to the front lines. His fighters were packed up three and four deep. He knew the crucial time would come in the first few minutes of fighting. If his first wave of attackers could not make it through the defenders then they were going to be in for a long and painful night. He was aware it was in his best interest to attack at night. There was a commotion in his ranks and Nicaro jumped on a hood of a jeep to see what was happening. Three military trucks pulled into a sea of civilians, and the mobs looked as if they were attacking the trucks.

Nicaro jumped down and grabbed a loaded AK-47 and he charged wildly at the three trucks. He was determined if the enemy were in his flanks, he was going to kill them before he died in the fighting. He charged forward until he realized no one was shooting with him. Instead, his fighters were cheering and holding up long tube type items over their heads as they yelled. A driver sitting on his fender of the vehicle yelled out something to the mob. He increased his pace for the three surrounded vehicles. When he made it over to them, the crowd realized it was their leader and they immediately made a path for him to get up to the first parked truck so he could see what just arrives in their defenses.

The driver on the fender jumped down, and he offered Nicaro one of the tubes he carried, and announced proudly. "Nicaro, we successfully attacked a military base and we located these weapons, sir. They are SA-7 Grail, man portable shoulder launched anti-aircraft missiles, sir."

"They are so small and light. Are you sure they're able to knock a plane out of the air for us?"

"Without a doubt, they have a five pound warhead, and the missiles can travel at Mach One point Five. The only shortcoming the missile has is its short range of two miles on a clear day."

"How does one aim one of the dom things?" Nicaro asked as he looked over the cylinder tube.

"It zeros in by using its infrared/heat seeking abilities against the attacking plane, Nicaro."

He remembers how the attacking aircraft came in when they dropped their bombs on the first attack against them, and how devastating the attacks were against his forces as he growled. "Let the dom planes come and this time we'll knock them out of the air before they can kill us. Then, we'll see how good those government fighters are when they have to fight us hand to hand." The driver held the tube up and over his head, and the gathered crowd cheered again.

Nicaro screamed over the shouts of the crowd. "How many of these launchers do you have at our disposal?" His words were drowned out by the crowd, so he repeated his question.

"We have fifteen boxes in each truck sir, with six launchers in each truck, and we also have another six boxes of extra missiles, with a dozen missiles in each crate for the weapons." The driver's words were now drowned out by the mob again, who were cheering at the amount of anti-aircraft missiles they had in their possession.

Nicaro screamed to try and get the crowd quieted down so he could get control over the situation. But it was useless because his fighters were too worked up to be silenced by mere words. He pulled his pistol out and fired three rounds in the air. Immediately, everyone quieted and stared at their leader. He ordered the driver to deploy the launchers to the frontline and give them out to the men in position there to hit their targets.

Navea rushed through the crowd and he went up to Nicaro. He told him Captain Sanguily was on the radio, demanding to know what the shooting in his lines was about.

Nicaro showed Navea the launchers and instructed him to tell the Captain he was forced to shoot a troublemaker talking his fighters into attacking them. He watched him run off quickly. He knew in less than three hours his fighters would start their last fight to free Cuba.

HAVANA, CUBA 9:35 P.M. EST. SEPTEMBER 27th, 1996

Presidente Alvarez was getting tired as he made plans to share Maria's delights. He glazed out over the dark capital and wherever he looked, everything seemed peaceful, almost too peaceful. The glare from the streetlights lit up the area with an eerie glow, few civilians walked around one was playing with a dog. He watched as soldiers ran the one with the dog off. He stretched as he mumbled. "Ahhh, it looks like it's going to be a peaceful night after all. One more and I might think about relaxing the curfew and things will get back to normal."

Unbeknownst to him, hundreds of civilians stealthily worked their way throughout the capital, taking up positions where they could attack the soldiers and military installations. The civilians moved in for the past few hours, and they had orders to begin their attack at exactly midnight. None were going to wait they were going to hit at the same time. All this took place in other cities and towns throughout the entire Island. This would be the first organized attack against the new military government by civilian fighters.

NICARO'S FORCES SURROUNDING THE CITIES OF SANTA CLARA AND CIENFUEGOS

The civilian leader Nicaro, found himself staring at his watch as it ticked off time, while he was trying to gain some kind of control over his rapid breathing. It was eleven thirty p.m., and all he could see were the many campfires from the government soldier's campsites a little over a half a mile from where he presently stood. It looked like the government troops had no idea his civilian fighters were only a few minutes away from attacking the soldier's positions.

Sanguily read the latest report from his surveillance craft. He wanted the pilot's opinion as he kept him on the radio. "Do you think the civilians are preparing to attack us?"

"Without a doubt they're coming Captain." The pilot reported back to the Captain with a grin.

"When do you think they'll hit us then sir?" the Captain asked as he looked to the civilians.

"Sir, I don't know what the hell's holding them back. With each pass I made over their positions, I saw hundreds more gathering on the frontlines, sir. They're coming and they're coming soon sir." The pilot offered.

Sanguily did not respond, instead he called Sanchez to his side and ordered him to send in the bomber aircraft equipped with night attack capabilities. He told him to order the aircraft to pound the civilian fighter's main line. He was hoping to break up the attack before they could launch it.

Sanchez replied the first of the bombers would be over the civilian fighters by midnight.

Both officers checked their watches to make certain they read the same time on both.

Nicaro's fighters broke out and charged into the span of no man's land separating the two massive Armies, and the first bomber aircraft appeared. He could only hear them, not see the aircraft. His fighters looked towards the night sky.

Streaks of thin flames crisscrossed the night sky as the AS-7 Grail missiles launched at their targets. The first five of seven Backfire bombers exploded in flight as they approached their ordered targets. The last two surviving aircraft made an attempt to bank to their left to try and outrun the small shoulder launch missiles. They exploded in balls of flames.

The civilian fighters cheered as they were charged up with renewed vigor for the attack.

"What happened?" Captain Sanguily screamed as he stared at the flames in the sky.

"Those sir, were our bomber aircraft. The dom civilians must have gotten their hands on some anti-aircraft missiles and that fooks us over bad sir." Sanchez griped as he watched the last of the flaming debris fall to the ground.

"What about our fighter planes mista? Send them in and let them pound the dirty civilian bastards, so they can soften them up for us. We have to do something, or these sonofabitches will be in our dom laps before you know it." The two officers were forced to duck as their artillery joined the engagement and opened fired on the charging hordes of civilians attacking them.

The scene unfolding was out of a nightmare, thousands of civilians charging. Thunderous explosions ripped into the ranks of the rampaging mob. Bodies were sent flying in the air, body parts showered down on the wave of humanity. Thousands of automatic weapons fired at them, and more fired at the defending troops. More planes came in, this time faster and smaller. Again, the sky was lit up by missile streaks as they sought the planes. Out of the twelve Migs that attacked, three completed the mission. The planes had an effect on the hordes of civilians as their cannon fire ripped into the leading elements. More than a hundred were mowed down by the attacking Mig aircraft.

Nicaro watched as the three planes did a high loop over end, and righted as they prepared to make a second run on the civilian attackers. The second attack never came, as nine SA-7s closed in on the Migs as they finished their turn. Three fireballs brightened the night sky. Nicaro turned to his fighters hundreds of them were climbing the defenses as they charged onto the battlefield.

The artillery was having little effect on the masses attacking the city defenders. Captain Sanguily was shocked at the losses suffered by the civilians, yet it did nothing to stop them from continuing the attack at them. He saw no alternative but to commit his tanks. He realized if he held them back any longer, he would not need them. The civilians would be in his defenses and all would be lost to the defenders. He barked at Sanchez, trying to force him to commit his reserves, including the tanks.

The artillery was joined by two hundred cannons from the tanks as they moved out. Rounds of high explosive and fragmentation shells landed in the civilian ranks. Bodies were flung in the air and come tumbling back to the earth, tripping more attackers as they charged forward on their attack. The area of no man's land was covered with blood and broken bodies. The area was harder for the attackers to cross because of the bodies they trampled over. The attack slowed down, but it was far from stopped.

Sanguily saw the first rays of hope when civilian fighters veered off to the left. He thought they were going to turn around and head into the oncoming fighter planes as they did when they first attacked his position. If they did, the results would be the same with a slight difference. This time, when the attackers ran into their own men and were forced to stop, he was not going to allow them to get away. He planned to send his troops out and eliminate all the civilian fighters caught in the middle, and then he would have his soldiers continue until they overran the civilian fortifications and wiped them all out.

Since the first civilian attack was beaten back, Sanguily cursed for not pursuing the fleeing civilian fighters, thus allowing them to reorganize and attack a second time. His hopes were dashed when he saw what they were up to. The turning mob got out of the way of another wave of attackers pouring into no man's land. The group that veered off removed many bodies with them, giving a clear corridor for this wave of attackers. Sanguily did not notice the ones who veered off, changed their direction and they were now attacking his weakest section of defense.

This second attack added to the large one coming down the throat of his defenders. Almost instantly, the left section of the revolutionary forces collapsed under the weight of the charging civilians. The fighting turned to hand to hand combat, with the civilians gaining, not because they were better trained, there was an endless sea of them being thrown at the military defenders.

Some of Sanguily's tanks came under attack as the advance elements of the civilians fired shoulder launched anti-tank AT-7 Saxhorn wire guided missiles at them. Three T-80 tanks came under fire, one took three hits to destroy the steel behemoth. Other tanks were hit, but all limped back to safety. The stunned Captain ordered his heavy weapons to concentrate fire on the missile launchers gathered in one area of trees. Mortars, grenade launchers and machine guns concentrated fire in the tree line, and anti-tank missiles ceased fired by the civilians.

Sanguily ordered some tanks and artillery pieces to cover his retreat to the center of the city. He hoped to deploy his forces in the buildings and resort to guerrilla warfare tactics of sniper fire with ambushes and man traps aimed at the civilians. The only thing he could hope for now was to slow down the rampaging civilians until his reinforcements arrived on the scene, or he received orders to pull back to a safer position. He called out to Major Trujillo, but he was unable to get through the bunched up ranks of soldiers and his military equipment.

The artillery pieces were setup on the other side of the city, and his tanks followed him in the streets, and they disappeared and setup again to wait for the attacking civilians to enter their kill zones. Tanks and armored vehicles were setup in such a way to protect the nuclear reactors until the last possible moment, before they were forced to abandon their posts and retreat.

The Captain moved back with his retreating troops while issuing ordering for his tanks and artillery pieces to continue firing into the so called no man's land, in an effort to break up the massive civilian Army attacking them. He knew this was a waste of time, because the attackers easily broke through his lines. He saw civilian fighters pouring through his defense and he ordered the artillery to concentrate their fire at the rupture in his ranks. He wanted to slow the attackers down so he could get his men out. He allowed tanks to fire into the no man's land.

Two Migs made a pass over the civilian hordes, dropping six five hundred pound bombs before escaping the scene, being chased by missiles. The aircraft attack appeared to slow the civilians down long enough for the government troops trapped by the breach to get out and rejoin the other troops setting up new defensive lines. Sanguily ordered his men to fall back into the city. There, he broke down his Army into seven separate fighting units. Each unit's officers laid out the new orders.

Their job now was to slow down the civilian attackers until the other government troops had a chance to setup another frontline of defense against them. Once again, the Captain tried to reach Captain Trujillo who was defending the town of Santa Clara. This time the radio was answered, and when he requested to speak with the Captain, the voice on the other end reported he would have to go to hell to speak with him. Captain Sanguily demanded to know who spoke. "Fulfencio Camacho, civilian fighter." The voice growled back at him. His fears were just confirmed, all Captain Trujillo's troops had been overrun by the attacking civilian hordes.

HAVANA, CUBA. SEPTEMBER 28th, 1996, 12:03 A.M.

The peace and serenity of the city of Havana was shaken, as a new series of devastating explosions took place in rapid succession. Presidente Alvarez jumped out of bed and ran to the window to see what was happening in the city. It looked like the entire skyline had been lit up by a series of massive fireballs rolling through the cloud cover. More explosions followed the first ones. Alvarez turned and was about to call for his guard in the hall when he spotted Maria behind him. She broke the bottle of wine they shared last night, and she was sneaking up behind him.

"What were you going to do with that broken bottle, witch? You heard me bitch, I asked you what you were going to do with that broken bottle?" he snarled at his once lover and future wife.

"I was going to rip your throat open, you devil you." She hissed in a harsh voice.

"You were huh? Madre de Dios, did you think you would've had the dom balls to go through with that threat against me, bitch?" Alvarez growled at her as he took a threatening stance against her. When she did not answer, he walked up to her and he growled in her face. "Come on you bitch! You wanted to rip my throat open. Here I am bitch. Go ahead and cut me if you dare, Maria! Come on bitch, cut me I said!" he barked as he even lifted his chin up, giving her a better shot at his throat then he hissed at her. "Yeah, I didn't think you'd have the guts to do it, bitch!"

Alvarez violently pulled the broken bottle from her hand and with a quick motion, he gave her an ugly, jagged wound on the side of her cheek with the broken glass edge.

She screamed from the pain, but Alvarez had not finished with her yet. He set on her as if she was a man, and he was fighting for his life. He beat her across the face and chest with a closed fist, and roared with anger until he beaten her unconscious. He continued to pound on the helpless body as if trying to beat her for everything that went wrong with his life, and with the revolution he started. When he was satisfied he punished her enough, he got up and dressed and headed for his office. All the while, more heavy explosions continued to rake the capital streets. The sound of small weapons fire could also be heard as his troops entered the fray now.

Alvarez entered his office in a huff and heard the roar of tanks as their engines growled to life, and the war machines moved on the roads. Another explosion ripped the night asunder.

He pressed the intercom and he screamed for Colonel Calvo to get over to his office.

Calvo entered the large office out of breath, and then he stared at his new leader.

"What the fook is happening out there, god dommit Colonel?" Alvarez barked at him.

THE PENTAGON, WASHINGTON D.C. 12:21 A.M.
SEPTEMBER 28th, 1996

General William Weidenbacher, the Chairman of the Joint Chiefs of Staff just woke to a phone call at home, informing him to report to the Pentagon, ASAP. It took ten minutes to get there, and as he entered his office he found CIA Director John Raincloud waiting.

"Arrr... I should've known it'll be you pushing the panic button, what's the matter, Director you need a fourth for bridge?" Weidenbacher snapped as he walked past the Native American, knocking his feet off his desk and he plopped in his chair and he moaned. "How many times do I hafta tell you to keep you feet off my damn desk? You want a drink?"

"Yes sir, by all means General." The large and full blooded Sioux replied with a slight smile on his lips as he stared back at the powerful and respected General.

"Say when Chief." The General remarked with a smirk as he stared back at the large man.

"When your fingers get wet, General Weidenbacher." The Chief grinned back at his friend.

"Okay pal, it's your ass on the line here, mister. Whatdaya got for me this time John?"

"General Weidenbacher, I have a number of latest reports from my operatives in Cuba. The whole Island erupted in violence at the same time, sir. I know I reported fighting, but this time no section on the

413

Island's free of it. I'm waiting for the latest reports to come in, but I don't think the fighting's going to stop until the troops put down the civilians, or the civilian overrun the military, which I seriously doubt will happen, sir. I read the reports stating the civilians are knocking warplanes out of the air. This means they have anti-aircraft weapons, making them a force to be reckoned with, sir. Other reports warn the civilians have anti-tank weapons. If something isn't done soon, I think it's going to break down and become an outright slaughter on both sides, sir."

"What do you suggest we do about it?" the General asked him as he looked into his eyes.

"I think we should get our troops on the damn Island immediately sir." The Director offered.

"Me too Mr. Raincloud, but the only way we'll accomplish that feat, is if we talk the Boss into allowing us to step up our invasion clock. I'll be busy setting out my plans for the man. I'll also check with my Intel people, and determine where to establish my beachheads on the damn Island. I want to know exactly where the heavier fighting is taking place on the Island, so our boys aren't dumped off in the middle of a hot free fire zone, Director Raincloud. I need to get as many of my people on the Island before either side knows we're there. Once I put everything together, I'll be back in touch with you, and then we'll see the Boss together, John."

"That's fine with me sir, I'll continue to gather information and we'll compare notes before we meet with him. Billy, I'm sorry I had to get you out of bed, but I thought this might be important and it shouldn't wait until tomorrow morning." Director Raincloud offered his friend.

"No need to apologize, its better this way because I plan to be meeting with the Boss by eight. Let me know if you find out anything more, and have your Intel work with my boys, so we're kept up to date over this mess. Fucking Cubans messing up my sleep on me, go John."

"I'm on my way General Weidenbacher." Director Raincloud offered as he left the office.

THE DEFENDING GOVERNMENT TROOPS INSIDE THE CITY OF CIENFUEGOS. 1:20 A.M. ON THE 28th, OF SEPTEMBER, 1996

Captain Sanguily's forces were being pressured on all sides by the civilian attackers. The Captain's men were routed out of their defensive positions as they tried to slow the advancing hordes. He had no other choice and ordered his artillery to stay ahead of his retreating forces to enable him to use his artillery to its best advantage. He instructed them to continue pounding the frontlines of the civilian attackers.

The Captain's troops resorted to a delay and attack action aimed at the civilians. He ordered his troops to fight long enough to cause the civilians to stop their forward advance, and then dig in to better defend themselves from the slaughter being dished out against them. Once he understood the civilians stopped coming at them, and now they were preparing to defend their present positions. He would have his troops leave their position while the civilians attacked the now un-defended area. He ordered his artillery units to zero in on the hunkered down civilian targets, and then pound them until he was able to setup his next defense positions against them.

As soon as the civilians realized what was happening, and the government troops opposing them moved out, and they were falling victim to horrendous artillery fire. Every time the civilians started an advance on them again, it was broken up by the artillery bombardment, thus neutralizing the current attack against the city defenders. The civilians began to try and change some of their attack on the government troops, in an attempt to stop some of the civilian death.

Once the civilians advanced again, Sanguily ordered his troops to take another stand and fire at the attacking civilian fighters, forcing them to repeat the whole process over again. The artillery rounds concentrated their fire on the dug in civilian fighters, and it was having a devastating effect on them. The bombardment killed hundreds of the civilians where they hid, while slowing down their forward advance down to a crawl, and causing a heavy death toll to mount.

Sanguily understood his only hope of saving this region of Cuba, was to have his artillery and tank fire concentrate on the civilian frontlines. This way they could devastate the untrained units until they tired of the slaughter, and ended up stopping their attack against the government troops. This would allow him the time needed to better organize a counterattack against them, and drive the civilian fighters out of the city and back in the hills where they belonged. Every soldier believed, no matter how badly outnumbered they were on the battlefield, if he had the power and will to counterattack, it could turn the tide of the war in their favor at a moment's notice.

The Captain's plan worked well, because he stopped all forward advance of the civilian enemy, and in some cases he turned them back completely. This gave his artillery units a larger target to concentrate their fire power on. Everywhere he looked, he saw dead and dying lying. The death on both sides were heavy, and when the artillery fire turn on a second target, the cries of the dying replaced the thunder of the guns. His heart was heavy, because no matter whose men were being mangled to death by the cannon fire, they were Cubans. He knew he had to continue on with his strategy of using the artillery against the attacking civilians, or he was going to lose the battle, and then Cuba would fall to the civilian hordes.

The pounding from the artillery started again, turning the nighttime sky into a shower of flying sparks, flames, shrapnel and dead body parts. Sanguily admitted his plan worked out pretty well so far. He had no way of knowing Nicaro requested the Commander who attacked the troops defending Santa Clara, to start a march to Cienfuegos, to attack the artillery units from the northwest of the city that would put the group of civilian attackers in their enemy flanks.

Nicaro hoped to have his second Army attack the artillery units out of his reach. He knew if he knocked out the artillery then he could beat the government defenders. Especially since he would have a second Army attacking the government troops from the west at the same time, once they eliminated the artillery. Nicaro reasoned in his mind what the troops would do once they realized they had no artillery to support them further, and a second huge civilian Army was presently marching on them from their lead. There was nothing worse than to be caught between two separate attacking Armies at the same time. This spelled the death of the trapped enemy Army unless the government troops surrendered quickly to his attacking forces.

Nicaro prayed to capture the artillery, tanks, and the armored vehicles mostly intact, so he could then use them on the capital when he attacked there. He knew that would be a tougher battle than the assault they were presently conducting against these two cities, and their military defenders. He could actually hear the fighting going on in the outskirts of the city from where he was standing, and he also knew his second Army finally arrived and joined the attack. He felt the effects as the artillery slacken its deadly fire on his civilian fighters already.

He was not the only one who noticed the artillery had diminished some. Sanguily tried to get in contact with his artillery support units, and when he could not raise them on the radio, he realized he lost hope of defeating the civilian hordes and keeping command of the two cities. Somehow, the civilians sidestepped the city and attacked his artillery units in his rear flanks. His troops were now trapped and they were going to be forced to stand where they were and fight to the death. Slowly, the noose closed around the necks of the revolutionary military troops, as the civilians worked their way successfully around them. They surrounded the soldiers and attacked them from all sides.

Radio complaints flooded Sanguily's unit. Every complaint reported the same thing, the civilian troublemakers were in their flanks, and his troops were taking a beating from them. After an hour of senseless fighting, some government troops were requesting permission to surrender to the civilians, reporting they were cut off.

Sanguily tried desperately to keep his troops strong by screaming out new orders at them, but he knew whatever he tried on them, it was hopeless for them and he was losing his own will to continue on with a senseless fighting and killing of Cubans. The Cuban Captain understood it was useless to continue on while so overwhelmingly outnumbered, and with many of his troops running out of ammunition. It was nothing short of pure insanity to keep fighting on against such odds. He looked to the Heavens for an answer and it came to him with machine gun fire now breaking out to his rear. He cursed angrily he cursed Castro, Alvarez, his mother, and God for allowing this to happen to Cuba, to him, and to his loyal troops. He knew he had no other choice in the matter and he reached for the radio.

"Nicaro, this is Captain Sanguily and I wish to speak with you at once sir. Come in Nicaro."

After a few moments of dead silence, his radio finally came back. "Captain Sanguily, this is Nicanor Navea, sir. Emil is busy at the moment, so he has ordered me to speak with you on his behalf. What is it you want to say to me, Captain Sanguily Sir?"

"What is it I want to say to you Nicanor Navea Sir? I want the fooking death and destruction to stop! We're killing Cuban people here and it has to stop immediate..." The Captain was cut off in mid sentence by the angry civilian fighter as he snapped at him.

"Captain Sanguily, allow me to get this straight in my foolish mind. Are you telling me you want to surrender your military forces to our civilian fighters, sir?" Navea snarled in his radio as nastily as he could utter his words at the stunned sounding Cuban Captain.

"If that's what it'll take to stop the god dom death of us Cubans, sir. Then yes Nicanor Navea Sir that is what I'm telling you, sir." Sanguily replied to the civilian leader in a snap to his own tone of voice this time around.

"Then say the dom words to me, Captain. Say the god dom words I await coming from your foul and lying lips, sir." Navea barked savagely at him over the radio.

"Come on Nicanor, stop the fooking death will you please. These are our god dom people dying in this fighting, sir." The Cuban Captain suddenly roared into the radio.

"Say the god dom words then, and it'll stop the fooking dying as you say, Captain Sanguily!" Navea barked right back at him again over the radio.

"Very well Navea, if that's what it'll take for us to stop this god dom death, sir. I surrender to you and your forces sir." Sanguily hissed at him over the radio this time.

"Do you speak for all your foul troops you have fighting us, Captain Sanguily?" Nicanor Navea asked the young Cuban Captain, hoping he was hearing his words correctly.

"Yes. I speak for all the troops defending this one city, Navea." Sanguily snarled back at him.

"Then give the fooking order to your troops to lay down their arms and stop firing at us, dommit. Once the shooting stops from your side it'll stop from mine at the same time, Captain Sanguily. Order your Military units to raise the white flags above their worthless heads. Any area without a white flag of surrender flying, will receive fire from my people until they comply with my demands, Captain. Once we're sure you stopped the killing we'll follow suite and stop firing on your troops from our side. From now, any further death of Cuban peoples will rest solely upon your head alone, Captain." The civilian Navea broke off the communication at this point.

Sanguily pleaded in his radio for his units to stop their firing at the civilians, he instructed his troops to lay down their arms and raise white flags over their present positions. His troops were then told to sit tight until the civilian leaders told them what to do next. Slowly, so painstakingly slow, did the weapon fire start to slacken down, and then stopped all together from both sides of the fighting. Shouts replaced the weapon fire as the civilian fighters took command of the government troops, disarming them and grouping the soldiers out in any open areas. Out of the two hundred thousand government troops he started out with, Sanguily was down to a fighting force of less than fifty thousand soldiers alive and well enough to continue fighting if ordered.

The true leader of the civilians, Nicaro ordered a splinter group of his fighters to break off, and they were to head for the twin nuclear reactors of the city. He instructed his fighters not to harm the reactors in any way, shape or form, or the technicians controlling the reactors.

He ordered his people to take control, and instruct the technicians to start a hot shut down of the power producing machines. He did order his men to engage any troops who tried to hinder their mission. These orders were to be carried out even if a cease fire was in effect. Nicaro impressed on his fighters he wanted these two dangerous machines left intact and in good working order.

Nicaro then made his way to the center of the city with Navea walking by his side. They were looking for Captain Sanguily in the mess of government prisoners. When he found him, Nicaro walked up to him and warned the man angrily and in no uncertain terms. "Captain Sanguily, do you remember my last warning to you. I told you if you tried to deceive me in any way, I'd kill you on the spot when I set eyes upon you, sir." Nicaro did not say another word as he removed his pistol, and aimed it at Sanguily's head and fired.

Sanguily saw he was about to die and he snapped to attention, and then he stared in his executioner's eyes, and waited for death to wrap its icy fingers around his soul as if he was actually daring the civilian leader to kill him.

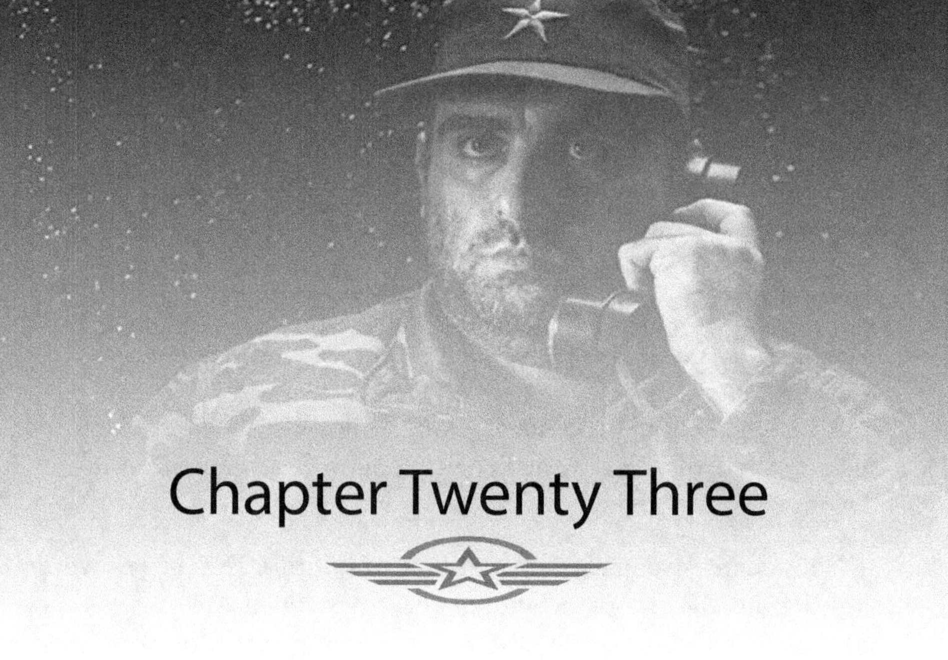

Chapter Twenty Three

Presidente Carlos Rafael Hernandez Alvarez returned to his office in a huff, after nearly beating Maria to death moments ago. Colonel Calvo waited for him. He stormed across the room and plopped down in his seat and snarled at his officer. "Well, what the hell is happening at Cienfuegos? I warn you sir, it better not be bad news or it could cost you your cursed head." The thunder of cannon fire echoed throughout the Palace walls.

Havana was in the midst of an assault by the civilian hordes rampaging wildly through the streets of the city. The civilians attacked government troops on their dash through the capital. Hundreds of dead and dying lay scattered about as the fighting continued unchecked. The troops pulled in the tanks and artillery to deal with the out of control mobs. They were ordered to shoot anyone on the streets. Armor vehicles with loud speakers roamed the streets of Havana, ordering the civilians to remain in their homes until the fighting was over. The message warned the civilians caught on the streets were subject to arrest, and will be shot if resisting the authorities.

Alvarez looked out his window in time to see the effects of an exploding steel monster once his main battle tank. He saw a mob of civilians climbing all over the machine of war, and they were attacking the tank with fire bombs and hand grenades. Alvarez turned away and looked at Colonel Calvo and stared at him.

"That is right Presidente Alvarez the civilians have grenades now, even some anti-tank and anti-aircraft weapons, sir. They're slowly becoming better armed than we are, sir."

Alvarez glared at the smug looking Colonel as he went deep in thought. Suddenly, he repeated the question. "You didn't inform me how our troops defending the two cities are doing."

"Presidente Alvarez, I hate to inform you of this. But the last word I heard from the troops defending the cities stated their lines were crumbling, and it looked like the civilians were going to overrun their positions."

Alvarez let out his breath in a hiss and snarled. "When was the last time you heard anything from the defenders of the cities, sir?"

Calvo checked his watch, and replied to Alvarez. "Fifteen minutes ago sir."

"By the Christ Child, do you not think it's about time you tried to find out what is happening over there, sir? We desperately need to remain in command of these two cities, or all is lost to us, you fool." He exploded as he jumped to his feet and then he walked back over to the window.

Calvo spoke into a radio and while he was waiting for a response, he warned Alvarez. "Presidente Sir, I don't think you should stand so near the window, not with the lights on sir."

He spun around and he growled at his Colonel. "Sweet Lord Jesus, are you telling me I'm no longer safe in my own god dom office, Colonel?"

"I'm not saying any such thing I just suggested you shouldn't take any chances while the unrest in the city is taking place. Why tempt faith..." His conversation was interrupted by the voice on the radio.

After a few seconds he looked at Alvarez and reported. "Presidente, Santa Clara has fallen and Cienfuegos is crumbling."

Alvarez sat down hard and he spoke in a low, controlled, almost scary tone. "By the Holy Father, is there a chance of us sending enough troops down there to save Cienfuegos from falling into the hands of the god dom civilians, Colonel?"

"Not a chance in hell sir. I believe it's far too late for us to try and save either of the two cities, sir. It's lost and now we have to protect the capital city."

As if to emphasize the Colonel's last statement, the Palace lights flickered and then went out. Both men heard the emergency generator roar to life. Calvo looked at his President and said in a disgusted voice. "Presidente Alvarez Sir, you can take this as a signal that Cienfuegos has fallen to the civilian attackers, and they shut down the reactors."

"How long before the capital falls to these bastard fighters then, Colonel Calvo Sir?"

"I figure we should be able to hold on for the rest of the night, but when dawn comes I fear the civilians will attack in force. Then, who knows. Hours, days, surely not week's sir."

"We'll not be able to hold them off and get control over them, Colonel?" he asked with concern of his Colonel. In his mind he was refusing to believe all was lost to his new revolution.

"Not a chance the civilians are attacking in massive and uncontrolled waves, and we cannot kill them quick enough to make a difference in the outcome of the war, Presidente Alvarez Sir."

"That is it then, God curse me to hell I wasted my last breath of these ingrates who refuse to allow me to command Cuba and make their lives better for the fools. Here is what I want you to do, hurry down and get on that dom radio and get our attack units in Israel and the Arab nations in gear, sir. I want them to create the same kind of hell that's taking place on this god dom foul Island, sir. I want the eyes of the world off our necks and drawn over to the Middle East, while we set the cursed missiles in place. Then we'll make our demands known to the people of Cuba, and the rest of the world at the same time, Colonel Calvo."

Calvo did not move a muscle as he stared at the raving Cuban President. He did not know if this was the right road to travel on. He was torn between trying to talk sense into the civilian leaders, or try to make Alvarez seek help of the United States to stem the tide of death engulfing the capital and Cuba.

Alvarez pounded his fist heavily on his desk in a rage and he stormed at his officer. "Colonel Calvo! God curse you to death, do you have shit packed in your worthless ears? I thought I just issued you an order, sir?"

"You did sir, but I was giving you time to change your mind, before I carried the orders out. Sir, you must give these orders more thought. Once they're issued, they cannot be resented or stopped. We have..."

Alvarez pointed his finger at Colonel Calvo's chest and he snorted at him. "I gave this matter all the thought I intend to give it. I issued my orders and I expect you to carry them out as I issued them to you, immediately Colonel!"

Calvo slowly stood and saluted Alvarez as he headed out the office. Alvarez stopped him by calling to him. "Colonel have my armored vehicle stand by to transport me to Guanahacabibes. I'm planning to take Maria with me to that dom bunker. I suggest you make plans to follow me there once you start our plans in motion."

"Fine!" the Colonel snapped sharply at the fuming Presidente of Cuba.

Colonel Calvo was shoved aside by an excited Vice Presidente Lazaro Prio Socarras Cabrisas, who came stormed in Alvarez's office while offering him at the same time. "Presidente Alvarez Sir, this is wrong. Something has gone terribly wrong with the Revolution, sir. I must protest the way you're handling the civilians of this Island. These are our people, our civilians being slaughtered by our military and armor. I demand this dom fighting come to a halt, sir. We must stop killing the civilians before there are no more civilians alive on the entire Island. We ha..."

Alvarez was surprised by Cabrisas and his actions. He showed little if any sign of his wounds. He was obviously having a problem breathing, but he still stood erect, and looked like he was moving with ease. The wounds did little to take the passion of his convictions from the strength and tone of his voice. He stared at the huge man who looked as if he had grown wider, as Cabrisas drew a breath.

"What do you suggest I do? Order my troops to lay down their arms and allow the civilian mobs to slaughter them? I can't do as you ask, you ask the impossible Cabrisas. Leave me, I have work to accomplish." He snapped, as he interrupted Cabrisas, and he glared at the angry man.

"Bullshit! Bullshit! What could be more pressing than to stop the slaughter of the Cuban civilians of this country, Presidente Carlos Alvarez Sir?" he suddenly roared back at Alvarez.

"You're beginning to bore me which is dangerous on your part, Cabrisas. I told you I have work to do sir." Alvarez repeated, he still refused to address Cabrisas with the title of Vice Presidente because he no longer regarded him as the Vice Presidente of Cuba..

"Like what and, don't deceive me, I know everything taking place on this Island. Alvarez please, we have to stop the slaughter of our civilians. We have to search out the leaders of these civilians and speak with them. We have to get them to stop their advance on the capital, and in return we shall promise we'll stop firing on them just as long as they stay where they are, sir."

"I have work to do on Guanahacabibes, mista." Alvarez replied with much bitterness in his voice, and he removed some papers from the lower drawers of his desk, dumping them on top.

"What could be so dom important on that isolated section of the Island? That area is nothing more than a garbage dump and a place for criminals to hide from the law." Vice Presidente Cabrisas complained as he wiped his brow.

"Why Cabrisas, I thought you said you know everything taking place on the Island of Cuba. If you were so in tune with your Island and these dom civilians and know everything as you say, you would know about the missiles we're preparing for flight there, sir." Calvo said in a bragging tone of voice, this time the Colonel did not address Cabrisas as the Vice Presidente.

Vice Presidente Cabrisas spun around so fast Calvo thought he was going to strike him, but Cabrisas wanted to face the one speaking to him. He stared at the Colonel as he milled over what he said. His face showed the fear and recognition of the importance of the Colonel's last statement as he groaned at the military officer. "Oh sweet Jesus, don't tell me the great fool Castro hid some of the Russian God awful missiles in that lowly wilderness of the Island. Of course he did that would be the only area on the whole island where a secret of this magnitude would be hidden without becoming public knowledge."

Vice Presidente Cabrisas turned away from Calvo and faced Alvarez and pointed his finger at his face and warned him angrily. "Don't tell me you intend to use the cursed weapons of the hated devil. Alvarez, you can do nothing but disassemble them and their hated warheads, and get their parts off our Island as quickly as possible. If you don't do this, they could be the cause a terrible reaction from the United States, if the Americans discover we're in possessions of them God cursed weapons on the Island, sir."

Alvarez ignored his pleas as he continued to stack his many files on top of his desk.

"Oh God, you're going to be so foolish as to dare threaten the United States with the dom things, as Castro had once intended to do. Alvarez, do you not understand how the Americans will respond to such threats? They'll burn Cuba to nuclear ash and cinder, killing everyone on the Island, sir. You cannot be so foolish as to dare to threaten the United States with these weapons of mass destruction, knowing how they'll respond to those threats. It'll spell the end of Cuba as a nation, Alvarez!"

"By God in Heaven, it's Presidente Alvarez to you, and if it makes any difference, that is exactly what I intend to do with the dom things. If the Americans destroy Cuba in the process, so be it. Cuba has no future without my leadership to guide them. The way the civilians are treating me and my Revolution, shows me they don't deserve to live, and I'll do what I can to gain control over the civilians of this foul country." Alvarez stared at the shaking Cabrisas.

"Presidente Alvarez, you stand as much of a chance of stopping the winds of fate, as you do of controlling the United States and her might. What powers do you possess to control the United States? Not even the awesome power of the Soviet Union could conquer the will of America and her people. Alvarez, I beg you to think of what you're threatening before you do something foolish. Something that'll does not stop or reversed once the wheels of the monster are in motion..."

"I warned you once Cabrisas. The next time you refer to me as Alvarez, I shall have you shot for your crime against me, sir." He hissed as he slammed a file on his desk, sending the contents flying across the room.

"You wouldn't dare, not even you are capable of such treachery." Cabrisas snapped as he straightened up and he stared at the President, favoring his right side where he was wounded.

"I'm growing tired of arguing with you, Cabrisas. I'm angered by the civilian fools of this miserable country and their reaction to my Revolution to set them free as it is and now you're arguing with me as well. Arr... I'll teach everyone on this dom Island the error of their ways, when they go up against me and my beliefs." Alvarez produced a pistol from the desk drawer and aimed it at Cabrisas's chest and he fired three times point blank at him.

Cabrisas's body jerked as the bullets tore into his chest, and he came to rest sprawled out lying on the Persian rug. Alvarez walked over to Cabrisas as he struggled for breath and he said. "It's about time everyone living on this fooking Island realizes I'm the man, the dom Presidente of Cuba, and my word is the law here god dommit."

Calvo joined Alvarez as he fired the final bullet into Cabrisas's brain.

"He's dead." Calvo announced with a grin on his face and he looked at Alvarez.

"I know this fool. Did I not give you orders to carry out, Colonel Calvo?"

"Yes sir." He announced with little care in his tone for the dead Vice-Presidente.

"Then why are you not carrying them out as you were ordered, Colonel Calvo?"

"Right away." Calvo headed out of the Presidente's office on the third floor of the Palace, and rushed to his office and picked up his phone and dialed the local radio station. He ordered the person to play a record at the top of the hour. He looked at his watch, it was two forty seven a.m. that meant he had to wait for another thirteen minutes before his teams operating in Israel and the selected Arab nations would hear the recording, and know they were to carry out their missions.

The first Cuban attack team scheduled to go in action was the one prepared to hit the Israeli resort. Once this attack was completed, the teams scheduled to attack the Arab states would then go active one after the other. The first attack would occur twenty hours after the opening attack on Israel, followed by another three hours later. The last attack was scheduled to begin three hours after the least attack took place.

Calvo understood he could not attack the Arab nations too quickly after the attack on Israel, or no one would believe the Israeli's were retaliating for the attack on their country by the supposed Arab attackers. He was pleased the well hated Jews and the foul Arabs could not get along even with themselves, or this part of his plan would never be successful. They would never get the missiles in position without the Americans knowing about them and reacting against them first.

A HILLSIDE OVERLOOKING HAIFA AND A CLUB MED RESORT

Sergeant Quintana, known as Abdul Jabbar Abdul Agazadeh to the team members, and his twenty six Arab acting fighters were prepared to descend on the uncaring group of vacationers enjoying the sun in Israel.

Quintana shaded his eyes with his hand as he looked to a cloudless sky, and his radioman monitored the radio station. His heart skipped a beat as he heard the first words of the recording. He dared not breathe until the song was completed. Then, as ordered, the same record was repeated. He looked to his Second in Command and announced. "Looks like we'll carry out what we were trained for. Call everyone together so I can brief them at the same time, and we can get on with our attack."

While the Second in Command organized the rest of his troops, Quintana drew a map in the sand, and he went over the plan with the other soldiers of his group. He split up his group in three separate units, with his unit coming straight on at the resort, and the other two units would attack from other angles of the resort. This would leave only the Ocean area free from his attack. Quintana's solution to this problem was simple he was merely going to put off his attack until noontime, when he believed everyone on the resort would be going for lunch.

The Cuban Sergeant sent in four fighters armed with pistols, they would walk the beach and once the attack began, they would pick up any stragglers they came across. The four soldiers would force anyone they found on the beach to the lunchroom area. There, they were going to keep all the vacationers locked up until they carried out their final orders, and then they would kill them all. The four soldiers were to shoot anyone who gave them the slightest bit of trouble.

Once Quintana finished scratching his marks in the sand completing his map, he made certain everyone knew their orders and what was expected of them. They were then sent to their units to prepare them for attack. Quintana checked his watch, 10:43 a.m. and he ordered. "You have an hour to get your people to their assigned positions. We begin our attack at noon. Anyone not in position by this time will have me to answer too after the attack has been completed. I'll not accept failure! Good luck." Quintana snapped as he glared at each fighter, before giving them the final word. Remember why we were trained, and what we'll accomplish for the sake of Cuba. We have to be successful, if we want to return to Cuba as heroes. Let's move out people."

Quintana watched as his soldiers split up into three separate attack units. His force was to remain behind and allow the two smaller groups to move out first, because they had a larger area to cover, before they could get set in position. Quintana's group remained perched on the high ground, and he watched what was going on at the resort. Through field glasses he saw the people swimming in the warm waters of the Mediterranean Sea. Two pleasure boats pulled people on skies. Thirty one guests lay on recliners on the beach. Quintana tried to get a good count of the visitors but, when the count went over fifty, he gave up.

The Sergeant kept a close eye open for any Israeli troops appearing at or near the resort, he knew they were in the area, but he had not seen any sign of them. A bus pulled up then went through the gate and stopped. He watched the three people climbed off and headed for the dining area. A second sightseeing bus was coming on the compound behind the first bus. This one was empty and went right through the gate and parked by the first bus.

The Sergeant observed as much of the compound as he could see, and he saw many civilians playing or lying on the sand, get up and make their way to the dining area. He turned to one of his men and said. "This is going to be easier than I thought. The lambs head for the slaughter without worry. By the time we attack, all should be in one place for us, One." Quintana called each of his attackers by numbers rather than names for fear of making a mistake, and calling them by their Cuban names. "One, you better get ready to move out. We have to get in position, remember, your duty is to cut off all communications going and coming from the resort, so you better start now. You remember where the communications hut is located on the resort, fool?"

The soldier called One nodded in reply, and he slid down the side of the hill carefully. Every attacker was out of view of anyone in the resort. Quintana's heart stopped beating as he watched some Israeli military jeeps heading down the road along the waterfront. His mind raced, had someone spotted and turned them in? Had a Jew noticed his men? Or was it dumb luck Jew soldiers showed up? Quintana kept an eye on the jeeps until they passed the main gate of the resort. He breathed easier when he realized the jeeps headed for the Lebanon, Israeli border. He kept them under surveillance until the jeeps were completely out of sight.

The Sergeant checked his watch again, eleven thirty one a.m. and he decided to get off the hillside, or he would never be in position for the opening attack. Quintana slid down the slope until he was hiding in a drainage ditch across from the main entrance of the resort. His eleven fighters fanned out and waited word to move out. Each attacker checked his AK-47 and chambered a round, and made sure they were in the proper working order. They chose the Russian weapons to further the deception they were Arabs.

Each member of the group hand signaled Quintana they were in place. Each attacker knew where they were to be, and what his target was. Quintana gave a signal then watched as One charged across the road then snuck onto the resort. He watched until One was out of sight. One was given five minutes to render the communications hut useless, before the attack began. Quintana checked his watch again, 11:54. He cursed, the time crawled by slowly and he knew his men were ready to go, and the longer it took to go in action, the less sharp their edge would be.

The second hand hit the noon time hour mark. Quintana stretched his neck out to see if he could spot Number One. He had not returned, and he did not hear any weapon fire, so he was certain One was successful in shutting down the communication systems of the resort.

When the second hand reached twelve, weapons fire erupted on two sides of the resort as his fighters attacked. They waited with Quintana until he charged across the road. The attackers bolted through the main gate, killing the guard in the tower. Quintana left one fighter to man the gate, and to turn away anyone who showed up later. He was to report the resort closed while conducting a cleaning of the complex. Something that was not unusual. The Sergeant's men checked the huts, forcing anyone found in them to run for the lunchroom. In one hut the attackers broke in on a pair making love, and they refused to allow the couple to dress as they shoved them out of the room.

When the weapon fire broke out on the resort, many vacationers thought it was the Israeli soldiers running a training exercise in the hills which they sometimes did. But when the supposed Arab fighters poured through the doors, the vacationers began paying attention to the commotion taking place throughout the resort. Nine of Quintana's fighters turned up in the lunchroom at the same time he arrived on the resort property. He emptied a clip of twenty rounds in the ceiling as he roared at the vacationers. "Everyone on the floor! Down on the floor or die!" He slammed another clip home and then he fired at the ceiling again as he repeated. "Everyone down now!"

Screams from the scared civilians filled the lunchroom as everyone left their tables, and fell to the floor as they were instructed to do. A young woman looked up and she got Quintana's attention and she cried to him. "Sir, I'm a Swedish citizen. I'm not a Jew sir."

"Talk again and I kill you." Quintana screamed as he fired three more rounds in the floor, feet before the blonde woman's face that screamed hysterically, and she covered her head with her hands. More vacationers were pushed into the lunchroom, as his men found more outside, some of them knew what was happening and tried to hide. Number One killed three Club Med workers who tried to make their way to the communications hut to call for help.

By the time everyone was herded into the lunchroom, the total of civilians climbed to one hundred and three souls, mostly women. His forces killed sixteen of them, mostly men.

Quintana sat on a table and casually ate an apple, paying little attention to the civilians lying on the floor. Screams of terror and women weeping filled the room, there were eleven children. When Quintana had enough of the apple and the screams and crying, he got up and fired once more at the ceiling. This caused the quiet ones to scream now.

"Everyone in this room, listen to my words and you might live through this, but I'll not repeat myself. Break one of my commands and you'll die. In case you do not know it by now, we're Arabs and we are here to send a message to the Jews running this foul country..."

A number of people called out. "I'm not a Jew. We're not Jews. Most of us are not Jews."

Again, Quintana fired his weapon as he roared at his hostages, this time only two rounds went off before it ran out. "Shut up. I didn't ask question. No one talk unless ask question. Talk without asked to, and by the will of Allah, you'll die. Everyone shut up! Stop crying or I'll cut you." He barked at the blonde begging for her life. She would not be still, so he walked over to her and slammed his boot against her forehead. She was knocked unconscious, and he warned the others. "I order everyone shut up, and that what you do. Anyone speaks again and you die. That goes for cry too."

Quintana watched a few of the women tried desperately to protect their children. One cradled her child's head to her bosom, but the boy would have none of it as he tried to look at the man with the gun. He walked over to him put his fingers under the lads chin, forcing him to look up and he asked the child. "You not afraid?"

"Yes I am." The young child said while he looked directly into Quintana's staring eyes.

"Then why do you look at me so and not hide from me?" Quintana asked.

"Because my father told me to look into the eyes of your enemy and your fears will be few to worry about." The boy snapped back proudly at the angry looking man.

"Your father is a very brave man. You must be proud of him? How old are you young one? It is good for me to speak to a young soldier who is not afraid."

"I'm twelve years old." Again, the child looked directly into Quintana's eyes.

"And, you very brave also. The ones to live in this world are the brave soldier. What is father job young one?"

"He's a Marine." The child replied proudly to the much taller and angry sounding stranger.

"American?" Quintana snapped as he carefully eyed the young man again.

The boy nodded yes as proudly as he could back at the man holding the gun.

"Well son, you shall live to see your father this I promise. Number Three, take this boy along with rest of the children, and lock them in first aide room. Allah does not make war on children no matter who children they be. Young man you go with this man, you be safe, this I promise."

"What about my mother? I will not go without her." The child growled defiantly at him.

"David, you'll do as the man tells you to do. Don't worry about me I'll be fine son."

Quintana ignored the mother as any Arab man would, because women meant nothing to them, as he grumbled at the child again. "Your father has trained you well young man. You act like an Arab young man, train by respect mother and father." Quintana turned to the boy's mother and said. "You and rest of mother go with you children. Allah doesn't make war on good families. Our war is with Jew, and we continue the war until they off Arab land. Three, take mother and children to first aid building and lock them there. You protect them and make sure nothing happens to them. We'll be off this foul installation quickly, when our demands are met by the hatful Jews of this country."

Quintana motioned Three to move the children and mothers out of the room with a jerk of his weapon. He waited until they were out of the lunchroom. He did not allow the fathers to accompany their families. Once they were gone, he got up and he walked over to the woman he kicked in the face and pulled her by her hair. Groggy and sobbing, she allowed herself to be pulled to her feet, she was a young woman. The Sergeant violently shook her by her hair as he barked in her face, spittle spraying all over her face and he ordered her in one word. "Strip!"

The woman stared at the angry looking Quintana, but she did not move a muscle.

"I said strip, and that what you do as ordered!" He slapped her across the face knocking her to one knee. Then he was on her, ripping her clothes from her body. "I thought European slut like go with no clothes." He roared at her, and when she was naked he yanked her to her feet and added. "All women stand and strip. Do now or die." He fired in the air, but he did not let go of the other woman's hair. He was forcing her to stand by his side and watch as the other women began to remove their clothes.

Many scared women did as they were told, but some hesitated momentarily, mostly the younger women of the late teenage years. This hesitation brought a severe reprisal against them. They were felled on by the soldiers who beat them with their weapons. Once the women were beaten senseless, their clothes were ripped from their bodies.

An Israeli man stood and snarled at the leader of the attackers. "What the hell is the meaning of this? Since when do Arabs force women to undress? I must protes..." Three bullets ended the Israeli's protest. The death of the man seemed to remove the defiance from the rest of the group as they stripped.

"When I tell you stand this you do, and you stand until told do next." Quintana growled as he glared at each of the naked women, and added to his warning. "You'll put hands by you sides and stand straight up."

The women did so. Quintana ordered the Israeli workers taken out to the pool area of the resort. There, their hands were tied behind their backs and they were forced to kneel facing the pool water. Their legs were tied to their hands so it was impossible for them to move. Two terrorists started down the line of Jewish workers, each from the opposite ends, working their way to the middle of the workers, and they cut the throats of the workers then shoving and sending them tumbling in the water. Quintana felt most, if not all the workers were Jews.

Quickly, the once sparkling clear water of the large pool turned red as the helpless Jewish workers were sent tumbling into the warm waters of the pool. Twenty one workers in all were slaughtered in the same terrible manner with their throats slit. The attackers stayed by the pool side until the kicking and struggling from the dying workers ended, and their bodies slowly started to float towards the surface of the blood red water.

In the lunchroom, Quintana ordered the male prisoners up to their feet now and he then ordered them strip also. The few who refused were shot, causing the women to cry again.

"Stop cry!" he barked at them as he walked over to a shaking woman, and beat her for no reason. The sobbing woman cringed on the floor trying to fend off any further blows as best as she could with her arms and legs. A second woman went to her aid and she was attacked by Quintana as savagely. He was angry they would dare to ignore him, the man standing over them with a weapon held at the ready. His anger got the best of him and he fired before thinking, killing the both women.

Two men from the resort made a move on Quintana, they were killed by other attackers standing guard over them. When the men were naked, they were ordered to surround the large columns of the room, four to each post supporting the roof structure. Once there, they were handcuffed to each other making every male helpless to protect themselves. Quintana smiled as he realized he had everyone under his control. What woman would try to run away if naked he reasoned? The men, they were another problem, they were going to die slowly, and there was nothing they could do to avoid their death. One of Quintana's men walked up to him and said. "Abdul Jabbar Abdul Agazadeh, Allah Akbar. We are successful sir." He fired in the air. This was followed by a number of his attackers doing the same, forcing the women to cover their ears.

Quintana nodded to his Number Five soldier for following his orders. Five was instructed to use the Arab names and the way the Arabs usually addressed their God by. Quintana knew he was going to leave enough of the women alive to report to the Jew rescuers who would eventually save them. The women would tell of the Arab names they heard used by the attackers, and the Arab mannerisms used by the well known terrorists.

Quintana took a drink as he milled over his strategy. He knew he had to follow his orders to the letter and be as savage as possible to those he was going to kill, but killing a bunch of naked women would be hard, even for him. He studied the defenseless women standing in the open area. In his mind he separated the ones he would allow to be raped and tortured to death, from those who he would allow to live. He wanted to allow the younger women to live, but there were not enough older women to satisfy his men, and show the world just how savage the Arabs were.

He pointed at one woman after the other. The women selected were moved from the rest, and they were forced to stand in a corner. The women who remained were manhandled over to the support columns where they were handcuffed to them. These women were molested as the attackers went about their duty of pinning them to the columns. Once they were helpless, the men attacked them in earnest until Quintana/Agazadeh cursed at his people, and then he yelled at the men to leave the youngest ones alone.

Once his soldiers moved away from the helpless women, they set on those still standing in the corner of the building. They were beaten and kicked to the floor then raped.

The men pinned to the columns roared curses at the terrorists as they moved against the helpless women. When the soldiers grew tired of the women, they turned their attention on the men. Two attackers walked over to the first column and they cut the men with bayonets. First, they were satisfied to cut their arms and legs, but when one of the terrorists cut a man's organ off, the killing began. Some captives were partially filleted as the soldiers cut skin from their legs. Others had their throats slit and were allowed to bleed to death slowly. Others had gaping holes drilled in their bodies by the heavy bayonets, and then they were left to die as well.

While all this was going on in the lunchroom, the women pinned to the other support columns began to beg not to have the same fate happen to them. They did not realize until the last moment they were the lucky ones picked to live through this terrible nightmare.

As the thought to be Arab attackers killed the men from the resort, they continued to use Arabic phrases in an attempt to try and convince the survivors they were indeed Arab terrorists attacking them. When the men were dead or dying, the attackers turned on the women. The same fate had fallen on them. The terrorists hacked at them with dull bayonets they stabbed, sliced and ripped at the unprotected female bodies. Three hours after the attack began, sixty five bodies lay savagely hacked to death in the lunchroom, more dead by the pool and bodies also lay spread throughout the rest of the resort. The eighteen women left alive to attest to the savage attack were left naked and chained to the columns. Many screamed until their minds found temporary peace in the dark world of insanity. Twenty women and children locked in the first aid hut were alive and luckily, they didn't have to witness the butchery going on inside main building of the resort.

As quickly as they first appeared on the resort property, the attackers disappeared back into the mountains. They had their orders and each man knew where they were to meet up in the desert. The last action required of Sergeant Quintana before he left, was to make his way to the communications hut of the resort and Number One. He entered the building and One asked him. "I heard screaming, is the deed done Sergeant Quintana Sir?"

"Yes it is." He replied to his second in command, as he stared back at him.

The Cuban soldier known as Number One to the rest of the group of attackers breathed a deep sigh of relief as he complained. "I'm god dom glad I was spared that ugly duty, sir. I don't know if I would've been able to kill women and unarmed civilians. It's not the soldier's way."

"Maybe not, but we're bound to follow our orders no matter what they are. I want you to raise the Jew's headquarters. You have the numbers and the words you need to say to the Jew who'll respond to your call?" Quintana asked.

"Yes. I have them with me Sergeant." One held up a small slip of paper in his fingers.

"Good, get it done." Quintana ordered, ignoring the slip of One calling him Sergeant.

Without further words from his control, Number One quickly keyed the radio and said into it in an extremely excited tone of voice. "Eliza, Moses, Abraham, Joshua, One, One, Seven. Emergency, emergency, emergency. Oh, by the power of God there is an emergency here at the resort, sir." The attacker Number One was the only attacker in Quintana's entire group of soldiers who spoke fluent Hebrew with the proper accent.

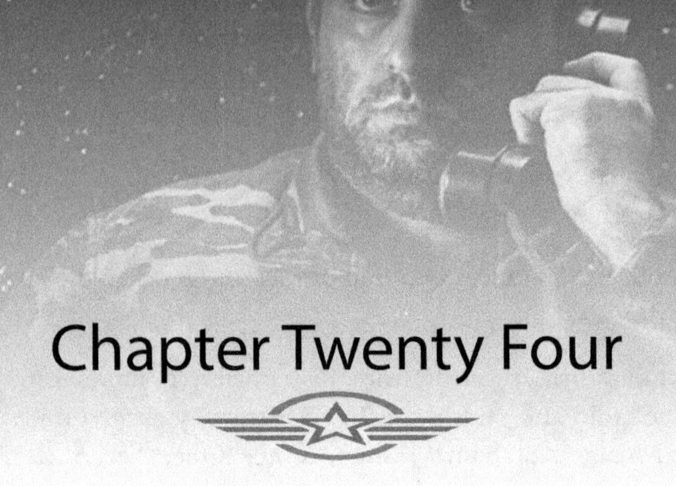

Chapter Twenty Four

A rather jovial voice laughed on the radio at him. "Okay EMAJ One, One, Seven. What is this so called emergency of yours, mister? Did someone fall into the warm Mediterranean waters again on you, mister?" The operator knew from the call numbers that had just come in, that the station was the one attached to the Club Med resort stationed in Haifa.

"I have an emergency here sir. The resort is under attack by a large number of unknown guerrillas at this time, sir. We need help sir they're killing everyone visiting the damn resort. Oh God no, please don't kill me. Please, I want to live, please don't kill me." Number One did not use the call numbers for the second time, and he was making like he was about to be killed by one of the terrorists, as he cried out into the radio now. To carry out this charade even further, Quintana fired on full automatic out the shattered window of the small communication's hut, just as Number One let go of the radio key, making the radio go dead in the middle of the weapon fire and his frantic cries.

The once jovial Jewish Lieutenant monitoring the radio was up on his feet, and he excitedly screamed in the dead machine. "EMAJ-One, One, Seven report. EMAJ-One, One, Seven. I order you to report to me you damn fool you! Report to me at once, god dammit you report to me!"

Others working in the communications room gathered around the angry operator. A Major came out of his office and rushed to the radio operator and asked the Lieutenant. "What's the problem here?"

"Major, I received an emergency report from EMAJ-One, One, Seven, sir. He reported a large number of possible Arab guerrillas attacked the Club Med resort at Haifa, Major. He also reported the attackers were killing everyone visiting the resort, Major. I heard automatic weapons fire in the background then the radio went dead as we talked and the weapon fire started, sir."

"Give me that damn thing will you, Lieutenant. EMAJ-One, One, Seven. Come in."

There was no reply from the other end of the communication, so the concerned Major tried his call a second time to the resort. "EMAJ-One, One, Seven. This is Command and I'm ordering you to report in at once, mister. Report this minute soldier." The Major then covered over the receiver mouthpiece with his hand and barked at the Lieutenant standing by his side looking upset.

"Get a pair of god damn helicopters out there, mister. Tell them to approach the fucking resort carefully. Warn them to be on the alert for a possible terrorist attack against them as they come in. The pilots are to be prepared for an attack. Tell them I don't want them going in there like an American Rambo assault team, in case this report is a bunch of shit mister. Get it done man."

Then the excited Major went back to the radio and tried again. "EMAJ-One, One, Seven. Report before I come and give you a hell of a kick in the seat of your pants soldier."

The Lieutenant was back to the Major's side and reported. "Sir, I scrambled a pair of AH-64 A Peten Apache attack helicopters from Tsvah Haganah, sir. Their ETA's fifteen minutes out, sir."

"Okay, patch me through to the Joshua Forces guarding the damn border at Lebanon, sir." The Major next ordered the Lieutenant as he stared at him.

"Done, they're on net three for you already sir." He informed the Major.

The Israeli Major switched over to the next net on the radio frequency so he could better communicate with his ground forces in the surrounding area of his control. The Commander of the Joshua Forces was waiting for his call to come in already.

"Colonel Ben-Eliezer, you're ordered to cut free a patrol of your specialized troops and get them on the move to the damn resort area at Club Med. I received word some fucking Arab terrorists might have attacked us there sir, and your troops are the closest ones I have in the surrounding area to help assist me on this one, sir. Get going and once there inform me of what you find there. If this is a joke, I'll skin the fool who started it alive Colonel."

"Right away sir, any idea on the number of terrorist we might be facing here, Major."

"Report back to me the instant you find out anything at this damn resort, Colonel. I have nothing on the number of possible terrorists involved in this attack at the moment, sir. I'll report to you if I find out anything as your troops head for the resort." The fuming Jewish Major warned the concerned sounding Israeli Colonel.

"Right away sir, the troops are on the way to the site as we speak, Major." He replied in the radio to his Commanding Officer for the moment even though he outranked the officer.

The Major broke off the connection and watched the clock slowly pass the time. The helicopters were seconds away from their target area now. Static still filled the speaker as the Major waited for the first reports to come in.

TWO AMERICAN MADE APACHE HELICOPTERS

HEADING FOR THE RESORT AT HAIFA

The pair of Israeli helicopters slowly circled the resort in a low orbit, and as far as the pilots could tell, they saw nothing amiss on the resort. So, the pilot of the lead helicopter reported to his Commander. "Sh'hafit Leader to Command, sir. We made our first pass over the target area sir, and from what we can see so far sir. Everything seems normal at the resort sir. No one is running around and taking shots at us at this time, sir."

"You're instructed to make another complete pass over the entire resort complex, sir. If you feel nothing is wrong with the damn place, you're instructed to set down across the road from the resort. Then you'll get that radio happy EMAJ operator, and beat his ass black and blue, soldier." The Major growled angrily into the radio, feeling he was being played for a fool by the resort's radio operator this time.

"Roger, copy last, I'll follow my orders as received Major. I'm beginning my second pass over the complex and will report once my second pass has been completed, Major. Over."

"Leave the damn radio channel opened this time sir. I want to hear everything going on there the instant it takes place, sir." The Major ordered the pilot of the lead Apache attack helicopter.

"Roger that last as received Major. We're coming in from the east side for the resort at this time and will be heading due west, sir. Everything looks okay so far sir. Passing over the outer fence, and heading for center of the compound, sir. Hey, what's that? Co-pilot, is that what I think it is lying there, sir?" the pilot of the helicopter replied to his commander for this mission.

"What the hell are you seeing, mister?" the Major barked into the radio this time as he was forced to wait for the helicopter pilot's reply to his last request.

"I can't tell for sure Major, it looks like we have a body lying in the middle of the pathway, sir. We're passing over the pool area of the complex and then we plan to head for the main section of the complex... Oh God! Major, we have people down sir. We have many dead in the pool, sir. Hell sir, it looks like quite a few dead, sir. The water's stained red with blood. I can't get a good count on the dead Major, but there are over fifteen bodies I see floating in the pool." The pilot's report was cut off by the pilot of the second helicopter.

"Sh'hafit Two, I have three down on the path leading to the main part of the resort complex sir. What are my orders, we have civilians down sir?" The second helicopter pilot requested from his Commanding Officer.

"Are you taking fire from the complex, sir?" The Major growled into the radio.

"Negatory on that last. We're not taking incoming fire. I repeat no enemy fire sir."

"Can you set down anywhere? I have Joshua ground troops heading for your position at present time, sir. They should be arriving your location within seven minutes. I repeat, seven minutes sir. Over." The Israeli Major roared in the radio.

"No problem setting my helicopter down sir. What are our orders once we're on the ground, Major? Do you want us to enter the resort? Over." The pilot asked over the radio.

"Yes, I want you to arm yourselves and enter the resort. You're ordered to kill any terrorists you find on the damn site, if you cannot take them as prisoners first. I want you to report when you know what's happening there. I need information god dammit." The Major shouted in the radio as he squeezed the mike locked in his hands as if he wanted to crush it.

"Understood orders as received, will report moment I know what the hell's going on. Over."

The two Israeli helicopters touched down on the sandy beach area of the plush resort, and the two Israeli pilots and co-pilots jumped out of their war machines, and made their way towards the main building of the complex. The two pilots were armed with automatic weapons, and the co-pilots were left behind so they could work the heavy weapons systems of the Apache helicopters, if the pilots came under attack from possible terrorist hunkered down on the resort.

The pilots jumped from one cover to another as they cautiously headed for the main building of the complex. They stopped by the main door, one on each side of it, and the first pilot went through the double doors, and he ended up lying on the floor with his weapon held at the ready. His eyes searching the area and focused on the horrible scene displayed before his eyes, and he wished he was blind because of what he was witnessing.

Both aviators stood by the door staring in stunned disbelief at the mayhem they discovered in the building. A few vacationers were still alive and chained to the main support columns of the building. The pilots were dumb struck by the ugly scene, because they never expected to see such savagery used against helpless people, civilians at that. It was unlike the Arabs to be so animalistic on their attack on the civilians of their country. What struck the pilots most was, everyone was naked and some of their sex organs terribly mutilated. The Arabs believed if the body was not whole, it could never be allowed into Paradise. That's why they rarely dismembered their victims. This attack was new to the Israeli pilots. One pilot left in silence to make his report.

"What did you find in there sir?" the co-pilot asked his pilot as he headed for his machine.

"You don't want to know what we found in there. Sh'hafit One to Command. Over."

"It's about time you checked in, mister. What did you find out there sir?"

"Sir, most civilians are dead in the main building of the resort, Commander. They're worse than dead sir, they were butchered alive Commander. Sir, they did terrible things to their bodies before they killed them, Commander." The shaken pilot reported to his Commander, as he tried to get his breathing under control.

"Any sign of the terrorists still in the area, Lieutenant? Are they on the resort site, mister?" The fuming Major demanded from his pilot, as he stared at the mike locked in his hands. In his mind, he was hoping to trap some terrorists at the resort site.

"None I can see Commander, the attackers obviously fled the scene, sir. They must have left before we arrived on scene to assist any survivors, sir." The pilot reported over the radio.

"How many survivors did you find at the resort? There are survivors, right? There always are some alive to tell what the damn terrorists done to them, and how it was done mister."

"Commander, so far we have found eighteen women alive in the building sir, they were chained naked to the columns of the structure. The other pilot's trying to free them as we speak, sir. I heard screaming and calling out for help from another section of the complex, Commander. But I haven't checked this area of the resort out as of yet. Sir, this is a bad one, a very bad one sir. I think we better get someone over here with special recording equipment, sir. So we can make a record of the slaughter, Commander. It's a real bad one here this time, sir."

"Understood, help's on the way. You're instructed to secure the entire complex then you'll take damn good care of those survivors, get them off the damn site as soon as possible. Wave down any passing civilians to help you with the survivors, I don't want any of them in that damn complex when our troops arrive at the site. Lieutenant, we have to be careful here. We could be facing an international incident on this one. There's probably dead from every country of the world on that complex, and that's why I want you to handle the survivors with kid gloves sir.

"Feed them and get them drunk if you have to, but take care of them. I'll dispatch more support helicopters immediately, troop carriers this time. I'll flood the entire area with troops. I want these sonofabitches caught before they're able to escape back into Arab land, and we can't get at them, sir. I dispatched a number of jets to your position, and I'll assign them to hunt down these bastards who done this against us, sir."

"Then you think the attackers came from Lebanon, Commander?"

"Where the hell else do you think the sonofabitches came from, fool!" the Major barked at him over the radio.

CIA HEADQUARTERS, LANGLEY VIRGINIA.

SATURDAY, SEPTEMBER 28th, 1996. 8:20 A.M. EST

The attack on the Club Med resort in Haifa, Israel ended twenty minutes before first words of the attack reached CIA Director John Raincloud's desk. He read the report and drew air in between his teeth in a rush as he pressed the intercom and told his secretary to phone General Weidenbacher at once, and inform him he was on the way over to his office immediately.

He walked into the General's office and announced. "Ahhh John, your secretary said you were on the way over here. What can I do for you?" General Weidenbacher said as he replaced the receiver. He spotted the Blue Border Report clutched in the Director's hands, and knew some where the shit had hit the fan.

John threw the Top Secret report on the General's desk and let out his air and tried to calm his rattled nerves.

"Do you want me to take the time to read it, or are you going to give me a verbal report, John?"

"How do you want it General Weidenbacher? It's a bad one Billy."

"You know I don't like reading of these longwinded reports of yours, sir."

"I'll begin the report for you then sir. Israel, twelve noon their time, a large number of obvious Arab terrorists attacked the Club Med resort at Haifa, sir. The first reports state there are many deaths involved in this latest attack, sir. That's about the bulk of the report, sir. Other than reporting the Israeli Command dispatched troops helicopters to the resort."

"Whattt?" General Weidenbacher grunted as he rose to his feet and he stared at the Director.

"It's true, I had operatives go to this location, and they reported something big took place at the resort. My operatives stated numerous ambulances and emergency evacuation helicopters are on the scene. The resort's reported to be crawling with Israeli soldiers, and there's a report of weapon fire in the hills surrounding the resort, sir."

"Jesus Christ John. Do you know what this shit means to us, dammit?"

"Fraid I do General Weidenbacher." The CIA Director grumbled at the officer.

"Were there Americans killed in this attack John?"

"Dunno for sure at this time General, reports coming in are sketchy at best. I have an operative trying to compile a list of the dead and wounded, sir." Director John Raincloud reported with a deep sigh as he let out his breath slowly.

"Then there are some survivors at the resort I take it?" Weidenbacher mumbled as he let his breath out.

"Reports of a few, yes sir. The death toll was placed at over seventy though, General."

"Man, these Arabs don't give a shit how many people they kill anymore, do they John?"

"Fraid not sir." The Director replied to the General's complaint.

"I guess we better let the Boss know of what's going on in Israeli, John." He reached for the phone and called the White House staff secretary, as soon as it was answered, he said. "Hello, this is General Weidenbacher. I have to speak with the President immediately."

"Good day General Weidenbacher Sir. Please hold the line while I switch your call over to the President, sir. He's in the Oval Office General Weidenbacher Sir."

After a series of loud clicks and tones, the President's voice came in over the phone.

"Yes General Weidenbacher, it's a beautiful day today sir. What can I do for you sir?"

"Mr. President. I'm afraid we have to meet. I have a Blue Border Report to discuss…"

"General, I have a full schedule of appointments for the day." The President interrupted him.

"With all due respect Mr. President, I'm sorry sir, but I'm afraid you'll have to cancel some of your scheduled meetings for the day sir. This is extremely important Mr. President."

"What the hell could be so damn important to make me cancel my scheduled appointments for the day, General Weidenbacher?"

"Mr. President, there was a terrorist attack on a Club Med vacation resort in Israel, sir. First reports state there were at least sixty killed in the attack, and more wounded. Some survivors though Mr. President." The General changed the number of the dead, he wanted to underestimate the dead because he knew how the Jewish Army was when it came down to counting the dead from a terrorist attack against their people. They always added numbers to it to make it look worse than it was.

President Cole was stunned and he dropped in his chair to steady himself, while looking in the phone as if trying to see the General on the other end. He was sure he gone mad. "Jesus Christ General, you sure know how to fuck up my day mister. Okay, get that Sioux pal of yours and get your asses here, STAT. I'll assemble the others and have them here by the time you two arrive…"

"Mr. President, I think we should meet in the Situation Room, sir." Weidenbacher offered.

"You feel this action will have that far reaching an effect on the media and us, General?"

"Mr. President Sir, I have no idea. But judging by the fact this group of terrorists decided to attack a resort, I have to think they were after a larger target than killing a bunch of Jews and civilians, sir."

"Like who General Weidenbacher?" President Cole barked at his General.

"Dunno for certain sir. They could have been a visiting dignitary or two, possibly even some Americans, or even European VIPs the attackers might have been after, Mr. President. Their target could have been anyone in the damn world, sir."

"Okay General Weidenbacher, the Situation Room it is, in ten minutes sir."

THE SITUATION ROOM UNDER THE WHITE HOUSE, WASHINGTON

D.C. 8:40 A.M. EST SATURDAY, SEPTEMBER 28th, 1996

The air was refreshing as the General walked into the room constructed seventy five feet below the ground under the East Wing of the White House. The President, Vice President, Secretary of State, along with the National Security Director and Secretary of Defense were present for the meeting. Manning, the Civilian Advisor was scheduled to arrive within fifteen minutes.

President Albert Cole was pacing behind his seat as he usually did when he was upset and waiting for a meeting to start. He was walking off some of his steam as he waited for everyone to report in for the latest emergency meeting as he cracked his knuckles at the same time. When General Weidenbacher and Director Raincloud entered the room, he barked at them. "Have you two gathered any new information on what the fucks. Err... sorry Maria. Anything more on what the hell's happening in Israel, General Weidenbacher? I want to know a helluva lot more than you two reported so far."

"Not at the moment Mr. President, but I ordered all further reports to be transferred to this office the moment they come in sir. The same goes for any of Director Raincloud's reports as well, sir."

Director Raincloud passed his reports out to each member as President Cole continued to speak with the General.

"Fine, fine..." President Cole was interrupted by Norman Griffin.

"What the hell's happening in Israel now, Mr. President?" the National Security Advisor Norman Griffin asked the upset President.

"We have reports stating there was a terrorist attack there, Norm. It was directed at a vacation resort in the Haifa region of the country, sir. Many civilians visiting the site are reported dead and wounded, sir." The President replied to Norman.

"Any reports as to who these terrorists might belong to, Mr. President?" the Secretary of Defense, Jerry Levenhagen asked as he held the President in his stare.

"The first reports in state the attackers were definitely Arab, possibly the Shiite Muslim group of Hezbollah, sir. We have one report from a survivor stating the attackers spoke Arab, and they definitely acted like Arab attackers, sir." The President replied to the Secretary mater of factly.

There was a chuckle, but a quick glare from the President stopped it. The conversation was interrupted when a report came in. The General asked the Marine guard to receive it for him.

As General Weidenbacher listened to the report, he was visibly shaken. When it was completed he hung up, but he had to rest his hand on the console of the station for few moments so he could gather himself a little. President Cole was stunned to see his General so shaken by the report.

"What the hell is it now General?" The President asked his military officer in a harsh tone.

General Weidenbacher turned and looked at the President, but he was still unable to speak.

"I'm waiting for a reply General Weidenbacher!" the President demanded.

"Mr. President, I don't know how else to say this sir. The terrorists were animals, they not only kill seventy souls, but they took time to torture them, sir." Weidenbacher took a quick breath to help calm his rattled nerves.

"Torture them? How? What the hell do you mean by torturing them, General? Since when do Arab terrorists take time to torture anyone for God sake?" The badly shaken and extremely upset Vice President Mary Hirshfield demanded from him.

"Ma'am, these bastards took their time torturing the vacationers, Ma'am." Weidenbacher answered without looking at her.

Ms. Hirshfield slowly rose to her feet as she repeated her words, while she stared intensely at the military officer, and then she snapped again. "General Weidenbacher! I asked you what the hell you meant by torturing their hostages, and I don't want to be forced to repeat myself again mister." The young Jewish woman was angry as hell as she leaned her hands flat on the desk before her, and she cautiously eyed the shaken General harshly.

"Ma'am I don't know, the first report states many were cut, raped, and otherwise tortured and injured before they were slaughtered by the attackers, Ma'am."

"You know, this is like asking seven blind men to describe an elephant, sir. Cut in what manner of the word, soldier? I'm tired of having to repeat myself, General Weidenbacher." Vice President Mary Hirshfield growled as she looked to the American Leader for his help with the obviously stalling military officer.

General William Weidenbacher looked at the stunned looking young Jewish woman as if she was only interested in hearing the morbid details of the terrorist attack. She saw the look and recognized it for what it was. She declared angrily at the officer. "General Weidenbacher, I can see you have no idea why I asked you this question, sir. I'm not a ghoul, I only ask so I can be certain these attackers were Arabs. Arab terrorists have certain standards they always adhere to sir, and they never deviate from these practices for a moment. If you don't mind, I'd dearly like to know how these civilians were cut, sir."

"Sorry Ma'am, but it's pretty tough stuff if you really want to know. Are you absolutely certain you want to hear this, Ma'am?"

"I'm capable of taking it. My mother survived the death camps during World War Two, sir."

The General nodded slowly and said. "Very well Ma'am. The men had their throats slit, others were skinned, and others had their sex organs cut away..."

"And the women sir?" Hirshfield interrupted him, "what about the women, General?"

"Err, I'm terribly sorry Ma'am, but they were raped by these asses, some had their breasts hacked off while they were alive, while others were cut in most savage of ways. Pardon me Ma'am. There were some left alone, handcuffed to columns and for the most part unharmed."

Director Raincloud interrupted the General's words as he offered. "Ma'am, the terrorists killed the workers by the pool. They were Jew workers, the terrorists slit their throats and shoved them in the pool with their hands tied behind their backs, leaving them to drown or bleed to death while struggling in the water, Ma'am."

Weidenbacher saw the Vice President was turning green, and she had to sit as Raincloud continued to explain the tortures the civilians went through during the terrorist attack to her.

"Any Americans killed in this attack, General Weidenbacher?" Griffin asked.

"At least a dozen, it was a slaughter, sir." Director Raincloud offered as he answered for the still shaken General.

The President sat back as he studied both Weidenbacher and Raincloud. He breathed out and growled at them. "Okay people, obviously we have a situation on our hands, and I need input."

"I don't think these sonofabitches were Arabs." Hirshfield snapped angrily.

"Why the hell do you think that, Mary?" the President asked as he looked at his Vice President as if she did not know what she just said.

"I agree with the Vice President on this one, sir." Weidenbacher added, but his words were ignored by President Cole as he stared at Mary while waiting for her answer.

"I have a problem over how this attack was carried out against those poor souls Al. Arabs would never dismember anyone, sir. It goes against their beliefs sir. The Arabs never stoop so low as to rape any female captive, especially if one of them might be a Jew. I see many incongruities between this attack and other known Arab attacks on Israel and her people, sir. The Arabs would never take the time to do half of the crap they had done here, sir."

President Cole turned to Weidenbacher and asked. "And, you happen to agree with Mary, sir?"

"Completely sir, something smells rotten in Denmark if you were to ask me, Mr. President. True, the Arabs might be crazy sonofabitches, and they have been known to carry out attacks on innocent civilians, but they never resorted to raping women, least wise, not I'm aware of, sir. I have problems believing this attack was carried out by Arabs, sir. The Vice President covered all but one of them sir. Since when do Arab terrorists leave witnesses behind to testify to who the attackers were, especially since none were killed in the attack, sir? No one would have any idea who the attackers were if they eliminated everyone at the Jewish resort, Mr. President Sir."

"Come on General, the bastards are capable of doing anything. As to leaving witnesses, maybe they grew tired of the killing sir. Christ, they have to have some heart or conscience."

"With all due respect Mr. President, I agree with General Weidenbacher, and Vice President Hirshfield on most of the points the Vice President made sir. By taking the bits and pieces of information under consideration, I'm forced to believe there's a possibility someone else might be responsible for this attack, and they're trying to pin the tag on the Arabs for some reason, Mr. President. Something that's easy believed in view of many of their past actions carried out against Israel by the Arab terrorist groups, sir." The Secretary of Defense concluded in a flat tone of voice to his boss.

"Like who! I have to have someone to bring under suspicion, before I can eliminate any Arab nations, sir. These fools brought this crap down on themselves by conducting, and condoning other terrorist actions against the world, and by not giving a shit on the outcome of their actions."

"I wish I knew Mr. President, I'd hate like hell to think how the Israelis will react if they think this action was carried out by Arabs. The ramifications could split the Israeli government in two, with the radical faction demanding war against Arab states, all of them. They'd gain the support for this demand with the moderate faction that's voting to refrain from attacks on the Arab neighbors. This thing could blossom into an all out war involving all the Middle Eastern nations with a possibility of a nuclear exchange between Israel, Iraq, and also Saudi Arabia.

"I'm certain if it started, Israel would take the opportunity to include Lebanon and Iran in their attack, because the Iranian back terrorists attacks on Israeli lands. The Israeli's have long memories, and they'll seek to wreak revenge on anyone who attacked her country or civilians in the past. We know each of these countries is in possession of nuclear weapons, and each of these states having the means of launching and hitting any of these countries in the region, sir." Vice President Hirshfield asserted to the others attending the meeting.

"Jesus H. Christ Mary." The President moaned as he got angry and he ran his fingers through his hair and he rested his head in his hands and moaned. "General Weidenbacher, I need to hear from you sir. If you believe these terrorists weren't Arabs in origin, just a pack of animals made to look like Arabs. Then who the hell do you think they were sir? And, what the hell were they up to here? And, what are our next moves, General?"

Weidenbacher thought for a moment and offered. "Mr. President Sir, I have no idea who the hell these attackers were, or might be. But I believe I know what their attack was about sir. I believe it was an attempt by some government to start trouble between the Arabs and Israelis. Probably to disrupt the peace talks being held between Israel, Jordan, and Egypt with Syria, sir."

"Jesus, you're right, that has to be the reason sir. This changes the picture for us. I want you to forget about Cuba for the time being. I don't mean to stop training of the exiles at Bragg, I mean we have to turn our attention to the Middle East until this situation is under control..."

"Mr. President, I'm concerned on how the Israeli's are going to react once they have time to digest this attack, sir. I'd hate like hell to be an Arab living in Israel or the surrounding Arab countries when Israel responds to this latest attack against them, sir. You know who they'll go after, Iran, then Syria, then Iraq. They'll probably refrain from attacking the other Arab states until they go over the information." Griffin offered the President.

Before the President responded, Levenhagen added. "I think the Israelis will go after the Islamic militant cell operating in Lebanon, especially Hezbollah, with escalating hostilities taking place in the region for many years, Mr. President. Evidently, what the perpetrators wanted to accomplish, sir."

"You're right Jerry." The President moaned as he straightened up and he keyed the intercom.

"Yes sir." Another Marine manning the station replied to the American Leader.

"Get me the Secretary of the Navy here right away. Tell him to bring his papers with him sir."

"Yes Sir Mr. President." The Marine guard replied sharply to his Commander in Chief.

President Cole turned to Weidenbacher and offered him. "I guess we'll have to change direction in midstream. I'm going to split the Atlantic Fleet and have some ships head for the Mediterranean. I don't know where the rest are standing post sir, so we're forced to wait for the Secretary to arrive. Coffee people?"

Moments later, a slightly out of breath Secretary of the Navy rushed into the Situation Room, he plopped down in a chair and placed his briefcase on the table and sighed deeply.

"Sorry Admiral Richardson for rushing you like I did, sir. But we have an emergency situation on our hands sir. Dennis, I'm sure you know everyone here so I won't waste time introducing you to everyone, sir?" the President offered.

The Secretary nodded to the members attending the meeting and then he turned his attention back to the American Leader.

"Very well Admiral, I find myself having to flood the Med with warships, sir. The hot spot's going to be Israel sir. Where are our Fleets stationed in this region of the world, sir? I ordered your Atlantic Fleet to split their forces, with half steaming for the Med, sir. You got the floor Dennis."

Before the Admiral rose to speak, he opened his briefcase and removed a paper and started. "Mr. President, I have the Med Fleet underway with twenty four support ships, and a land attack force of nine thousand soldiers, mostly Marines in the Task Force, sir. This group consists of two Aircraft Carriers, the CVN-69 USS Dwight D. Eisenhower and CVN-74 USS Stennis. I can pull the CVN-71 USS Theodore Roosevelt from her station in the Adriatic, she's doing guard duty for the Bosnia action, sir. I can have the Indian Ocean Fleet steam up the Red Sea and get in the Med in fifteen hours, if you feel you want that many ships in the region sir. This Fleet's constructed around the two Aircraft Carriers the CVN..."

"I'm not interested in the Carriers, have them set sail. I want that many ships in the area in case the shit hits the fan? Does this hurt our protection in the Indian Ocean?"

"Err... not really Mr. President, I can always split up the Pacific Fleet though, and have one of the Carrier Groups pick up the slack for the Indian Ocean Fleet, while I'm at it, sir."

"That's a good idea, order it done. I should've had the Secretary of the Air Force report for this meeting, dammit. I want him to put all American and NATO bases on full alert status, sir. His aircraft are to be loaded down for bear and ready to respond at a moment's notice to any situation occurring in the Middle East, sir. Dammit, what the hell was I thinking here?"

"With all due respect Mr. President, I can handle that through my Chief of Staff of the Air Force, General Luther Claiborne, sir." Weidenbacher offered to the upset American Leader.

"Very well, do it. General, you're free to pull any ground forces up you need for this one, and have them moved to this region. All you have to do is order it, and it shall be done. You don't need written permission from me and I'll handle Congress."

"Fine sir, I'll pull our rapid response forces out of Saudi Arabia, and have the soldiers moved onto the amphibious ships currently stationed in the Med group. I hope the Iraqi's are not the ones who instigated this mess, because I'll be allowing the Persian Gulf states to fall victim to them if they're the one."

"Understood General, we have to take some chances I'm afraid, sir. If the Iraqi's use this opportunity to attack Saudi Arabia we'll settle up with them later, once we established some stability in the Middle East again. It's that simple General."

General Weidenbacher nodded to the President as he smiled back at him.

"Mr. President, I want to know what you intend to do about this latest attack on Israel, sir?" Vice President Hirshfield snapped then added. "We have to let the world know we have evidence the attack wasn't carried out by Arabs, sir. This has to be done before the hard-liners of Israel force the government to send troops out after the bastards who they might believe slaughtered their children."

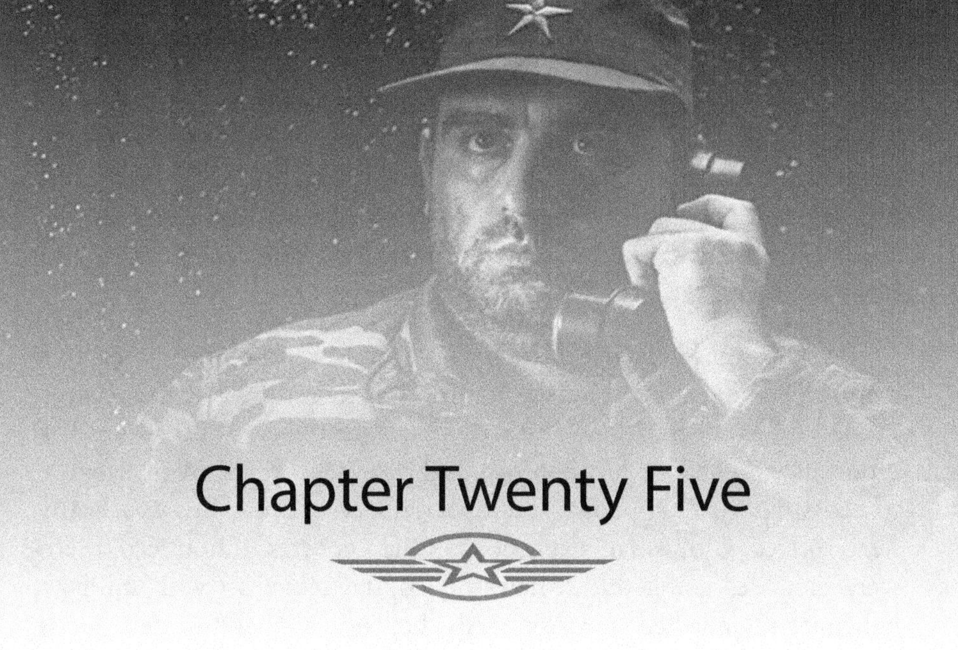

Chapter Twenty Five

The Club Med resort was being flooded with Israeli troops, many battle hardened soldiers leaned against their vehicles. Some cried, shocked by the scope of incursion carried out against the civilians at the resort. Other soldiers were hot as they demanded permission to head into the hills and search for the perpetrators of the savage attack on their citizens. Helicopters scoured the hills and surrounding area near the resort. Some American Military Units joined the search for the fleeing terrorists. Slowly, word of the raid was released, and reporters from every nation in the world made their way to the resort in Israel, hoping to be the first to get pictures of the horror. Israeli helicopters protecting the vacation resort forced two news helicopters out of the airspace over the site. Bodies were tagged and bagged, with many of them being removed from the resort. The non-Israeli dead were boxed and then sent back to their respective countries.

A horde of Jewish males moved in and washed the blood from the floor and walls of the structure of the resort. They collected what blood they could, had it blessed and then buried. What had been the scene of horror hours before, now looked like a military resort where nothing more than a fight broken out in it.

Reporters flooded Haifa, looking for information. They were not unsuccessful in learning anything from the Israeli soldiers who took over the complex. Slowly, media people were allowed in, the pool was still full of blood stained waters, and it became the focal point of the news reporters.

The air over Haifa was criss crossed by a fleet of military attack and troop helicopters. There was a commotion in the hills as helicopters headed off to the location. The activity caught the eyes of the horde of reporters who headed for their cars and own helicopters, in an attempt to see what was happening there. Sound of weapon fire was heard next, mixed with small explosions. One reporter announced there were grenades going off. A news helicopter, mixed in with military helicopters, reported an American helicopter crew located men, apparently Arabs carrying weapons, and they were trying to flee from the area in haste.

Helicopters landed, and weapon fire increased for a short time. Then they lifted off again, each heading for a different area. This was done to confuse the reporters, so they would not know which machine to follow next. The news helicopter with the military machines reported three terrorists were captured alive, and another five were killed in the quick but hard hitting firefight. Speculation ran wild with many reporters making statements from five to over a hundred terrorists were engaged in action in the hills over Haifa, and a running gun battle was being carried out by the Israeli soldiers against the terrorists. The terrorists were said to be anything from Arab, to African, or Spanish, European to Russian. Reports flashed to every corner of the world.

An American EH-60C Blackhawk helicopter CR-17-119 was the one who had the two live terrorists trapped in a shallow cave and taken prisoners. One was wounded, the craft headed for the closest Israeli military command stationed at Et Tira. The American craft was followed by three Israeli helicopters that joined the Americans as they neared Et Tira. After it was given permission to land, a small Army of Israeli soldiers surrounded the craft and the two Arab speaking prisoners were rushed inside a barracks. There, the interrogation began first; the two were beaten and deprived of food, water, and sleep. The Americans allowed to witness the interrogation, were aware the Israeli interrogators were getting nowhere with the terrorists, and they had to resort to using increased violence on their two prisoners.

One of the Americans asked if he could have a shot at breaking the two prisoners, and he was given permission to try. He ordered the prisoners separated, and started on the one hurt the least. The American removed his K-bar knife he used as last resort during close in fighting. The Lieutenant leaned close to the suspected Arab prisoner and sneered in a threatening voice at him. "You speak English huh pal?"

The terrorist remained looking straight ahead of himself, paying little if any attention to the American soldier threatening him with the deadly edge of his knife.

The Lieutenant leaned forward and ran the edge of the knife along the side of the terrorists jaw, drawing blood in three different spots on his face, but the terrorist refused to flinch and the American inquisitor barked at the two Israeli soldiers assisting his interrogation of the prisoner. "Stand this piece of shit and depants the bastard. Then we'll see how brave he is for crap sake."

When the prisoner was naked from the waist down, the Lieutenant moved on him. He rested the edge of the razor sharp K-bar under the prisoners scrotum and lifted the knife while keeping steady pressure on the prisoners cherished parts. Then he growled in the scared man's face, his breath moving the prisoner's hair. "Okay scumbag, if you don't understand English then I suggest you learn real quick or you can kiss these little babies here bye."

The terrorist glared at the American, but the look showed he understood the threat.

"One more time scumbag then I'll cut you. Who gave you the damn orders for the attack?"

Not even a flinch came from the now extremely angry looking prisoner.

The American lifted a little harder with the knife, and the prisoner had to get on his toes to avoid losing his future and the Lieutenant warned him. "I suggest you speak, I'm getting kinda tired of holding this knife on you, pal. I asked you who gave the orders for this attack. Speak, or I'll give these babies back to you in your fucking hand, buster."

Still not a flinch from him and when the Lieutenant relaxed the pressure, the prisoner went off his toes, and turned and sneered. The American lost control and smashed the prisoner with a fist, knocking him unconscious. "Shit, the scumbag's good. Leave him on the floor and bring in the other guy, but cover this one's nuts. I want the other guy to think I just cut his balls off."

The second prisoner was brought in, his eyes opened wide when he saw his partner lying unconscious on the floor.

"Take his pants off." The American Officer ordered the two Israelis with him.

When this was done, the American Lieutenant used the same procedure with the same results. Nothing from the prisoner, he left and sat down with the Israeli Commander and complained. "I don't know how to break these stinking bastards, sir. They're damn good sir. They seem to be well trained and don't give a shit what happens to them after their attack, sir."

"Have no fear Lieutenant, we'll break them easy enough sir. I sent for a doctor sir. We'll get the information from the prisoners when he gets here. He has drugs that'll loosen their tongues. But I don't think the prisoners are Arabs, sir. Both men have been cut, and no Arabs would ever allow themselves to be circumcised, sir."

"How's that Commander Sir?" The American asked the other military officer standing with him with some surprise lacing his tone this time.

"Besides them being circumcised, it's a rather simple deduction to make, sir. You don't know the ways of the Arabs like we understand them, sir. When you threatened to cut his balls as you called them, off and there was no reaction from him. According to what these Islamic militants believe, there's no way in hell an Arab can get into Paradise if his body is not whole. This bugger didn't blink an eye, sir. I think these bastards are trying to pass for bloody Arabs on us, sir. And, that's what I'm going to put down in my report to headquarters, sir. Especially over the circumcised thing sir." The Israeli General offered the American Officer.

"Who do you think he is then sir?" The American asked with some concern in his voice.

"I have no idea who he might be or who he's working for. And, I have less of an idea why they attacked this vacation resort like they have done against us, sir. But I'll promise you this much though, sir. I'll find out why they did attack..." Their conversation was interrupted when there was a commotion in the interrogation room and then shots rang out.

The American and the Israeli ran in the room, only to see the bodies of the two terrorists sprawled out on the floor. Three soldiers stood ready, still aiming their weapons at the bodies.

"What the fuck happened here dammit?" the Israeli General roared at the guards.

The Sergeant assisting the interrogation snapped to attention and reported. "General, the terrorist we believed to be unconscious, sprang to his feet and made a lunge for the Corporal's weapon, sir. He wrestled it away and he fired at him, sir. We were forced to react, General. I fired at the one with the weapon, and the second terrorist took this opportunity and attacked the other Corporal, sir. I was forced to kill him as well sir."

"Great, that's great. Now we'll never know who the hell was behind this attack against us. What is the status of the other two wounded terrorists, mister?"

"They both died on the operating table. It seems they took something to kill themselves with."

"Dammit to hell and back Sergeant." The Israeli General cursed as he glared at the soldier.

The American made his excuses and left the interrogation area, he reported to his Commander of the sentiment of the Israeli, and he informed command of the deaths of the two prisoners.

THE SITUATION ROOM UNDER THE WHITE HOUSE, WASHINGTON D.C.

The Marine manning the radio console in the Situation Room during the meeting, reported. "General Weidenbacher Sir, there's flash traffic coming in for you sir."

The President gave Weidenbacher a slight nod. A second later he was listening to the reporter and then he offered to his Command in Chief. "Mr. President Sir, one of our helicopter crews on a special training mission in Israel, came across some of the terrorists. Some prisoners were taken in alive sir, but there was an accident and the terrorists were killed in a brief scuffle while in custody sir. The pilot reported the Israeli Officer in command of interrogation shares our beliefs, the terrorists weren't Arabs sir. The pilot stated the Israeli Officer believed this strongly enough to include the same in his report back to his own headquarters, sir."

"That's great. The jerks couldn't get the information from the prisoners. General, I have to ask this question sir. Do you think Israel will act before the evidence is in on the terrorist's origin?"

"I don't know for certain sir. I don't know how to read them any longer. They seem to have the knack to do the opposite of what I think they're going to do next. I just don't know sir."

All eyes went over to the Vice President as they waited for her opinion on the situation.

Vice President Hirshfield smiled as she pointed to herself and remarked. "Why the hell are the lot of you fools looking at me for? Just because I'm a Jew, doesn't mean I know what they're going to do, guys."

"Venture an opinion on what you think they might do, young lady." The President ordered.

Ms. Hirshfield thought for a second then offered to the staring President. "Albert, I think they'll go after the Arabs in Lebanon, sir. I'm surprised they haven't done so already, sir."

"Christ Almighty and the Saints too." The President moaned at no one in particular. "I guess we'll have to sit by and see how the hell long it takes before they do something now."

TYRE, LEBANON 8 A.M. SUNDAY,SEPTEMBER 29th, 1996

Exactly twenty hours after the attack on the Club Med resort in Haifa, a second cell of Cuban terrorists attacked the largest Islamic Mosque as their morning prayers were concluded.

Fifteen heavily armed Israeli speaking gun men poured into the Mosque through the three main doors of the building. The attackers sprayed the occupants with automatic weapon fire, killing fifty Muslim Fundamentalists as they knelt on their prayer rugs praising the Almighty Allah. Even the Muslim priest was killed in the attack as he prayed over the coffin believed to be that of Muhammad himself.

Not a soul was spared in the savage attack as the gun fire continued, carrying itself outside the Mosque. The fake Israeli attackers shot anyone they came across they threw a number of explosive satchel charges inside the Mosque as they charged down the side streets. The attackers continued to shoot at anyone in their path, screaming out Hebrew words of hate at the Arabs they slaughtered. "This is for the attack on Israel." Was heard as a second attacker added to his cry "Death to any Arab who attacks Israel or her people!"

These threats were answered by the Arabs vowing to avenge this attack. With a thunderous explosion, the Mosque was lifted off its foundation, turning while in air. The building crashed to earth, crumbling as it did so, and burying everyone inside under tons of concrete and tiles.

The attackers believed to be Israeli soldiers climbed aboard the armored vehicles covered with the Israeli markings, and rumbled down the streets, heading towards the Israeli border. The leader of this terrorist cell ordered the three vehicles to pull off the road once he was certain no one was following them. Then he ordered his men to get out of their Israeli uniforms and dress in the Arab robes hidden in the machines. Then they casually walked back to Tyre, but not before setting fire to the abandoned metal war machines.

By the time the disguised Arabs returned to the city, it was mayhem. Hundreds of Arab men ran through the streets of Tyre, armed and firing their weapons in the air. Women screamed and cried in hatred as they cared for their dead and wounded brother and sisters by the destroyed Mosque. The men continued shooting in the air wildly while screaming. "Death to all Jews!"

The leader of this cell stopped an Arab man and asked him. "Brother of Allah, what has just happened here?"

"Jews, Jews have attacked us while we prayed. Death to all hated Jews of the world. Brothers, arm yourselves with weapons and come with us on our holy war into the Jew land."

"Brother of Allah, we have no weapons to begin our attack against the lowly Jews, sir. We have ventured far too pray on this morning."

"Fools, dung eating fools, you can no longer pray in this city of Allah. Our Mosque has been destroyed by the Jews. Look at what they done to us, take my weapons and turn it on Jews who committed this crime against Allah, I'll get another. Follow brothers, because we'll avenge the death of our people. Death to all Jews!" He repeated as he quickly disappeared into the masses.

THE SITUATION ROOM UNDER THE WHITE HOUSE, WASHINGTOND.C. 12:23 A.M. EST SUNDAY, SEPTEMBER 29th, 1996

Everyone attending the meeting over the situation developing in the Middle East and Israel was exhausted, but the President refused to end the meeting until they worked out the particulars on where and how many troops, ships and equipment was to be deployed to keep the lid on the Middle East situation. The President was in contact with the Russian President, and the Chinese Chairman, to appraise them of the situation in the Middle East, and what their opinions were on the identity of the unknown attackers. President Albert Cole informed the Heads of States of the NATO Alliance, and any other country that might have an interest in the situation. It was advantageous the meeting went on so long, because everyone was in position to receive the latest report from the Middle East.

President Cole was about to call an end for the meeting when another report came in. After listening to it, General Weidenbacher turned to the American Leader and offered. "Mr. President Sir, I received the first report of an Israeli response attack carried out in Tyre, inside Lebanon. It was a bad one sir."

"Jesus H. Christ, these damn Israeli's, couldn't they have waited until we gathered the information that would've proved the attackers weren't Arabs, dammit. What the hell did they hit?" the American President groaned at his military officer.

"The Israelis hit a Muslim Mosque during prayer sessions. The thought to be Israeli attackers slaughtered all in the Mosque, and hit any Arabs they came across on the streets while planting explosive charges, they destroyed the entire Mosque, sir."

"Why the hell did they have to destroy a Mosque? Don't they understand the best way to give an Arab a cause is to destroy a Mosque? Christ sake, during Desert Storm we made certain we stayed away from any Mosques in that country. Even though we knew damn well Saddam used many Mosques to hide his aircraft and tanks, and weapons and his soldiers in. What the hell's wrong with them Jews?" This time the President did not give a glance to his Vice President.

Ms. Hirshfield interrupted President Cole angry words by offering. "Albert, I'll tell you what is wrong with the Jews. They didn't commit this attack. The Israeli Command knows to give a Mosque a wide berth. This is more evidence the attacks aren't carried out by Arabs or Jews. Look at the form the attacks took, Jews attacking a Mosque, Arabs torturing civilians, not caring if they're killing Jews or Americans. No,

I know these attacks weren't carried out by those being blamed for it, sir."

As if to strengthen the Vice President's position, another report came in from the Israeli Prime Minister, informing President Cole in no instant, did any Israeli troops or civilians engage in the attack on the Mosque. When the Marine read the report, the President sat deeper in his chair.

"Jesus! I can't believe this. Who the hell is behind these damn attacks, and what do they hope to gain by the damn things?" President Cole ran his hands over his head and drew in a huge gulp of air, and then ordered. "General Weidenbacher, I want answers, and I'll have them before anyone leaves this damn room. You better get in touch with your snoops, and find out what's going on, before we lose the Middle East, and who knows what else, to war."

IN THE MOUNTAIN VILLAGE OF DHIBAN, JORDAN11 A.M. SUNDAY, SEPTEMBER 29th, 1996

Ricardo Carlos Serantes, known by his Jewish name of Shmulik Buzali, and his group of Cuban terrorists prepared for their attack on a small Arab village in Jordan. The attackers waited until most of the men of the village headed for work, before they attacked the sleepy Arab village. The latest count on who were left was twenty five women, and a number of men too old to work in the fields. The streets of the village were crawling with children of all young ages.

The attack was going to be carried out on foot, and the fast hitting attackers were to enter the village from the two ends, and were to work their way through it, killing anyone they came across. They were dressed in Israeli uniforms, and carried Jewish made weapons and spoke Hebrew. Sergeant Serantes gave his men the orders to kill everyone as they came out of the rugged hills. He waited at the north end of the village as he and his men took up their position before the second group got set in position at the southern end of the town. Serantes decided not to attack until he heard the first shots being fired by the second group of his terrorists.

At exactly eleven twenty, Serantes grew concerned about the second group of his attackers. He was about to send a runner out when the first shots were heard, automatic weapon fired on the southern section of the village was being fired. The Sergeant yelled out in Hebrew. "Kill all of the enemy Arabs of Israeli lands!"

His men instantly charged into the village, their machine guns blazing before them as they picked and chose their targets, killing children running for their homes. Next, the women were targeted for slaughter as they charged out of their homes to save the children from the hail of bullets fired at them. The few old men in the village, tried to attack the thought to be Israeli soldiers, slaughtering the children and women of their village by firing their single shot antique long rifles. Any weapon fired at the attackers brought a hail of bullets on the shooter in reply.

Once everyone was killed in the village, Serante's attackers set out a number of explosives in all the buildings. When the charges were set, the terrorists gathered on the street. Once everyone was accounted for, the Sergeant ordered the charges to detonate in an hour. That would give them time need to get to the vehicles, ditch the Israeli uniforms, dress as Arabs and head for the Iraqi border and the safety offered them there. He knew when the charges went off in the village. The male workers who left for work earlier would hear the explosions, and then come running.

Serantes gave the order and the timer was set, and then the attackers ran off for the hills and their vehicles. At exactly twelve noon, a series of rattling explosions rocked the Jordanian village from one end to the other. The workers in the field jumped then they looked in the direction of their village. Columns of thick black smoke rose tumbling in the noontime sky. The workers ran for the village, many crying, because they knew they lived in a most violent time and region of the world, and they could be set upon at any time by a horde of criminals and murders.

The excited Arab men poured into the destroyed village from the north, and they found the slaughtered bodies of their loved ones left lying on the streets, or shot and left to die mixed in with the rubble of what was once their homes. Panic and mayhem replaced the peace and harmony of the day. Phone and radio calls from the village to the capital were intercepted by news agencies throughout the world and a flood of reporters descended on the village.

The first news reporters to make it out to the scene of the terrorist attack were not kind to Israeli nation. They placed the blame squarely upon the shoulders of the Israeli soldiers, without gathering enough information to be any kind of accurate about the terrorist attackers, or their statements to the world. One woman of the village was found alive, and her husband was able to force her to say that a group of Israeli soldiers attacked the village before she died on him.

Reporters had a field day training their cameras on the crying Arab men, as they lifted the bodies of their loved ones, and then placed them in wood coffins. The coffins were lifted over their heads and sent through the growing crowds of excited Arab men and women who descended on the tiny village. The reporters trained their cameras on a number of Israeli flags being burned not only in the village, but in Amman, Iran, Libya and Iraq. Riots took place in Egypt and Saudi Arabia, all protesting the Israeli attacks on the Arab states. The Arabs called for open war against the Jew state, and all who backed her.

Hordes of reporters continued to show the terrible grief of the loving Arabs as they clawed through the rubble with their bare hands, looking for their missing loved ones buried under tons of rubble. Not one building was left standing, and no further survivors were found in the rubble of the small Arab village.

THE WHITE HOUSE, WASHINGTON D.C.4 A.M. EST ON THE 29th, OF SEPTEMBER 1996

President Albert Cole called the Situation Room meeting to a quick end, he hoped to get himself some needed sleep, before he was dragged before the media to answer questions on what was taking place in the Middle East. He just finished brushing his teeth and was preparing to join his wife in bed, when the scared White House Chief of Staff aide lightly tapped on the door to his room. The President washed the toothpaste out of his mouth, and then came out of the bathroom and he headed for the door to his living quarters in the White House.

"This better be important my friend! I was turning in for the night, mister." The upset American Leader warned the aide with a half smile.

"I'm terribly sorry for disturbing you Mr. President Sir, we received a flash message from an operative working in Jordan, and General Weidenbacher and Director Raincloud already arrived, and they're waiting for you downstairs, Mr. President Sir. I placed them in the Oval Office, sir."

"Very well, tell them I'm on my way down, dammit." The President grumbled at his aide.

His wife faced her husband and asked. "Can't this wait until morning? You need sleep honey."

"It can't wait I have to respond to all incoming flash traffic immediately my lady. Keep the bed warm for me, love." President Cole lightly tapped his wife on her rear end and smiled at her.

"That's not all I'll be keeping warm for when you get back, honey." She offered him.

"Sure, make it harder for me to leave you now, dear." He moaned to his wife.

They shared a laugh as he slipped in his robe and then headed for the Oval Office. When he entered his favorite room, General Weidenbacher and Director Raincloud stood up and nodded at the exhausted looking American Leader.

"Be seated gentlemen please. Whaddaya have for me General Weidenbacher Sir?"

President Cole looked a real mess, with puffed up bags building under his blood shot eyes, his hair was tousled and uncombed, and one collar of his pajamas was sticking out from under his robe, and his slippers were dragging on the floor. With his shoulders hunched over like they were, he looked like he had aged ten years over the past twenty four hours. He took a cigar and then he lit it and he offered one to the other two men in the room.

Both of them refused the offered cigars which caused the President to snap at the both of them. "You two will take one of these damn things and you'll enjoy them. If I have to be down here, I want to enjoy a smoke, and you have to as well. This way I can blame the two of you for the stink of cigar smoke on my robe, gentlemen." The President smirked at the two respected men.

All three men laughed as Weidenbacher added to the seated and grinning President of the United States, as he replied calmly. "The First Lady still won't allow you to smoke, sir?"

"Naw, she's losing her sense of humor lately, sir. Makes one wonder that the hell is running this place around here anyhow, sir. Okay General, what happened to bring the two of you here to the White House this late, sir?" The American Leader complained at his military officer.

"Mr. President Sir, I'm afraid there's been another attack in the Middle East moments ago sir, and it was..." The General was cut off by the President as he moaned back at him.

"Arrr... Christ, who the hell got it this time, General Weidenbacher. Jew or Arab State, sir?"

"Another attack against the Arabs sir, committed by a group of attackers supposed to be Israeli soldiers, Mr. President Sir."

"God dammit! How bad this time General?" the President snarled as he let out his breath.

"Terrible, really bad sir, a small village in Jordan was razed to the ground by the attackers, sir. All residents were outright slaughtered by this new band of attac..."

"Excuse me General Weidenbacher, but I believe you're making a mistake on your report to the President, sir." Director Raincloud offered.

Both President Cole and General Weidenbacher looked at the large Director in surprise.

"General Weidenbacher, only the women and children of the village were killed in the attack, sir. The men were in the fields working for the day, sir. The attackers destroyed every building in the village though sir. Reports state the attackers were dressed in Israeli military uniforms, and spoke Hebrew fluently, sir."

President Cole allowed his cigar burn out resting in the astray as he stared at the ceiling, searching for answers to these problems he was facing in the Middle East and he groused. "What the hell's going on over there General, dammit? All these damn attacks can't have been carried out by some other government, sir. It's has to be the Arabs and Israeli's going at each other's throats again. Well General, what the hell are we going to do about this new mess taking place in the Middle East, sir?"

"With all due respect Mr. President Sir, most of our ships are set in position, and some of the other Arab nations are protesting the presence of the ships positioned near their countries, sir. But I don't give a shit about their gripes at this point, sir. I think Egypt will control her people and so will Saudi Arabia, sir. It's Iran, Iraq, and now Jordan and Syria I'm most concerned about, sir."

"What do the Israeli's say about this second attack, General Weidenbacher Sir?"

"They swear they had nothing to do with it sir. Israel's Command is offering to have Mossad investigate the circumstances of the attacks, so they can find out who is responsible for the terrorist actions, sir." The powerful military officer replied to his Commander in Chief.

"What the hell's the damn Arabs response to the Israeli's offer for this latest mess, General Weidenbacher Sir?" the President moaned as he suddenly let his breath out in a rush this time.

"The Lebanese are dead set against it sir. But the Jordanians seem responsive enough to it, sir. King Hussian's still trying to keep the peace talks on track, even after this latest attack, sir."

"He's a good man General Weidenbacher. Remind me to make a trip to Jordan so we can meet again once this damn mess is all over with, General."

The General nodded, surprised President Cole told him to remind him to go to Jordan to visit with the king of that country in the near future.

"I don't know. Do you think this was the last of the attacks, sir? Or do you think these asses that have us chasing all over the Middle East are planning to hit again? If so, where sir?"

"Mr. President Sir, they'll go once more, possibly twice. Why shouldn't they? They have us reacting to shadows, and the world's choosing up sides, if war breaks out in the Middle East..."

"Where do you think they'll hit the next time, sir?" President Albert Cole snapped back at the General while fighting desperately to try and keep his eyes open for the meeting.

Director Raincloud took a quick breath then he replied to the exhausted American Leader. "Err... Mr. President Sir, I believe they'll hit somewhere else in Israel again, and soon at that, sir. Whoever is behind these attacks has the Arabs worked up in a lather sir. Another such attack by the Israeli's should push their anger beyond the controlling point, sir. It's going to be one helluva mess if anyone tries to attack Israel again, Mr. President."

"General Weidenbacher, can we get any of our troops on shore in Israel at this time, sir?"

"Sure, just give me the word and tell me where you want them to land, Mr. President."

"Oh brother, I don't know what to do now I'm afraid, General Weidenbacher Sir." The President moaned at his military officer.

"I'm hoping to know something more positive by early this morning, Mr. President."

"Good, keep at it sir. How are the reporters handling all this crap General?"

"Not well I'm afraid, sir. They backed off on their assault of the Israeli's over the attack inside Lebanon sir, but they're still dumping on Israel for the latest attack in Jordan, Mr. President. It seems everyone's siding with Jordan on this one sir. I believe it's because Jordan was instrumental in getting the peace talks back on track again, sir."

"Yeah, I can understand that sir, how long has it been since this latest attack had taken place in any of the countries in the Middle East or Israel, General Weidenbacher?" the President grumbled as he ran his fingers through what hair he had left.

"Two and a half hours ago I believe Mr. President." The General replied.

"That's just fricking great General. I wonder how long we'll have to wait before the next attack goes down on us, General Weidenbacher Sir." The American Leader griped as he pushed the intercom button and said into the machine.

"Yes, Paul we could sure use a bit of coffee and maybe some cakes in here, young man. It looks like we're going to be in here for quite a while longer, mister." The President let go of the button, and then he asked the General if he thought he should get the rest of team together to finish up with this latest meeting over the Middle East situation.

The answer came back confidently as a strong yes from the concerned looking General.

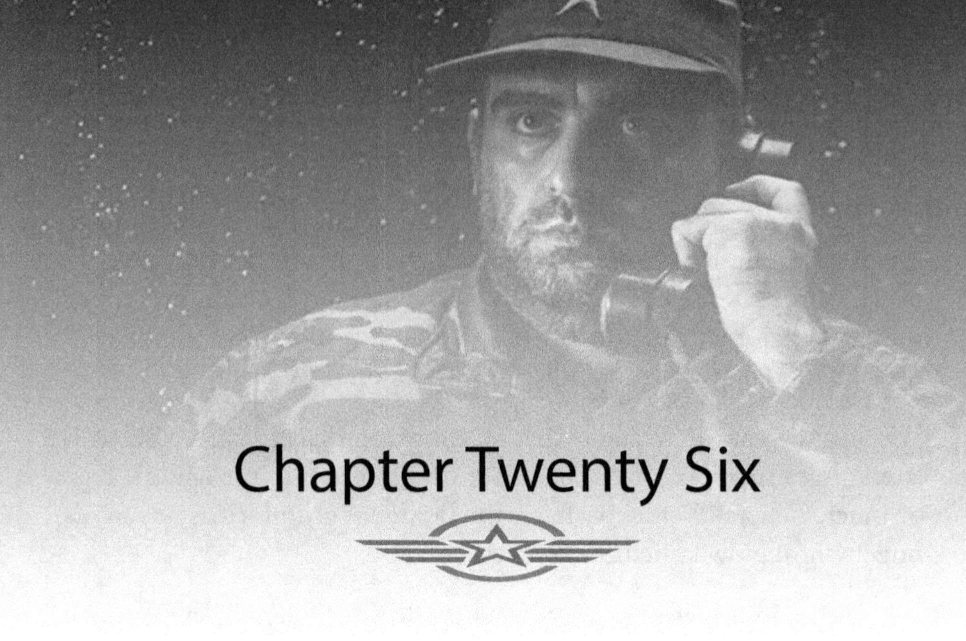

Chapter Twenty Six

EL QARYATEIN, SYRIA 2 P.M. SUNDAY,
SEPTEMBER 29th, 1996

In a narrow mountain pass that was half way between the Syrian cities of Damascus and El Quayatein, the last Cuban terrorist cell made their final plans for the next attack. Jacinto Crabb Mella, known as the Jew, Bin Tamin Aloni in this region, had trouble getting his attackers set in position at the designated time and area. He fallen well behind his appointed schedule, and he resorted to screaming at his attackers to have them pick up their pace. From his position, he picked up the railroad tracks leading from Damascus to El Quayatein and beyond.

He wanted to have his explosive charges on the tracks set, but he was forced to remain in the mountains as a number of Syrian military patrols worked their way down the railroad tracks. Jacinto had to send a team up the mountain to keep an eye for other Syrian patrols. The last thing he needed was to have a Syrian patrol sneak up on them while they were setting the charges on the railroad tracks. His target was the three o'clock train bringing mountain visitors to their homes from the Syrian capital city. It was estimated at this time of day, the train would be the most crowded.

Jacinto was about to give the signal for his attackers to move off for their attack when his lookout reported another Syrian patrol coming down the tracks from El Qaryatein in the north. Jacinto had to call his terrorists back then they hunker down and waited for the third patrol to pass their position. Jacinto glared at the six man patrol as they slowly and carefully walked the tracks, kicking at stones and taking shots at fleeing rabbits, and any other critters of the desert the soldiers stirred up walking the train tracks. The patrol stopped moving and sat down for a moment and sip water, one scanning the mountain where Jacinto's men hid with his field glasses.

His attackers ducked as a Syrian soldier scanned the area where they were hiding. The other five Syrian soldiers were bullshitting and laughing as they sipped water and smoked. One produced a magazine and passed it around, causing the patrol members to laugh and point at the pictures of the naked women. Jacinto picked up his glare resistant field glasses and focused in on the Syrian patrol. He smiled when he realized one of the guys produced an illegal Playboy magazine, and the soldiers were gawking at the naked women. He knew if they were caught with it, they might be blinded by a hot poker.

The guy passing the magazine around checked his watch then said something to the rest of the soldiers, and they got up and started down the tracks in the direction of Damascus again.

Jacinto called his lookout over the radio and asked him if he saw any more Syrian patrols coming down the line of railroad tracks. After a few seconds, the lookout reported to his leader there were no other patrols within a five mile distance in either direction of them on the tracks besides the one slowly leaving their area. He asked about the Syrian patrol that left the area. The lookout reported they were being picked up by a helicopter, and it was heading off to the south.

This statement caused more concern for the leader of the terrorist group, because he knew the soldiers could be back in the area quickly with a helicopter at their disposal. He decided to split up his force for this attack. He was going to have three units of two attackers each go to the railroad tracks, plant the charges and beat it back to the mountain area. He understood he could not go down to the tracks in force because he had to leave a flanking unit to protect the attacking units planting the explosives on the tracks. He never thought this operation would be plagued with so many problems.

The small group of Cuban born terrorists moved out while Jacinto checked his watch, it was a quarter to three and he searched the hills looking for the first signs of the train heading for its pending doom on the tracks. He spotted nothing then he looked down the mountain side and picked up a number of his attackers cautiously working their way towards the railroad tracks. One unit was already working on planting their explosive charge under the tracks.

He ordered the attackers to set the charges under the sand and cover them over to make it look like nothing was amiss. He had the charges wrapped up in Israeli flags, and he ordered the men to drop empty Israeli cigarette packages around at the foot of the mountain. He had to leave some telltale evidence behind Israel was responsible for the sabotage of the railroad system.

Jacinto watched with anticipation and concern, it was taking too long for the saboteurs to get to the tracks, let alone set their destructive charges. The attackers had to get back to the mountains, and the safety they provided them. After what seemed like an eternity, the terrorists finished setting their explosives then they headed for the mountains. No sooner did the last team member start up the mountain than a Russian built Syrian helicopter came in from the northeast. The helicopter passed by and showed no signs they were looking for anything out of the ordinary. Nor did it show any signs of spotting his attackers.

Jacinto cursed because he believed this section of Syria was mostly unpopulated, and he could escape from the area easily. He had no idea the other two attacks on the Arab countries caused the King of Syria to increase his country's military readiness. The King ordered more military patrols to protect the aqueduct systems of Syria, and their airports and rail systems, and communication facilities. The aqueducts were the most important target in Syria, and the best protected. Jacinto was aware of this, and it was why he decided to go after the aqueducts only as a last resort.

Cuban Presidente Carlos Rafael Hernandez Alvarez wanted to use the water aqueducts of the targeted Arab nations as a final target, it was certain to cause open war. He would resort to this action if the three attacks did not cause the proper response, getting the eyes of the United States off what he was doing on the Cuban Peninsula.

The leader of the terrorist demolition teams reported to Jacinto his charges were set in place and read to go off, and it would take a dog to locate them the way he had them hid by the railroad tracks. Jacinto relaxed before ordering his attackers to make it over the mountain range to the safety offered them from the nation of Iraq. He wanted to remain to observe the destruction of the Jordanian train. He had his people remove their Israeli uniforms, and bury them deep then they were ordered to get back in the robes of the Arab desert travelers. So they could make their escape from Syria into Iraq on the other side of the mountain range.

The Cuban terrorist leader watched them work their way to safety over the mountain top. His attention was brought back to the tracks, and he checked his watch as his impatience grew in his aching body. It was two minutes to three, and he was surprised he had not seen any signs of the train coming as yet.

There was no way he could have known the train was being detained at the Syrian town of Busra while it was searched for hidden bombs, or Israeli saboteurs. When the train was searched and found to be in order, it was allowed to continue fifteen minutes late.

As the time crawled on slowly, Jacinto became concerned the train had not reached his position yet. The Cuban terrorist wondered if the train schedule had been changed, he was not aware of. He stretched his neck, looking down the length of the tracks for smoke from the train's struggling engine.

Suddenly, he heard the engine before the train came in view. He flipped the red cover off the radio controlled detonation device then held his finger over the firing switch while he waited until most of the train cars were over the three planted charges his attackers set.

He wanted to destroy as much of the slow moving train as possible, to increase the effect of the terrorist attack against it and the civilians on the train. He smiled as he watched the train labor slowly towards his position, and the explosives that would destroy the unsuspecting train, and hopefully killing enough Syrian civilians to set the entire Middle East in the flames of war.

Finally, the train was in the right location and at that moment he pushed the button. The train was assaulted by three earth shattering powerful explosions that lifted the train from the tracks and sent it tumbling to earth with many cars ending up lying on their sides and crushing some passengers.

Three patrolling Syrian troop helicopters came over the crest of the mountains on the side of the pass where Jacinto hid. A number of secondary explosions ripped through what was left of the destroyed train, sending train cars tumbling along the ground and spilling its human cargo along the way. Then the train came to rest lying on the dead and dying crushed under the train cars. More explosions adding to the destruction, the train engine exploded with the rumble of a thunderstorm. Fires and smoke attacked the survivors as they tried to crawl out of the destroyed cars. Screams of those being burned alive in the wreckage filled the air.

The three Soviet made Syrian helicopters veered off to their left then circled and worked their way back to the exploding train. But the helicopters did not set down this time. The machines kept heading for the mountains area instead.

Jacinto realized the pilots had no interest in the wreckage of the train they were looking for him and his attackers. He snubbed out his Israeli made cigarette then threw the Israeli made radio control in the narrow path in plain sight. He made for the crest of the mountain as cautiously as he could climb up the mountain. He was careful to use the shadows of the rocks for cover as he moved up the mountain.

The three helicopters split up and worked their way up the mountain slope. At one point, one helicopter stopped and hovered then opened up with a 12.5 mm machine gun, and the pilot did not stop firing until the pilot saw it was a mountain goat he slaughtered. The helicopter went back to sliding up the slope of the mountain, checking out any would be hiding places. At one point, one helicopter flew over Jacinto's spot, he was forced to drop down into a narrow crevice, getting skinned up while doing so.

He had no idea his unit was forced to hunker down. A Syrian patrol work the flat area at the foot of the mountains they were hiding in, making sure no one tried to cross the border between Syria and Iraq. The patrol heard the explosions echoing through the valley, and the troops stared at the mountains to see what it was.

The three helicopters made it to the top of the mountain where Jacinto hid, and they spotted the patrol on the other side of the mountains and made for the troops. The pilot informed the Commander of the foot patrol of the attack on the train and told him they were looking for the terrorists who attacked the rail system. The foot patrol took positions and called for reinforcements to aid them. The helicopters went back up the mountain because the pilots knew the saboteurs could not have gotten out of the area as quickly as the helicopters arrived on scene.

The lead pilot believed he had the attackers trapped on the mountain, and he was not going to allow them to get away. The controlling pilot decided to call for more choppers and troops to search the mountain. When the three helicopters reached the mountain top, they hovered and dropped off four soldiers in each machine, so they could search the mountain for the terrorists.

News reporters and journalists monitoring the radio reports of the Arab nations while waiting for the next shoe to fall picked up the report of the destroyed train. They begged for permission to be allowed into Syria to cover this breaking story, but the Syrian government refused to allow anyone to cross over the border.

Jacinto made the crest of the mountain and bumped into half of his attackers as they tried to make it to the safety of the other side of the mountain, and the border of Iraq. The terrorists reported to Jacinto Syrian patrols were in position, and they spotted a number of armored vehicles traveling at a high speed towards their location. Jacinto ordered them to line up with him, and they checked their ammunition then the attackers took up defending positions in the underbrush.

THE WHITE HOUSE, 6 A.M. EST. SUNDAY,SEPTEMBER 29th, 1996

After the meeting with General Weidenbacher and Director Raincloud, President Cole got an hour's worth of sleep, before his White House aide tapped on his door again.

It was his wife who jumped out of bed and marched to the door, opening it a crack she barked at the aide. "For God sake Paul, Al just fell asleep. What do you want now?"

"I understand that Ma'am, but General Weidenbacher's requesting a private audience with the President, Ma'am." The aide replied to the First Lady.

"General Weidenbacher's getting to be a pain in the ass lately, Paul. What the hell does he want did he tell you, young man? I'm not waking Albert up unless this is an emergency, mister. For the love of God Paul, he needs his sleep dammit." The President's wife was getting upset with the young aide around as she glared at him.

"I understand this and I agree with you Ma'am, but the General has informed me this was another emergency in the Middle East, Ma'am." The Presidential aide offered in his own defense to the President's angry wife.

"I don't give a shit how much of an emergency the General says it is Paul. You tell the General I told him to go to hell, because I'm not waking the President for him under no circumstances. I simply will not..."

A hand covered the First Lady's arm resting on the door to their apartment, and she turned to see her husband standing behind her. President Albert Cole smiled at his wife as he said. "It is okay honey I'll handle this one myself, honey. Why don't you go back to bed, there's no sense the both of us losing our sleep over this mess, dear." The President smiled pleasantly at his wife and then he spoke to his aide.

"Paul, have the General shown to the LBJ library. There's no reason for us being uncomfortable while discussing the latest attacks. Have coffee and cake sent up for us." He winked at his Chief aid. He knew the President wanted to have a cigar with his coffee.

"Paul, I'll take care of the coffee while my husband's meeting with Weidenbacher. You worry about getting the President's cigar please." The First Lady smiled at the young man.

President Cole smiled at his wife as he said. "I guess I can't hide anything from you."

"No! So you might as well stop trying to get away with it, mister. There's not a man born to this earth that can pull the wool over a woman's eyes and get away with it, you know my husband. You don't think I knew you were still smoking those damn things whenever you held meetings in your office with either the General or Director, dear? I have some news for you mister, you stank from the smoke and it was more than if the others were smoking in front of you. Now, get out of the way so I can get coffee for you and the General, my darling. Do you mind if I sit in on the meeting with you this time dear. I'll never be able to go back to sleep now honey. Not without you lying by my side that is."

"You might as well, you probably know more of what's going on than I do honey."

General William Weidenbacher was shown to the esteem library, and there he waited for President Cole to arrive, who entered and he complained at his officer. "Well General, it seems like we done this same shit on this night, sir. I just fell asleep you know General Weidenbacher."

The General gave out with a nervous laugh, especially when he noticed the President's wife enter the room behind her husband. The First Lady placed a tray on the table then she made herself comfortable on an overstuffed wingchair. She glared at the General for a brief moment as she warned him in no uncertain terms. "I don't like you waking Albert so much lately sir, he needs his sleep General."

"Sorry Ma'am, but this is extremely important Ma'am, and I felt the President needed to know about it Ma'am." The actually concerned looking General replied to the First Lady.

President Cole shot a look at his wife, and she knew if she wanted to stay while they spoke, she was going to have to be still. Once he was certain he had his wife under some kind of control, he looked to the General and asked. "Okay, where the hell did the next attack take place, General?" The President was taking it for granted another terrorist attack took place somewhere in the Middle East, and the General was there to inform him of the attack.

"Syria, Mr. President Sir." The General replied a little surprised of the President's remark.

"God dammit General, I can't believe this shit for a damn minute sir."

EL QARYATEIN, SYRIA

A horde of Arab rescue workers descended on the affected area lying between the Syrian cities of El Qaryatein and En Nebk, where the destroyed train lay in flaming ruins. Troops and military helicopters flooded the area of the latest attack. Then the Syrian soldiers fanned out into the surrounding mountain area, searching for the attackers who planted and set off the explosive charges that destroyed the train that had killed so many Syrian civilians and visitors to the country. The soldiers were hoping to find some remaining evidence to prove to the rest of the world who the attackers were.

The United States offered to send in her huge military transport aircraft loaded with all sorts of medical and emergency supplies, to help aid with survivors and injured. But the Syrian King politely, but not so politely told America to go to hell again.

Jacinto saw a large number of soldiers climbing the mountain side feet apart, and they were working their way right towards his position. He whispered to his second. "Does everyone have grenades with them, and do they understand their orders? I don't want anyone taken alive, or our mission will be compromised."

"Yes sir, they know if trapped they're to use them to take their life and many of the enemy."

"Good, because it looks like we're not going to get out of this one alive, my brother." Jacinto replied as he kept a close watch on the soldiers who seemed like they were coming right at him.

His attention was glued to the troops massing by the destroyed train, but he did not realize more soldiers were working their way up the other side of the mountain, and they were about to make the crest of the mountain with the soldiers dropped off by the helicopters about where he was hiding. The first two terrorists were spotted and a nasty firefight took place. Machine guns fired, grenades exploded, and the troops quickly overran the small enemy position. Only one of the terrorists was captured still alive.

Jacinto stretched his neck while trying to see what was going on at the crest of the mountain top. Suddenly, a large squad of soldiers pounced down on his location. His attackers were captured without a single shot fired at the soldiers. The terrorists were beaten by the angry soldiers then dragged from their hiding places. In less than an hour, fifteen of the thirty five attackers were captured alive, and were dragged out of the hills, the rest of the terrorist were dead trying to resist the Syrian captors. The living terrorists were transported to Damascus for interrogation.

THE WHITE HOUSE, 7:10 A.M. EST

General Weidenbacher entered the library and smiled at the President's wife after she warned him, she was angry he was waking her husband the second time tonight. He was surprised she was being allowed to sit in on the briefing. "Mr. President, I have an unofficial death toll of the attack on the train disaster."

President Cole did not answer right off he instead looked at the seated General.

"Mr. President, the death toll was placed at over three hundred and fifty dead, with many more wounded and dying, sir."

His wife gave a cry as she covered her mouth with her hand, and sobbed over the loss of life.

"You all right, honey?" President Cole demanded as he looked at his shaken wife.

She shook her head yes as she dabbed at her eyes with a cloth and then she let out a sigh.

"Jesus H. Christ General, it must have been one helluva charge to do that much damage to a damn train. Were they able to capture any terrorists alive I hope?" the President asked as he placed his attention on the General who disturbed his sleep.

The General's face broke out into a sort of a grin as he replied to the President's question. "Yes Sir Mr. President, I picked up a number of reports stating at least ten terrorists were captured alive, and they're in the process of being transported to Damascus for interrogation by some of their own special ops people, sir."

President Cole let out with a whistle as he offered. "I'm damn glad I'm not one of those asses who allowed themselves to be captured, and they're now in the Syrian's hands, General."

"Yes sir, you can bet the bank on it they don't look too good by now, Mr. President."

The levity ended when President Cole asked. "General, what are you doing about learning the identities of these terrorists? Does anything point to them being Jews or Arabs, sir?"

Director Raincloud entered the library just as the President asked that question of the General, and he offered to answer for the President.

"I placed every Agent I had free on the case, sir. I even enlisted certain members of Mossad and Shin Bet, Israeli's Secret Police, along with some KGB Agents. Every Agent agreed without assumption the attacks were being carried out by a third person for some reasons unknown. The Agents are committed to searching for the organization responsible. They're monitoring all suspected nations and their militaries for signs of anything out of the ordinary, sir."

"What about the situation taking place in Cuba, General? We can't forget about that mess, sir." President Cole asked, remembering that problem was still going on.

"Radio Marti, that's a Radio Free European type radio station, is still broadcasting certain code messages out to my Agents in the field in Cuba, sir. Their orders were to prepare for an invasion by the exile forces, Mr. President. These Agents are organizing Cuban resistance fighters against the new revolutionary government being run by this Colonel Rafael Hernandez Alvarez nut, sir. The Agents were ordered to step up their sabotage attacks against government forces, and or installations sir. Everything pertaining to Cuba and our invasion is being coordinated through the Joint Task Force Headquarters out of Key West, Florida sir, as per previous instructions sir."

"Good then getting back to the mess occurring in the Middle East John, are any of your Agents zeroing in on any specific nation yet who might have been behind these attacks against the Arab states and Israeli, sir? I want to know the moment they located the smoking gun Director Raincloud, and I mean the exact moment sir!" President Cole warned the CIA Director as he gave his wife another look to make sure she was holding up okay.

"It looks like the fingers are beginning to point at a few nations, but nothing discovered yet to enable us to single out any one of them, sir." Director Raincloud offered.

"And, you're not willing to venture any opinion of the suspected culprit as of this time, are you Director Raincloud?" the American Leader asked as he glanced at the General.

Director Raincloud smiled as he replied to the American Leader's question. "Mr. President, opinions are like assholes, everyone has one, but that's not to say they're the right one." The CIA Director turned red because of his comment as he remembered the President's wife was in the room, and he used gutter language in her present. He turned to her and nodded and offered. "Please forgive my insensitivity to your presence I forgot you were attending this meeting."

The First Lady smiled as she replied to the Director. "That was an interesting aphorism you used, John. I'll remember that one when I'm dealing with the media or the pain in the neck interest groups, John." Her remark broke up the uneasiness, and it gave President Cole a chance to ask his next question of the Director.

"Director Raincloud, how the hell are the Israelis taking this anti-Israeli rhetoric crap being leveled against them over this mess, sir? Since these terrorist attacks on the Arabs targets and their country started."

Director John Raincloud allowed the General to field this question as he turned to the powerful military officer and sort of smirked at him.

"I guess I got the ball I see." He offered and then began his reply. "Mr. President, the Israelis aren't taking this well. The Jews are reacting too much of it, as if they believe they're about to be attacked by Arab countries. Every Arab nation is being ripped apart from within by protests aimed against Israel, demonstrators demanding action be taken against them, sir. Anyone not against the Jews in the Arab nations is being attacked by the rioters. I'm sure the attack on the Mosque was the straw that broke the camel's back. The attacks on Arab countries adding salt to the wound."

"That's all well and good General, but you didn't answer the question to my satisfaction, sir. What actions are the Israelis taking, dammit?"

"Got ya sir." The General put his thumb up, and continued his explanation. "The Israelis ordered their military base at Teh Nof on full alert, as well as the three other airbases. Ichilov hospital at Tel Aviv is to stand by to receive wounded. Sir, every airbase throughout Israel is on full alert now. The Patriot missile systems we sold to them are also up and on line. I have a report stating the missile base at Zah Haria was placed on Red Alert. That places Israel's nuclear capability on the ready standby. I received reports stating the 679th Reserve Armor Brigade was brought up on full alert, along with the 77th and the 109th Armor Battalions, and also the 7th Armor Brigade, sir. The Israeli's activated the IDF (Israeli Defense Forces) on the Southern, Eastern and Northern frontiers. In essence Mr. President, the Israeli's placed their entire nations on full war time alert, sir.

"Any attack on Israel will bring down the full weight of the Israeli military response, sir. She's trying to enlist help from her allies, including us, Mr. President. Israel's also ordering her able bodied male and female civilians to report to their assigned military bases. It was further reported Israel has mechanics working on the Syrian and Egyptian tanks they confiscated during the Arab, Israeli wars of the past, Mr. President. It looks like they're reading themselves for any controlling factors, sir."

"And, you agree with Israel's moves so far, General?" the President asked him.

"Completely agree with their moves so far, Mr. President." The General replied.

"How the hell are the Arabs reacting to the Israeli military buildup, General Weidenbacher?"

"In much the same manner as we would respond to any other nation preparing to attack us, sir. Each nation is mobilizing their militaries, they ordered their military up on full alert, and have pulled in civilians for strengthening up their Armies. Saudi Arabia issued orders for all our military personnel to leave the country within twenty four hours, and any personnel remaining will be placed under arrest until this present situation has concluded. Mr. President, the Saudis confiscated much of our military equipment on their soil, sir.

"I received assurances this was carried out to ensure the Saudis we wouldn't intervene in any military conflict between Saudi Arabia and Israel, by using our military equipment in their country for Israel's defense. I'm praying no one goes off half cocked on this one sir, or the

Middle East could erupt in total war, sir. If this happens, I don't think the world would remain on the sidelines for long without choosing sides, Mr. President."

"Do I understand you right General? Are you trying to say we might find ourselves locked in another World War over this matter?" the President declared angrily as he stared deeply into his eyes for a second.

"Yes sir, on the scale of the last World War, but with one difference, sir. Nuclear weapons will be employed this time, and that'll make it impossible for anyone to stay neutral if this war comes to tradition, sir."

"Then we have no alternative left opened but to prevent this damn situation from happening, General." The President barked as he stared at the General.

"With every fiber of our being, Mr. President." The General replied to the angry President

President Cole let out his breath in a sigh as he bitched. "General, both you and Director Raincloud better locate the people responsible for this shit. I hope to God it isn't the Jews and Arabs, or we'll never avert a war in the Middle East. If one happens, we're going to be forced to resign ourselves to a total effort trying to contain the fighting to the Middle East to keep it from spreading to the rest of the world at all costs. General, if you find out who is responsible, I want you to bring down the full, and I mean the full weight of our combined forces on their necks, sir. I'll give you the power to destroy the offending nation's entire country if necessary, sir. I want the heads of the bastards who hung this crap on my front door, sir." The American Leader pounded his fist on the table, sending his cup of coffee flying across the room. His wife jumped up to clean the mess.

"Leave the shit alone. If that's the worst thing that happens here, I want the damn stain to remain for all history. To remind me and the next Presidents who'll follow me, how close we came to fighting another World War. You'll inform the staff not to clean it honey." The President was hot as he jumped up.

His wife stood, frightened for his health she fought back tears, but she had no idea who she would be shedding them for, her husband, or the civilians who would lose their lives if fighting broke out in the Middle East. She excused herself and left the men to speak in private.

HAVANA, CUBA, 7:21 A.M. EST.SUNDAY, SEPTEMBER 29th, 1996

Presidente Carlos Rafael Hernandez Alvarez removed his files and his personal belongings from the Presidential office as he prepared for the trip to Guanahacabibes, and the long range nuclear tipped missiles. He was determined to use them as a threat to enlist the United States in his ongoing fight for power over the tiny Cuban Island. He was sure once the United States was aware of the weapons of mass destruction in his possession, they would do anything in their power to stop them from being launched at their country, even if it meant the Americans coming to his aid.

A massive explosion on the parade grounds forced Colonel Alvarez to duck behind his desk. He crawled to the window and looked out only to see one of his massive T-80 tank lying on its side, with flames roaring out of the open hatches. His attention was brought back to his office when Colonel Carlos Calvo rushed in and called out. "Presidente Alvarez, I was afraid you might have been injured in the last blast, sir." He looked at all the glass lying everywhere in the large room and was amazed if he found the President still alive the office.

"These dom civilians are a pain in my ass, sir. Colonel Calvo, do we have troops left from the defenders of Santa Clara and Cienfuegos action, sir?" Alvarez asked as he got off the floor and was angry because he was using generators to provide electric power for the Palace. Elsewhere throughout the rest of the capital and Island as far as he knew, there was no electric. The darkness gave the civilian troublemakers the forum to run their attacks against his government from.

"Yes sir, we have quite a large force of soldiers who escaped from the ring of the civilian fighters. They're making their way to Matanzas as of now, where I ordered them to make their last stand. Each of the troops was ordered to fight to the last man."

"Who is commanding the troops at Matanzas, Colonel Calvo?"

"Me! I'm planning to take over command of all soldiers at Matanzas myself, sir."

"You! No way. I need you at Guanahacabibes with the missiles and myself, Colonel."

"I assure you sir, everything you'll need you have at your fingers tips down there Presidente Alvarez. If I can hold off, or defeat the bulk of the civilian forces marching on the capital as we talk. You can return to Havana the conquering hero you should be sir, and you'll still have the missiles as your trump card when it comes time for us to deal with the Americans, Presidente Alvarez."

"By the Blessed Virgin Mary, you'll do this for me, Colonel?"

"Yes my Presidente, I'll fight with every soldier I have at my command, sir. I'll turn these dom civilian fighters away from the capital and save Havana for you. Then I shall continue my attacks on the civilian troublemakers until I completely cleanse the Island of the civilian Army. Then, at last, you'll take your rightful position as the new Presidente of Cuba, and you'll deal with the loathsome Americans any way you see fit, sir."

Alvarez walked over to Calvo and hugged and kissed him on both cheeks then he said. "Colonel Calvo, by the Holy Father, if you can accomplish this feat of destroying the civilian Armies, you shall join me at the seat of power over Cuba as my Vice Presidente, sir."

"Presidente Alvarez, have no fear of my victory over these lowly civilian troublemakers, sir. I shall defeat the foolish civilian's fighters to the last one of them fools, sir. Think of it sir, since when would a bunch of unorganized, cursed and misguided civilians troublemakers defeat me, one of the greatest military commander outside of yourself of course, to have every walked upon the soil of Cuba, Presidente Alvarez." The bragging Cuban Colonel offered to him.

"True, true. Colonel, I'll never be able to put in words how I feel about your offer, your loyalty your patriotism to me. I swear by the sacred Madonna, your name will be renowned in the history of Cuba." Alvarez announced as he turned, and then he worked on his files again.

Calvo stared at the Presidente of Cuba for a moment. He knew with one bullet, he could bring Cuba out of a civil war. He decided against it, knowing the reason he planned to lead the troops to defend the last stronghold, before the civilian Army could march through the streets of capital of Havana. He planned to organize the remaining troops, and make peace with the civilian horde, and then he would turn his Army and use them to attack the soldiers Alvarez was transferring to the Guanahacabibes Peninsula. He also intended to inform the civilian leaders of Alvarez's plan to use the threat of the nuclear missiles against the United States.

The wise Colonel would stop Alvarez, and he would use his victory to power him to the Presidency over Cuba with civilian and American backing. Who would not back the soldier responsible for saving the world from a nuclear holocaust? He believed his involvement with Alvarez would be overlooked, after he helped to destroy the missiles. The military units he sent to Israel and the Arab states would most certainly be destroyed, or absorbed by the host nations by the time he finished off Alvarez and his missiles and nuclear warhead. Either way, there was one place he would come out on, the top, once he carried out his attack on Alvarez's Armies.

The Colonel watched Alvarez working on emptying his desk and file cabinets in haste, all the time the streets of Havana was a scene of heavy fighting. A second explosion outside the Palace grounds, made Alvarez look up and complain at his officer. "Madre de Dios, are you still here Colonel Calvo? Check on the troops gathering at Matanzas? See if they reached the dom city, sir. Should you not be down there and organizing the defense of that city, Colonel Calvo?"

Calvo smiled at the Presidente. "I was planning to check on their situation sir."

"For the love of God then do it Colonel Calvo!" Alvarez barked at the officer.

THE DEFEATED TROOPS FROM CIENFUEGOS AND SANTA CLARA

Sergeant Rosendo Omnibuses was in command of the unorganized troops who escaped the destruction when the two Cuban cities fell to the horde of attacking civilian Armies. Whatever government troops left with him, were involved fighting a delaying action, as they made for the next city of defense, Matanzas.

Omnibuses was doing a good job holding off the civilian fighters, he got away with plenty of ammunition along with some armor and artillery, and these weapons were all that was standing between him and the civilians taking command of more than half of Cuba. His hope was the aircraft that attacked the frontlines of the civilian Armies in an attempt to turn them back, but the civilians kept marching on them.

Emil Nicaro split up his Army in two separate fronts, one controlled by him and the other by Navea, his two Armies marched on Matanzas from two sides. He had the retreating revolutionary Army outflanked, but Nicaro decided he would fight his last fight in the streets of Matanzas. Nicaro sent a splinter Army out to attack the airbase to his north, in an effort to stop any aerial attacks against his civilian Army.

Colonel Calvo left Havana with his Paratroopers. He was not willing to take too much of a risk when it came time to talk with the civilian leader. He knew if he had a large enough Army behind him the civilian leader would be willing to talk peace with him rather than fight his soldiers.

Calvo's troops roared into the city of Matanzas at about the same time the leading elements of Sergeant Rosendo's government troops flooded into the city from the east side. The two Armies met in the middle of the city. The Colonel informed the Sergeant of his plans, and he agreed to join with him. Sergeant Rosendo Omnibuses was willing to do anything that would save his skin. The Colonel took command of both Armies, and had the troops set up defensive positions, while he waited for the civilian leader to make contact with him. He was confident he could talk sense with the civilian. Rosendo knew the name of the civilian and he reminded the Colonel.

495

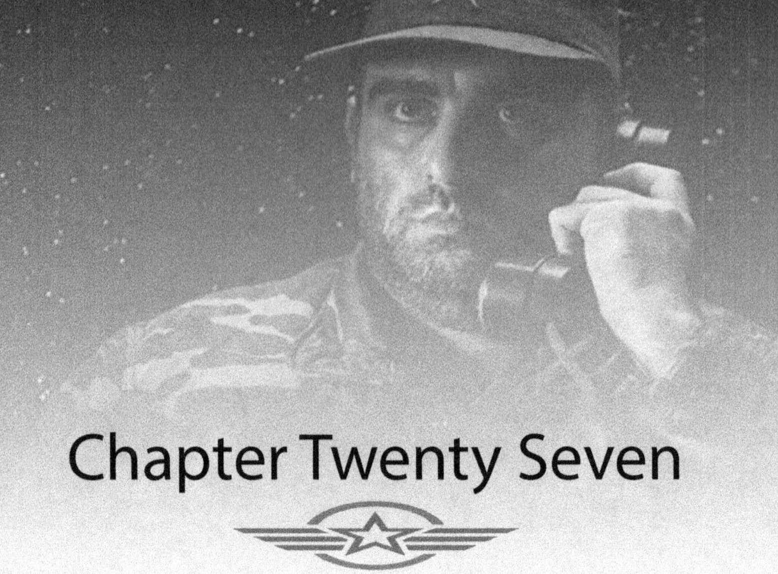

Chapter Twenty Seven

HAVANA, CUBA 10:35 A.M. SUNDAY, SEPTEMBER 29th, 1996

Presidente Carlos Rafael Hernandez Alvarez emptied his office of everything he wanted to take with him, and his aides loaded his belongings into one of the armor vehicles he chose to use as his command vehicle. He smiled when he saw Maria was inside the idling war machine for him, and he bitched at her. "By the Holy Madonna, we shall be at my new military base within an hour or so. There, we'll be able to start our new lives together, foul woman."

"If I had my way about it, your worthless life would be over this moment, you cursed pig you." She raised her hands that were tied together, and made her fingernails come out as she swiped the air before her face.

"You devil born bitch, how dare you threaten me in this manner. I don't like it one bit, and if you continue with this foolishness, you'll live long enough to regret it, woman." Alvarez kicked out with his foot, catching her in the side and knocking the wind out from her lungs as he added to his threat. "You'll be happy to be my mistress, Maria."

Before he left, Alvarez checked on the arming of the missiles. He was assured everything was proceeding as scheduled. He remembered how he smiled when he was informed American warships took up positions off Cuba's coast, but they left when the attacks in Israel began. The few remaining ships had also moved out, but he knew they were still in the area.

Alvarez's vehicle bucked violently as the engine engaged, and the machine started out of the capital. He had fifteen T-80 tanks, and thirty armored vehicles in his column. He left the bulk of his troops behind to defend the capital, and to protect their flank for as long as possible.

THE SECLUDED GUANAHACABIBES PENINSULA, CUBA

The technicians trained by the Russian engineers before they left the Island, successfully moved a few of the missiles around indie the bunker, and they installed the six reentry warheads into each weapon of mass destruction delivery system. They then placed two of the nuclear armed missiles into the underwater silos. It was hard work and the technicians decided to arm the other two missiles, before proceeding with the placing of the missiles in the silos. Another driving factor in this decision was the sun was up and it backed off the fog and mist of the night. The technicians did not want to chance moving anymore of the missiles out in the day light conditions. They preferred to move the missiles under the cover of darkness, as they done with the other two massive missiles.

Other technicians worked on slaving (ordering) the two placed missiles to the control and launch computers in the bunker. So far, everything was green with the commands, with the computers linking up with the missiles, and the missiles responding to the computers orders.

THE UNITED STATES CRUISER CGN-41 ARKANSAS ON STATION TWENTY MILES FROM THE COAST OF CUBA. 2:10 A.M. SUNDAY, SEPTEMBER 29th, 1996

The American Navy Cruiser CGN-41 Arkansas, was holding her position twenty miles off the lighthouse on Cado Corrientes in Cuba, and she started her surveillance of Haiti as ordered. The surveillance computer was set on maximum, and the operator scanned the irregular shoreline of Haiti, registering no unusual activity on the Island. On his follow through scan, he allowed the computer to make a three hundred and sixty degree sweep of the region. The Cayman and Grand Cayman were quiet, but when his probe passed through the southern tip of Cuba including the Guanahacabibes Peninsula, the radar operator picked up unusual activity happening there.

The immediately called his Commander to his radar screen, and pointed to the activity on the Island as he offered. "Lieutenant, I'm picking up movement on Cuba, coordinates 31R by 78C."

The concerned Lieutenant moved closer to the radar operator and he rested his hand on his back as he watched the scope finish its run and grumbled. "Unusual activity on Cuba you say mister. Anything happening on Cuba is an unusual event, my friend. Hmmm, I see what you mean, that's a lot of activity in that secluded region of Cuba. What the hell do you think they're up to down there? I don't like the looks of this activity."

"Dunno sir, do you think they're aware of our invasion plan, sir? I peg it as activity, but not much movement. Maybe it's some of their government Army trying to escape the Island before we come after them, sir."

"Don't be an ass, mark the location on the threat map then ship a report out to Task Force Whiskey, X-ray stationed on Key West. Cuba's their baby to deal with and we might as well let them figure out what the hell the Cubs are up to. We're ordered to keep Haiti under the magnifying glass."

"Aye sir. Should I send it out over the open key, or on the secured line, Lieutenant?"

"What's in your brain, saltwater? Since when do we send anything out in open key from this surveillance ship, mister? Code it."

"Aye Lieutenant. Quebec, November R73 to Whiskey, X-ray 23, stand by to receive a Level Two communication from QNR 73. Flash! Flash! Over." The operator placed his call out.

"Whiskey X-ray 23 to QNR 73. We're ready to receive your flash traffic on Two, Seven, sir. Let her fly sir. Over."

"Roger that last Whiskey X-ray 23. Beginning my Flash transmission now sir. End of Flash transmission, sir. Over."

"Received as sent, will advise when decision on flash traffic is made, sir. Over."

The Sergeant who received the coded Flash message, unscrambled the jumble of dots, dashes and numbers. His Commander came over and watched as the younger man worked.

"Whaddaya got soldier?" he asked the Sergeant as he continued to decode the communication.

"Arrr... it seems a long boy (slang for Cruiser) picked up some unusual activity they want us to check out for them, sir. It looks like it has something to do with Cuba, Lieutenant."

"Very good, keep me advised Sergeant." The officer ordered his operator sharply.

"Stick around for a moment sir. I should have it done in a moment. Yep, it's about Cuba alright, Lieutenant. Hmmm, seems the Cruiser picked up what they're reporting as unusual activity in sector 31R by 78C on the Island of Cuba, sir."

The Lieutenant looked at his wall map and complained at the Sergeant. "That's the Guanahacabibes Peninsula area okay. What the hell could these damn fools be doing out there on that arm pit of hell, fishing mister?"

"That's about all I could imagine they might be doing down there myself, Lieutenant."

"Agreed, but if this action has the Navy's short hairs on edge. We better send it to Command, STAT it, and let the bigwigs get someone over that spot, and see what the hell's going on there for themselves. If it's anything at all which I seriously doubt. Send a second request out to Beal for an SR-91 flyover on same coordinates, Sergeant." The Lieutenant controlling this unit ordered the Sergeant.

"Right away Lieutenant." The Sergeant sent out the request as ordered immediately.

BEAL AIRFORCE BASE, MARYVILLE CALIFORNIA.3:15 A.M. SUNDAY, SEPTEMBER 29th, 1996

Command Headquarters stationed at Beal Airforce Base Airman Carl Levit was commanding the radio. Levit jumped as the request came in on him. "Captain, I have a request for an immediate flyover coming in, sir."

"Oh yeah, from who mister?" the Captain laughed, thinking someone just overstepped their bounds to send him such a request without going through the proper channels first.

"Whiskey, X-ray 23 sir." The airman reported with concern lacing his voice.

Captain Walsh, leaning back in his chair and relaxing from his boring day, almost fell over backwards when he heard who made the request for the flyover as he cried out. "Holy shit, Task Force HQ wants a fricking flyover? What are their coordinates, man?"

"31R by 78C sir." The operator replied to his Commander's request.

"Got ya Airman." The Captain said as he checked out the coordinates on his computer, and then he grumbled at the airman. "Christ, that's Cuba son. Better order S-21 out of the hanger."

"Roger that Captain." The Airman keyed the radio and then he ordered. "Scramble Flight Amble, Scramble Flight Amble. S-21's ordered scrambled for a flyover mission."

The doors of hanger twelve opened as the massive engines of the SR-91 roared and they flamed to life. The specially designed surveillance aircraft taxied from the building then aligned itself with Runway Five.

There, she built up her full military take off power until reaching takeoff thrust. A second later, she roared down the long runway.

Captain Walsh watched with pride as the twin shafts of flames disappeared in the blackness of the night. He left the window and went to his command station and keyed his radio and barked in the radio at the pilot of the Pathfinder flight. "Eagles Nest Pathfinder Flight 21. Come in. Over."

"Yeah Eagles Nest, this is Pathfinder One Commander. I copy your last transmission, sir. Go with your traffic, sir. Over."

"Pathfinder, you're instructed to a heading of 37R by 78C for a photo op. You're to take three rolls of film, one from the north heading south, another from the west heading east, and the last pass from the northeast heading southwest. I want a complete mosaic of the entire targeted area. Understood Pathfinder Commander? Over."

"Roger, copy that as received Eagle's Nest. A complete mosaic of the entire target area, will comply sir. Over." Pathfinder One then pulled the nose of his SR-91 into a steep climb while trading off sir speed for altitude heading fight for his hovering fuel tanker. Like the SR-71 before her, the SR-91 could not take off with her full load of fuel, or her fuel bladders would imploded. The fuel cells of the SR-91 had to expand because of the unnatural speeds the aircraft traveled at, until it sealed the upper section of the fuel tanks as they expanded from the heat raised by the friction of the aircraft slicing though the air. It was the only drawback, having to fuel the unusual aircraft while in mid-flight so soon after taking off.

After fueling, the pilot pushed the envelope until his aircraft pushed near Mach Five. In a matter of an hour and ten minutes time, the SR-91, branded 'The Hole in the Sky', closed in on its assigned target. The pilot picked up the shoreline of Cuba coming at him from the northeast, and he dropped down to Angels 65,000 feet. He lowered his aircraft's speed down to Mach Three point Five, the fastest speed he could travel and have his specially designed Kodak cameras film a crystal clear picture of the intended target area. The pilot carried out a simple maneuver until his plane headed to Cuba from the north heading south.

It took the pilot of the SR-91fifteen minutes to make his flight corrections and finish his second pass over the tiny Island of Cuba, and then another seventeen minutes to complete his ordered mission. The pilot was then ordered up to Texas for his second mid-flight refueling, once this was carried out, the pilot headed his aircraft back for Beal Airforce Base, taking the long way around to avoid anyone monitoring of his flight. If anyone detected his flight path, they could possibly discover his mission.

BEAL AIRFORCE BASE. MARYVILLE, CALIFORNIA 7:01 A.M. EST SUNDAY, SEPTEMBER 29th, 1996

The Pathfinder Flight Commander aligned his aircraft up with the blacked out runway. He touched down and taxied his secret black plane back to the specially built hanger. The folding doors closed silently behind the spy plane even before the engines were shutdown. The horde of technicians responsible for the aircraft moved in and removed the camera pods, one from the nose section the other from the mid-belly of the aircraft. The pods were placed on dollies and wheeled over to the lab where the film was removed, processed and developed. It took an hour for the technicians to develop the photos of Guanahacabibes Peninsula area of Cuba. Then, the painstaking work of scrutinizing the photos began. The technicians used microscopes and magnifying glasses to analyze what secrets were hidden on the photos.

PRESIDENTE CARLOS ALVAREZ'S MILITARY CARAVAN

Cuban Presidente Carlos Rafael Fernandez Alvarez's column of tanks and armored vehicles came under light arms fire twice, and they were only seven miles out of the capital. Every time he looked out of the gun ports of his armored vehicle, all he saw were fires raging and bodies lying on the ground, and civilians running in all directions carrying weapons or gas bombs. The bullets fired at his vehicle echoed throughout the machine, but they did no damage to it and it forced

Alvarez to bark at his driver. "Driver! For the love of God, did you pick up anything on Calvo's forces marching on Matanzas yet, mista?"

"Yes sir, he reported his forces entered Matanzas, and they've been successful linking up with the advance troops already stationed there, who fled from Santa Clara, sir."

"Madre de Dios, what about the soldiers from Cienfuegos? Where the devil are they, dommit?"

"Sir, Colonel Calvo reported in that no troops have been able to escape Cienfuegos, sir."

Alvarez was stunned he lost ten thousand troops defending Cienfuegos as he roared at his driver. "Impossible. I guarantee many of Captain Sanguily's troops made it to safety, and they're assembling, possibly to attack the civilians from its flanks. There's no way these dom civilians could destroy such a powerful force as his. Dommit, I knew I should've replaced that sonofabitch." In his mind, Alvarez could not believe he lost an Army of such strength, and he convinced himself of what he just said.

The driver had no illusions, he realized all was lost, and he was biding his time until he found a window of opportunity where he would strip his uniform then come back to Havana dressed as a civilian soldier.

COLONEL CARLOS CALVO'S FORCES TAKING UP POSITION FOR THE DEFENSE OF THE CUBAN CITY OF MATANZAS

Colonel Calvo screamed at his troops as they erected the defensive lines needed to ward off the civilian Army marching against them. The Colonel wanted to create an impenetrable defense around him and the rest of his defenders, in case he could not talk sense into the chosen civilian leader, Emil Nicaro. His first defense consisted of soldiers armed with AK-47 heavy assault weapons and mortars, along with some light weight 30 mm cannons.

Calvo's second defensive line was constructed of the heavier 100 and 120 mm cannons, heavy machine guns, and his back up troops armed with mortars, and rapid firing 60 mm grenade launchers with his older tanks. His last line of defense was strengthened with his newer T-72 and T-80 tanks, his complete complement of the D-20/152 mm, and the D-30/122 mm towed Howitzers, the M-46/130 mm guns, mortars, and the 2S3/152 mm self-propelled Howitzers, along with more mortars, and three rapid fire guns. Calvo ordered the mining of all roads leading into the city. He was determined if he could not talk sense to the civilian fighters he would stop them at any cost to him and his troops. If he could not stop them then he would make certain no civilian survivors would continue their march on to the capital, in his heart though he felt he owed this much to Presidente Carlos Alvarez.

Along the way, the Colonel drafted other troops who survived the attacks on the two Cuban cities to strengthen up his forces. He knew he was weakening the defenses behind him, opening his flanks to attacks by the civilian units, but if he was unable to stop the main civilian Army then the little Armies he allowed to survive behind him, would be of no concern to him and his troops, once they were destroyed by the civilian attackers.

It took the Colonel's troops over two hours to establish his defensive lines he demanded made up. Calvo then ordered his troops to hunker down and go on a one sleep, and one awake system while they waited for the civilian to arrive. He had limited information coming in, so he was unaware the civilian Army replaced their fighters lost in the attack on the two cities, and with every step they took, Nicaro's Army picked up another three fighters. They were coming from behind every bush, every destroyed building, and from ever wrecked vehicle, all wanting to fight the military who destroyed their villages and homes. Nicaro's Army was well over eight hundred thousand strong, and it was moving all across Cuba as one great mass of civilians fighting for their freedom of Cuba.

A radio call received from a scout, reporting to Colonel Calvo's command a small Army of civilian fighters were spotted moving in the northeastern section of the city. The scout was requesting orders.

Calvo's troops were under strict orders to hold their fire until they were ordered to do otherwise by the Colonel himself.

Calvo ordered the scout to raise the white flag, and he was hen to request direct contact with the civilian fighter's leader, Nicaro. The scout was fuming, but he did as ordered. The advance civilian units saw the white flag and they contacted Nicaro for instructions. They were ordered to take the two men standing under the white flag in custody, and bring them to him unharmed.

As Nicaro's civilian fighters continued their rapid march on the Cuban city of Matanzas, he did not stop his attacks on the other government troops he came across. He splintered off a small force of his fighters and ordered this unit to attack the bomber aircraft base on the Peninsula de Hicacos. He ordered them to destroy the Tu-22M Backfire, and the Tu-22 Blinder bombers left on the ground. He did not want his forces to be attacked by these bomber aircraft, they devastated his forces in the first fight, and he was going to do something to stop the aircraft from attacking his ground forces during this second confrontation.

Nicaro kept in contact with his units attacking the airbase. His Commander reported he had a count of the bombers reported to be in Castro, and now Alvarez's, airforce. He was surprised to hear they discovered a number of the Mig fighter aircraft parked on the airbase, and ordered his men to destroy the planes where they sat. This response was the reply to his Commander's request to try to take some of the aircraft intact to use them against the government defenders of the city of Matanzas, and then their supposed attack on the Cuban capital of Havana.

Nicaro understood he had no one in his massive Army who was qualified to fly the complicated Soviet made bomber aircraft, and he was not going to rely on the government pilots who already killed so many of his fighters in the battle for control of the two cities below. The civilians setup mortars, and zeroed in on the lead bomber planes on the runway, as if prepared to take off at a moment's notice. The rest of the civilians aimed at the other planes on the ground with automatic weapons. The three anti-aircraft triple A guns were also targeted for destruction on the opening salvos by the civilian attackers.

The Commander of the civilians picked out a number of machine gun nests setup to better protect the airbase from attack, and he scheduled them for destruction once the aircraft on the airbase were destroyed. The civilian Commander waited until his people nodded to acknowledge they were ready to begin the assault on the airbase, and then he looked at the three men and two women controlling the mortars. The civilian lifted his hand and took one last look at the planes on the runway then he lowered it. Five mortars fired at the same instant, and each plane erupted in fireballs. His machine gunners opened up at the same time, killing another three planes as his mortars reloaded. Quickly, one after the other, the planes on the airbase was destroyed by their mortar and machine gunfire.

Return fire from the airbase government defenders was heavy, and the civilian forces were cut in half, and when two tanks moved out from behind a building and pressed the action against his civilian attackers, the Commander of the civilians decided not to press the fight further against the airbase, and they flee the area for their lives, rather than allow his men to be slaughtered needlessly. He left knowing his orders were carried out, and his fighters destroyed the bomber and Mig aircraft, and rendered the airbase useless to receive, or prepare any of the aircraft for more attacks on the civilian Army.

Once the Commander and fighters were far enough away from the military airbase and he was sure none of the government defenders were coming after them, he reported to Nicaro the planes were destroyed. This information took the pressure off of Nicaro. Now he did not have to worry about any bomber aircraft beating on his men, all he had to concern himself with were the artillery and tanks if he wanted to overrun the military defenders of Matanzas, and make his way over to the heart of the capital city of Cuba.

After the revolutionary soldiers under the protection of the white flag were marched before him, Nicaro asked them what they wanted from him, and they replied Colonel Carlos Calvo wanted to meet with him in person. Nicaro jumped on the offer. The smug Colonel and

Nicaro met between the two Armies in the open field on either side of a table set up for this meeting on a small grassy knoll.

Calvo began speaking to the civilian like he was holding the upper hand in the fighting. "Nicaro, I know you're going to soon march over my god dom defenders, sir. So, I'm offering you the lives of many of your people who'll surely die in the battle when you try and attack my troop's positions, sir. I propose our two Armies unite, and together, we'll set Cuba free of this new madman in command of the country at this time sir."

Nicaro laughed as he replied to the officer in a sarcastic voice. "Why in the unholy hell should I allow you to join my civilian forces, Colonel Calvo? I have more than enough of my own men needed to take over all of Cuba as it is now, sir. I think all the people of Cuba have had their fill of being ruled by any of you god cursed military types, mista."

"You have no choice left opened to you and your people but to allow this Nicaro." Calvo fired back at the grinning civilian leader of the Cuban fighters.

"Ha, I have no choice do I you offer me, Calvo? In a pig's ear I don't have any choice left to me and my fighters, sir. Colonel, it's you who have no choice opened to him, and I'm sure that is why you're here talking to me, to try and save your own worthless hide. I don't need you to get your soldiers to join my fighters. All I have to do is offer them their lives, and they'll flock to me without you commanding them to do so."

Calvo laughed this time as he stared into the glaring eyes of the angry Nicaro.

"You doubt me and what I say is the truth I see, so I'll prove to you what I say is true." Nicaro bellowed out in a commanding tone. "To all the government defenders of Matanzas, I offer you life here. Lay down your cursed weapons and join forces with me and my fighters, and together we'll set Cuba free from all would be military leaders. I have a million men in the hills ready to attack you, if you want to see tomorrow's sunrise, I suggest you do as I ordered, and join my forces."

Nicaro lifted his hand, and instantly an ocean of humanity rose and shouted as they beat on anything that made noise.

The noise was deafening, and Calvo's troops staring at the massive civilian Army with their mouths hanging opened. At best, they had nine thousand government soldiers in their ranks pitted against such a mammoth assembly of civilian fighters.

Nicaro continued speaking to the government defenders as he lowered his hand, and his men quieted down, so their leader could speak to the Colonel's troops again. "I'm finished talking any more deals with any military type people of Cuba. I made two so far, and both were broken by your supposed leaders. From now on, I'll only speak to the soldiers themselves. The soldiers who'll soon die for this lowly fool seated before me, because he's too stupid to offer you your lives. I make this offer once to you government soldiers. Don't join forces with me and my fighters, and you'll end up like Calvo." Nicaro produced a pistol from under the table, and fired twice at Calvo's chest. He fell backwards, dead before he had a chance to react to this attack.

A cry rose up from the revolutionary Army, and again Nicaro lifted his arm. When all was quiet, he offered the soldiers their lives and he gave them an hour to decide their fate.

THE SECLUDED GUANAHACABIBES PENINSULA, CUBA

Presidente Carols Alvarez's column of government troops and military vehicles pulled up to the secret missile installation on the secluded peninsula. He jumped out of his machine, and dragged Maria out of it by her hair. As he pulled her below, she drew in her breath when she saw the missiles and the men working on them, and the control computers.

"What is the meaning of this bullshit, Carlos? What are you going to do with these hated weapons!" Maria roared at Alvarez as she glared at him.

Alvarez back handed her because of the way she spoke to him as he hissed. "Jesus Madonna, how come the missiles are not placed in position yet? By the Blessed Mother, I want to be prepared to fire them off by tonight at the god dom United States, fools."

The lead technician offered. "Presidente Alvarez Sir, we planned to install the warheads on the remaining missiles first then set them later tonight using the darkness to hide our actions, sir."

"The hell you will do that! May God curse you to the fires of hell. I want those dom missiles set in position now or you'll be killed, and you'll be replaced with soldiers who'll do as I order. I don't know how much longer the attack units operating in Israel and the Arab states will be able to hold out. I set them in motion to cover your action here, you pack of fools. I don't need to wait any longer for the cover of darkness to arrive to finish setting the missiles in their launch silos."

"But sir." The scared technician began to offer in his defense to the Presidente of Cuba.

"But nothing. By the Holy Madonna, you'll do as you were ordered, or you'll die here, god dommit." Alvarez snapped, and then he removed his pistol and aimed it at the lead technician.

DAMASCUS, SYRIA. SUNDAY, SEPTEMBER 29th, 1996.
THREE P.M.

The terrorist prisoners were marched through the streets of Damascus in chains, and they were brought to the prison where their interrogation began. The Cubans terrorists were not prepared for the techniques their captors employed against them to extract information. After five minutes of questioning, the interrogators knew these men they captured were not Israeli soldiers.

A representative from the United States was allowed to sit on the questioning of the prisoners, and he came to the same conclusion. The soldiers were not Israeli but no matter what the inquisitor did to their unprotected bodies, hot pokers, caning, making cuts on their arms and legs. They could not get the terrorists to reveal their true identifies, or who they were working for.

The CIA Agent grew bored with the torture of the prisoners, and reported to his control on the Syrian's failure to break the prisoners. He stated the attackers were definitely not Israeli soldiers.

The Syrian government started to listen to the United States civilian advisor, and they agreed to a number of meetings to be held between the leaders of Lebanon, Jordan, Israel and Syrian. The respected Jordanian King listened to everything uncovered on the group of terrorists, and he then ordered his nation to step down from a war footing against the Israeli nation.

The nation of Israel followed suit and ordered her troops to relax their war footing, thus forcing Lebanon and Syria to follow their lead, and step down from their war footing. The meetings between the three Arab nations and Israel began under United States control, although they were scheduled to take place in Arabia classified as an unthreatened Arab nation. The American President felt it would be more productive for all sides concerned, if the talks of peace were conducted in their native land, and Arabia was felt by all sides as a natural site to start the talks of peace between the nations of the Middle East involved in this latest military action.

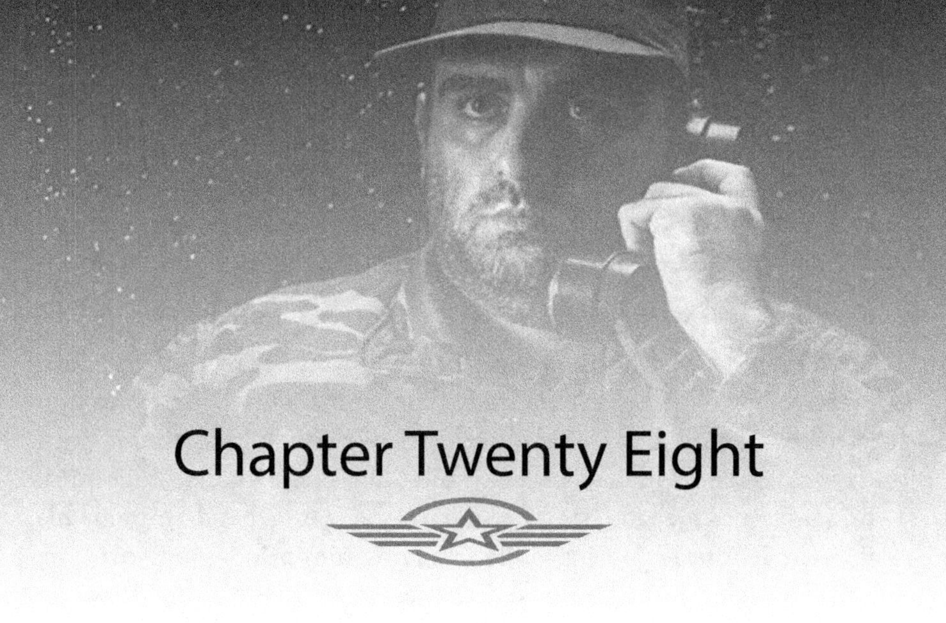

Chapter Twenty Eight

WASHINGTON D.C., THE WHITE HOUSE.
SUNDAY, SEPTEMBER 29th, 1996, 8 A.M. EST.

CIA Director John Raincloud requested the meeting to continue when he received word from his operative in Syria, that the Syrians did not believe the attackers were Israelis. He cleared his throat, and then began his words. "Err... Mr. President Sir, my operative was allowed to sit in on some questioning of the terrorist held by the Syrians, and he informed me the terrorists don't appear to be Israeli's..."

"This is great Director Raincloud! Who the hell are the bastards then, sir?" the American President roared at him.

"Unknown as of this time I'm afraid Mr. President, we're still trying to determine where these terrorists came from and who was sponsoring them." Director Raincloud replied flatly.

"What the hell do you mean by unknown, mister? How come you don't know who the hell they are and who is sending them out to attack these nations, sir? Director Raincloud, I order you to find out who these buggers owe their allegiance to sir, even if you have to have your operatives carry out the questioning of these damn terrorists, sir." President Albert Cole growled as he suddenly stood and stretched his arms.

"With all due respect Mr. President, but the Syrian examiners can do a much better job of questioning the prisoners than my people can do, sir. The Syrians are not bound by the laws of civility as my people are, Mr. President. You wouldn't want to know how the examination was being carried out. It'd definitely make you sick to your stomach sir."

"Perhaps so Director but nevertheless, I need not remind you until I locate the smoking gun here there'll be a possibility of war breaking out in the Middle East, sir. All we need is for one of these asses from either side going off half cocked, and they could plunge the entire world into utter chaos, sir." President Cole ran a hand through his hair as he let out his breath while searching him mind, going over the problems facing him. He looked at the General who seemed like he was in another world and grumbled at him. "General Weidenbacher! What about you, you're sitting there as if you're on vacation, sir. What are you doing about this mess?"

He jumped as his eyes focused on the angry President and replied. "Mr. President, the ships and our troops are in the war zone, and I believe the mere appearance of them was the determining factor that led the nations threatened, to sit down and talk things over sir."

"Yes, yes, how is that going along for us anyway, General Weidenbacher?"

"Well Mr. President, you have to understand sir. Both feuding sides agreed to a meeting to take place in Arabia, but not until next week, sir."

"You mean I'm going to be forced to sit on pins and needles until then, General?"

"Not really Mr. President, ever since the two sides offered to speak of peace, the nations in question dropped their war footings, sir. The only thing we still have to guard ourselves against, are the small groups of asses trying to take matters in their own hands, sir. This is the reason we're putting United Nations troops on all borders leading into Israel sir, to try and stop any rebel Arab group from attacking them, or the reverse sir. Mr. President, we're guarding the Arab nations from any right wing Israeli groups attacking their countries sir, and causing a war to break out sir." General Weidenbacher took a quick breath in.

President Cole took a swig of cold coffee and made a face. His weariness showed as he looked at the General, knowing he had something to ask, but it would not come to him. He pointed at the officer then groused. "General, there was something on the table, but it escapes me now."

"Cuba, Mr. President?" General Weidenbacher asked more in a question than an answer.

"Yes, yes of course, that's it sir. What the hell's happening down there for the love of God? Christ Almighty, I can't get over this crap. This world's getting to be nothing but trouble for me lately, sir. Well General, can you brief me on the happenings in Cuba, sir?"

"Mr. President, I was forced to cut a number of my support ships in half in the Cuban area sir, more than half really sir. But what I have left is still stationed within striking distance of Cuba, and I could have troops air dropped on the Island in fifteen minutes if I had to push the issue on the Island if things started to get out of hand and we..."

"Are these troops the damn exile troops we were training in the States you're speaking about before this mess in Israel started, sir?"

"Yes Mr. President, I have the 199th Cuban Infantry Freedom Force stacked up on the ship the Kearsarge, sir. I held back the Aircraft Carrier the United States and her support Task Force, she's going to anchor up for the invasion force to be..."

"Are these the troops you have standing by for this possible mission, General?" Norman Griffin asked the officer, the Security Director showed up a short while ago for the meeting, after the Vice President put out a call another meeting was taking place in the Oval Office. The other members were willing to allow Raincloud and Weidenbacher shoulder the bulk of the discussion. Everyone realized the President was not in a good mood, and no one wanted to have his wrath fall upon them.

"No Sir Mr. President, at this time I have three thousand Rapid Reactionary Force Marines on the Aircraft Carrier the United States, along with two thousand Marines on board the Wasp assault ship, sir. On the other ships with this Carrier Task Force, I have two Mechanized Brigades. Add this to the forty four Apache fast attack helicopters, and the seven Wings of aircraft on board the Carrier, I'd say we should be able to handle anything breaking out on the Cuban Island, sir."

"Great, I'm glad something's working out for us in this mess, sir. When do you plan to move on Cuba, General?" the President asked, showing more interest in his response.

"I don't know sir, I guess I was kind of holding back some until we knew for certain what's happening in the Middle East. I didn't want to commit these troops to action on Cuba, in case all hell broke out in the Middle East and these troops might have been needed there, Mr. President."

"That's a wise idea on your part, General. Don't move against Cuba until I give you the green light. I wish I could find that smoking gun, dammit." The American Leader bitched.

BEAL AIRFORCE BASE, MARYVILLE, CALIFORNIA.8:33 A.M. EST SUNDAY, SEPTEMBER 29th,1996 PST. (PACIFIC STANDARD TIME)

It took the Airforce technicians longer than it was expected to develop the SR-91's film, moments passed before the ones studying the photos showed any concern. On photo frame 54, there appeared to be something in the water, it looked like just a dry hole in the middle of a lake. The technician did everything in their power to try and enhance the picture, but whatever he did made the blotch look like a hole in the water which he knew was impossible. The rest of the photos showed nothing except for an unusual amount of workers milling about in the middle of the night. The spray from the nearby water hurt the clarity of the infrared pictures, many were blotchy, and some did not come out at all.

The technician called for the rest of the lab techs to keep an eye out for the section marked C-8 by M-1 and one found another photo of the area and he rushed it over to the lead technician. He studied the photo, the hole in the water was gone, but it looked like something was moved around under the water. After checking the shore he noticed tracks leading to the water and he mumbled more to himself. "I wonder what the hell these people are launching in the water. Could they have launched a mini-sub, dammit?"

The technician, who brought over the second photo, carried another. He placed it down on the table and he grumbled to the lead technician. "Sir, I found something and I don't know what to make of it sir. I never saw anything like it before and it has me baffled. Maybe you can make some light of the photo, sir."

After studying the photo, the lead technician came to the conclusion it looked identical to the first one, and he started to believe it was some kind of glitch in the film. He figured the angle of the shot and the obvious different position of this showed a hole in the water on the second pass by the spy plane.

It was not until the lead technician compared both photos together that he realized he had something on them. He saw the two holes in the water and they were in different locations in the area. They were close by, but yet apart. All the technicians in the lab gathered around the lead man, and they studied the pictures while giving their opinion of what the black spots might be in the water. No technician could come up with a believable response to what the black marks might be showing up on some pictures, or in the water. One technician offered the spots could be a fishing trap, but this suggestion was laughed off by the others, causing the lead technician to remark. "Why the hell would the Cubans use what obviously looks like lab technicians for fishing attempts, mister?"

This response caused the lab man to offer an excuse for the Cubans actions. "Maybe they're trying to do something with the fish. We know Cuba's having trouble feeding her people. Could they be trying to experiment on a certain species of fish to increase the catch, sir?"

The lead man though about this remark for a moment then he made his offering. "No Sam, I believe you're wrong on this one. The men are working much too close to shore for this to be some kind of a experimentation with fish. No, I believe this is something more sinister then that, sir. I think we're going to be forced to seek help from the outside on this one, people. Martha, please get me the FBI headquarters, see if they can send down one of their photo observations people. Someone more familiar with analyzing reconnaissance photos, please."

At five minutes of nine, a member of the FBI strolled through the doors and he picked up a cup and poured himself coffee. Then he looked at the technician and smirked as he asked. "Okay Billy, whaddaya got that's causing you an itch in your jockies, my old friend."

"Right here Carl." The two worked together before. Bill laid out the two photos on the table, and stood by as the FBI Agent checked them. "Hmmm, it looks to me as if they're some kind of holes in the damn water. What the hell are the asses up to down there?"

"I was kind of hoping you could tell me what they might be doing there, Bill." The lead lab technician mumbled as he continued to study the two photos in concern.

"Nope, never saw anything like these things before sir. You think it might be a chunk of metal under the water that's giving the appearance of a hole in it, sir?"

"That's a possibility Carl. I never gave that idea a thought myself, sir."

The technician who found the other picture added. "If that's true then how come it looks like there's no water inside the hole or even over it in the photo, sirs."

The FBI Agent leaned closer to the picture and he studied it again and then complained. "Holy shit Billy, I think he's right. I don't believe there's any water in the damn hole, sir."

"This is starting to bug the shit out of my ass, Carl." Bill moaned as he continued to study the picture, and he searched his mind to see if he saw anything like it before at the same time. He could pull up nothing and grumbled. "Christ Carl, I don't know what the hell to make of it dammit, but whatever the hell it is, it has to be bugging the crap out of the Navy people as well. They're the ones who requested the photo run to be taken in the first place, sir. They warned us they were certain something was going on down at the Guanahacabibes Peninsula in Cuba. And from the looks of it, we might have found the something they're so damn worried about, sir."

"Is that a fact? Then why don't you get one of their boys down here to help us out with this damn thing, sir. Maybe they can tell us what the hell the damn thing is." The FBI Agent offered.

"That's an idea, there's a Navy recruiter on the fourth floor of this building, sir. I believe he was an under the waves prick, a submariner I believe I heard it said. He's always bragging about being able to survive a nuclear war under the seas." Bill ordered the technicians to go over the pictures one last time. They were instructed to pay close attention to the area marked down as C-8, M-1, and then he left the lab for the nearby recruiter's office. Bill shared a coffee with Captain Elliot Wisemen while he explained to him what he had. They both waited until a Seaman came in to relieve the Captain before they left for the lab.

Fifteen minutes later, a Seaman came in to the recruiter's office and the Captain bitched at him. "You took your damn time getting here, mister."

The Seamen smiled as he hung up his coat and looked through the morning newspaper.

"I don't want you looking at that damn paper today, mister. While I'm gone from the office, clean up the place some, it's a mess in here mister. Go get some lifer's juice, (coffee) in here, and we need more paper for the copier. I don't know how long I'm going to be gone, so if you run out of things to do, you can always go through the requisition sheets, and make a list of everything I requested and didn't receive as yet, Seaman. We have to keep after these bastards, or we're going to be shit outta luck. They'll give our supplies to the one who cries louder than we do, mister."

"Aye, sir." Was the only thing the kid said while not looking up from the newspaper.

"Are you sure he was paying attention to you, Elliot?" Carl asked the Captain with a smirk.

"You bet'cha, he's a good man sir. He's going to make something of himself in this man's Navy soon. Let's get going." Captain Wisemen put his cover on, and they both headed out of his office together.

"Let's." Bill added as he followed the Navy Officer out his office and then down the stairs.

It took the two ten minutes to get over to the Beal Airforce Base. The FBI Agent was enjoying a second cup of coffee while the lab men continued to pour over the stack of recent recon pictures they had been developing, while Bill was out of the lab for the while.

"Anything new?" Carl bellowed as he poured coffee. When no one answered, he called out. "Break time, thirty minutes." Carl was surprised when none of the workers left, but instead they crowded around the table with the photos. Carl smiled. "Bunch of noise hens."

The Naval Captain moved close to the table as Carl lined up some pictures for him to study and announced. "Here's what's got us so baffled Captain." He handed the Navy man a powerful magnifying glass.

Elliot leaned on the table as he studied the photos in question then asked. "These all you got?"

"We have five hundred photos in all, but these few are the ones we're most interested in." Carl offered as he looked over the Captain's shoulder.

"Hmmm, there's two of them I see here you know, Carl." The Navy Officer offered calmly.

"Two of what, Captain?" Carl asked as he stared at him with concern.

"Hmmm, I don't know, they look like a submarine does when she's open to the air to receive her missile complement, sir. Yep, if I was a betting man, I'd swear to hell and back you people found a pair of underwater missile silos, sir. Where the hell did you guys locate the damn things? Russia?" the Captain asked as he put down the cup.

Carl had a stunned look on his face as he mumbled back at the Navy man. "Cuba sir!"

"Cuba! Man, you gotta be shitting me! Do you have any idea what a fucking discovery like this means to us for God's sake? Damn, the Cuban asshole got himself more god damn missiles on this fucking Island, and you can bet the bank on it they're nuclear in nature, sir. This is a national emergency, man! Have you notified anyone about these things yet, mister?" the stunned Captain was hot as he glared at the lead technician.

"Not yet sir, we didn't know what to make of them before you identified them for us, sir."

"Well man, you betta get on the damn horn then and tell someone about these damn things, and pretty damn quick while you're at it, no? At least the damn things are empty."

Carl looked to his technician. The Captain saw the look and said. "They're still empty right?"

"I don't know sir. There's another picture we discovered. Here you go Captain."

Captain Wisemen stared with his mouth hanging open at the new picture, because he knew right away what the tracks leading to the water meant. He plopped down heavily in a chair as he mumbled more to himself than anyone standing near him. "These sonofabitches just loaded the damn things with their miserable missiles. How many of the fucking things have you discovered on Cuba so far, sir?"

"Out of all the pictures we have, only these few shows anything in the water, sir."

"Son, you can bet your wife's virginity where there's two, there's more, sir. We gotta sterilize the entire region before the damn fools do something we won't like with the damn things. Where the hell's your phone, sir?" Elliot hissed as he looked around the room.

Carl pointed to his desk and they both charged after the phones at the same time. Captain Wisemen placed a call to Naval Headquarters, Washington D.C., while Carl placed his call to Headquarters at Atlantic Fleet, Norfork Virginia, where the requested SR-91 flight originated.

Elliot got through first by classifying his call as a Level One priority call to his Commander. He spoke with an Admiral Richie, and explained to him what he discovered on the spy photos, and he was told to hold the line. Seconds later he was speaking directly with the Chief of Naval Operations at the Pentagon. Major Vincent Guaglardi answered the phone. When Elliot explained what he found, he was again ordered to hold the line. Seconds later, he spoke to the man himself, Admiral Thomas Standlund of the Joint Chiefs of Staff.

After Elliot explained what was discovered on the photos, the stunned Admiral took down his information, and then ordered him to scramble fax the pictures to his office. While he waited, he ordered the Captain to report to the Pentagon when they finished speaking. He had to put the Captain on hold for a few moments while he answered a second emergency call.

This second call was from the lab technician, Carl Goodman. The Admiral had to cut off the excited man, and informed him he was speaking to Captain Elliot Wisemen standing next to the lab man. Embarrassed, Goodman hung up and punched the Naval Captain in the arm.

"What?" He moaned back at the grinning Carl as he stared back at him for a few seconds.

"We're speaking to the same fricking man in Washington at the moment Captain, dammit."

Elliot shrugged at Carl, but he had to cut off his conversation with the lab technician when the Admiral came back on the phone. The Admiral received the three pictures sent to him by Wisemen locked in his hand, and he complained at the Naval Officer. "Jesus Christ Almighty Captain, these god damn pictures are piss poor shots at best, mister. With all the damn money we're pouring into them damn ass expensive spy planes of yours sir, you'd think by now they'd be able to take better photos than these shits for us, Captain. I can barely make out anything clearly on the damn things, sir"

"Understood sir, but the technicians explained the pictures quality is poor, because they were taken by infrared cameras that are affected by salt water spray. I believe that the..."

"I don't give a good god damn shit about all that other crap, sir. Look Captain, I didn't ask you for a photo lesson, mister. I got the damn pictures so get your ass over here PDQ sir." The Admiral hung up and pressed the intercom and said into it. "Ahhh... Kathleen, where the hell's the damn Chairman at please?"

His secretary fumbled through a number of papers and replied. "Admiral Standlund, General Weidenbacher's at a scheduled meeting with the President sir. Seems he's been there all night as far as I can tell, sir."

"You better patch me through to him right away. I have a Level One Communication for him."

"Very well Admiral Standlund." The secretary did as she was ordered and within moments, she was speaking with the Marine soldier monitoring the console for the White House. The officer told her to hold the line for a moment while he notified the General he had a Level One coming in. The Marine left the console and walked over to the General and whispered in his ear. "General Weidenbacher Sir, you have a LO coming in sir."

"Yeah, from who?" he asked as he turned to the Marine leaning on him.

"Sir, Admiral Standlund's on the horn sir." The guard whispered low to him.

"Is there a problem here General Weidenbacher?" President Cole asked when he saw the concerned look on the General's face.

"I don't know yet Mr. President. It seems I have a Level One communication from Admiral Standlund, sir."

CIA Director John Raincloud stared at the General for a moment, because he understood what a call of this magnitude meant to them. The last one was placed when President Bush informed command he was committing the troops to the war in Iraq.

Without a word, Weidenbacher went over to the radio set. The Marine Major stiffened up as he offered. "General, it's a scrambled transmission transmitted by the Admiral, sir. The unscrambled report will come out on this machine for you sir. You'll have to answer that one."

He grabbed the phone. "Yeah Woody, whaddaya got for me sir?"

"General Weidenbacher, I had a troubling conversation with a Captain Wisemen at Beal, sir."

"What the hell's he doing at Beal, that's an Airforce Base, and he's a damn Navy puke, sir?"

"He was requested there by a lead lab technician General. It seems one of our Cruisers stationed on duty picked up something going on in Cuba sir, and he requested a flyover by one of our SR aircraft, sir. The lab boys were going over the pictures and they located what seems to be a pair of underwater missile silos. The Captain sent a series of photos along with his report to me, and he believed the silos to be missile bound sir. We have tracks made on the sand by a possible missile transports, and we believe the missiles were set in position in the silos just today, sir."

"Whattt! What you fuck are you trying to tell me here god dammit, Admiral Standlund Sir? How the fuck did the damn Cubans been able to pull this one off on us, sir."

All eyes at the meeting went to the upset General as he tried to keep his voice calm and low at the same time.

"Fraid so General, I have the pictures on hand and although they're piss poor in clarity, you can plainly see what he's talking about, and what's got him concerned about damn things sir. I had some on my men go over the photos also, and they agree with Elliot's assumption, sir."

"Jesus, I don't believe this shit. How the hell did the damn Cubans get their damn hands on a number of fucking missiles? They're nuclear I take it, Admiral?"

"Fraid so sir. At least that's what the Captain believes they are sir, and I agree with him sir."

President Cole was on his feet and he rushed over to the console and demanded to listen in on the conversation. The Marine opened a line making the Admiral ask. "What was that sir?"

"It's me Admiral Standlund Sir, our President and Commander In Chief, mister."

"He's on the other line Woody." Weidenbacher offered to the Admiral.

"Oh, hello sir. And how are you today Mr. President?" the Admiral asked him calmly.

"Never mind that what's this shit about the Cubans having nuclear missiles on the damn Island again, sir?" the President asked with concern lacing his voice

"Sorry sir, but I believe it's true, Mr. President." The Admiral offered to him.

"Where were they able to get their hands on these damn things for the love of God sir?" the American Leader demanded to know from the Admiral angrily.

"Mr. President, we believe they were probably secretly smuggled on the Island over the year's sir. One of my men believes the underwater silos were constructed during the original missile crisis of 1962 and we missed it, sir."

"Are these damn things you're speaking about that old, Admiral Standlund?"

"No Sir General Weidenbacher." The Admiral replied while fielding the questions from the President, and then the General at the same time. "We analyzed a series of tire tracks leading to the water, and we come to the conclusion the missiles in these underwater silos might be the mid-aged SS-18 model 4 type, with ten nuclear warheads apiece on them..."

"Are they are believed to be ICBM's Admiral Standlund Sir?" the President demanded.

"Could be sir, but I have to remind the President we're only speculating at this point as it is, sir. We have no clear pictures of the missiles in question as of yet, Mr. President."

"Well then, I suggest you get some pictures, so you're no longer speculating, Admiral. What the hell do you think I'm paying you for to get your best guess, mister? I want answers, and I want them now!" President Cole hung up and stomped to his desk, resting his head in his hands.

The General remained standing, and he was steaming as he roared. "How many of these damn things do you think these sonofabitches have down there, Woody?"

"General Weidenbacher, I had the lab techs go over all the pictures for a second time with a fine tooth comb, sir. They reported they have located a potential of at least six concrete covers in waters on the damn Peninsula, as deep as six feet in the water, sir. I believe they're right sir, we can count on a minimum of at least six missiles on Cuba, sir."

"Well that changes the picture a might, Admiral. Look Woody, I want you to stay in contact with me on this one, sir. I want to know the moment you can tell me what kind of missiles these pricks have down there, and how many of the damn things they have. Most importantly the number of warheads on each birds (missiles) and the range of the missiles, sir." With that said, the General broke off the communication with the Admiral and he turned to the President.

"Mr. President, it looks like we might have found our smoking gun sir. I believe the new Cuban military leader has created the diversions taking place in the Middle East and Israel to cover his tracks with these missiles. He successfully removed our eyes from his Island and had us aim them at the Middle East while he set these missiles in the silos, sir." The General offered in an extremely angry tone of voice.

"You don't mean to tell me Cuba was behind these attacks on Israel and the Arab States, sir?"

"I believe that might be the fact, Mr. President." General Weidenbacher offered.

"Explain this reasoning General Weidenbacher!" the President barked at him.

The rest of the members at the meeting leaned forward in their chairs to hear every word spoke by the General. None of them wanted to miss anything said by the General.

The Chairman of the Joint Chiefs of Staff rolled his eyes as he began speaking. "Mr. President, you have to realize what the hell's on Cuba, sir. Evidently, Castro was able to get his hands on a number of ICBM's he had smuggled onto the Island, when I don't know sir. These damn missiles were to be placed inside the underwater silos which were obviously build during the missile crisis of 62, and they sat dormant for all these years, sir. Mr. President, it was long believed Castro was able to hide a number of the older Russian missiles on his Island someplace, but we were never able to prove it until now, sir. I guess these missiles were smuggled onto the Island sometime in the past few years to replace the older and more unreliable missiles and warheads, or they were brought on the Island to fill these underwater silos, sir. Perhaps Castro never had any of the older missiles on the Island of Cuba until now sir."

"That's all fine, well, and good General. But it still doesn't explain the so called smoking gun theory you spoke of to my satisfaction, General. Why the hell would this new President of Cuba send out a number of terrorist to attack Israel, Jordan, Lebanon and Syria, sir? I don't understand this way of thinking even though you offered some idea why he ordered this, sir."

"I'm afraid it's simple to figure it out for yourself, Mr. President..."

The General was interrupted by an angry President. "Well then General why the hell don't you spell it out for this god damn simpleton sir. Because I don't see why the Cubans would ever carry out such severe attacks on innocent nations of the world, attacks that could have easily started a World War if the terrorist attacks were allowed to go on unchecked, General."

"I'm sorry for my poor choice of words Mr. President. With all due respect sir, if one was to look at what's taking place on Cuba sir, we'd understand the severe ramifications of the new Cuban President's actions, sir. Once he has the missiles set in their launch silos then he'd be holding a fist full of trump cards against us he would use to neutralize us by involving the nuclear weapons into the mix, sir. If we choose to use the path this new Cuban President is forcing us down, Russia, China and a host of other countries would be trying to stand on our damn throats to try and block us from retaliating against them with our own nuclear weapons. Sir, you can bet dollars to donuts if the Russians find out the new Cuban government installed the missiles in the underwater silos, they'd be doing everything under their power to get their noses in on some of the action, sir.

"We know Russia feels they could hold the upper hand against us, if they got some operating nuclear missiles on Cuban soil before we had a chance to react against them, sir. We know we dodged the damn bullet when we found out about the missiles they were installing on Cuba during the Kennedy Administration, sir. If we didn't find out about those damn things until they were installed and operational, the damn things would still be there and we'd be being held hostage by this little bastard of a country Mr. President, and Russia would still be a nuclear world power and a serious threat to the..."

President Cole let out his breath as he glared at the General and said. "I understand this General, but it still doesn't explain why the Cubans attacked Israel, and the Arab nations."

"Sorry Mr. President, but this new President of Cuba must know we have an active Task Force sitting off his shores, and he felt he had to install the missiles if he stood any chance of negotiating a compromise, a solution where he'd hold onto his power over the damn Island, sir. We know as well as he does, it's only a matter of time before these civilians takes over Cuba, and he'll find himself shit out of luck, sir.

"He must have understood if he tried to install the missiles in the silos while this Aircraft Carrier Task Force was in their waters, we would've known the instant one of these missiles were moved from its hiding place, and horsed into the damn silos. This Cuban President realized he had to create some kind of a diversion against us to get the eyes of the world away from his shores, and shifted onto another country, sir. Thus, the damn attacks on the Middle Eastern nation's sir." The General spread his hands apart and then shrugged at the upset President.

President Cole sat in stone silence and he staring in space. None of the others at the meeting dared to interrupt his thoughts. His breathing was controlled, but heavy. Vice President Hirshfield made a head movement to one of the Marines, and she whispered to the President."Mr. President, it's getting late, would you and the others care for a coffee break and something to eat, sir?"

The President shook his head to file away everything he was hearing from his officer, as he looked at the Marine manning the door, he finally replied. "Yes, it's getting later than you think, young man." He scanned the room and added. "Gentlemen, ladies." He looked at Ms' Hirshfield then to Maria Hernandez. "No one is going anywhere until we worked out what the hell we intend to do about this damn missile situation on Cuba, people. Bob, would you mind getting some coffee and sandwiches sent in here so we can continue on with this damn discussion. If anyone needs something stronger to give them added strength to carry on with this meeting, speak up." He went on showing he got his second wind again.

"General, I know our people feel strongly these holes are underwater missile silos, and this new Cuban President installed the missiles in. Err… how many of them are we talking about again, General?"

"The lab boys feel the Cuban technicians have installed at least two of the missiles in their launching silos so far, sir."

"Just two of them General?" the President moaned back at the officer.

"Yes Sir Mr. President." The General replied, knowing the President was pleased.

"Thank God only two of them. But I'm going to play the devil's advocate for the moment, General. No one brought me proof positive these holes in the water are underwater missile silos or even if the Cuban nut has any missiles under his control. This is going to buy me some time, sir. I'm not going to overreact until I'm positive the missiles do exist, and these holes are indeed missile silos, sir. General, this is what I suggest you do sir. I want you to flood this region with every spy plane and operative we have at our command.

"I want pictures, along with proof positive before I react against this one, sir. I don't think any of you could blame me for the course I'm taking. I'm not willing to pound the shit out of this end of Cuba, and then invade the damn Island unless I have the evidence to prove to the world this new Cuban government was preparing to use these nuclear weapons against the United States. General, have the Syrians had any luck breaking them terrorist sonsofbitches, sir? If we at least get evidence these terrorists originated in Cuba, I'd have that much I could react on, sir."

"As far as I know, they're still working on the damn terrorists, Mr. President."

"Dammit, I can't catch a damn break anywhere I twist and turn around here, General."

"Err… excuse me Mr. President, but I have something to offer in this conversation." CIA Director Raincloud spoke up.

"It's about time someone else picked up the ball and started to bounce it around a little. I was getting kind of tired of speaking to just the General at this meeting, people."

529

Chapter Twenty Nine

The President's words created a round of nervous laughter as Director Raincloud stood and he offered. "Mr. President, one of my operatives was able to infiltrate the Cuban civilian Armies' high command. She reported she made contact with Emil Hernandez Nicaro, and his Second in Command, Nicanor Hector Navea. What do you want me to do with her next, sir?"

"Director Raincloud, this is a stroke of luck. This means we can get at them sir."

"Yes sir, indeed it does Mr. President." Director Raincloud replied with a smile.

"Great, have her make contact with Nicaro, and inform him what we found on Guanbibies..."

"Guanahacabibes Peninsula Mr. President." Director Raincloud corrected the President.

"Whatever!" he snapped as he dismissed the correction with a simple wave of his hand and then he went on with is orders for the CIA Director. "Inform this operative she's to inform the civilian leader we'll invade the western section of this Peninsula, and then destroy the damn missiles and installation. I want this operative to offer our services to this civilian leader. Tell him we could coordinate our attack on this end of the Peninsula, while his civilian forces attack from the upper section of the Island, sir." The President looked at Raincloud while waiting for him to respond.

"Err... excuse me Mr. President, of course you understand this move would critically compromise my operative and place her life in extreme danger, if she follows these orders sir."

"Why is that Mr. Raincloud?" the President asked the CIA Director with some concern.

"Well Mr. President, suppose this civilian leader's not opened to our advances, and he takes it upon himself to kill my operative because she's a spy for the United States, sir?"

"I'm sure your operative knew the risks that came with her job, no Director Raincloud?"

"That's true enough I guess Mr. President. But if this Nicaro fellow kills her then I'll be losing an extremely important source of up to date information from Cuba sir, one I can ill afford to do without, Mr. President."

"I understand this John, but you have to understand the seriousness of this frigging situation, Director. If this operative's able to convince the civilian leader to allow us to join his cause, we'd be establishing communications with the next possible ruling party of Cuba, sir. Let alone possibly adverting a World War while we're at it, or at least stopping a messy Middle Eastern war, Director Raincloud."

"You're correct Mr. President, I'll inform her to make contact with Nicaro and let her know what she's supposed to offer him, if he allows us to help his fighters with his attempted takeover of Cuba, sir."

"Thank you, John. Please get it done then and get back to me as soon as possible sir."

Director Raincloud stood and headed for the console. Moments later he spoke with his operative in Cuba.

"General, how are you doing getting those damn spy planes over this Peninsula, sir?"

"I'm still working on it Mr. President." The General was by the radio, and he was in direct contact with Command of the Aircraft Carrier the United States sailing off the coast of Cayman Islands. "Yes, Captain Haverlin that's right sir. I want constant flights over the Cuban Guanahacabibes Peninsula from this point on sir. Take pictures of anything that moves, if a dog shits, I want a fucking 8x10 glossy of the product. Send the photos to station. S-1."

"Aye General Weidenbacher, I'm scrambling the flights as we speak, sir." Captain Haverlin was standing on the Pry-Fry deck of his Carrier, and he hit the panic button as his voice bellowed over the intercom. "All hands stand by. All OS-3 Officers report to their aircraft. B personnel report to your assigned stations. Fire watch to stations. All deck personnel prepare for immediate launch of aircraft. That is all."

Deck alarms blared throughout the massive Aircraft Carrier, as the observation and surveillance pilots rushed to their waiting planes sitting on the deck of the ship. The first aircraft to be launched was an E-2C Hawkeye radar aircraft to help coordinate the other air flights over the Island of Cuba. Next to launch was a pair of F-18 Hornets equipped with cameras to film every inch of the suspected target area on Cuba. Two other Hornet aircraft were lined up on the catapults, and they were scheduled to launch when the first Hornets ran out of film. Haverlin decided he was going to have a pair of planes over the requested area in question at all times, so he did not miss a second of any of the activity being carried out on the tiny Peninsula. He ordered the pilots of the Hornets to protect themselves by any means, if they came under attack in flight.

The pilots took this to mean they had permission to engage and destroy any Cuban planes sent to engage them. The pilots prayed for an enemy aircraft to appear, not since the Desert Storm action had an American flyer destroyed an enemy plane in combat, and these pilots felt it was long overdue to run up their score card.

Haverlin increased the air cap over his Aircraft Carrier at the same time, in case the Lion Flight ran into trouble, he wanted his defending aircraft airborne so they could react to any distress call sent out rapidly.

"Lion Flight Leader to Ironside entered Cuban air space. Am being tracked by two standard radar tracks. No threat and attack radar lockons. Ammo plus zero sir. Over."

"Roger, I copy that last. Understood. Have four Stingers up and waiting if you need help. Over." Stingers were slang for the fast attack Hornets flying air cover for the surveillance craft.

"Understood as stated, beacon on double, (double pulse mode on tracking beacon) am going to commence my first pass over the target area of the Island in two seconds. Repeat, two seconds sir. Am approaching target area at Angels Seven, (Seven thousand feet) at Mach Minus One to create best ATM (Air Target Mosaic). Check starboard, I thought I picked up something back there, sir. Over."

"Roger that, negative on suspected rear contact. Over." Was the reply from the airborne radar search aircraft. "Be advised you're naked in the sky, Lion Flight Leader. Over."

The Lion Flight Leader pilot aligned himself up with his set flight path as he dropped down through the cloud layer until he broke through, and had a clear shot at his target area. Lion Flight Leader saw a number of men working on a trailer. Some workers were in the water, but the pilot paid little attention to them. He was more interested in the trailer and what it contained on its back. The whole back of the truck was draped over by a heavy white canvass, but something was sticking out from the front and the back end of the tarpaulin.

"Weapons free." The lead pilot called out in his radio for his wingman to follow his order.

"Roger that, am arming my master control now. Over." His Wingman replied to the order.

As the Lion Flight Leader began his pass, he smiled as he watched the workers on the ground pointed at his approaching aircraft, and then they ran for cover as they screamed at the guards protecting them.

"Check Six." His Wingman warned him. This was a pilot's order for checking his rear position, to make certain no enemy planes were closing in on them from the tail end of the plane.

"Roger that, am clear on my six. Over." The leader replied in his radio after checking his six.

"Lion Flight Leader to Six Pack. It looks like we caught the ground turds with their pants down around their knees, sir. I'm concentrating my next approach on the large trailer sir, and then I'll hit the water where the men were working, sir Six Pack, I want you to concentrate your first pass a hundred yards off to my right side, sir. It looks like some of the workers ran into what looks to me like some sort of concrete bunker down there, sir. Starting my next photo run. Over."

"Six Pack to Lion Flight Leader. Copy your last as stated sir. State condition and good luck on your next run over target, sir. I'll keep you advised if anything changes on the situation on the ground, sir. Over."

"State is at Tiger Six Pack, I have more than sufficient fuel remaining in my aircraft to complete my mission as ordered. Over." The Lion Flight Leader pilot reported to his Wingman as he dipped his aircraft down, and his tracking radar started tracking his flight for him.

"Eye to Lion Flight Leader. Be advised, you're being targeted by enemy radar hits, sir. Possible Russian made interceptor missiles locking onto your heat feathers, sir. Be prepared to adopt evasive maneuvers. Over." Eye was the Hawkeye radar aircraft stationed off the coast of Cuba for the Hornet's added protection.

"No shit Eye, my damn threat board's screaming like a whore who hasn't gotten any in some days, sir. Cranking up my ECJ (Electronic countermeasures jamming) unit sir. Reporting my cameras is humming away like they're supposed to, sir."

As Lion Flight Leader's aircraft closed in on his target, what drew his attention became clearer until he cried out in an excited voice. "Oh my good God, it's a damn missile resting on the back of the truck, a big one sir."

"Lion Flight Leader to Ironside. The Cubans are placing what looks to me like an ICBM (Intercontinental Ballistic Missile) in a sort of underwater silo or something, sir. Over."

"Ironside to Lion Flight Leader. What state sir? What state sir? (Amount of fuel, ammo and oxygen remaining in the aircraft) Are you sucking bad fumes up your oxygen mask, sir? Over."

Nothing came back over the radio from the pilot of Lion Flight, forcing the Commander of the Aircraft Carrier to call to him over the radio a second time with concern lacing his tone.

"Come back with your last reply Lion Flight Leader. That was a direct order sir. Over."

"Six Pack to Ironside." Six Pack was Lion Flight Leader's Wingman for this flight. "Lion Leader's busy. Two SAM's fired and he's taking evasive action against them. Over."

"Roger that last Six Pack. I have an excited Captain on my hands, and he strangling me for info. He wants to know if you can verify what Lion Leader reported to base. Over."

"Roger his last as stated Ironside. Positive sighting on what is believed to be an ICBM missile on its missile transport system, sir. Have also picked up a concrete bunker type structure hidden well by heavy underbrush with what is believed to be second missile positioned in the doorway of the bunker and prepared to be moved out to another underwater silo. Am also picking up Triple A fire from the Island, sir." Six Pack watched as Lion Flight Leader did a quick barrel roll to his portside, and his plane then jump into a vertical rolling lift, and it went into a high speed yo-yo maneuver. All the while the Lion Flight Leader pilot made the evasive maneuvers, he popped chaff and flares off to help confuse the high speed SAM missiles charging at him.

The Six Pack pilot breathed a sigh of relief when he saw the first missile go after some spreading chaff, and then the second one go after a flare and followed it down to the earth before the missiles harmlessly exploded in the water off the Island.

"Six Pack to Ironside, Lion Flight Leader has successfully evaded two SAM missiles sir, and he's going into a turn to begin his second run on the intended target. Am requesting permission to engage the missiles and batteries on the ground. Over."

"Ironside to Six Pack. Negatory on your last request to attack the SAM missile sites on the ground, sir. You're instructed to take no further action against any ground installations on the Island until further noticed. Am scrambling six Stingers for added protection Lion Flight. You are instructed to make second runs over the target area. Then you're ordered to get the hell out of the area and back to the nest. Your information is more important to command than engaging enemy troops on the Island. Something is going to be done about those long range missiles, but I don't have the power to order it outright. Over."

"Roger that last as received Ironside. Will make two more runs as stated over the target area then clear the area and report back to nest. Over." The lead pilot of the Lion Flight reported to his Commander as he aligned his plane up with the target area again.

Haverlin made his way to his quarters on the Carrier to make an emergency call to the Pentagon in private via the special scrambled radio to S-1. After a series of loud clicks, he spoke directly with Weidenbacher on the radio.

"General Weidenbacher Sir, Captain Haverlin sir." the Captain started off his report.

"Good Captain Haverlin, I'm please you got back to me so quickly, I was about to call you myself, sir. What were you able to find out about the situation taking place on that damn Peninsula I won't try and pronounce the name of?" the Chairman of the Joint Chiefs of Staff asked the Captain with concern lacing his tone.

"General Weidenbacher, Lion Flight Leader's reporting they're picking up an ICBM missile presently stored on the back of a missile transporter vehicle, and there's a horde of Cuban workers moving said missile to the reported underwater silo, sir. The pilot has also reported the presence of a possible concrete bunker with a second missile stationed in the door..."

"Where's the pictures man? I need hard evidence for the Boss Man here, sir." The General growled at the Captain of the Carrier.

"My flight hasn't landed on the Carrier as yet, General. But I felt compelled to make a verbal report to you as soon as I found out this information, sir. When Lion Flight lands, I'll transmit the photos to you instantly, sir. My pilot reported catching an ICBM missile in the open, and has requested permission to attack said installation after they came under SAM attack from the defenders of the Island, General. I refused the permission to engage them at this time."

"That was a wise response, Captain. I don't want anyone attacking that damn installation, not until we find out how far along these assholes are with arming, and aiming those damn things at us, sir. Captain, prepare your ships for an all out invasion of that section of Cuba, sir. We're going to make direct contact with the damn Russians and see if they'll give us any information on how to jam the missile's launch commands, so we can block their launch from the ground sir. Captain, we know there are at least two of the missiles set into position and ready for firing sir.

"That's why I don't want anyone screwing around with that installation sir. Not until we can find out if the missiles have to be set into the fricking silos, or if they can be fired independently, and exactly what conditions are needed for that damn launching. We're not even sure what type of missiles we're going up against as yet, sir. There's a shit load of other crap we have to find out first, before we can react properly to this situation, sir. I want a copy of those damn photos the moment that plane decks down on your ship, sir. You did well Captain Haverlin Sir."

The General broke off the communication, and then he turned to the President and offered him in a calm tone. "With all due respect Mr. President, I'm certain you heard what transpired over the Island of Cuba with our Hornets, sir."

The exhausted and angry President of the United States sadly shook his head yes while putting a disgusted look on his face, and letting out his breath in a rush at the same time, before the extremely powerful and well respected General.

Director Raincloud piped. "Mr. President, I finished speaking with my operative in Cuba, and she assured me she'll be able to speak to Nicaro, sir."

"I don't give a shit about your damn spy or her life at the moment, Director Raincloud. I have a much more important mission on my hands to accomplish, sir. Okay everyone, out of my office while I make contact with the Russian President, people. I'm going to demand to know the exact frequency we need to broadcast to jam the damn launch orders for those missiles of theirs before they're able to launch the damn things at us. Then, I'm going to ream him a new asshole for selling the things to the Cubans in the first place. Okay, I suggest you people get some shuteye for yourselves while you can.

"I'm going to want everyone back in my office within two hours if not sooner, people. Be off with you now. Because once this thing starts, no one will be leaving this office until this situation has come to a conclusion." The upset American President stared at everyone who was in his office, until they all started to file out of the room quickly.

Everyone gathered for the meeting with the President shook their heads in compliance to the last order, and for what was going to be done with the Russian President from the American President, as the rest of them filtered out of the Oval Office to carry out their orders from their Commander In Chief. The Chairman of the Joint Chiefs of Staff wanted to get back to his office for a change, to see if he could find out any new information for himself privately. Director Raincloud went along with him to his office.

The President yawned as he reached for the phone, he was exhausted. He dialed the private number for the Russian President and within moments, he was speaking with him. The American Leader did not mince his words as he growled at the Russian Leader. "President Tkachenko, I have been informed by my Intelligence people your country placed a number of nuclear tipped long range missiles on Cuba soil again. I'm requesting, no check that last statement. I'm demanding the radio frequencies needed to enable my people to interrupt their launch cycle, sir."

Russian President Tkachenko laughed as he mildly protested he had no idea what the frequencies were, nor did he have anything to do with any missiles that might be on Cuba soil. President Tkachenko was interrupted and he was forced to ask the American to remain on the line while he conferred with his associates.

After a few seconds of intense arguing, the Russian President returned to his call from the American Leader and offered. "Ahhh, President Cole, I have been informed these missiles you speak of, do certainly exist on Cuba soil, sir. But these missiles you speak of were sent to Cuba long before I took over the Presidency of Russia, sir. I must admit I'm shocked and deeply distressed over this most disturbing information, sir. I assure you Mr. President, I shall do everything in my power to find this requested information, and I'll severely punish the ones responsible for sending these missiles to Cuba. I, we both learned valuable lessons from the last time our missiles were sent to this rebel land, sir."

President Cole ignored the niceties from the Russian as he fired back. "President Tkachenko, I must inform you I have plans to invade Cuba within the next five hours, sir. With, or without this requested information I'm going to act. I must further warn you, if any Russian missiles are somehow launched at the United States, I shall regard this action as a preemptive strike by your country against the United States, and I'll react accordingly to this attack on my country, sir. President Tkachenko, your country has everything to lose and nothing to gain by withholding this needed information I seek from your government and your military personnel, sir." President Cole paused for effect.

There was a hesitation and then the Russian President replied calmly. "Russia has no intention of attacking the United States in any way, shape, or form sir. We have come too far to turn the clock back to the Cold War days. Any problems facing our two countries can be worked out to the satisfaction of both nations. I'm at a loss to explain how these missiles found their way to Cuba without..."

"That part of this mess doesn't concern me at this particular time, President Tkachenko. Right now, my most pressing needs are for the scrambling code for those damn missiles. My second problem is; I want to know what Russia intends to do once my invasion force lands on Cuba and stops the slaughter taking place on the Island, sir."

"Err... Mr. American President Albert Cole Sir, I assure you Russia has no intention of blocking any invasion of the Cuban Island by your troops under these trying circumstances, sir. But we'll react if your troops go too far with their invasion of Cuba, sir. Let me get this right before I respond further to your words, sir. It's your intention to have some of your brave troops invade Cuba to eliminate the missile situation and nothing more, sir? You have no intention of installing a new government more favorable to the United States, sir?"

"That and the other reasons, we intend to invade the Island of Cuba, President Tkachenko Sir."

"Such as why, Mr. American President?" the concerned Russian Leader asked him.

"Such as stopping the damn slaughter of the civilians on the Island by heavily armed government troops as I stated, President Tkachenko. Also, allowing a working government to takeover of the Island country, one with Cuba and her people's best interests in mind, sir. Also, to repatriate the thousands of exile Cubans living in the United States and elsewhere throughout the world, sir. President Tkachenko, there are many other reasons for American troops to enter Cuba, sir. I'm certain you're aware of most of them at this point as I am, Mr. President."

"Err... American President Cole, I'll have to take this latest request under advisement with my Generals and other advisors, sir. I don't know how the members of Parliament are going to react to any such an aggression taken by the United States against one of Russia's allies, sir."

President Cole lost his temper he was struggling to control since the conversation began with the Russian President. "Russia's allies shit! President Tkachenko, you don't care what happens to Cuba. She's as much a thorn in your side as she is to us, and the other Caribbean nations. I believe if you look at what's happening in Cuba, you'll realize something has to be done to stop the slaughter on the Island, sir."

"Perhaps, but nevertheless I'll have to discuss this with other members of my government."

"You do that, but you better also warn them we're going into Cuba in less than five hours time, and it's up to you as to how much of the country would be left after we invade it, sir. If you refuse to give me the codes to stop the missiles from being launched at my country then I'll have no alternative but to consider a surgical nuclear strike to eliminate these nuclear tipped Russian made missiles before they're launched at the United States, or elsewhere sir."

"This is a serious statement and threat you issued to my nation, Mr. American President Sir."

"President Tkachenko, how the hell do you think your military would react if the United States was instrumental in placing a number of nuclear weapons and their delivery systems within ninety miles of your shore, and you had information these missiles were armed and prepared to be fired at your nation by a madman who caused a savage war to take place in his own country?"

"This is nonsense I believe you're offering me, Mr. American President. The missiles were never placed in their launch silos, and you're worried..."

"All of a sudden, you seem to know a helluva lot more about these damn missiles than you first lead on, Mr. President."

"Ahhh… Mr. American President, I'm merely reading from an old file that was brought to me, sir. It states the missiles are being stored on the Island, and they don't have their nuclear warheads installed on them. Now, you tell me some under trained Cuban technicians installed the warheads to the missiles, and the missiles were place in their launch tubes, sir. Mr. American President, I don't know what to believe now, sir." The Russian Leader smirked into the phone.

"Well let me assure you President Tkachenko, two missiles are set in their launch silos, and a third is in the process of being loaded into its launch silo as we speak, sir. I have the photos." The America President paused.

"This is serious, very serious indeed to understand, Mr. American President. If it's as you say it is then I'd have no course left open, but to back up your request to attack Cuba. Mr. American President, I shall leave you now and check out what you stated to me. If it's as you stated then I shall give you the scramble codes for said missiles, and I'll further support any action you decide to take against the missiles, or this old rebel leader sir. Ahhh... Mr. President, I assure you sir, the missiles were never to be set into their launch silos, sir. This is a breach of trust and their orders by the Cuban government, and Castro will have a lot to answer to me for, sir."

"President Tkachenko, I must inform you Castro is dead, and Cuba is being run by a Colonel Carlos Rafael Hernandez Alvarez, and he's the man setting the your damn nuclear tipped missiles into their launch tubes, sir."

There was nothing but silence on the other end of the phone line for a number of moments.

"Are you still there President Tkachenko?" the American Leader asked into the phone.

"Yes, I'm here Mr. President, but I shall go. I'll be back to you in a moment sir."

It did not take long for the Russian Leader to get back to President Cole and he offered in an excited voice. "Mr. American President, I believe all you told me is true, and Russia will back any decision you make in dealing with this rebel Island of Cuba, sir. Russia and the

United States have come much too far in the past few years, to allow a new rebel and backwards nation such as Cuba is, to interrupt our advances and future progress, sir. I'll get you the scrambling codes before you attack the installation, sir. I'll not allow the missiles to be launched at your nation you have my solemn word on this matter, sir."

"Thank you for this reassuring offer from you and your Administration, President Tkachenko." Both leaders of the two most powerful nations in the world, broke off their connection with each other and they both attended to their own work.

The Chairman of the Joint Chiefs of Staff came back to the Oval Office holding a file as he tapped on the open door.

"Come in General. What's that sir?" President Cole snapped as he looked up from his desk.

"They're the latest photos of Cuba sir, shot by the Hornets from the Carrier United States, sir."

"Let me see the damn things General." The President picked up the photos as he leaned back in his chair and he studied them then offered hotly. "Well General there's no fucking denying they're Russian ICBM missiles alright. How many do you feel this Cuban ass has again, sir? By the way General, I just got off the phone with the Russian President, sir. He promised he was going to give us the scramble codes for his damn missiles, to allow us to disrupt them from being launched at the United States, sir."

"Six missiles in all were detected sir and that's fantastic news, it makes our job a helluva lot easier to carry out, sir."

"You sound pretty positive of the number of missiles down there, General."

"Yes, allow me to show you what the latest pictures depict, Mr. President. Here, sir, here, here, here, here and here. These circles on the photos are the underwater launch silos, sir. We went over the photos with a fine tooth comb and were unable to locate any further concrete caps under the water in the area. This is why I'm positive there are only six missiles in all, sir."

"Any chance they might have some other silos on the Island somewhere else, sir?"

"Not a chance in hell of that Mr. President. We have confidential information the new Cuban President has fled the capital, and he's somewhere on the Peninsula in question, sir. It seems he's intending to use the missiles as his last stand, sir. Mr. President, I believe he's ready to use them to either force the civilian Army back, or force us to respond by destroying the Island. We believe he's in a win all or nothing situation." General Weidenbacher took a seat.

"Are you telling me we're dealing with a possibly unstable character here, sir?"

"Without a doubt Mr. President, a very unstable character that has six nuclear tipped long range ICBM missiles under his thumb, and it looks like he's intending to use them."

"Then we're going to stop him before he pushes that button against us, sir. Where the hell's Director Raincloud at, General Weidenbacher? I need his ass here right now dammit!" the President announced in a rather confident yet slightly angry tone of voice to the General.

"Mr. President, he's outside in the waiting room, sir."

"Why the hell didn't he come in with you General? Get his ass in here toot Sweet sir. I want to know what his operatives are doing in dealing with that civilian ass marching on Havana, sir."

The General got up and went out to get CIA Director John Raincloud.

NICARO'S MOBILE HEADQUARTERS,HEADING
TOWARDS HAVANA

Emil Nicaro sat in his command vehicle as it came to a jolting stop, and an excited female was let in. He was pleased at how it went with the government troops so far, once he killed Colonel Calvo. Ninety percent of the Colonel's troops voted to go with him. The ones he left behind vowed not to attack his civilian fighters, and to allow the fate of Cuba work itself out on its own. The remaining government Army stationed in Matanzas was out of the picture. Nicaro and his civilians were heading towards the capital, traveling at forty miles an hour. Now, Nicaro found himself staring at a beautiful Cuban woman as he asked her. "Yes, what is it I can do for you?"

"Mr. Nicaro, I'm Donna Maria Hernandez Saladrigas, sir." The woman replied.

"Yes." Emil Nicaro offered calmly as he sat up straight and he stared back at this young beauty while rubbing his stubble covered chin. Navea glared at her as she struggled to stay in the chair. Donna Maria knew her life was on the line as the war machine rumbled on to Havana. "What is it you have to speak with me that is so important it caused the stopping of my machine?"

"Emil Nicaro, I work for the American government, sir." The woman announced as she dared to speak who she was working for.

Navea moved to draw his pistol, but Nicaro stopped him by taking his arm and saying to his Second in Command. "I was wondering how long it would take for the dom Americans to make contact with me. Speak, my time is precious. I want to know what the United States has to offer me I cannot attain for myself."

"Nicaro, my government ordered me to inform you of what it has uncovered resting on your Island sir. What is hidden on the Guanahacabibes Peninsula sir? Years ago, Castro hid a number of nuclear, multi tipped ballistic missiles on Cuban soil, sir. This new Revolutionary Presidente has discovered where these missiles were hidden after all this time, and he has set them up for launching at my country. We believe he's going to use them as a threat against your fighters, or against the United States itself, or even both sir.

"Mr. Nicaro, if Presidente Alvarez launches those nuclear tipped missiles at the United States, my country will have no alternative but to respond with her weapons of mass destruction, in an all out effort to destroy these missiles before they leave the ground and strike anywhere within the boundaries of the United States, sir. What I'm telling you is, if Colonel Carlos Rafael Fernandez Alvarez is unsuccessful in stopping your fighters, he's more than willing to see the entire Island of Cuba burn to death in a nuclear hell, sir."

Navea moved his head in a nodding motion at her, and then he made a spitting sound as he barked angrily. "How do we know what you're saying, is true woman? Allow me to remind you of something young lady. The United States has been known to lie to further her own causes."

Donna Saladrigas reached in her pocket and removed the only picture she was sent of the activities happening on the small Cuban Peninsula, and she offered it to Nicaro. Her movement caused Navea to draw his pistol and aim it at her chest. This time Nicaro did not stop him, he feared she might be reaching for a weapon because he did not cave in to her demands. When he saw she removed a picture, he put his hand in Navea's face and he ordered him to back off.

Nicaro took the photo and studied it, with Navea looking over his shoulder. "What is this you show me woman? It looks like a dom hole in the water. Is this what the great America is trying to convince us, are nuclear missiles? Young woman, your government will have to go further than this, to make me believe a mere spot on a dom picture is a nuclear missile aimed at their great country." Navea spat angrily, and he dismissed the photo with a wave of his hand.

"Navea, be still will you for a second and allow me a moment to think." Nicaro growled at him.

Navea stared at his Commander then complained. "Don't tell me you're going to believe this farfetched story from a dom American spy. I say we kill her, and continue with our mission as planned of setting Cuba free of all military rule, sir." Navea aimed his pistol at the American female again who glared at him, daring him to shoot her. Nicaro put his hand up, grabbing the barrel of the weapon and pulled it down again.

"Navea, it's true I don't see any nuclear tipped missiles in this photo. However, my loyal friend, it does show me something I never saw in our waters before. If this hole in the water doesn't have something to do with any cursed missiles then perhaps you can explain what I'm looking at in this picture." Nicaro offered Navea the photo, but he refused to take it as he bitched again at him.

"I have no idea what it might be on that photo. It could be something the Americans superimposed on the picture..."

"Navea, you have to have faith in something my friend. Have we not discussed speaking to the Americans on many occasions in the past, especially if we found ourselves beaten back by government troops? I look on this as a God send. We know sooner or later we're going to win this final war to plague Cuba, and the Americans want to help by offering to fighting on our side. What more can we ask for from the Americans, or anyone else in this world for that matter. Navea, I'm going to override you on this worry, and allow the Americans to help us, if they so choose to assist us. And, if they need our help in return, we'll give it to them willingly." Nicaro turned back to the female American operative and said. "Young woman, what is it your government wants from us?"

Donna Maria let out the breath in a relieved sigh and she replied. "Nicaro, my government wants to invade your Island in the Guanahacabibes region sir. Our forces, consisting of many exiled Cubans, will attack this installation containing the Russian missiles, sir. We'll assume the responsibility for the missiles and what happens to them when, and after we attack. My government will not hold Cuba or any of your fighters responsible for the actions of this new Revolutionary President, if we're allowed to attack this installation..."

"There, you see Nicaro, it's as I told you all along this was nothing more than a plan devised by the untrustworthy Americans so they could invade our Island. You see how the cursed fools plan against us constantly. See, how the Americans intend to bring the cowardly exile fools back to our Island, and once the American troops are allowed to take a hold on the Guanahacabibes Peninsula. They'll do everything in their dom power to bring these cursed coward exiles that chose to run from Cuba to safety in the United States rather than stand and fight with us for her freedom. Where were the exiles when our citizens suffered under the thumb of Castro?

"You don't have to answer my question because I'll tell you where they were. They spent their time sitting on the dom beaches in the United States, safe and sound while we were being slaughtered by the thousands by Castro and his thugs. Now, they'll come marching back to Cuba after scores of us have laid down their lives to free Cuba, and takeover. We'll again find ourselves standing on the outside looking in. We'll be powerless to do anything about the dom exiles once they're on our Island receiving America's support. The United States will get what it wanted all along, someone running Cuba they can control. I say we kill this American female spy, and send a letter to the American government stating, thanks, but no thanks. Nicaro, you have to believe it's a..."

"Navea, will you be still. With all your chattering, I cannot think properly my friend."

"But Nicaro, you cannot believe anything this female spy says to you. Nicaro..."

"God dommit Navea! For the love of God, will you be still so I can think please."

Navea glared at Nicaro as he studied the photo a second time then he turned to Navea and offered. "I'm sorry to bark at you so, but you have to allow me the space to make a decision. Arrr... Navea, I know you're not going to like my judgment on this situation. But it'll remain as I said. We'll allow the Americans to help us, and in return we'll help them. I'm not afraid to allow the worthless exiles back on our Island. Think Navea, if we beat back the government troops which numbered nearly a million men, what challenge would a force of a couple thousand exile troops offer against us?"

"How many American troops will be involved in this invasion force?" Navea spat at him.

"That was a good question Navea. When you take the time to think with your mind and not your anger, you make good sense." Nicaro turned to the woman and asked. "How many American soldiers will be involved in this?"

"I cannot answer that for certain, because I don't know. From what I was led to believe, America was going to allow the exile forces do most fighting for their country, and the American troops were going to intervene if the exiles got bogged down, or if there was a possibility of their being overra..."

"You see Nicaro, it's like I warned you!" Navea exploded and threw his hands in the air and continued with his anger. "The dom Americans are poised to attack our Island in force, if their puppet fighters run in trouble. Does this trouble include our troops also, if we're forced to lock horns with the cowardly exiles?"

Nicaro looked at the American Agent and waited for her to respond to Navea's warning.

"Nicaro, let me assure you the full weight of the United States military will back your government once it's firmly established on your Island, sir. The only reason the United States wanted the exiles to be a dominate actor in this invasion, is because she's hoping the exiles will linkup with the civilian resistance fighters, meaning yourselves. Between the two civilian forces, you should be able to establish a true, working Cuban government, run by only Cuban civilians, with no military members. Nicaro, if for any reason you choose to ignore the exiles in your government, so be it sir. That's your decision to make, and is on your conscience sir. We'll not try to change it, all my country wants is for you to allow the exiles who want to move back to Cuba, to be able to do so, sir." The Agent shrugged, and then added. "It's that simple sir."

Nicaro smiled at the agent as he offered her. "It'll be as I stated. We'll work together, but on my terms. I'll stop my convoy for fifteen minutes. While we're stopped, I'll allow you to get in touch with who you have to speak with to have my request carried out by your invasion troops. Tell your government I want some of your soldiers air dropped to our position. I'll hold these men as my wards for lack of a better term. If there's any treachery on America's part, it'll cost the lives of these soldiers. Stop this machine and order my fighters to take this time to eat and rest for a while. We'll fight again in a short time."

Nicaro's vehicle came to a sliding stop, and he allowed the agent to use his radio to communicate with her control in the United States. After a few moments, the agent turned to Nicaro and said. "The soldiers you wanted are in the air as we speak, Nicaro. Where do you want them deposited, sir?"

"We shall stay right where we are until the American plane finds us, and they shit out these fine soldiers of yours. I'll remain still for one hour. After that time, if the American soldiers are not here the deal will be off and you'll be dead. I'll piss on your body for daring to lie to me."

She turned back to the radio and relayed the request then broke off the communication and informed the civilian. "Nicaro the soldiers will be overhead in fifteen minutes or so, sir."

"Good, then we shall wait for your brave soldiers to arrive, woman. Would you care for something to eat or drink? We have plenty of provisions to choose from, more than most of our civilians have to survive on, woman."

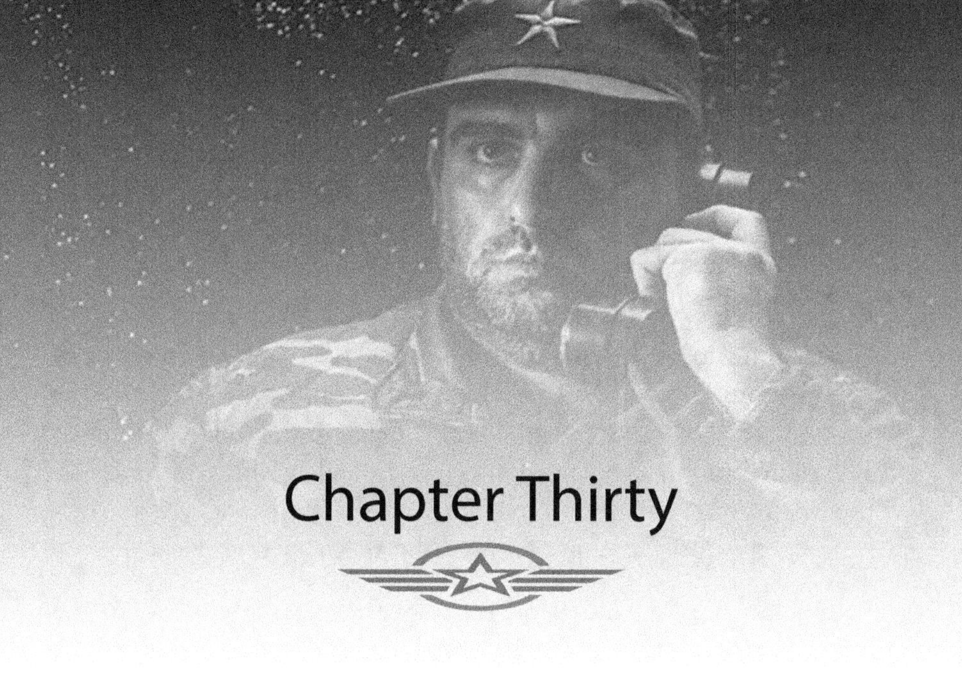

Chapter Thirty

THE ISLAND OF JAMAICA

Corporal Robert Walker, and the few American soldiers scheduled to take part in the invasion of Cuba, were cut away from the rest of their troops then transferred from the Carrier United States, to Jamaica where a C-17 Globemaster transport aircraft waited for the soldiers on the tarmac of the airfield. Walker's troops were the ones elected to be air dropped to the civilian forces on Cuba. He took a few of the exile fighters with him as interpreters. The Mutt was bitching all the way, complaining he was a foot soldier not bird shit.

Walker and his troops strapped themselves in the metal chairs as the transport aircraft lifted off the civilian runway heading out on its mission. In minutes, the plane along with two Hornet fighter aircraft as escorts was humming towards Cuba. The C-17 turned on its approach, and the troops were ordered to prepare to jump out of the opening tail ramp of the lumbering war plane while in flight.

Again, the Mutt complained causing Walker to snap at him. "Put a sock in it will ya Homes and do as you're ordered for once in your wasted life, old buddy."

The Corporal was going to be the first to jump so he stared at the red blinking light, waiting for it to turn green. When it did, he yelled to the other soldiers with him. "The first one down gets Sally suck'em Silly from Philly for the whole night to do with what he will, people."

The Mutt watched him go and he yelled. "The last dick out sucks shit outta a dead dog's ass."

The chutes looked like large white flower blooms drifting slowly to the earth seven thousand feet below the soldiers. Walker saw the column of armored vehicles parked off the side of their target highway, and he pulled on his control lines to make the drift chute move closer to the line of war machines. He landed on the road with a thud then ran a few steps until his chute released the air trapped under it.

The Mutt almost landed on top of Walker as he crashed to the ground, cursing all the way as he yelled. "Hey Homes, get outta the way or I'm gonna land in your stinking pocket."

The civilian fighters rushed out and gave the Americans a hand wrestling with the flowing chutes, as the other soldiers landed safely on the road. The group was rushed over to Nicaro, but before they were allowed to speak to him, Walker's soldiers were relieved of their weapons.

Nicaro came out of his machine and offered the one he thought was in command of the other soldiers his hand.

Walker took it and said. "I guess you're the main Home Boy I'm supposed to hook up with."

Nicaro looked at Walker as if he was speaking a foreign language.

The exile fighter Walker took with him as interpreter, moved closer to the Cubans. The exile smiled as he offered it was a form of American street slang the weird looking soldier was speaking, causing Nicaro to chuckle a bit and he informed Walker he spoke English.

"Okay man, what's the fricking scoop then sir? When do I get my fucking weapons back sir? I feel naked without them, sir. A soldier without a weapon is just another damn civilian. If you want some damn good fighters on your side then you betta give me my cap gun back, and get the hell outta my way, sir." He grunted in his poor Spanish as he stretched, shook his arm to get the stiffness out of it then he stared at Nicaro.

"Your weapons? Why were your weapons taken from you? What good is a soldier to me if he is unarmed? Miguel, give these Americans their weapons back. Err..."

"Corporal Robert Walker, betta known as Road Kill, at your service sir. What are my orders, sir?" he clicked his heels as he bowed slightly to the grime covered civilian before him.

"A Corporal, I was hoping for Officers to join us, mister." Navea grumbled nastily.

"There are no Officers involved in the whole damn invasion force, buddy. All Officers work from the cheap seating behind all grunts, sir." Walker replied just nastily to the other civilian who glared at him for no reason.

"Okay Walker." Nicaro began to speak with the American soldier, but he cut him off sharply.

"Road Kill if you don't mind sir." He retorted with a grin to the civilian leader.

"Road Kill? Very well Road Kill, you and your soldiers will join forces with me and the rest of my people on the advance line. American, if you fight as well as you brag then we should win this war by night fall at the latest, sir." Nicaro added, causing everyone standing with him to laugh as the Americans were lead into Nicaro's armored vehicle. The Cuban exiles accompanying Walker's group, were lead to a second machine to separate them.

THE WHITE HOUSE, WASHINGTON D.C. 10:30 A.M. EST SUNDAY, SEPTEMBER 29th, 1996

President Albert Cole was tired and angry as hell the Russian Leader had not got back to him yet, because he was locked in of the Oval Office for hours. He enjoyed one and a half hours of sleep since the Situation Room meeting broke up. General Weidenbacher,

Director Raincloud, the Secretary of State, National Security Director, Vice President, Secretary of Defense, and two Senators were with him. General Weidenbacher had General Claiborne, his Air Force Chief of Staff, along with the Chief of Naval Operations, and his Senior Military Officer present. The General had a phone line set up between the Oval Office and the Pentagon, and he was running his operations from the President's office for the time being.

President Cole just lit up a cigar when the phone rang, and the Marine guard announced. "Mr. President Sir, it's the Russian President on the line for you sir."

The American Leader grabbed the phone as if he was going to choke it, as he stabbed his cigar out in the astray. "President Tkachenko! I was worried you were going to fight me on this one, sir." He said while laboring to breathe, as he waited for the Russian to reply.

"Mr. American President Cole, I'm sorry it took me this time to get back to you, sir. But I had to make certain what you told me was true. I'm sorry to inform you sir, but everything is the truth. It's true we delivered six SS-18 ICBMs, but this was done long before I came to office and without my knowledge or agreement I add. I never knew these missiles existed until you informed me of them. It's also true this new Cuban President, Colonel Carlos Rafael Fernandez Alvarez, has moved these missiles from their bunkers, and is in process of setting them in their launch silos. Mr. President, I don't know if these Cuban technicians have the knowledge or the capabilities to launch the missiles, there are no Russian technicians helping these Cuban rebels, of this I assure you. I issued orders for my Agents working in Cuba, to make sure these missiles never leave the svinaya (fucking) ground, sir. My operatives are preparing to attack the installation if nece..."

"They can't do that President Tkachenko!" President Cole bellowed in the phone receiver.

"I cannot, and why can I not do as I offered you, Mr. American President?"

"Because President Tkachenko they have at least two missiles set in the silos as we speak, sir."

"I was unaware of this Mr. American President Sir." The Russian Leader stopped speaking to the American and said. "How come I was not aware of this fact?" the Russian President was heard yelling at someone obviously in his office.

"I told you of this already, never mind President Tkachenko. You have to stop that hit squad dammit..." The angry American Leader interrupted the Russian.

"Mr. American President, I already issued the order to back my operatives off. I know they could no longer attack if there was a possibility of the Cuban fools launching any missiles, if they came under attack. I'm afraid the entire area the missiles are in, will have to be erased from the face of the earth. Mr. President, it'll take three hours for my technicians to realign our missiles, for us to hit the area with one of our ICBMs. My technicians assured me one missile will be more than enough to take care of this entire situation, sir."

"That's too damn long. They'll be launched long before then. President Tkachenko, what about the codes? I fear this is our only hope. If we can stop the Cubans from launching the damn things, I have the forces set in position to eliminate the Cuban leader, and take care of the missiles at the same time, sir."

"Err... Mr. President, this request for the scramble codes has cost me much distress and arguments with my military leaders, sir. I must inform you many of my Generals are set against my releasing these codes to you. They warn me once your government knows our codes, even if we change them, you'll figure out our process of developing the scramble codes, and this information would render our nuclear capabilities useless to us. This would give your country controlling power over my country. I don't know what to do sir. I have to respect my General's opinion..."

"President Tkachenko, you have to understand what the outcome might be if this new Cuban leader launches these damn missiles you gave him, sir. Have you explained this to your Generals, sir?" President Cole growled in the phone at the Russian President.

"This I have done sir. But yet my Commanders continue to stand their ground on our national securities, sir. They pointed out what the United States would be able to do to Russia, if she was in command of our scramble codes, sir. Mr. President what would you do if the roles were reversed? Would you be so willing to give us the scramble codes for your nuclear missiles, if we asked for them? Knowing it would render your nuclear fleet useless to you, if you launched your missiles at Russia, sir." The Russian Leader was doing everything in his power to avoid giving the scramble codes to the American Leader.

"Sure I would be upset, it's understandable, but I'd give you the damn codes if it meant saving thousands of civilian lives. President Tkachenko, if you won't give me the damn codes, how about getting some of your people in position to transmit the codes to the missiles themselves, sir. This way, we won't know what they are or how you arrived at the codes, and you'll be able to stop the missiles, and yet still maintain your nation's secrets sir."

There was a fierce conversation held off the line. President Cole could tell Russian President was having a heated discussion with a number of men, probably his Generals. After five minutes, he was back on the line. "Ahhh, Mr. President, this I can do. But my Generals wants to know what your troops intend to do with our missiles, once we render them useless to this new rebel Cuban fool who created these problems for us, sir?"

"We'll destroy the damn things, President Tkachenko." President Cole snapped at him.

"But not before you studied them, and you removed our military secrets, sir."

"If we do this then Russia will have no one to blame but itself. After all President Tkachenko, it wasn't the United States who installed these damn missiles on Cuban soil again, and going against the agreements to both our countries. And, it isn't Russian cities being threatened by the damn things either. Of course we intend to remove the missiles and their warheads from Cuban soil, and have them brought to the United States where they'll be safely dismantled and rendered helpless. Yes it's true any secrets hidden in the missiles will become public information, sir. Maybe in this manner we can start protecting these damn things like they should be protected, along with their damn secrets, until we're able to trust one another. Then the missiles and their damn warheads can be destroyed once and for all." President Cole snapped, growing increasingly angry with the constant stalling Russian Leader.

The Russian understood he had no choice but to agree with anything the American Leader offered. He knew he was caught with his fingers in the honey as he replied. "Mr. President, how do you want to handle this? I can have my General flown to Cuba in seven hours..."

"That's no good, we plan to jump off sooner than that, and we'll need the missiles shutdown before we attack, or I'm going to be forced to change my plans and go in with my missiles, sir."

"Nuclear missiles I assume you're speaking about, Mr. President Sir?"

"You're damn right they'll be nuclear missiles. What choice would I have opened to my actions? I have to stop the missiles your people installed in Cuba before they're fully operational and launched in any manner I deem fit, sir."

"I see, but you have to understand Russia no longer has such travel means at her disposal, sir."

"President Tkachenko, I can have one of my aircraft land in Moscow, pick up your General and have him flown out to Jamaica in one and a half hours. I can delay my attack until that time sir. If you can have the General ready by this time then tell me where you want my plane to land, sir." The President covered the mouth piece, and then he barked at General Weidenbacher.

"General Weidenbacher, I want you to get hold of Beal and inform them I want an SR-91 up and heading for Moscow at full power ten minutes ago. Tell the pilot he's going to pick up some Russian General then he's to get his ass over to Jamaica where I can have him shipped out to the Aircraft Carrier and do his act."

Weidenbacher tapped his forehead with a finger, and then he headed for the console.

"Mr. President, how can you possibly do this great feat you speak of? All my Generals assured me it's impossible to accomplish what you offer in so short a time. No aircraft made could travel at the speeds it would take to travel this distance, in so short a period of time Mr. President." The Russian Leader offered, not believing his own words.

"President Tkachenko, the SR-91 can do it and it's in the air heading for Moscow International Airport, sir. Will your General be ready by then sir?"

"Yes Mr. President, but my General still assures me this is impossible to accomplish, and I'm sorry to offer but he also warns me you must be drunk or dreaming, sir."

"Maybe I am Mr. President, but you have the General at the Moscow Airport in fifteen minutes, and you'll see if I'm drunk or dreaming or not. President Tkachenko, you have to clear the Russian air space for my aircraft. I don't want your gunners taking pot shots at my aircraft and possibly damaging it."

"I'll do as you requested Mr. President. But my Generals still thinks you're talking through your hat, sir." The Russian Leader complained as he broke off the connection.

EMIL NICARO'S CVILIAN FORCES ON THE OUTSKIRTS OF HAVANA

Nicaro, with Corporal Walker by his side, watched as the civilians spread throughout the streets of Havana. Nicaro and Walker were surprised there was no weapon fire, or little if any resistance from what they believed had to be a substantial Army of revolutionary defenders supposed to be deployed in the city. They expected the government defenders to hinder their rapid progress.

Fifteen minutes into the deployment of the civilians in the capital, the first weapon fire started. It wasn't heavy though, just a few machine guns and rifles trading rounds with each other. Nicaro said something to Navea in Spanish, and he disappeared. Walker grinned as he leaned closer to Emil Nicaro and said. "Yes sir and I agree it's stinking strange there's no defenders bugging our asses yet, sir."

"Ahhh American Corporal, you understand Spanish very good for an American huh?"

"Some. Dealing with so many Latino's in America, you're bound to pick up their lingo sir."

"Good, let's get to my machine. We're going to take a ride to the Presidential Palace. Somewhere in the city, there have to be government soldiers waiting to attack us, Road Kill."

The five mile trip from the outskirts of the city to the Presidential Palace was covered quickly. Nicaro engaged in talk with the American, he was curious about the workings of the American military. After many questions answered by Walker, Nicaro asked him. "You surprise me Corporal, you surround yourself with black, and half black men. Are you not going against the flow of your country's beliefs? I was lead to believe there were many racial problems still troubling the United States, and her people?"

"That's a load of shit man, it's the same blood the same mud, the color is green sir. There's no time for that kinda crap sir. You got a problem about being round brothers, sir?"

"No, I never did, nor will I ever have problems working with a black man, sir."

"Good, that last reply will allow you to live another day." Walker glared at the civilian fighter.

Nicaro glared just as hard at the American, angry he dared to speak to him in such a foul manner. Then he decided to let it go, turning to stare out the front window as he went in thought. After a moment, Nicaro asked another question bothering him. "What about the gay soldiers in your Army and your government's no tell policy towards them? In Cuba, we have no such problem with gay soldiers, sir."

Walker stared at the civilian and then snapped. "What the hell are ya doing, writing a fucking book or sumthin? Or are you fishing around for something to bitch about my country. If you wanna know what I think arr..., it's a good solution to a shitty situation. Don't get me wrong, I believe every American should be free to do what the fuck he or she wants. Slip it to whomever. But I feel if your lifestyle goes against the grain, keep it to yourself. Hell, I like eating pussy, but I ain't gonna go round wearing a button bragging bout it. Does that answer your question?"

"Fully, I must say you have an interesting and colorful way to express yourself with words, Corporal." Nicaro replied as he went back to staring out of the window, deciding he asked enough questions.

Now, it was Walker's turn to be the inquisitor. "Say Nicaro, how are the supporters of Castro old regime taking to the damn fighting between your forces and the government troops, sir?"

"Castro's supporters are refusing to lift a weapon against the government forces, but I'm as glad to say they're not attacking us either, Corporal. I believe they want to sit on the sidelines in hopes we knock each other off so they can step in and take the government for themselves. Or I guess they figure if they don't have Castro to lead them they'll allow anyone, even the Americans to come in and take over the nation for them, sir."

Throughout the rest of the trip through the streets of Havana, the war machine sped by while taking little incoming small arms rounds. The thick metal hide of the machine came to a sliding stop on the grass field beside the paved parking lot that serviced the Palace elite. A dozen armored vehicles pulled up, each sliding on the grass. Hundreds, then thousands of civilians came out of the woodwork and surrounded the Palace and took up defensive positions. Every once in a while, small arms fire would break out but it ended quickly.

Nicaro got out of the machine first, followed by Walker and the rest. Navea was still on his mission, so Nicaro's third in command, Miguel Hernandez Machado, moved to his side. The civilians encircled Nicaro, and ushered him in the building after it had been given the once over. They had to make sure there were no bombs or booby traps left behind by the government troops who fled the city before Nicaro's civilians arrived in the capital. Nicaro was lead up to the third floor where it was known Castro had his private office and held meetings. He was hoping beyond hope Castro had not been killed, when the revolutionaries attacked the Palace.

When Nicaro entered the room, he could see it had been sprayed by automatic weapons fire. There were two dark reddish brown stains on the carpet by the side of the desk he knew was blood and grumbled. "I guess Castro is part of Cuba's history now. Perhaps it's better off this way. I wouldn't have liked to take that man a prisoner in his own country, sir."

Nicaro turned to a Cuban fighter standing by his side and issued orders to the man, and then he turned to Walker and announced. "Ahhh Corporal, it seems your presence has brought me luck, yes great luck. It appears the defending troops have fled the capital, or took to wearing civilian clothes to avoid detection and arrest. No matter, I don't care what they're doing, as long as they're not shooting at my men. I'm going to organize my main fighters, and then we're going to turn our attention to the last strong hold of revolutionary troops on the entire Island, the Guanahacabibes Peninsula.

"I must tell you Corporal from the United States, it's believed this Revolutionary Presidente we chase from the capital has taken this Peninsula as his last strong hold on Cuba. We defeat him there, and Cuba is free of all would be military leaders. I have information that shows he has ships there, and he's intending to make a get-a-way to someplace in Central America, and he'll then disappear in the jungles. Corporal, I don't care where he goes, as long as he leaves this country before I find him, and he never dares to set foot in Cuba again, as long as I'm alive. If he does this, I'll have his evil head for the destruction he has caused to Cuba and all her children."

"What about the damn missiles, sir?" Walker asked as he checked his M-16 rifle to make certain he had a round chambered in the weapon.

"I heard little about the supposed missiles from your female American spy. But I haven't witnessed anything that makes me believe they exist on Cuban soil, Corporal. I allowed you to accompany me on this battle, so I could keep a close eye on the American forces that shall attack the Peninsula from the south of the Island. But, as I stated Corporal, I don't care if this self proclaimed Presidente Alvarez gets off the Island alive. Soon, he and his forces are going to find they're trapped between two separate Armies, and he'll have no course of action open, but to give up or flee the Island. Either way I win and Cuba is free at long last sir."

Walker paid little attention to the bullshit Nicaro was spewing as he reached in his pocket and removed seven photos taken by a second flight of Hornets. They were given to him before he left the Aircraft Carrier and he asked the civilian. "Didn't the damn Agent show you any stinking pictures of the damn thing? I know she was issued a number of photos before she was ordered to make contact with you, sir."

"Yes Corporal, your female Agent shown me a picture taking by one of your spy planes that the United States has flying over our country. They showed me what looked like a simple hole in the water, and she tried to make me believe this hole was an underwater missile silo prepared for ICBM's. That is why I sent Navea out to bring her to the Palace, where she'll be safe until the fighting is over."

"Then you're still not convinced these missiles exist in Cuba, Homes?"

Nicaro could not understand why this American kept referring to him as a home, but he allowed him to get away with it, until he figured out if it was a derogatory term or not, as he shook his head no to Corporal's question.

"Okay Homes take a gander at these babies, and see if you still don't believe this Alvarez dick got control of some damn nuclear tipped missiles, Nicaro." Walker handed the photos to civilian, and he waited for him to look them over. Nicaro's eyes opened as he stared at the missile caught in the open resting on a missile transporter. It was covered by a canvass that was being moved towards the water, to a hole he saw in the picture shown to him by the female agent.

"By the Virgin it's true. Madre de Dios, where have the weapons of the devil come from?"

"Where the fuck do you think they came from Nicaro. Russia!" Walker growled at him.

"Then may Russia be damned to hell for her sins committed against humanity, and this country, sir." Nicaro snarled at both Corporal Walker and Russia at the same time.

DAMASCUS, SYRIA

The pictures of the missiles and other evidence the United States accumulated showing Cuban troops might be responsible for attacks occurring in the Middle East. Were sent to the CIA Agent helping with the interrogation of the remaining Cuban supposed Arab prisoners captured in the mountains in Syria.

Jacinto Crabb Mella sat handcuffed to a heavy wooden high back chair bolted to the cement floor, and he was surrounded by armed and seething Syrian soldiers. He no longer looked like the once proud Cuban operative he was, smiling when he pushed the button to destroy the Syrian train hours ago. Now, he sat naked chained in the chair, his left eye swollen closed and his lip split open, and three teeth missing. He had a broken left arm, and three fingers on his right hand were smashed. Every finger nail on his hands was missing, pulled out in an effort to gain the truth from the terrorist. Three toes were cut off, and as his fingers the toenails were ripped out.

A doctor was busy breaking the prisoner's molars by forcing a common nail in his mouth then resting the nail against his back teeth then smashing the nail with a hammer. The doctor was instructed to work on the terrorist's penis and testicles next, if the pain from the destroyed teeth did not break his will. Then ice cold water was prepared to be forcibly pumped in the prisoners destroyed mouth, to create unending pain to the destroyed teeth and exposed nerves. Everything the doctor tried against the terrorist was designed to break the resistance offered by the terrorist who still refused to speak.

The American Agent came in the room and went to the Syrian General controlling the interrogation. He showed the General the photos and asked if he would be allowed to address the prisoner and show him the pictures. The Syrian resented the intrusion of the American, but he allowed him to approach the prisoner under his watchful eye.

Once Jacinto was shown the evidence of the pictures the agent had, he was informed another prisoner admitted they were ordered out by the new President of Cuba to kill the Arabs and Jews alike. When he was promised freedom if he spoke, he gave in and began babbling away. Once he talked, everything about his mission, about his specialized training and those who ordered him in action, poured out from his destroyed mouth in a rush.

Word the terrorists admitted they were Cuban troops trained by Fidel Castro, and sent in action by the new President of Cuba was flashed to the United States then the rest of the world.

GUANAHACABIBES PENINSULA, CUBA

Carlos Alvarez was informed his hit teams were taken prisoner, and they admitted they were Cubans and sent to attack Israel and the Arab nations under his orders. He realized there was no longer any escape for him. The American government would hunt him down no matter where he hid. He knew his life was over and he made up his mind he was going to take Cuba, and as much of the United States as he could to his grave. In a rage, he grabbed the technician and squeezed his neck and roared in his face. "How many god dom missiles are ready to be launched at the United States, and how soon?"

"Four are set in position, the fifth is minutes from being ready for position in its launch silo, and the sixth missile will take two hours before it's ready to be moved out and set for launch."

"The last missile is out of the question, I don't even want you wasting time with it. I order you to end all work on that missile. By the hand of God." Colonel Alvarez roared as he lifted his hand to God and added. "I'll launch the dom missiles the moment you completed work on the fifth missile. Five will be more than enough for me to leave my impression on the Americans and their precious cities, and the world. All your foul efforts are to be placed on the last missiles, in ten minutes I countdown for the destruction of most of the United States and all Cuba. It'll teach all who come after me that Cuba was not to be taken lightly, or to be toyed with either.

"I blame all that happens, on the dom Americans and their trade embargo against Cuba for all these years. To think Castro allowed Cuba to wallow in the dregs of his hatred for so long, that it has lead to this. An ending I never would've considered if it wasn't for the dom civilian fighters marching on my troops. I'll teach all those who went against me that I too, was not to be taken lightly. Work! Work on the remaining missile before I have your cursed head. I want to launch now." Alvarez growled as he smashed the technician across his face with the back of his hand and snarled. "Work!"

THE CIVILIAN TROOPS ENTERING THE CAPITAL, HAVANA

After studying the photos of the missiles for a few moments, Nicaro decided to splinter his forces in two groups. He was going to allow a number of fighters to enter the city, just enough to gain control over it and keep it under control. The rest of his fighters were going to be placed on the highway heading for the Guanahacabibes Peninsula, and the missile installation there, at their fastest speed. Nicaro believed Walker when he warned they had to do everything possible to stop Alvarez from launching the missiles, if he wanted to save Cuba from a nuclear death.

Nicaro offered Walker and the rest of the Americans with him, his best civilian fighters, and the fastest of his machines, and then he sent the attack team of two hundred and fifty men on a fast ride to the installation at the end of the Peninsula. He was putting his faith in the American trained soldiers, to make his fighters operate at their best ability. Nicaro made sure this Army was equipped with his best weapons.

Word was sent out by his radio operators to all civilian fighters attacking the government troops of Colonel Cienfuegos's 1st Armor Division. All these fighters were ordered to give his convoy easy and safe access through the entire Peninsula region, and to back any civilian fighters if they came under attack. He also ordered his operators to inform the civilians on the Peninsula to join forces with this fast moving unit of fighters, and to help them in any way to attack the secret installation they were heading for.

Even though Nicaro hated to remain in the capital, he knew it was his place to be there. He had to gain control over the capital, and stop the fighting taking place in the streets. He made contact with Colonel Cienfuegos, to see if he could talk the last government troops into ending the fighting. He hoped Cienfuegos' troops would join him in saving Cuba from the death if the missiles were fired on the United States. He never considered Alvarez might have targeted one of the missiles for Havana, such a thought never entered his mind. With Navea gone, he placed Machado in command of the soldiers sent to attack the base on the tip of the Peninsula.

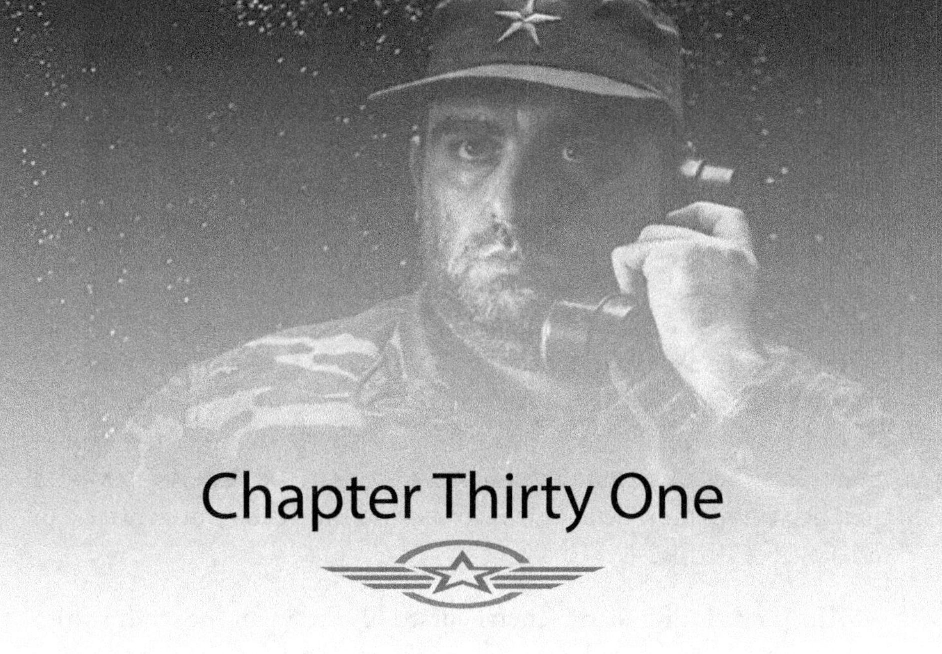

Chapter Thirty One

THE SR-91 STARLIGHT FLIGHT LANDING IN JAMAICA

The SR-91 Starlight surveillance and reconnaissance aircraft landed on the civilian airbase in Jamaica in broad daylight. All unauthorized personnel were ordered away from the base, and the Jamaican police stopped anyone from taking pictures of the strange looking aircraft as it landed. When it touched down, flares were fired off to shield the secret aircraft from photographers. The SR-91 was pulled into a hanger then the doors closed. There were no secrets held from the Russians, not with the spy plane landing in Russia, and now with the Russian General the lone passenger in the plane. Anything the Russians wanted to know about the once top secret aircraft was seen firsthand by this officer.

The Russian, the American pilot and co-pilot, and navigator were rushed into a secured room where a Naval Officer waited for them. The Russian stomped pugnaciously into the office as the Airmen were given leave time, and the Russian was made comfortable while he waited for his second ride. His metal suitcase held tightly in his crossed arms and guarded with his life.

The Russian sat in the lone chair in the room, and appeared to be scared to death to move. He glared harshly at any American soldiers who walked in the office, or passed by the open door. A Lieutenant smiled, but the angry Russian General ignored the kind offer of friendship from the officer, and he glared back at him.

General Mashennikova hated all Americans alike he always had and always would until he died. Mashennikova understood English well, but refused to speak it outside his country. His was the voice the American President heard on the phone, arguing with his President. He was set against giving the Americans the codes to his missiles, afraid once they had one, even though it was easy to change, they would figure out how they came to choose the codes. The Americans would then be able to neutralize their ICBMs, and then they would attack an indefensible Russia.

The powerful Russian General cursed his President for sending him to help the Americans, he cursed more when he found out the new Cuban rebel leader aimed the missiles he sent to Cuba, at the United States and here he sat. Sent to help the Americans by showing them how to defeat the missiles he hoped would one day destroy American cities, before Russia attacked the United States in the future. He was aware his former boss, Leonid Brezhnev, supervised his smuggling of the nuclear missiles to Cuba, would never have issued such orders to him to help the Americans, no matter what the outcome was.

The Russian's angry scowl deepened more when Naval Officers stormed through the door. They gave him a quick glance as they reported to the desk Lieutenant. "Majors Parks and Williams reporting in sir, we're here to pick up the happy looking chap over there, sir."

Lieutenant Johnson warned the two officers. "Better be careful of him, the bugger might understand English, sir."

"Let's find out if he does or not, I'm sure security would want to know if the bastard understands our lingo. "Hey, hey you over there. Yes you with the briefcase in your hands."

When the angry Russian looked at the speaker, Major Parks continued with his words. "You want a good piece of ass sir? There's plenty of lose pussy hanging around this little Island that would be more than happy to spread them for a snappy looking Russian Officer like you sir. Especially such a fine looking specimen like yourself, sir."

When no facial change occurred, Parks turned to the Lieutenant and said. "See, the bugger has no idea what the fuck we're talking about man. He's harmless enough I guess sir."

"Maybe so, but I suggest you watch your Ps and Qs around him, Major. I still don't trust any of them as far as I can throw them, sir. And, I have never known any Russian to be harmless, unless he's a dead one, sir. Even then I wouldn't be too sure about them, Major."

None of the soldiers noticed the smirk that crossed the Russian's lips as they conversed about women and trusting Russians. His smirk was more over his ability to make them believe he had not understood them. He was happy he was one up on the Americans and could not understand how they could be so lax around their enemy. He listened to their conversation.

"Say Lieutenant, you got anyone around here who can communicate with this one here for us sir? We gotta get him on our plane and then out to the ship after that, A-SAP sir."

"Sure thing, say Capt, we got to get this Russian Officer on the move for the Major, sir."

Captain Koshkin, a Ukrainian nodded at the Russian as he told him what was going on.

The three American Officers stared at the two Russians busy speaking their gibberish with one of them remarking. "Look at the bastards, once an Ivan always a fucking Ivan man. You're right you can never trust a stinking Ruskie, sir." The three Americans laughed as the Captain glared at them and barked. "Are any of you turds going to show this Russian where you want him, sirs? All you have to do is wave, and he'll follow you. I warn you, you better treat him as you would any General, or I'll have your balls for tie tacks."

The two young flyers snapped to attention and saluted the Captain. "Understood sir."

"Very well, I suggest you get on your way. We have a situation to unravel here sir."

"Yes sir." The pilot snapped as he walked over to the Russian and motioned for him to stand up. Once standing, the pilot waved for him to follow them. "Major, that's not necessary, his name's General Mashennikova, but he's been kind enough to allow you shits to call him by his first name. Vladimir sir, it'll be easier for him to understand you're referring to him, when you need his to do something for you sir."

The co-pilot was in the Sikorsky built MH-53E Sea Dragon helicopter, and the machine was spooling while waiting for the pilot and his Russian cargo to arrive. The Russian looked over the massive machine and admired its fine construction. Fifteen minutes later, they were hovering six feet over the rolling deck of the Carrier United States.

The Russian tried to memorize everything he saw of the helicopter, but there was so much to see he found it impossible to remember anything he saw of the helicopter. He cursed under his breath, because it was his belief Russia should have built a few of these floating airbases for their Navy, instead of the halfassed Carriers they wasted their time constructing. They were unable to accept a Mig fighter landing on it, because they had no arresting wire systems on the ships, and the runway was too short for landing on.

Three American Officers were there to meet the Russian General while hunched over to avoid contact with the spooling rotor blades, and they rushed him for the ship's Island structure, and the safety it afforded them from the harsh elements assaulting the massive ship. They ushered the elderly Russian Officer to the Control Center, the heartbeat of the Aircraft Carrier. There, Captain Charles Haverlin waited with a Russian interpreter. As the Russian Officer sat down, Haverlin offered him a shot of Vodka that he greedily drank then he held his glass out for a refill.

Seaman First Class Sergie Kostikov smiled as he bowed politely, and offered the Russian General the refill then announced he would be the translator for the meeting for them.

General Mashennikova glared at the smiling man and angrily snapped at him. "You speak good Russian, you act like good Russian soldier, you smell like good Russian soldier, why are you not killing these American pigs like all good Russians should instead aiding the fools?"

The Seaman's face reddened and he could only stare back at the fearsome looking Russian while glaring at him. He dared not respond to his remark against him and his country. Because he feared what he might say to the angry pig and the terrible wrath of his Captain if he dared to curse at their Russian visitor like he wanted to. All he could do was smile meekly at the Russian soldier and hold his temper in check.

The old Russian continued to glare at the young man, and then he snapped at the American again in a hot tone of voice. "I thought so you are a Blagarodnaya Sabaka (Noble Dog) for your Amirikanskaya masters. You're a Svinaya Mudnya (Fucking Shit). The sight of you makes me sick to my stomach you dog, Ukhaditye (Go away). Leave my sight before I break your traitorous neck with my bare hands."

The Captain picked up the Seaman's stress and said. "Seaman Kostikov, is there a problem?"

"It seems our new friend doesn't like the fact I'm working for the American Navy, sir." The Seaman replied to his Commanding Officer with a smirk.

"Can he understand us Seaman?" the Captain asked.

"I doubt it sir." The Seaman replied, not sure of his answer though to the Captain.

"Fine, then he can go and fuck himself along with his damn Russian Bear, Seaman." The Captain growled hotly. "You'll relay everything I say to him, and what he says back to me immediately, word for word Seaman. Don't omit anything said from either side, do you understand Seaman? If he has a fucking problem with this arrangement, he can go to hell and I'll blow the end of Cuba to oblivion, along with his precious missiles and anything else Russian there. You'll tell him everything I tell you to say."

"Understood sir, and I'll do as ordered, Captain. Word for word, sir."

"Good then you ask the General if he has the power to scramble these fucking missile launching codes, Seaman. Err.... omit the fucking for now son."

Everyone at the meeting laughed except for the Russian, who stared straight ahead as if he was trying to ignore everyone in the room. He was trying to control the rage he was feeling for the men surrounding him.

The Seaman asked the questions as instructed, and he received a verbal tongue lashing from the angry Russian. Once he was through, Captain Haverlin asked. "What's up his ass?"

"Captain Haverlin Sir, the Russian said he'll listen to me as I translate your words for him, but he'll not answer directly me sir. He offered he'll direct his answers only to you sir, and I can translate them if I care to, Captain. Or I could stand here and die for all he cares, sir." The Seaman replied to his Commanding Officer.

"Look mister, I don't have the time for this bullshit. Inform the dopey bastard I don't give a rat's ass who he likes and dislikes here, or who he'll answer or not speak to, son. I want fucking answers dammit! And, leave the damn slang in this time, mister." The fuming Captain of the Carrier ordered the Seaman in no uncertain terms.

The Russian stared at the Captain as the Seaman spoke. Haverlin saw the Russian's eyes open, and then his lips part as he smiled. "Da, Da, Peytye." (Yes, yes, drink) He held out his glass.

"Seaman, can this popinjay scramble the damn missile codes for us, or not son?"

The Russian responded without waiting for the translation. "Kaneshna Da! (Yes of course) I can scramble the codes." He realized his mistake instantly and snapped his mouth shut, but it was too late. Everyone in of the CIC now understood he could understand English.

The Seaman and Captain looked at each other and smirked, as the Seaman snapped at the Captain. "Be careful with this one, Captain Haverlin. This sonofabitch obviously understands English well sir. I believe he's screwing with us a little on this one, Skipper."

Haverlin glared at the Russian and growled angrily. "General Mashennikova, if you're able to speak English and understand, I suggest you do so. It'll make it easier for both of us to communicate, sir."

The Russian stared straight ahead as if he was not able to understand the Captain's words.

"General Mashennikova I don't have the fucking time to waste with you on this shit, sir. Either you understand and speak English or you don't sir, there's no half way about it sir. Look sir, I'll make out my report either way on you, and if you're fucking with me. It's going to be your ass that'll be on the line when you get back to Russia, and they read my report about you stating we couldn't communicate with you, buster." Haverlin moved to his left until he looked directly into the Russian Officer's eyes while he waited for the answer from his last statements.

General Mashennikova moved his head then he locked eyes with the angry American Captain. He stared at him for a few moments before grinning. The smile was marred by rotted and missing teeth, and his grin allowed his terrible breath to escape. "Ahhh, General..."

"Captain, sir." The skipper corrected the large Russian as he smiled at him.

"It should be General..." The Russian offered, but he was cut off by the Captain again.

"Thanks for the raise in rank but I'm not here to have any smoke blown up my ass either, sir." Haverlin snapped back at the Russian.

"My English no too very good please. I understand better much than speak it. I'll to speak you language if you speak slow, if it help much for you better, Captain." The Russian smiled.

"It'll help me plenty sir. Why didn't you let me know you could understand English, General? It woulda saved me a lot of time trying to locate someone who spoke Russian, sir."

The Russian shrugged at the Captain then put a smirk on his lips and stared at the Captain of the Carrier.

"The hell with the bullshit General!" Haverlin growled then continued with his words. "Okay General Mashennikova, I need to know what you'll need to help you communicate with your damn missiles on Cuba. I can give you direct access to my computers, my radar and radio for jamming purposes, if they'll be of assistance to you, sir. Anything you'll need, I believe I have it here and it's at your disposal, sir."

The Russian continued to stare at the Commander and Haverlin believed he might have spoken too quick for the Russian to follow his words. The Russian looked at him with his mouth open just as Haverlin was going to repeat himself again.

The Russian's mouth snapped shut and the grin returned as he replied to Haverlin. "Amirikanski Captain, everything I need I have inside my case, sir. We Ruskies not dumb as think we be before, sir. We more than capable of build computer on par Amirikanski computer, sir. We're not helpless, and we're capable defend ourselves and Motherland, sir. We once again be major power in world, you will see soon sir."

"Look General, that's politics and I'm not a fucking politician. I don't have the time for a commercial at this time sir. All I asked you was what you needed to help you communicate with your damn missiles, sir. Nothing else General, I don't give a rat's stinking ass about your damn county's military philosophy, sir. That's for another meeting and another time sir. If you have everything you need with you sir then all I need to know is how close to the damn Island do you have to be to communicate with the damn missile's computers, sir?"

The Russian was in no hurry to answer the question of the American Naval Officer. Nor was he in any hurry to scramble the missile codes. He hoped he could waste enough time before he had to act. The Russian was hoping against hope the rebel Cuban President would launch the missiles before he could scramble the codes. He did not care he was so near to ground zero, he would lose his life when the United States retaliated against the Cuban launch. He was willing to give up his life to destroy more than a quarter of the United States. The Russian shifted his weight in his chair as he moved the briefcase to the floor then slid it between his legs.

"Is that getting heavy for you General? I can have one of my Seamen carry it for you, if you would like, General." Haverlin offered politely to the Russian Officer.

The Russian grinned as he replied to the Captain. "Amirikanskaya Captain, I connect to case by this wire, sir. If I become how you say, err… disconnect from my case and the electronic impulse interrupt for one second, case will explode and control computer, myself, and anyone in fifteen feet of me be killed instantly. I have to protect National Security of my country. I have…"

"What the hell's wrong with you sir?" Haverlin roared as he jumped up and glared at the Russian as he continued to thunder at him. "How dare you bring a bloody booby trapped briefcase on board my god damn ship, sir? Suppose you went through one of my explosive detection machines and it went off, sir. My men would've fallen on you like white on rice sir, before I had a chance to react, and your wire control could have been disconnected and you would've failed your mission, and your country sir. Christ sake man."

The Russian nodded to the American as he admitted. "Perhaps, stupid on my part to bring explosive charge on board you ship. I should warn you of fact before enter you ship, Captain."

"Arr… that's a load of crap if you ask me sir, we're getting side tracked here, dammit. I order you to disarm that explosive charge immediately. Then we'll go back to the question at hand I asked you before, and I'll repeat myself so you'll understand me perfectly, sir. General Mashennikova, how close do you have to be to the damn Island for your computer to work properly, for it to scramble the codes?"

The Russian thought for a moment, it looked like he was going over figures in his mind, because his lips were moving as if he was talking to himself. Suddenly, he looked at Haverlin and replied. "My computer has limit range. I work from platform no more away from target missile of 16.2 kilometers which is ten of you miles."

"For Christ sake, why the fuck didn't you tell me this crap before I was forced to ask for it, dammit. This is going to bring me into Cuban territorial waters, not to mention it'll take nearly twenty minutes to sail to the closest position sir." The Captain grabbed the mike as if he was angry at it and barked in to. "Bridge to Conn."

"Conn Aye sir." The Seaman replied to his Commanding Officer over the radio.

"Get underway immediately we have to make for the Cuban coast, son. Work out the shortest course and distance. We have to be within ten miles of the target area, ten minutes ago."

"Conn to Captain, the water's awful shallow in that region of the Island and we have..."

"I don't give a rat's ass if you have to ground her, get me to within ten miles of the fucking coast of that damn Island on the fastest course possible. Increase air cap to ten aircraft in case those bastards send out aircraft once we enter their damn waters, mister. Err... Seaman, if you have to ground her, you better make damn sure we're well within the ten mile limit before you do so, or you'll be swimming your way back to the States, son. Do I make myself clear mister?"

"Crystal clear Skipper, sir." The Seaman replied to the Captain's last orders sharply.

Haverlin gave a thought of dumping the Russian into a helicopter, and have it land in the shallow water off the Cuban Island so the Russian popinjay could transmit his command to his missiles, and put a quick end to this threat aimed at the United States. The Captain gave a thought back to the Cuban missile crisis. He was a Lieutenant then, and he remembered hoping President Kennedy would give the word to level Cuba, because if he had they would not be going through this mess now. He always felt President Kennedy allowed Castro and his followers off the hook too easily. Of course, he realized he was not privy to all the information about the situation, and his decision was decided strictly on a military basis. Not a political one.

Both men felt the power of the Carrier as she quickly got underway under them.

"Might as well relax General, this is going to take us a while, sir. Would you like something to eat or drink sir?" Haverlin asked the Russian.

The Russian gave a smirk as he snuggled in his chair and asked. "Peytye!" (Drink)

"You're not going to get drunk on me mister? This thing's too important for that sort of shit, General." The Captain bitched as he poured the Russian another glass of Vodka.

"Neyt!" (No) The Russian enjoyed the feeling of the ultimate power the massive Aircraft Carrier exuded under him. He saw the Captain watching his every move and felt at a disadvantage as he asked the Captain. "What proof you have Cuba do anything with missile we left on Island, Captain?"

Without answering the Russian's question, the Captain looked at a Second Lieutenant who produced the latest pictures taken of the activities going on in the secluded section of the Cuban Peninsula. He spread the three dozen photos on the table before the angry looking Russian.

The General leaned forward, moving his case to between his legs so he could see the photos better. Haverlin pointed to a photo capturing the fifth missile sitting in the open on the transport machine, and the opened silo in the water as he stated. "This is one of your damn ICBM missiles being lowered into the concrete launching tube, sir. It was by sheer luck we happened to pick up this action before it was completed, General. Otherwise, we wouldn't have known jack shit about these damn nuclear tipped missiles of theirs, until it was too late for everyone concerned with the damn things, General. I can't believe you guys had the stupidity to give these backassward people more nuclear tipped missiles again, General Mashennikova Sir."

The Russian's chest swelled with pride as he studied the one photo clearly showing the Russian made ICBM missile he was instrumental in getting on the Island, being lifted by the transport's onboard crane, he checked the next set of photos and they showed the missile being lowering into the underwater silo. The last picture showed it set in place, and a flood of Cuban technicians making the necessary electrical hookups from the missiles to the hookups on the concrete sides of the silo. The Russian knew this missile would be ready for launching well before the American Carrier arrived in position, and before he could transmit the scrabble codes to them. He found himself subconsciously urging the Cuban technicians on their task to complete the launch capabilities of this last missile.

"How soon will this missile be ready for the launching, General Mashennikova Sir?"

The Russian looked to the American Office for a moment before he replied. "We be plenty time to stop launch." He lied.

Haverlin leaned against the wall of his ship as he took a breath in, he was relieved by the Russian's words. Even though he was relaxing, he never took his eyes off the Russian for a second. Something about the prick was rubbing him the wrong way, but he was unable to put his finger on what was bothering him about the large Russian. All he knew was he wanted to keep the Russian talking as long as possible, so he could figure out what it was about him that irritated him so much. Haverlin rubbed his chin as he thought of another question. "Err... General, with your computer, will you know if the Cubans try to launch the missiles once they're scrambled?"

"Da! I'll know whatever they try do to launch missiles after I scrambled the launch codes." The Russian replied to the concerned looking American.

"Yes, how so General?" the Captain asked, trying to keep the conversation going.

"No understand you last remark." The Russian said to the Captain as he looked at him.

"Oh, I wanted to know how you'd know if the Cubans try a launch the missiles, that's all."

"It simple Captain, I display board produce launch number. Once change number, any attempt to launch missile with old code make number flash on screen, change my number. A red light flash as request missile launch control board destroyed, so missile no long allow launch free. It what believe you call it, a safe precaution, an off button, Captain."

The Captain remained leaning against the wall as he made another statement to the Russian. "Well sir, I don't know how this electronic crap works, sir. All I know is I push the button, and things move around here, sir." Haverlin let out his breath as he added as if an afterthought. "We have to stop this launch, General Mashennikova Sir."

"My dalzhni sdyelat." (We must do it) The Russian looked at the Captain again.

"Yeah, whatever the hell that means." Haverlin mumbled more to himself.

CORPORAL ROBERT WALKER'S COLUMN

Corporal Robert Walker's column of armored vehicles entered the Cuban town of La Fe, at the end of the highway they traveled on. From here they would have to travel on the narrow roads till they reached the dirt roads on their way out to La Bejada, and the missile installation there. No sooner did the last vehicle turn off the highway, than the first vehicle erupted into a shower of flames and sparks. It was hit by an anti-tank shoulder launched missile, fired from the jungle's edge running along the road they turned onto.

Walker grabbed the mike and roared in it. "Disperse, scatter. Get under cover dammit. Dismount people."

Walker troops tumbled out of the rearend of the vehicle, even before the ramp was down all the way, and they rolled in the underbrush off the side of the road. The Corporal looked for muzzle flashes from the enemy's weapons. The left side of the road was one mass of weapon flashes now.

"Fire, fire, fire, for Christ sake, they're on our left fucking right quarter, man. Return fire or they're gonna get the best of us, dammit." Walker yelled as the Mutt, and the rest of the soldiers he was with, who opened fire with automatic weapons on the government attackers hiding in the bush. Walker had a good idea on how many men would be in the government's force they would be going against, but he was taking no chances of it. This attack might be a diversion against them created to cover up for a larger attack coming their way later on.

He pulled the radio from the vehicle and dished out orders for the Cuban tanks to open fire on the attackers in the bush. None of the Cuban tankers understood English, so they held their fire. Machado took the radio and translated Walker's orders then the tankers reacted to the orders. Machado explained to Walker. "My men will not take any orders from you. Anything you want them to do, you have to tell me, and I'll order my soldiers to do as you requested, Corporal."

"Understood man, have the tankers concentrate their damn fire on the edge of the tree line to our left. Let them pump the shells in there, working their way deeper in the woods with each volley they fire, until these pricks break off their attack. Have the rest of the heavy weapons open up on the same area. We have to break off their attack before they develop a fricking foothold against us, and we'll be forced to abandon our vehicles and pull back and regroup. Then we're fucked out of the damn ball game, we'll never get at those missiles before they're launched."

"I understand your orders Corporal." Machado issued Walker's orders again for the Cubans.

When the tanks opened up, the fire from the bush almost stopped, the attackers knew they had it. Walker heard the attackers run through the jungle to get out of the hail of death ripping the jungle and hidden troops apart. Round after round of tank fire plowed into the attacker's position as they abandoned them. Machado heard the attackers run and laughed as he slapped Walker on his back. "You did well for an American soldier, Corporal."

"Yep, them mutherfakkas sure took off like their assholes were shitting sparks. You and your people did well for a bunch of Cubans. We betta move on while we still can sir." Walker grumbled at the Cuban fighters as he looked around for the Mutt.

"First, we shall check on the wounded. Cubans don't allow our wounded die in the bush like animals, Corporal." Machado mumbled as he began to check on the many wounded of both sides as other Cubans join him with working on the fallen Cuban civilians and soldiers alike.

"Suit your fucking self pal, but you betta remember one thing here, buddy. We're working against a set time line. If your damn pals down there launch their missiles at my country, we're all gonna be fricking toast on this stinking Island of yours, buddy."

Machado ignored Walker's crude warning aimed at him as he ordered his men out from their hiding places, and then he told them to check for wounded on both sides.

This part of battle always seemed to amaze Walker. He wondered how ironic war was. Less than a few minutes ago, everyone connected with his column was trying his or her damnedest to kill the other sonofabitches attacking them. But now, with the fires of war still burning in the bush, the attacked moved out and they checked on the welfare of their attackers. Everything was being done for the wounded from both sides. Even the Mutt and two other Americans tried to help the medics get to an attacker trapped under a machine.

Corporal Robert Walker stretched his neck and saw the guy was in bad shape, and he knew there was no hope for the prick to live with the wounds he received. Yet he stared in wonderment as the Mutt and the rest of his men, and two Cuban fighters and their medic worked feverishly to try and save the trapped soldier.

Walker did not suffer from any illusions of compassion though, because his compassion was for his troops, and his troops and his country alone, and for the mission they were on. Nothing else mattered jack shit to him until he finished his mission. Yes, he would do anything in his power to try and save one of his guys, but he would march over any enemy wounded until the battle was won, and his mission completed. Then, he might find some compassion for the injured enemy, maybe.

The trapped revolutionary screamed in terrible pain whenever the civilian medic tried to move him out from under the destroyed war machine's treads. Walker shook his head and muttered at no one in particular standing around him. "Yep, war's one real fucked up way of getting ones damn point across to your stinking enemy."

One of the Cubans made his way to Walker's side and produced a long, well made roach from his pocket, and then he smiled at Walker as he held the roach in his hand and showed it to the American soldier. Walker smiled as he announced. "Hey Homes, now you're talking in fricking words I can understand, buster. Toke one of them fucking babies up for us man."

The Cuban had no idea what the American said, and he cared less as he lit up the roach. He drew in a lung full of smoke and blew the smoke out slowly over his head. He then gave a shudder as he offered Walker a hit from the joint. Walker sucked in the smoke and it made his toes curl. It was good shit.

Other Cubans gathered around the two man and took hits from the joint.

The Mutt came back to Walker's group and announced sadly the trapped enemy soldier died, and there was no way for them to help him before he died.

Walker smiled at his lifelong sidekick, and then offered him a hit from the half cooked roach.

The Mutt smiled as he took a drag then announced through a series of hacking coughs and watering eyes. "Man that's some good shit you got there man. Where the hell didja get your hands on this shit, man?" he complained as he wiped his eyes from the choking fit his body was going through. He wiped at his stinging eyes for a second, and continued to laugh, causing the rest of the soldiers and civilians near him to join in on his laughing and joking around.

Corporal Theodore Irvington heard the Mutt choking and the laughter it caused, and he knew what the men had and plowed through the group and he grabbed the roach from the Mutt's hand and took a hit from it. He drew in a huge lung full of smoke, and coughed it out of his body.

It was Walker's turn to take another hit from the joint being passed between the soldiers and civilians when the soldier branded Glue, barged into the group of mixed soldiers and civilians, and interfered with the direction the roach was traveling in, and Walker complained at him angrily. "Hey Homes, you're fucking up the damn rotation, asshole. Its puff, puff then give it up, you little prick. Or you can move to the uther end of the group and take your stinking chances of not ending up with another hit from the damn thing, Homes." Walker glared at the soldier.

Irvington laughed and said. "That'll be the day I don't get a hit from a stinking joint, ground pounder." He blew the smoke out through his nose and passed the roach on to Walker who stabbed it with a pin to hold the now hot roach, and get a safe hit from it without burning the end of his fingers. He struggled to get a good hit from it this time.

Blade, Corporal McKinnon and Wire, Private Delorenzo, joined the group now sort of hanging around near one of the parked vehicles. Walker looked at the newcomers then he grumbled at the two soldiers. "You guys are too late, dick faces. That's the last hit offa this baby that anyone's gonna get offa it, man. You know what they say, you snooze you lose, Homes."

"Lose shit wiseguy, you just take a gander at this big baby I got me here, man." Wire snapped at Walker with a wide grin on his lips as he produced his own roach, and lit it up and passed it around the circle jerk, with each soldier taking a pull from it. Each soldier was taking this time to relax while building up their strength for the next, and sure to be upcoming fight they were about to enter in this mini war taking place on the Island of Cuba.

Machado grabbed Walker by the shoulder and he turned him to the side towards the civilian warrior as he told the American in broken English. "We're done there's nothing else for us to gain hanging around this death and destruction longer than necessary, Corporal. I lost seven men to this fight, and our attackers lost thirty of their proud warriors. A good trade if you ask me American. Most enemy dead were torn apart by our cannon and machine guns and as to all Cubans, this was sad to witness, American. It was a wise way to fight our attackers off, but it was also a savage way for us to kill good Cuban people following their orders from their Presidente as all good soldiers must do, sir."

Walker was exhausted and pissed in general, and he dumped it off on the Cuban bitching at him. "Hey Homes, in case you don't know it yet buddy, war is hell man. You wanna attack other soldiers with your stinking fighters then you betta be prepared to kill in the most savage of ways, or you're gonna lose every time. And, you betta also have a damn good supply of mummy bags (body bags) with you when the fighting is over, pal. Would you rather have more of your guys lying on the stinking ground dead and wounded, than the other guy's soldiers killed, man? Then there's uther ways to fight off your..."

"Perhaps you're right Corporal." Machado interrupted, "but it still does not mean I have to like the way we killed our own brothers and sisters."

Walker was on a roll and he was not going to get off his soap box that easily, as he continued his gripe at the Cuban fighter, staring him in his eyes. "Listen up Homes, the second you start like killing soldiers, no matter whose soldiers they are. Then you're no longer a fucking soldier following your damn orders for your stinking government, buster. You made the giant leap forward from being a stinking soldier, all the way over to being a fricking murderer, and that's when you get on the bad side of my stinking ass, soldier."

The upset Corporal glared at the big civilian Cuban fighter still staring at him as intensely as if he was trying to understand his words. The Cuban fighter knew Walker was correct, but he would never tell him so to his face though.

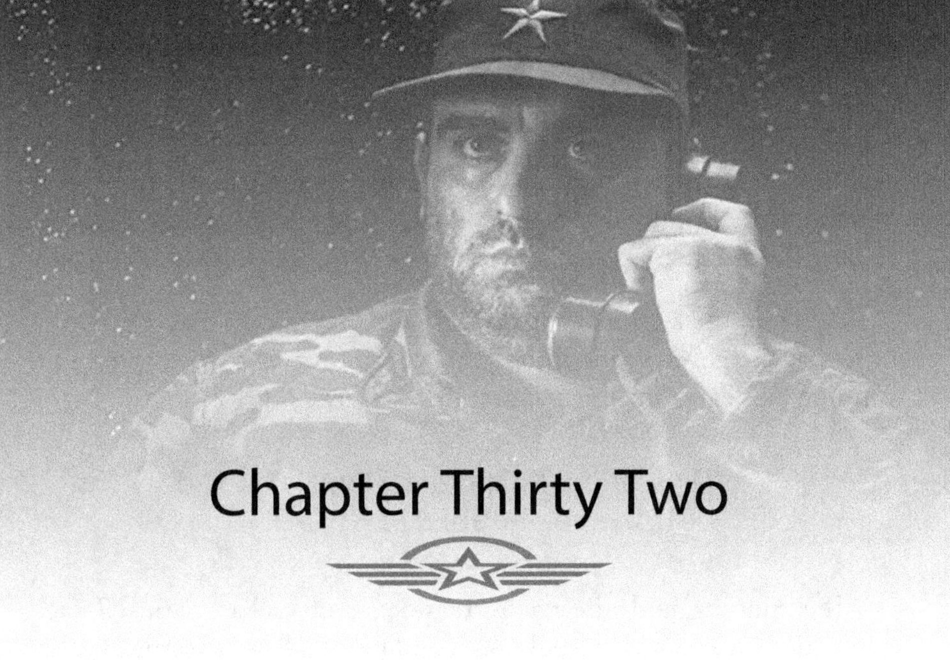

Chapter Thirty Two

Throughout most of Cuba, the civilian forces fought Colonel Carlos Rafael Fernandez Alvarez's Armies to a standstill. Everywhere on the Island, the government troops laid down their arms and called a halt to the fighting ripping Cuba apart by the two feuding sides. Negotiations began between Nicaro and the Commander of the Cuban troops stationed in Havana. It was not long before a ceasefire was instigated, and the fighting in the capital stopped for the most part, except for the last section of the Island still locked in the throngs of battle.

Nicaro was elected by the masses to run the country until he was able to organize a polling challenge, where the free people of Cuba would elect their next Presidente to govern Cuba's future and fate. It was offered they would be allowed to vote for the men and few women who would be running for the new Presidency of Cuba. Or they would be allowed to write in the name of the man or the woman they would want to govern Cuba. For the moment, the civilian fighters were ignoring what was still happening on the secluded small Peninsula. The other nations of the world followed suit with Russia leading the way. Canada, England, Italy, Spain and the People's Republic of China offered to send in representatives to aid in the organization of the free elections for the people of Cuba.

The United States announced she was dropping the trade embargos against the Cuban nation, and she was loading a number of cargo ships with all matters of provisions and medical supplies to help the civilians recover from the devastating effects of the latest war in their country.

While all the kindness was occurring in Havana and the large cities of Cuba, the government troops and civilian forces were engaging in running battles on the Guanahacabibes Peninsula.

THE MISSILE INSTALLATION ON THE GUANAHACABIBES PENINSULA

The running and already ex Presidente of Cuba, Carlos Rafael Fernandez Alvarez was in a wild rage, and lost it when he learned of the collapse of the capital of Havana. He was further infuriated when he was informed a peace was declared for Cuba, except for the Peninsula region, and there was a large civilian Army heading for their position. Alvarez was informed an American Aircraft Carrier was making way towards Cuban territorial waters. He screamed out a stream of orders, and one after the other, he was informed it was impossible for them to be carried out. His most important order was for his Cuban Airforce to engage the American Aircraft Carrier, and their orders were left hanging in the air. None of his officers wanted to be the one to tell the once Presidente he no longer had an active airforce or a working Army. They just stood by and watched him lose his sanity.

The officers felt it was safer to go through the motions of ordering Alvarez's Airforce to engage the American ship. Alvarez turned his wrath lose on the technicians, accusing them of dragging their feet preparing the missiles for launch. He grew so angry at them he pulled his pistol and fired on two technicians he believed were doing nothing to further his cause. By this move, he served warning on the remaining technicians they better step it up, or the same fate would befall them.

Alvarez remained standing in the center of the concrete bunker, his pistol locked in his hands, and it was held over his head as he scanned the faces staring at him in silence as he roared at them. "By the Holy Father, what the hell is wrong with all of you lazy people? Has everyone forgotten how to take orders from their leader? I want those dom missiles launched in ten minutes, or by the Holy Madonna you'll all lose your worthless lives in this concrete tomb." Alvarez fired two rounds in the ceiling to accentuate his warning, causing everyone to duck.

Maria stood near the last missile stored in the bunker staring angrily at Alvarez's back. She was amazed she allowed herself to fall in love with such a madman as he was who was far worse than Castro ever was. She glared at him, trying to will death upon him, but it did her no good.

A soldier felt sorry for her and he untied her hands because they were turning blue on the woman. She was basically given freedom to move around in the concrete bunker, but always under the cautious eyes of some troops who shared life in the bomb proof shelter with her.

Maria was fighting back tears as she listened to Alvarez continue to rant and rave at everyone in the bunker with them, his voice echoing throughout the concrete structure. She knew if he launched the god awful missiles, Cuba would be burned out of existence when the United States retaliated against her. She felt her chest grow heavy, and her breathing labored as she searched her mind for a solution. She knew she had to try something to try and change Alvarez's mind, or all would be lost for her beloved Island nation. She decided to try and reason with him by using some feelings he once held for her, as she stepped closer to the raving wild man with the gun in his hands, and fire burning in his wild eyes.

Alvarez caught the movement out of the corner of his eye and spun around and aimed the pistol at Maria's chest. She had to show no fear as she spoke to her once lover in an calm and begging voice.

"Presidente Alvarez, Carlos, please, if my love has ever meant anything to you in the past. I beg of you to think of what you're proposing to do with the cursed missiles. Think of the death they'll cause to our county and her people if you fire them at the United States, my love. I beg of you to reconsider these orders. So far, nothing you done cannot be repaired, changed, but if you fire the missiles, the world will change forever, and they'll blame it on you. Presidente

Alvarez please, think before you do something that cannot be stopped." She lowered herself to her knees and clasped her hands together as if in prayer, as she stared at Alvarez for a moment. She looked deeply in his eyes and saw nothing looking back at her, it was at this point she reached out and took his left hand in hers.

Alvarez stared hard and long at the young pleading woman he once loved. She hung on to his left arm as she begged him not to launch the missiles at the United States. For a brief second, he weakened but he caught himself. He grew angry as he thought of her words. He slammed her against the side of her head with his right hand holding the gun as he snarled at her. "Think of the others, this is bullshit bitch maybe it's time some of them thinks of my feelings, before this whole miserable country decides to turn its back on me! I'm the god dom Presidente of Cuba, and all its god dom troops.

"How was I to know these lowly ungrateful motherless bastards were happy living under Castro's rule and thumb? I guess I should've considered weighing this fact before I reacted against him. Even though the bearded cochino was a devil, maybe he wasn't that much of a Devil in Paradise. If only the Americans would have backed off their dom trade embargo, and they had dealt with Castro in a better manner. Maybe he would have lightened up on his people, and I wouldn't have attacked him."

"All that doesn't matter now, Carlos please. What matters most is not to launch those hated missiles at the United States and stop the fighting in Cuba." She offered while lying on the floor where she was knocked down to from the blow. She rubbed the side of her face, blood seeped in her eye from a slight gash on the side of her forehead, and she tasted the warm liquid.

Alvarez stared at her with a wild look blazing in his eyes as he roared at her. "Enough, enough dommit! By all the Saints that are Holy, who the hell are you to offer me guidance, bitch? If I wanted your opinion, I would've asked you for it, woman! You're a bitch trying to remove me from my rightful place as the new Presidente of Cuba." Alvarez barked as he stooped down and he took a threatening stance over the prone, frail woman.

"Please Alvarez, we have to start thinking about what is good for Cuba and her children..."

"Enough I said, may God curse you to the fires of hell of eternity, it's enough I say!" Alvarez yelled as he slammed her against the head with a fist, knocking her unconscious. He looked at Maria for a brief second, and then said. "Look, look at what you made me do, dommit. I told you to shut your filthy mouth, did I not woman? I swear to the Holy Madonna, it's your fault bitch." Alvarez looked around the bunker until he spotted a soldier who looked like he had nothing to do and growled at him. "You, pick her up and lay her on that cursed table and make her comfortable, fool."

The soldier gave his weapon to a second soldier as he picked up Maria's limp body. He laid her on the table, and tried to make her as comfortable as possible.

"By God that's enough touching that lowly bitch, get away from her god dom body!" Alvarez demanded as he made a threatening gesture for the soldier to move with his sidearm.

The soldier jumped away from her and then he went back to his guard post.

THE AMERICAN AIRCRAFT CARRIER THE UNITED STATES

Captain Haverlin moved to his command chair on the bridge, and directed the ship through the shallow waters nearing Cuba. A Navigator and Seaman were calling out the depth of the water under the keel of the ship as it plowed towards the ten mile limit of the Cuban Island. Haverlin looked over his shoulder and barked at Seaman Kostikov. "You better get General Mashennikova to the CIC (Combat Information Center) so he can increase his computers output. I'll be down the moment I know my ship's safe. Boatswain, G.Q."

The Boatswain Mate jumped up after being ordered by the Captain and replied. "Aye, aye sir." He turned to the ships intercom and keyed it, and blew his whistle and bellowed in it. "General Quarters, General

Quarters. All hands man your battle station. This is not a drill. I repeat this is not a drill. Fire details man your substations. General Quarters, General Quarters." The Boatswain Mate repeated his message again.

Sirens and alarms wailed throughout the ship, as it sprang in life with hordes of Sailors and Marines running in every direction. Aircraft were moved on the flight deck as ready air cap aircraft launched from three catapults. All water tight doors were dogged down, and all non-essential items were stored so they would not become a problem if the ship came under attack.

Seaman Kostikov looked at the angry Russian sitting in his chair, and asked him. "General Mashennikova, if you would be so kind as to follow me sir."

The old man tucked his computer briefcase under his arm as the two Marine guards moved to either side as he followed the Seaman into the bowels of the ship. He was amazed the Sailors did not bang into one another as they dashed for their battle station. Subconsciously, the Russian was counting to see how long it was before the Carrier was fully battle ready.

The General entered the CIC Chamber and was bathed in the soft, warm glow of red lights. He listened as one after the other, the Sailors checked in, informing the Captain their stations were manned and ready for action. There was barely enough room to stand in the CIC, as the Seaman lead the Russian to the main computer he demanded access to. The Seaman backed off a step and watched as the Russian opened the lid of his case then he removed a thick stack of wires and laid them out with great care on the tabletop. One of the ship's electronic engineers was assisting the Russian with his work on the wires who the Russian told him in poor English where each of the wires had to be hooked up to the computer. Seaman Kostikov stood by ready to help the engineer if he did not understand what the Russian wanted from him. So far, they were working pretty well together, and he had no reason to step in.

Seaman Kostikov saw the Russian was taking his time hooking the computer up, as well as avoiding making requests that might speed things along. He knew the fifth missile was set, and the Cuban technicians were linking up the external wires to the missile and controlling computers. He was about to head for the Captain to report his findings, when Haverlin walked in the CIC. He slapped the Seaman on his back and asked. "How's the turd doing now?"

"Captain Haverlin I think he's fucking with us, sir. I feel he's deliberately stalling work sir."

"Why in the hell would he want to do that for, Seaman?" the Captain asked with concern.

"Maybe he wants the fucking... err... sorry for my poor choice of words, sir."

"C'mon man, I'm more interested in your damn opinion than your fucking apology, son."

"Yes sir, I think the puke wants the Cubans to launch the missiles sir. Maybe we're looking at the turd responsible for getting the missiles to Cuba in the first place, sir."

"Christ sake." The Captain moaned at the Seaman before he added. "What the hell should I do dammit, stop the fuck and takeover his damn machine and call for the codes from Russia myself? How the hell am I going to trust this POS. (piece of shit) Suppose he fucks up the computer and it gives the damn Cubans the time to launch the missiles, dammit. I guess I have to get in contact with command" The ship's Captain left the CIC heading for communications and demanded a Code One scramble be transmitted. "Transmit it through the Telstar System, son."

In moments, Haverlin was speaking to Admiral Standlund, the Chief of Naval Operations at the Pentagon. The Captain explained his fears to the Admiral and he told Haverlin he would get back to him. The Admiral placed a call to General Weidenbacher, reported to be in a meeting with the President in the Oval Office.

General William Weidenbacher was listening to Director John Raincloud's assumption of the situation taking place in Cuba when the Marine guard informed him he had a Code One call. Everyone stopped speaking until Weidenbacher was off the phone, and the President snapped at him. "What is it, more bad news General?"

"Mr. President Sir, it seems the Russian Officer is stalling sir. Captain Haverlin feels he's trying to wait and see if the Cubans are going to launch the missiles, sir."

"He is is he, well I shall see about this stack of bullshit, General." President Albert Cole growled as he picked up the phone and connected with the Russian President. After a heated exchange between the two powerful leaders, President Cole gave the Russian President the means to make contact with his General on board the Aircraft Carrier. When he hung up, he turned to the General and offered. "I just cooked his eggs. How are our soldiers doing with the Cuban forces?"

"Great Mr. President, they had three separate engagements so far, but the column's minutes away from their objective, sir." The General announced proudly.

"How's this lead man you sent out there, err... Corporal... err... What was his name General?"

"Corporal Robert Walker, sir." The General offered to the seated President of America.

"Yes, Corporal Walker. I don't know much about him, I hope he's as good as you say he is."

"He's a fine soldier, one of our best, sir. He's the type of soldier who'd swallow a hand full of rounds, so he could fart death and destruction from his asshole as he charged forward, sir. His ego's so large it's about to file for independent statehood, Mr. President."

Everyone at the meeting chuckled over the General's remark to the President.

"He's that good, huh General? Is he going to get the missiles before they're launched, sir?"

"If anyone can stop them from being launched, he sure can, sir. I have complete trust in him sir." Weidenbacher replied proudly as he smiled back at the American Leader now.

"You better, because it's your ass if he fails, sir." President Cole warned as he glared at him.

THE AMERICAN AIRCRAFT CARRIER THE UNITED STATES

Everyone stationed inside the CIC of the Carrier intently watched the Russian continue to fumble about with the stack of wires from the computer first then he began to screw around with the display panel. A second Seaman was in contact with the Carrier's ready air cap group flying over the Carrier, moving the aircraft over the ship's security and defensive zone. His voice was the only one heard speaking in the CIC, as the rest of the Sailors watched the Russian working on the computer system. The Russian moved his chair to the table and began to play with something from his briefcase as if time was not important to him.

Captain Haverlin entered the CIC and studied the Russian as he slowly set up his computer. He stood next to Seaman Kostikov and leaned to him and offered. "I see what you mean about this prick stalling us."

Seaman Kostikov smiled back at the wise Captain as he nodded.

A Seaman manning the radio announced. "Hey Skipper, I have an incoming radio message for General Vladimir Mashennikova, something like that, sir. The calls originating from Russia, sir. The talker identifies himself as Russian President Tkachenko, sir."

The Captain said. "Man, the President cooked this fool's ass. I can't believe he was able to get a reaction so quickly from the Ruskies, son. Patch the call over to table three for me please."

"Aye sir and I'm patching the call over to table three right away, sir."

Haverlin made his way to the Russian with Kostikov in tow and he announced. "General Mashennikova, you have a call from your President, sir. I guess he wants to wish you good luck."

Mashennikova stared at the smiling Captain as Kostikov translated everything he said, in case the Russian missed something.

Haverlin watched as the Russian picked up the phone as if it weighed a ton and instantaneously became uncomfortable as he replied. "Da, President Tkachenko. General Mashennikova sir."

"Da, Kaneshna Da (Yes, yes of course) you are, you old fool!" the Russian President said.

"Da, my dalzhni sdyelat, (Yes, we must do it) for the Americans, sir." The General replied.

"Da, ochin' khsroshi chilavyek." (Yes, he is a good man) The President said.

"Da, Da. mozhit." (Yes, yes maybe) The Russian General replied, not giving in just yet.

"If you don't do as they need, you'll be sent to Sibirski, (Siberia) General Mashennikova!"

"Da, Kaneshna Da!"(Yes, yes of course) "I understand what you want from me, sir."

Haverlin watched the Russian turn green then red as he spoke to his President. After he hung up, he cursed. "Svinaya Sumashedshaya Idiyot!" (Fucking mad idiot)

"Is there a problem General Mashennikova Sir?" Haverlin asked as he rocked back and forth on his heels with his hands tucked neatly behind his back.

"No Captain, I shall be prepared transmit the scramble message to missile in two minutes, sir." Under his breath, the fuming Russian was burning up inside as he cursed this smiling American. He also cursed the Russian President and the Cuban fool in control of his missiles. He was trying to actually will the stupid man to launch the missiles before he scrambled the codes. He hooked up the last of the wires to the computer, and he stared at the computer as the blue screen came to life with a bright flash then the board was covered with a series of running numbers.

The Russian's hands flew over the keyboard as he entered his access codes, and then he punched up the launch codes for this particular ICBM missile series. He picked the code numbers under the SS-19 series, and pulled them up on the computer screen. He was tempted to punch the wrong set of numbers into the computer in an attempt to stall for more time, but remembered what his President threatened him and his family in Russia, if he failed on his assigned mission.

General Mashennikova looked at the three code groups for the three different SS-19 missiles series. His fingers hesitated for a moment over the keyboard before he pushed the set of codes in. The computer flashed the numbers as it pulled up the launch codes for these particular missiles. Once they were up, his fingers pounded away on the keys. The Russian altered the launch codes for this one missile group. Once he changed the launch code for the SS-19 missile system, he turned to Haverlin and said. "Captain, I successfully altered the launch code number, once I press this one key, order will be transmitted to the missiles automatically, and the missiles in the Cuban hands will be rendered unable to be launch, sir. It take technicians years to locate new launch codes I set up, sir."

Everything said to the Russian by his President moments ago was translated from a secured tapped line, and a hard copy was sent to the Captain. He read it while the Russian changed the launch codes for these missiles. Whatever the Russian said to the Captain not understood, was translated by the Seaman by his side. He leaned over and whispered in his ear, evaluating the Russian's actions.

Unbeknownst to the Russian, his worse fears had been realized. All his supposed secret commands to the computer were unscrambled by a set of specialized computers designed for this purpose on board the Aircraft Carrier. The United States now had the means to scramble the launch codes for every single SS-19 model Three missile system throughout Russia, if she so chose and it would take only a matter of a few minutes, until the computer whizzes would figured out the entire Russian missile launch code control system. Soon, the United States military would be able to scramble the launch codes for the entire fleet of their ICBMs based in Russia and elsewhere in the rest of the world.

"What's our present position Seaman?" the Captain demanded from his Navigator.

"Nine point three miles from Guanahacabibes, sir." The Navigator called out from his seat.

Haverlin turned to the Russian and offered. "What the fuck are you waiting for sir? Push the damn button that'll scramble the launch codes, General." The Captain let the Russian know in no short terms he knew he was stalling.

The Russian understood his command without waiting for a translation, and flinched with anger at having to do the Americans bidding. He wished this button controlled the entire Russian ICBM fleet, and he was unleashing its destruction on the United States, instead of saving America's ass. He cursed his President one last time as he pushed the computer button. The computer went crazy as the scramble code numbers were transmitted to the missile launch computers stationed on Cuban soul.

Haverlin ordered the invasion force based on his ship in action.

LA BAJADA, THE GUANAHACABIBES PENINSULA, CUBA

At the Cuban town of La Bejada, Colonel Carlos Alvarez was pleased as he watched the fifth missile being lowered into its concrete launch tube. He set a number of explosive charges under the remaining warheads in the bunker. He was that determined to destroy the Island of Cuba by any means at his disposal.

Alvarez ran back in the bunker and watched as the technicians hooked up a flood of wires to the main computer system, and he pulled up a command order slaving the last missile's computer system to the bunker's launch and command main computer system. He moved closer to the command computer until he was looking over the technicians shoulder as he ordered the computer.

"How long before I'm able to launch the god dom missiles at the United States, fool?"

The technician did not look up as he replied. "In less than ten minute's Presidente Sir."

"Good, don't waste time speaking to me further you great fool. Get it done." Alvarez took a second to look around the bunker. With five of the missiles out of the control room and bunker, there was plenty of room to move around now. He looked at Maria who was still lying on the desk, but she was conscious at least. She leaned up on an elbow, and glared at him with all the hatred she could muster locked in her eyes.

Alvarez's cheeks flushed with anger, and his first impulse was to go and beat her for her insolence aimed at him. But he decided against this move for fear it might serve to upset the other soldiers. He had a thought and he ordered the technicians to remove the warheads from the remaining missile, and set them up outside with the charges. He thought if he and the chosen men accompanying him would close themselves in the bunker, maybe they could survive the nuclear holocaust about to hit his country.

"It has started El Presidente," The technician announced sadly. "I started the missiles on their final launch orders, sir. You can see what is taking place outside if you wish sir."

Alvarez ran up the steps of the bunker and watched as the underwater silo shrouds lifted until they were above the waterline. Heavy motors were heard as the pumps drained off the remaining sea water from the shrouds. Next, the massive lids of the silos lifted, exposing the missiles.

Alvarez ran downstairs and yelled. "For the love of God, how much longer you fool?"

"It'll take the missiles at least an hour to build up the heat necessary to enable us to launch them." The technician flinched as he spoke his words, fearful of Alvarez's reaction against them.

"God curse you to hell, an hour. By the Blessed Virgin, why was I not told of this delay?"

"Begging your pardon El Presidente Sir, but when we discussed the possibility of launching the missiles. Do you not remember my telling you the missiles were a cold start launch system, and the missiles needed nearly a full hour before they could be launched?"

"Yes, yes of course I remember the dom conversation we had back then, you fool. Is there any way we can speed up this process of launching the dom missiles?"

"We're doing everything in our power to accomplish this feat my Presidente. All we can do now is stand by and watch as the missiles go through their launch orders until they reach the zero number on the computer, sir. Then they'll be off sir."

"Yeah, yeah, I know this fool." Alvarez bitched at him as he ran outside to watch the missiles.

The technician watched the countdown clock as it clicked off the minutes, it read forty nine.

The heavy lead lined doors leading to the inside of the bunker slowly began to close with orders from the countdown computer as it secured the complex.

Now the time to launch read out read forty four minutes left to launching the missiles.

The other technicians who set the charges under the ten nuclear warheads outside the bunker, ran down the stairs as the first door slammed shut behind them.

The clock now read thirty nine minutes until the launch time was achieved.

Maria hopped down from the table and stood on wobbly legs, trying to get her balance.

Alvarez lit a cigar and blew the smoke over his head as if he was angry with the smoke.

A soldier leaned close to Alvarez and asked. "My President, what about the troops above?"

It was now down to thirty one minutes left until launch could be achieved.

"By all the Saints Holy, don't concern yourself with them worthless fools out there, you dom fool. They shall have the honor of laying down their lives for their country and Presidente. It's the same fate that should be suffered by all loyal soldiers to their leaders and country."

The countdown clock read twenty seven minutes to launch time.

Alvarez looked around the underground complex. There were three women in the room with him, and over a hundred soldiers locked inside the bunker.

THE UNITED STATES FORCES STATIONED OFF THE COAST OF CUBA

Captain Haverlin went on the massive deck of his warship and looked to the sky, he counted fifteen huge Globemaster transport planes heading for Cuba in formation. He looked out to the sea and saw a large number AAAV, Advanced Amphibious Assault Vehicles charging through the shallow waters of the Bay of Corrientes that lead to La Bejada and missile installation. Each AAAV carried twelve soldiers. Everywhere he looked, he saw United States Naval crafts heading north. His flight deck was crawling with activity, as it went through the motions of an Alpha launch alert. This meant every able aircraft on the ship was going to be launched for action.

Next, a formation of fast attack Apache helicopters flew over his Carrier blinking their lights in a salute to the grounded Carrier. Following the Apache helicopters was a fleet of Sikorsky H-60 Blackhawk troop carriers. The C-17 Globemasters carried the exile Cuban forces, but the Captain knew it was an all or nothing operation, and he was sending everything he had under his command at the Island. He was going to stop the missiles. In the back of his mind, he was scared the Russian might have pulled something off, and he was not willing to take anything for granted. If the Cuban technicians realized they were messing with the missiles, they would be inclined to launch what they had on line already.

Haverlin's fists balled up as he cursed the Russian under his breath, and he silently urged his troops on with his mind. The fighter warplanes marshaling off the fantail of the Carrier, grouped together and as one turned north and headed for Cuba's shoreline. The adrenaline wore off as the Captain realized he done everything humanly possible to get his troops and war equipment to the Island, and the rest was up to the fighting men and women of his country. It was their responsibility to stop the nuclear tipped missiles from launching.

INSIDE THE CONCRETE BUNKER AT LA BEJADA, CUBA

Alvarez leaned on one of the technician's shoulders as they watched the countdown clock ticking the time away. His eyes betrayed the madness that took over his body. Most troops in the bunker moved close to the walls where they felt the most protection was.

The countdown clock read twenty two minutes to launch time.

Alvarez had no idea Cuban soldiers trapped with him were cursing him. They wanted to kill him and then stop the launching of the dreaded missiles at the United States, and give up to the civilians marching for their installation. Alvarez did not know what was stopping these troops from reacting, neither did they.

Alvarez jumped as the last lead coated door slammed shut with a bang. They were sealed in the bunker. He was content to allow Cuba to her fate, even if it meant the total destruction of the Island. He cursed the clock for moving so slow, staring at it he tried to will the time to move faster.

The countdown clock read twenty minutes to launch time.

The technician tried to relax as he stared at the clock then mumbled. "Presidente Alvarez, there is nothing left for us to do but wait until the engines are charged."

"Is there anything the Americans or anyone else can do to stop the launch for the dom missiles, mista?"

"The Americans cannot do anything to stop the launching of the missiles, Presidente. They're helpless to stop the launching of the missiles sir."

Suddenly, the technician looked in the eyes of Alvarez and his soul chilled. The sheer madness was taking him over and his eyes were red with wildness as they darted back and forth in his skull. The technician did not want to launch the missiles, and decided to plead his case. "Presidente Alvarez, we're the only ones on the face of the earth who can stop the launch of the missiles from this point, sir. This is something I wish you'd consider sir. If we launch the missiles, we would barely hurt the United States, but Cuba, Cuba would be erased from the face of the earth.

"Cuba would be burned to a nuclear cinder, and all who live on her land would be a memory to history, my Presidente. Sir, I beseech you to reconsider the launching of the missiles, sir. If the United States learns we have the missiles on our Island, she'll do anything in her power to strike a bargain with you, my Presidente. Think Presidente Alvarez, you could demand the United States land her troops on our Island to help your troops put down the civilian unrest ripping our country apart, sir. There are many other avenues open to you rather then launching the missiles at the United States. I hope you..."

Presidente Alvarez grabbed the man by the throat and roared. "Everyone on this dom Island has had their cursed chance to avoid their foul death by backing me and my Presidency, you fool. But what did they choose as their fate?" Alvarez screamed at the technician as he slowly lost consciousness as he continued to strangle him. "They're the ones who chose to betray me, betray the trust I placed in their future and loathsome fates. No one on this cursed Island deserves to live for another day longer, and I'm going to see to it no one does."

Alvarez took the technician by the throat and shook him violently, and when he lost consciousness, he released his grasp on his throat and growled. "You'll not offer me any more of your dom suggestions, fool!

You'll keep your foul mouth shut unless I ask you a question. Your duty is to control this countdown of the dom missiles and nothing more. When the missiles are on their way then and only then you shall be free to do whatever you chose to do you see fit. To pick the manner of your death if you like." Alvarez slammed his fist down on the console as the countdown clock registered seventeen minutes from launch time.

The technician struggled desperately to catch his breath while gasping for air for his starved lungs, and he was leaning over the counter when the countdown clock on his console unexpectedly went wild before his eyes. He froze in place as he watched the clock go from seventeen to ninety eight minutes to launch then down to twenty one again then up to seventy four minutes remaining. Suddenly, the countdown clock blinked then it went black. The scared technician's fingers danced with blinding speed over the keyboard of the computer, in an effort to bring up the data backup systems on the console's screen, but his actions were to no avail.

Alvarez saw the technician was having trouble with the computer system, and he barked at the scared technician. "What the hell is it now? Did the Americans do something to interfere with our launching of the missiles, dommit?"

"That's impossible Presidente Alvarez there's nothing the Americans could do that would interfere with the launching of the missiles at this point, sir. I believe it's a glitch on the computer's countdown clock because these systems are so old, and the mains are still up and running true as instructed, sir."

"I swear by the Holy Madonna, for your sake it better be as you say." Alvarez hissed at the scared man as he watched the technician trying to pull up the data backup systems.

Suddenly, the entire bunker complex was shaken by a tremendous series of explosions from outside its thick walls. Alvarez went to the explosion proof window and looked out. The charges set under the extra warheads had gone off, but the warheads were moved from the charges before they detonated under the warheads. Heavy automatic weapon fire was heard next, and Alvarez continued to watch until he saw a number of armored vehicles and tanks plow their way out of the jungle onto his once secret complex.

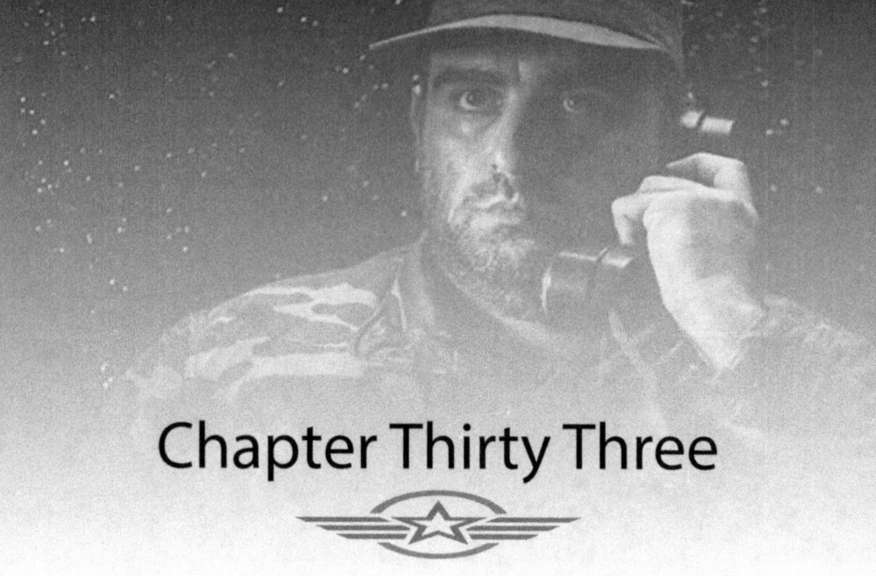

Chapter Thirty Three

CORPORAL ROBERT WALKER'S MILITARY COLUMN

Corporal Robert Walker jumped out of the back of the vehicle with his weapon spraying death at any soldier dressed in a regular Cuban military uniform. The rest of his men were behind him with their weapons firing. The revolutionary troops outside the bunker were locked in the fight of their lives.

Walker had orders if he could not get to the missiles before they were launched at the United States, he was to jump in the silos and cut the electric wires leading to the massive harbingers of death with the ax he had in his gear. The Corporal, along with the Mutt, Private Frank Hall, McKinnon, Delorenzo and Irvington, charged the missile silos with abandonment, and after dropping their weapons on the ground. The soldiers jumped into the cylinder shaped watertight missile silos and went to work.

Delorenzo took a round in the arm, but he did not allow it to stop him as he jumped the ten feet to the grate level where the wires came out of the concrete wall, and they hooked up to the missile. He and Walker's men cut, ripped, and disconnecting any wires they found leading to the sides of the missiles they were trying to stop from being launched at their country.

Walker received burns on his hands as he yanked the heating tube for the missile's fuel out of the side of the bird. He heard the engines kick back and the exhaust from the tail of the machine lessened and he announced in a booming voice. "My fucking bird's dead man." After he yelled his warning he looked after his burnt hands.

The Mutt was the next one to scream out. "My bird's deader than a fucking doorknob, man."

The other three American soldiers confirmed the demise of their missiles.

Walker had a tough time shimmying up the ten feet to the ground level from inside the missile silo. The silos smelt like rotting fish, and the walls were covered with slim and also covered with mold and other stuff that made the walls slippery. Once he struggled to the surface, he was amazed at what he saw happening. Hundreds of American Marines poured onto the Island from every direction. The exile Cuban paratroopers landed on the installation site, and they scattered out, and engaging the remaining government troops they happened across. AAAV's came ashore faster than Walker could count them, and as their tail ramps dropped, more Marines poured out of them and contiguously engaged the remaining enemy troops.

Walker got nipped in the ear when a bullet flew by his head, as he retrieved his weapon on the ground when he dropped it when he went after the missiles. He rolled out of the watertight shroud and found himself standing in about five feet of water. Bullets sprayed the water around him as he hustled for the shore. A round ripped through the sleeve of his uniform, but it did not do damage to him, but a second round took a nick out of his chin.

"Jesus Christ man, where the hell are these miserable fucks hiding at for the love of God?" Walker bellowed out as he emptied his clip of rounds from his weapon in the direction of the incoming fire. From out of nowhere, the Mutt was by his side, and the two American Marine rushed for the shore to help out their fellow soldiers as he yelled at the Mutt over the sounds of battle. "Where the fuck's the rest of our damn shits at around here, man?"

"Delorenzo's had it man, I saw him take a stinking round to the fucking head man. He was dead before he hit the water, Walker. McKinnon took one in the shoulder as well, and he's down but he's alive. I left him inside the damn missile shroud, man. Irvington's okay the last time I saw the dumb prick, he was working his way towards the shoreline from over that way, man." The Mutt pointed east, and he received a round through his hand for his trouble.

"Yeeeeooowww, the sonofabitch tagged my sagging ass, man. I don't believe this crap for a stinking minute, Homes. I just got hit man, I don't fucking believe it man. I'm gonna get that sorry sonofabitch then I'm gonna put my fricking foot up his ass until he can't breathe no more. Then I'm gonna take one giant shit on his stinking face, Homes." The Mutt roared at the sky as he checked his wound.

"Let me get a look at it for ya will ya. Arr.... it's not that bad, I believe you'll live." Walker laughed as he pulled Mutt to shore because his hand was messed up. They went behind an AAAV's and fired at the enemy from the cover of the metal monster. Walker fired from the right, he leaned back to slam another clip in his weapon when he got tagged in the leg. He was pitched back from the force of the round hitting him, and he rolled on the ground until he came to a stop against the Mutt.

The Mutt saw the blood pumping from the wound in a steady stream and he stabbed his finger in the bloody opening then he screamed out at the top of his lungs. "Medic, medic, I need a fucking medic over here double quick man." He looked around until he saw a medic making his way towards them. "Over here scumbag, I gots me a fucking man down and hurt bad, man."

The medic was forced to dive onto Walker and the Mutt as a spray of bullets dotted the ground he was running on. The Mutt snarled at the medic. "Hey Homes, what the fuck's wrong with you buddy? I gots me a hurt man here stupid and you're jumping all over the two of us, stupid." He complained as he shoved the medic off his shoulder then he glared at him for a moment.

The medic ignored the Mutt as he told the concerned soldier. "Here, let me check him out will ya. Yep, he hasta be nicked in the artery soldier. You did wise jamming your finger in there, or he would probably have bled to death by the time I got to him. Hey man, you're hit in the hand."

"Never mind my stinking ass he's hurt worse than I am. You just take care of him before I hop you in the stinking ass, buster." The Mutt snapped at the medic.

"Okay soldier, and I want you to listen up soldier and follow my orders closely, I want you to pull your finger out of the wound slowly, don't twist the fucking thing while coming out, maybe we'll be lucky and the artery's closed. But first, I'm going to apply a tourniquet to his leg, in case the artery healed itself. I don't want it to be hit by a surge of blood and have it rip open again. Okay, I have the tourniquet in place, now move your finger out nice and slow, straight out, it is important man. I want you to be careful as you remove your finger from the wound and what I told you to do, soldier."

The Mutt removed his finger out of the wound as he was instructed by the medic, when it was out blood started oozing out of the wound again. "It's no good, it's still bleeding like shit, fucker." The Mutt barked back at the medic, scared that Walker might die on him.

"Take it easy fellow. That's just trapped blood coming out. I'm going to back off on the pressure on the tourniquet in a few moments and we'll see what's up, man."

Walker drifted in and out of consciousness for a combination of reasons. He lost a lot blood, and he was suffering from exhaustion, shock, and from being beaten all over his body.

The medic slowly released pressure and immediately the blood poured out of the wound. "Ahhh... shit, it's no good man. The damn artery musta been nicked good. I'm gonna hafta evac his ass the hell outta here pronto. Radio, I need a radio, man."

A second soldier made his way to the medic and asked. "Whaddaya got man."

"He's hit in the artery in the damn leg man. I gotta get him out to the ship immediately. They have to go in there and get the bleeder or he's gonna bleed to death."

"Got ya." The radio operator made the call and reported. "I have an evac helo on the way in. In a few minutes this guy's going to be safe and sound on the ever loving Carrier." The radio operator then disappeared into the battle, as someone else screamed for a radio.

The medic checked Mutt's wound, he remarked it was a fat shot, (flesh wound). He made sure no bones were broken, he cleaned it and wrapped it in a field dressing. He smiled at Mutt as he leaned against the parked AAAV war machine and tapped out a cigarette, lit one and offered it to the Mutt as he asked. "You wanna go to the Carrier so they can look at your hand, or do you wanna stick around until this little fracas is over with, buddy?"

"Fuck that shit buddy, I'm not that bad hurt my friend. If I was to go out to the Carrier with a small wound, they'd pitch my ass overboard and make me swim back to this frigging Island." The Mutt turned serious. "Hey Homes, I wanna thank ya for working so good on my pal there. My name's the Mutt, his is Road Kill." He offered the medic his good hand.

"Glad to meet ya Mutt, my name's Richard Drumback, and my friends, what I have of them anyway, call me Blood Clot, man. I guess it kinda comes with the territory I figure man."

"Got ya loud and clear Homes." The Mutt smiled at his new friend and medic.

Their conversation was interrupted by a Blackhawk helicopter hovering over them. Fifteen fresh soldiers jumped out of both sides of the chopper, and the machine lowered until it was hovering a foot above the ground. The door guard yelled out at the soldiers hiding behind one of the armored vehicles. "What's his fucking problem?" As he took Walker by the shoulder then he hoisted him in the chopper. A second man slammed Walker in a chair and strapped him in, taking care with his leg though.

"He's hit in the leg artery, it's a bleeder. You gotta release the pressure from the tourniquet every fifteen minutes for a minute or so, or he could end up losing his fricking leg, man."

"That's bullshit fellow. In five minutes he's going to be on the damn operating table."

Blood Clot slammed his hand loudly on the side of the chopper and the pilot lifted off. By the time the Mutt returned to the fighting, it was turning into a mop up operation. Most government troops had given up to the new soldiers. The Mutt worked himself over to a group of Marines who looked like they were preparing to assault the last obstacle of the operation. The heavy six inch thick lead lined steel bunker doors. He plopped down in the hole and spoke to the Sergeant issuing orders for the other soldiers around him. "Hey Sarge, I'm in on the game you're planning to do here man."

"Who the fuck are you and where the hell did you come from, mud skipper? You smell like shit man." The soldier in command of the Marines barked at him nastily.

Hall announced his name as if it was going to open doors for him. "I'm the Mutt, Homes."

"The Mutt? You look like a fucking mutt, buddy. Who the fuck were you assigned to shitbird? Who's your Commanding Officer, buster?"

"I was air dropped to the civilian fighters who began this damn mess. My group disabled the stinking missiles in the water."

"Got ya, you walking sand bag. We were ordered to keep our eyes open for you slugs when we landed on this stinking Island, man. Any trouble with the Cuban fuckers, buddy?"

"Naw, they're okay squirts for a bunch of foreigners, man." The Mutt smirked at him.

Everyone laughed as the Sergeant grumbled at the soldier. "In case you're not aware of it man. You're the foreigner here, asshole. You're free to linkup with us if you wanna, pal. We're going to pop these doors and level everyone inside that fucking dump. You hurt bad?" The Sergeant asked as he nodded towards the Mutt's hand.

"Didja ever see anyone hurt good? Let's do it Homes. I'm hot and ready to rock, man."

Irvington saw the Mutt head for the group of Marines and he linked up with him. He rolled on the ground over to the Mutt's side and bitched. "Hey Homes, I'm glad you made it through that bunch of shit, man. You see McKinnon hanging around anywhere? He was hurt and I lost sight of the dopey puke." The Mutt snapped while keeping his eyes glued to the doors to the bunker.

"Yeah Homie, he bought the big dirt nap. I saw him get hit in the arm and go down. He stayed inside the shroud trying to get a field dressing on his wound when a cannon round hit it square on. I saw him go tumbling into the air and the way he landed on the ground. No way in hell would he have been able to survive that one, he was done for it man. His head never came outta the fucking water again, Mutt."

"Shit, I kinda liked that turd. I was gonna make him part of my group if we all made it outta this mess alive." The Mutt griped at him.

"What about me Homes?" Irvington snapped back at the Mutt as he pointed to his own chest.

"Relax you made the group the moment you gave me a hard time in the Colonel's office back in the real world, man."

"Enough bullshitting people, we're gonna do it man. Theo? Engineers get out there, set your charges for a minute and then bug the hell outta the damn area. The rest of you motherless turds, we're going to charge in there the moment those doors are blown apart, people. Any questions with your orders as received, bullet stoppers?"

No one offered anything back to the man giving them the orders.

"Good, let's go and do it people." The Sergeant growled as he checked his weapon.

INSIDE THE BUNKER

Alvarez ran around the bunker like a wild man, screaming at anyone who crossed his path. He kicked a soldier out of his way as he grabbed a technician and screamed in his face. "Blessed Lord Jesus, I thought you told me the dom Americans could do nothing to stop the cursed launching of my missiles, mista? What the hell happened out there, you fool?"

"I don't know El Presidente. I believe somehow, someone was able to scramble the launch order, sir." The frightened technician replied as he continued to watch the clock. When the time passed for the launch to go and there was still no sign of the missiles doing so, he knew the missiles were tampered with from some other sources beyond his knowledge and control, and he was unable to launch the missiles at the United States. He let out a sigh, knowing Cuba would be allowed to live, despite this madman screaming at him.

"Madre de Dios, you lied you son of a milkless whore! As God is my judge, you lied. I swear by the Holy Madonna, you'll pay dearly for this lie. You'll rue the day your father mixed his seed with your whore of a mother. By the Blessed Virgin I swear, answer me truly. Is all lost or is there still a way for me to launch my missiles, mista?"

The technician hesitated for a second and Alvarez slammed him across his face with the back of his hand, and screamed at him again. "Answer me god dommit!"

"Presidente Alvarez, there's no other way I know of that would allow me to launch the missiles, sir. I have no control over them any longer sir. Someone has somehow changed the launch numbers, and it would take me a lifetime to figure out the new launching numbers."

"Then you're no longer of use to me and my Revolution, fool." Alvarez hissed as he drew his pistol and he held it two inches from the forehead of the technician. With the roar of thunder, the Cuban pulled the trigger, sending the nine mm chunk of lead into the technician's head.

Many trapped soldiers mumbled angrily as they watched Alvarez cold bloodedly killed the unarmed civilian technician. All of a sudden, Alvarez felt threatened by the soldiers who moved around him and he roared at them. "By the hand of God, what is this? Any of you motherless bastards have a problem with the way I'm running this cursed country? Lord give me mercy speak up or hold your dom water."

The wildly raving Alvarez held his pistol at the ready while pointing it at each and every soldier in the concrete bunker, as he went from one scared face to another of the soldiers standing in the shadows of the bunker walls and he roared at them. "By the Blessed Virgin, I didn't think so, a bunch of spineless fools I aligned myself with I see. God curse us all to hell, we better prepare ourselves, the soldiers attacking us are sure to turn their attention on the bunker next. Take up your positions and prepare to repel the hated attackers as they enter my bunker."

Alvarez watched as his soldiers moved the heavy metal desks, file cabinets, a number of steel tables, and whatever else they could more or hide behind to better defend the bunker and themselves. He saw Maria standing by the desk she laid on, and a soldier shoved her aside and he pulled the heavy metal desk over until it was in line with the two steel doors protecting them from the attackers outside. He flipped the desk on its side then the soldier hid behind it as he aimed his weapon at the set of doors and waited.

Alvarez kept an eye on Maria, he saw her left eye swollen about closed, and her once beautiful lips were swollen and cut, and the side of her face was puffy and an angry red. For a second he felt sorry for what he done to her. But of everyone locked in the bunker, he found himself fearing her the most. He glared at her until she looked at him. As soon as her eyes connected with his, she sat on the concrete floor and she crossed her legs under her, and placed her head in her arms. Alvarez could tell she was crying. "Ahhh, at least she's no longer a threat against me and my plans a crying female is not to be feared by anyone." He mumbled as he turned his attention back to the technicians.

"You, over there is this devil's born bastard telling me the truth? Is there no other way for us to regain control over my god dom missiles out there?" Alvarez barked savagely at a second technician as he leveled his pistol right at the other worker as he waited for his reply.

"He spoke the truth El Presidente Sir." The scared lab tech replied, and when he noticed Alvarez move the pistol and aim it at his chest, he realized he had to say something or he was going to die. "Presidente Alvarez, there is always a chance though sir."

Alvarez relaxed his arm as he snapped at the technician. "Yes and what is this one chance you speak of, mista? It's your only chance to live, you fool."

"Presidente Alvarez! It's yet possible we may have lost only temporary control over the missiles and launch capabilities, sir. There's still a slight chance they could come back on line in a short time, sir. We'll have to wait and see if this happens, Presidente." The scared to death lab technician was reaching for anything that might stop this madman from killing him like he did to the other man.

"You think this is possible, mista?" Alvarez suddenly barked at the technician.

"I swear by all that's holy sir. This is a possibility. All we have to do is to maintain the computers on line, and once this jamming stopped, we'll be able to launch the missiles. We know the missiles are already heated up, and they could be launched immediately, by merely pushing the launch button as soon as we get control of them again, sir."

"By all of the Saints, this is good news from your foul lips." Alvarez grumbled as he paced the bunker in a wild rage again, slowly calming down he added. "Then all is not lost. All I have to do is be patient and there's a chance I can launch the dom missiles at the United States." Suddenly, Alvarez's disposition changed. He looked around the bunker until he found Maria's guard.

"Melba, make coffee, enough for everyone. The American troops cannot get at us as long as we're inside this dom building. We're safe until the missiles come back on line. Let the foolish soldiers outside kill each other, so when our missiles are launched we can go out and reclaim whatever is left of Cuba. We'll survive, by God, this I swear to my loyal troops with me today." Alvarez lifted his right hand up to God, to sort of seal the pact he made with Him.

The soldier keeping watch looking out of the blast proof window, had to duck back as an approaching American soldier saw him, and he opened fire on his image in the glass. The window cracked but did not shatter by the rounds that struck it. The Cuban soldier tried to locate the American soldier who marched up to the doors. He knew the Americans had to be up to something. When he could not locate him, he cried out the alarm to the other soldiers inside the bunker.

"Presidente Alvarez, an American soldier was starting down the staircase sir, and when he saw me he fired, making it impossible for me to see what he's up to outside, sir."

The once Cuban President ran the twenty feet separating him from the blast proof window and heavy doors. Alvarez could not see anything outside the fractured glass. With the sun bouncing off the cracks, he could see nothing outside. Alvarez turned back to the soldiers bunching up behind him until he found the Lieutenant he was looking for. "You, by God, yes you there you dom fool." He pointed to him with his pistol still in his hand. "What do you think the American soldiers are up to out there, mista?"

"If I were them, I'd be trying to get in here by any means possible, Presidente Alvarez Sir. I'd place explosive charges against the doors then blast them open, sir."

Alvarez jumped two feet in the air and spun around in mid air. He screamed like a wounded bear, cursing everything from the Saints, to the Americans and Castro. He stormed back to the center of the bunker and killed three more technicians, one at a time slowly.

It was here Maria decided to make a move against her once lover and Colonel. She ran over to a soldier staring at the bewildering scene unfolding before his eyes, and she pulled his field knife free of his belt. She then wildly charged at Alvarez's back as he fired at another one of the cowering and unarmed technicians, and she plunged the knife deep into the center of his back then she pulled it out and stepped away from him as she continued to hold the knife in her hands.

The stunned Alvarez roared out in pain and spun around then he stared at his once lover. Blood trickled down her chin and dripped onto her slender neck. His eyes were wild then slowly, he lowered his arm and aimed his pistol at her forehead. He smiled at her as he said to Maria. "Ahh... my beloved bitch, Maria. I should've known it'd be your hand that would swing the foul knife of death into my back, woman. I should've known this all along my dear it'd be you who betrays me the most. At least you'll not live long enough to enjoy what you have done to me, bitch. You'll not live long enough to see me die like you desire, bitch. I'll send you to meet your bastard of a father dwelling in the fires of hell where you belong, woman. I hate you I hate all who gone against what I was trying to do for Cuba, and her children."

Alvarez pulled the trigger of his pistol, and the deafening sound of metal striking bare metal filled the deafening silence of the massive concrete bunker. But that was all heard. Alvarez's weapon was empty of bullets.

Maria stood with her eyes closed tight with tears streaming down her filthy cheeks, while feeling the coldness of the barrel of the gun pressed so hard against her head. She flinched and her eyes closed tighter when she heard the metal click that sounded like the loudest thing she ever heard in her life, but no bullet struck her head. Uncontrolled rage instantly filled her soul and body at the same instant, as she screamed a roar of pure hatred as if she just lost her mind. Then she charged wildly at Alvarez a second time, raising her hands over her head then bringing them down and plunging the knife locked so tightly between her hands, deep in Alvarez's chest, once, twice, then a third time. All with a sickening thud, and her roaring in rage at the dying man.

The slowly dying Carlos Rafael Hernandez Alvarez locked his hands around Maria's slender neck, and squeezed it with his remaining might, but his strength rapidly seeped from his body until she was able to shake free of his dying grasp. His body slowly slid down hers and all the while he sagged to the floor his eyes locked on her eyes, as his hands clutched at Maria's body. When Alvarez was lying on the ground struggling to breathe, he looked up once more and said in a weak strained voice. "It takes a true and trusted friend to stab you in the front as you done to me. Maria, I love you dear."

His eyes closed for the last time in his life, as he continued to stare at his once lover.

"Dirty bastard, you love only your wasted self." Maria roared as she kicked him hard in the face. Then, she turned to the other soldiers in the bunker and hissed at them. "Does everyone here want to die in this hellhole with this madman, or do you want to put an end to the fighting happening on Cuba, god dommit?"

No soldiers moved since Maria made her charge at the madman's back. Everyone wanted to do the same thing, but they were frozen in place with fear of the madman. Maria stood over Alvarez's body, her dress covered with his blood, and when Alvarez body slid down the length of her body, his reaching hands ripped her dress here and there, making her look almost as wild as he was acting. She began to scream at the stunned looking not moving soldiers. "We have to give up before the Americans blow up the bunker, killing all of us in here, dommit."

These words seem to have done the trick, because three of the soldiers charged for the steel doors, and they released the heavy dead bolts that locked them shut and in place.

OUTSIDE THE CONCRETE BUNKER

The Mutt, Private Frank Hall kept the American engineers covered as they placed the satchel charges that would have blown open the bunker doors, against them. The engineers placed a charge at each of the four corners of the doors on their hinges, and then they placed two more charges on the center of the doors by their handles. It took the soldiers over five minutes to place the charges correctly against the double doors then to set them to blow in one minute at the same exact time. Then the engineers ran up the concrete stairs and dropped down on each side of the concrete staircase that offered them protection from the pending explosions, and they covered their heads with their arms and waited for the explosives to go off.

The Mutt was aiming his weapon down the staircase, and he was the first one to notice the metal double doors slowly open as he yelled out. "Hold up on the fucking charges, hey Sarge, they're coming the fuck outta their damn rathole in the wall, man."

The Sergeant jumped up and saw the soldiers coming out of the bunker with their hands held over their heads and he roared. "They're giving up. Engineers, they're giving up. Stop them damn charges."

The engineers jumped up and charged down the staircase, pushing the fleeing Cuban soldiers coming out of the bunker out of the way as they rushed to the fuses, and cut the lines. The Mutt, the Sergeant and a number of other American soldiers and Cuban exiles charged towards the bunker doors. The exile troops pulled the government soldiers up the steps, and herded them to a safe place for processing and securing, while the other soldiers charged in the bunker to secure it.

The Mutt and Sergeant allowed the exiles to deal with the rush of government troops pouring out of the bunker begging not to be killed in broken English and Cuban.

The Mutt was the first one to get inside the concrete bunker, once there he saw the lone woman kind of half standing, and slouching over in the center of the bunker, and she was crying over a downed soldier laying on the floor by her feet. There was another body lying on the floor, it was that of a woman. The Mutt did not know Melba charged Maria's back when she killed the President, but one of the soldiers stopped her by stabbing her before she got at the young woman. Other of the charging American soldiers rushed to the computers and shut them down then they disconnected the electrical power to the computers for extra safety.

The Mutt, along with a fellow Marine confidently walked over to the slumping and exhausted looking woman, as the Mutt growled at her nastily. "What the fuck happened to you honey? Who the hell are you anyway, bitch?" As he reached out to help support her weight in his hands as Maria almost collapsed in his arms as she let out with a sigh, and she tried to reply to the American soldier.

Maria mustered the remaining strength she could gather still in her exhausted, bloody and battered body, and she pulled away from the American soldier who snarled at her so savagely, and defiantly growled at him. "I am Maria Ibarra, and I was the lover of this last Devil of Paradise. This piece of filthy lying at my feet is the man I mean, American Soldier."

Maria motioned with her head towards the body lying on the floor by her feet. "This thing laying here is Colonel Carlos Alvarez, the so called new Presidente of Cuba, sir."

"You fucking kill'em honey?" the Marine Sergeant asked the shaking young and pretty Cuban woman angrily. "That was real fucking cold blooded of you there baby."

The Sergeant shook his head slowly as he looked at the body of the dead Cuban Colonel. His body was a mess, with three large, gaping holes ripped in the front of his body, obviously caused by a military field knife. There was no denying the Colonel was dead. The exhausted Marine Sergeant turned his attention back to the woman covered from head to toe with the fresh blood of the dead Colonel, and watched the woman in the torn dress as she stared into his wondering eyes with a blank stare.

Maria did not reply, instead, she allowed the field knife still locked in the death grip in her hand to fall to the ground at her feet. Then, she collapsed to the floor in exhaustion, sitting down heavily on her rear end she lowered her head, and took in a deep breath as she tried to get her breathing under control. The Mutt stared at the woman as she struggled to breath, he smiled at her, it was the only thing he could thing of doing.

9 798893 892406